DANGEROUS WOMEN

DANGEROUS WOMEN

EDITED BY

GEORGE R. R. MARTIN

AND

GARDNER DOZOIS

TOR®

A TOM DOHERTY ASSOCIATES BOOK
NEW YORK

DANGEROUS WOMEN

Copyright © 2013 by George R. R. Martin and Gardner Dozois

A Tor Book
Published by Tom Doherty Associates, LLC
175 Fifth Avenue
New York, NY 10010

www.tor-forge.com

Tor® is a registered trademark of Tom Doherty Associates, LLC.

Library of Congress Cataloging-in-Publication Data

Martin, George R. R., editor of compilation.
    Dangerous women / George R.R. Martin and Gardner Dozois, ed. — First Edition.
        p. cm.
    ISBN 978-0-7653-3206-6 (hardcover)
    ISBN 978-1-4299-5596-6 (e-book)
    1. Women—Fiction.   2. Fantasy fiction.   I. Dozois, Gardner R., editor of compilation.   II. Title.
    PS648.W6D36 2013
    813'.010832042—dc23

                                                            2013018473

Tor books may be purchased for educational, business, or promotional use. For information on bulk purchases, please contact Macmillan Corporate and Premium Sales Department at 1-800-221-7945, extension 5442, or write specialmarkets@macmillan.com.

Printed in the United States of America

0 9 8 7 6 5 4

Copyright Acknowledgments

To Jo Playford, my dangerous minion.

—George R. R. Martin

Contents

DANGEROUS WOMEN

Introduction by Gardner Dozois

Genre fiction has always been divided over the question of just *how* dangerous women are.

In the real world, of course, the question has long been settled. Even if the Amazons are mythological (and almost certainly wouldn't have cut their right breasts off to make it easier to draw a bow if they *weren't*), their legend was inspired by memory of the ferocious warrior women of the Scythians, who were very much *not* mythological. Gladiatrix, women gladiators, fought other women—and sometimes men—to the death in the arenas of Ancient Rome. There were female pirates like Anne Bonny and Mary Read, and even female samurai. Women served as frontline combat troops, feared for their ferocity, in the Russian army during World War II, and serve so in Israel today. Until 2013, women in the U.S. forces were technically restricted to "noncombat" roles, but many brave women gave their lives in Iraq and Afghanistan anyway, since bullets and land mines have never cared whether you're a noncombatant or not. Women who served as Women Airforce Service Pilots for the United States during World War II were also limited to noncombat roles (where many of them were nevertheless killed in the performance of their duties), but Russian women took to the skies as fighter pilots, and sometimes became aces. A Russian female sniper during World War II was credited with more than fifty kills. Queen Boudicca of the Iceni tribe led one of the most fearsome revolts ever against Roman authority, one that was almost successful in driving the Roman invaders from Britain, and a young French peasant girl inspired and led the troops against the enemy so successfully that she became famous forever afterwards as Joan of Arc.

On the dark side, there have been female "highwaymen" like Mary Frith and Lady Katherine Ferrers and Pearl Hart (the last person to ever rob a stagecoach); notorious poisoners like Agrippina and Catherine de Medici, modern female outlaws like Ma Barker and Bonnie Parker, even female serial killers like Aileen Wuornos. Elizabeth Báthory was said to have bathed in the blood of virgins, and even though that has been called into question, there is no doubt that she tortured and killed dozens,

perhaps hundreds, of children during her life. Queen Mary I of England
had hundreds of Protestants burnt at the stake; Queen Elizabeth of
England later responded by executing large numbers of Catholics. Mad
Queen Ranavalona of Madagascar had so many people put to death that
she wiped out one-third of the entire population of Madagascar during her
reign; she would even have you executed if you appeared in her dreams.

Popular fiction, though, has always had a schizophrenic view of the
dangerousness of women. In the science fiction of the 1930s, '40s, and '50s,
women, if they appeared at all, were largely regulated to the role of the
scientist's beautiful daughter, who might scream during the fight scenes
but otherwise had little to do except hang adoringly on the arm of the hero
afterwards. Legions of women swooned helplessly while waiting to be rescued by the intrepid jut-jawed hero from everything from dragons to the
bug-eyed monsters who were always carrying them off for improbable
purposes either dietary or romantic on the covers of pulp SF magazines.
Hopelessly struggling women were tied to railroad tracks, with nothing
to do but squeak in protest and hope that the Good Guy arrived in time to
save them.

And yet, at the same time, warrior women like Edgar Rice Burroughs's
Dejah Thoris and Thuvia, Maid of Mars, were every bit as good with the
blade and every bit as deadly in battle as John Carter and their other male
comrades, female adventuresses like C. L. Moore's Jirel of Joiry swash-
buckled their way through the pages of *Weird Tales* magazine (and blazed
a trail for later female swashbucklers like Joanna Russ's Alyx); James H.
Schmitz sent Agents of Vega like Granny Wannatel and fearless teenagers
like Telzey Amberdon and Trigger Argee out to battle the sinister menaces and monsters of the spaceways; and Robert A. Heinlein's dangerous
women were capable of being the captain of a spaceship or killing enemies
in hand-to-hand combat. Arthur Conan Doyle's sly, shady Irene Adler
was one of the only people ever to outwit his Sherlock Holmes, and probably one of the inspirations for the legions of tricky, dangerous, seductive,
and treacherous "femmes fatale" who featured in the works of Dashiell
Hammett and James M. Cain and later went on to appear in dozens of
films noir, and who still turn up in the movies and on television to this
day. Later television heroines such as Buffy the Vampire Slayer and Xena,
Warrior Princess, firmly established women as being formidable and deadly
enough to battle hordes of fearsome supernatural menaces, and helped to

inspire the whole subgenre of paranormal romance, which is sometimes unofficially known as the "kick-ass heroine" genre.

Like our anthology *Warriors*, *Dangerous Women* was conceived of as a cross-genre anthology, one that would mingle every kind of fiction, so we asked writers from every genre—science fiction, fantasy, mystery, historical, horror, paranormal romance, men and women alike—to tackle the theme of "dangerous women," and that call was answered by some of the best writers in the business, including both new writers and giants of their fields like Diana Gabaldon, Jim Butcher, Sharon Kay Penman, Joe Abercrombie, Carrie Vaughn, Joe R. Lansdale, Lawrence Block, Cecelia Holland, Brandon Sanderson, Sherilynn Kenyon, S. M. Stirling, Nancy Kress, and George R. R. Martin.

Here you'll find no hapless victims who stand by whimpering in dread while the male hero fights the monster or clashes swords with the villain, and if you want to tie *these* women to the railroad tracks, you'll find you have a real fight on your hands. Instead, you will find sword-wielding women warriors; intrepid women fighter pilots and far-ranging spacewomen; deadly female serial killers; formidable female superheroes; sly and seductive femmes fatale; female wizards; hard-living bad girls; female bandits and rebels; embattled survivors in postapocalyptic futures; female private investigators; stern female hanging judges; haughty queens who rule nations and whose jealousies and ambitions send thousands to grisly deaths; daring dragonriders; and many more.

Enjoy!

Joe Abercrombie

As the sizzlingly fast-paced and action-packed story that follows demonstrates, sometimes chasing a fugitive can be as dangerous for the pursuers as for the pursued—particularly when the quarry has no place left to run. . . .

Joe Abercrombie is one of the fastest-rising stars in fantasy today, acclaimed by readers and critics alike for his tough, spare, no-nonsense approach to the genre. He's probably best known for his First Law trilogy, the first novel of which, *The Blade Itself*, was published in 2006; it was followed in subsequent years by *Before They Are Hanged* and *Last Argument of Kings*. He's also written the stand-alone fantasy novels *Best Served Cold* and *The Heroes*. His most recent novel is *Red Country*. In addition to writing, Abercrombie is also a freelance film editor and lives and works in London.

SOME DESPERADO

Shy gave the horse her heels, its forelegs buckled, and, before she had a notion what was happening, she and her saddle had bid each other a sad farewell.

She was given a flailing instant aloft to consider the situation. Not a good one at a brief assay, and the impending earth gave her no time for a longer. She did her best to roll with the fall—as she tried to do with most of her many misfortunes—but the ground soon uncurled her, gave her a fair roughing up, and tossed her, flopping, into a patch of sun-shrivelled scrub.

Dust settled.

She stole a moment just to get some breath in. Then one to groan while the world stopped rolling. Then another to shift gingerly an arm and a leg, waiting for that sick jolt of pain that meant something was broke and her miserable shadow of a life would soon be lost in the dusk. She would've welcomed it, if it meant she could stretch out and not have to run any more. But the pain didn't come. Not outside of the usual compass, least-ways. As far as her miserable shadow of a life went, she was still awaiting judgment.

Shy dragged herself up, scratched and scuffed, caked in dust and spitting out grit. She'd taken too many mouthfuls of sand the last few months but she'd a dismal premonition that there'd be more. Her horse lay a few strides distant, one foamed-up flank heaving, forelegs black with blood. Neary's arrow had snagged it in the shoulder, not deep enough to kill or even slow it right off, but deep enough to make it bleed at a good pace. With her hard riding, that had killed it just as dead as a shaft in the heart.

There'd been a time Shy had got attached to horses. A time—despite reckoning herself hard with people and being mostly right—she'd been uncommon soft about animals. But that time was a long time gone. There wasn't much soft on Shy these days, body or mind. So she left her mount to its final red-frothed breaths without the solace of her calming hand and ran for the town, tottering some at first, but quickly warming to the exercise. At running, she'd a heap of practice.

"Town" was perhaps an overstatement. It was six buildings, and calling them buildings was being generous to two or three. All rough lumber and an entire stranger to straight angles, sun-baked, rain-peeled, and dust-blasted, huddled about a dirt square and a crumbling well.

The biggest building had the look of a tavern or brothel or trading post or more likely all three amalgamated. A rickety sign still clung to the boards above the doorway but the name had been rubbed by the wind to just a few pale streaks in the grain. *Nothing, nowhere,* was all its proclamation now. Up the steps two by two, bare feet making the old boards wheeze, thoughts boiling away at how she'd play it when she got inside, what truths she'd season with what lies for the most likely recipe.

There's men chasing me! Gulping breath in the doorway and doing her best to look beyond desperate—no mighty effort of acting at that moment, or any occupying the last twelve months, indeed.

Three of the bastards! Then—provided no one recognised her from all the bills for her arrest—*They tried to rob me!* A fact. No need to add that she'd robbed the money herself from the new bank in Hommenaw in the company of those three worthies plus another since caught and hung by the authorities.

They killed my brother! They're drunk on blood! Her brother was safe at home where she wished she was, and if her pursuers were drunk, it would likely be on cheap spirits as usual, but she'd shriek it with that little warble in her throat. Shy could do quite a warble when she needed one, she'd practiced it 'til it was something to hear. She pictured the patrons springing to their feet in their eagerness to aid a woman in distress. *They shot my horse!* She had to admit it didn't seem overpowering likely that anyone hard-bitten enough to live out here would be getting into a sweat of chivalry, but maybe fate would deal her a winning hand for once.

It had been known to happen.

She blundered through the tavern's door, opening her mouth to serve up the tale, and stopped cold.

The place was empty.

Not just no one there, but nothing there, and for damn sure no winning hand. Not a twig of furniture in the bare common room. A narrow stairway and a balcony running across the left-hand wall, doorways yawning empty upstairs. Chinks of light scattered where the rising sun was seeking out the many gaps in the splitting carpentry. Maybe just a lizard skittering away into the shadows—of which there was no shortage—and a bumper harvest of dust, greying every surface, drifted into every corner. Shy stood there a moment just blinking, then dashed back out along the rickety stoop and to the next building. When she shoved the door, it dropped right off its rusted hinges.

This one hadn't even a roof. Hadn't even a floor. Just bare rafters with the careless, pinking sky above, and bare joists with a stretch of dirt below, every bit as desolate as the miles of dirt outside.

She saw it now as she stepped back into the street with vision unhindered by hope. No glass in the windows, or wax paper, even. No rope by the crumbling well. No animals to be seen—aside from her own dead horse, that was, which only served to prove the point.

It was a dried-out corpse of a town, long since dead.

Shy stood in that forsaken place, up on the balls of her bare feet as though she was about to sprint off somewhere but lacked the destination, hugging herself with one arm while the fingers of the other hand fluttered and twitched at nothing, biting on her lip and sucking air fast and rasping through the little gap between her front teeth.

Even by recent standards, it was a low moment. But if she'd learned anything the last few months, it was that things can always get lower. Looking back the way she'd come, Shy saw the dust rising. Three little grey trails in the shimmer off the grey land.

"Oh, hell," she whispered, and bit her lip harder. She pulled her eating knife from her belt and wiped the little splinter of metal on her dirty shirt, as though cleaning it might somehow settle the odds. Shy had been told she had a fertile imagination, but even so, it was hard to picture a more feeble weapon. She'd have laughed if she hadn't been on the verge of weeping. She'd spent way too much time on the verge of weeping the last few months, now that she thought about it.

How had it come to this?

A question for some jilted girl rather than an outlaw with four thousand marks offered, but still a question she was never done asking. Some desperado! She'd grown expert on the desperate part but the rest remained a mystery. The sorry truth was that she knew full well how it came to this—the same way as always. One disaster following so hard on another that she just bounced between 'em, pinging about like a moth in a lantern. The second usual question followed hard on the first.

What the fuck *now*?

She sucked in her stomach—not that there was much to suck in these days—and dragged the bag out by the drawstrings, coins inside clicking together with that special sound only money makes. Two thousand marks in silver, give or take. You'd think that a bank would hold a lot more—they told depositors they always had fifty thousand on hand—but it turns out you can't trust banks any more than bandits.

She dug her hand in, dragged free a fistful of coins, and tossed the money across the street, leaving it gleaming in the dust. She did it like she did most things these days—hardly knowing why. Maybe she valued her life a lot higher'n two thousand marks, even if no one else did. Maybe she hoped they'd just take the silver and leave her be, though what she'd do once she was left be in this corpse town—no horse, no food, no weapon—she hadn't thought out. Clearly she hadn't fixed up a whole plan, or not one that would hold too much water, leastways. Leaky planning had always been a problem of hers.

She sprinkled silver as if she was tossing seed on her mother's farm, miles and years and a dozen violent deaths away. Whoever would've thought she'd miss the place? Miss the bone-poor house and the broke-down barn and the fences that always needed mending. The stubborn cow that never gave milk and the stubborn well that never gave water and the stubborn soil that only weeds would thrive in. Her stubborn little sister and brother too. Even big, scarred, softheaded Lamb. What Shy would've given now to hear her mother's shrill voice curse her out again. She sniffed hard, her nose hurting, her eyes stinging, and wiped 'em on the back of her frayed cuff. No time for tearful reminiscences. She could see three dark spots of riders now beneath those three inevitable dust trails. She flung the empty bag away, ran back to the tavern, and—

"Ah!" She hopped over the threshold, bare sole of her foot torn on a loose nail head. The world's nothing but a mean bully, that's a fact. Even when you've big misfortunes threatening to drop on your head, small ones still take every chance to prick your toes. How she wished she'd got the chance to grab her boots. Just to keep a shred of dignity. But she had what she had, and neither boots nor dignity were on the list, and a hundred big wishes weren't worth one little fact—as Lamb used to boringly drone at her whenever she cursed him and her mother and her lot in life and swore she'd be gone in the morning.

Shy remembered how she'd been then, and wished she had the chance now to punch her earlier self in the face. But she could punch herself in the face when she got out of this.

She'd a procession of other willing fists to weather first.

She hurried up the stairs, limping a little and cursing a lot. When she reached the top she saw she'd left bloody toe prints on every other one. She was working up to feeling pretty damn low about that glistening trail leading right to the end of her leg, when something like an idea came trickling through the panic.

She paced down the balcony, making sure to press her bloody foot firm to the boards, and turned into an abandoned room at the end. Then she held her foot up, gripping it hard with one hand to stop the bleeding, and hopped back the way she'd come and through the first doorway, near the top of the steps, pressing herself into the shadows inside.

A pitiful effort, doubtless. As pitiful as her bare feet and her eating knife and her two-thousand-mark haul and her big dream of making it back home to the shit-hole she'd had the big dream of leaving. Small chance those three bastards would fall for that, even stupid as they were. But what else could she do?

When you're down to small stakes, you have to play long odds.

Her own breath was her only company, echoing in the emptiness, hard on the out, ragged on the in, almost painful down her throat. The breath of someone scared near the point of an involuntary shitting and all out of ideas. She just couldn't see her way to the other side of this. She ever made it back to that farm she'd jump out of bed every morning she woke alive and do a little dance, and give her mother a kiss for every cuss, and never snap at her sister or mock Lamb again for being a coward. She promised it, then wished she was the sort who kept promises.

She heard horses outside, crept to the one window with half a view of the street, and peered down as gingerly as if she was peering into a bucket of scorpions.

They were here.

Neary wore that dirty old blanket cinched in at the waist with twine, his greasy hair sticking up at all angles, reins in one hand and the bow he'd shot Shy's horse with in the other, the blade of the heavy axe hanging at his belt as carefully cleaned as the rest of his repugnant person was beyond neglect. Dodd had his battered hat pulled low, sitting his saddle with that round-shouldered cringe he always had around his brother, like a puppy expecting a slap. Shy would have liked to give the faithless fool a slap right then. A slap for starters. Then there was Jeg, sitting up tall as a lord in that long red coat of his, dirt-fringed tails spread out over his big horse's rump, hungry sneer on his face as he scanned the buildings, that tall hat which he thought made him look quite the personage poking off his head slightly crooked, like the chimney from a burned-out farmstead.

Dodd pointed to the coins scattered across the dirt around the well, a couple of 'em winking with the sun. "She left the money."

"Seems so," said Jeg, voice hard as his brother's was soft.

She watched them get down and hitch their mounts. No hurry to it. Like they were dusting themselves off after a jaunt of a ride and looking forward to a nice little evening among cultured company. They'd no need to hurry. They knew she was here, and they knew she was going nowhere, and they knew she was getting no help, and so did she.

"Bastards," Shy whispered, cursing the day she ever took up with them. But you have to take up with someone, don't you? And you can only pick from what's on offer.

Jeg stretched his back, took a long sniff and a comfortable spit, then drew his sword. That curved cavalry sword he was so proud of with the clever-arsed basketwork, which he said he'd won in a duel with a Union officer, but that Shy knew he'd stolen, along with the best part of everything else he'd ever owned. How she'd mocked him about that stupid sword. She wouldn't have minded having it to hand now, though, and him with only her eating knife.

"Smoke!" bellowed Jeg, and Shy winced. She'd no idea who'd thought that name up for her. Some wag had lettered it on the bills for her arrest and now everyone used it. On account of her tendency to vanish like smoke, maybe. Though it could also have been on account of her tendencies to stink like it, stick in folks' throats, and drift with the wind.

"Get out here, Smoke!" Jeg's voice clapped off the dead fronts of the buildings, and Shy shrank a little further into the darkness. "Get out here and we won't hurt you too bad when we find you!"

So much for taking the money and going. They wanted the price on her too. She pressed her tongue into the gap between her teeth and mouthed, "Cocksuckers." There's a certain kind of man, the more you give him, the more he'll take.

"We'll have to go and get her," she heard Neary say in the stillness.

"Aye."

"I told you we'd have to go and get her."

"You must be pissing your pants with joy over the outcome, then, eh?"

"Said we'd have to get her."

"So stop pointing it out and get it done."

Dodd's wheedling voice. "Look, the money's here, we could just scrape this up and get off, there ain't no need to—"

"Did you and I really spring from between the same set o' legs?" sneered Jeg at his brother. "You are the stupidest bastard."

"Stupidest," said Neary.

"You think I'm leaving four thousand marks for the crows?" said Jeg. "You scrape that up, Dodd, we'll break the mare."

"Where do you reckon she is?" asked Neary.

"I thought you was the big tracker?"

"Out in the wild, but we ain't in the wild."

Jeg cocked an eyebrow at the empty shacks. "You'd call this the highest extent of civilisation, would you?"

They looked at each other a moment, dust blowing up around their legs, then settling again.

"She's here somewhere," said Neary.

"You think? Good thing I got the self-described sharpest eyes west of the mountains with me, so I don't miss her dead horse ten fucking strides away. Yes, she's here somewhere."

"Where do you reckon?" asked Neary.

"Where would you be?"

Neary looked about the buildings and Shy jerked out of the way as his narrowed eyes darted over the tavern.

"In that one, I reckon, but I ain't her."

"Course you ain't fucking her. You know how I can tell? You got bigger tits and less sense. If you was her, I wouldn't have to fucking look for her now, would I?"

Another silence, another dusty gust. "Guess not," said Neary.

Jeg took his tall hat off, scrubbed at his sweaty hair with his fingernails, and jammed it back on at an angle. "You look in there, I'll try the one next to it, but don't kill the bitch, eh? That'll half the reward."

Shy eased back into the shadows, feeling the sweat tickling under her shirt. To be caught in this worthless arsehole of a place. By these worthless bastards. In bare feet. She didn't deserve this. All she'd wanted was to be somebody worth speaking of. To not be nothing, forgotten on the day of her death. Now she saw that there's a sharp balance between too little excitement and a huge helping too much. But like most of her lame-legged epiphanies, it had dawned a year too late.

She sucked air through the little gap between her teeth as she heard Neary creaking across the boards in the common room, maybe just the metal rattle of that big axe. She was shivering all over. Felt so weak of a sudden she could hardly hold the knife up, let alone imagine swinging it. Maybe it was time to give up. Toss the knife out the door and say, "I'm coming out! I'll be no trouble! You win!" Smile and nod and thank 'em for their betrayal and their kind consideration when they kicked the shit out of her or horsewhipped her or broke her legs and whatever else amused them on the way to her hanging.

She'd seen her share of those and never relished the spectacle. Standing there tied while they read your name and your crime, hoping for some last reprieve that wouldn't come while the noose was drawn tight, sobbing for mercy or hurling your curses and neither making the slightest hair of difference. Kicking at nothing, tongue stuck out while you shat yourself for the amusement of scum no better'n you. She pictured Jeg and Neary, up front in the grinning crowd as they watched her do the thief's dance at rope's end. Probably arrayed in even more ridiculous clothes secured with the reward money.

"*Fuck* them," she mouthed at the darkness, lips curling back in a snarl as she heard Neary's foot on the bottom step.

She had a hell of a contrary streak, did Shy. From when she was a tot, when someone told her how things would be, she immediately started thinking on how she'd make 'em otherwise. Her mother had always called her mule stubborn, and blamed it on her Ghost blood. "That's your damn Ghost blood," as though being quarter savage had been Shy's own choice rather than on account of her mother picking out a half-Ghost wanderer to lie with who turned out—no crashing surprise—to be a no-good drunk.

Shy would be fighting. No doubt she'd be losing, but she'd be fighting.

She'd make those bastards kill her and at least rob 'em of half the reward. Might not expect such thoughts as those to steady your hand, but they did hers. The little knife still shook, but now from how hard she was gripping it.

For a man who proclaimed himself the great tracker, Neary had some trouble keeping quiet. She heard the breath in his nose as he paused at the top of the steps, close enough to touch if it hadn't been for the plank wall between them.

A board groaned as he shifted his weight and Shy's whole body tensed, every hair twitching up. Then she saw him—not darting through the doorway at her, axe in his fist and murder in his eyes, but creeping off down the balcony after the bait of bloody footsteps, drawn bow pointed exactly the wrong way.

When she was given a gift, Shy had always believed in grabbing it with both hands rather than thinking on how to say thank you. She dashed at Neary's back, teeth bared and a low growl ripping at her throat. His head whipped around, the whites of his eyes showing and the bow following after, the head of the arrow glinting with such light as found that abandoned place.

She ducked low and caught him around the legs, shoulder driving hard into his thigh and making him grunt, her hand finding her wrist and clamping tight under Neary's arse, her nose suddenly full of the horse-and-sour sweat stink of him. The bowstring went, but Shy was already straightening, snarling, screaming, bursting up, and—big man though he was—she hoisted Neary right over the rail as neat as she used to hoist a sack of grain on her mother's farm.

He hung in the air a moment, mouth and eyes wide with shock, then he plummeted with a breathy whoop and crashed through the boards down below.

Shy blinked, hardly able to believe it. Her scalp was burning and she touched a finger to it, half expecting to feel the arrow stuck right in her brains, but she turned and saw it was in the wall behind her, a considerably happier outcome from her standpoint. Blood, though, sticky in her hair, tickling at her forehead. Maybe the lath of the bow scratched her. Get that bow, she'd have a chance. She made a step towards the stairs, then stopped dead. Jeg was in the doorway, his sword a long, black curve against the sun-glare of the street.

"Smoke!" he roared, and she was off down the balcony like a rabbit, following her own trail of bloody footprints to nowhere, hearing Jeg's heavy boots clomping towards the stairs. She hit the door at the end full tilt with her shoulder and burst into the light, out onto another balcony behind the building. Up onto the low rail with one bare foot—better to just go with her contrary streak and hope it somehow carried her through than to pause for thought—and she jumped. Flung herself writhing at a ramshackle balcony on the building across the narrow lane, as if flapping her hands and feet like she was having a fit might carry her further.

She caught the rail, wood smashing her in the ribs, slipped down, groaning, clawing for a grip, fought desperately to drag herself up and over, felt something give—

And with a groan of tortured wood the whole weather-blasted thing tore from the side of the building.

Again Shy was given a flailing instant aloft to consider the situation. Again not good, at a brief assay. She was just starting to wail when her old enemy the ground caught up with her—as the ground always will—folded up her left leg, spun her over, then smashed her in the side and drove her wind right out.

Shy coughed, then moaned, then spat more grit. That she had been right about her earlier sandy mouth not being her last was scant comfort. She saw Jeg standing on the balcony where she'd jumped. He pushed his hat back and gave a chuckle, then ducked back inside.

She still had a piece of the rail in her fist, well rotted through. A little like her hopes. She tossed it away as she rolled over, waiting again for that sick pain that told her she was done. Again it didn't come. She could move. She worked her feet around and guessed that she could stand. But she thought that she might leave that for now. Chances were she'd only get to do it one more time.

She floundered clear of the tangle of broken wood against the wall, her shadow stretching out towards the doorway, groaning with pain as she heard Jeg's heavy footsteps inside. She started wriggling back on her arse and her elbows, dragging one leg after, the little knife blade hidden up behind her wrist, her other fist clutching at the dirt.

"Where are you off to?" Jeg ducked under the low lintel and into the lane. He was a big man, but he looked a giant right then. Half a head taller than Shy, even if she'd been standing, and probably not much short of twice her weight, even if she'd eaten that day. He strutted over, tongue wedged into his lower lip so it bulged out, heavy sword loose in his hand, relishing his big moment.

"Pulled a neat trick on Neary, eh?" He pushed the brim of his hat up a little to show the tan mark across his forehead. "You're stronger'n you look. That boy's so dumb he could've fallen without the help, though. You'll be pulling no tricks on me."

They'd see about that, but she'd let her knife say it for her. Even a little knife can be a damned eloquent piece of metal if you stick it in the right place. She scrambled back, kicking up dust, making it look like she was trying to push herself up, then sagging back with a whimper as her left leg took her weight. Looking badly hurt was taking no great effort of acting. She could feel blood creeping from her hair and tickling her forehead. Jeg stepped out of the shadow and the low sun shone in his face, making him squint. Just the way she wanted it.

"Still remember the day I first put eyes on you," he went on, loving the sound of his own bleating. "Dodd come to me, all excited, and said he met Smoke, her whose killer's face is on all them bills up near Rostod, four thousand marks offered for her capture. The tales they tell on you!" He gave a whoop and she scrambled back again, working that left leg underneath her, making sure it would work when she needed it. "You'd think you was a demon with two swords to a hand the way they breathe your name. Picture my fucking *disappointment* when I find you ain't naught but a scared girl with gappy teeth and a powerful smell o' piss about her." As if Jeg smelled of summer meadows! He took another step forward, reaching out for her with one big hand. "Now, don't scratch; you're worth more to me alive. I don't want to—"

She flung the dirt with her left hand as she shoved up hard with her right, coming to her feet. He twisted his head away, snarling as the dust showered across his face. He swung blind as she darted at him low and the sword whipped over her head, wind of it snatching at her hair, weight of it turning him sideways. She caught his flapping coat tail in her left hand and sank her eating knife into his sword shoulder with the other.

He gave a strangled grunt as she pulled the knife clear and stabbed at him again, blade ripping open the arm of his coat and the arm inside it too, almost cutting into her own leg. She was bringing up the knife again when his fist crunched into the side of her mouth and sent her reeling,

bare feet wrestling with the dirt. She caught hold of the corner of the
building and hung there for a moment, trying to shake the light from her
skull. She saw Jeg a pace or two off, bared teeth frothy with spit as he tried
to fumble the sword from his dangling right hand into his left, fingers
tangled with the fancy brass basketwork.

When things were moving fast, Shy had a knack for just doing, without
thoughts of mercy, or thoughts of outcomes, or thoughts of much at all.
That was what had kept her alive through all this shit. And what had
landed her in it in the first place, for that matter. Ain't many blessings
aren't mixed blessings, once you got to live with them, and she'd a curse for
thinking too much after the action, but that was another story. If Jeg got a
good grip on that sword she was dead, simple as that, so before she'd quite
stopped the street spinning she charged at him again. He tried to free an
arm but she managed to catch it with her clawing left hand, pressing up
against him, holding herself steady by his coat as she punched wildly with
the knife—in his gut, in his ribs, in his ribs again—her snarling at him and
him grunting at her with every thump of the blade, the grip slippery in her
aching hand.

He got hold of her shirt, stitches tearing as the arm half-ripped off,
tried to shove her away as she stabbed him again but there was no strength
in it, only sent her back a step. Her head was clearing now and she kept
her balance, but Jeg stumbled and dropped on one knee. She lifted the
knife up high in both hands and drove it right down on that stupid hat,
squashing it flat, leaving the blade buried to the handle in the top of Jeg's
head.

She staggered back, expecting him just to pitch onto his face. Instead he
lurched up suddenly like a camel she'd once seen at a fair, the brim of his hat
jammed down over his eyes to the bridge of his nose and the knife handle
jutting straight up.

"Where you gone?" The words all mangled as if his mouth was full of
gravel. "Smoke?" He lurched one way, then the other. "Smoke?" He shuffled at her, kicking up dust, sword dangling from his bloody right hand,
the point scratching grooves in the dust around his feet. He reached up
with his left, fingers all stretched out stiff but the wrist all floppy, and
started prodding at his hat like he had something in his eye and wanted to
wipe it clear.

"Shmoke?" One side of his face was twitching, shuddering, fluttering in a most unnatural way. Or maybe it was natural enough for a man with a knife lodged through his brains. "Thmoke?" There was blood dripping from the bent brim of his hat, leaving red streaks down his cheek, his shirt halfway soaked with it; but he kept coming on, bloody right arm jerking, hilt of his sword rattling against his leg. "Thmoe?" She backed away, staring, her own hands limp and all her skin prickling, until her back hit the wall behind her. "Thoe?"

"Shut your mouth!" And she dived at him with both palms, shoving him over backwards, sword bouncing from his hand, bloody hat still pinned to his head with her knife. He slowly rolled over, onto his face, right arm flopping. He slid his other hand underneath his shoulder as though he'd push himself up.

"Oh," he muttered into the dust. Then he was still.

Shy slowly turned her head and spat blood. Too many mouthfuls of blood the last few months. Her eyes were wet and she wiped them on the back of her trembling hand. Couldn't believe what had happened. Hardly seemed she'd had any part in it. A nightmare she was due to wake from. She pressed her eyes shut, and opened them, and there he still lay.

She snatched in a breath and blew it out hard, dashed spit from her lip, blood from her forehead, caught another breath and forced it free. Then she gathered up Jeg's sword, gritting her teeth against the urge to spew, rising in waves along with the thumping pain in the side of her face. Shit, but she wanted to sit down! Just *stop*. But she made herself turn away. Forced herself up to the back door of the tavern. The one Jeg had come through, still alive, a few moments before. Takes a lifetime of hard work to make a man. Only takes a few moments to end one.

Neary had dragged himself out of the hole his fall had put through the floorboards, clutching at his bloody trouser leg and looking quite put out about it. "Did you catch that fucking bitch?" he asked, squinting towards the doorway.

"Oh, no doubt."

His eyes went wide and he tried to drag himself towards his bow, not far out of reach, whimpering all the way. She hefted Jeg's big sword as she got close, and Neary turned over, eyes wide with terror, holding up one desperate arm. She hit it full-blooded with the flat of the sword and he moaned, clutching it to his chest. Then she hit him across the side of the head and rolled him over, blubbering, into the boards. Then she padded past him, sliding the sword through her belt, picked up the bow, and dragged some arrows from his quiver. She made for the door, stringing one as she went, and peered out into the street.

Dodd was still scraping coins from the dust and into the bag, working his way towards the well. Insensible to the fates of his two companions. Not as surprising as you might suppose. If one word summed up Dodd, it was "insensible."

She padded down the steps of the tavern, near to their edges where they were less likely to give a warning creak, drawing the bow halfway and taking a good aim on Dodd, bent over in the dust with his back to her, a dark sweat patch down the middle of his shirt. She gave some long, hard consideration to making that sweat patch the bull's-eye and shooting him in the back right there. But killing a man isn't easy, especially after hard consideration. She watched him pick up the last coin and drop it in the bag, then stand, pulling the drawstrings, then turn, smiling. "I got the—"

They stayed there awhile. He crouched in the dusty street, bag of silver in one hand, uncertain smile lit up in the sun, but his eyes looking decidedly scared in the shadow of his cheap hat. She on the bottom step of the tavern, bloody bare feet, bloody split mouth, bloody hair plastered across her bloody forehead, but the bow good and steady.

He licked his lips, swallowed, then licked them again. "Where's Neary?"

"In a bad way." She was surprised by the iron in her voice. Sounded like someone she didn't even know. Smoke's voice, maybe.

"Where's my brother?"

"In a worse."

Dodd swallowed, sweaty neck shifting, starting to ease gently backwards. "You kill him?"

"Forget about them two and stop still."

"Look, Shy, you ain't going to shoot me, are you? Not after all we been through. You ain't going to shoot. Not me. Are you?" His voice was rising higher and higher, but still he edged back towards the well. "I didn't want this. It weren't my idea!"

"Course not. You need to think to have an idea, and you ain't up to it. You just went along. Even if it happened to mean me getting hung."

"Now, look, Shy—"

"Stop still, I said." She drew the bow all the way, string cutting tight into her bloody fingers. "You fucking deaf, boy?"

"Look, Shy, let's just talk this out, eh? Just talk." He held his trembly palm up like that might stop an arrow. His pale blue eyes were fixed on her, and suddenly she had a memory rise up of the first time she met him, leaning back against the livery, smiling free and easy, none too clever but plenty of fun. She'd had a profound lack of fun in her life since she'd left home. You'd never have thought she left home to find it.

"I know I done wrong, but . . . I'm an idiot." And he tried out a smile, no steadier than his palm. He'd been worth a smile or two, Dodd, at least to begin with, and though no artist of a lover, had kept the bed warm, which was something, and made her feel as if she weren't on her own on one side with the whole rest of the world on the other, which was something more.

"Stop still," she said, but more softly now.

"You ain't going to shoot me." Still he was edging back towards the well. "It's me, right? Me. Dodd. Just don't shoot me, now." Still going. "What I'm going to do is—"

She shot him.

It's a strange thing about a bow. Stringing it, and drawing it, and nocking the arrow, and taking your aim—all that takes effort, and skill, and a decision. Letting go the string is nothing. You just stop holding it. In fact, once you've got it drawn and aimed, it's easier to let fly than not to.

Dodd was less than a dozen strides distant, and the shaft flitted across the space between them, missed his hand by a whisker and stuck silently into his chest. Surprised her, the lack of a sound. But then, flesh is soft. 'Specially in comparison to an arrowhead. Dodd took one more wobbly pace, like he hadn't quite caught up with being arrow-stuck yet, his eyes going very wide. Then he blinked down at the shaft.

"You shot me," he whispered, and he sank to his knees, blood already spreading out on his shirt in a dark oval.

"Didn't I bloody warn you!" She flung the bow down, suddenly furious with him and with the bow too.

He stared at her. "But I didn't think you'd do it."

She stared back. "Neither did I." A silent moment, and the wind blew up one more time and stirred the dust around them. "Sorry."

"Sorry?" he croaked.

Might've been the stupidest thing she'd ever said, and that with some fierce competition, but what else could she say? No words were going to take that arrow out. She gave half a shrug. "I guess."

Dodd winced, hefting the silver in one hand, turning towards the well. Shy's mouth dropped open, and she took off running as he toppled sideways, hauling the bag into the air. It turned over and over, curving up and starting to fall, drawstrings flapping, Shy's clutching hand straining for it as she sprinted, lunged, fell . . .

She grunted as her sore ribs slammed into the wall around the well, right arm darting down into the darkness. For a moment she thought she was going in after the bag—which would probably have been a fitting conclusion—then her knees came back down on the dirt outside.

She had it by one of the bottom corners, loose canvas clutched by broken nails, drawstrings dangling as dirt and bits of loose stone filtered down around it.

Shy smiled. For the first time that day. That month, maybe.

Then the bag came open.

Coins tumbled into the darkness in a twinkling shower, silver pinging and rattling from the earthy walls, disappearing into the inky nothingness, and silence.

She straightened up, numb.

She backed away slowly from the well, hugging herself with one hand while the empty bag hung from the other.

She looked over at Dodd, lying on his back with the arrow sticking straight up from his chest, his wet eyes fixed on her, his ribs going fast. She heard his shallow breaths slow, then stop.

Shy stood there a moment, then doubled over and blew puke onto the ground. Not much of it, since she'd eaten nothing that day, but her guts clenched up hard and made sure she retched up what there was. She shook so bad she thought she was going to fall, hands on her knees, sniffing bile from her nose and spluttering it out.

Damn, but her ribs hurt. Her arm. Her leg. Her face. So many scrapes, twists, and bruises, she could hardly tell one from another: her whole body was one overpowering fucking throb.

Her eyes crawled over to Dodd's corpse, she felt another wave of sickness and forced them away, over to the horizon, fixing them on that shimmering line of nothing.

Not nothing.

There was dust rising there. She wiped her face on her ripped sleeve one more time, so filthy now that it was as like to make her dirtier as cleaner.

She straightened, squinting into the distance, hardly able to believe it. Riders. No doubt. A good way off, but as many as a dozen.

"Oh, hell," she whispered, and bit her lip. Things kept going this way she'd soon have chewed right through the bloody thing. "Oh, hell!" And Shy put her hands over her eyes and squeezed them shut and hid in self-inflicted darkness in the desperate hope she might have somehow been mistaken. Would hardly have been her first mistake, would it?

But when she took her hands away, the dust was still there. The world's a mean bully, all right, and the lower down you are, the more it delights in kicking you. Shy put her hands on her hips, arched her back, and screamed up at the sky, the word drawn out as long as her sore lungs would allow.

"Fuck!"

The echoes clapped from the buildings and died a quick death. No answer came. Perhaps the faint droning of a fly already showing some interest in Dodd. Neary's horse eyed her for a moment, then looked away, profoundly unimpressed. Now Shy had a sore throat to add to her woes. She was obliged to ask herself the usual questions.

What the fuck now?

She clenched her teeth as she hauled Dodd's boots off and sat in the dust beside him to pull them on. Not the first time they'd stretched out together in the dirt, him and her. First time with him dead, though. His boots were way too loose on her, but a long stride better than no boots at all. She clomped back into the tavern in them.

Neary was making some pitiable groans as he struggled to get up. Shy kicked him in the face and down onto his back, plucked the rest of the arrows from his quiver, and took his heavy belt knife too. Back out into the sun and she picked up the bow, jammed Dodd's hat onto her head, also somewhat on the roomy side but at least offering some shade as the sun got up. Then she dragged the three horses together and roped them into a string—quite a ticklish operation, since Jeg's big stallion was a mean bastard and seemed determined to kick her brains out.

When she'd got it done, she frowned off towards those dust trails. They were headed for the town, all right, and fast. With a better look, she reckoned on about nine or ten, which was two or three better than twelve but still an almighty inconvenience.

Bank agents after the stolen money. Bounty hunters looking to collect her price. Other outlaws who'd got wind of a score. A score that was currently in the bottom of a well, as it happened. Could be anyone. Shy had an uncanny knack for making enemies. She found that she'd looked over at Dodd, facedown in the dust with his bare feet limp behind him. The only thing she had worse luck with was friends.

How had it come to this?

She shook her head, spat through the little gap between her front teeth, and hauled herself up into the saddle of Dodd's horse. She faced it away from those impending dust clouds, towards which quarter of the compass she knew not.

Shy gave the horse her heels.

Megan Abbott

Megan Abbott was born in the Detroit area, graduated from the University of Michigan with a B.A. in English literature, received her Ph.D. in English and American literature from New York University, and has taught literature, writing, and film at New York University and the State University of New York at Oswego. She published her first novel, *Die a Little,* in 2005, and has since come to be regarded as one of the foremost practitioners of modern noir mystery writing, with the *San Francisco Chronicle* saying that she was poised to "claim the throne as the finest prose stylist in crime fiction since Raymond Chandler." Her novels include *Queenpin,* which won the Edgar Award in 2008, *The Song Is You, Bury Me Deep,* and *The End of Everything.* Her most recent novel is *Dare Me.* Her other books include, as editor, the anthology *A Hell of a Woman: An Anthology of Female Noir* and a nonfiction study, *The Street Was Mine: White Masculinity in Hardboiled Fiction and Film Noir.* She lives in Forest Hills, New York, and maintains a website at meganabbott.com.

In the subtle yet harrowing story that follows, she shows us that there are some things that you just can't get over, no matter how hard you try—and some insights into the hearts of even those we love the most that you can't unsee once you see them.

MY HEART IS EITHER BROKEN

He waited in the car. He had parked under one of the big banks of lights. No one else wanted to park there. He could guess why. Three vehicles over, he saw a woman's back pressed against a window, her hair shaking. Once, she turned her head and he almost saw her face, the blue of her teeth as she smiled.

Fifteen minutes went by before Lorie came stumbling across the parking lot, heels clacking.

He had been working late and didn't even know she wasn't home until he got there. When she finally picked up her cell, she told him where she was, a bar he'd never heard of, a part of town he didn't know.

"I just wanted some noise and people," she had explained. "I didn't mean anything."

He asked if she wanted him to come get her.

"Okay," she said.

On the ride home, she was doing the laughing-crying thing she'd been doing lately. He wanted to help her but didn't know how. It reminded him of the kinds of girls he used to date in high school. The ones who wrote in ink all over their hands and cut themselves in the bathroom stalls at school.

"I hadn't been dancing in so long, and if I shut my eyes no one could see," she was saying, looking out the window, her head tilted against the window. "No one there knew me until someone did. A woman I didn't know. She kept shouting at me. Then she followed me into the bathroom stall and said she was glad my little girl couldn't see me now."

He knew what people would say. That she was out dancing at a grimy pickup bar. They wouldn't say she cried all the way home, that she didn't know what to do with herself, that no one knows how they'll act when something like this happens to them. Which it probably won't.

But he also wanted to hide, wanted to find a bathroom stall himself, in another city, another state, and never see anyone he knew again, especially his mother or his sister, who spent all day on the Internet trying to spread the word about Shelby, collecting tips for the police.

Shelby's hands—well, people always talk about baby's hands, don't they?—but they were like tight little flowers and he loved to put his palm over them. He never knew he'd feel like that. Never knew he'd be the kind of guy—that there even were kinds of guys—who would catch the milky scent of his daughter's baby blanket and feel warm inside. Even, sometimes, press his face against it.

It took him a long time to tug off the dark red cowboy boots she was wearing, ones he did not recognize.

When he pulled off her jeans, he didn't recognize her underwear either. The front was a black butterfly, its wings fluttering against her thighs with each tug.

He looked at her and a memory came to him of when they first dated, Lorie taking his hand and running it along her belly, her thighs. Telling him she once thought she'd be a dancer, that maybe she could be. And that if she ever had a baby she'd have a C-section, because everyone knew what happened to women's stomachs after, *not to mention what it does down there,* she'd said, laughing, and put his hand there next.

He'd forgotten all this, and other things too, but now the things kept coming back and making him crazy.

He poured a tall glass of water for her and made her drink it. Then he refilled it and set it beside her.

She didn't sleep like a drunk person but like a child, her lids twitching dreamily and a faint smile tugging at her mouth.

The moonlight coming in, it felt like he watched her all night, but at some point he must have fallen asleep.

When he woke, she had her head on his belly, was rubbing him drowsily.

"I was dreaming I was pregnant again," she murmured. "It was like Shelby all over again. Maybe we could adopt. There are so many babies out there that need love."

———

They had met six years ago. He was working for his mother, who owned a small apartment building on the north side of town.

Lorie lived on the first floor, where the window was high and you could see people walking on the sidewalk. His mother called it a "sunken garden apartment."

She lived with another girl and sometimes they came in very late, laughing and pressing up against each other in the way young girls do, whispering things, their legs bare and shiny in short skirts. He wondered what they said.

He was still in school then and would work evenings and weekends, changing washers on leaky faucets, taking out the trash.

Once, he was in front of the building, hosing down the garbage cans with bleach, and she rushed past him, her tiny coat bunched around her face. She was talking on the phone and she moved so quickly he almost didn't see her, almost splashed her with the hose. For a second he saw her eyes, smeary and wet.

"I wasn't lying," she was saying into the phone as she pushed her key into the front door, as she heaved her shoulders against it. "I'm not the liar here."

One evening not long after, he came home and there was a note under the door. It read:

> *My heart is either broken or I haven't paid the bill.*
> *Thx, Lorie, #1-A*

He'd read it four times before he figured it out.

She smiled when she opened the door, the security chain across her forehead.

He held up his pipe wrench.

"You're just in time," she said, pointing to the radiator.

No one ever thinks anything will ever happen to their baby girl. That's what Lorie kept saying. She'd been saying that to reporters, the police, for every day of the three weeks since it happened.

He watched her with the detectives. It was just like on TV except nothing like on TV. He wondered why nothing was ever like you thought it would be and then he realized it was because you never thought this would be you.

She couldn't sit still, her fingers twirling through the edges of her hair. Sometimes, at a traffic signal, she would pull nail scissors from her purse and trim the split ends. When the car began moving, she would wave her hand out the window, scattering the clippings into the wind.

It was the kind of careless, odd thing that made her so different from any girl he ever knew. Especially that she would do it front of him.

He was surprised how much he had liked it.

But now all of it seemed different and he could see the detectives watching her, looking at her like she was a girl in a short skirt, twirling on a bar stool and tossing her hair at men.

"We're gonna need you to start from the beginning again," the male one said, and that part was like on TV. "Everything you remember."

"She's gone over it so many times," he said, putting his hand over hers and looking at the detective wearily.

"I meant you, Mr. Ferguson," the detective said, looking at him. "Just you."

They took Lorie to the outer office and he could see her through the window, pouring long gulps of creamer into her coffee, licking her lips.

He knew how that looked too. The newspapers had just run a picture of her at a smoothie place. The caption was "What about Shelby?" They must have taken it through the front window. She was ordering something at the counter, and she was smiling. They always got her when she was smiling. They didn't understand that she smiled when she was sad. Sometimes she cried when she was happy, like at their wedding, when she cried all day, her face pink and gleaming, shuddering against his chest.

I never thought you would, she had said. *I never thought I would. That any of this could happen.*

He didn't know what she meant, but he loved feeling her huddled against him, her hips grinding against him like they did when she couldn't hold herself together and seemed to be holding on to him to keep from flying off the earth itself.

"So, Mr. Ferguson," the detective said, "you came home from work and there was no one home?"

"Right," he said. "Call me Tom."

"Tom," the detective started again, but the name seemed to fumble in his mouth like he'd rather not say it. Last week he'd called him Tom. "Was it unusual to find them gone at that time of day?"

"No," he said. "She liked to keep busy."

It was true, because Lorie never stayed put and sometimes would strap Shelby into the car seat and drive for hours, putting 100 or 200 miles on the car.

She would take her to Mineral Pointe and take photos of them in front of the water. He would get them on his phone at work and they always made him grin. He liked how she was never one of these women who stayed at home and watched court shows or the shopping channels.

She worked twenty-five hours a week at the Y while his mother stayed with Shelby. Every morning, she ran five miles, putting Shelby in the jogging stroller. She made dinner every night and sometimes even mowed the lawn when he was too busy. She never ever stopped moving.

This is what the newspapers and the TV people loved. They loved to take pictures of her jogging in her short shorts and talking on the phone in her car and looking at fashion magazines in line at the grocery store.

"What about Shelby?" the captions always read.

They never understood her at all. He was the only one.

"So," the detective asked him, rousing from his thoughts, "what did you do when you found the house empty?"

"I called her cell." He had. She hadn't answered, but that wasn't unusual either. He didn't bother to tell them that. That he'd called four or five times and the phone went straight to voice mail and it wasn't until the last time she picked up.

Her voice had been strange, small, like she might be in the doctor's office, or the ladies' room. Like she was trying to make herself quiet and small.

"Lorie? Are you okay? Where are you guys?"

There had been a long pause and the thought came that she had crashed the car. For a crazy second he thought she might be in the hospital, both of them broken and battered. Lorie was a careless driver, always sending him texts from the car. Bad pictures came into his head. He'd dated a girl once who had a baby shoe that hung on her rearview mirror. She said it was to remind her to drive carefully, all the time. No one ever told you that after you were sixteen.

"Lorie, just tell me." He had tried to make his voice firm but kind.

"Something happened."

"Lorie," he tried again, like after a fight with her brother or her boss, "just take a breath and tell me."

"Where did she go?" her voice came. "And how is she going to find me? She's a little girl. She doesn't know anything. They should put dog tags on them like they did when we were kids, remember that?"

He didn't remember that at all, and there was a whirr in his head that was making it hard for him to hear.

"Lorie, you need to tell me what's going on."

So she did.

She said she'd been driving around all morning, looking at lawn mowers she'd found for sale on Craigslist. She was tired, decided to stop for coffee at the expensive place.

She saw the woman there all the time. They talked online about how expensive the coffee was but how they couldn't help it. And what was an Americano, anyway? And, yeah, they talked about their kids. She was pretty sure the woman said she had kids. Two, she thought. And it was only going to be two minutes, five at the most.

"What was going to be five minutes?" he had asked her.

"I don't know how it happened," she said, "but I spilled my coffee, and it was everywhere. All over my new white coat. The one you got me for Christmas."

He had remembered her opening the box, tissue paper flying. She had said he was the only person who'd ever bought her clothes that came in boxes, with tissue paper in gold seals.

She'd spun around in the coat and said, *Oh, how it sparkles.*

Crawling onto his lap, she'd smiled and said only a man would give the mother of a toddler a white coat.

"The coat was soaking," she said now. "I asked the woman if she could watch Shelby while I was in the restroom. It took a little while because I had to get the key. One of those heavy keys they give you."

When she came out of the restroom, the woman was gone, and so was Shelby.

———

He didn't remember ever feeling the story didn't make sense. It was what happened. It was what happened to them, and it was part of the whole impossible run of events that led to this. That led to Shelby being gone and no one knowing where.

But it seemed clear almost from the very start that the police didn't feel they were getting all the information, or that the information made sense.

"They don't like me," Lorie said. And he told her that wasn't true and had nothing to do with anything anyway, but maybe it did.

He wished they could have seen Lorie when she had pushed through the front door that day, her purse unzipped, her white coat still damp from the spilled coffee, her mouth open so wide, all he could see was the red inside her, raw and torn.

Hours later, their family around them, her body shuddering against him as her brother talked endlessly about Amber Alerts and Megan's Law and his criminal justice class and his cop buddies from the gym, he felt her pressing into him and saw the feathery curl tucked in her sweater collar, a strand of Shelby's angel-white hair.

By the end of the second week, the police hadn't found anything, or if they did they weren't telling. Something seemed to have shifted, or gotten worse.

"Anybody would do it," Lorie said. "People do it all the time."

He watched the detective watch her. This was the woman detective, the one with the severe ponytail who was always squinting at Lorie.

"Do what?" the woman detective asked.

"Ask someone to watch their kid, for just a minute," Lorie said, her back stiffening. "Not a guy. I wouldn't have left her with a man. I wouldn't have left her with some homeless woman waving a hairbrush at me. This was a woman I saw in there every day."

"Named?" They had asked her for the woman's name many times. They knew she didn't know it.

Lorie looked at the detective, and he could see those faint blue veins showing under her eyes. He wanted to put his arm around her, to make her feel him there, to calm her. But before he could do anything, she started talking again.

"Mrs. Caterpillar," she said, throwing her hands in the air. "Mrs. Linguini. Madame Lafarge."

The detective stared at her, not saying anything.

"Let's try looking her up on the Internet," Lorie said, her chin jutting and a kind of hard glint to her eyes. All the meds and the odd hours they were keeping, all the sleeping pills and sedatives and Lorie walking through the house all night, talking about nothing but afraid to lie still.

"Lorie," he said. "Don't—"

"Everything always happens to me," she said, her voice suddenly soft and strangely liquid, her body sinking. "It's so unfair."

He could see it happening, her limbs going limp, and he made a grab for her.

She nearly slipped from him, her eyes rolling back in her head.

"She's fainting," he said, grabbing her, her arms cold like frozen pipes. "Get someone."

The detective was watching.

"I can't talk about it because I'm still coping with it," Lorie told the reporters who were waiting outside the police station. "It's too hard to talk about."

He held her arm tightly and tried to move her through the crowd, bunched so tightly, like the knot in his throat.

"Is it true you're hiring at attorney?" one of the reporters asked.

Lorie looked at them. He could see her mouth open and there was no time to stop her.

"I didn't do anything wrong," she said, a hapless grin on her face. As if she had knocked someone's grocery cart with her own.

He looked at her. He knew what she meant—she meant leaving Shelby for that moment, that scattered moment. But he also knew how it sounded, and how she looked, that panicky smile she couldn't stop.

That was the only time he let her speak to reporters.

Later, at home, she saw herself on the nightly news

Walking slowly to the TV, she kneeled in front of it, her jeans skidding on the carpet, and did the oddest thing.

She put her arms around it, like it was a teddy bear, a child.

"Where is she?" she whispered. "Where is she?"

And he wished the reporters could see this, the mystifying way grief was settling into her like a fever.

But he was also glad they couldn't.

It was the middle of the night, close to dawn, and she wasn't next to him.

He looked all over the house, his chest pounding. He thought he must be dreaming, calling out her name, both their names.

He found her in the backyard, a lithe shadow in the middle of the yard.

She was sitting on the grass, her phone lighting her face.

"I feel closer to her out here," she said. "I found this."

He could barely see, but moving closer saw the smallest of earrings, an enamel butterfly, caught between her fingers.

They had had a big fight when she came home with Shelby, her ears pierced, thick gold posts plugged in such tiny lobes. Her ears red, her face red, her eyes soft with tears.

"Where did she go, babe?" Lorie said to him now. "Where did she go?"

He was soaked with sweat and was pulling his T-shirt from his chest.

"Look, Mr. Ferguson," the detective said, "you've cooperated with us fully. I get that. But understand our position. No one can confirm her story. The employee who saw your wife spill her coffee remembers seeing her leave with Shelby. She doesn't remember another woman at all."

"How many people were in there? Did you talk to all of them?"

"There's something else too, Mr. Ferguson."

"What?"

"One of the other employees said Lorie was really mad about the coffee spill. She told Shelby it was her fault. That everything was her fault. And that Lorie then grabbed your daughter by the arm and shook her."

"That's not true," he said. He'd never seen Lorie touch Shelby roughly. Sometimes it seemed she barely knew she was there.

"Mr. Ferguson, I need to ask you: Has your wife had a history of emotional problems?"

"What kind of question is that?"

"It's a standard question in cases like this," the detective said. "And we've had some reports."

"Are you talking about the local news?"

"No, Mr. Ferguson. We don't collect evidence from TV."

"Collecting evidence? What kind of evidence would you need to collect about Lorie? It's Shelby who's missing. Aren't you—"

"Mr. Ferguson, did you know your wife spent three hours at Your Place Lounge on Charlevoix yesterday afternoon?"

"Are you following her?"

"Several patrons and one of the bartenders contacted us. They were concerned."

"Concerned? Is that what they were?" His head was throbbing.

"Shouldn't they be concerned, Mr. Ferguson? This is a woman whose baby is missing."

"If they were so concerned, why didn't they call me?"

"One of them asked Lorie if he could call you for her. Apparently, she told him not to."

He looked at the detective. "She didn't want to worry me."

The detective looked back at him. "Okay."

"You can't tell how people are going to act when something like this happens to you," he said, feeling his head dipping. Suddenly his shoulders felt very heavy and he had these pictures of Lorie in his head, at the far corner of the long black lacquered bar, eyes heavy with makeup and filled with dark feelings. Feelings he could never touch. Never once did he feel sure he knew what she was thinking. That was part of it. Part of the throb in his chest, the longing there that never left.

"No," he said, suddenly.

"What?" the detective asked, leaning forward.

"She has no history of emotional problems. My wife."

It was the fourth week, the fourth week of false leads and crying and sleeping pills and night terrors. And he had to go back to work or they wouldn't make the mortgage payment. They'd talked about Lorie returning to her part-time job at the candle store, but somebody needed to be home, to be waiting.

(Though what, really, were they waiting for? Did toddlers suddenly toddle home after twenty-seven days? That's what he could tell the cops were thinking.)

"I guess I'll call the office tomorrow," he said. "And make a plan."

"And I'll be here," she said. "You'll be there and I'll be here."

It was a terrible conversation, like a lot of those conversations couples have in dark bedrooms, late into the night, when you know the decisions you've been avoiding all day won't wait anymore.

After they talked, she took four big pills and pushed her face into her pillow.

He couldn't sleep and went into Shelby's room, which he only ever did at night. He leaned over the crib, which was too small for her but Lorie wouldn't use the bed yet, said it wasn't time, not nearly.

He put his fingers on the soft baby bumpers, festooned with bright yellow fish. He remembered telling Shelby they were goldfish, but she kept saying *Nana, nana,* which was what she called bananas.

Her hands were always covered with the pearly slime of bananas, holding on to the front of Lorie's shirt.

One night, sliding his hand under Lorie's bra clasp, between her breasts, he felt a daub of banana even there.

"It's everywhere," Lorie had sighed. "It's like she's made of bananas."

He loved that smell, and his daughter's forever-glazed hands.

At some point, remembering this, he started crying, but then he stopped and sat in the rocking chair until he fell asleep.

In part, he was relieved to go back to work, all those days with neighbors and families and friends huddling in the house, trading Internet rumors, organizing vigils and searches. But now there were fewer family members, only a couple friends who had no other place to go, and no neighbors left at all.

The woman from the corner house came late one evening and asked for her casserole dish back.

"I didn't know you'd keep it so long," she said, eyes narrowing.

She seemed to be trying to look over his shoulder, into the living room. Lorie was watching a show, loudly, about a group of blond women with tight lacquered faces and angry mouths. She watched it all the time; it seemed to be the only show on TV anymore.

"I didn't know," the woman said, taking her dish, inspecting it, "how things were going to turn out."

———

you sexy, sexy boy, Lorie's text said. *i want your hands on me. come home and handle me, rough as u like. rough me up.*

He swiveled at his desk chair hard, almost like he needed to cover the phone, cover his act of reading the text.

He left the office right away, driving as fast as he could. Telling himself that something was wrong with her. That this had to be some side effect of the pills the doctor had given her, or the way sorrow and longing could twist in her complicated little body.

But that wasn't really why he was driving so fast, or why he nearly tripped on the dangling seat belt as he hurried from the car.

Or why he felt, when he saw her lying on the bed, flat on her stomach and head turned, smiling, that he'd burst in two if he didn't have her. If he didn't have her then and there, the bed moaning beneath them and she not making a sound but, the blinds pulled down, her white teeth shining, shining from her open mouth.

It felt wrong but he wasn't sure why. He knew her, but he didn't. This was her, but a Lorie from long ago. Except different.

The reporters called all the time. And there were two that never seemed to leave their block. They had been there right at the start, but then seemed to go away, to move on to other stories.

They came back when the footage of Lorie coming out of Magnum Tattoo Parlor began appearing. Someone shot it with their cell phone.

Lorie was wearing those red cowboy boots again, and red lipstick, and she walked right up to the camera.

They ran photos of it in the newspaper with the headline: *A Mother's Grief?*

He looked at the tattoo.

The words *Mirame quemar* written in script, wrapping itself around her hip.

It covered just the spot where a stretch mark had been, the one she always covered with her fingers when she stood before him naked.

He looked at the tattoo in the dark bedroom, a band of light coming from the hallway. She turned her hip, kept turning it, spinning her torso so he could feel it, all of it.

"I needed it," she said. "I needed something. Something to put my fingers on. To remind me of me.

"Do you like it?" she asked, her breath in his ear. The ink looked like it was moving.

"I like it," he said, putting his fingers there. Feeling a little sick. He did like it. He liked it very much.

Late, late into that night, her voice shook him from a deep sleep.

"I never knew she was coming and then she was here," she was saying, her face pressed in her pillow. "And I never knew she was going and now she's gone."

He looked at her, her eyes shut, dappled with old makeup.

"But," she said, her voice grittier, strained, "she was always doing whatever she wanted."

That's what he thought she said. But she was sleeping, and didn't make any sense at all.

"You liked it until you thought about it," she said. "Until you looked close at it and then you decided you didn't want it anymore. Or didn't want to be the guy who wants it."

He was wearing the new shirt she had bought for him the day before. It was a deep, deep purple and beautiful and he felt good in it, like the unit manager who all the women in the office talked about. They talked about his shoes and he always wondered where people got shoes like that.

"No," he said. "I love it. But it's just . . . expensive."

That wasn't it, though. It didn't seem right buying things, buying anything, right now. But it was also how colorful the shirt was, the sheen on it. The bright, hard beauty of it. A shirt for going out, for nightclubs, for dancing. For those things they did when they still did things: vodka and pounding music and frenzied sex in her car.

The kind of drunken sex so messy and crazy that you were almost shy around each other after, driving home, screwed sober, feeling like you'd showed something very private and very bad.

Once, years ago, she did something to him no one had ever done and he couldn't look at her afterward at all. The next time he did something to her. For a while, it felt like it would never stop.

"I think someone should tell you about your wife," the e-mail said. That was the subject line. He didn't recognize the address, a series of letters and digits, and there was no text in the body of the e-mail. There was only a photo of a girl dancing in a bright green halter top, the ties loose and dangling.

It was Lorie, and he knew it must be an old picture. Weeks ago, the newspapers had gotten their hands on some snapshots of Lorie from her late teens, dancing on tabletops, kissing her girlfriends. Things girls did when they were drinking and someone had a camera.

In those shots, Lorie was always posing, vamping, trying to look like a model, a celebrity. It was a Lorie before he really knew her, a Lorie from what she called her "wild girl days."

But in this picture she didn't seem to be aware of the camera at all, seemed to be lost in the thrall of whatever music was playing, whatever sounds she was hearing in her crowded head. Her eyes were shut tight, her head thrown back, her neck long and brown and beautiful.

She looked happier than he had ever seen her.

A Lorie from long ago, or never.

But when he scrolled further down, he saw the halter top riding up her body, saw the pop of a hip bone. Saw the elegant script letters: *Mirame quemar.*

That night, he remembered a story she had told him long ago. It seemed impossible he'd forgotten it. Or maybe it just seemed different now, making it seem like something new. Something uncovered, an old sunken box you find in the basement smelling strong and you're afraid to open it.

It was back when they were dating, when her roommate was always around and they had no place to be alone. They would have thrilling bouts in his car, and she loved to crawl into the backseat and lie back, hoisting a leg high over the headrest and begging him for it.

It was after the first or second time, back when it was all so crazy and confusing and his head was pounding and starbursting, that Lorie curled against him and talked and talked about her life, and the time she stole four Revlon eyeslicks from CVS and how she had slept with a soggy-eared stuffed animal named Ears until she was twelve. She said she felt she could tell him anything.

Somewhere in the blur of those nights—nights when he, too, told her private things, stories about babysitter crushes and shoplifting Matchbox cars—that she told him the story.

How, when she was seven, her baby brother was born and she became so jealous.

"My mom spent all her time with him, and left me alone all day," she said. "So I hated him. Every night, I would pray that he would be taken away. That something awful would happen to him. At night, I'd sneak over to his crib and stare at him through the little bars. I think maybe I figured I could think it into happening. If I stared at him long enough and hard enough, it might happen."

He had nodded, because this is how kids could be, he guessed. He was the youngest and wondered if his older sister thought things like this about him. Once, she smashed his finger under a cymbal and said it was an accident.

But she wasn't done with her story and she snuggled closer to him and he could smell her powdery body and he thought of all its little corners and arcs, how he liked to find them with his hands, all the soft, hot places on her. Sometimes it felt like her body was never the same body, like it changed under his hands. *I'm a witch, a witch.*

"So one night," she said, her voice low and sneaky, "I was watching him through the crib bars and he was making this funny noise."

Her eyes glittered in the dark of the car.

"I leaned across, sticking my hands through the rails," she said, snaking her hand towards him. "And that's when I saw this piece of string dangling on his chin, from his pull toy. I starting pulling it, and pulling it."

He watched her tugging the imaginary string, her eyes getting bigger and bigger.

"Then he let out this gasp," she said, "and started breathing again."

She paused, her tongue clicking.

"My mom came in at just that moment. She said I saved his life," she said. "Everyone did. She bought me a new jumper and the hot-pink shoes I wanted. Everyone loved me."

A pair of headlights flashed across them and he saw her eyes, bright and brilliant.

"So no one ever knew the real story," she said. "I've never told anyone."

She smiled, pushing herself against him.

"But now I'm telling you," she said. "Now I have someone to tell."

"Mr. Ferguson, you told us, and your cell phone records confirm, that you began calling your wife at 5:50 p.m. on the day of your daughter's disappearance. Finally, you reached her at 6:45. Is that right?"

"I don't know," he said, this the eighth, ninth, tenth time they'd called him in. "You would know better than me."

"Your wife said she was at the coffee place at around five. But we tracked down a record of your wife's transaction. It was at 3:45."

"I don't know," he said, rubbing at the back of his neck, the prickling there. He realized he had no idea what they might tell him. No idea what might be coming.

"So what do you think your wife was doing for three hours?"

"Looking for this woman. Trying to find her."

"She did make some other calls during that time. Not to the police, of course. Or even you. She made a call to a man named Leonard Drake. Another one named Jason Patrini."

One sounded like an old boyfriend—Lenny someone—the other he didn't even know. He felt something hollow out inside him. He didn't know who they were even talking about anymore, but it had nothing to do with him.

The female detective walked in, giving her partner a look.

"Since she was making all these calls, we could track her movements. She went to the Harbor View Mall."

"Would you like to see her on the security camera footage there?" the female detective asked. "We have it now. Did you know she bought a tank top."

He felt nothing.

"She also went to the quickie mart. The cashier just IDed her. She used the bathroom. He said she was in there a long time and when she came out, she had changed clothing.

"Would you like to see the footage there? She looks like a million bucks."

She slid a grainy photo across the desk. A young woman in a tank top and hoodie tugged low over her brow. She was smiling.

"That's not Lorie," he said softly. She looked too young, looked like she looked when he met her, a little elfin beauty with a flat stomach and pigtails and a pierced navel. A hoop he used to tug. He'd forgotten about that. She must have let it seal over.

"I'm sure this is tough to hear, Mr. Ferguson," the male detective said. "I'm sorry."

He looked up. The detective did look very sorry.

"What did you say to them?" he asked.

Lorie was sitting in the car with him, a half block from the police station.

"I don't know if you should say anything to them anymore," he said. "I think maybe we should call a lawyer."

Lorie was looking straight ahead, at the strobing lights from the intersection. Slowly, she lifted her hand to the edges of her hair, combing them thoughtfully.

"I explained," she said, her face dark except for a swoop of blue from the car dealership sign, like a tadpole up her cheek. "I told them the truth."

"What truth?" he asked. The car felt so cold. There was a smell coming from her, of someone who hasn't eaten. A raw smell of coffee and nail polish remover.

"They don't believe anything I say anymore," she said. "I explained how I'd been to the coffee place twice that day. Once to get a juice for Shelby and then later for coffee for me. They said they'd look into it, but I could see how it was on their faces. I told them so. I know what they think of me."

She turned and looked at him, the car moving fast, sending red lights streaking up her face. It reminded him of a picture he once saw in a *National Geographic* of an Amazon woman, her face painted crimson, a wooden peg through her lip.

"Now I know what everyone thinks of me," she said, and turned away again.

It was late that night, his eyes wide open, that he asked her. She was sound asleep, but he said it.

"Who's Leonard Drake? Who's Jason whatever?"

She stirred, shifted to face him, her face flat on the sheet.

"Who's Tom Ferguson? Who is he?

"Is that what you do?" he asked, his voice rising. "Go around calling men."

It was easier to ask her this than to ask her other things. To ask her if she had shaken Shelby, if she had lied about everything. Other things.

"Yes," she said. "I call men all day long, I go to their apartments. I leave my daughter in the car, especially if it's very hot. I sneak up their apartment stairs."

She had her hand on her chest, was moving it there, watching him.

"You should feel how much I want them by the time they open their doors."

Stop, he said, without saying it.

"I have my hands on their belts before they close the door behind me. I crawl onto their laps on their dirty bachelor's sofas and do everything."

He started shaking his head, but she wouldn't stop.

"You have a baby, your body changes. You need something else. So I let them do anything. I've done everything."

Her hand was moving, touching herself. She wouldn't stop.

"That's what I do while you're at work. I wasn't calling people on Craigslist, trying to replace your lawn mower. I wasn't doing something for you, always for you."

He'd forgotten about the lawn mower, forgotten that's what she'd said she'd been doing that day. Trying to get a secondhand one after he'd gotten blood blisters on both hands using it the last time. That's what she'd said she was doing.

"No," she was saying, "I was calling men, making dates for sex. That's what I do since I've had a baby and been at home. I don't know how to do anything else. It's amazing I haven't been caught before. If only I hadn't been caught."

He covered his face with his hand. "I'm sorry. I'm sorry."

"How could you?" she said, a strangle in her throat. She was tugging all the sheet into her hands, rolling it, pulling off him, wringing it. "How could you?"

He dreamt of Shelby that night.

He dreamt he was wandering through the blue-dark of the house and when he got to Shelby's room, there was no room at all and suddenly he was outside.

The yard was frost-tipped and lonely looking and he felt a sudden sadness. He felt suddenly like he had fallen into the loneliest place in the world, and the old toolshed in the middle seemed somehow the very center of that loneliness.

When they'd bought the house, they'd nearly torn it down—everyone said they should—but they decided they liked it; the "baby barn," they'd called it, with its sloping roof and faded red paint.

But it was too small for anything but a few rakes and that push lawn mower with the sagging left wheel.

It was the only old thing about their house, the only thing left from before he was there.

By day, it was a thing he never thought about at all anymore, didn't notice it other than the smell sometimes coming off it after rain.

But in the dream it seemed a living thing, neglected and pitiful.

It came to him suddenly that the lawn mower in the shed might still be fixed, and if it were, then everything would be okay and no one would need to look for lawn mowers and the thick tug of grass under his feet would not feel so heavy and all this loneliness would end.

He put his hand on the shed's cool, crooked handle and tugged it open.

Instead of the lawn mower, he saw a small black sack on the floor of the shed.

He thought to himself in the way you do in dreams: *I must have left the cuttings in here. They must be covered with mold and that must be the smell so strong it—*

Grabbing for the sack, it slipped open, and the bag itself began to come apart in his hands.

There was the sound, the feeling of something heavy dropping to the floor of the shed.

It was too dark to see what was slipping over his feet, tickling his ankles.

Too dark to be sure, but it felt like the sweet floss of his daughter's hair.

He woke already sitting up. A voice was hissing in his head: *Will you look in the shed? Will you?*

And that was when he remembered there was no shed in the backyard anymore. They'd torn it down when Lorie was pregnant because she said the smell of rot was giving her headaches, making her sick.

The next day the front page of the paper had a series of articles marking the two-month anniversary of Shelby's disappearance.

They had the picture of Lorie under the headline: *What Does She Know?* There was a picture of him, head down, walking from the police station yesterday. The caption read: "More unanswered questions."

He couldn't read any of it, and when his mother called he didn't pick up.

All day at work, he couldn't concentrate. He felt everyone looking at him.

When his boss came to his desk, he could feel the careful way he was being talked to.

"Tom, if you want to leave early," he said, "that's fine."

Several times he caught the administrative assistant staring at his screen saver, the snapshot of Lorie with ten-month-old Shelby in her Halloween costume, a black spider with soft spider legs.

Finally he did leave, at three o'clock.

Lorie wasn't in the house and he was standing at the kitchen sink, drinking a glass of water, when he saw her through the window.

Though it was barely seventy degrees, she was lying on one of the summer loungers.

Headphones on, she was in a bright orange bikini with gold hoops in the straps and on either hip.

She had pushed the purple playhouse against the back fence, where it tilted under the elm tree.

He had never seen the bikini before, but he recognized the sunglasses, large ones with white frames she had bought on a trip Mexico she had taken with an old girlfriend right before she got pregnant.

Gleaming in the center of her slicked torso was a gold belly ring.

She was smiling, singing along to whatever music was playing in her head.

That night he couldn't bring himself to go to bed. He watched TV for hours without watching any of it. He drank four beers in a row, which he had not done since he was twenty years old.

Finally, the beer pulled on him, and the Benadryl he took after, and he found himself sinking at last onto their mattress.

At some point in the middle of the night, there was a stirring next to him, her body shifting hard. It felt like something was happening.

"Kirsten," she mumbled.

"What?" he asked. "What?"

Suddenly she half sat up, her elbows beneath her, looking straight ahead.

"Her daughter's name was Kirsten," she said, her voice soft and tentative. "I just remembered. Once, when we were talking, she said her daughter's name was Kirsten. Because she liked how it sounded with Krusie."

He felt something loosen inside him, then tighten again. What was this?

"Her last name was Krusie with a *K*," she said, her face growing more animated, her voice more urgent. "I don't know how it was spelled, but it was with a *K*. I can't believe I just remembered. It was a long time ago. She said she liked the two *K*s. Because she was two *K*s. Katie Krusie. That's her name."

He looked at her and didn't say anything.

"Katie Krusie," she said. "The woman at the coffee place. That's her name."

He couldn't seem to speak or even move.

"Are you going to call?" she said. "The police?"

He found he couldn't move. He was afraid somehow. So afraid he couldn't breathe.

She looked at him, paused, and then reached across him, grabbing for the phone herself.

As she talked to the police, told them, her voice now clear and firm, what she'd remembered, as she told them she would come to the station, would leave in five minutes, he watched her, his hand over his own heart, feeling it beating so hard it hurt.

———

"We believe we have located the Krusie woman," the female detective said. "We have officers heading there now."

He looked at both of them. He could feel Lorie beside him, breathing hard. It had been less than a day since Lorie first called.

"What are you saying?" he said, or tried to. No words came out.

Katie-Ann Krusie had no children, but told people she did, all the time. After a long history of emotional problems, she had spent a fourteen-month stint at the state hospital following a miscarriage.

For the past eight weeks she had been living in a rental in Torring, forty miles away with a little blond girl she called Kirsten.

After the police released a photo of Katie-Ann Krusie on Amber Alert, a woman who worked at a coffee chain in Torring recognized her as a regular customer, always ordering extra milk for her babies.

"She sure sounded like she loved her kids," the woman said. "Just talking about them made her so happy."

The first time he saw Shelby again, he couldn't speak at all.

She was wearing a shirt he'd never seen and shoes that didn't fit and she was holding a juice box the policeman had given her.

She watched him as he ran down the hall toward her.

There was something in her face that he had never seen before, knew hadn't been there before, and he knew in an instant he had to do everything he could to make it gone.

That was all he would do, if it took him the rest of his life to do it.

The next morning, after calling everyone, one by one, he walked into the kitchen to see Lorie sitting next to Shelby, who was eating apple slices, her pinkie finger curled out in that way she had.

He sat and watched her and Shelby asked him why he was shaking and he said because he was glad to see her.

It was hard to leave the room, even to answer the door when his mother and sister came, when everyone started coming.

Three nights later, at the big family dinner, the Welcome Home dinner for Shelby, Lorie drank a lot of wine and who could blame her, everyone was saying.

He couldn't either, and he watched her.

As the evening carried on, as his mother brought out an ice cream cake for Shelby, as everyone huddled around Shelby, who seemed confused and shy at first and slowly burst into something beautiful that made him want to cry again—as all these things were occurring—he had one eye on Lorie, her quiet, still face. On the smile there, which never grew or receded, even when she held Shelby in her lap, Shelby nuzzling her mother's wine-flushed neck.

At one point he found her standing in the kitchen and staring into the sink; it seemed to him she was staring down into the drain.

It was very late, or even early, and Lorie wasn't there.

He thought she had gotten sick from all the wine, but she wasn't in the bathroom either.

Something was turning in him, uncomfortably, as he walked into Shelby's room.

He saw her back, naked and white from the moonlight. The plum-colored underpants she'd slept in.

She was standing over Shelby's crib, looking down.

He felt something in his chest move.

Then, slowly, she kneeled, peeking through the crib rails, looking at Shelby.

It looked like she was waiting for something.

For a long time he stood there, five feet from the doorway, watching her watching their sleeping baby.

He listened close for his daughter's high breaths, the stop and start of them.

He couldn't see his wife's face, only that long white back of hers, the notches of her spine. *Mirame quemar* etched on her hip.

He watched her watching his daughter, and knew he could not ever leave this room. That he would have to be here forever now, on guard. There was no going back to bed.

Cecelia Holland

Cecelia Holland is one of the world's most highly acclaimed and respected historical novelists, ranked by many alongside other giants in that field such as Mary Renault and Larry McMurtry. Over the span of her thirty-year career, she's written more than thirty historical novels, including *The Firedrake, Rakóssy, Two Ravens, Ghost on the Steppe, The Death of Attila, Hammer for Princes, The King's Road, Pillar of the Sky, The Lords of Vaumartin, Pacific Street, The Sea Beggars, The Earl, The Kings in Winter, The Belt of Gold*, and more than a dozen others. She also wrote the well-known science fiction novel *Floating Worlds*, which was nominated for a Locus Award in 1975, and of late has been working on a series of fantasy novels, including *The Soul Thief, The Witches' Kitchen, The Serpent Dreamer, Varanger*, and *The King's Witch*. Her most recent books are the novels *The High City, Kings of the North*, and *The Secret Eleanor*.

In the high drama that follows, she introduces us to the ultimate dysfunctional family, whose ruthless, clashing ambitions threw England into bloody civil war again and again over many long years: King Henry II, his queen, Eleanor of Aquitaine, and their eight squabbling children. All deadly as cobras. Even the littlest one.

NORA'S SONG

Nora looked quickly around, saw no one was watching, and slipped away between the trees and down the bank to the little stream. She knew there would be no frogs to hunt; her brother had told her that when the trees had no leaves, the streams had no frogs. But the water glittered over bright stones and she saw tracks printed into the damp sand. She squatted down to pick a shiny bit from the stream. It wouldn't be pretty when it dried out. Behind her, her little sister Johanna slid down the bank in a rush.

"Nora! What do you have?"

She held out the pebble to her sister and went on a little way along the trickle of water. Those tracks were bird feet, like crosses in the damp sand. She squatted down again, to poke at the rocks, and then saw, in the yellow gritty stream bank, like a little round doorway, a hole.

She brushed aside a veil of hairy roots, trying to see in; did something live there? She could reach her hand in to find out, and in a quick tumble of her thoughts she imagined something furry, something furry with teeth, the teeth snapping on her hand, and tucked her fist against her skirt.

From up past the trees, a voice called, "Nora?"

That was her new nurse. She paid no attention, looking for a stick to probe the hole with; Johanna, beside her, went softly, "Ooooh," and on all fours leaned toward the burrow. Her skirt was soaked from the stream.

"Nora!" Another voice.

She leapt up. "Richard," she said, and scrambled up the bank, nearly losing a shoe. On the grassy edge, she pulled the shoe back on, turned and helped Johanna up behind her, and ran out through the bare trees, onto the broad open ground.

Her brother was striding toward her, smiling, his arms out, and she ran to him. She had not seen him since Christmas, the last time they had all been together. He was twelve years old, a lot older than she was, almost grown up. He bundled her into his arms and hugged her. He smelled like horses. Johanna came whooping up and he hugged her too. The two nurses, red in the face, were panting along behind them, their skirts clutched up in their hands. Richard straightened, his blue eyes blazing, and pointed across the field.

"See? Where Mother comes."

Nora shaded her eyes, looking out across the broad field. At first she saw only the crowded people, stirring and swaying all around the edges of the field, but then a murmur swept through them, and on all sides rose into a roar. Far down there, a horse loped up onto the field and stopped, and the rider raised one hand in salute.

"Mama!" Johanna cried, and clapped.

Now the whole crowd was yelling and cheering, and, on her dark grey horse, Nora's Mama was cantering along the sideline, toward the wooden stand under the plane trees, where they would all sit. Nora swelled, full to bursting; she yelled, "Hooray! Hooray, Mama!"

Up there, by the stand, a dozen men on foot went forward to meet the woman on the horse. She wheeled in among them, cast her reins down, and dismounted. Swiftly she climbed onto the platform, where two chairs waited, and stood there, and lifted her arm, turning slowly from one side to the other to greet the cheering crowd. She stood straight as a tree, her skirts furling around her.

Above the stand, suddenly, her pennant flapped open like a great wing, the Eagle of Aquitaine, and the thunderous shouting doubled.

"Eleanor! Eleanor!"

She gave one last wave to the crowd, but she had seen her children running toward her, and all her interest turned to them. She stooped, holding her arms out toward them, and Richard scooped Johanna into his arms and ran toward the platform. Nora went up the steps at the side. Coming to the front, Richard set Johanna at their mother's feet.

Their mother's hands fell on them. Nora buried her face in the Queen's skirts.

"Mama."

"Ah." Their mother sat down, holding Johanna slightly away from her;

she slid her free arm around Nora's waist. "Ah, my dear ones. How I've missed you." She kissed them both rapidly, several times. "Johanna, you're drenched. This won't do." She beckoned, and Johanna's nurse came running. Johanna squealed but was taken.

Still holding Nora against her, Eleanor leaned forward and leveled her gaze on Richard, leaning with his arms folded on the edge of the platform in front of her.

"Well, my son, are you excited?"

He pushed away from the platform, standing taller, his face flaming, his fair hair a wild tangle from the wind. "Mother, I can't wait! When will Papa get here?"

Nora leaned on her mother. She loved Richard too, but she wished her mother would pay more heed to her. Her mother was beautiful, even though she was really old. She wore no coif, only a heavy gold ring upon her sleek red hair. Nora's hair was like old dead grass. She would never be beautiful. The Queen's arm tightened around her, but she was still tilted forward toward Richard, fixed utterly on Richard.

"He's coming. You should get ready for the ceremony." She touched the front of his coat, lifted her hand to his cheek. "Comb your hair, anyway."

He jiggled up and down, vivid. "I can't wait. I can't wait. I'm going to be Duke of Aquitaine!"

The Queen laughed. A horn blew, down the pitch. "See, now it begins. Go find your coat." She turned, beckoned to a page. "Attend the Lord Richard. Nora, now . . ." She nudged Nora back a step so that she could run her gaze over her from head to toe. Her lips curved upward and her eyes glinted. "What have you been doing, rolling in the grass? You're my big girl now; you have to be presentable."

"Mama." Nora didn't want to be the big girl. The idea reminded her that Mattie was gone, the real big girl. But she loved having her mother's attention, she cast wildly around for something to say to keep it. "Does that mean I can't play anymore?"

Eleanor laughed and hugged her again. "You will always be able to play, my girl. Just different games." Her lips brushed Nora's forehead. Nora realized she had said the right thing. Then Eleanor was turning away.

"See, here your father comes."

A ripple of excitement rose through the crowd like the wind in a dry field, turned to a rumble, and erupted into a thunderous cheer. Down the pitch came a column of riders. Nora straightened, clapping her hands together, and drew in a deep breath and held it. In the center of the horsemen, her father rode along, wearing neither crown nor royal robes, and yet it seemed that everything bowed and bent around him, as if nobody else mattered but him.

"Papa."

"Yes," Eleanor said, under her breath. "The kingly Papa." She drew her arm from Nora and sat straighter on her chair.

Nora drew back; if she got behind them, out of sight, they might forget her, and she could stay. Richard had not gone away, either, she saw, but lingered at the front of the royal stand. Her father rode up and swung directly from his saddle to the platform. He was smiling, his eyes narrow, his clothes rumpled, his beard and hair shaggy. He seemed to her like the king of the greenwood, wild and fierce, wreathed in leaves and bark. All along this side of the field, on either side of the booth, his knights rode up in a single rank, stirrup to stirrup, facing the French across the field. The king stood, throwing a quick glance that way, and then lowered his gaze to Richard, standing stiff and tall before him.

"Well, sirrah," their father said, "are you ready to shiver a lance here?"

"Oh, Papa!" Richard bounced up and down. "Can I?"

Their father barked a laugh at him, looking down on him from the height of the booth. "Not until you can pay your own ransoms when you lose."

Richard flushed pink, like a girl. "I won't lose!"

"No, of course not." The King waved him off. "Nobody ever thinks he'll lose, sirrah." He laughed again, scornful, turning away. "When you're older."

Nora bit her lip. It was mean to talk to Richard that way, and her brother drooped, kicked the ground, and then followed the page down the field. Suddenly he was just a boy again. Nora crouched down behind her mother's skirts, hoping her father did not notice her. He settled himself in the chair beside the Queen's, stretched his legs out, and for the first time turned toward Eleanor.

"You look amazingly well, considering. I'm surprised your old bones made it all the way from Poitiers."

"I would not miss this," she said. "And it's a pleasant enough ride." They didn't touch, they didn't give each other kisses, and Nora felt a little stir of worry. Her nurse had come up to the edge of the platform and Nora shrank deeper into Eleanor's shadow. Eleanor paid the king a long stare. Her attention drifted toward his front.

"Eggs for breakfast? Or was that last night's supper?"

Startled, Nora craned up a little to peer at him: his clothes were messy but she saw no yellow egg. Her father was glaring back at her mother, his face flattened with temper. He did not look down at his coat. "What a prissy old woman you are."

Nora ran her tongue over her lower lip. Her insides felt full of prickers and burrs. Her mother's hand lay on her thigh, and Nora saw how her mother was smoothing her skirt, over and over, with hard, swift, clawing fingers.

Her nurse said, "Lady Nora, come along now."

"You didn't bring your truelove," the Queen said.

The King leaned toward her a little, as if he would leap on her, pound her, maybe, with his fist. "She's afraid of you. She won't come anywhere near you."

Eleanor laughed. She was not afraid of him. Nora wondered what that was about; wasn't her mother the King's truelove? She pretended not to see her nurse beckoning her.

"Nora, come now!" the nurse said, loudly.

That caught her mother's attention, and she swung around, saw Nora there, and said, "Go on, my girl. Go get ready." Her hand dropped lightly to Nora's shoulder. "Do as you're bid, please." Nora slid off the edge of the platform and went away to be dressed and primped.

Her old nurse had gone with Mattie when Nora's big sister went to marry the Duke of Germany. Now she had this new nurse, who couldn't brush hair without hurting. They had already laced Johanna into a fresh gown, and braided her hair, and the others were waiting outside the little tent. Nora kept thinking of Mattie, who had told her stories, and sung to her when she had nightmares. Now they were all walking out onto the field for the ceremony, her brothers first, and then her and Johanna.

Johanna slipped her hand into Nora's, and Nora squeezed her fingers tight. All these people made her feel small. Out in the middle of the field everybody stood in rows, as if they were in church, and the ordinary people were all gathered closely around, to hear what went on. On either side banners hung, and a herald stood in front of them all, watching the children approach, his long shiny horn tipped down.

On big chairs in the very middle sat her father and mother and, beside them, a pale, weary-looking man in a blue velvet gown. He had a little stool for his feet. She knew that was the King of France. She and her sister and brothers went up before them, side by side, and the herald said their names, and as one they bowed, first to their parents and then to the French king.

There were only five of them now, with Mattie gone, and their baby brother still in the monastery. Henry was oldest. They called him Boy Henry because Papa's name also was Henry. Then there was Richard, and then Geoffrey. Mattie would have been between Boy Henry and Richard. After Geoffrey was Nora, and Johanna, and, back with the monks, baby John. The crowd whooped and yelled at them, and Richard suddenly raised his arm up over his head like an answer.

Then they were all shuffled around into the crowd behind their parents, where they stood in line again. The heralds were yelling in Latin. Johanna leaned on Nora's side. "I'm hungry."

Two steps in front of them on her chair, Eleanor glanced over her shoulder, and Nora whispered, "Ssssh." All the people around them were men, but behind the King of France a girl stood, who looked a little older than Nora, and now Nora caught her looking back. Nora smiled, uncertain, but the other girl only lowered her eyes.

A blast of the horn lifted her half off the ground. Johanna clutched her hand. One of Papa's men came up and began to read from a scroll, Latin again, simpler than the Latin the monks had taught her. What he read was all about Boy Henry, how noble, how good, and, at a signal, her oldest brother went up before the two kings and the Queen. He was tall and thin, with many freckles, his face sunburnt. Nora liked the dark green of the coat he wore. He knelt before his father and the French king, and the heralds spoke and the kings spoke.

They were making Boy Henry a King too. He would be King of England now, just as Papa was. In her mind suddenly she saw both Henrys trying to jam together into one chair, with one crown wrapped around their two heads, and she laughed. Her mother looked over her shoulder again, her eyes sharp and her dark brows drawn into a frown.

Johanna was shuffling from one foot to the other. Louder than before, she said, "I'm hungry."

"Sssh!"

Boy Henry got up from his knees, bowed, and came back around among the children. The herald said Richard's name and he sprang forward. They were proclaiming him Duke of Aquitaine. He would marry the daughter of the French king, Alais. Nora's eyes turned again toward the strange girl among the French. That was Alais. She had long brown hair and a sharp little nose; she was staring intently at Richard. Nora wondered what it felt like, looking for the first time on the man you knew you would marry. She imagined Alais kissing Richard and made a face.

In front of her, sitting stiff on her chair, the Queen pulled her mouth down at the corners. Her mother didn't like this, either.

Until she was old enough to marry Richard, Alais would live with them, his family. Nora felt a stir of unease: here was Alais come into a strange place, as Mattie was gone off into a strange place, and they would never see her again. She remembered how Mattie had cried when they told her. But Mama, he's so *old*. Nora pressed her lips together, her eyes stinging.

Not to her. This wouldn't happen to her. She wouldn't be sent away. Given away. She wanted something else, but she didn't know what. She had thought of being a nun, but there was so little to do.

Richard knelt and put his hands between the long, bony hands of the King of France, and rose, his head tipped forward as if he already wore a coronet. He was smiling wide as the sun. He moved back to the family and the herald spoke Geoffrey's name, who was now to be Duke of Brittany, and marry some other stranger.

Nora hunched her shoulders. This glory would never come to her, she would get nothing, just stand and watch. She glanced again at the Princess Alais and saw her looking down at her hands, sad.

Johanna suddenly yawned, pulled her hand out of Nora's, and sat down.

Now up before them all came somebody else, his hands wide, and a big, strong voice said, "My lord of England, as we have agreed, I ask you now to receive the Archbishop of Canterbury, and let you be restored to friendship, end the quarrel between you, for the good of both our kingdoms, and Holy Mother Church."

The crowd around them gave up a sudden yell, and a man came up the field toward the kings. He wore a long black cloak over a white habit with a cross hanging on his chest. The stick in his hand had a swirly top. A great cry went up from the people around them, excited. Behind her, somebody murmured, "Becket again. The man won't go away."

She knew this name, but she could not remember who Becket was. He paced up toward them, a long, gaunt man, his clothes shabby. He looked like an ordinary man but he walked like a lord. Everybody watched him. As he came up before her father, the crowd's rumbling and stirring died away into a breathless hush. In front of the King, the gaunt man knelt, set his stick down, and then lay on the ground, spreading himself like a mat upon the floor. Nora shifted a little so she could see him through the space between her mother and her father. The crowd drew in closer, leaning out to see.

"My gracious lord," he said in a churchy voice, "I beg your forgiveness for all my errors. Never was a prince more faithful than you, and never a subject more faithless than I, and I am come asking pardon not from hopes of my virtue but of yours."

Her father stood up. He looked suddenly very happy, his face flushed, his eyes bright. Face to the ground, the gaunt man spoke on, humble, beseeching, and the King went down toward him, reaching out his hands to lift him up.

Then Becket said, "I submit myself to you, my lord, henceforth and forever, in all things, save the honor of God."

The Queen's head snapped up. Behind Nora somebody gasped, and somebody else muttered, "Damn fool." In front of them all, halfway to Becket, his hands out, Papa stopped. A kind of pulse went through the crowd.

The King said sharply, "What is this?"

Becket was rising. Dirt smeared his robe where his knees had pressed the ground. He stood straight, his head back. "I cannot give up the rights of God, my lord, but in everything else—"

Her Papa lunged at him. "This is not what I agreed to."

Becket held his ground, tall as a steeple, as if he had God on his shoulder, and proclaimed again, "I must champion the honor of the Lord of Heaven and earth."

"*I* am your Lord!" The King wasn't happy anymore. His voice boomed across the field. Nobody else moved or spoke. He took a step toward Becket, and his fist clenched. "The kingdom is *mine*. No other authority shall rule there! God or no, kneel, Thomas, give yourself wholly to me, or go away a ruined man!"

Louis was scurrying down from the dais toward them, his frantic murmuring unheeded. Becket stood immobile. "I am consecrated to God. I cannot wash away that duty."

Nora's father roared, "I am King, and no other, you toad, you jackass, no other than me! You owe everything to me! *Me!*"

"Papa! My lord—" Boy Henry started forward and their mother reached out and grabbed his arm and held him still. From the crowd, other voices rose. Nora stooped and tried to make Johanna stand up.

"I won't be disparaged! Honor *me,* and me alone!" Her father's voice was like a blaring horn, and the crowd fell quiet again. The King of France put one hand on her Papa's arm and mouthed something, and Papa wheeled around and cast off his touch.

"Henceforth, whatever comes that he chooses not to abide, he will call it the Honor of God. You must see this! He has given up nothing; he will pay me no respect—not even the respect of a swine for the swineherd!"

The crowd gave a yell. A voice called, "God bless the King!" Nora looked around, uneasy. The people behind her were shuffling around, drawing back, like running away slowly. Eleanor was still holding fast to Boy Henry, but now he whimpered under his breath. Richard was stiff, his whole body tipped forward, his jaw jutting like a fish's. The French king had Becket by the sleeve, was drawing him off, talking urgently into his ear. Becket's gaze never left Nora's father. His voice rang out like the archangel's trumpet.

"I am bound to the Honor of God!"

In the middle of them all, Nora's father flung up his arms as if he would take flight; he stamped his foot as if he would split the earth, and shouted, "Get him out of here before I kill him! God's Honor! God's round white backside! Get him away, get him gone!"

His rage blew back the crowd. In a sudden rush of feet, the French king and his guards and attendants bundled Thomas away. Nora's father was roaring again, oaths and threats, his arms pumping, his face red as raw meat. Boy Henry burst out of Eleanor's grasp and charged him.

"My lord—"

The King spun around toward him, his arm outstretched, and knocked him down with the back of his hand. "Stay out of this!"

Nora jumped. Even before Richard and Geoffrey started forward, Eleanor was moving; she reached Boy Henry in a few strides, and as he leapt to his feet, she hurried him off. A crowd of her retainers bustled after her.

Nora stood fast. She realized that she was holding her breath. Johanna had finally gotten up and wrapped her arms around Nora's waist, and Nora put her arms around her sister. Geoffrey was running after the Queen;

Richard paused, his hands at his sides, watching the King's temper blaze. He pivoted and ran off after his mother. Nora gasped. She and Johanna were alone, in the middle of the field, the crowd far off.

The King saw them. He quieted. He looked around, saw no one else, and stalked toward them.

"Go on—run! Everybody else is abandoning me. Run! Are you stupid?"

Johanna shrank around behind Nora, who stood straight and tucked her hands behind her, the way she stood when priests talked to her. "No, Papa."

His face was red as meat. Fine sweat stood on his forehead. His breath almost made her gag. He looked her over and said, "Here to scold me, then, like your rotten mother?"

"No, Papa," she said, surprised. "You are the King."

He twitched. The high color left his face like a tide. His voice smoothed out, slower. He said, "Well, one of you is true, at least." He turned and walked off, and as he went, he lifted one arm. From all sides his men came running. One led Papa's big black horse and he mounted. Above all the men on foot surrounding him, he left the field. After he was gone, Richard trotted up across the grass to gather in Nora and Johanna.

"Why can't I—"

"Because I know you," Richard said. "If I let you run around, you'll get in trouble." He lifted her up into the cart, where already Johanna and the French girl sat. Nora plunked down, angry; they were only going up the hill. He could have let her ride his horse. With a crack of the whip, the cart began to roll, and she leaned back against the side and stared away.

Beside Nora, Alais said, suddenly, in French, "I know who you are."

Nora faced her, startled. "I know who you are too," she said.

"Your name is Eleonora and you're the second sister. I can speak French and Latin and I can read. Can you read?"

Nora said, "Yes. They make me read all the time."

Alais gave a glance over her shoulder; their attendants were walking along behind the cart, but nobody close enough to hear. Johanna was standing up in the back corner, throwing bits of straw over the side and leaning out to see where they fell. Alais said quietly, "We should be friends, because we're going to be sisters and we're almost the same age." Her gaze ran thoughtfully over Nora from head to toe, which made Nora uncomfortable; she squirmed. She thought briefly, angrily, of this girl taking Mattie's place. Alais said, "I'll be nice to you if you're nice to me."

Nora said, "All right. I—"

"But I go first, I think, because I am older."

Nora stiffened and then jumped as a cheer erupted around her. The cart was rolling up the street toward the castle on the hill, and all along the way, crowds of people stood screaming and calling. Not for her, not for Alais; it was Richard's name they shouted, over and over. Richard rode along before them, bareheaded, paying no heed to the cheers.

Alais turned to her again. "Where do you live?"

Nora said, "Well, sometimes in Poitiers, but—"

"My father says your father has everything, money and jewels and silks and sunlight, but all we have in France is piety and kindness."

Nora started. "We are kind." But she was pleased that Alais saw how great her father was. "And pious too."

The sharp little face of the French princess turned away, drawn, and for the first time her voice was uncertain. "I hope so."

Nora's heart thumped, unsteady with sympathy. Johanna was scrabbling around on the floor of the cart for more things to cast out, and Nora found a little cluster of pebbles in the corner and held them out to her. On Nora's other side, Alais was staring down at her hands now, her shoulders round, and Nora wondered if she were about to cry. She might cry, if this happened to her.

She edged closer, until she brushed against the other girl. Alais jerked her head up, her eyes wide, startled. Nora smiled at her, and between them their hands crept together and entwined.

They did not go all the way up to the castle. The cheering crowd saw them along the street and onto a pavement, with a church on one side, where the cart turned in the opposite direction from the church and went down another street and through a wooden gate. Over them now a house loomed, with wooden walls, two rows of windows, a heavy overhang of roof. Here the cart stopped and they all got out. Richard herded them along through the wide front door.

"Mama is upstairs," he said.

They had come into a dark hall, full of servants and baggage. A servant led Alais away. Nora climbed the steep, uneven stairs, tugging Johanna along by the hand. Johanna was still hungry and said so every step. At the top of the stairs was one room on one side and another on the other side, and Nora heard her mother's voice.

"Not yet," the Queen was saying; Nora went into the big room and saw her mother and Boy Henry at the far side; the Queen had her hand on his arm. "The time is not yet. Don't be precipitous. We must seem to be loyal." She saw the girls, and a smile twitched over her face like a mask. "Come, girls!" But her hand on Boy Henry's arm gave him a push away. "Go," she said to him. "He will send for you; better you not be here. Take Geoffrey with you." Boy Henry turned on his heel and went out.

Nora wondered what "precipitous" meant; briefly she imagined a cliff, and people falling off. She went up to her mother and Eleanor hugged her.

"I'm sorry," her mama said. "I'm sorry about your father."

"Mama."

"Don't be afraid of him." The Queen took Johanna's hands and spoke from one to the other. "I'll protect you."

"I'm not—"

Her mother's gaze lifted, aimed over Nora's head. "What is it?"

"The King wants to see me," Richard said, behind Nora. She felt his hand drop onto her shoulder.

"Just you?"

"No, Boy and Geoffrey too. Where are they?"

Nora's mother shrugged, her whole body moving, shoulders, head, hands. "I have no notion," she said. "You should go, though."

"Yes, Mama." Richard squeezed Nora's shoulder and he went away.

"Very well." Eleanor sat back, still holding Johanna by one hand. "Now, my girls." Nora frowned, puzzled; her mother did know where her other brothers were, she had just sent them out. Her mother turned to her again. "Don't be afraid."

"Mama, I'm not afraid." But then she thought, somehow, that her mother wanted her to be.

Johanna was already asleep, curled heavy against Nora's back. Nora cradled her head on her arm, not sleepy at all. She was thinking about the day, about her splendid father and her beautiful mother, and how her family ruled everything, and she was one of them. She imagined herself on a big horse, galloping, and everybody cheering her name. Carrying a lance with a pennon on the tip, and fighting for the glory of something. Or to save somebody. Something proud, but virtuous. She caught herself rocking back and forth on her imaginary horse.

A candle at the far end cast a sort of twilight through the long narrow room; she could see the planks of the wall opposite and hear the rumbling snore of the woman asleep by the door. The other servants had gone down to the hall. She wondered what happened there that they all wanted to go. Then, to her surprise, someone hurried through the dark and knelt by her bed.

"Nora?"

It was Alais. Nora pushed herself up, startled, but even as she moved, Alais was crawling into the bed.

"Let me in, please. Please, Nora. They made me sleep alone."

She could not move to make room because of Johanna, but she said anyway, "All right." She didn't like sleeping alone, either: it got cold, sometimes, and lonely. She pulled the cover back, and Alais crept into the space beside her.

"This is an ugly place. I thought you all lived in beautiful places."

Nora said, "We don't live here." She snuggled back against Johanna, and without waking, her little sister murmured and shifted away, giving her more room, but Alais was still jammed up against her. She could smell the French girl's breath, meaty and sour. Rigid, she lay there wide awake. She would never fall asleep now.

Alais snuggled into the mattress; the ropes underneath creaked. In a whisper she said, "Do you have boobies yet?"

Nora twitched. "What?" She didn't know what Alais meant.

"Bumps, silly." Alais shifted, pulling on the covers, banging into her. "Breastses. Like this." Her hand closed on Nora's wrist and she pulled, brushing Nora's hand against Alais' chest. For an instant, Nora felt a soft roundness under her fingers.

"No." She tried to draw her hand out of Alais' grip, but Alais had her fast.

"You're just a baby."

Nora got her hand free, and squirmed fiercely against Johanna, trying to get more room. "I'm a big girl!" *Johanna* was the baby. She struggled to get back the feeling of galloping on the big horse, of glory, pride, and greatness. She blurted out, "Someday I'm going to be king."

Alais hooted. "Girls aren't kings, silly! Girls are only women."

"I mean, like my mother. My mother is as high as a king."

"Your mother is wicked."

Nora pushed away, angry. "My mother is *not*—"

"Sssh. You'll wake everybody up. I'm sorry. I'm sorry. It's just everybody says so. I didn't mean it. You aren't a baby." Alais touched her, pleading. "Are you still my friend?"

Nora thought the whole matter of being friends to be harder than she had expected. Surreptitiously, she pressed her palm against her own bony chest.

Alais snuggled in beside her. "If we're to be friends, we have to stay close together. Where are we going next?"

Nora pulled the cover around her, the thickness of cloth between her and Alais. "I hope to Poitiers, with Mama. I hope I will go there, the happiest court in the whole world." In a flash of temper she blurted out, "Any place would be better than Fontrevault. My knees are so sore."

Alais laughed. "A convent? They put me in convents. They even made me wear nun clothes."

Nora said, "Oh, I hate that! They're so scratchy."

"And they smell."

"*Nuns* smell," Nora said. She remembered something her mother said. "Like old eggs."

Alais giggled. "You're funny, Nora. I like you a lot."

"Well, you have to like my mother too, if you want to go to Poitiers."

Again, Alais' hand came up and touched Nora, stroking her. "I will. I promise."

Nora cradled her head on her arm, pleased, and drowsy. Maybe Alais was not so bad after all. She was a helpless maiden, and Nora could defend her, like a real knight. Her eyelids drooped; for an instant, before she fell asleep, she felt the horse under her again, galloping.

Nora had saved bread crumbs from her breakfast; she was scattering them on the windowsill when the nurse called. She kept on scattering. The little birds were hungry in the winter. The nurse grabbed her by the arm and towed her away.

"Come here when I call you!" The nurse briskly stuffed her headfirst into a gown. Nora struggled up through the mass of cloth until she got her head out. "Now sit down so I can brush your hair."

Nora sat; she looked toward the window again, and the nurse pinched her arm. "Sit still!"

She bit her lips together, angry and sad. She wished the nurse off to Germany. Hunched on the stool, she tried to see the window through the corner of her eye.

The brush dragged through her hair. "How do you get your hair so snarled?"

"Ooow!" Nora twisted away from the pull of the brush, and the nurse wrestled her back onto the stool.

"Sit! This child is a devil." The brush smacked her hard on the shoulder. "Wait until we get you back to the convent, little devil."

Nora stiffened all over. On the next stool, Alais turned suddenly toward her, wide-eyed. Nora slid off the stool.

"I'm going to find my Mama!" She started toward the door. The nurse snatched at her and she sidestepped out of reach and moved faster.

"Come back here!"

"I'm going to find my Mama," Nora said, and gave the nurse a hard look, and pulled the door open.

"Wait for me," said Alais.

The servingwomen came after them; Nora went on down the stairs, hurrying, just out of reach. She hoped her Mama was down in the hall. On the stairs, she slipped by some servants coming up from below and they got in the nurses' way and held them back. Alais was right behind her, wild-eyed.

"Is this all right? Nora?"

"Come on." Gratefully she saw that the hall was full of people; that meant her mother was there, and she went in past men in long stately robes, standing around waiting, and pushed in past them all the way up to the front.

There her mother sat, and Richard also, standing beside her; the Queen was reading a letter. A strange man stood humbly before her, his hands clasped, while she read. Nora went by him.

"Mama."

Eleanor lifted her head, her brows arched. "What are you doing here?" She looked past Nora and Alais, into the crowd, brought her gaze back to Nora, and said, "Come sit down and wait; I'm busy." She went back to the letter in her hand. Richard gave Nora a quick, cheerful grin. She went on

past him, behind her Mama's chair, and turned toward the room. The
nurses were squeezing in past the crowd of courtiers, but they could not
reach her now. Alais leaned against her, pale, her eyes blinking.

In front of them, her back to them, Eleanor in her heavy chair laid the
letter aside. "I'll give it thought."

"Your Grace." The humble man bowed and backed away. Another, in a
red coat, stepped forward, a letter in his hand. Reaching for it, the Queen
glanced at Richard beside her.

"Why did your father want to see you last night?"

Alais whispered, "What are you going to do?" Nora bumped her with
her elbow; she wanted to listen to her brother.

Richard was saying, "He asked me where Boy was." He shifted his
weight from foot to foot. "He was drunk."

The Queen was reading the new letter. She turned toward the table on
her other hand, picked up a quill, and dipped it into the pot of ink. "You
should sign this also, since you are Duke now."

At that, Richard puffed up, making himself bigger, and his shoulders
straightened. The Queen turned toward Nora.

"What is this now?"

"Mama." Nora went up closer to the Queen. "Where are we going? After
here."

Her mother's green eyes regarded her; a little smile curved her lips.
"Well, to Poitiers, I thought."

"I want to go to Poitiers."

"Well, of course," her Mama said.

"And Alais too?"

The Queen's eyes shifted toward Alais, back by the wall. The smile flattened out. "Yes, of course. Good day, Princess Alais."

"Good day, your Grace." Alais dipped into a little bow. "Thank you, your
Grace." She turned a bright happy look at Nora, who cast her a broad look of
triumph. She looked up at her mother, glad of her, who could do anything.

"You said you'd protect us, remember?"

The Queen's smile widened, and her head tipped slightly to one side.
"Yes, of course. I'm your mother."

"And Alais too?"

Now the Queen actually laughed. "Nora, you will be dangerous when
you're older. Yes, Alais too, of course."

On the other side of the chair, Richard straightened from writing, and Eleanor took the letter from him and the quill also. Nora lingered where she was, in the middle of everything, wanting her mother to notice her again. Richard said, "If I'm really Duke, do I give orders?"

The Queen's smile returned; she looked at him the way she looked at no one else. "Of course. Since you are Duke now." She seemed to be about to laugh again; Nora wondered what her Mama thought was funny. Eleanor laid the letter on the table and the quill jigged busily across it.

"I want to be knighted," her brother said. "And I want a new sword."

"As you will, your Grace," her mother said, still with that little laugh in her voice, and gave him a slow nod of her head, like bowing. She handed the letter back to the man in the red coat. "You may begin this at once."

"God's blessing on your Grace. Thank you." The man bobbed up and down like a duck. Someone else was coming forward, another paper in his hand. Nora bounced on her toes, not wanting to go; the nurses were still waiting, standing grimly to the side, their eyes fixed on the girls as if a stare could pull them within reach. She wished her mother would look at her, talk to her again. Then, at the back of the hall, a hard, loud voice rose.

"Way for the King of England!"

Eleanor sat straight up, and Richard swung back to his place by her side. The whole room was suddenly moving, shifting, men shuffling out of the way, flexing and bending, and up through the suddenly empty space came Nora's Papa. Nora went quickly back behind the Queen's chair to Alais, standing there by the wall.

Only the Queen stayed in her chair, the smile gone now. Everybody else was bent down over his shoes. The King strode up before Eleanor, and behind him the hall quickly emptied. Even the nurses went out. Two of her father's men stood on either side of the door, like guards.

"My lord," the Queen said, "you should send ahead; we would be more ready for you."

Nora's Papa stood looking down at her. He wore the same clothes he had the day before. His big hands rested on his belt. His voice grated, like walking on gravel. "I thought I might see more if I came unannounced. Where are the boys?" His gaze flicked toward Richard. "The other boys."

The Queen shrugged. "Will you sit, my lord?" A servant hurried up with a chair for him. "Bring my lord the King a cup of wine."

The King flung himself into the chair. "Don't think I don't know what you're doing." His head turned; he had seen Nora, just behind the Queen, and his eyes prodded at her. Nora twitched, uncomfortable.

"My lord," Eleanor said, "I am uncertain what you mean."

"You're such a bad liar, Eleanor." The King twisted in the chair, caught Nora by the hand, and dragged her up between their two chairs, in front of them both. "This little girl, now, she spoke very well yesterday, when the rest of you ran off. I think she tells the truth."

Standing in front of them, Nora slid her hands behind her back. Her mouth was dry and she swallowed once. Her mother smiled at her. "Nora has a mind. Greet your father, dear."

Nora said, "God be with you, Papa."

He stared at her. Around the black centers, his eyes were blue like plates of sky. One hand rose and picked delicately at the front of her dress. Inside the case of cloth, her body shrank away from his touch. He smoothed the front of her dress. Her mother was twisted in her chair to watch. Behind her, Richard stood, his face gripped in a frown.

"So. Just out of the convent, are you? Like it there?"

She wondered what she was supposed to say. Instead, she said the truth. "No, Papa."

He laughed. The black holes got bigger and then smaller. "What, you don't want to be a nun?"

"No, Papa, I want—" To her surprise, the story had changed. She found a sudden, eager courage. "I want to be a hero."

Eleanor gave a little chuckle, and the King snorted. "Well, God gave you the wrong stature." His gaze went beyond her. "Where are you going?"

"Nowhere, my lord," Richard said in a cool voice.

The King laughed again, so that his teeth showed. He smelled sour, like old beer and dirty clothes. His eyes watched Nora, but he spoke to her mother.

"I want to see my sons."

"They are alarmed," the Queen said, "because of what happened with Becket."

"I'll deal with Becket. Keep out of that." The servant came with the cup of wine and he took it. Nora shifted her feet, wanting to get away from them, the edges of their words like knives in the air.

"Yes, well, how you deal with Becket is getting us all into some strange places," her mother said.

"God's death!" He lifted the cup and drained it. "I never knew he had such a hunger for martyrdom. You saw him. He looks like an old man already. This is a caution against virtue, if it turns you into such a stork."

Her mother looked off across the room. "No, you are right. It does no service to your justice when half the men in the kingdom can go around you."

He twisted toward her, his face clenched. "Nobody goes around me."

"Well," she said, and faced him, her mouth smiling, but not in a good way. "It seems they do."

"Mama," Nora said, remembering how to do this. "With your leave—"

"Stay," her father said, and, reaching out, took her arm and dragged her forward, into his lap.

"Nora," her mother said. Beyond her, Richard took a step forward, his eyes wide. Nora squirmed, trying to get upright on her father's knees; his arms surrounded her like a cage. The look on her mother's face scared her. She tried to wiggle free, and his arms closed around her.

"Mama—"

The Queen said, her voice suddenly harsh, "Let go of her, sir."

"What?" the King said, with a little laugh. "Aren't you my sweetheart, Nora?" He planted a kiss on Nora's cheek. His arms draped around Nora; one hand stroked her arm. "I want my sons. Get my sons back here, woman." Abruptly, he was thrusting Nora away, off his lap, back onto her feet, and he stood up. He crooked his finger at Richard. "Attend me." His feet scraped loud on the floor. Everybody was staring at him, mute. Heavily, he went out the door, Richard on his heels.

Nora rubbed her cheek, still damp where her father's mouth had pressed; her gaze went to her mother. The Queen reached out her arms and Nora went to her and the Queen held her tight. She said, "Don't be afraid. I'll protect you." Her voice was ragged. She let Nora go and clapped her hands. "Now we'll have some music."

Feathers of steam rose from the tray of almond buns on the long wooden table. Nora crept down the kitchen steps, staying close by the wall, and swiftly ducked down under the table's edge. Deeper in the kitchen, someone was singing, and someone else laughed; nobody had noticed her. She reached up over the side of the table and gathered handfuls of buns, dumping them into the fold of her skirt and, when her skirt was full, swiftly turned and scurried back up the steps and out the door.

Just beyond the threshold, Alais hopped up and down with delight, her eyes sparkling, her hands clasped together. Nora handed her a bun. "Quick!" She started toward the garden gate.

"Hey! You girls!"

Alais shrieked and ran. Nora wheeled, knowing that voice, and looked up into Richard's merry eyes.

"Share those?"

They went into the garden and sat on a bench by the wall, and ate the buns. Richard licked the sweet dust from his fingers.

"Nora, I'm going away."

"Away," she said, startled. "Where?"

"Mama wants me to go find Boy and Geoffrey. I think she's just getting me away from Papa. Then I'm going to look for some knights to follow me. I'm duke now, I need an army." He hugged her, laid his cheek against her hair. "I'll be back."

"You're so lucky," she burst out. "To be duke. I'm nobody! Why am I a girl?"

He laughed, his arm warm around her, his cheek against her hair. "You won't always be a little girl. You'll marry someday, and then you'll be a queen, like Mama, or at least a princess. I heard them say they want you to marry somebody in Castile."

"Castile. Where's that?" A twinge of alarm went through her. She looked up into his face. She thought that nobody was as handsome as Richard.

"Somewhere in the Spanish Marches." He reached for the last of the buns, and she caught his hand and held on. His fingers were all sticky.

"I don't want to go away," she said. "I'll miss you. I won't know anybody."

"You won't go for a while. Castile—that means castles. They fight the Moors down there. You'll be a Crusader."

She frowned, puzzled. "In Jerusalem?" In the convent, they had always been praying for the Crusade. Jerusalem was on the other side of the world, and she had never heard it called Castile.

"No, there's a Crusade in Spain too. El Cid, you know, and Roland. Like them."

"Roland," she said, with a leap of excitement. There was a song about

Roland, full of thrilling passages. She tilted her face toward him again. "Will I have a sword?"

"Maybe." He kissed her hair again. "Women don't usually need swords. I have to go. I just wanted to say good-bye. You're the oldest one left at home now, so take care of Johanna."

"And Alais," she said.

"Oh, Alais," he said. He took her hand. "Nora, listen, something is going on between Mama and Papa, I don't know what, but something. Be brave, Nora. Brave and good." His arm tightened a moment and then he stood and walked away.

"When will we be in Poitiers?" Alais said happily. She sat on a chest in the back of the wagon and spread her skirts out.

Nora shrugged. The carts went very slowly and would make the journey much longer. She wished they would let her ride a horse. Her nurse climbed in over the wagon's front, turned, and lifted Johanna after her. The drover led the team up, the reins bunched in his hands, turned the horses' rumps to the cart, and backed them into the shafts. Maybe he would let her hold the reins. She hung over the edge of the wagon, looking around at the courtyard, full of other wagons, people packing up her mother's goods, a line of saddled horses waiting.

The nurse said, "Lady Nora, sit down."

Nora kept her back to her, to show she didn't hear. Her mother had come out of the hall door, and at the sight of her everybody else in the whole courtyard turned toward her as if she were the sun; everybody warmed in that light. Nora called, "Mama!" and waved, and her mother waved back.

"Lady Nora! Sit!"

She leaned on the side of the wagon. Beside her, Alais giggled and poked her with her elbow. A groom was bringing the Queen's horse; she waved away someone waiting to help her and mounted by herself. Nora watched how she did that, how she kept her skirts over her legs but got her legs across the saddle anyway. Her Mama rode like a man. She would ride like that. Then, from the gate, a yell went up.

"The King!"

Alais on the chest twisted around to look. Nora straightened. Her father on his big black horse was riding in the gate, a line of knights behind him, mailed and armed. She looked for Richard, but he wasn't with them. Most of the knights had to stay outside the wall because there was no room in the yard.

Eleanor reined her horse around, coming up beside the wagon, close enough that Nora could have reached out and touched her. The horse sidestepped, tossing its head up. His face dark, the King forced his way through the crowd toward her.

She said, "My lord, what is this?"

He threw one wide look all around the courtyard. His face was blurry with beard and his eyes were rimmed in red. Nora sat quickly down on the chest. Her father spurred his horse up head to tail with her mother's.

"Where are my sons?"

"My lord, I have no notion, really."

He stared at her, furious. "Then I'll take hostages." He twisted in his saddle, looking back toward his men. "Get these girls!"

Nora shot to her feet again. "No," the Queen said, forcing her way between him and the wagon, almost nose to nose with him, her fist clenched. "Keep your hands off my daughters." Alais reached out and gripped Nora's skirt in her fist.

He thrust his face at her. "Try to stop me, Eleanor!"

"Papa, wait." Nora leaned over the side of the wagon. "We want to go to Poitiers."

The King said evilly, "What *you* want." Two men had dismounted, were coming briskly toward the wagon. He never took his gaze off her mother.

The Queen's horse bounded up between the men and the cart. Leaning closer to the King, she spoke in a quick low voice. "Don't be foolish, my lord, on such a small matter. If you push this too hastily, you will never get them back. Alais has that handsome dowry; take her."

"Mama, no!" Nora stretched her arm out. Alais flung her arms around her waist.

"Please—please—"

The Queen never even looked at them. "Be still, Nora. I will deal with this."

"Mama!" Nora tried to catch hold of her, to make her turn and look. "You promised. Mama, you promised she would come with us!" Her fingers grazed the smooth fabric of her mother's sleeve.

Eleanor struck at her, hard, knocking her down inside the wagon. Alais gave a sob. The King's men were coming on again, climbing up toward them. Nora lunged at them, her fists raised.

"Get away! Don't you dare touch her!"

From behind, someone got hold of her and dragged her out of the way. The two men scrambled up over the side of the wagon and fastened on the little French princess. They were dragging her up over the side. She cried out once and then was limp, helpless in their arms. Nora wrenched at the arm around her waist, and only then she saw it was her mother holding her.

"Mama!" She twisted toward Eleanor. "You promised. She doesn't want to go."

Eleanor thrust her face down toward Nora's. "Be still, girl. You don't know what you're doing."

Behind her, the King was swinging his horse away. "You can keep that one. Maybe she'll poison you." He rode off after his men, who had Alais clutched in their grip. Other men were lifting out Alais' baggage. They were hauling her off like baggage. Nora gave a wordless cry. With a sharp command, her father led his men on out the gate again, taking Alais like a trophy.

Her arm still around Nora's waist, Eleanor was scowling after the King. Nora wrenched herself free and her mother turned to face her.

"Well, now, Nora. That was unseemly, wasn't it."

"Why did you do that, Mama?" Nora's voice rang out, high-pitched and furious, careless who heard.

"Come, girl," her mother said, and gave her a shake. "Settle yourself. You don't understand."

With a violent jerk of her whole body, Nora wrenched away from her mother. "You said Alais could come." Something deep and hard was gathering in her, as if she had swallowed a stone. She began to cry. "Mama, why did you lie to me?"

Her mother blinked at her, her forehead crumpled. "I can't do everything." She held out her hand, as if asking for something. "Come, be reasonable. Do you want to be like your father?"

Tears were squirting from Nora's eyes. "No, and not like *you*, either, Mama. You promised me, and you lied." She knocked aside the outstretched hand.

Eleanor recoiled; her arm rose and she slapped Nora across the face. "Cruel, ungrateful child!"

Nora sat down hard. She poked her fists into her lap, her shoulders hunched. Alais was gone; she couldn't save her after all. It didn't matter that she hadn't really liked Alais much. She wanted to be a hero, but she was just a little girl, and nobody cared. She turned to the chest and folded her arms on it, put her head down, and wept.

Later, she leaned up against the side of the wagon, looking down the road ahead.

She felt stupid. Alais was right: she couldn't be a king, and now she couldn't even be a hero.

The nurses were dozing in the back of the wagon. Her mother had taken Johanna away to ride on her saddle in front of her, to show Nora how bad she had been. The drover on his bench had his back to her. She felt as if nobody could see her, as if she weren't even there.

She didn't want to be a king anyway if it meant being mean and yelling and carrying people off by force. She wanted to be like her mother, but her *old* mother, the good mother, not this new one, who lied and broke promises, who hit and called names. Alais had said, "Your mother is wicked," and she almost cried again, because it was true.

She would tell Richard when he came back. But then in her stomach something tightened like a knot: *if* he came back. Somehow the whole world had changed. Maybe even Richard would be false now.

"You'll be a Crusader," he had said to her.

She didn't know if she wanted that. Being a Crusader meant going a long, long way and then dying. "Be good," Richard had said. "Be brave." But she was just a little girl. Under the whole broad blue sky, she was just a speck.

The wagon jolted along the road, part of the long train of freight heading down toward Poitiers. She looked all around her, at the servants walking along among the carts, the bobbing heads of horses and mules, the heaps of baggage lashed on with rope. Her mother was paying no heed to her, had gone off ahead, in the mob of riders leading the way. The nurses were sleeping. Nobody was watching her.

Nobody cared about her anymore. She waited to disappear. But she didn't.

She stood, holding on to the side to keep from falling. Carefully, she climbed up over the front of the wagon onto the bench, keeping her skirts over her legs, and sat down next to the drover, who gawked down at her, a broad, brown face in a shag of beard.

"Now, my little lady—"

She straightened her skirts, planted her feet firmly on the kickboard, and looked up at him. "Can I hold the reins?" she said.

Melinda Snodgrass

A writer whose work crosses several mediums and genres, Melinda M. Snodgrass has written scripts for television shows such as *Profiler* and *Star Trek: The Next Generation* (for which she was also a story editor for several years), a number of popular SF novels, and was one of the cocreators of the long-running Wild Card series, for which she has also written and edited. Her novels include *Circuit, Circuit Breaker, Final Circuit, The Edge of Reason, Runespear* (with Victor Milán), *High Stakes, Santa Fe,* and *Queen's Gambit Declined.* Her most recent novel is *The Edge of Ruin,* the sequel to *The Edge of Reason.* Her media novels include the Wild Cards novel *Double Solitaire* and the Star Trek novel *The Tears of the Singers.* She's also the editor of the anthology *A Very Large Array.* She lives in New Mexico.

Here she takes us to a distant planet to show us that even in a society where spaceships thunder through the night and aliens mingle with humans on crowded city streets, some of the games you might run into go *way* back.

THE HANDS THAT ARE NOT THERE

Glass met glass with dull, tuneless clunks as the human bartender filled orders. A Hajin waitress with a long and tangled red mane running down her bare back clicked on delicate hooves through the bar delivering drinks. The patrons were a surly lot, mere shadows huddled in the dark dive, and carefully seated at tables well away from each other. No one talked. Substituting for conversation were commentators calling the action of a soccer game playing on the wall screen over the bar. Even those voices were growling rumbles because the sound was turned down so low. The odors of spilled beer and rancid cooking oil twisted through the smoke, but they and the tobacco smells were trumped by the scents of despair and simmering anger.

This dank hole was a perfect match for Second Lieutenant Tracy Belmanor's mood. He had picked it because it was well away from the spaceport and he was unlikely to meet any of his shipmates. He should have been happy. He had graduated from the Solar League's military academy only last month and had been assigned to his first posting. Problem was, his fellow classmates had walked out as newly minted first lieutenants, but such was not the case for the lowborn tailor's son who had attended the academy on a scholarship. When he had received his insignia, he'd stared down at the stars and single bar and realized that he was one rung below his aristocratic classmates, even though his grades had been better, his performance in flight the equal of any of them save Mercedes, whose reflexes and ability to withstand high gee had put them all to shame. When he'd looked up at the commandant of the High Ground, Vice Admiral Sergei Arrington Vasquez y Markov, the big man had casually delivered the explanation, totally unaware how insulting it had been.

"You must understand, Belmanor, it wouldn't do for you to be in the position

of issuing orders to your classmates, especially to the Infanta Mercedes. This way you will never hold the bridge solo, and so be spared the embarrassment."

The implication that *he* would be embarrassed to issue an order to high-born assholes, including the Emperor's daughter, had ignited his too-quick temper. *"I'm sure that will be a great comfort to me as I'm dying because one of those idiots wrecked the ship."* But of course he hadn't said that. The unwary words had been at the edge of his teeth, but after four years being drilled in protocol and the chain of command, he managed to swallow the angry retort. Instead he had saluted and managed a simple "Yes, sir." At least he hadn't thanked Markov for the insult.

Later, he wondered why he hadn't spoken up. Cowardice? Was he really intimidated by the FFH? That was a terrible thought, for it implied that he *did* know his place. If he was honest with himself, that was why he hadn't attended the postgraduation ball. He knew that none of Mercedes's ladies-in-waiting would have accepted him as escort. He couldn't bring a woman of his own social strata. And Mercedes was the daughter of the Emperor, and no one could ever know what they had shared, or that Tracy loved her and that she loved him.

So he didn't go to the ball. Instead, he stood on the Crystal Bridge on Ring Central and watched Mercedes, out of uniform and a vision in crimson and gold, enter the ballroom on the arm of Honorius Sinclair Cullen, Knight of the Arches and Shells, Duke de Argento, known casually as Boho, and Tracy's nemesis and rival. It should have been Tracy at her side. But that could never be.

Tracy took a long pull on his whiskey, draining the glass. It was cheap liquor and it etched pain down his throat, and settled like a burning coal in his gut. Unlike the other morose and uncommunicative patrons, Tracy had chosen to sit at the bar. The bartender, a big man, the stripes on his apron imperfectly hiding the grime, nodded at Tracy's empty glass.

"Another?"

"Sure. Why the hell not?"

"You've really been hammering these down, kid." Tracy looked up and was surprised by the kindness in the man's brown eyes. "You gonna be able to find your way back to your ship?" Whiskey gurgled into the glass.

"Maybe it would be better if I didn't."

A rag emerged from the apron pocket and wiped down the steel surface of the bar. "You don't wanna do that. The League hangs deserters."

Tracy downed the drink in one gulp, and fought back nausea. He shook his head. "Not me. They wouldn't look for me. They'd be glad the Embarrassment has been quietly swept under the rug."

"Look, kid, you got troubles. I can see that."

"Wow, you always this perceptive?"

"Cut the attitude," but the words were said mildly and with a faint smile. "Look, if you want feel better about the state of the galaxy and your place in it, you should talk to *that* guy. It may all be bullshit, but Rohan's got one hell of a story."

Tracy looked in the direction of the pointing finger and saw a portly man of medium height seated at a corner table and cuddling an empty glass. His dark hair was streaked with grey, and his forehead overly large due to the receding hairline. The bartender moved to the far end of the bar and started filling the empty glasses on the Hajin's tray. Tracy looked again at the slumped man. On impulse, he snatched up his glass and walked over to the table.

Jerking a thumb over his shoulder at the bartender, Tracy said, "He says you've got a good story that's going to put everything in perspective for me." Tracy kicked out a chair and sat down. He half hoped that the man would object and start a fight. Tracy was in the mood to hit somebody, and here on Wasua, unlike at the High Ground, a fight wouldn't turn into a stupid duel. Tracy touched the scar at his left temple, a gift from Boho. A closer look at the man revealed the unlikeliness of a fight breaking out. There was no muscle beneath the fat, and dark, puffy bags hung beneath his eyes.

"Loren doesn't believe me," Rohan said. "But it's all true." Alcohol slurred the words, but Tracy could hear the aristocratic accent of a member of the Fortune Five Hundred. God knew he could recognize it. He'd been listening to it for four damn years. He even feared he'd begun to ape it.

"Okay, I'll bite: What's all true?"

The tip of the man's tongue licked at his lips. "I could tell the story better with something to wet my throat," he said.

"Okay, fine." Tracy went back to the bar and returned with a bottle of bourbon. He slammed it down between them. "There. Now I've paid for the tale. So go on, amaze me."

Rohan drew himself up, but the haughtiness of the movement was undercut when he began swaying in his chair. A pudgy hand grabbed the edge of the table and he stabilized. "I am more, much more than I seem."

"Okay." Tracy drew out the word.

The man looked around with exaggerated care. "I have to be careful. If they knew I was talking . . ."

"Yes?"

The man drew a finger across his throat. He leaned across the table. His breath was a nauseating mix of booze and halitosis. "What I'm going to tell you could shake the foundations of the League."

The drunk poured himself a drink, tossed it back, and continued. "But it happened—all of it—and it's all true. Listen and learn, young man." Rohan refilled his glass, topped off Tracy's, and saluted with his glass. This time he settled for a sip rather than a gulp. Rohan sighed and no longer seemed focused on the young officer.

"It all started when one of my aides arranged a bachelor party. . . ."

If a strip club could ever be considered tasteful, Rohan assumed that this one fit that bill. Not that he was an expert. This was his first time in such an establishment, where human women flaunted themselves, much to the fury of the Church. So why had he agreed to join his staff at a stag party in honor of Knud's upcoming nuptials? The answer came easily. *Because my wife's latest lover is the same age as my daughter, and this one was just too much.* So his presence in the Cosmos Club was—what? Payback? And how likely was it that Juliana would ever find out? Surpassingly small. And that she would care? Smaller yet.

He blushed as a nearly naked hostess, her breasts and mons outlined with a jeweled harness, took their coats and, with the graceful hand gestures of a trained courtesan, ushered them over to the smiling maître d', a handsome man with a spade beard and sparkling black eyes. He led the group through tall double doors and into the club proper. The lighting in the main room was subdued, but recessed spotlights struck fire from the slowly rotating platforms that held beautiful, naked women. The platforms were shaped like spiral galaxies, the stars formed by faux diamonds. Rohan stared at the rounded buttocks of the girls and wondered what those behinds looked like after a long night seated on the platforms. Between the platforms was a stage made of clear glass. A crystal pole thrust up, an aggressive statement, from the center of the stage.

Waitresses dressed—no, make that accented—with the same kind of jeweled harness worn by the hostess moved between the tables, serving drinks and food. Rohan saw a Brie en croûte garnished with sour cherries go past on a tray, and the aromas from the kitchen were as good as anything he'd smelled in the city's finest restaurants. His belly gave a growl of appreciation. Yes, definitely an upscale establishment, catering to the wealthy and wellborn of the FFH. Another anomaly struck him. There were no aliens present. The waitstaff were all humans, an expensive affectation. Rohan assumed that in the bowels of the kitchen, Hajin and Isanjo labored as dishwashers, but the image presented to the paying customers was aggressively human.

John Fujasaki had reserved a circular booth at the edge of the stage. An ice-filled champagne bucket and the expected bottle were already waiting. As the party arranged themselves, the maître d' opened the bottle with a discreet *pop* and filled their glasses. The upholstery was plush, made from neural fabric that sensed the tension in Rohan's lower back and began to massage the spot. The floating holo table displayed a constantly shifting view of spectacular astronomical phenomenon. Rohan stared, mesmerized, as a blossoming supernova tried to consume his drink.

John Fujasaki, the instigator of this outing, leaned in close to Rohan and murmured, "You're blushing, sir." Laughter hung on the words.

"I'm not accustomed to seeing this much . . . female . . . flesh," he murmured back.

"Pardon my saying so, but you need to get out more" was the response. Then John turned away to respond to another comment.

Rohan watched the bubbles rising in his glass and wondered what the young aide would think if he knew that his boss did frequent less reputable establishments in Pony Town that catered to humans with a taste for the alien and the exotic. Then the hypocrisy of his anger at his wife over her infidelity struck him. He fell back on the age-old defense: whoring was expected of men, and no woman should place a cuckoo in her husband's nest. The excuses rang hollow.

John tapped his glass with a spoon. The young men fell silent and Fujasaki stood up. "Well, here's to Knud. Those of us who've avoided the wedded state think he's mad, and those who have entered the bonds of matrimony also think he's mad. But at least for tonight we'll put aside

such worries and concentrate on sending him off in style. So, a toast to
Knud on his final night of freedom, and may it be memorable!" John
cried.

There were calls of "Here, here!" from around the table; glasses were
clinked, drained, and refilled. Knud, smiling but with a hint of worry in the
back of his eyes, laid a hand over his glass. "Now, go easy, fellas. I have to be
in reasonably good shape tomorrow."

"Not to worry, Knud," Franz said. "You're with *us*."

"And *that's* why I'm worried."

A waitress took their dinner orders. Booze continued to flow. Rohan
found himself thinking about the inflation numbers from the Wasua star
system. That made him switch from champagne to bourbon. A live band
began to play, and girl after girl in various and creative outfits took to the
stage. The creative outfits were shed in time to the pulsing music, and
the ladies were all very . . . Rohan searched for a word and settled on "flexible." Almost all the tables were filled now, parties of men with sweat
gleaming on their faces, stocks and ties loosened, coats removed. Girls
settled into laps and ran tapering fingers through their marks' hair. The
roar of conversation was basso and primal.

A quintet of five girls was dancing and singing on the stage to an old
SpaceCom marching song, but with some interesting new lyrics. The
sprightly music had Rohan first humming along and then singing along,
but it was frustrating that the girls couldn't get the beat right. They were
late. He began to conduct vigorously, and felt his elbow connect with
something.

"Whoa!" shouted Fujasaki. There was a large wet stain on the front of
his trousers.

"He's drunk," Rohan vaguely heard someone say.

"So what? We're all drunk," Franz replied.

"Yeah, but he's the Chancellor, what if—" Bret, a newly hired aide
began.

"Relax. They sweep the place regularly and keep the press out," John
replied.

"Yeah, relax, Bret. We're having fun. *I'm* fun. I'm . . . I'm just made of
fun!" Rohan shouted.

The five ladies went trooping off the stage, their sassy little buttocks wiggling provocatively. "Where are they going?" Rohan asked. "Where are all the lovely ladies going?" he repeated, and felt a tightness in his chest at the sadness of it all.

"Gone to housewives everyone," Franz said.

"What an awful waste," Rohan groaned. "We need an expert commission—girls keep turning into wives. It's a scandal. We need an investiga—"

A drum roll cut through his slurring words. All the lights in the club went out save for a single stabbing spotlight pinning the stage. Into that cone of light leaped a girl. She seemed to be flying, so high was her *grand jeté*, and the long cloak flowing behind her added to the illusion of flight. The music resumed, a primitive, urgent beat. She stood front and center, her features covered by an elaborate mask and headdress. All that could be seen was an unnaturally pointed chin and the glitter of her eyes. She caught the edges of the cloak with long claws set with light-emitting diodes, and dropped it to reveal an elaborate costume, far more concealing than was usual for a stripper. Rohan wondered if the claws were sewn into gloves?

She began to dance. No harsh gyrating and suggestive posing. She danced with breath-catching grace. Her arms wove patterns, and the diodes left streaks of multicolored fire in the air around her. Layers began to fall away. The crowd shouted its approval as each piece of clothing fell. Another slithered to the stage floor and a long silky tail covered with sleek red and white fur unfolded and wove around her like a dancing snake. The shouts became roars.

The girl danced in close to her sweating admirers. Hands groped for her like blind babies seeing the tit, but she always eluded them. Unless those reaching hands held credit spikes. Those she allowed to be thrust into the credit deck that adorned the low-slung belt that clasped her waist. Rohan sat rigid, fingers gripping the edge of the table, willing her to remove the mask. *Show me . . . show me . . .* She approached their table. The young men leaned across the table, spikes extended like some commercial metaphor for sex. Rohan couldn't move. He just watched as another layer fell away to reveal pale cream and red fur that covered her flanks and belly and rose like a spear point between her breasts. There was a gasp from the audience.

John fell back against the booth. "The Pope's holy whickerbill!" he breathed.

The music quickened in tempo. Fire sparked from the tips of her long claws, the jewels and bells on the mask and headdress set up a hysterical ringing. She spun, faster and faster, then another great leap took her back center stage. Legs widely braced, hands cupping her breasts. She slowly slid them up her chest, across her neck, lifted the mask and headdress and flung them aside. She was alien and yet familiar. Rohan devoured her features. Noting the tiny upturned nose with flaring nostrils, pricked ears thrusting through the wild tumble of cream and red curls. They were tufted on each point. Cat eyes of emerald green.

"An alien," Bret said, and his voice held both disgust and lust.

Blackout.

The lights came up. The stage was empty. Excited conversation danced around the table.

"Cosmetic surgery?"

"No. Gotta be one of those Cara half-breeds."

"Thought we killed all of them."

"Should have. Disgusting."

"Hey, turn out the lights, close your eyes, and think of it as exotic underwear," John said with a laugh.

The room seemed to be ballooning and receding about Rohan. His heart thundered in his chest, and his breath came in short pants. An erection nudged urgently at his fly. He staggered out of the booth.

"Sir?"

"Are you all right?"

"Where are you going?"

He didn't answer.

"Wait," Tracy said. "A Cara/human half-breed? There's no such thing. First off, it's illegal." The young officer pointed at the Hajin waitress. "And second, our equipment might line up, but there's no way we'd produce offspring."

Rohan waved an admonishing finger at him. "Ah, but remember that the Cara were master geneticists. They'd been blending genes from every known alien race long before humans arrived on the scene. They were eager to add us to the mix, and couldn't believe that the League was serious when the ban on alien-human comingling was put in place."

Tracy took a sip of his drink. He knew from his studies that the Cara had no physical norm. They tailored bodies to suit a given situation. They changed sex on a whim. For thousands of years, they had been harvesting, mixing, and manipulating the genetic material from every race they met. A task easily accomplished, since the Cara spent their lives aboard vast trading ships that traveled between systems, or in the shops supplied by those ships. For the Cara, the greatest sin was uniformity. They believed that diversity was the key to survival and advancement. It had all been horrifying to the humans, and human purity became an obsession. Most genetic research and manipulation was outlawed for fear that the Cara might find a way to affect the basic human genome. Tracy said as much to Rohan.

The older man shook his head. "Yes, but that didn't discourage the Cara. They found volunteers, disaffected humans hostile to the League, and produced several thousand half-breeds." He picked up his glass and set it down over and over. Linking the circles formed by condensation into a concentric pattern.

"So, why make this girl look so different?" Tracy asked. "They could have made the offspring look like anything. Even exactly like a human."

Rohan looked up. "And that was their mistake. That's what they should have done. Instead, they tried to temper any backlash by tweaking the genes to make the children attractive to humans. Or at least what they thought would be attractive. They had noticed that we like cats. Hence Sammy." Rohan refilled his glass and took a long pull. "What they didn't realize was that it would make the kids just that much more horrifying."

"But you weren't disgusted by . . . Sammy?"

"Samarith, her full name was Samarith. And no, I wasn't disgusted, but I had a taste for the exotic. They knew that. And used it."

Rohan's stomach was roiling, his head pounding. Swaying, he made his way through the anteroom and out onto the street. The sea-tinged air cleared his head somewhat. He found the corner of the building and went looking for the stage door.

What are you doing? the rational part of his mind wailed.

"I'm going to compliment her on her dancing," he said aloud.

And ask about her life. Explore her thoughts. Share her dreams. Fuck her blind.

He found the side entrance and entered. Inside, the smell of sweat and rancid makeup seeped from the walls and hung in the air. Rohan swallowed hard and tried to find his way past the lighting control panel. He turned down a hall and found himself pressed against the wall as a gaggle of girls came hurrying past, heading for the stage. In the confines of that narrow space, they rubbed against him. He could feel the warmth of their bare skin even through his clothes, and his erection hardened again. He found another hallway, but this one was guarded by a tall man with a pendulous belly. Rohan tried to walk past and was blocked. The bouncer's exposed biceps displayed military tattoos and muscle now overlaid with fat. The overhead lights gleamed on his shaved head.

"Where do you think you're going?"

"I wish to see the young lady who just finished performing."

"You and every other aristo . . ." The man glanced down at Rohan's crotch. "Who stores his brains in his cock."

Rohan gaped at him. "My good man, you can't address me in that way."

"Yeah, I can. And if you want to see Sammy, it'll cost you." He thrust his hips forward, displaying his credit deck. It didn't have the same effect as when the dancers did it. Rohan dithered, remembered that gamine little face, unlimbered his credit spike, and paid.

"Where can I find her?" Rohan asked.

"Follow your prick. It seems to be doing a pretty good job as a dousing rod."

The bouncer stepped aside and Rohan walked down the hall, checking each room as he came to it. Giggles and a couple of lewd invitations were received as he opened and closed doors. Hers was the fifth dressing room he checked. She was dressed in a deep-green robe and seated at a dressing table. The bottom drawer had been pulled out and she rested a bare foot on it. The robe had fallen aside, revealing the shapely leg almost up to the hip. Smoke from the stim she held languidly in one hand swirled like a halo about the tips of her pricked ears. She raked him with a long glance from those amazing green cat eyes.

"How much did you pay?"

"I beg your pardon?"

"To Dal. How much did you pay him to get back here?"

"Three hundred."

"You got taken. He would have let you in for half that."

"I'll remember that next time." Samarith lit a new stim and regarded him. Rohan shifted uncomfortably from foot to foot.

"Don't you want to know why I'm here?" he finally asked.

She let her gaze drift down to his crotch. "You're giving me a moderately sized hint." His erection deflated. "Awww, I broke it," she drawled.

"I wanted to invite you to supper," Rohan said.

"Courtship first? Well, that's a change." She stood and stubbed out her stim. "There's a pretty good place in Pony Town that serves late."

"I was going to take you to the French Bakery." It was the capital's best restaurant. He thought it would impress her.

She laughed. "You're such an idiot. Kind of sweet, but an idiot." He gaped at her. "It's better if I keep a low profile."

"Your profile wasn't very low tonight," Rohan shot back.

"This is a strip joint. It may be frequented by your set, but it's still a strip joint. Waving me around in public wouldn't be good for either of us. And who are you, by the way? Which scion of a decaying noble house are you?"

"How do you even know I'm FFH?"

"Oh, please." Scorn etched the words.

He thought about his job and the stress that it carried. He thought about his cold and distant wife. "Can't I just be Rohan for tonight?"

She cocked her head to the side, an endearing sight, and considered him. Her tone was gentler as she said, "All right. I'll call you Han, and you can call me Sammy, and tonight we'll pretend we aren't who and what we are."

"And after tonight?" Rohan asked.

"That depends on how tonight turns out."

Rohan allowed Sammy to issue directions to his Hajin chauffeur, Hobb. Neither he nor Hobb intimated by word or action that they were familiar with the area. But he knew it well. His favorite massage spa was just a few streets over. It was a place where men with his tastes could feel the touch of the exotic. He liked the way the soft play of fur and the rough pads of an Isanjo masseuse tickled his skin and kneaded his muscles.

That night the summer heat had broken and it was pleasant to be outside. Humans, Hajin, Isanjo, Tiponi Flutes, and Slunkies roamed the streets listening to musicians performing on street corners. They played games of chance or skill—everything from chess, to craps, to a swaying grove of Flutes playing their incomprehensible stick game. Diners lingered in the restaurants. Lovers cuddled on benches in a small park, while the elderly sat and contemplated the ships lifting off from the Cristóbal Colón spaceport. Hobb opened the flitter doors for them. Rohan stepped out and felt the rumble underfoot as another spaceship leaped skyward. The fire from engines was a red-orange scar ripping the darkness. For a brief moment, it almost eclipsed the light from the nebula floating overhead.

The long lines and evident elegance of the flitter drew more than a few looks. "I'll call you when we're ready to be picked up," he said softly to Hobb. The Hajin bowed his long bony head, revealing his golden mane between his collar and hat. Rohan turned to Sammy. She wore slim-legged pants tucked into high boots, and a silk top of varying shades of green and blue that was tied in interesting ways to make it drape and flow. The cream and red hair tumbled over her shoulders. She drew looks. Rohan struggled for breath.

"So, where would you like to eat?" he asked.

"There." She pointed at an Isanjo restaurant. Potted trees dotted the space with webs of rope slung between them. Isanjo, using hands, their prehensile feet, and their tails darted along the woven lines. Somehow none of the items on the trays tilted, slipped, or fell.

They settled into woven rope chairs, and a waiter slithered down the trunk of the tree next to their table. His order pad hung on his neck along with a credit deck. "Drinks?" he asked, the muzzle making him lisp the word.

"Champagne," Rohan said.

"Actually, I don't like champagne," Sammy said.

"Oh. Your pardon. What would you like?"

"Tequila."

The waiter turned dark, wide eyes to Rohan. Their blackness against the gold of his fur made them seem fathomless and terribly alien. "I'll drink what the lady is drinking," Rohan said, making it an act of gallantry. With a bouncing leap, the creature was up the tree, gripping the ropes and racing away.

"You just full of courtesy, aren't you?" Sammy asked. "Do you even like tequila?"

"Well enough."

"What do you drink at home?" she asked, fixing those emerald cat eyes on him.

"Champagne, martinis. In the summer months I'll drink the occasional beer or gin and tonic. Wine with dinner. Why do you ask?"

"How often do you drink?"

"Every night," he blurted before he could help himself. "And why the interrogation? You sound like my doctor."

"Do you drink to relax or to forget? Or both?"

"You make too much of this. I drink because . . . I enjoy a drink in the evenings. That's all." Though he found himself remembering the night five weeks ago when he'd heard Juliana's tinkling laugh as she flirted with the young officer who was currently inhabiting her bed. He had drunk himself into insensibility that night.

Another Isanjo landing next to the table caused Rohan to start and pulled him from his brooding reverie. A bowl of dipping sauce and pieces of bread were slapped down on the table. The pungent scent of the sauce set Rohan's eyes and mouth to watering.

"You were drunk tonight," Sammy said, and popped a piece of bread into her mouth. "Otherwise you would never have come backstage."

"Do you rate your charms so low?"

"I rate your sense of propriety a good deal higher" was the dry reply.

"Well, you're probably right about that," Rohan admitted.

"So, why did you come?"

"Because you're beautiful. . . . And . . . and I'm lonely."

"And do you think two bodies clashing in the dark will alleviate that?" she asked.

He was embarrassed to discover that his throat had gone tight. He swallowed past the lump, coughed, and said, "Are you propositioning me, young woman?" He hoped his tone was as light as the words.

"No. You have to do that. I still have some pride left. Not a lot, but some."

"You find your . . . er . . . profession to be demeaning?" The look of contempt and incredulity almost cut. He looked away from those blazing green eyes. "Well, I think you answered that question."

Sammy shrugged. "It's this state religion of yours. Women are either Madonnas or whores."

"And which are you?" he asked, deciding to hit back.

It was the right move. She gave him an approving smile. "Whichever you want."

"Oh, I doubt that. I think you're not at all accommodating," Rohan said.

Their drinks arrived. She lifted hers and smiled at him over the rim of her glass. "For an aristo, you're not at all stupid."

"Thank you. And for a stripper you're not at all common."

They clinked glasses. She sipped. Suddenly nervous, he threw his back in a single gulp. "Whoa, slow down there, *caballero*. Otherwise I'll be carrying you out of here."

"My driver would handle that," Rohan said.

"Yes, but he can't handle propositioning me," Sammy retorted. She picked up her menu. "Shall we order? I'm famished."

She made love as well as she stripped.

Rohan rolled off her with a gasp and a groan. Shudders still shook his body. She sat up, straddled him, and raked her mane of hair back off her face. She drew a forefinger down his nose, traced the line of his lips, stroked his neck, and then rubbed his paunch. Futilely, Rohan tried to suck in his gut. She chuckled deep in her throat, and Rohan felt his penis try to respond, then collapse in defeat.

He had wanted her so badly by the time they reached her apartment deep in Stick Town, where the Flutes congregated. He had ripped off her clothes and shoved her down on the bed. Then, with clumsy fingers, he'd freed the clasps on his shirt, ripped loose his belt, pulled down the zipper, skinned his trousers over his hips, and fallen onto her. There had been little foreplay.

He reached up and gently touched that gamine little face. "I'm sorry. That probably wasn't very good for you."

"I'm sure there will be an opportunity for you to make it up to me," she said softly, and bent forward to kiss his lips. She tasted of vanilla with a hint of tequila on the back of her tongue.

He rubbed his hands across her groin, and stopped when his fingers hit deep, twisting scars beneath the silken fur. How had he not felt them earlier? Too absorbed in his own pleasure and the sensations sweeping through his body. She froze and stared down at him.

"What—?" he began.

"I was on Insham." He yanked back his hands as if he's been the one who had applied the knife and cut away her ovaries. "Of course, I'm one of the lucky ones. Neutered beats dead." The words were flat, matter-of-fact.

He found himself making excuses, offering the party line. "It was the actions of one overzealous admiral. The government never . . . we stopped it as soon as word reached us."

"But not before three thousand seven hundred and sixty-two children were killed. Do you know how many are left?" He stared up at her, at the glitter in her eyes, and shook his head. "Two hundred and thirty-eight."

"You know the exact count?" It was inane, but he couldn't think of anything else to say.

"Oh yes."

"How did you . . . ?"

"One of your soldiers saved me. Me and a few other children. He guarded the nursery, shot and killed other SpaceCom troops who weren't so . . . squeamish."

"You think that's the only reason he acted?" Rohan asked. "Maybe he knew it was barbaric and immoral. Can't you give us humans that much credit?"

"You humans started it." She pressed her lips together, as if holding back more words. "But perhaps you're right." She paused, lost in some memory. "I always wonder what happened to him. Did your government court-martial and execute him for refusing an order?"

Rohan couldn't continue to meet her gaze. He turned his head on the pillow, catching a scent of lilac as his stubbled cheek rasped across the silky material of the pillowcase. "No. All the troops, and there were a number of them who refused the order," he added defensively, "were allowed to resign from the service without prejudice."

"I'm glad. I would hate to think he died for an act of mercy."

They were both silent for a long time. "None of you would have suffered if the Cara had just obeyed the law."

Sammy smiled and drew her finger down the bridge of his nose. "And if they had, I wouldn't be here, and you wouldn't be lying, sated, in my bed."

There was no answer to that. He struggled to sit up past the curve of his belly and kiss her. She made it easy by lying down next to him and cradling his dick in her hands. Her head was on his shoulder, hair tickling his chin, breath warm against his neck. Tentatively he asked, "Do you hate us?"

"What a silly question." She paused. "Of course I hate you." The words landed like a blow. "Oh, not 'you' as in *you*. Humans in general, yes. You personally, no. Humans are mean, violent monkeys, and the galaxy would be better off if you'd never crawled off your rock, but *you* seem to be all right."

"You're half human."

"Which means that I'm at least half as mean. You should keep that in mind," she said, her voice catching on a little chuckle.

"I'll keep that in mind," Rohan mumbled as sleep fell on his eyelids as soft as snowflakes. He drowsily thought back over the evening, the quick steps of her tiny, arched feet, the play of muscles in her belly. The memories and the heat of her skin pressed against his had his dick hardening again. He remembered the flash of light from her claws. Unease banished torpor. "Those were gloves, right? The claws, I mean. They were sewn onto gloves."

There was a sharp pricking against the soft skin of his penis. His eyes snapped open, and he tried to peer past the bulge of his gut, but to no avail. He pushed up on his elbows, the pinpricks becoming stabs of pain. "Shit!" he yelled as he saw the extruded claws inset with the diodes. The razor-sharp tips pressed against the pink, wrinkled skin of his rapidly deflating dick.

"No. They're real."

He stared up at her, now deeply frightened. She retracted the claws, then she fell onto his chest, hair spread like a cloak across them both. He took her hand in his and inspected her fingers, trying to see how the claws were sheathed. He noticed that the pads on the tips of her fingers were completely smooth, but then she kissed him hard, her tongue demanding,

THE HANDS THAT ARE NOT THERE

forcing past his teeth. His erection returned, and all thought about her odd hands was driven from his head.

"I won't hurt you, Han," she murmured against his mouth. "That much I promise."

Tracy stared, stricken. "We . . . SpaceCom . . . killed . . . children?"

"Yes. All but a handful." Rohan refilled his glass. "I wasn't lying to Sammy, it really did start with an overly pious and deeply bigoted admiral." He shrugged. "And some good came from the revulsion that shook the League once word of the butchery got out. The laws on aliens were relaxed somewhat."

"Was this why the Cara vanished?" Tracy asked.

"Yes. Within days of the slaughter, the Cara were gone. Their shops standing empty, the freighters drifting abandoned and stripped in space or laying derelict on various moons and asteroids, as if a great storm had swept through and tossed them aground." Rohan looked around the bar with the exaggerated care of the profoundly drunk. He leaned in across the table and whispered, the words carried on alcohol-laden breath, "They could still be all around us, and we wouldn't even know it."

There was a prickling between Tracy's shoulder blades, as if hostile eyes or something more lethal were being leveled at him. "That's stupid. Space is big. They probably just went someplace else. Got away from us. Went back to their home world. We never found it."

"In what? They abandoned their ships."

Tracy found himself reevaluating the sullen drinkers, the jovial bartender, the waitress. Did each face hide a murderous hatred?

Rohan resumed his story.

For their two-month anniversary, Rohan gave Sammy an emerald-and-gold necklace. It was a massive thing, reminiscent of an Egyptian torque from Old Earth, and it seemed to bend her slender neck beneath its weight. He had bought it originally for Juliana, but she had never worn it, disparaging it as gaudy and more what she would have expected from some jumped-up, nouveau riche trader than a member of the FFH.

"So, I get your wife's castoffs?" Sammy asked with a crooked little smile.

"No . . . that's not . . . I never—"

Sammy stopped the stammered words with a soft hand across his mouth. "I don't mind. It's beautiful, and it's rather appropriate. I got her cast-off husband."

They were at his small hunting lodge in the mountains, enjoying a rare snowfall. The only light in the bedroom was provided by the dancing flames in the stone fireplace. Outside, the wind sighed in the trees like a woman's sad cries.

Sammy sat up and twined her fingers through his. "Why did you marry her? Was it arranged? Did you ever care for her?"

"I was a replacement. Her fiancé was lost along with his ship. No bodies, no debris, just a ship and her complement of spacers gone. After an appropriate period of mourning, her father approached my father. I was the dull number cruncher. I was never going to equal Juliana's dashing SpaceCom captain."

"Tell me about your father. Is he still alive?"

Hours passed. He told her about his family, the estate in the Grenadine star system. His sisters. His younger brother. His hobbies, favorite books, taste in music. Occasionally she asked a question, but mostly she listened, head resting on his shoulder, hand stroking his chest. He talked of his daughter, Rohiesa, the one good thing that had come from his marriage.

He poured himself out to her. His hopes and dreams, his secret shames and deepest desires. She never judged, just listened. Only the fire seemed to object with an occasional sharp snap as flame met resin.

Over the next month, his need for Sammy rose to the level of an addiction. He left work early, returned home at dawn, if at all. The conversations continued. Unlike Juliana, Sammy seemed genuinely interested in his economic theories as well as the name of his old fencing master.

Some nights he couldn't see her. He had to escort Juliana and Rohiesa to various soirees. The final night had began that way, at the first grand ball of the season.

The walls and ceiling of the enormous ballroom of Lord Palani's mansion seemed to have vanished and been replaced with the glitter of stars and the varicolored swirl of nebulas. The effect was spectacular and utterly terrifying. Guests clustered near the center of the room, avoiding the seeming emptiness all around them. It made it difficult for those who did wish to dance to actually dance. Lady Palani was in a rage, as evidenced by her pinched nostrils and compressed lips. One of the young Misses Palani was in tears. Tomorrow's gossip would be filled with talk of the Palani disaster. Rohan handed his empty plate to a passing Hajin servant and snagged a glass of champagne from yet another. His host approached, his long face had drooped into even more lugubrious lines.

Rohan gestured at the holographic effect. "It's quite . . . stunning."

Palani took a long pull of champagne. "Stunning price tag, too, and everyone's terrified. But they insisted." He gave a sad shake of his head. "There's no accounting for what mad notion will seize them."

Rohan correctly interpreted this as a reference to Lady Palani and the couple's five daughters. It also brought back the memory of a conversation he'd had with Sammy only three day before.

They had been walking in the Royal Botanical Garden, Sammy pausing frequently to touch and sniff the flowers. He loved to watch her: each gesture was a sonnet, each step a song. She had gently stroked the petals on a rose and turned back to him. He had tucked her arm through his and as they strolled he had casually mentioned how a friend's daughter was at a discreet clinic after a very public and embarrassing breakdown at a Founder's Day picnic.

She had glanced up at him, the glitter back in those strange eyes. "Are you surprised? You keep your women mewed up and deny them any kind of meaningful activity. I'm surprised more of them don't go nuts. You give them nothing to think about or talk about beyond family and gossip. You never let them do anything but plan parties or attend parties, run households and raise children."

"That's a schedule that would kill most men," Rohan said with a ponderous attempt at humor. "Thus proving you are the stronger sex, Sammy."

"On Earth, before the Expansion, women were lawyers, doctors, soldiers, presidents, and captains of industry."

"And space is hostile, and most planets difficult and dangerous to colonize. Women are our most precious possession. Men can produce a million sperm, but it requires a woman to gestate and deliver a child." Rohan's voice had risen and his breath had gone short. He wondered at his own vehemence and defense of the system. And why had he brought up De Varga's daughter? Because he feared for his own Rohiesa?

"And those days are gone. Your conservatism will be the death of the League, Han. The Cara were right about one thing. Adapt and change . . . or die."

"Rohan?"

"What? Ah, beg pardon. I was drifting."

"I was just asking about the inflation figures," Palani repeated.

"Ugly, but let's not mar the evening with such talk," Rohan said, and moved away.

He risked a surreptitious glance at the chrono set in the sleeve of his evening jacket. *Forty minutes.* It seemed like he'd been here for an eternity. Just a few more and he should be able to slip away and join Sammy at the street festival in Pony Town. He imagined the pungent scents of chile and roasting meats, passionate music from the street musicians, bodies moving in wild abandon to the primal beat and thrum of guitars. The imagined music clashed with the lovely but formal dance music provided by the orchestra hidden in an overhead alcove. Rohan deposited his champagne flute and moved toward the doors. To hell with it, he couldn't wait any longer.

Juliana intercepted him. The hand-sewn sequins on her formfitting dress flashed as she moved, echoing the glitter from the diamonds tucked into her dark curls. "You're not leaving, are you?"

"Umm . . . yes."

"You abandon me for your whore?" Her voice was rising, the words starting to penetrate through the stately measures of the music.

"What are you talking about?" He knew it wouldn't work. He was a terrible liar. He resorted to pleading. "For God's sake, don't make a scene."

"And why not? You're making a spectacle of yourself with this alien *puta.*"

"How—"

"Bret's wife had it from Bret. She told her mother. It's all over Campo Royale and you're a laughingstock."

"You had already assured that with your parade of lovers!" he spat back, finally saying aloud what had lain between them and rubbed like sand in his craw.

"At least mine are *human.*"

People were starting to stare. Rohan looked around at the gawking faces, the soft-footed servants, the elaborate clothes. Steel bands seemed to close around him, penning him in, holding him fast. The cry of the guitars in the streets of the Old City seemed faint and far away.

"No," he said, not certain what he was rejecting, but rejecting it all the same.

He heard Juliana screaming imprecations after him as he trod down the curving crystal staircase.

He found her in the streets among the beribboned stalls that sold jewelry and pottery, perfumes and scarves. The roar of voices mingled with the music; fat sizzled as it fell from roasting meats onto the wood beneath. He clung to Sammy and buried his head against her shoulder.

She brushed his hair back with a gentle hand. "What's happened?"

"Juliana knows. They all know. They'll make me give you up." He choked. "And I can't. I can't."

"Come," she said, and, taking his hand, she led him through the rollicking crowds where humans and aliens could dance and feast together, and perhaps even fall in love.

She took him back to her apartment. She prepared him a drink. He slammed it down, only realizing after that there was an odd taste. The room began ballooning and receding around him.

"I'm sorry, Han, I wish we could have had a little more time together." Her voice seemed to echo and be coming from a vast distance. Then there was darkness.

The first return to consciousness brought with it an awareness of the chill of a metal surface against bare back, buttocks, and legs. He knew he was naked and cold, and that nausea roiled his gut. He felt gloved hands pressing against his arms and the bite of a needle, then Sammy's voice murmured soothing words and her hand stroked his hair. He dropped back into darkness.

A bright pinpoint of light glaring directly into his eye was the next memory. The light shifted from his right eye to his left and was snapped off. Concentric circles of blue and red obscured his vision as he tried to focus after being nearly blinded. This was followed by hard pressure against the tips of his fingers. Another needle prick and he slipped away again.

When he awoke he was in Sammy's apartment, lying on a bed frame without mattress, sheets, or cover. He staggered out of bed and stood swaying in the middle of the bedroom. His eyes felt crusty; slowly the disjointed memories returned. He looked down at the crook of his elbow. There was a small red dot like the bite of a steel insect. His clothes were dumped on a chair in the corner of the room. He searched the pockets and found them empty. His keys, wallet, and comm were gone. Even his comb and monogrammed handkerchief had been taken.

"Just a thieving whore," he said, testing out the words, and then recoiled at the unfamiliar sounds issuing from his throat. He had gone from a light baritone to a deep bass. His throat felt sore and his mouth was desert dry. That's why he sounded so strange.

Pressure on his bladder sent him into the bathroom. As he relieved himself it started to penetrate: every vestige of Sammy was gone. No toothbrush, no hairbrush, no makeup, even the delicate perfume bottle he'd bought her—all gone. But if it had been nothing more than a con, why had she waited so many months and through so many encounters before robbing him? He staggered to the sink to wash his hands and splash his face, and recoiled from the image in the mirror.

A stranger looked back at him.

The frightened eyes staring out at him were now a pale grey. His hair was dark and straight rather than reddish and curly. His forehead was much higher because this alien hair seemed to be rapidly retreating toward the back of his neck. His skin tone was decidedly darker. Nose larger and bulbous on the tip. Ears clipped closer to his skull. His real ears had been rather protuberant. He looked down. His belly was larger, and the birthmark on his left hip was gone. He stumbled back to the toilet and vomited until he was reduced to dry heaves.

Whimpering, he returned to the sink, rinsed out his mouth, and gulped down water. Then stared at his hands. His wedding ring and the heavy signet ring with the family crest were missing. His gut twisted again, but he managed to keep from hurling. Back in the bedroom, he snatched up his clothes with trembling hands and started to dress. Because of his weight gain, he couldn't close the top clasp on his trousers, and the straining buttons on his shirt gapped open enough to reveal skin.

He left the bedroom and found the living room to be equally void of any trace of the occupant. On an impulse, he checked the kitchen. All the dishes, utensils, and food were gone. In this room he was more aware of a faint disinfectant smell, as if every surface had been washed down with bleach.

He made his way down the stairs and out into the street, where he stood blinking in the sunlight. He had lost a night. Then he realized that heat and humidity pounded at his head and shoulders. Sweat bloomed in his armpits and went rolling down his sides. It was high summer. When he'd come looking for Sammy the night of the ball it had been a cool fall night. Dear God, he had lost *months*!

He needed to get home. But how to accomplish that journey loomed monumental. No money, no comm, no proof that he was who he claimed to be. Not even a face. He guessed it was about twenty miles from Pony Town to the Cascades and his mansion. He didn't think he could walk one mile, much less twenty. Still, he wouldn't know until he tried. He walked away from the building. He tried not to, but he looked back several times until its salmon-colored stucco was hidden by other structures.

Two hours later his feet were a mass of stabbing pain, and he felt the wetness of a burst blister. He saw the glowing shield that indicated a police station and realized that he was an idiot. He had been kidnapped, assaulted, surgically altered. The police would help him. They would call his home, Hobb would arrive with the flitter, and he would be whisked away from all this. And the hue and cry would be raised for Sammy. Rohan swallowed bile. It was unfortunate but necessary. The creature deserved nothing less. He walked into the precinct house.

"I need to report a crime," he announced to the desk sergeant.

The man didn't even look up, just pushed over an etablet. "Write it up. Bring it back when you're done."

When he presented his name and title in his aristocratic accent, the man became a good deal more attentive. His eyes did narrow with suspicion as he studied the ill-fitting clothing, but the sergeant offered coffee and water. It would never do to offend if Rohan really was a member of the FFH.

Mollified, Rohan settled into a chair and typed up his experiences. The beverages were supplied and the desk sergeant sent the report up to his superiors. A few minutes later a captain arrived. He walked up to stand in front of Rohan and called over his shoulder to the desk clerk.

"Don't follow politics, do you, Johnson? This is not the Chancellor."

"As I indicated in my report, my appearance has been altered," Rohan said.

"And I just talked to the Chancellor's office. According to John Fujasaki, the Chancellor's aide, the Conde is in a meeting with the Prime Minister. Now, get out of here and try your con someplace else."

Rohan just kept staring up at the officer, trying to process the words. His removal was then expedited by the arrival of two burly officers, who frog-marched him out of the building.

Panic lay like a stone on his chest. Rohan gasped for breath. He stood on the sidewalk, blocking the flow of humanity and staring back at the police station. Eventually he resumed his slow march toward home.

He was getting odd looks because of his formal, too-small evening attire in the middle of the day, and his limping progress wasn't helping. A Hajin message runner gave him a somewhat sympathetic look. Rohan gathered his nerve and approached the alien.

"Excuse me. I've been robbed, and I need to make a call. May I borrow your comm? If you'll give me your name, I'll see that you're compensated once I have access to my funds."

The Hajin handed over his comm. "Of course." The creature ducked his head, his forelock veiling his eyes. "And you don't have to pay me."

The sudden kindness in the midst of the nightmare had tears stinging his eyes. "Thank you." Rohan forced the words past the lump in his throat. He took the offered comm and called his private line at the Exchequer. John answered.

"Chancellor's office, Fujasaki speaking."

"John," Rohan said. "John, listen. I'm in a nightmare. I think—"

"Who is this?"

"It's Rohan. I know it sounds incredible—"

The line went dead. Numbly, Rohan handed back the comm to the Hajin. "Thank you," he said automatically. One should always show respect to one's inferiors.

He turned and continued walking.

At the house, he didn't even attempt to explain the situation to the butler. Instead he shoved the elderly Hajin aside and ran, panting, up the long, curving staircase. Behind him were rising cries of alarm. He raced through Juliana's mirrored and gold-inlaid dressing room. Her Isanjo maid clutched a discarded ball gown against her chest and gazed at Rohan from wide, frightened eyes.

"Where is she? Where's my wife?"

The creature reverted to her alien nature and went swarming up the drapes to cower on the rod. The large golden eyes shifted toward the bedroom door.

Rohan stormed through. He was met with the sight of an expanse of bare white back, a few freckles on the shoulders. The man propped himself on his forearms, his doughy behind pumping in an age-old dance. A woman's soft cries emerged from among the tumbled pillows.

Juliana opened her eyes, looked at Rohan, and let out a piercing scream. The man who had been plowing her gave a grunt and pulled out.

"What in the hell?" he roared, and now Rohan finally saw his face.

It was him.

"The authorities arrived and took away the *madman*. I kept trying to make them understand. To realize that the Cara had placed an agent at the very heart of government. No one would listen. I would show them articles that proved what the impostor was doing, sending money to companies that I knew were fronts for the aliens. An audit would have revealed that funds were missing, redirected, but they wouldn't listen. Eventually, I realized if I ever wanted to be released I had to end my accusations. I also knew that in the sanatorium I was at greater risk of being assassinated. I needed to get free. Once I was released, I headed to the outer worlds. Here I tell the story to people like you." He rose to his feet, swaying. "I am Rohan Danilo Marcus Aubrey, Conde de Vargas, and I adjure you to act! Inform your superiors. Alert them to the danger!"

He seemed to have expended all his strength in the ringing call to arms. The drunk dropped heavily into his chair and his head nodded toward his chest.

Disgusted by his gullibility, and out the cost of a bottle, Tracy pushed back violently from the table. The shriek of the chair legs on the floor brought Rohan, or whatever his name might be, out of his stupor. The drunk belched and raised his head.

"Wha . . . ?"

"Nice. What a scam. He"—Tracy jerked a thumb at the bartender—"sells more booze, and you get to drink for free."

"Wha . . . ?" the grifter repeated.

"The Conde de Vargas is Prime Minister. Second only to the Emperor in power." Tracy tapped the name into the comm set in his jacket sleeve. "*This* is the *real* Rohan." Tracy thrust his arm under the man's nose, showing him the photos.

He waved a pudgy hand in a vague circle, indicating his visage. "I told you. They stole my face, my life . . . my wife . . . he made her love him again, or maybe love him for the first time."

Tracy shook his head and headed for the door.

"Wait!" the drunk called. The young officer looked back, and the drunken Scheherazade gave Tracy a desperate look. "Your duties will take you all over League space. If you see her tell her . . . tell her . . ." His voice was thick with unshed tears and an excess of booze. "I never saw Sammy again, and I need to . . . need to . . ." The man began to sob. "I love her," Rohan said brokenly. "Love her so much."

Embarrassment, pity, and fury warred for primacy. Tracy embraced the anger. Clapping slowly, Tracy said, "Nice touch."

The young officer stepped out into the darkness. The cold air cleared his head a bit, but he was still very drunk. He stared at the distant glow of the spaceport. Follow through on his threat? Go AWOL? He was only twenty-one. Was it worth risking a noose to walk away from casual insults and petty condescension? He realized that he could far too easily become that pathetic drunk in the bar, telling fantastic stories for the price of a drink.

I saved the heir to the throne from a scandal that might have rocked the League. We shared a secret love. I know that Mercedes de Arango, the Infanta, loves me, the tailor's son.

But his story was *true*, not like that bit of farrago to which he'd just been treated.

And your story is any less fantastic?

No, Rohan's—or whatever his name was—his story couldn't be true. If it was, then he, Tracy Belmanor, second lieutenant in the Imperial Fleet, was privy to a secret that would not just rock the League but destroy it. He peered suspiciously into the shadowy depths of the alley to his left and saw nothing beyond the hulking shadow of a garbage container. But what if they were there, hiding among them, watching, waiting, listening? What if they decided they needed to silence him?

Tracy broke into a run and didn't stop until he reached the ship. The outer hatch cycled closed and he leaned, panting, against the bulkhead. Inside the steel-and-resin bulwark of the warship, his panic receded. How foolish. The whole thing had been a scam. Sammy didn't exist. The Cara weren't hiding among them. Human males were still at the apex of power.

It had just been a story.

Jim Butcher

New York Times bestseller Jim Butcher is best known for the Dresden Files series, starring Harry Dresden, a wizard for hire who goes down some very mean streets indeed to do battle against the dark creatures of the supernatural world, and who is one of the most popular fictional characters of the twenty-first century to date; he even had his own TV show. The Dresden Files books include *Storm Front, Fool Moon, Grave Peril, Summer Knight, Death Masks, Blood Rites, Dead Beat, Proven Guilty, White Night, Small Favor, Turn Coat,* and *Changes.* Butcher is also the author of the swashbuckling sword and sorcery Codex Alera series, consisting of *Furies of Calderon, Academ's Fury, Cursor's Fury, Captain's Fury,* and *Princeps' Fury.* His most recent books are *First Lord's Fury,* the new Codex Alera novel, and *Ghost Story,* a Dresden Files novel. There's also a collection of stories featuring Harry Dresden, *Side Jobs: Stories from the Dresden Files.* Coming up is a new Dresden Files novel, *Cold Days.* Butcher lives in Missouri with his wife, his son, and a ferocious guard dog.

Butcher flabbergasted everyone by killing Harry Dresden off at the end of *Changes.* (The next novel, *Ghost Story,* was told from the point of view of Harry's ghost!) Here Harry's young protégé, trying to carry on the fight against the forces of darkness *without* Harry, finds that she has some very big shoes to fill, and that she'd better fill them *fast*—or die.

BOMBSHELLS

I miss my boss.

It's been most of a year since I helped him die, and ever since then I've been the only professional wizard in the city of Chicago.

Well, okay. I'm not, like, officially a wizard. I'm still sort of an apprentice. And no one really pays me, unless you count the wallets and valuables I lift from bodies sometimes, so I guess I'm more amateur than professional. And I don't have a PI license like my boss did, or an ad in the phone book.

But I'm all there is. I'm not as strong as he was, and I'm not as good as he was. I'm just going to have to be enough.

So anyway, there I was, washing the blood off in Waldo Butters' shower.

I did a lot of living outdoors these days, which didn't seem nearly as horrible during the summer and early autumn as it had during the arctic chill of the previous superwinter. It was like sleeping on a tropical beach by comparison. Still, I missed things like regular access to plumbing, and Waldo let me clean up whenever I needed to. I had the shower heat turned all the way up, and it was heaven. It was kind of a scourgey, scoury heaven, but heaven nonetheless.

The floor of the shower turned red for a few seconds, then faded to pink for a while as I sluiced the blood off. It wasn't mine. A gang of Fomor servitors had been carrying a fifteen-year-old boy down an alley toward Lake Michigan. If they'd gotten him there, he'd have been facing a fate worse than death. I intervened, but that bastard Listen cut his throat rather than give him up. I tried to save him while Listen and his buddies ran. I failed. And I'd been right there with him, feeling everything he did, feeling his confusion and pain and terror as he died.

Harry wouldn't have felt that. Harry would have saved the day. He would have smashed the Fomor goons around like bowling pins, picked the kid up like some kind of serial-movie action hero, and taken him to safety.

I missed my boss.

I used a lot of soap. I probably cried. I had begun ignoring tears months ago, and at times I honestly didn't know when they were falling. Once I was clean—physically, anyway—I just stood there soaking up the heat, letting the water course all over me. The scar on my leg where I'd been shot was still wrinkled, but the color had changed from purple and red to angry pink. Butters said it would be gone in a couple of years. I was walking normally again, unless I pushed myself too hard. But yikes, my legs and various pieces needed to get reacquainted with a razor, even with medium-blond hair.

I was going to ignore them, but . . . grooming is important for keeping one's spirits up. A well-kept body for a well-kept mind and all that. I wasn't a fool. I knew I wasn't exactly flying level lately. My morale needed all the boost it could get. I leaned out of the shower and swiped Andi's pink plastic razor. I'd pay Waldo's werewolf girlfriend back for it later.

I wrapped up about the same time as the hot water ran out, got out of the shower, and toweled off. My things were in a pile by the door—some garage-sale Birkenstocks, an old nylon hiker's backpack, and my bloodied clothes. Another set gone. And the sandals had left partial tracks in blood at the scene, so I'd have to get rid of them, too. I was going to have to hit another thrift store at this rate. Normally, that would have cheered me up, but shopping just wasn't what it used to be.

I was carefully going over the tub and floor for fallen hairs and so on when someone knocked. I didn't stop scanning the floor. In my line of work, people can and will do awful things to you with discarded bits of your body. Not cleaning up after yourself is like asking for someone to boil your blood from twenty blocks away. No, thank you.

"Yes?" I called.

"Hey, Molly," Waldo said. "There's, uh . . . there's someone here to talk to you."

We'd prearranged a lot of things. If he'd used the word "feeling" at any point in his sentence, I would have known there was trouble outside the door. Not using it meant that there wasn't—or that he couldn't see it. I slipped on my bracelets and my ring and set both of my wands down where I could snatch them up instantly. Only then did I start putting clothes on.

"Who?" I called.

He was working hard not to sound nervous around me. I appreciated the effort. It was sweet. "Says her name is Justine. Says you know her."

I did know Justine. She was a thrall of the vampires of the White Court. Or at least a personal assistant to one and the girlfriend of another. Harry always thought well of her, though he was a big goofy idiot when it came to women who might show the potential to become damsels in distress.

"But if he was here," I muttered to myself, "he'd help her."

I didn't wipe the steam off the mirror before I left the bathroom. I didn't want to look at anything in there.

Justine was a handful of years older than me, but her hair had turned pure white. She was a knockout, one of those girls all the boys assume are too pretty to approach. She had on jeans and a button-down shirt several sizes too large for her. The shirt was Thomas's, I was certain. Her body language was poised, very neutral. Justine was as good at hiding her emotions as anyone I'd ever seen, but I could sense leashed tension and quiet fear beneath the calm surface.

I'm a wizard, or damned close to it, and I work with the mind. People don't really get to hide things from me.

If Justine was afraid, it was because she feared for Thomas. If she'd come to me for help, it was because she couldn't get help from the White Court. We could have had a polite conversation that led up to that revelation, but I had less and less patience for the amenities lately, so I cut to the chase.

"Hello, Justine. Why should I help you with Thomas when his own family won't?"

Justine's eyes bugged out. So did Waldo's.

I was getting used to that reaction.

"How did you know?" Justine asked quietly.

When you're into magic, people always assume anything you do must be connected to it. Harry always thought that was funny. To him, magic was just one more set of tools that the mind could use to solve problems. The mind was the more important part of that pairing. "Does that matter?"

She frowned and looked away from me. She shook her head. "He's missing. I know he left on some kind of errand for Lara, but she says she doesn't know anything about it. She's lying."

"She's a vampire. And you didn't answer my first question." The words came out a little harsher and harder than they'd sounded in my head. I tried to relax a little. I folded my arms and leaned against a wall. "Why should I help you?"

It's not like I wasn't planning to help her. But I knew a secret about Harry and Thomas few others did. I had to know if Justine knew the secret, too, or if I'd have to keep it hidden around her.

Justine met my eyes with hers for a moment. The look was penetrating. "If you can't go to family for help," she said, "who can you turn to?"

I averted my eyes before it could turn into an actual soulgaze, but her words and the cumulative impression of her posture, her presence, her *self*, answered the question for me.

She knew.

Thomas and Harry were half brothers. She'd have gone to Harry for help if he was alive. I was the only thing vaguely like an heir to his power around these parts, and she hoped I would be willing to step into his shoes. His huge, stompy, terrifying shoes.

"You go to friends," I said quietly. "I'll need something of Thomas's. Hair or fingernail clippings would be . . ."

She produced a zip-closed plastic bag from the breast pocket of the shirt and offered it to me without a word. I went over and picked it up. It had a number of dark hairs in it.

"You're sure they're his?"

Justine gestured toward her own snow-white mane. "It's not like they're easy to confuse."

I looked up to find Butters watching me silently from the other side of the room. He was a beaky little guy, wiry and quick. His hair had been electrocuted and then frozen that way. His eyes were steady and worried. He cut up corpses for the government, professionally, but he was one of the more savvy people in town when it came to the supernatural.

"What?" I asked him.

He considered his words before he spoke—less because he was afraid of me than because he cared about not hurting my feelings. That was the reverse of most people these days. "Is this something you should get involved in, Molly?"

What he really wanted to ask me was if I was sane. If I was going to help or just make things a lot worse.

"I don't know," I said honestly. I looked at Justine and said, "Wait here." Then I got my stuff, took the hairs, and left.

The first thing Harry Dresden ever taught me about magic was a tracking spell.

"It's a simple principle, kid," he told me. "We're creating a link between two similar things out of energy. Then we make the energy give us an indicator of some kind, so that we can tell which way it's flowing."

"What are we going to find?" I asked.

He held up a rather thick grey hair and nodded back toward his dog, Mouse. He should have been named Moose. The giant, shaggy temple dog was pony-sized. "Mouse," Harry said, "go get lost and we'll see if we can find you."

The big dog yawned and padded agreeably toward the door. Harry let him out and then came over to sit down next to me. We were in his living room. A couple of nights before, I had thrown myself at him. Naked. And he'd dumped a pitcher of ice water over my head. I was still mortified— but he was probably right. It was the right thing for him to do. He always did the right thing, even if it meant he lost out. I still wanted to be with him so much, but maybe the time wasn't right yet.

That was okay. I could be patient. And I still got to be with him in a different way almost every day.

"All right," I said when he sat back down. "What do I do?"

In the years since that day, the spell had become routine. I'd used it to find lost people, secret places, missing socks, and generally to poke my nose where it probably didn't belong. Harry would have said that went with the territory of being a wizard. Harry was right.

I stopped in the alley outside Butters's apartment and sketched a circle on the concrete with a small piece of pink chalk. I closed the circle with a tiny effort of will, drew out one of the hairs from the plastic bag, and held it up. I focused the energy of the spell, bringing its different elements together in my head. When we'd started, Harry had let me use four different objects, teaching me how to attach ideas to them, to represent the different pieces of the spell, but that kind of thing wasn't necessary. Magic all happens inside the head of the wizard. You can use props to make things simpler, and in truly complex spells they make the difference between impossible and merely almost impossible. For this one, though, I didn't need the props anymore.

I gathered the different pieces of the spell in my head, linked them together, infused them with a moderate effort of will, and then with a murmured word released that energy down into the hair in my fingers. Then I popped the hair into my mouth, broke the chalk circle with a brush of my foot, and rose.

Harry always used an object as the indicator for his tracking spells—his amulet, a compass, or some kind of pendulum. I hadn't wanted to hurt his feelings, but that kind of thing really wasn't necessary, either. I could feel the magic coursing through the hair, making my lips tingle gently. I got out a cheap little plastic compass and a ten-foot length of chalk line. I set it up and snapped it to mark out magnetic north.

Then I took the free end of the line and turned slowly, until the tingling sensation was centered on my lips. Lips are extremely sensitive parts of the body, generally, and I've found that they give you the best tactile feedback for this sort of thing. Once I knew which direction Thomas was, I oriented the chalk line that way, made sure it was tight, and snapped it again, resulting in an extremely elongated V shape, like the tip of a giant needle. I measured the distance at the base of the V.

Then I turned ninety degrees, walked five hundred paces, and repeated the process.

Promise me you won't tell my high school math teacher about it, but after that I sat down and applied trigonometry to real life.

The math wasn't hard. I had the two angles measured against magnetic north. I had the distance between them in units of Molly-paces. Molly-paces aren't terribly scientific, but for purposes of this particular application, they were practical enough to calculate the distance to Thomas.

Using such simple tools, I couldn't get a measurement precise enough to know which door to kick down, but I now knew that he was relatively nearby—within four or five miles, as opposed to being at the North Pole or something. I move around the city a lot, because a moving target is a lot harder to hit. I probably covered three or four times that on an average day.

I'd have to get a lot closer before I could pinpoint his location any more precisely than that. So I turned my lips toward the tingle and started walking.

Thomas was in a small office building on a big lot.

The building was three stories, not huge, though it sat amidst several much larger structures. The lot it stood upon was big enough to hold something a lot bigger. Instead, most of it was landscaped into a manicured lawn and garden, complete with water features and a very small, very modest wrought-iron fence. The building itself showed a lot of stone and marble in its design, and it had more class in its cornices than the towers nearby had in their whole structures. It was gorgeous and understated at the same time; on that block, it looked like a single, small, perfect diamond being displayed amidst giant jars of rhinestones.

There were no signs outside it. There was no obvious way in, beyond a set of gates guarded by competent-looking men in dark suits. Expensive dark suits. If the guards could afford to wear those to work, it meant that whoever owned that building had money. Serious money.

I circled the building to be sure, and felt the tingling energy of the tracking spell confirming Thomas's location; but even though I'd been careful to stay on the far side of the street, someone inside noticed me. I could feel one guard's eyes tracking me, even behind his sunglasses. Maybe I should have done the initial approach under a veil—but Harry had always been against using magic except when it was truly necessary, and it was way too easy to start using it for every little thing if you let yourself.

In some ways, I'm better at the "how" of magic than Harry was. But I've come to learn that I might never be as smart as him when it came to the "why."

I went into a nearby Starbucks and got myself a cup of liquid life and started thinking about how to get in. My tongue was telling me all about what great judgment I had when I sensed the presence of supernatural power rapidly coming nearer.

I didn't panic. Panic gets you killed. Instead I turned smoothly on one heel and slipped into a short hallway leading to a small restroom. I went inside, shut the door behind me, and drew my wands from my hip pocket. I checked the energy level on my bracelets. Both of them were ready to go. My rings were all full up, too, which was about as ideal as things could get.

So I ordered my thoughts, made a small effort of will, whispered a word, and vanished.

Veils were complex magic, but I had a knack for them. Becoming truly and completely invisible was a real pain in the neck: passing light completely through you was a literal stone-cold bitch, because it left you freezing cold and blind as a bat to boot. Becoming unseen, though, was a different proposition entirely. A good veil would reduce your visibility to little more than a few flickers in the air, to a few vague shadows where they shouldn't be, but it did more than that. It created a sense of ordinariness in the air around you, an aura of boring unremarkability that you usually only felt in a job you didn't like, around three thirty in the afternoon. Once you combined that suggestion with a greatly reduced visible profile, remaining unnoticed was at least as easy as breathing.

As I vanished into that veil, I also called up an image, another combination of illusion and suggestion. This one was simple: me, as I'd appeared in the mirror a moment before, clean and seemingly perky and toting a fresh cup of creamy goodness. The sensation that went with it was just a kind of heavy dose of me: the sound of my steps and movement, the scent of Butters's shampoo, the aroma of my cup of coffee. I tied the image to one of the rings on my fingers and left it there, drawing from the energy I'd stored in a moonstone. Then I turned around, with my image layered over my actual body like a suit made of light, and walked out of the coffee shop.

Once outside, the evasion was a simple maneuver, the way all the good ones are. My image turned left and I turned right.

To anyone watching, a young woman had just come out of the store and gone sauntering down the street with her coffee. She was obviously enjoying her day. I'd put a little extra bounce and sway into the image's movements, to make her that much more noticeable (and therefore a better distraction). She'd go on walking down that street for a mile or more before she simply vanished.

Meanwhile, the real me moved silently into an alleyway and watched.

My image hadn't gone a hundred yards before a man in a black turtleneck sweater stepped out of an alley and began following it—a servitor of the Fomor. Those jerks were everywhere these days, like roaches, only more disgusting and harder to kill.

Only . . . that was just too easy. One servitor wouldn't have set my instinct alarms to jingling. They were strong, fast, and tough, sure, but no more so than any number of creatures. They didn't possess mounds of magical power; if they had, the Fomor would never have let them leave in the first place.

Something else was out there. Something that had wanted me to be distracted, watching the apparent servitor follow the apparent Molly. And if something knew me well enough to set up this sort of diversion to ensnare my attention, then it knew me well enough to find me, even beneath my veil. There were a really limited number of people who could do that.

I slipped a hand into my nylon backpack and drew out my knife, the M9 bayonet my brother had brought home from Afghanistan. I drew the heavy blade out, closed my eyes, and turned quickly with the knife in one hand and my coffee in the other. I flicked the lid off the coffee with my thumb and slewed the liquid into a wide arc at about chest level.

I heard a gasp and oriented on it, opened my eyes, and stepped toward the source of the sound, driving the knife into the air before me at slightly higher than the level of my own heart.

The steel of the blade suddenly erupted with a coruscation of light as it pierced a veil that hung in the air only inches away from me. I stepped forward rapidly through the veil, pushing the point of the knife before me toward the suddenly revealed form behind the veil. She was a woman, taller than me, dressed in ragged (coffee-stained) clothes, but with her long, fiery autumn hair unbound and wind tossed. She twisted to one side, off balance, until her shoulders touched the brick wall of the alley.

I did not relent, driving the blade toward her throat—until at the last second, one pale, slender hand snapped up and grasped my wrist, quick as a serpent but stronger and colder. My face wound up only a few inches from hers as I put the heel of one hand against the knife and leaned against it slightly—enough to push against her strength, but not enough to throw me off balance if she made a quick move. She was lean and lovely, even in the rags, with wide, oblique green eyes and perfect bone structure that could only be found in half a dozen supermodels—and in every single one of the Sidhe.

"Hello, Auntie," I said in a level voice. "It isn't nice to sneak up behind me. Especially lately."

She held my weight off of her with one arm, though it wasn't easy for her. There was a quality of strain to her melodic voice. "Child," she breathed. "You anticipated my approach. Had I not stopped thee, thou wouldst have driven cold iron into my flesh, causing me agonies untold. Thou wouldst have spilled my life's blood upon the ground." Her eyes widened. "Thou wouldst have killed me."

"I wouldst," I agreed pleasantly.

Her mouth spread into a wide smile, and her teeth were daintily pointed. "I have taught thee well."

Then she twisted with a lithe and fluid grace, away from the blade and to her feet a good long step away from me. I watched her and lowered the knife—but I didn't put it away. "I don't have time for lessons right now, Auntie Lea."

"I am not here to teach thee, child."

"I don't have time for games, either."

"Nor did I come to play with thee," the Leanansidhe said, "but to give thee warning: thou art not safe here."

I quirked an eyebrow at her. "Wow. Gosh."

She tilted her head at me in reproof, and her mouth thinned. Her eyes moved past me to look down the alley, and she shot a quick glance behind her. Her expression changed. She didn't quite lose the smug superiority that always colored her features, but she toned it down a good deal, and she lowered her voice. "Thou makest jests, child, but thou art in grave peril—as am I. We should not linger here." She shifted her eyes to mine. "If thou dost wish to brace this foe, if thou wouldst recover my Godson's brother, there are things I must tell thee."

I narrowed my eyes. Harry's Faerie Godmother had taken over as my mentor when Harry died, but she wasn't exactly one of the good faeries. In fact, she was the second in command to Mab, the Queen of Air and Darkness, and she was a bloodthirsty, dangerous being who divided her enemies into two categories: those who were dead, and those in which she had not yet taken pleasure. I hadn't known that she knew about Harry and Thomas—but it didn't shock me.

Lea was a murderous, cruel creature—but as far as I knew, she had never lied to me. Technically.

"Come," said the Leanansidhe. She turned and walked briskly toward the far end of the alley, gathering a seeming and a veil around her as she went, to hide herself from notice.

I glanced back toward the building where Thomas was being held, ground my teeth, and followed her, merging my veil with hers as we left.

We walked Chicago's streets unseen by thousands of eyes. The people we passed all took a few extra steps to avoid us, without really thinking about it. It's important to lay out an avoidance suggestion like that when you're in a crowd. Being unseen is kind of pointless if dozens of people keep bumping into you.

"Tell me, child," Lea said, shifting abruptly out of her archaic dialect. She did that sometimes, when we were alone. "What do you know of svartalves?"

"A little," I said. "They're from northern Europe, originally. They're small and they live underground. They're the best magical craftsmen on earth; Harry bought things from them whenever he could afford it, but they weren't cheap."

"How dry," the faerie sorceress said. "You sound like a book, child. Books frequently bear little resemblance to life." Her intense green eyes glittered as she turned to watch a young woman with an infant walk by us. "What do you *know* of them?"

"They're dangerous," I said quietly. "Very dangerous. The old Norse gods used to go to them for weapons and armor and they didn't try to fight them. Harry said he was glad he never had to fight a svartalf. They're also honorable. They signed the Unseelie Accords and they uphold them. They have a reputation for being savage about protecting their own. They aren't human, they aren't kind, and only a fool crosses them."

"Better," the Leanansidhe said. Then she added, in an offhand tone, "Fool."

I glanced back toward the building I'd found. "That's their property?"

"Their fortress," Lea replied, "the center of their mortal affairs, here at the great crossroads. What else do you recall of them?"

I shook my head. "Um. One of the Norse goddesses got jacked for her jewelry—"

"Freya," Lea said.

"And the thief—"

"Loki."

"Yeah, him. He pawned it with the svartalves or something, and there was a big to-do about getting it back."

"One wonders how it is possible to be so vague and so accurate at the same time," Lea said.

I smirked.

Lea frowned at me. "You knew the story perfectly well. You were . . . tweaking my nose, I believe is the saying."

"I had a good teacher in snark class," I said. "Freya went to get her necklace back, and the svartalves were willing to do it—but only if she agreed to kiss each and every one of them."

Lea threw her head back and laughed. "Child," she said, a wicked edge to her voice, "remember that many of the old tales were translated and transcribed by rather prudish scholars."

"What do you mean?" I asked.

"That the svartalves most certainly did not agree to give up one of the most valuable jewels in the universe for a society-wide trip to first base."

I blinked a couple of times and felt my cheeks heat up. "You mean she had to . . ."

"Precisely."

"*All* of them?"

"Indeed."

"Wow," I said. "I like to accessorize as much as the next girl, but that's over the line. Way over. I mean, you can't even *see* the line from there."

"Perhaps," Lea said. "I suppose it depends upon how badly one needs to recover something from the svartalves."

"Uh. You're saying I need to pull a train to get Thomas out of there? 'Cause . . . that just isn't going to happen."

Lea showed her teeth in another smile. "Morality is amusing."

"Would you do it?"

Lea looked offended. "For the sake of another? Certainly not. Have you any idea of the obligation that would incur?"

"Um. Not exactly."

"This is not my choice to make. You must ask yourself this question: Is your untroubled conscience more valuable to you than the vampire's life?"

"No. But there's got to be another way."

Lea seemed to consider that for a moment. "Svartalves love beauty. They covet it the way a dragon lusts for gold. You are young, lovely, and . . . I believe the phrase is 'smoking hot.' The exchange of your favors for the vampire, a straightforward transaction, is almost certain to succeed, assuming he still lives."

"We'll call that one plan B," I said. "Or maybe plan X. Or plan XXX. Why not just break in and burgle him out?"

"Child," the Leanansidhe chided me. "The svartalves are quite skilled in the Art, and this is one of their strongholds. *I* could not attempt such a thing and leave with my life." Lea tilted her head to one side and gave me one of those alien looks that made my skin crawl. "Do you wish to recover Thomas or not?"

"I wish to explore my options," I said.

The faerie sorceress shrugged. "Then I advise you to do so as rapidly as possible. If he yet lives, Thomas Raith might count the remainder of his life in hours."

I opened the door to Waldo's apartment, shut and locked it behind me, and said, "Found him."

As I turned toward the room, someone slapped me hard across the face.

This wasn't a "Hey, wake up" kind of slap. It was an openhanded blow, one that would have really hurt if it was delivered with a closed fist. I staggered to one side, stunned.

Waldo's girlfriend, Andi, folded her arms and stared at me through narrowed eyes for a moment. She was a girl of medium height, but she was a werewolf and she was built like a pinup model who was thinking about going into professional wrestling. "Hi, Molly," she said.

"Hi," I said. "And . . . ow."

She held up a pink plastic razor. "Let's have a talk about boundaries."

Something ugly way down deep inside me somewhere unsheathed its claws and tensed up. That was the part of me that wanted to catch up to Listen and do things involving railroad spikes and drains in the floor. Everyone has that inside them, somewhere. It takes fairly horrible things to awaken that kind of savagery, but it's in all of us. It's the part of us that causes senseless atrocities, that makes war hell.

No one wants to talk about it or think about it, but I couldn't afford that kind of willing ignorance. I hadn't always been this way, but after a year fighting the Fomor and the dark underside of Chicago's supernatural scene, I was somebody else. That part of me was awake and active and constantly pushing my emotions into conflict with my rationality.

I told that part of me to shut up and sit its ass down.

"Okay," I said. "But later. I'm kind of busy."

I started to brush past her into the room, but she stopped me short by placing a hand against my sternum and shoved me back against the door. It didn't look like she was trying but I hit the wood firmly.

"Now's good," she said.

In my imagination, I clenched my fists and counted to five in an enraged scream. I was sure Harry had never had to deal with this kind of nonsense. I didn't have time to lose, but I didn't want to start something violent with Andi, either. I'd catch all kinds of hell if I threw down. I allowed myself the pleasure of gritting my teeth, took a deep breath, and nodded. "Okay. What's on your mind, Andi?"

I didn't add the words "you bitch" but I thought them really loud. I should probably be a nicer person.

"This is not your apartment," Andi said. "You don't get to roll in and out of here whenever you damned well please, no matter the hour, no matter what's going on. Have you even stopped to think about what you're doing to Butters?"

"I'm not doing anything to Butters," I said. "I'm just borrowing the shower."

Andi's voice sharpened. "You came here today covered in blood. I don't know what happened, but you know what? I don't care. All I care about is what kind of trouble you might draw down onto other people."

"There was no trouble," I said. "Look, I'll buy you a new razor."

"This isn't about property or money, Christ," Andi said. "This is about respect. Butters is there for you whenever you need help, and you barely do so much as to thank him for it. What if you'd been followed here? Do you have any idea how much trouble he could get into for helping you out?"

"I wasn't followed," I said.

"Today," Andi said. "But what about next time? You have power. You can fight. I don't have what you do, but even I can fight. Butters can't. Whose shower are you going to use if it's his blood all over you?"

I folded my arms and looked carefully away from Andi. In some part of my brain I knew that she had a point, but that reasoning was coming in a distant second to my sudden urge to slap her.

"Look, Molly," she said, her voice becoming more gentle. "I know things haven't been easy for you lately. Ever since Harry died. When his ghost showed up. I know it wasn't fun."

I just looked at her without speaking. Not easy or fun. That was one way to describe it.

"There's something I think you need to hear."

"What's that?"

Andi leaned forward slightly and sharpened her words. "Get over it."

The apartment was very quiet for a moment, and the inside of me wasn't. That ugly part of me started getting louder and louder. I closed my eyes.

"People die, Molly," Andi continued. "They leave. And life goes on. Harry may have been the first friend you lost, but he won't be the last. I get that you're hurting. I get that you're trying to step into some really big shoes. But that doesn't give you the right to abuse people's better natures. A *lot* of people are hurting lately, if you didn't notice."

If I didn't notice. God, I would absolutely *kill* to be able not to notice people's pain. Not to live it beside them. Not to sense its echoes hours or days later. The ugly part of me, the black part of my heart, wanted to open a psychic channel to Andi and *show* her the kind of thing I went through on a regular basis. Let *her* see how she would like my life. And we'd see if she was so righteous afterward. It would be wrong, but . . .

I took a slow breath. No. Harry told me once that you can always tell when you're about to rationalize your way to a bad decision. It's when you start using phrases such as "It would be wrong, but . . ." His advice was to leave the conjunction out of the sentence: "It would be wrong." Period.

So I didn't do anything rash. I didn't let the rising tumult inside me come out. I spoke softly. "What is it you'd like me to do, exactly?"

Andi huffed out a little breath and waved a vague hand. "Just . . . get your head out of your ass, girl. I am not being unreasonable here, given that my boyfriend gave you a key to his freaking apartment."

I blinked once at that. Wow. I hadn't even really considered that aspect of what Butters had done. Romance and romantic conflict hadn't exactly been high on my list lately. Andi had nothing to worry about on that front . . . but I guess she didn't have way too much awareness of people's emotions to tip her off to that fact. Now I could put a name to some of the worry in her. She wasn't jealous, exactly, but she was certainly aware of the fact that I was a young woman a lot of men found attractive, and that Waldo was a man.

And she loved him. I could feel that, too.

"Think about him," Andi said quietly. "Please. Just . . . try to take care of him the way he takes care of you. Call ahead. If you'd just walked in covered with blood next Saturday night, he would have had something very awkward to explain to his parents."

I most likely would have sensed the unfamiliar presences inside the apartment before I got close enough to touch the door. But there was no point in telling Andi that. It wasn't her fault that she didn't really understand the kind of life I lived. Certainly, she didn't deserve to die for it, no matter what the opinion of my inner Sith.

I had to make my choices with my head. My heart was too broken to be trusted.

"I'll try," I said.

"Okay," Andi said.

For a second, the fingers of my right hand quivered, and I found the ugly part of me about to hurl power at the other woman, blind her, deafen her, drown her in vertigo. Lea had shown me how. But I reeled the urge to attack back under control. "Andi," I said instead.

"Yes?"

"Don't hit me again unless you intend to kill me."

I didn't mean it as a threat, exactly. It was just that I tended to react with my instincts when things started getting violent. The psychic turbulence of that kind of conflict didn't make me fall over screaming in pain anymore, but it did make it really hard to think clearly over the furious roaring of ugly me. If Andi hit me like that again . . . well. I wasn't completely sure how I would react.

I'm not Mad Hatter insane. I'm pretty sure. But studying survival under someone like Auntie Lea leaves you ready to protect yourself, not to play well with others.

Threat or not, Andi had seen her share of conflict, and she didn't back down. "If I don't think you need a good smack in the face, I won't give you one."

Waldo and Justine had gone out to pick up some dinner, and got back about ten minutes later. We all sat down to eat while I reported on the situation.

"Svartalfheim," Justine breathed. "That's . . . that's not good."

"Those are the Norse guys, right?" Butters asked.

I filled them in between bites of orange chicken, relaying what I had learned from the Leanansidhe. There was a little silence after I did.

"So . . ." Andi said after a moment. "The plan is to . . . boink him free?"

I gave her a look.

"I'm just asking," Andi said in a mild voice.

"They'd never sell," Justine said, her voice low, tight. "Not tonight."

I eyed her. "Why not?"

"They concluded an alliance today," she said. "There's a celebration tonight. Lara was invited."

"What alliance?" I asked.

"A nonaggression pact," Justine said, "with the Fomor."

I felt my eyes widen.

The Fomor situation just kept getting worse and worse. Chicago was far from the most preyed-upon city in the world, and they had still made the streets a nightmare for those of even modest magical talent. I didn't have access to the kind of information I had when I was working with Harry and the White Council, but I'd heard things through the Paranet and other sources. The Fomor were kind of an all-star team of bad guys, the survivors and outcasts and villains of a dozen different pantheons that had gone down a long time ago. They'd banded together under the banner of a group of beings known as the Fomor, and had been laying quiet for a long time—for thousands of years, in fact.

Now they were on the move—and even powerful interests like Svartalfheim, the nation of the svartalves, were getting out of the way.

Wow, I was so not wizard enough to deal with this.

"Lara must have sent Thomas in for something," Justine said. "To steal information, to disrupt the alliance somehow. Something. Trespassing would be bad enough. If he was captured spying on them . . ."

"They'll have a demonstration," I said quietly. "They'll make an example."

"Couldn't the White Court get him out?" Waldo asked.

"If the White Court seeks the return of one of their own, it would be like admitting they sent an agent in to screw around with Svartalfheim," I said. "Lara can't do that without serious repercussions. She'll deny that Thomas's intrusion had anything to do with her."

Justine rose and paced the room, her body tight. "We have to go. We have to do something. I'll pay the price; I'll pay it ten times. We have to *do* something!"

I took a few more bites of orange chicken, frowning and thinking.

"Molly!" Justine said.

I looked at the chicken. I liked the way the orange sauce contrasted with the deep green of the broccoli and the soft white contours of the rice. The three colors made a pleasant complement. It was . . . beautiful, really.

"They covet beauty like a dragon covets gold," I murmured.

Butters seemed to clue in to the fact that I was onto something. He leaned back in his chair and ate steadily from a box of noodles, his chopsticks precise. He didn't need to look to use them.

Andi picked up on it a second later and tilted her head to one side. "Molly?" she asked.

"They're having a party tonight," I said. "Right, Justine?"

"Yes."

Andi nodded impatiently. "What are we going to do?"

"We," I said, "are going shopping."

I'm kind of a tomboy. Not because I don't like being a girl or anything, because for the most part I think it's pretty sweet. But I like the outdoors, and physical activities, and learning stuff and reading things and building things. I've never really gotten very deep into the girly parts of being a girl. Andi was a little bit better at it than me. The fact that her mother hadn't brought her up the way mine had probably accounted for it. In my house, makeup was for going to church and for women with easy morals.

I know, I know: the mind boggles at the contradiction. I had issues way before I got involved with magic, believe me.

I wasn't sure how to accomplish what we needed in time to get to the party, but once I explained what we needed, I found out that when it came to being a girly girl, Justine had her shit wired tight.

Within minutes a town car picked us up and whisked us away to a private salon in the Loop, where Justine produced a completely unmarked, plain white credit card. About twenty staff members—wardrobe advisors, hairdressers, makeup artists, tailors, and accessory technicians—leapt into action and got us kitted out for the mission in a little more than an hour.

I couldn't really get away from the mirror this time. I tried to look at the young woman in it objectively, as if she was someone else, and not the one who had helped kill the man she loved and who had then failed him again by being unable to prevent even his ghost from being destroyed in its determination to protect others. That bitch deserved to be run over by a train or something.

The girl in the mirror was tall and had naturally blond hair that had been rapidly swirled up off of her neck and suspended with gleaming black chopsticks. She looked lean, probably too much so, but had a little too much muscle tone to be a meth addict. The little black dress she wore would turn heads. She looked a little tired, even with the expertly applied makeup. She was pretty—if you didn't know her, and if you didn't look too hard at what was going on in her blue eyes.

A white stretch limo pulled up to get us, and I managed to dodder out to it without falling all over myself.

"Oh my God," Andi said when we got in. The redhead stuck her feet out and wiggled them. "I love these shoes! If I have to wolf out and eat somebody's face, I am going to cry to leave these behind."

Justine smiled at her but then looked out the window, her lovely face distant, worried. "They're just shoes."

"Shoes that make my legs and my butt look awesome!" Andi said.

"Shoes that hurt," I said. My wounded leg might have healed up, but moving around in these spiky torture devices was a new motion, and a steady ache was spreading up through my leg toward my hip. The last thing I needed was for my leg to cramp up and drop me to the ground, the way it had kept doing when I first started walking on it again. Any shoes with heels that high should come with their own safety net. Or a parachute.

We'd gone with similar outfits: stylish little black dresses, black chokers, and black pumps that proclaimed us hopeful that we wouldn't spend much time on our feet. Each of us had a little Italian leather clutch, too. I'd put most of my magical gear in mine. All of us had our hair up in styles that varied only slightly. There were forged Renaissance paintings which had not had as much artist's attention as our faces.

"It just takes practice wearing them," Justine said. "Are you sure this is going to work?"

"Of course it is," I said calmly. "You've been to clubs, Justine. The three of us together would skip the line to any place in town. We're a matched set of hotness."

"Like the Robert Palmer girls," Andi said drily.

"I was going to go with Charlie's Angels," I said. "Oh, speaking of"—I opened the clutch and drew out a quartz crystal the size of my thumb—"Bosley, can you hear me?"

A second later, the crystal vibrated in my fingers and we heard Waldo's faint voice coming from it. "Loud and clear, Angels. You think these will work once you get inside?"

"Depends on how paranoid they are," I said. "If they're paranoid, they'll have defenses in place to cut off any magical communications. If they're murderously paranoid, they'll have defenses in place that let us talk so that they can listen in, and then they'll kill us."

"Fun," Butters said. "Okay, I've got the Paranet chat room up. For what it's worth, the hivemind is online."

"What have you found out?" Andi asked.

"They'll look human," Waldo replied. "Their real forms are . . . well, there's some discussion, but the basic consensus is that they look like aliens."

"Ripley or Roswell?" I asked.

"Roswell. More or less. They can wear flesh forms, though, kind of like the Red Court vampires did. So be aware that they'll be disguised."

"Got it," I said. "Anything else?"

"Not much," he said. "There's just too much lore floating around to pick out anything for sure. They might be allergic to salt. They might be supernaturally OCD and flip out if you wear your clothes inside out. They might turn to stone in sunlight."

I growled. "It was worth a shot. Okay. Keep the discussion going, and I'll get back to you if I can."

"Got it," he said. "Marci just got here. I'll bring the laptop with me and we'll be waiting for you on the east side of the building when you're ready to go. How do you look, Andi-licious?"

"Fabulous," Andi said confidently. "The hemlines on these dresses stop about an inch short of slutty nymphomaniac."

"Someone take a picture," he said cheerfully, but I could hear the worry in his voice. "I'll see you soon."

"Don't take any chances," I said. "See you soon."

I put the crystal away and tried to ignore the butterflies in my stomach.

"This isn't going to work," Justine murmured.

"It is going to work," I told her, keeping my tone confident. "We'll breeze right in. The Rack will be with us."

Justine glanced at me with an arched eyebrow. "The Rack?"

"The Rack is more than just boobs, Justine," I told her soberly. "It's an energy field created by all living boobs. It surrounds us, penetrates us, and binds the galaxy together."

Andi started giggling. "You're insane."

"But functionally so," I said, and adjusted myself to round out a little better. "Just let go your conscious self and act on instinct."

Justine stared blankly at me for a second. Then her face lightened and she let out a little laugh. "The Rack will be with us?"

I couldn't stop myself from cracking a smile. "Always."

The limo joined a line of similar vehicles dropping people off at the entrance to the svartalf stronghold. A valet opened our door, and I swung my legs out and tried to leave the car without flashing everyone in sight. Andi and Justine followed me out, and I started walking confidently toward the entrance with the other two flanking me. Our heels clicked in near unison, and I suddenly felt every eye in sight swivel toward us. A cloud of thought and emotion rolled out in response to our presence— pleasure, mostly, along with a mixed slurry of desire, outright lust, jealousy, anxiety, and surprise. It hurt to feel all of that scraping against the inside of my head, but it was necessary. I didn't sense any outright hostility or imminent violence, and the instant of warning I might get between sensing an attacker's intention and the moment of attack might save our lives.

A security guard at the door watched us intently as we approached, and I could feel the uncomplicated sexual attraction churning through him. He kept it off his face and out of his voice and body, though. "Good evening, ladies," he said. "May I see your invitations?"

I arched an eyebrow at him, gave him what I hoped was a seductive smile, and tried to arch my back a little more. Deploying the Rack had worked before. "You don't need to see our invitation."

"Um," he said. "Miss . . . I kind of do."

Andi stepped up beside me and gave him a sex-kitten smile that made me hate her a little, just for a second. "No you don't."

"Uh," he said, "yeah. Still do."

Justine stepped up on my other side. She looked more sweet than sexy, but only barely. "I'm sure it was just an oversight, sir. Couldn't you ask your supervisor if we might come to the reception?"

He stared at us for a long moment, clearly hesitant. Then one hand slowly went to the radio at his side and he lifted it to his mouth. A moment later a slight, small man in a silk suit appeared from inside the building. He took a long look at us.

The interest I'd felt from the guard was fairly normal. It had just been a spark, the instinct-level response of any male to a desirable female.

What came off of the new guy was . . . it was more like a road flare. It burned a thousand times hotter and brighter, and it kept *on* burning. I'd sensed lust and desire in others before. This went so much deeper and wider than mere lust that I didn't think there was a word for it. It was . . . a vast and inhuman yearning, blended with a fierce and jealous love, and seasoned with sexual attraction and desire. It was like standing near a tiny sun, and I suddenly understood exactly what Auntie Lea had been trying to tell me.

Fire is hot. Water is wet. And svartalves are suckers for pretty girls. They could no more change their nature than they could the course of the stars.

"Ladies," the new guy said, smiling at us. It was a charming smile, but there was something distant and disquieting in his face all the same. "Please, wait just a moment for me to alert my other staff. We would be honored if you would join us."

He turned and went inside.

Justine gave me a sidelong look.

"The Rack can have a powerful influence over the weak-minded," I said.

"I'd feel better if he hadn't left on a Darth Vader line," Andi breathed. "He smelled odd. Was he . . . ?"

"Yeah," I whispered back. "One of them."

The man in the silk suit reappeared, still smiling, and opened the door for us. "Ladies," he said, "I am Mister Etri. Please, come inside."

———

I had never in my life seen a place more opulent than the inside of the svart-alves' stronghold. Not in magazines, not in the movies. Not even on *Cribs*.

There were tons of granite and marble. There were sections of wall that had been inlaid with precious and semiprecious stones. Lighting fixtures were crafted of what looked like solid gold, and the light switches looked like they'd been carved from fine ivory. Security guards were stationed every twenty or thirty feet, standing at rigid attention like those guys outside Buckingham Palace, only without the big hats. Light came from everywhere and from nowhere, making all shadows thin and wispy things without becoming too bright for the eyes. Music drifted on the air, some old classical thing that was all strings and no drumbeat.

Etri led us down a couple of hallways to a vast cathedral of a ballroom. It was absolutely palatial in there—in fact, I was pretty sure that the room shouldn't have *fit* in the building we'd just entered—and it was filled with expensive-looking people in expensive-looking clothing.

We paused in the entry while Etri stopped to speak to yet another security guy. I took the moment it offered to sweep my gaze over the room. The place wasn't close to full, but there were a lot of people there. I recognized a couple of celebrities, people you'd know if I told you their names. There were a number of the Sidhe in attendance, their usual awe-inspiring physical perfection muted to mere exotic beauty. I spotted Gentleman Johnnie Marcone, the head of Chicago's outfit in attendance, with his gorilla Hendricks and his personal attack witch, Gard, floating around near him. There were any number of people who I was sure weren't people; I could sense the blurring of perception in the air around them as if they were cut off from me by a thin curtain of falling water.

But I didn't see Thomas.

"Molly," Justine whispered, barely audible. "Is he . . . ?"

The tracking spell I'd focused on my lips was still functioning, a faint tingle telling me that Thomas was nearby, deeper into the interior of the building. "He's alive," I said. "He's here."

Justine shuddered and took a deep breath. She blinked slowly, once, her face showing nothing as she did. I felt the surge of simultaneous relief and terror in her presence, though, a sudden blast of emotion that cried out for her to scream or fight or burst into tears. She did none of that, and I turned my eyes away from her in order to give her the illusion that I hadn't noticed her near meltdown.

In the center of the ballroom, there was a small, raised platform of stone, with a few stairs leading up onto it. Upon the platform was a podium of the same material. Resting on the podium was a thick folio of papers and a neat row of fountain pens. There was something solemn and ceremonial about the way it was set up.

Justine was looking at it, too. "That must be it."

"The treaty?"

She nodded. "The svartalves are very methodical about business. They'll conclude the treaty precisely at midnight. They always do."

Andi tapped a finger thoughtfully on her hip. "What if something happened to their treaty first? I mean, if someone spilled a bunch of wine on it or something. That would be attention getting, I bet—maybe give a couple of us a chance to sneak further in."

I shook my head. "No. We're guests here. Do you understand?"

"Uh. Not really."

"The svartalves are old-school," I said. "*Really* old-school. If we break the peace when they've invited us into their territory, we're violating our guest right and offering them disrespect as our hosts—right out in the open, in front of the entire supernatural community. They'll react . . . badly."

Andi frowned and said, "Then what's our next move?"

Why do people keep asking me that? Is this what all wizard types go through? I'd probably asked Harry that question a hundred times, but I never realized how hard it was to hear it coming toward you. But Harry always knew what to do next. All I could do was improvise desperately and hope for the best.

"Justine," I said, "do you know any of the players here?"

As Lara Raith's personal assistant, Justine came in contact with a lot of people and not-quite-people. Lara had so many fingers in so many pies that I could barely make a joke about it, and Justine saw, heard, and thought a lot more than anyone gave her credit for. The white-haired girl scanned the room, her dark eyes flicking from face to face. "Several."

"All right. I want you to circulate and see what you can find out," I said. "Keep an eye out. If you see them sending the brute squad after us, get on the crystal and warn us."

"Okay," Justine whispered. "Careful."

Etri returned and smiled again, though his eyes remained oddly, unsettlingly without expression. He flicked one hand and a man in a tux floated over to us with a tray of drinks. We helped ourselves, and Etri did, too. He lifted his glass to us and said, "Ladies, be welcome. To beauty."

We echoed him and we all sipped. I barely let my lips touch the liquid. It was champagne, really good stuff. It fizzed and I could barely taste the alcohol. I wasn't worried about poison. Etri had quite diffidently allowed us to choose our glasses before taking one of his own.

I was actually more worried about the fact that I'd stopped to consider potential poisoning, and to watch Etri's actions carefully as he served us. Is it paranoid to worry about things like that? It seemed reasonable to me at the time.

Man, maybe I'm more messed up than I thought I was.

"Please, enjoy the reception," Etri said. "I'm afraid I must insist on a dance with each of you lovely young ladies when time and duty shall allow. Who shall be first?"

Justine gave him a Rack-infused smile and lifted her hand. If you twisted my arm, I'd tell you that Justine was definitely the prettiest girl in our little trio, and Etri evidently agreed. His eyes turned warm for an instant before he took Justine's hand and led her out onto the dance floor. They vanished into the moving crowd.

"I couldn't do this ballroom stuff anyway," Andi said. "Not nearly enough booty bouncing. Next move time?"

"Next move time," I said. "Come on."

I turned the follow the tingle in my lips and the two of us made our way to the back side of the ballroom, where doors led deeper into the facility. There were no guards on the doors, but as we got closer, Andi's steps started to slow. She glanced over to one side, where there was a refreshments table, and I saw her begin to turn toward it.

I caught her arm and said, "Hold it. Where are you going?"

"Um," she said, frowning. "Over there?"

I extended my senses and felt the subtle weaving of magic in the air around the doorway, cobweb fine. It was a kind of veil, designed to direct the attention of anyone approaching it away from the doorway and toward anything else in the room. It made the refreshment table look yummier. If Andi had spotted a guy, he would have looked a lot cuter than he actually was.

I'd been having a powerful faerie sorceress throwing veils and glamours at me for almost a year, building up my mental defenses, and a few months ago I'd gone twelve rounds in the psychic boxing ring with a heavyweight champion necromancer. I hadn't even noticed the gentle magical weaving hitting my mental shields.

"It's an enchantment," I told her. "Don't let it sway you."

"What?" she asked. "I don't feel anything. I'm just hungry."

"You wouldn't feel it," I said. "That's how it works. Take my hand and close your eyes. Trust me."

"If I had a nickel for every time a bad evening started with a line like that," she muttered. But she put her hand in mine and closed her eyes.

I walked her toward the doorway and felt her growing more tense as we went—but then we passed through it and she let out her breath explosively, blinking her eyes open. "Wow. That felt . . . like nothing at all."

"It's how you recognize quality enchantment," I said. "If you don't know it's got you, you can't fight it off." The hallway we stood in looked much like any in any office building. I tried the nearest door and found it locked. So were the next couple, but the last was an empty conference room, and I slipped inside.

I fumbled the crystal out of my little clutch and said, "Bosley, can you hear me?"

"Loud and clear, Angels," came Waldo's voice. Neither of us used real names. The crystals were probably secure, but a year with Lea's nasty trickery as a daily feature of life had taught me not to make many assumptions.

"Were you able to come up with those floor plans?"

"About ninety seconds ago. The building's owners filed everything with the city in triplicate, including electronic copies, which I am now looking at, courtesy of the hivemind."

"Advantage, nerds," I said. "Tell them they did good, Boz."

"Will do," Waldo said. "These people you're visiting are thorough, Angels. Be careful."

"When am I not careful?" I said.

Andi had taken up a guard position against the wall next to the door, where she could grab anyone who opened it. "Seriously?"

I couldn't help but smile a little. "I think our lost lamb is in the wing of the building to the west of the reception hall. What's there?"

"Um . . . offices, it looks like. Second floor, more offices. Third floor, more offi—hello there."

"What'd you find?"

"A vault," Waldo said. "Reinforced steel. Huge."

"Hah," I said. "A reinforced-steel vault? Twenty bucks says it's a dungeon. We start there."

"Whatever it is, it's in the basement. There should be a stairway leading down to it at the end of the hallway leading out of the reception hall."

"Bingo," I said. "Stay tuned, Bosley."

"Will do. Your chariot awaits."

I put the crystal away and began putting on my rings. I got them all together, then began to pick up my wands, and realized that I couldn't carry them in each hand while also carrying the little clutch. "I knew I should have gone for a messenger bag," I muttered.

"With that dress?" Andi asked. "Are you kidding?"

"True." I took the crystal out and tucked it into my décolletage, palmed one of the little wands in each hand, and nodded to Andi. "If it's a vault or a dungeon, there will be guards. I'm going to make it hard for them to see us, but we might have to move fast."

Andi looked down at her shoes and sighed mournfully. Then she stepped out of them and peeled the little black dress off. She hadn't been wearing anything underneath. She closed her eyes for a second and then her form just seemed to blur and melt. Werewolves don't do dramatic, painful transformations except right at first, I've been told. This looked as natural as a living being turning in a circle and sitting down. One moment Andi was there, and the next there was a great russet-furred wolf sitting where she'd been.

It was highly cool magic. I was going to have to figure out how that was done, one of these days.

"Don't draw blood unless it's absolutely necessary," I said, stepping out of my own torturous shoes. "I'm going to try to make this quick and painless. If there's any rough stuff, not killing anyone will go a long way with the svartalves."

Andi yawned at me.

"Ready?" I asked.

Andi bobbed her lupine head in a sharp, decisive nod. I drew the concealing magic of my top-of-the-line veil around us, and the light suddenly went dim, the colors leaching out of the world. We would be almost impossible to see. And anyone who came within fifty or sixty feet of us would develop a sudden desire for a bit of introspection, questioning their path in life so deeply that there was practically no chance we'd be detected as long as we were quiet.

With Andi walking right beside me, we stole out into the hallway. We found the stairwell Waldo had told us about, and I opened the door to it slowly. I didn't go first. You can't do much better than having a werewolf as your guide, and I'd worked with Andi and her friends often enough in the past year to make our movements routine.

Andi went through first, moving in total silence, her ears perked, her nose twitching. Wolves have incredible senses of smell. Hearing, too. If anyone was around, Andi would sense them. After a tense quarter of a minute, she gave me the signal that it was all clear by sitting down. I eased up next to her and extended my senses, feeling for any more magical defenses or enchantments. There were half a dozen on the first section of the stairwell—simple things, the sorcerous equivalent of trip wires.

Fortunately, Auntie Lea had shown me how to circumvent enchantments such as these. I made an effort of will and modified our veil, and then I nodded to Andi and we started slowly down the stairs. We slipped through the invisible fields of magic without disturbing them, and crept down to the basement.

I checked the door at the bottom of the stairs and found it unlocked.

"This seems way too easy," I muttered. "If it's a prison, shouldn't this be locked?"

Andi let out a low growl, and I could sense her agreement and suspicion.

My mouth still tingled, much more strongly now. Thomas was close. "Guess there's not a lot of choice here." I opened the door, slowly and quietly.

The door didn't open onto some kind of dungeon. It didn't open up to show us a vault, either. Instead, Andi and I found ourselves staring at a long hallway every bit as opulent as those above, with large and ornate doors spaced generously along it. Each door had a simple number on it, wrought in what looked like pure silver. Very subdued lighting was spaced strategically along its length, leaving it comfortably dim without being dark.

Andi's low growl turned into a confused little sound and she tilted her head to one side.

"Yeah," I said, perplexed. "It looks like . . . a hotel. There's even a sign showing fire escape routes on the wall."

Andi gave her head a little shake, and I sensed enough of her emotions to understand her meaning. *What the hell?*

"I know," I said. "Is this . . . living quarters for the svartalves? Guest accommodations?"

Andi glanced up at me and flicked her ears. *Why are you asking me? I can't even talk.*

"I know you can't. Just thinking out loud."

Andi blinked, her ears snapping toward me, and she gave me a sidelong glance. *You heard me?*

"I didn't so much hear you as just . . . understand you."

She leaned very slightly away from me. *Just when I thought you couldn't get any more weird and disturbing.*

I gave her a maliciously wide smile, and the crazy eyes I used to use to scare my kid brothers and sisters.

Andi snorted and then began testing the air with her nose. I watched her closely. Her hackles rose up and I saw her crouch down. *There are things here. Too many scents to sort out. Something familiar, and not in a good way.*

"Thomas is close. Come on." We started forward, and I kept my face turned directly toward the tingling signature of my tracking spell. It began to bear to the right, and as we got to the door to room 6, the tingle suddenly swung to the very corner of my mouth, until I turned to face the doorway directly. "Here, in six."

Andi looked up and down the hall, her eyes restless, her ears trying to swivel in every direction. *I don't like this.*

"Too easy," I whispered. "This is way too easy." I reached out toward the doorknob and stopped. My head told me this situation was all wrong. So did my instincts. If Thomas was a prisoner being held by Svartalfheim, then where were the cages, the chains, the locks, the bars, the guards? And if he wasn't being held against his will . . . what *was* he doing here?

When you find yourself in a situation that doesn't make any sense, it's usually for one reason: you have bad information. You can get bad information in several ways. Sometimes you're just plain wrong about what you learn. More often, and more dangerously, your information is bad because you made a faulty assumption.

Worst of all is when someone deliberately feeds it to you—and, like a sucker, you trust her and take it without hesitation.

"Auntie," I breathed. "She *tricked* me." Lea hadn't sent me into the building to rescue Thomas—or at least not only for that. It was no freaking coincidence that she'd taught me how to specifically circumvent the magical security the svartalves were using, either. She'd had another purpose in bringing me here, on this night.

I replayed our conversation in my mind and snarled. Nothing she told me was a lie, and all of it had been tailored to make me reach the wrong conclusion—that Thomas had to be rescued and that I was the only one who would do it. I didn't know why the Leanansidhe thought I needed to be where I was, but she sure as hell had made sure I would get there.

"That conniving, doublespeaking, treacherous *bitch*. When I catch up with her, I'm going to—"

Andi let out a sudden, very low growl, and I shut up in the nick of time.

The door from the upstairs opened, and that bastard Listen and several turtlenecks started walking down the hall toward us.

Listen was a lean and fit-looking man of middling height. His hair was cropped military short, his skin was pale, and his dark eyes looked hard and intelligent. The werewolves and I had tried to bring him down half a dozen different times, but he always managed to either escape or turn the tables and make us run for our lives.

Vicious bad guys are bad enough. Vicious, resourceful, ruthless, professional, *smart* bad guys are way worse. Listen was one of the latter and I hated his fishy guts.

He and his lackeys were dressed in the standard uniform of the Fomors' servitors: black slacks, black shoes, and a black turtleneck sweater. The high neck of the sweater covered up the gills on both sides of their necks, so that they could pass as mortals. They weren't, or at least they weren't anymore. The Fomor had changed them, making them stronger, faster, and all but immune to pain. I'd never managed to set up a successful ambush before, and now one had fallen right into my lap. I absolutely *ached* to avenge the blood I'd washed from my body early that very day.

But the servitors had weird minds, and they kept getting weirder. It was damned difficult to get into their heads the way I would need to do, and if that first attack failed in close quarters like these, that crew would tear Andi and me apart.

So I ground my teeth. I put my hand on Andi's neck and squeezed slightly as I crouched down beside her, focusing on the veil. I had to damp down on the introspection suggestion: Listen had nearly killed me a few months before, when he noticed a similar enchantment altering the course of his thoughts. That had been damned scary, but I'd worked on it since then. I closed my eyes and spun the lightest, finest cobwebs of suggestion that my gifts could manage while simultaneously drawing the veil even tighter around us. The light in the hallway shrunk to almost nothing, and the air just over my skin became noticeably cooler.

They came closer, Listen clearly in the lead, walking with swift and silent purpose. The son of a bitch passed within two feet of me. I could have reached out and touched him with my hand.

None of them stopped.

They went down the hall to room 8, and Listen pushed a key into a door. He opened it and he and his buddies began to enter the room.

This was an opportunity I couldn't pass up. For all the horror the Fomor had brought to the world since the extinction of the Red Court, we still didn't know why they did what they did. We didn't know what they wanted, or how they thought their current actions would get it for them.

So I moved in all the silence the past year had taught me the hard way, and stalked up to the line of servitors passing into the chamber. After a startled second, Andi joined me, just as quietly. We just barely slipped through the door before it shut.

No one looked back at us as we passed into a palatial suite, furnished as lavishly as the rest of the building. In addition to the half dozen turtlenecks in Listen's party, another five were standing around the room in a guard position, backs straight, their arms clasped behind them.

"Where is he?" Listen asked a guard standing beside a door. The guard was the biggest turtleneck there, with a neck like a fireplug.

"Inside," the guard said.

"It is nearly time," Listen said. "Inform him."

"He left orders that he was not to be disturbed."

Listen seemed to consider that for a moment. Then he said, "A lack of punctuality will invalidate the treaty and make our mission impossible. Inform him."

The guard scowled. "The lord left orders that—"

Listen's upper body surged in a sudden motion, so fast that I could only see it *as* motion. The big guard let out a sudden hiss and a grunt, and blood abruptly fountained from his throat. He staggered a step, turned to Listen, and raised a hand.

Then he shuddered and collapsed to the floor, blood pumping rapidly from a huge and jagged wound in his neck.

Listen dropped a chunk of meat the size of a baseball from his bare, bloody fingers, and bent over to wipe them clean on the dead turtleneck's sweater. The blood didn't show against the black. He straightened up again and then knocked on the door.

"My lord. It is nearly midnight."

He did it again exactly sixty seconds later.

And he repeated it three more times before a slurred voice answered, "I left orders that I was not to be disturbed."

"Forgive me, my lord, but the time is upon us. If we do not act, our efforts are for nothing."

"It is not for you to presume what orders may or may not be ignored," said the voice. "Execute the fool who allowed my sleep to be disturbed."

"It is already done, my lord."

There was a somewhat mollified grunt from the far side of the door, and a moment later it opened, and for the first time I saw one of the lords of the Fomor.

He was a tall, extremely gaunt being, yet somehow not thin. His hands and feet were too large, and his stomach bulged as if it contained a basketball. His jowls were oversized as well, his jaws swollen as if he had the mumps. His lips were too wide, too thick, and too rubbery looking. His hair look too flattened, too limp, like strands of seaweed just washed up onto shore, and on the whole he looked like some kind of gangling, poisonous frog. He was dressed only in a blanket draped across his shoulders. Ew.

There were three women in the room behind him, naked and scattered and dead. Each had livid purple bruises around her throat and glassy, staring eyes.

The turtlenecks all dropped to the floor in supplication as the Fomor entered, though Listen only genuflected upon one knee.

"He is here?" asked the Fomor.

"Yes, my lord," Listen said, "along with both of his bodyguards."

The Fomor croaked out a little laugh and rubbed his splay-fingered hands together. "Mortal upstart. Calling himself a Baron. He will pay for what he did to my brother."

"Yes, my lord."

"No one is allowed to murder my family but me."

"Of course, my lord."

"Bring me the shell."

Listen bowed and nodded to three of the other turtlenecks. They hurried to another door and then emerged, carrying between them an oyster shell that must have weighed half a ton. The thing was monstrous and covered in a crust of coral or barnacles or whatever those things are that grow on the hulls of ships. It was probably seven feet across. The turtlenecks put it down on the floor in the middle of the room.

The Fomor crossed to the shell, touched it with one hand, and murmured a word. Instantly, light blossomed all across its surface, curling and twisting in patterns or maybe letters which I had never seen before. The Fomor stood over it for a time, one hand outstretched, bulbous eyes narrowed, saying something in a hissing, bubbling tongue.

I didn't know what he was doing, but he was moving a lot of energy around, whatever it was. I could feel it filling the air of the chamber, making it seem tighter and somehow harder to breathe.

"My lord?" asked Listen abruptly. "What are you doing?"

"Making a present for our new allies, of course," the Fomor said. "I can hardly annihilate the svartalves along with everyone else. Not yet."

"This is not according to the plans of the Empress."

"The Empress," spat the Fomor, "told me that I ought not harm our new allies. She said nothing of the puling scum attending their festivities."

"The svartalves value their honor dearly," Listen said. "You will shame them if their guests come to harm whilst under their hospitality, my lord. It could defeat the point of the alliance."

The Fomor spat. A glob of yellowy, mucus-like substance splattered the floor near Listen's feet. It hissed and crackled against the marble floor. "Once the treaty is signed, it is done. My gift will be given to them in the moments after: I will spare their miserable lives. And if the rest of the scum turn against the svartalves, they will have no choice but to turn to *us* for our strength." He smirked. "Fear not, Listen. I am not so foolish as to destroy one of the Empress' special pets, even in an accident. You and your fellows will survive."

I suddenly recognized the tenor of energy building up in the giant shell on the floor and my heart just about stopped.

Holy crap.

Lord Froggy had himself a *bomb*.

Like, right *there*.

"My life belongs to my masters, to spend as they will, my lord," Listen said. "Have you any other instruction?"

"Seize whatever treasure you might from the dead before we depart."

Listen bowed his head. "How efficacious do you anticipate your gift to be?"

"The one I made for the Red Court in the Congo was deadly enough," Lord Froggy said, a smug tone in his voice.

My heart pounded even harder. During its war with the White Council, the Red Court had used some kind of nerve gas on a hospital tending wounded wizards. The weapon had killed tens of thousands of people in a city far smaller and less crowded than Chicago.

My bare feet felt tiny and cold.

Lord Froggy grunted and fluttered his fingers, and the bomb-shell vanished, hidden by a veil as good as anything I could do. The Fomor lord abruptly lowered his hand, smiling. "Bring my robes."

The turtlenecks hurriedly dressed Lord Froggy in what might have been the tackiest robe in the history of robekind. Multiple colors wavered over it in patterns like the ripples on water, but seemed random, clashing with one another. It was beaded with pearls, some of them the size of big supermarket gumballs. They put a crown-like circlet on his head after that, and then Lord Froggy and company headed out the door.

I crouched as far to the side as I could, almost under the minibar, with Andi huddling right beside me, holding my veil in tight. Lord Froggy blew right by me, with the turtlenecks walking in two columns behind him, their movements precise and uniform—until one of the last pair stopped, his hand holding the door open.

It was Listen.

His eyes swept the room slowly, and he frowned.

"What is it?" asked the other turtleneck.

"Do you smell something?" Listen asked.

"Like what?"

"Perfume."

Oh, crap.

I closed my eyes and focused on my suggestion frantically, adding threads of anxiety to it, trying to keep it too fine for Listen to pick up on.

After a moment, the other turtleneck said, "I've never really liked perfume. We should not be so far from the lord."

Listen hesitated a moment more before he nodded and began to leave.

"Molly!" said Justine's voice quite clearly from the crystal tucked into my dress. "Miss Gard freaked out about two minutes ago and all but carried Marcone out of here. Security is mobilizing."

Sometimes I think my life is all about bad timing.

Listen whirled around toward us at once, but Andi was faster. She bounded from the floor into a ten-foot leap and slammed against the doorway, hammering it closed with the full weight of her body. In a flickering instant, she was a naked human girl again, straining against the door as she reached up and manually snapped its locks closed.

I fished the crystal out of my dress and said, "There's a bomb on the premises, down in the guest wing. I repeat, a *bomb* in the guest wing, in the Fomor Ambassador's quarters. Find Etri or one of the other svartalves and tell them that the Fomor is planning to murder the svartalves' guests."

"Oh my God," Justine said.

"Holy crap!" chimed in Butters.

Something heavy and moving fast slammed into the door from the other side, and it jumped in its frame. Andi was actually knocked back off of it a few inches, and she reset herself, pressing her shoulder against it to reinforce it. "Molly!"

This was another one of those situations in which panic can get you killed. So while I wanted to scream and run around in circles, what I did was close my eyes for a moment as I released the veil and take a slow, deep breath, ordering my thoughts.

First: if Froggy and the turtlenecks managed to get back into the room, they'd kill us. There were already at least four dead bodies in the suite. Why not add two more? And, all things considered, they'd probably be able to do it. So, priority one was to keep them out of the room, at least until the svartalves sorted things out.

Second: the bomb. If that thing went off, and it was some kind of nerve agent like the Red Court used in Africa, the casualties could be in the hundreds of thousands, and would include Andi and Thomas and Justine—plus Butters and Marci, waiting outside in the car. The bomb had to be disarmed or moved to somewhere safe. Oh, and it would probably need to be not invisible for either of those things to happen.

And three: rescue Thomas. Can't forget the mission, regardless of how complicated things got.

The door boomed again.

"Molly!" Andi screamed, her fear making her voice vibrant, piercing.

"Dammit," I growled. "What would Harry do?"

If Harry was here, he would just hold the stupid door shut. His magic talents had been, like, superhero strong when it came to being able to deliver massive amounts of energy. I'm fairly sure he could have stopped a speeding locomotive. Or at least a speeding semitrailer. But my talents just didn't run to the physical.

Harry had once told me that when you had one problem, you had a problem—but when you had several problems, you might also have several solutions.

I stood up and dropped my wands into my hands, gripping them hard. I faced the doorway and said, "Get ready."

Andi flashed me a glance. "For what?"

"To open the door," I said. "Then shut it behind me."

"*What?*"

"Close your eyes. Go on three," I said, and bent my knees slightly. "One!"

The door rattled again.

"Two!"

"Are you insane?" Andi demanded.

"Three!" I screamed, and sprinted for the door, lifting both wands.

Andi squeezed her eyes shut and swung the door open, and I deployed the One Woman Rave.

Channeling the strength of my will, light and sound burst from the ends of the two wands. Not light like from a flashlight—more like the light of a small nuclear explosion. The sound wasn't loud like a scream, or a small explosion, or even the howl of a passing train. It was like standing on the deck of one of those old World War II battleships when they fired their big guns—a force that could stun a full-grown man and knock him on his ass.

I charged ahead with a wall of sound and furious light leading the way, and burst into the hall among the scattered forms of the startled, dazed turtlenecks.

And then I started playing nasty.

A few seconds later, the scattered turtlenecks were all on their feet again, though they looked a little disoriented and were blinking their eyes. Down the hallway, one of the turtlenecks was helping Lord Froggy to his feet, his lank hair disheveled, his robes in disarray. His ugly face was contorted in fury. "What is happening here, Listen?" he demanded. He was screaming at the top of his lungs. I doubt his ears were working very well.

"My lord," Listen said, "I believe this is more of the work of the Ragged Lady."

"What!? Speak up, fool!"

Listen's cheek twitched once. Then he repeated himself in a shout.

Froggy made a hissing sound. "Meddling bitch," he snarled. "Break down that door and bring me her *heart*."

"Yes, my lord," Listen said, and the turtlenecks grouped up around the door to room 8 again.

They didn't use any tools. They didn't need any. They just started kicking the door, three of them at a time, working in unison, driving the heels of their shoes at the wood. In three kicks, cracks began to form and the door groaned. In five, it broke and swung in loosely on its hinges.

"Kill her!" snarled Lord Froggy, pacing closer to the broken door. "*Kill her!*"

All but two of the turtlenecks poured into the room.

From behind my renewed veil, I figured the timing was about right to discontinue my illusion just as the door bounced back after they'd rushed through it. The silver numeral 8 hanging on the door blurred and melted back into a silver numeral 6.

Lord Froggy's eyes widened in sudden, startled realization.

One of the turtlenecks flew back out the door to room 6 and smashed into the wall on the far side. He hit like a rag doll and flopped off it to the ground. There was a body-shaped outline in cracked marble and flecks of fresh blood left on the wall behind him.

And from the other side of the broken door, Thomas Raith, vampire, said, "It's Listen, right? Wow. Did you clowns ever pick the wrong room."

"We made a mistake," Listen said.

"Yes. Yes, you did."

And things started going crunch and thump in the room beyond.

Lord Froggy hissed and swiveled his bulgy head around on his gangly neck. "Ragged bitch," he hissed. "I know you are here."

This time, I knew exactly what Harry would do. I lifted my sonic wand and sent my voice down to the far end of the hall, behind him. "Hi there, Froggy. Is it as hard as it looks, holding up villain clichés, or does it come naturally to you?"

"You *dare* mock *me*?" the Fomor snarled. He threw a spiraling corkscrew of deep green energy down the hall, and it hissed and left burn marks upon everything it touched, ending at the doors. When it hit *them*, there was a snarling, crackling sound, and the green light spread across their surface in the pattern of a fisherman's net.

"Hard to do anything else to a guy with a face like yours," I said, this time from directly beside him. "Did you kill those girls, or did they volunteer once they saw you with your shirt off?"

The Fomor snarled and swatted at the air beside him. Then his eyes narrowed, and he started muttering and weaving his spatulate fingers in complicated patterns. I could feel the energy coming off of him at once, and knew exactly what he was trying to do—unravel my veil. But I'd been playing that game with Auntie Lea for months.

Lord Froggy hadn't.

As his questing threads of magic spread out, I sent out whispers of my own power to barely brush them, guiding them one by one out and around the area covered by my veil. I couldn't afford to let him find me. Not like that, anyway. He wasn't thinking, and if I didn't get him to, it was entirely possible that he'd be too stupid to fool.

I couldn't have him giving up and leaving, either, so when I was sure I'd compromised his seeking spell I used the sonic wand again, this time directly above his head. "This kind of thing really isn't for amateurs. Are you sure you shouldn't sit this one out and let Listen give it a shot?"

Lord Froggy tilted his head up and then narrowed his eyes. He lifted a hand, spat a hissing word, and fire leapt up from his fingers to engulf the ceiling above him.

It took about two seconds for the fire alarm to go off, and another two before the sprinkler system kicked in. But I was back at the door to room

& when the falling water began to dissolve my veil. Magic is a kind of energy, and follows its own laws. One of those laws is that water tends to ground out active magical constructs, and my veil started melting away like it was made of cotton candy.

"Hah!" spat the Fomor, spotting me. I saw him send a bolt of viridian light at me. I threw myself facedown to the floor and it passed over me, splashing against the door. I whipped over onto my back, just in time to raise a shield against a second bolt and a third. My physical shields aren't great, but the Fomor's spell was pure energy, and that made it easier for me to handle. I deflected the bolts left and right, and they blasted chunks of marble the size of bricks out of the walls when they struck.

Lord Froggy's eyes flared even larger and more furious that he'd missed. "Mortal cow!"

Okay, now. That stung. I mean, maybe it's a little shallow, and maybe it's a little petty, and maybe it shows a lack of character of some kind that Froggy's insult to my appearance got under my skin more effectively than attempted murder.

"*Cow?*" I snarled as water from the sprinkler system started soaking me. "I *rock* this dress!"

I dropped one of my wands and thrust my palm out at him, sending out an invisible bolt of pure memory, narrowed and focused with magic, like light passing through a magnifying glass. Sometimes you don't really remember traumatic injuries, and my memory of getting shot in the leg was pretty blurry. It hadn't hurt so much when I actually got shot and I'd had a few things occupying my attention. Mostly, I'd just felt surprised and then numb—but when they were tending the wound in the helicopter, later, now *that* was pain. They'd dug the bullet out with forceps, cleaned the site with something that burned like Hell itself, and when they'd put the pressure bandage on it and tightened the straps, it hurt so bad that I'd thought I was going to die.

That's what I gave to Lord Froggy, with every bit of strength I could muster.

He wove a shield against the attack, but I guess he wasn't used to handling something so intangible as a memory. Even with the falling water weakening it, I felt the strike smash through his defense and sink home, and Froggy let out a sudden, high-pitched shriek. He staggered and fell heavily against the wall, clutching at his leg.

"Kill her!" he said, his voice two octaves higher than it had been a moment before. "Kill her, kill her, kill her!"

The remaining pair of turtlenecks in the hallway plunged toward me.
A wave of fatigue from my recent efforts, especially that last one, almost
held me pinned to the floor—but I scrambled to my feet, lurched to the
door to room 8, and pounded against it with one fist. "Andi! Andi, it's
Molly! Andi, let me—"

The door jerked open and I fell into the room. I snapped my legs up into
a fetal curl, and Andi slammed the door shut behind me and hit the locks.

"What the *hell*, Molly?" she demanded. Andi was soaking wet, along
with everything else in the room—including the Fomor's bomb.

I got up and scrambled toward it. "I couldn't take apart the veil over the
bomb from the outside," I panted. "We didn't have time to build up a fire,
and I can't call up enough of my own to set off the alarms. I had to get
Froggy to do it for me."

The door shuddered under more blows from the turtlenecks.

"Hold them off," I told her. "I'll disarm the bomb."

"Can you *do* that?" Andi asked.

"Piece of cake," I lied.

"Okay," Andi said. She grimaced. "I'm going to smell like wet dog all
night."

She turned to face the door in a ready position as I reached the giant
shell. I forced the battering enemies at the door out of my thoughts and
focused my complete attention on the shell before me. Then I extended
my senses toward it and began feeling out the energy moving through it.

There was a *lot* of energy involved in this thing, power stored up inside
and ready to explode. A thin coating of enchantment lined the shell's ex-
terior, kind of the magical equivalent of a control panel. The water was
eroding it slowly, but not fast enough to start melting the core enchantment and dispersing the stored energy. But if I didn't move fast, the water
would destroy the surface enchantment and make it impossible for *anyone*
to disarm the bomb.

I closed my eyes and put one hand out over the shell like Froggy had
done. I could feel the energy of the shell reaching up to my fingers, ready
to respond, and I began pouring my own energy down into it, trying to
feel it out. It was a straightforward spell, nothing complicated, but I didn't
know what anything did—it was like having a remote control for the TV,

if someone had forgotten to label any of the buttons. I couldn't just start pushing them randomly.

On the other hand, I couldn't *not* do it, either.

It would have to be an educated guess.

On a TV remote, the power button is almost always a little apart from the others, or else somehow centered. That's what I was looking for—to turn the bomb off. I started eliminating all the portions of the spell that seemed too complex or too small, narrowing my choices bit by bit. It came down to two. If I guessed wrong . . .

I burst out into a nervous giggle. "Hey, Andi. Blue wire or red wire?"

A turtleneck's foot smashed a hole in the door, and Andi whipped her head around to give me an incredulous look. "Are you fucking *kidding* me?" she shouted. "Blue, you *always* cut the blue!"

Half of the door broke down and crashed to the floor. Andi blurred into her wolf form and surged forward, ripping at the first turtleneck as he tried to come in.

I turned my attention back to the bomb and picked the second option. I focused my will on it. It took me a couple of tries, because I was freaking terrified, and pants-wetting fear is generally not conducive to lucidity.

"Hey, God," I whispered. "I know I haven't been around much lately, but if you could do me a solid here, it would be really awesome for a lot of people. Please let me be right."

I cut the blue wire.

Nothing happened.

I felt a heavy, almost paralytic surge of relief—and then Lord Froggy hopped over the two turtlenecks struggling with Andi and smashed into me.

I went down hard on the marble floor, and Froggy rode me down, pinning me beneath his too-gaunt body. He wrapped the fingers of one hand all the way around my neck with room enough for them to overlap his thumb, and squeezed. He was hideously strong. My breath stopped instantly and my head began to pound, and my vision to darken.

"Little *bitch*," he hissed. He started punching me with his other hand. The blows landed on my left cheekbone. They should have hurt, but I think something was wrong with my brain. I registered the impact but everything else was swallowed by the growing darkness. I could feel myself struggling, but I didn't get anywhere. Froggy was way, way stronger than he looked. My eyes weren't focusing very well, but I found myself staring down a dark tunnel toward one of the dead girls on the bedroom floor, and the dark purple band of bruising around her throat.

Then the floor a few feet away rippled, and an odd-looking grey creature popped up out of it.

The svartalf was maybe four-six and entirely naked. His skin was a mottled shade of grey, and his eyes were huge and entirely black. His head was a little larger than most people's and he was bald, though his eyebrows were silvery-white. He did look kind of Roswellian, only instead of being super-skinny he was built like a professional boxer, lean and strong—and he carried a short, simple sword in his hand.

"Fomor," said the svartalf calmly. I recognized Mister Etri's voice. "One should not strike ladies."

Froggy started to say something, but then Etri's sword went snicker-snack, and the hand that was choking the life out of me was severed cleanly from the Fomor's wrist. Froggy screamed and fell away from me, spitting words and trying to summon power as he scrambled away on three limbs.

"You have violated guest right," Etri continued calmly. He made a ges-ture and the marble beneath Lord Froggy turned suddenly liquid. Froggy sank about three inches, and then the floor hardened around him again. The Fomor screamed.

"You have attacked a guest under the hospitality and protection of Svartalfheim," he said, his tone of voice never changing. The sword swept out again and struck the nose from Froggy's face, spewing ichor every-where and drawing even more howling. Etri stood over the fallen Fomor and looked down at him with absolutely no expression on his face. "Have you anything to say on your own behalf?"

"No!" Froggy screamed. "You cannot do this! I have harmed none of your people!"

There was a pulse of rage from Etri so hot that I thought the falling water would burst into steam when it struck him. "Harmed us?" he said quietly. He glanced at the shell and then back at Froggy with pure con-tempt. "You would have used our alliance as a pretext to murder innocent thousands, making us your accomplices." He crouched down to put his face inches from Froggy's, and said in a calm, quiet, pitiless voice, "You have stained the honor of Svartalfheim."

"I will make payment!" Froggy gabbled. "You will be compensated for your pains!"

"There is but one price for your actions, Fomor. And there are no negotiations."

"No," Froggy protested. "No. NO!"

Etri turned away from him and surveyed the room. Andi was still in wolf form. One of the turtlenecks was bleeding out onto the marble floor, the sprinklers spreading the blood into a huge pool. The other was crouched in a corner with his arms curled around his head, covered in bleeding wounds. Andi faced him, panting, blood dripping from her reddened fangs, a steady growl bubbling in her chest.

Etri turned to me and offered me his hand. I thanked him and let him pull me up to a sitting position. My throat hurt. My head hurt. My face hurt. It's killing me, nyuk, nyuk, nyuk. C'mere, you.

You know you've been punched loopy when you're doing a one-person Three Stooges routine in your internal monologue.

"I apologize," Etri said, "for interfering in your struggle. Please do not presume that I did so because I thought you unable to protect yourself."

My voice came out in a croak. "It's your house, and your honor that was at stake. You had the right."

The answer seemed to please him and he inclined his head slightly. "I further apologize for not handling this matter myself. It was not your responsibility to discover or take action against this scum's behavior."

"It was presumptuous of me," I said. "But there was little time to act."

"Your ally alerted us to the danger. You did nothing improper. Svartalfheim thanks you for your assistance in this matter. You are owed a favor."

I was about to tell him that no such thing was necessary, but I stopped myself. Etri wasn't uttering social pleasantries. This wasn't a friendly exchange. It was an audit, an accounting. I just inclined my head to him. "Thank you, Mister Etri."

"Of course, Miss Carpenter."

Svartalves in security uniforms, mixed with mortal security guards, came into the room. Etri went to them and quietly gave instructions. The Fomor and his servitors were trussed up and taken from the room.

"What will happen to them?" I asked Etri.

"We will make an example of the Fomor," Etri said.

"What of your treaty?" I asked.

"It was never signed," he said. "Mostly because of you, Miss Carpenter. While Svartalfheim does not pay debts which were never incurred, we appreciate your role in this matter. It will be considered in the future."

"The Fomor don't deserve an honorable ally."

"It would seem not," he said.

"What about the turtlenecks?" I asked.

"What of them?"

"Will you . . . deal with them?"

Etri just looked at me. "Why would we?"

"They were sort of in on it," I said.

"They were property," said the svartalf. "If a man strikes you with a hammer, it is the man who is punished. There is no reason to destroy the hammer. We care nothing for them."

"What about them?" I asked, and nodded toward the dead girls in the Fomor's chamber. "Do you care what happened to them?"

Etri looked at them and sighed. "Beautiful things ought not be destroyed," he said. "But they were not our guests. We owe no one for their end and will not answer for it."

"There is a vampire in your custody," I said, "is there not?"

Etri regarded me for a moment and then said, "Yes."

"You owe me a favor. I wish to secure his release."

He arched an eyebrow. Then he bowed slightly and said, "Come with me."

I followed Etri out of the suite and across the hall to room 6. Though the door was shattered, Etri stopped outside of it respectfully and knocked. A moment later, a female voice said, "You may enter."

We went in. It was a suite much like the Fomor's, only with way more throw pillows and plush furniture. It was a wreck. The floor was literally covered with shattered furniture, broken décor, and broken turtlenecks. Svartalf security was already binding them and carrying them from the room.

Listen walked out on his own power, his hands behind his back, one of his eyes swollen halfway shut. He gave me a steady look as he went by, and said nothing.

Bastard.

Etri turned toward the curtained door to the suite's bedroom and spoke.

"The mortal apprentice who warned us has earned a favor. She asks for the release of the vampire."

"Impossible," answered the female voice. "That account has been settled."

Etri turned to me and shrugged. "I am sorry."

"Wait," I said. "May I speak to him?"

"In a moment."

We waited. Thomas appeared from the doorway to the bedroom dressed in a black terry-cloth bathrobe. He'd just gotten out of the shower. Thomas was maybe half an inch under six feet tall, and there wasn't an inch of his body that didn't scream sex symbol. His eyes were a shade of deep crystalline blue, and his dark hair hung to his wide shoulders. My body did what it always did around him, and started screaming at me to make babies. I ignored it. Mostly.

"Molly," he said. "Are you all right?"

"Nothing a bucket of aspirin won't help," I said. "Um. Are you okay?"

He blinked. "Why wouldn't I be?"

"I thought . . . you know. You'd been captured as a spy."

"Well, sure," he said.

"I thought they would, uh. Make an example of you?"

He blinked again. "Why would they do that?"

The door to the bedroom opened again, and a female svartalf appeared. She looked a lot like Etri—tiny and beautiful, though she had long silver hair instead of a cueball. She was wearing what might have been Thomas's shirt, and it hung down almost to her ankles. She had a decidedly . . . smug look about her. Behind her, I saw several other sets of wide, dark eyes peer out of the shadowy bedchamber.

"Oh," I said. "*Oh*. You, uh. You made a deal."

Thomas smirked. "It's a tough, dirty job. . . ."

"And one that is not yet finished," said the female svartalf. "You are ours until dawn."

Thomas looked from me to the bedroom and back and spread his hands. "You know how it is, Molly. Duty calls."

"Um," I said. "What do you want me to tell Justine?"

Again he gave me a look of near incomprehension. "The truth. What else?"

———

"Oh, thank goodness," Justine said as we were walking out. "I was afraid they'd have starved him."

I blinked. "Your boyfriend is banging a roomful of elfgirls and you're *happy* about it?"

Justine tilted her head back and laughed. "When you're in love with an incubus, it changes your viewpoint a little, I think. It isn't as though this is something new. I know how he feels about me, and he needs to feed to be healthy. So what's the harm?" She smirked. "And besides. He's *always* ready for more."

"You're a very weird person, Justine."

Andi snorted, and nudged me with her shoulder in a friendly way. She'd recovered her dress and the shoes she liked. "Look who's talking."

After everyone was safe home, I walked from Waldo's apartment to the nearest parking garage. I found a dark corner, sat down, and waited. Lea shimmered into being about two hours later and sat down beside me.

"You tricked me," I said. "You sent me in there blind."

"Indeed. Just as Lara did her brother—except that my agent succeeded where hers failed."

"But why? Why send us in there?"

"The treaty with the Fomor could not be allowed to conclude," she said. "If one nation agreed to neutrality with them, a dozen more would follow. The Fomor would be able to divide the others and contend with them one by one. The situation was delicate. The presence of active agents was intended to disrupt its equilibrium—to show the Fomor's true nature in a test of fire."

"Why didn't you just tell me that?" I asked.

"Because you would neither have trusted nor believed me, obviously," she said.

I frowned at her. "You should have told me anyway."

"Do not be ridiculous, child." Lea sniffed. "There was no time to humor your doubts and suspicions and theories and endless questions. Better to give you a simple prize upon which to focus—Thomas."

"How did you know I would find the bomb?"

She arched an eyebrow. "Bomb?" She shook her head. "I did not know what was happening in any specific sense. But the Fomor are betrayers. Ever have they been, ever will they be. The only question is what form their treachery will take. The svartalves had to be shown."

"How did you know I would discover it?"

"I did not," she said. "But I know your mentor. When it comes to meddling, to unearthing awkward truths, he has taught you exceedingly well." She smiled. "You have also learned his aptitude for taking orderly situations and reducing them to elemental chaos."

"Meaning what?" I demanded.

Her smile was maddeningly smug. "Meaning that I was confident that whatever happened, it would not include the smooth completion of the treaty."

"But you could have done everything I did."

"No, child," Lea said. "The svartalves would never have asked me to be their guest at the reception. They love neatness and order. They would have known my purposes were not orderly ones."

"And they didn't know that about me?"

"They cannot judge others except by their actions," Lea said. "Hence their treaty with the Fomor, who had not yet crossed their paths. My actions have shown me to be someone who must be treated with caution. You had . . . a clean record with them. And you are smoking hot. All is well, your city saved, and now a group of wealthy, skilled, and influential beings owes you a favor." She paused for a moment and then leaned toward me slightly. "Perhaps some expression of gratitude is in order."

"From me, to you?" I asked. "For that?"

"I think your evening turned out quite well," Lea said her eyebrows raised. "Goodness, but you are a difficult child. How he manages to endure your insolence I will never know. You probably think you have earned some sort of reward from me." She rose and turned to go.

"Wait!" I said suddenly.

She paused.

I think my heart had stopped beating. I started shaking, everywhere. "You said that you know Harry. Not knew him. Know. Present tense."

"Did I?"

"You said you don't know how he manages to put up with me. Manages. Present tense."

"Did I?"

"Auntie," I asked her, and I could barely whisper. "Auntie . . . is Harry . . . is he alive?"

Lea turned to me very slowly, and her eyes glinted with green, wicked knowledge. "I did not say that he was alive, child. And neither should you. Not yet."

I bowed my head and started crying. Or laughing. Or both. I couldn't tell. Lea didn't wait around for it. Emotional displays made her uncomfortable.

Harry. Alive.

I *hadn't* killed him.

Best reward ever.

"Thank you, Auntie," I whispered. "Thank you."

Carrie Vaughn

New York Times bestseller Carrie Vaughn is the author of a wildly popular series of novels detailing the adventures of Kitty Norville, a radio personality who also happens to be a werewolf and who runs a late-night call-in radio advice show for supernatural creatures. The Kitty books include *Kitty and the Midnight Hour, Kitty Goes to Washington, Kitty Takes a Holiday, Kitty and the Silver Bullet, Kitty and the Dead Man's Hand, Kitty Raises Hell, Kitty's House of Horrors, Kitty Goes to War,* and *Kitty's Big Trouble.* Her other novels include *Voices of Dragons,* her first venture into young adult territory, and a fantasy, *Discord's Apple.* Vaughn's short work has appeared in *Lightspeed, Asimov's Science Fiction, Subterranean, Inside Straight* (a Wild Cards novel), *Realms of Fantasy, Jim Baen's Universe, Paradox, Strange Horizons, Weird Tales, All-Star Zeppelin Adventure Stories,* and elsewhere. Her most recent books include the novels *After the Golden Age* and *Steel;* a collection, *Straying from the Path;* a new Kitty novel, *Kitty Steals the Show;* and a collection of her Kitty stories, *Kitty's Greatest Hits.* Coming up is another new Kitty novel, *Kitty Rocks the House.* She lives in Colorado.

In the vivid and compelling story that follows, she takes us to the front lines in Russia during the darkest days of World War II for the story of a young woman flying the most dangerous of combat missions, who is determined to do her duty as a soldier and keep flying them, even if it kills her—which it very well might.

RAISA STEPANOVA

My Dear Davidya:

If you are reading this, it means I have died. Most likely been killed fighting in service of the glorious homeland. At least I hope so. I have this terrible nightmare that I am killed, not in the air fighting Fascists, but because a propeller blade falls off just as I am walking under the nose of my Yak and cuts my head off. People would make a good show of pretending to mourn, but they'd be laughing behind my back. My dead back, so I won't notice, but still, it's the principle of the thing. There'd certainly be no Hero of the Soviet Union for me, would there? Never mind, we will assume I perished gloriously in battle.

Please tell all the usual to Mama and Da, that I am happy to give my life in defense of you and them and Nina and the homeland, as we all are, and that if I must die at all I'm very happy to do it while flying. So don't be sad for me. I love you.

Very Sincerely: Raisa

"Raisa!" Inna called from outside the dugout. "We're up! Let's go!"
"Just a minute!" She scribbled a last few lines.

P.S. My wingman, Inna, will be very upset if I am killed. She'll think it's her fault, that she didn't cover me. (It won't be true because she's a very good pilot and wingman.) I think you should make an effort to comfort her at the very first opportunity. She's a redhead. You'll like her. Really like her, I mean. I keep a picture of you in our dugout and she thinks you're handsome. She'll weep on your shoulder and it will be very romantic, trust me.

"Raisa!"

Raisa folded the page into eighths and stuffed it under the blanket on her cot, where it was sure to be found if she didn't come back. David's name and regiment were clearly written on the outside, and Inna would know what to do with it. She grabbed her coat and helmet and ran with her wingman to the airfield, where their planes waited.

The pair of them flew out of Voronezh on a routine patrol and spotted enemy planes even before reaching the front. Raisa breathed slow to keep her heart from racing, letting the calm spread to her hands to steady them, where they rested on the stick.

"Raisa, you see that? Two o'clock?" Inna's voice cracked over the radio. She flew behind and to the right—Raisa didn't have to look to know she was there.

"Yes." Raisa squinted through the canopy and counted. More planes, dark spots gliding against a hazy sky, seemed to appear as she did so. They were meant to be patrolling for German reconnaissance planes, which only appeared one or two at a time. This—this was an entire squadron.

The profile of the planes clarified—twin propellers, topside canopy, long fuselage painted with black crosses. She radioed back to Inna, "Those are Junkers! That's a bombing run!"

She counted sixteen bombers—their target could have been any of the dozens of encampments, supply depots, or train stations along this section of the front. They probably weren't expecting any resistance at all.

"What do we do?" Inna said.

This was outside their mission parameters, and they were so far outnumbered as to be ridiculous. On the other hand, what else were they supposed to do? The Germans would have dropped their bombs before the 586th could scramble more fighters.

"What do you think?" Raisa answered. "We stop them!"

"With you!"

Raisa throttled up and pushed forward on the stick. The engine rumbled and shook the canopy around her. The Yak streaked forward, the sky a blur above her. A glance over her shoulder, and she saw Inna's fighter right behind her.

She aimed at the middle of the German swarm. Individual bombers became very large very quickly, filling the sky in front of her. She kept on, like an arrow, until she and Inna came within range.

The bombers scattered, as if they'd been blown apart by a wind. Planes at the edges of the formation peeled off, and ones in the middle climbed and dived at random. Clearly, they hadn't expected a couple of Russian fighters to shoot at them from nowhere.

She picked one that had the misfortune to evade right into her path, and focused her sights on it. She fired a series of rounds from the 20mm cannon, missed when the bomber juked out of range. She cursed.

Rounds blazed above her canopy; a gunner, shooting back. She banked hard, right and up, keeping a watch out for collisions. Dicey, maneuvering with all this traffic. The Yak was fast—she could fly circles around the Junkers and wasn't terribly worried about getting shot. But she could easily crash into one of them by not paying close enough attention. All she and Inna really had to do was stop the group from reaching its target, but if she could bring down one or two of them in the meantime . . . One second at a time, that was the only way to handle the situation. Stay alive so she could do some good.

The enemy gunner fired at her again, then Raisa recognized the sound of another cannon firing. A fireball expanded and burned out at the corner of her vision—a Junker, one of its engines breaking apart. The plane lurched, off balance until it fell in an arc, trailing smoke. It waggled once or twice, the pilot trying to regain control, but then the bomber started spinning and it was all over.

Inna cried over the radio, "Raisa! I got him, I got him!" It was her first kill in battle.

"Excellent! Only fifteen more to go!"

"Raisa Ivanovna, you're terrible."

The battle seemed to drag, but surely only seconds had passed since they scattered the formation. They couldn't engage for much longer before they'd run out of ammunition, not to mention fuel. The last few shots had to count, then she and Inna ought to run. *After* those last few shots, of course.

Raisa caught another target and banked hard to follow it. The bomber climbed, but it was slow, and she was right on it. By now her nerves were singing and instinct guided her more than reason. She squeezed hard on the trigger before the enemy was fully in her crosshairs, but it worked, because the Junker slid into the line of fire just as her shots reached it. She put holes across its wings and across its engine, which sparked and began pouring smoke. The plane could not survive, and sure enough, the nose tipped forward, the whole thing falling out of control.

Inna cheered for her over the radio, but Raisa was already hunting her next target. So many to choose from. The two fighters were surrounded, and Raisa should have been frightened, but she could only think about shooting the next bomber. And the next.

The Junkers struggled to return to formation. The loose, straggling collection had dropped five hundred meters from its original altitude. If the fighters could force down the entire squadron, what a prize that would be! But no, they were running, veering hard from the fighters, struggling to escape.

Bombs fell from the lead plane's belly, and the others followed suit. The bombs detonated on empty forest, their balloons of smoke rising harmlessly. They'd scared the bombers into dropping their loads early.

Raisa smiled at the image.

With nothing left in their bomb bays and no reason to continue, the Junkers peeled off and circled back to the west. Lighter and faster now, they'd be more difficult for the fighters to catch. But they wouldn't be killing any Russians today, either.

Raisa radioed, "Inna, let's get out of here."

"Got it."

With Inna back on her wing, she turned her Yak to the east, and home.

"That makes three confirmed kills total, Stepanova. Two more, and you'll be an ace."

Raisa was grinning so hard, she squinted. "We could hardly miss, with so many targets to pick from," she said. Inna rolled her eyes a little, but was also beaming. She'd bagged her first kill, and though she was doing a very good job of trying to act humble and dignified *now*, right after they'd landed and parked she'd run screaming up to Raisa and knocked her over with a big hug. Lots of dead Germans and they'd both walked away from the battle. They couldn't have been much more successful than that.

Commander Gridnev, a serious young man with a face like a bear, was reviewing a typed piece of paper at his desk in the largest dugout at the

101st Division's airfield. "The squadron's target was a rail station. A battalion of infantry was there, waiting for transport. They'd have been killed. You saved a lot of lives."

Even better. Tremendous. Maybe Davidya had been there and she'd saved him. She could brag about it in her next letter.

"Thank you, sir."

"Good work, girls. Dismissed."

Out of the commander's office, they ran back home, stumbling in their oversized men's flight suits and jackets and laughing.

A dozen women shared the dugout, which if you squinted in dim light seemed almost homelike, with wrought iron cots, wool bedding, whitewashed walls, and wooden tables with a few vases of wildflowers someone had picked for decorations. The things always wilted quickly—no sunlight reached inside. After a year of this—moving from base to base, from better conditions to worse and back again—they'd gotten used to the bugs and rats and rattling of distant bombing. You learned to pay attention to and enjoy the wilted wildflowers, or you went mad.

Though that happened sometimes, too.

The second best thing about being a pilot (the first being the flying itself) was the better housing and rations. And the vodka allotment for flying combat missions. Inna and Raisa pulled chairs up close to the stove to drive away the last of the chill from flying at altitude and tapped their glasses together in a toast.

"To victory," Inna said, because it was tradition and brought luck.

"To flying," Raisa said, because she meant it.

At dinner—runny stew and stale bread cooked over the stove—Raisa awaited the praise of her comrades and was ready to bask in their admiration—two more kills and she'd be an ace; who was a better fighter pilot, or a better shot, than she? But it didn't happen quite like that.

Katya and Tamara stumbled through the doorway, almost crashing into the table and tipping over the vase of flowers. They were flushed, gasping for breath as if they'd been running.

"You'll never guess what's happened!" Katya said.

Tamara talked over her: "We've just come from the radio operator; he told us the news!"

Raisa's eyes went round and she almost dropped the plate of bread she was holding. "We've pushed them back? They're retreating?"

"No, not that," Katya said, indignant, as if wondering how anyone could be so stupid.

"Liliia scored two kills today!" Tamara said. "She's got five now. She's an ace!"

Liliia Litviak. Beautiful, wonderful Liliia, who could do no wrong. Raisa remembered their first day with the battalion, and Liliia showed up, this tiny woman with the perfect face and bleached blond hair. After weeks of living in the dugouts, she still had a perfect face and bleached blond hair, looking like some American film star. She was so small, they thought she couldn't possibly pilot a Yak, she couldn't possibly serve on the front. Then she got in her plane and she *flew*. Better than any of them. Even Raisa had to admit that, but not out loud.

Liliia painted *flowers* on the nose of her fighter, and instead of making fun of her, everyone thought she was so *sweet*.

And now she was a fighter ace. Raisa stared. "Five kills. Really?"

"Indisputable! She had witnesses; the news is going out everywhere. Isn't it wonderful?"

It was wonderful, and Raisa did her best to act like it, smiling and raising a toast to Liliia and cursing the Fascists. They ate dinner and wondered when the weather would change, if winter had a last gasp of frigid cold for them or if they were well into the merely chilly damp of spring. No one talked about when, if ever, the war might be done. Two years now since the Germans invaded. They'd not gotten any farther in the last few months, and the Soviets had made progress—recapturing Voronezh for one, and moving forward operations there. That was something.

But Inna knew her too well to let her go. "You were frowning all the way through dinner," she said, when they were washing up outside, in darkness, before bed. "You didn't hide it very well."

Raisa sighed. "If I'd been sent to Stalingrad, I'd have just as many kills as she does. I'd have more. I'd have been an ace months ago."

"If you'd been sent to Stalingrad, you'd be dead," Inna said. "I'd rather have you here and alive."

Frowning, she bit off her words. "We're all dead. All of us on the front, we're all here to die; it's just a matter of when."

Inna wore a knit cap over her short hair, which curled up over the edges.

This, along with the freckles dotting her cheeks, made her look elfin. Her eyes were dark, her lips in a grim line. She was always solemn, serious. Always telling Raisa when her jokes had gone too far. Inna would never say a bad word about anyone.

"It'll be over soon," she said to Raisa under the overcast sky, not even a dim lantern to break the darkness, lest German reconnaissance flights find them. "It has to be over soon. With the Brits and Americans pounding on the one side and us on the other, Germany can't last for long."

Raisa nodded. "You're right, of course you're right. We just have to hold on as long as we can."

"Yes. That's exactly right."

Inna squeezed her arm, then turned back to the dugout and a cot with too-thin blankets and the skittering of rats. Sometimes Raisa looked around at the dirt and the worn boots, the tired faces and the lack of food, and believed she'd be living like this for the rest of her life.

Raisa arrived at the command dugout for a briefing—a combat mission, she hoped, and a chance for her next two kills—but one of the radio operators pulled her aside before she could go in.

She and Pavel often traded information. She'd give him the gossip from the flight line, and he'd pass on any news he'd heard from other regiments. He had the most reliable information from the front. More reliable than what they could get from command, even, because the official reports that trickled down were filtered, massaged, and manipulated until they said exactly what the higher-ups wanted people like her to know. Entire battalions had been wiped out and no one knew because the generals didn't want to damage morale, or some such nonsense.

Today Pavel seemed pale, and his frown was somber.

"What is it?" she asked, staring, because he could only have bad news. Very bad, to come seek her out. She thought of David, of course. It had to be about David.

"Raisa Ivanovna," he said. "I have news . . . about your brother."

Her head went light, as if she were flying a barrel roll, the world going upside down around her. But she stood firm, didn't waver, determined to get through the next few moments with her dignity intact. She could do this, for her brother's sake. Even though *she* was supposed to die first. The danger she faced in the air, flying these death traps against Messerschmitts, was so much greater. She'd always felt so sure that *she* would die, that David would have to be the one to stand firm while he heard the news.

"Tell me," she said, and her voice didn't waver.

"His squadron saw action. He . . . he's missing in action."

She blinked. Not the words she was expecting. But this . . . the phrase hardly made sense. How did a soldier just *disappear*, she wanted to demand. David wasn't like an earring or a slip of paper that one wandered the house searching for. She felt her face turn furrowed, quizzical, looking at Pavel for an explanation.

"Raisa—are you all right?" he said.

"Missing?" she repeated. The information and what it meant began to penetrate.

"Yes," the radio operator answered, his tone turning to despair.

"But that's . . . I don't even know what to say."

"I'm so sorry, Raisa. I won't tell Gridnev. I won't tell anyone until official word comes down. Maybe your brother will turn up before then and it won't mean anything."

Pavel's hangdog look of pity was almost too much to take. When she didn't reply, he walked away, trudging through the mud.

She knew what he was thinking, what everyone would think, and what would happen next. No one would say it out loud—they didn't dare—but she knew. Missing in action; how much better for everyone if he had simply died.

Comrade Stalin had given the order soon after the war began: "We have no prisoners of war, only traitors of the motherland." Prisoners were collaborators, because if they had been true patriots they would have died rather than be taken. Likewise, soldiers missing in action were presumed to have deserted. If David did not somehow reappear in the Soviet army, he would be declared a traitor, and his family would suffer. Their parents and younger sister would get no rations or aid. Raisa herself would most likely be barred from flying at the very least. They'd all suffer, even though David was probably lying dead at the bottom of a bog somewhere.

She pinched her nose to hold the tears back and went into the dugout for whatever briefing the commander had for the flight. She mustn't let on that anything was wrong. But she had a hard time listening that morning.

David wasn't a traitor, but no matter how much she screamed that truth from the mountaintops, it didn't matter. Unless he appeared—or a body were found, proving that he'd been killed in action—he'd be a traitor forever.

Terrible, to wish a body would be found.

She had a sudden urge to take up a gun—in her own two hands, even, and not in the cockpit of her plane—and murder someone. Stalin, perhaps.

If anyone here could read her mind, hear her thoughts, she'd be barred from flying, sent to a work camp, if not executed outright. Then her parents and sister would be even worse off, with *two* traitors in the family. So, she should not think ill of Stalin. She should channel her anger toward the real enemy, the ones who'd really killed David. If he were dead. Perhaps he wasn't dead, only missing, like the report said.

Inna sat beside her and took her arm. "Raisa, what's wrong? You look like you're going to explode."

"It's nothing," Raisa answered in a whisper.

She kept writing letters to David as if nothing had happened. The writing calmed her.

> *Dear Davidya:*
>
> *Did I mention I have three kills now? Three. How many Germans have you killed? Don't answer that, I know you'll tell me, and it'll be more, and I know it's harder for you because you have to face them with nothing but bullets and bayonets, while I have my beautiful Yak to help me. But still, I feel like I'm doing some good. I'm saving the lives of your fellow infantry. Inna and I stopped a whole squadron from completing its bombing run, and that's something to be proud of.*
>
> *I'm so worried about you, Davidya. I try not to be, but it's hard.*
>
> *Two more kills and I'll be an ace. Not the first woman ace, though. That's Liliia Litviak. Amazing Liliia, who fought at Stalingrad. I don't begrudge her that at all. She's a very good pilot, I've seen her fly. I won't even claim to be better. But I'm just as good, I know I am. By the way, you should know that if you see a picture of Litviak in the papers (I hear the papers are making much of her, so that she can inspire the troops or some such thing) that Inna is much*

prettier. Hard to believe, I know, but true. After my next two kills, I wonder if they'll put my picture in the paper? You could tell everyone you know me. If you're not too embarrassed by your mouse-faced little sister.

I've gotten a letter from Mama, and I'm worried because she says Da is sick again. I thought he was better, but he's sick all the time, isn't he? And there isn't enough food. He's probably giving all his to Nina. It's what I would do. I'm afraid Mama isn't telling me everything, because she's worried that I can't take it. You'd tell me, wouldn't you?

You'd think I had enough to worry about, that I wouldn't worry about home, too. They can take care of themselves. As I can take care of myself, so do not worry about me. We have food, and I get plenty of sleep. Well, I get some *sleep. I hear the bombing sometimes, and it's hard to think they won't be here next. But never mind.*

Until I see you again, Raisa

Like dozens of other girls, Raisa had written a letter to the famous pilot Marina Raskova asking her how she could fly for the war. Comrade Raskova had written back: I am organizing a battalion for women. Come.

Of course Raisa did.

Da had been angry: he wanted her to stay home and work in a factory—good, proud, noble work that would support the war effort just as much as flying a Yak would. But her mother had looked at him and quietly spoken: Let her have her wings while she can. Da couldn't argue with that. Her older brother, David, made her promise to write him every day, or at least every week, so he could keep an eye on her. She did.

Raisa was assigned to the fighter regiment, and for the first time met other girls like herself who'd joined a local flying club, who had to fight for the privilege of learning to fly. At her club, Raisa had been the only girl. The boys didn't take her seriously at first, laughed when she showed up wanting to take the classes to get her license. But she kept showing up to every session, every meeting, and every class. They had to let her join. Truth to tell, they didn't take her seriously even after she soloed and scored better on her navigation test than any of the boys. She never said it out loud, but what made Raisa particularly angry was the hypocrisy of it all. The great Soviet experiment with its noble egalitarian principles that was meant to bring equality to all, even between men and women, and here the boys were, telling her she should go home, work in a factory with other women, get married, and have babies, because that was what women were supposed to do. They weren't meant to fly. They *couldn't* fly. She had to prove them wrong over and over again.

Thank goodness for Marina Raskova, who proved so much for all of them. When she died—a stupid crash in bad weather, from what Raisa heard—the women pilots were afraid they'd be disbanded and sent to factories, building the planes they ought to be flying. Raskova and her connections to the very highest levels—to Stalin himself—were the only things keeping the women flying at the front. But it seemed the women had proven themselves, and they weren't disbanded. They kept flying, and fighting. Raisa pinned a picture of Raskova from a newspaper to the wall of their dugout. Most of the women paused by it now and then, offering it a smile, or sometimes a frown of quiet grief. More dead pilots had lined up behind her since.

"I want a combat mission, not scut work," Raisa told Gridnev. Didn't salute, didn't say "sir." They were all equal Soviet citizens, weren't they?

He'd handed her flight its next mission outside the dugout, in a blustery spring wind that Raisa hardly noticed. They were supposed to report to their planes immediately, but she held back to argue. Inna hovered a few yards away, nervous and worried.

"Stepanova. I need pilots for escort duty. You're it."

"The flight plan takes us a hundred miles away from the front lines. Your VIP doesn't need escorting, he needs babysitting!"

"Then you'll do the babysitting."

"Commander, I just need those next two kills—"

"You need to serve the homeland in whatever fashion the homeland sees fit."

"But—"

"This isn't about you. I need escort pilots; you're a pilot. Now go."

Gridnev walked away before she did. She looked after him, fuming, wanting to shout. She wouldn't get to kill anything flying as an *escort*.

She marched to the flight line.

Inna ran after her. "Raisa, what's gotten into you?"

Her partner had asked that every hour for the last day, it seemed like. Raisa couldn't hide. And if she couldn't trust Inna, she couldn't trust anyone.

"David's missing in action," Raisa said, and kept walking.

She opened her mouth, properly shocked and pitying, as Pavel had done. "Oh—oh no. I'm so sorry."

"It's nothing. But I have to work twice as hard, right?"

They continued to their planes in silence.

Raisa's hands itched. They lay lightly on the stick, and she didn't have to do much to keep steady. The air was calm, and they—Inna, Katya, and Tamara were in the other fighters—were flying in a straight line, practically. But she wanted to shoot something. They weren't told who it was in the Li-2 they guarded, not that it would have mattered. But she imagined it might be Stalin himself. She wondered if she'd have the courage to radio to him, "Comrade, let me tell you about my brother . . ." But the higher-ups wouldn't tap a flight of women pilots from the front to protect the premier. It wasn't him.

Not that their VIP needing guarding. Out here, the most dangerous thing she faced was the other pilots slipping out of formation and crashing into her. *That* would be embarrassing.

Just before they'd left, the radio operator had brought news that Liliia had scored another kill. *Six* confirmed kills. The Germans seemed to be lining up for the privilege of being shot down by beautiful Liliia. And here Raisa was, miles and miles from battle, playing at guarding.

If she died in battle, heroically, with lots of witnesses, leaving behind an indisputable body, perhaps she might help recover David's reputation. If she were a hero—an ace, even—he could not be a traitor, right?

She stretched her legs and scratched her hair under her leather helmet. Another couple of hours and they'd land and get a hot meal. That was one consolation—they were flying their charge to a real base with real food, and they'd been promised a meal before they had to fly back to Voronezh. Raisa wondered if they'd be able to wrap some up to stuff in their pockets and take back with them.

Scanning the sky around her, out to the horizon, she didn't see so much as a goose in flight. The other planes—the bullet-shaped Yaks and the big Lisunov with its two wing-mounted engines and stocky frame—hummed around her, in a formation that was rather stately. It always amazed her, these great beasts of steel and grease soaring through the air, in impossible defiance of gravity. The world spread out below her, wide plains splotched in beige and green, trimmed by forests, cut through with the winding path of a creek. She could believe that nothing existed down there—a clean, new land, and she was queen of everything she could see, for hundreds and hundreds of miles. She sailed over it without effort. Then she'd spot a farm, rows of square fields that should have been green with the new growth of crops but instead held blackened craters and scraps of destroyed tanks.

If she focused on the sound of the engine, a comforting rattle that flowed through the skin of the fuselage around her, she wouldn't think so much about the rest of it. If she tipped her head back, she could watch blue sky passing overhead and squint into the sun. The day was beautiful, and she had an urge to open her canopy and drink in the sky. The freezing wind would thrash her at this altitude, so she resisted. The cockpit was warm and safe as an egg.

Something outside caught her eye. Far off, across the flat plain they soared over, to where sky met earth. Dark specks moving against the blue. They were unnatural—they flew too straight, too smoothly to be birds. They seemed far away, which meant they had to be big—hard to tell, without a point of reference. But several of them flew together in the unmistakable shape of airplanes in formation.

She turned on the radio channel. "Stepanova here. Ten o'clock, toward the horizon, do you see it?"

Inna answered. "Yes. Are those bombers?"

They were, Raisa thought. They had a heavy look about them, droning steadily on rather than racing. The formation was coming closer, but still not close enough to see if they had crosses or stars painted on them.

"Theirs or ours?" Katya said.

"I'll find out," Raisa said, banking out of formation and opening the throttle. She'd take a look, and if she saw that black cross, she'd fire.

A male voice intruded, the pilot of the Li-2. "Osipov here. Get back here, Stepanova!"

"But—"

"Return to formation!"

The planes were *right there*, it would just take a *second* to check—

Inna came on the channel, pleading, "Raisa, you can't take them on your own!"

She could certainly try. . . .

Osipov said, "A squadron has been notified and will intercept the unknown flight. We're to continue on."

They couldn't stop her . . . but they could charge her with disobeying orders once she landed, and that wouldn't help anyone. So she circled around and returned to formation. Litviak was probably getting to shoot someone today. Raisa frowned at her washed-out reflection in the canopy glass.

Dear Davidya:

I promised to write you every day, so I continue to do so.

How are you this time? I hope you're well. Not sick, not hungry. We've taken to talking about eating the rats that swarm the dugouts here, but we haven't gotten to the point of actually trying it. Mostly because I think it would be far too much work for too little reward. The horrid beasts are as skinny as the rest of us. I'm not complaining, though. We've gotten some crates of canned goods—fruits, meat, milk—from an American supply drop and are savoring the windfall. It's like a taste of what we're fighting for, and what we can look forward to when this mess is all over. It was Inna who said that. Beautiful thought, yes? She keeps the whole battalion in good spirits all by herself.

I ought to warn you, I've written a letter to be sent to you in case I die. It's quite grotesque, and now you'll be terrified that every letter you get from me will be that one. Have you done that, written me a letter that I'll only read if you die? I haven't gotten one, which gives me hope.

I'm very grateful Nina isn't old enough to be on the front with us, or I'd be writing double the grotesque letters. I got a letter from her talking about what she'll do when she's old enough to come to the front, and she wants to fly like me and if she can't be a pilot she'll be a mechanic—my mechanic, even. She was very excited. I wrote her

*back the same day telling her the war will be over before she's old
enough. I hope I'm right.*

Love and kisses, Raisa

Another week passed with no news of David. Most likely he was dead.
Officially, he had deserted, and Raisa supposed she had to consider that
he actually had, except that that made no sense. Where would he go? Or
maybe he was simply lost and hadn't made his way back to his regiment
yet. She wanted to believe that.

Gridnev called her to the operations dugout, and she presented herself
at his desk. A man, a stranger in a starched army uniform, stood with him.

The air commander was grim and stone-faced as he announced, "Stepanova, this is Captain Sofin." Then Gridnev left the room.

Raisa knew what was coming. Sofin put a file folder on the desk and sat
behind it. He didn't invite her to sit.

She wasn't nervous, speaking to him. But she had to tamp down on a
slow, tight anger.

"Your brother is David Ivanovich Stepanov?"

"Yes."

"Are you aware that he has been declared missing in action?"

She shouldn't have known, officially, but it was no good hiding it. "Yes,
I am."

"Do you have any information regarding his whereabouts?"

Don't you have a war you ought to be fighting? she thought. "I assume he
was killed. So many are, after all."

"You have received no communication from him?"

And what if he found all those letters she'd been writing *him* and
thought them real? "None at all."

"I must tell you that if you receive any news of him at all, it's your duty
to inform command."

"Yes, sir."

"We will be watching closely, Raisa Stepanova."

She wanted to leap across the table in the operations dugout and strangle
the little man with the thin moustache. Barring that, she wanted to cry,
but didn't. Her brother was dead, and they'd convicted him without evidence or trial.

What was she fighting for, again? Nina and her parents, and even Davidya. Certainly not this man.

He dismissed her without ever raising his gaze from the file folder he studied, and she left the dugout.

Gridnev stood right outside the door, lurking like a schoolboy, though a serious one who worried too much. No doubt he had heard everything. She wilted, blushing, face to the ground, like a kicked dog.

"You have a place here at the 586th, Stepanova. You always will."

She smiled a thanks but didn't trust her voice to say anything. Like observing that Gridnev would have little to say in the matter, in the end.

No, she had to earn her innocence. If she gathered enough kills, if she became an ace, they couldn't touch her, any more than they could tarnish the reputation of Liliia Litviak. If she became enough of a hero, she could even redeem David.

Winter ended, but that only meant the insects came out in force, mosquitoes and biting flies that left them all miserable and snappish. Rumors abounded that the Allied forces in Britain and America were planning a massive invasion, that the Germans had a secret weapon they'd use to level Moscow and London. Living in a camp on the front, news was scarce. They got orders, not news, and could only follow those orders.

It made her tired.

"Stepanova, you all right?"

She'd parked her plane after flying a patrol, tracing a route along the front, searching for imminent attacks and troops on the move—perfectly routine, no Germans spotted. The motor had grumbled to stillness and the propeller had stopped turning long ago, but she remained in her cockpit, just sitting. The thought of pulling herself, her bulky gear, her parachute, logbook, helmet, all the rest of it, out of the cockpit and onto the wing left her feeling exhausted. She'd done this for months, and now, finally, she wasn't sure she had anything left. She couldn't read any numbers on the dials, no matter how much she blinked at the instrument panel.

"Stepanova!" Martya, her mechanic, called to her again, and Raisa shook herself awake.

"Yes, I'm fine, I'm coming." She slid open the canopy, gathered her things, and hauled herself over the edge.

Martya was waiting for her on the wing in shirt and overalls, sleeves rolled up, kerchief over her head. She couldn't have been more than twenty, but her hands were rough from years of working on engines.

"You look terrible," Martya said.

"Nothing a shot of vodka and a month in a feather bed won't fix," Raisa said, and the mechanic laughed.

"How's your fuel?"

"Low. You think she's burning more than she should?"

"Wouldn't surprise me. She's been working hard. I'll look her over."

"You're the best, Martya." The mechanic gave her a hand off the wing, and Raisa pulled her into a hug.

Martya said, "Are you sure you're all right?" Raisa didn't answer.

"Raisa!" That was Inna, walking over from her own plane, dragging her parachute with one arm, her helmet tucked under her other. "You all right?"

She wished people would stop asking that.

"Tired, I think," Martya answered for her. "You know what we need? A party or a dance or something. There are enough handsome boys around here to flirt with." She was right: the base was filled with male pilots, mechanics, and soldiers, and they were all dashing and handsome. The odds were certainly in the women's favor. Raisa hadn't really thought of it before.

Inna sighed. "Hard to think of flirting when you're getting bombed and shot at."

Martya leaned on the wing and looked wistful. "After the war, we'll be able to get dressed up. Wash our hair with real soap and go dancing."

"After the war. Yes," Inna said.

"After we *win* the war," Raisa said. "We won't be dancing much if the Fascists win."

They went quiet, and Raisa regretted saying anything. It was the unspoken assumption when people talked about "after the war": of course they'd win. If they lost, there wouldn't be an "after" at all.

Not that Raisa expected to make it that far.

> *Davidya:*
> *I've decided that I'd give up being a fighter ace if it meant we could both get through the war alive. Don't tell anyone I said that;*

*I'd lose my reputation for being fierce, and for being hideously jeal-
ous of Liliia Litviak. If there's a God, maybe he'll hear me, and
you'll come walking out of the wilderness, alive and well. Not dead
and not a traitor. We'll go home, and Mama and Da and Nina will
be well, and we can forget that any of this ever happened. That's my
dream now.*

    *I've still got that letter, the hideous one I wrote for you in case I
die. I ought to burn it, since Inna doesn't have anyone to send it to
now.*

Your sister, Raisa

An alarm came at dawn.

By reflex, she tumbled out of her cot, into trousers and shirt, coat and
boots, grabbing gloves and helmet on the way out of the dugout. Inna was
at her side, running toward the airstrip. Planes were already rumbling
overhead—scouts returning from patrol.

Mechanics and armorers were at the planes—all of them. Refueling,
running chains of ammunition into cannon and machine guns. This was
big. Not just a sortie, but a battle.

There was Commander Gridnev addressing them right on the field. The
mission: German heavy bombers had crossed the front. Fighters were being
scrambled to intercept. He'd be flying this one himself, leading the first
squadron. First squadron launched in ten minutes and would engage any
fighters sent with the attack. Second squadron—the women's squadron—
would launch in fifteen and stop the bombers.

The air filled with Yak fighters, the drone of their engines like the buzz
of bees made large.

No time to think, only to do, as they'd done hundreds of times before.
Martya helped Raisa into her cockpit, slapped the canopy twice after
closing it over her, then jumped off the wing to yank the chocks out from
under the tires. A dozen Yaks lined up, taxiing from the flight line to wait
their turn on the runway. One after another after another . . .

Finally, Raisa's turn came, and she was airborne. It was a relief, being
in the air again, where she could *do* something. Up here, when someone
attacked, she could dodge. Not like being on the ground when the bombs
fell. She'd rather have a stick in her hand, a trigger under her finger. It felt
right.

Glancing back through the canopy, Raisa found Inna on her wing, right where she should be. Her friend gave her a broad salute, and Raisa waved back. Once the squadron was airborne, they settled into an echelon formation, following Gridnev's squadron up ahead. They'd all flown with Gridnev's men; they'd all had months to get used to each other. Men or women, didn't make a difference, and most men realized that sooner or later. Which was something of a revelation if she stopped to think about it. But no one had time to stop and think about it. All she needed to know was that Aleksei Borisov liked diving to the left and would loop above if he got into trouble; Sofia Mironova was a careful pilot and tended to hang back; Valentina Gushina was fast, very good in combat; Fedor Baurin had the keenest eyesight. He'd spot their target before anyone else.

The Yaks flew on in loose formation, ready to break and engage as soon as the target was sighted. Raisa scanned the skies in all directions, peering above and over her shoulders. The commander had the coordinates; he'd estimated twenty minutes until contact. They should be in sight of them any minute now. . . .

"There!" Baurin called over the radio. "One o'clock!"

Gridnev came on the channel. "Steady. Remain in formation."

She saw the enemy, sunlight flashing off canopies, airplanes suspended in the air. Hard to judge scale and distance; her own group was traveling fast enough that the enemy planes seemed to be standing still. But they were approaching, rapidly and inexorably.

While the heavy bombers continued on, straight and level, a handful of smaller planes broke off from the main group—a squadron of fighters as escort.

Well, this was going to be interesting.

On the commander's orders, they spread out and prepared to engage. Raisa opened the throttle and sped ahead, planning to overshoot the fighters entirely: Their goal was preventing those bombers from reaching their target. Her Yak dipped down, yawed to the left, roared onward.

A flight of Messerschmitts rocketed overhead. Gunfire sounded. Then they were gone.

Inna had followed her, and the bombers lay ahead of them, waiting. They had a short time to be as disruptive as they could before those Messers came back around, no matter how much the others were able to keep them occupied.

As soon as she was within range, she opened fire. The rattle from the cannon shook her fuselage. Nearby, another cannon fired; Raisa traced the smoke of the shells from behind her toward the Junkers: Inna had fired as well.

The bombers dropped back. And the fighters caught up with her and Inna. Then chaos.

She watched for stars and crosses painted on the fuselages, marking friend or foe. They chased each other in three dimensions, until it was impossible to track them all, and she began to focus on avoiding collision. The Messers were torpedo shaped, sleek and nimble. Formidable. Both sets of pilots had had two years of war to gain experience. The fight would end only when one side or the other ran out of ammunition.

They had to bring down those bombers, if nothing else.

The others had the same idea, and the commander ordered them to their primary target, until the bombers scattered, just to get out of the way of the dogfights. Now the Messers had to worry about hitting their charges by accident. That made them more careful; it might give the Yaks an edge.

The grumble of engines, of props beating the air, filled the sky around her. She'd never seen so many planes in the air at once, not even in her early days of training at the club.

She looped around to the outside and found a target. The pilot of the fighter had targeted a Yak—Katya's, she thought—and was so focused on catching her that he was flying straight and steady. First and worst mistake. She found him in her sights and held there a second, enough to get shots off before tipping and diving out of the way before someone else targeted her.

Her shells sliced across the cockpit—right through the pilot. The canopy shattered, and there was blood. She thought she saw his face, under goggles and flight cap, just for a moment—a look of shock, then nothing. Out of control now, the Me-109 tipped nose down and fell into a spiraling descent. The sight, black smoke trailing, the plane falling, was compelling. But her own trajectory carried her past in an instant, showing blue sky ahead.

"Four!" Raisa gave a shout. Four kills. And surely with all these targets around she could get her fifth. Both of them for David.

Other planes were falling from the sky. One of the bombers had been hit and still flew, with one engine pouring billows of smoke. Another fighter sputtered, fell back, then dropped, trailing fire and debris— Aleksei, that was Aleksei. Could he win back control of his injured plane? If not, did he have time to bail out? She saw no life in the cockpit; it was all moot. Rather than mourn, she set her jaw and found another target. So many of them, she hardly knew where to look first.

Over the radio, Gridnev was ordering a retreat. They'd done damage; time to get out while they could. But surely they'd only been engaged a few minutes. The motor of her Yak seemed tired; the spinning props in front of her seemed to sputter.

A Messerschmitt came out of the sun overhead like a dragon.

A rain of bullets struck the fuselage of her Yak, sounding like hail. Pain stabbed through her thigh, but that was less worrisome than the bang and grind screeching from the engine. And black smoke suddenly pouring from the nose in a thick stream. The engine coughed; the propeller stopped turning. Suddenly her beautiful streamlined Yak was a dead rock waiting to fall.

She held the nose up by brute force, choked the throttle again and again, but the engine was dead. She pumped the pedals, but the rudder was stuck. The nose tipped forward, ruining any chance she had of gliding toward earth.

"Raisa, get out! Get out!" Inna screamed over the radio.

Abandoning her post, no, never. Better to die in a ball of fire than go missing.

The nose tipped further forward, her left wing tipped up—the start of a dive and spin. Now or never. Dammit.

Her whole right leg throbbed with pain, and there was blood on her sleeve, blood spattered on the inside of the canopy, and she didn't know where it had come from. Maybe from that pilot whose face she'd seen, the one looking back at her with dead eyes behind his goggles. Instinct and training won over. Reaching up, she slammed open the canopy. Wind struck her like a fist. She unbuckled her harness, worked herself out of her seat; her leg didn't want to move. She didn't jump so much as let the Yak fall away from her, and she was floating. No—she was falling. She pulled the rip cord, and the parachute billowed above her, a cream-colored flower spreading its petals. It caught air and jerked her to a halt. She hung in the harness like so much deadweight. Deadweight, ha.

Her plane was on fire now, a flaming comet spinning to earth, trailing a corkscrew length of black smoke. Her poor plane. She wanted to weep, and she hadn't wept at all, this whole war, despite everything.

The battle had moved on. She's lost sight of Inna's plane but heard gunfire in the tangle of explosions and engine growls. Inna had covered her escape, protecting her from being shot in midair. Not that that would have been a tragedy—she'd die in combat, at least. Now she didn't know which side of the line the barren field below her was on. Who would find her, Russians or Nazis? *No prisoners of war, only traitors. . . .*

The worst part was not being able to do anything about it. Blood dripped from her leg and spattered in the wind. She'd been shot. The dizziness that struck her could have been the shock of realization or blood loss. She might not even reach the ground. Would her body ever be found?

The sky had suddenly gotten very quiet, and the fighters and bombers swarmed like crows in the distance. She squinted, trying to see them better.

Then Raisa blacked out.

Much later, opening her eyes, Raisa saw a low ceiling striped with rows of wooden roof beams. She was in a cot, part of a row of cots, in what must have been a makeshift field hospital bustling with people going back and forth, crossing rows and aisles on obviously important business. They were speaking Russian, and relief rushed through her. She'd been found. She was home.

She couldn't move, and decided she didn't much want to. Lying mindlessly on the cot and blankets, some distance from the pain she was sure she ought to be feeling, seemed the best way to exist, for at least the next few minutes.

"Raisa! You're awake!"

A chair scooted close on a concrete floor, and a familiar face came into view: David. Clean-shaven, dark hair trimmed, infantry uniform pressed and buttoned, as if he was going to a parade and not visiting his sister in hospital. Just as he was in the formal picture he'd sent home right after he signed up. This must be a dream. Maybe this wasn't a hospital. Maybe it was heaven. She wasn't sure she'd been good enough.

"Raisa, say something, please," he said, and with his face all pinched up he looked too worried to be in heaven.

"Davidya!" She needed to draw two breaths to get the word out, and her voice scratched surprisingly. She licked dry lips. "You're alive! What happened?"

He gave a sheepish shrug. "My squad got lost. We engaged a Panzer unit in the middle of the forest, and a sudden spring snowstorm pinned us down. Half of us got frostbite and had to drag the other half out. It took weeks, but we made it."

All this time . . . he really was just lost. She wished Sofin were here so she could punch him in the face.

"I'd laugh at all the trouble you caused, but my chest hurts," she said.

His smile slipped, and she imagined he'd had an interview with someone very much like Sofin after he and his squad limped back home. She wouldn't tell him about her own interview, and she would burn those letters she'd written him as soon as she got back to the airfield.

"It's so good to see you, Raisa." He clasped her hand, the one that wasn't bandaged, and she squeezed as hard as she could, which wasn't very, but it was enough. "Your Commander Gridnev got word to me that you'd been hurt, and I was able to take a day to come see you."

She swallowed and the words came slowly. "I was shot. I had to bail out. I don't know what happened next."

"Your wingman was able to radio your location. Ground forces moved in and found you. They tell me you were a mess."

"But I got my fourth kill, did they tell you that? One more and I'll be an ace." Maybe not the first woman fighter ace, or even the second. But she'd be one.

David didn't smile. She felt him draw away, as the pressure on her hand let up.

She frowned. "What?"

He didn't want to say. His face had scrunched up, his eyes glistening—as if *he* was about to start crying. And here she was, the girl, and she hadn't cried once. Well, almost once, for her plane.

"Raisa, you're being medically discharged," he said.

"What? No. I'm okay, I'll be okay—"

"Both your legs are broken, half your ribs are cracked, you've dislocated your shoulder, you have a concussion and been shot twice. You can't go back. Not for a long time, at least."

She really hadn't thought she'd been so badly hurt. Surely she'd have known if it was that bad. But her body still felt so far away. . . . She didn't know anything. "I'll get better—"

"Please, Raisa. Rest. Just rest for now."

One more kill, she only needed one more. . . . "Davidya, if I can't fly, what will I do?"

"Raisa!" A clear voice called from the end of the row of cots.

"Inna," Raisa answered, as loud as her voice would let her.

Her wingman rushed forward, and when she couldn't find a chair, she knelt by the cot. "Raisa. Oh, Raisa, look at you, wrapped up like a mummy." She fussed with the blankets, smoothed a lock of hair peeking out from the bandage around Raisa's head, and then fussed with the blankets some more. Good, sweet Inna.

"Inna, this is my brother, David."

Her eyes widened in shock, but Raisa didn't get a chance to explain that, yes, "missing" sometimes really meant missing, because David had stood in a rush and offered his chair to Inna, but she shook her head, which left them both standing on opposite sides of the cot, looking at each other across Raisa. Belatedly, Inna held out her hand. David wiped his on his trouser leg before shaking hers. What a David thing to do.

"Raisa's told me so much about you," Inna said.

"And she's told me about you in her letters."

Inna blushed. Good. Maybe something good would come out of all this.

She ought to be happy. She'd gotten her wish, after all.

Raisa stood on the platform, waiting for the train that would take her away from Voronezh. Her arm was still in a sling, and she leaned heavily on a cane. She couldn't lift her own bags.

Raisa had argued with the military about the discharge. They should have known she wouldn't give in—they didn't understand what she'd had to go through to get into the cockpit in the first place. That was the trick: she kept writing letters, kept showing up, over and over, and they couldn't tell her no. In a fit of fancy, she wondered if that was what had brought David home: She'd never stopped writing him letters, so he had to come home.

When they finally offered her a compromise—to teach navigation at a training field near Moscow—she took it. It meant that even with the cane and sling, even if she couldn't walk right or carry her own gear, she still wore her uniform, with all its medals and ribbons. She still held her chin up.

But in the end, even she had to admit she wouldn't fly again—at least, not in combat.

"Are you sure you'll be all right?" Inna had come with her to the station to see her off. David had returned to his regiment, but she'd overheard the two of them exchanging promises to write.

"I'm fine, really."

Inna's eyes shone as if she might cry. "You've gone so quiet. I'm so used to seeing you run around like an angry chicken."

Raisa smiled at the image. "You'll write?"

"Of course. Often. I'll keep you up to date on all the gossip."

"Yes, I want to know exactly how many planes Liliia Litviak shoots down."

"She'll win the war all by herself."

No, in a few months Raisa would read in the newspaper that Liliia was declared missing in action, shot down over enemy territory, her plane and body unrecovered. First woman fighter ace in history, and she'd be declared a deserter instead of a hero. But they didn't know that now.

The train's whistle keened, still some distance away, but they could hear it approach, clacking along its tracks.

"Are you *sure* you'll be okay?" Inna asked, with something like pleading in her eyes.

Raisa had been staring off into space, something she'd been doing a lot of lately. Wind played with her dark hair, and she looked out across the field and the ruins of the town to where the airfield lay. She thought she heard airplanes overhead.

She said, "I imagined dying in a terrible crash, or shot down in battle. I'd either walk away from this war or I'd die in some gloriously heroic way. I never imagined being . . . crippled. That the war would keep going on without me."

Inna touched her shoulder. "We're all glad you didn't die. Especially David."

"Yes, because he would have had to find a way to tell my parents."

She sighed. "You're so *morbid*."

The train arrived, and a porter came over to help with her luggage. "Be careful, Inna. Find yourself a good wingman to train."

"I'll miss you, my dear."

They hugged tightly but carefully, and Inna stayed to make sure Raisa limped her way onto the train and to her seat without trouble. She waved at Raisa from the platform until the train rolled out of sight.

Sitting in the train, staring out the window, Raisa caught sight of the planes she'd been looking for: a pair of Yaks streaking overhead, on their way to the airfield. But she couldn't hear their thrumming engines over the sound of the train. Probably just as well.

Joe R. Lansdale

Prolific Texas writer Joe R. Lansdale has won the Edgar Award, the British Fantasy Award, the American Horror Award, the American Mystery Award, the International Crime Writer's Award, and six Bram Stoker Awards. Although perhaps best known for horror/thrillers such as *The Nightrunners, Bubba Ho-Tep, The Bottoms, The God of the Razor,* and *The Drive-In,* he also writes the popular Hap Collins and Leonard Pine mystery series—*Savage Season, Mucho Mojo, The Two-Bear Mambo, Bad Chili, Rumble Tumble, Captains Outrageous*—as well as Western novels such as *Texas Night Riders* and *Blood Dance,* and totally unclassifiable cross-genre novels such as *Zeppelins West, The Magic Wagon,* and *Flaming London.* His other novels include *Dead in the West, The Big Blow, Sunset and Sawdust, Act of Love, Freezer Burn, Waltz of Shadows, The Drive-In 2: Not Just One of Them Sequels,* and *Leather Maiden.* He has also contributed novels to series such as Batman and Tarzan. His many short stories have been collected in *By Bizarre Hands; Tight Little Stitches in a Dead Man's Back; The Shadows, Kith and Kin; The Long Ones; Stories by Mama Lansdale's Youngest Boy; Bestsellers Guaranteed; On the Far Side of the Cadillac Desert with Dead Folks; Electric Gumbo; Writer of the Purple Rage; A Fist Full of Stories; Steppin' Out, Summer, '68; Bumper Crop; The Good, the Bad, and the Indifferent; For a Few Stories More; Mad Dog Summer and Other Stories; The King and Other Stories; Deadman's Road;* an omnibus, *Flaming Zeppelins: The Adventures of Ned the Seal;* and *High Cotton: Selected Stories of Joe R. Lansdale.* As editor, he has produced the anthologies *The Best of the West, Retro Pulp Tales, Son of Retro Pulp Tales, Razored Saddles* (with Pat LoBrutto), *Dark at Heart: All New Tales of Dark Suspense from Today's Masters* (with his wife Karen Lansdale), *The Horror Hall of Fame: The Stoker Winners,* and the Robert E. Howard tribute anthology *Cross Plains Universe* (with Scott A. Cupp). An anthology in tribute to Lansdale's work is *Lords of the Razor.* His most recent books are two new Hap and Leonard novels, *Devil Red* and *Hyenas;* the novels *Deranged by Choice* and *Edge of Dark Water;* a new collection, *Shadows West* (with John L. Lansdale); and, as editor, two new anthologies, *Crucified Dreams* and *The Urban Fantasy Anthology* (with Peter S. Beagle). He lives with his family in Nacogdoches, Texas.

Here he introduces us to the best bad girl ever, a woman who has the mojo, the black doo-doo, and the silent dog whistle over every man she meets; a woman like a bright red apple with a worm in the center, one who could make a priest go home and cut his throat if he saw her walking down the street. In short, a character that only Lansdale could write.

WRESTLING JESUS

First they took Marvin's sack lunch, then his money, and then they kicked his ass. In fact, he felt the ass whipping, had it been put on a scale of one to ten, was probably about a fourteen. However, Marvin factored in that some of the beating had been inconsistent, as one of his attackers had paused to light a cigarette, and afterwards, two of them had appeared tired and out of breath.

Lying there, tasting blood, he liked to think that, taking in the pause for a smoke and the obvious exhaustion of a couple of his assailants, points could be taken away from their overall performance, and their rating would merely have been nine or ten instead of the full fourteen.

This, however, didn't help his ribs one little bit, and it didn't take away the spots swimming before his eyes just before he passed out from the pain. When he awoke, he was being slapped awake by one of the bullies, who wanted to know if he had any gold teeth. He said he didn't, and the thug insisted on seeing, and Marvin opened his mouth, and the mugger took a look.

Disappointed, the thug threatened to piss in his mouth or fuck him, but the thug and his gang were either too tired from beating him to fuck him, or weren't ready to make water, because they started walking away, splitting up his money in fourths as they walked. They had each made about three dollars and twenty cents, and from his backpack they had taken a pretty good ham sandwich and a little container of Jell-O. There was, however, only one plastic spoon.

Marvin was beginning to feel one with the concrete when a voice said, "You little shits think you're something, don't ya?"

Blinking, Marvin saw that the speaker was an old man, slightly stooped, bowlegged, with white hair and a face that looked as if it had once come apart and been puzzled back together by a drunk in a dark room with cheap glue. His ear—Marvin could see the right one—contained enough hair to knit a small dog sweater. It was the only visible hair the man had that was black. The hair on his head was the color of a fish belly. He was holding up his loose pants with one hand. His skin was dark as a walnut and his mouth was a bit overfull with dentures. One of his pants pockets was swollen with something. Marvin thought it might be his balls: a rupture.

The gang stopped in their tracks and turned. They were nasty-looking fellows with broad shoulders and muscles. One of them had a large belly, but it was hard, and Marvin knew for a fact they all of them had hard fists and harder shoes. The old man was about to wake up dead.

The one who had asked Marvin if he had any gold teeth, the hard belly, looked at the old man and said, as he put down Marvin's stolen backpack, "You talking to us, you old geezer?"

"You're the only shit I see," said the old man. "You think you're a real bad man, don't you? Anyone can beat up some pussy like this kid. My crippled grandma could, and she's been dead some twenty years. Kid's maybe sixteen; what are you fucks—twenty? You're a bunch of cunts without any hair on your slit."

Marvin tried to crawl backwards until he was out of sight, not wanting to revive their interest in him, and thinking he might get away while they were killing the old man. But he was too weak to crawl. Hard Belly started strutting toward the old man, grinning, preening.

When he was about six feet away, the old man said, "You gonna fight me by yourself, Little Shit? You don't need your gang to maybe hold me?"

"I'm gonna kick out any real teeth you got, you old spic," said Hard Belly.

"Ain't got no real ones, so have at it."

The boy stepped in and kicked at the old man, who slapped his leg aside with his left hand, never taking the right away from holding up his pants, and hit him with a hard left jab to the mouth that knocked him down and made his lips bleed. When Hard Belly tried to get up, the old man made with a sharp kick to the windpipe. Hard Belly dropped, gagging, clutching at his throat.

"How's about you girls? You up for it, you little cunts?"

The little cunts shook their heads.

"That's good," said the old man, and pulled a chain out of his pocket.

That had been the bulk in his pocket, not a ruptured nut. He was still holding his pants with his other hand.

"I got me an equalizer here. I'll wrap this motherfucker around your head like an anchor chain. Come over here and get Mr. Butt Hole and take him away from me, and fast."

The three boys pulled Mr. Butt Hole, aka Hard Belly, to his feet, and when they did, the old man pushed his face close to Hard Belly's and said, "Don't come back around here. I don't want to see you no more."

"You'll be sorry, spic," said Hard Belly, bubbling blood over his lips and down his chin.

The old man dropped the chain on the ground and popped Hard Belly with a left jab again, breaking Hard Belly's nose, spewing blood all over his face.

"What the fuck you got in your ears?" the old man said. "Mud? Huh? You got mud? You hear me talkin' to you? Adios, asshole."

The three boys, and Hard Belly, who was wobbling, made their way down the street and were gone.

The Old Man looked down at Marvin, who was still lying on the ground.

"I've had worse beatings than that from my old mother, and she was missing an arm. Get the hell up."

Marvin managed to get his feet under him, thinking it a feat equal with building one of the Great Pyramids—alone.

"What you come around here for?" the old man said. "Ain't nobody around here but shits. You look like a kid might come from someplace better."

Marvin shook his head. "No," he said. "I'm from around here."

"Since when?"

"Since a week ago."

"Yeah? You moved here on purpose, or you just lose your map?"

"On purpose."

"Well, kid, you maybe better think about moving away."

There was nothing Marvin wanted to do more than move. But his mother said no dice. They didn't have the money. Not since his father died. That had nipped them in the bud, and quite severely, that dying business. Marvin's dad had been doing all right at the factory, but then he died and since then their lives had gone downhill faster than a little red wagon stuffed full of bricks. He and his mom had to be where they were, and there was nothing else to be said about it. A downgrade for them would be a cardboard box with a view. An upgrade would be lifts in their shoes.

"I can't move. Mama doesn't have the money for it. She does laundry."

"Yeah, well, you better learn to stand up for yourself, then," said the old man. "You don't, you might just wake up with your pants down and your asshole big as a dinner plate."

"They'd really do that?"

"Wouldn't put it past them," said the old man. "You better learn to fight back."

"Can you teach me?"

"Teach you what?"

"To fight."

"I can't do it. I have to hold my pants up. Get yourself a stick."

"You could teach me, though."

"I don't want to, kid. I got a full-time job just trying to stay breathing. I'm nearly eighty fucking years old. I ought to been feeding the worms five years ago. Listen up. You stay away from here, and if you can't . . . well, good luck, boy."

Holding his pants with one hand, the old man shuffled away. Marvin watched him go for a moment, and then fled. It was his plan to make it through the week, when school would turn out for the summer, and then he'd just stay in the apartment and never leave until school started up in the fall. By then, maybe he could formulate a new plan.

He hoped that in that time the boys would have lost interest in punching him, or perhaps been killed in some dreadful manner, or moved off themselves. Started a career, though he had a pretty good idea they had already started one—professional thugs.

He told his mother he fell down. She believed him. She was too preoccupied with trying to keep food on the table to think otherwise, and he didn't want her to know anyway. Didn't want her to know he couldn't take care of himself, and that he was a walking punching bag. Thing was, she wasn't too alert to his problems. She had the job, and now she had a boyfriend, a housepainter. The painter was a tall, gangly guy that came over and watched TV and drank beer, then went to bed with his mother. Sometimes, when he was sleeping on the couch, he could hear them back there. He didn't remember ever hearing that kind of thing when his dad was alive, and he didn't know what to think about it. When it got really loud, he'd wrap his pillow around his ears and try to sleep.

During the summer he saw some ads online about how you could build your body, and he sent off for a DVD. He started doing push-ups and sit-ups and a number of other exercises. He didn't have money for the weights the DVD suggested. The DVD cost him what little money he had saved, mostly a nickel here, a quarter there. Change his mother gave him. But he figured if his savings kept him from an ass whipping, it was worth every penny.

Marvin was consistent in his workouts. He gave them everything he had, and pretty soon his mother mentioned that he seemed to be looking stronger. Marvin thought so too. In fact, he actually had muscles. His arms were knotted and his stomach was pretty flat, and his thighs and calves had grown. He could throw a jab and a cross now. He found a guide on-line for how to do it. He was planning on working on the uppercut next, maybe the hook, but right now he had the jab and the cross down.

"All right," he said to the mirror. "Let them come. I'm ready."

After the first day of school in the fall, Marvin went home the same way he had that fateful day he had taken a beating. He didn't know exactly how he felt about what he was doing. He hoped he would never see them again on one hand, and on the other, he felt strong now, felt he could handle himself.

Marvin stuck his hand in his pocket and felt for the money he had there. Not much. A dollar or so in change. More money saved up from what his mother gave him. And he had his pack on his back. They might want that. He had to remember to come out of it, put it aside if he had to fight. No hindrances.

When he was where it happened before, there was no one. He went home feeling a bit disappointed. He would have enjoyed banging their heads together.

On his third day after school, he got his chance.

There were only two of them this time: Hard Belly, and one of the weasels that had been with him before. When they spotted him, Hard Belly smiled and moved toward Marvin quickly, the weasel trailing behind as if looking for scraps.

"Well, now," Hard Belly said as he got closer. "You remember me?"

"Yes," Marvin said.

"You ain't too smart, are you, kid? Thought you had done moved off. Thought I'd never get a chance to hit you again. That old man, I want you to know, he caught me by surprise. I could have kicked his ass from Monday to next Sunday."

"You can't whip me, let alone him."

"Oh, so, during the summer, you grew a pair of balls."

"Big pair."

"Big pair, huh. I bet you I can take that pack away from you and make you kiss my shoes. I can make you kiss my ass."

"I'm going to whip your ass," Marvin said.

The bully's expression changed, and Marvin didn't remember much after that.

He didn't come awake until Hard Belly was bent over, saying, "Now kiss it. And pucker good. A little tongue would be nice. You don't, Pogo here, he's gonna take out his knife and cut your dick off. You hear?"

Marvin looked at Hard Belly. Hard Belly dropped his pants and bent over with his hands on his knees, his asshole winking at Marvin. The weasel was riffling through Marvin's backpack, strewing things left and right.

"Lick or get cut," Hard Belly said.

Marvin coughed out some blood and started to try and crawl away.

"Lick it," Hard Belly said. "Lick it till I feel good. Come on, boy. Taste some shit."

A foot flew out and went between Hard Belly's legs, caught his nuts with a sound like a beaver's tail slapping on water. Hard Belly screamed, went forward on his head, as if he were trying to do a headstand.

"Don't never do it, kid," a voice said. "It's better to get your throat cut."

It was the old man. He was standing close by. He wasn't holding his pants this time. He had on a belt.

Pogo came at the old man and swung a wild right at him. The old man didn't seem to move much but somehow he went under the punch, and when he came up, the uppercut that Marvin had not practiced was on exhibition. It hit Pogo under the chin and there was a snapping sound, and

Pogo, the weasel, seemed to lose his head for a moment. It stretched his neck like it was made of rubber. Spittle flew out of Pogo's mouth and Pogo collapsed on the cement in a wad.

The old man wobbled over to Hard Belly, who was on his hands and knees, trying to get up, his pants around his ankles. The old man kicked him between the legs a couple of times. The kicks weren't pretty, but they were solid. Hard Belly spewed a turd and fell on his face.

"You need to wipe up," the old man said. But Hard Belly wasn't listening. He was lying on the cement, making a sound like a truck trying to start.

The old man turned and looked at Marvin.

"I thought I was ready," Marvin said.

"You ain't even close, kid. If you can walk, come with me."

Marvin could walk, barely.

"You got some confidence somewhere," the old man said. "I seen that right off. But you didn't have no reason for it."

"I did some training."

"Yeah, well, swimming on dry land ain't the same as getting into it. There's things you can do that's just in the air, or with a partner that can make a real difference, but you don't get no feel for nothing. I hadn't come along, you'd have been licking some ass crack and calling it a snow cone. Let me tell you, son. Don't never do that. Not unless it's a lady's ass and you've been invited. Someone wants to make you do something like that, you die first. You do that kind of thing once, you'll have the taste of shit in your mouth for the rest of your life."

"I guess it's better than being dead," Marvin said.

"Naw, it ain't neither. Let me tell you. Once I had me a little dog. He wasn't no bigger than a minute, but he had heart big as all the outdoors. Me and him took walks. One day we was walking along—not far from here, actually—and there was this German shepherd out nosing in some garbage cans. Rough-looking old dog, and it took in after my little dog. Mike was his name. And it was a hell of a fight. Mike wouldn't give. He fought to the death."

"He got killed?"

"Naw. The shepherd got killed."

"Mike killed the shepherd?"

"Naw. 'Course not. I'm jerking you. I hit the shepherd with a board I picked up. But the lesson here is you got to do your best, and sometimes you got to hope there's someone around on your side with a board."

"You saying I'm Mike and you're the guy with the board?"

"I'm saying you can't fight for shit. That's what I'm saying."

"What happened to Mike?"

"Got hit by a truck he was chasing. He was tough and willing, but he didn't have no sense. Kind of like you. Except you ain't tough. And another drawback you got is you ain't a dog. Another thing, that's twice I saved you, so you owe me something."

"What's that?"

"Well, you want to learn to fight, right?"

Marvin nodded.

"And I need a workout partner."

The old man's place wasn't far from the fight scene. It was a big, two-story concrete building. The windows were boarded over. When they got to the front door, the old man pulled out a series of keys and went to work on several locks.

While he did that, he said, "You keep a lookout. I got to really be careful when I do this, 'cause there's always some asshole wanting to break in. I've had to hurt some jackasses more than once. Why I keep that two-by-four there in the can."

Marvin looked. There was indeed a two-by-four stuffed down inside a big trash can. The two-by-four was all that was in it.

The old man unlocked the door and they went inside. The old man flicked some lights and everything went bright. He then went to work on the locks, clicked them into place. They went along a narrow hall into a wide space—a very wide space.

What was there was a bed and a toilet out in the open on the far wall, and on the other wall was a long plank table and some chairs. There was a hot plate on the table, and above and behind it were some shelves stuffed with canned goods. There was an old refrigerator, one of those bullet-shaped things. It hummed loudly, like a child with a head injury. Next to the table was a sink, and not far from that was a shower, with a once-green curtain pulled around a metal scaffold. There was a TV under some posters on the wall and a few thick chairs with the stuffing leaking out.

There was a boxing ring in the middle of the room. In the ring was a thick mat, taped all over with duct tape. The sun-faded posters were of men in tights, crouched in boxing or wrestling positions. One of them said, "Danny Bacca, X-Man."

Marvin studied the poster. It was a little wrinkled at the corners, badly framed, and the glass was specked with dust.

"That's me," the old man said.

Marvin turned and looked at the old man, looked back at the poster.

"It's me before wrinkles and bad knees."

"You were a professional wrestler?" Marvin said.

"Naw, I was selling shoes. You're slow on the upbeat, kid. Good thing I was out taking my walk again or flies would be having you for lunch."

"Why were you called X-Man?"

"'Cause you got in the ring with me, they could cross you off the list. Put an X through your name. Shit, I think that was it. It's been so long ago, I ain't sure no more. What's your name, by the way?"

"Marvin."

"All right, Marvin, let's you and me go over to the ring."

The old man dodged through the ropes easily. Marvin found the ropes were pulled taut, and he had more trouble sliding between them than he thought. Once in the ring, the old man said, "Here's the thing. What I'm gonna do is I'm gonna give you a first lesson, and you're gonna listen to me."

"Okay."

"What I want—and I ain't fucking with you here—is I want you to come at me hard as you can. Try and hit me, take me down, bite my ear off. Whatever."

"I can't hurt you."

"I know that."

"I'm not saying I'm not willing," Marvin said. "I'm saying I know I can't. You've beat a guy twice I've had trouble with, and his friends, and I couldn't do nothing, so I know I can't hurt you."

"You got a point, kid. But I'm wantin' you to try. It's a lesson."

"You'll teach me how to defend myself?"

"Sure."

Marvin charged, ducking low, planning to try and take the old man's feet. The old man squatted, almost sitting on his ass, and threw a quick uppercut.

Marvin dreamed he was flying. Then falling. The lights in the place were spotted suddenly. Then the spots went away and there was only brightness. Marvin rolled over on the mat and tried to get up. His eye hurt something awful.

"You hit me," he said when he made a sitting position.

The old man was in a corner of the ring, leaning on the ropes.

"Don't listen to shit like someone saying 'Come and get me.' That's foolish. That's leading you into something you might not like. Play your game."

"You told me to."

"That's right, kid, I did. That's your first lesson. Think for yourself, and don't listen to some fool giving you advice, and like I said, play your own game."

"I don't have a game," Marvin said.

"We both know that, kid. But we can fix it."

Marvin gingerly touched his eye. "So, you're going to teach me?"

"Yeah, but the second lesson is this. Now, you got to listen to every goddamn word I say."

"But you said . . ."

"I know what I said, but part of lesson two is this: Life is full of all kinds of contradictions."

It was easy to get loose to go to practice, but it wasn't easy getting there. Marvin still had the bullies to worry about. He got up early and went, telling his mother he was exercising at the school track.

The old man's home turned out to be what was left of an old TB hospital, which was why the old man bought it cheap, sometime at the far end of the Jurassic, Marvin figured.

The old man taught him how to move, how to punch, how to wrestle, how to throw. When Marvin threw the X-Man, the old guy would land lightly and get up quickly and complain about how it was done. When the workout was done, Marvin showered in the big room behind the faded curtain and went home the long way, watching for bullies.

After a while, he began to feel safe, having figured out that whatever time schedule the delinquents kept, it wasn't early morning, and it didn't seem to be early evening.

When summer ended and school started up, Marvin went before and after school to train, told his mother he was studying boxing with some kids at the Y. She was all right with that. She had work and the housepainter on her mind. The guy would be sitting there when Marvin came home evenings. Sitting there looking at the TV, not even nodding when Marvin came in, sometimes sitting in the padded TV chair with Marvin's mother on his knee, his arm around her waist, her giggling like a schoolgirl. It was enough to gag a maggot.

It got so home was not a place Marvin wanted to be. He liked the old man's place. He liked the training. He threw lefts and rights, hooks and uppercuts, into a bag the old man hung up. He sparred with the old man, who, once he got tired—and considering his age, it seemed a long time—would just knock him down and go lean on the ropes and breathe heavily for a while.

One day, after they had finished, sitting in chairs near the ring, Marvin said, "So, how am I helping you train?"

"You're a warm body, for one thing. And I got this fight coming up."

"A fight?"

"What are you, an echo? Yeah. I got a fight coming up. Every five years me and Jesus the Bomb go at it. On Christmas Eve."

Marvin just looked at him. The old man looked back, said, "Think I'm too old? How old are you?"

"Seventeen."

"Can I whip your ass, kid?"

"Everyone can whip my ass."

"All right, that's a point you got there," the old man said.

"Why every five years?" Marvin asked. "Why this Jesus guy?"

"Maybe I'll tell you later," the old man said.

Things got bad at home.

Marvin hated the painter and the painter hated him. His mother loved the painter and stood by him. Everything Marvin tried to do was tainted by the painter. He couldn't take the trash out fast enough. He wasn't doing good enough in school for the painter, like the painter had ever graduated so much as kindergarten. Nothing satisfied the painter, and when Marvin complained to his mother, it was the painter she stood behind.

The painter was nothing like his dad, nothing, and he hated him. One day he told his mother he'd had enough. It was him or the painter.

She chose the painter.

"Well, I hope the crooked painting son of a bitch makes you happy," he said.

"Where did you learn such language?" she asked.

He had learned a lot of it from the old man, but he said, "The painter."

"Did not," his mother said.

"Did too."

Marvin put his stuff in a suitcase that belonged to the painter and left. He waited for his mother to come chasing after him, but she didn't. She called out as he went up the street, "You're old enough. You'll be all right."

He found himself at the old man's place.

Inside the doorway, suitcase in hand, the old man looked at him, nodded at the suitcase, said, "What you doing with that shit?"

"I got thrown out," Marvin said. Not quite the truth, but he felt it was close enough.

"You mean to stay here? That what you're after?"

"Just till I get on my feet."

"On your feet?" the X-Man said. "You ain't got no job. You ain't got dick. You're like a fucking vagabond."

"Yeah," Marvin said. "Well, all right."

Marvin turned around, thinking maybe he could go home and kiss some ass, maybe tell the painter he was a good guy or something. He got to the door and the old man said, "Where the fuck you going?"

"Leaving. You wanted me to, didn't you?"

"Did I say that? Did I say anything like that? I said you were a vagabond. I didn't say something about leaving. Here. Give me the goddamn suitcase."

Before Marvin could do anything, X-Man took it and started down the hall toward the great room. Marvin watched him go: a wiry, balding, white-haired old man with a slight bowlegged limp to his walk.

One night, watching wrestling on TV, the old man, having sucked down a six-pack, said, "This is shit. Bunch a fucking tough acrobats. This ain't wrestling. It ain't boxing, and it sure ain't fighting. It's like a movie show or something. When we wrestled in fairs, we really wrestled. These big-ass fuckers wouldn't know a wrist lock from a dick jerk. Look at that shit. Guy waits for the fucker to climb on the ropes and jump on him. And what kind of hit is that? That was a real hit, motherfucker would be dead, hitting him in the throat like that. He's slapping the guy's chest high up, that's all. Cocksuckers."

"When you wrestled, where did you do it?" Marvin asked.

The old man clicked off the TV. "I can't take no more of that shit. . . . Where did I wrestle? I rode the rails during the Great Depression. I was ten years old on them rails, and I'd go from town to town and watch guys wrestle at fairs, and I began to pick it up. When I was fifteen, I said I was eighteen, and they believed me, ugly as I was. I mean, who wants to think a kid can be so goddamn ugly, you know. So by the end of the Great Depression I'm wrestling all over the place. Let me see, it's 1992, so I been doing it awhile. Come the war, they wouldn't let me go because of a rupture. I used to wrap that sucker up with a bunch of sheet strips and go and wrestle. I could have fought Japs bundled up like that if they'd let me. Did have to stop now and then when my nuts stuck out of the rip in my balls. I'd cross my legs, suck it up and push them back in, cinch up those strips of sheet, and keep on keeping on. I could have done that in the war, but they was all prissy about it. Said it'd be a problem. So I didn't kill no Japs. I could have, though. Germans. Hungarians. Martians. I could kill anybody they put me in front of. 'Course, glad I didn't in one way. Ain't good to kill a man. But them son of a bitches were asking for it. Well, I don't know about the Hungarians or the Martians, but the rest of them bastards were.

"I learned fighting by hard knocks. Now and then I met some guys knew a thing or two, and I picked it up. Some of them Jap tricks and the like. I had folks down in Mexico. So when I was in my twenties, I went there and became a wrestler for money."

"Wasn't that fake?"

The old man gave Marvin a look that made the water inside Marvin's body boil.

"There was them that put on shows, but then there was us. Me and Jesus, and ones like us. We did the real thing. We was hitting and kicking and locking and throwing. Look at this."

The old man jerked up a sleeve on his sweatshirt. There was a mark there like a tire track. "See that. Jesus bit me. I had him in a clench and he bit me. Motherfucker. 'Course, that's what I'd have done. Anyway, he got loose on account of it. He had this technique—the Bomb, he called it, how he got his nickname. He'd grab you in a bear hug, front or back, lift you up and fall back and drive your head into the mat. You got that done to you once or twice, you felt like your ears were wiggling around your asshole. It was something. Me, I had me the step-over-toe-hold. That was my move, and still is."

"Did you use it on Jesus?"

"Nope. He got the Bomb on me. After the Bomb I thought I was in Africa fucking a gorilla. I didn't know my dick from a candlewick."

"But you're still wrestling him?"

"Haven't beat him yet. I've tried every hold there is, every move, every kind of psychology I know, and nothing. It's the woman. Felina Valdez. She's got the mojo on me, the juju, the black doo-doo, and the silent dog whistle. Whatever there is that makes you stupid, she's got it on me."

Marvin didn't follow any of that, but he didn't say anything. He drank his glass of tea while X-Man drank another beer. He knew he would come back to the subject eventually. That's how he worked.

"Let me tell you about Felina. She was a black-eyed maiden, had smooth, dark skin. A priest saw her walking down the street, he'd go home and cut his throat. First time I seen her, that stack of dynamite was in a blue dress so tight, you could count the hairs on her thingamajig.

"She was there in the crowd to watch the wrestling. She's in the front row with her legs crossed, and her dress is slithering up to her knee like a snake creeping, and I'm getting a pretty good look, you see. Not seeing the vine-covered canyon, but I'm in the neighborhood. And looking at that broad, I'm almost killed by this wrestler named Joey the Yank. Guy from Maine who takes my legs out from under me and butts me and gets me in an arm bar. I barely manage to work out of it, get him and throw him and latch on my step-over-toe-hold. I put that on you, you pass through

time, baby. Past and future, and finally you're looking at your own goddamn grave. He tapped out.

"Next thing I know, this blue-dress doll is sliding up next to me, taking
my arm, and, well, kid, from that point on I was a doomed man. She
could do more tricks with a dick than a magician could with a deck of
cards. I thought she was going to kill me, but I thought too it was one hell
of a good way to go. Hear what I'm saying?"

"Yes, sir," Marvin said.

"This is all kind of nasty talk for a kid, ain't it?"

"No, sir," Marvin said.

"Fuck it. You're damn near eighteen. By now you got to know about
pussy."

"I know what it is," Marvin said.

"No, kid. You talk like you know where it is, not what it is. Me, I was
lost in that stuff. I might as well have let her put my nuts in a vise and
crank it. She started going to all my fights. And I noticed something
pretty quick. I gave a great performance, won by a big margin, the loving
was great. It was a mediocre fight, so was the bedding. I had it figured.
She wasn't so much in love with me as she was a good fight and my finishing move, the step-over-toe-hold. She had me teach it to her. I let her
put it on me one time, and kid, I tell you, way she latched it, I suddenly
had some mercy for all them I'd used it on. I actually had to work my way
out of it, like I was in a match, 'cause she wasn't giving me no quarter.
That was a cheap price to pay, though, all that savage monkey love I was
getting, and then it all come apart.

"Jesus beat me. Put the Bomb on me. When I woke up I was out back of
the carnival, lying on the grass with ants biting me. When I came to myself,
Felina was gone. She went with Jesus. Took my money, left me with nothing
but ant bites on my nuts."

"She sounds shallow."

"As a saucer, kid. But once she slapped that hoodoo on me, I couldn't
cut myself loose. Let me tell you, it was like standing on the railroad tracks
in the dark of night, and you can see a train coming, the light sweeping
the tracks, and you can't step off. All you can do is stand there and wait
for it to hit you. One time when we were together, we're walking in Mexico City, where I had some bouts, and she sees a guy with a wooden cage
full of pigeons, six or seven of them. She has me buy all of them, like we're

gonna take them back to the States. But what she does is she takes them back to our hotel room. We had to sneak them in. She puts the cage on an end table and just looks at the birds. I give them some bread, you know, 'cause they got to eat, and I clean out their cage, and I think: this girl is one crazed bird lover. I go and take a shower, tell her to order up some dinner.

"I take my time in there. Shit and shave, good hot shower. When I come out, there she is, sitting at one of those little push tables room service brings up, and she's eating fried chicken. Didn't wait on me, didn't say boo. She was like that. Everything was about her. But right then I learned something else. I saw that cage of birds, and they were all dead. I asked her what happened to the birds, and she says, 'I got tired of them.'

"I went and looked, and their necks was wrung."

"But why?" Marvin asked.

The old man leaned back and sucked his beer, took his time before he spoke. "I don't know, kid. Right then I should have thrown my shit in a bag and got the hell out of there. But I didn't. It's like I told you about those train tracks. Christ, kid. You should have seen her. There wasn't never nothing like her, and I couldn't let her go. It's like you catch the finest fish in the world, and someone's telling you to throw it back, and all you can think about is that thing fried up and laid out on a bed of rice. Only it ain't really nothing like that. There ain't no describing it. And then, like I said, she went off with Jesus, and every day I get up my heart burns for her. My mind says I'm lucky to be shed of her, but my heart, it don't listen. I don't even blame Jesus for what he done. How could he not want her? She belonged to whoever could pin the other guy to the mat. Me and him, we don't fight nobody else anymore, just each other. Every five years. If I win, I get her back. I know that. He knows that. And Felina knows that. He wins, he keeps her. So far, he keeps her. Its best he does. I ought to let it go, kid, but I can't."

"She really that bad?"

"She's the best bad girl ever. She's a bright red apple with a worm in the center. Since that woman's been with Jesus, he left a wife, had two of his children die, one in a house fire that happened while he was out, and Felina gave birth to two babies that both died within a week. Some kind of thing happens now and then. Cradle death, something like that. On top of that, she's screwed just about everyone short of a couple of eunuchs, but she stays with Jesus, and he keeps her. He keeps her because she has a power, kid. She can hold you to her tight as liver cancer. Ain't no getting away from that bitch. She lets you go, you still want her like you want a drink when you're a drunk."

"The way you mentioned the fire and Jesus's kids, the two babies that died . . . you sounded like—"

"Like I didn't believe the fire was no accident? That the babies didn't die naturally? Yeah, kid. I was thinking about that cage full of pigeons. I was thinking about how she used to cut my hair, and how she had this little box she had with her, kept it in the purse she carried. I seen her wrap some hair into the knot of a couple twisted pipe cleaners. Oh, hell. You already think I'm nuts."

Marvin shook his head. "No. No, I don't."

"All right, then. I think she really did have the hoodoo on me. I read somewhere that people who know spells can get a piece of your hair and they can use that as part of that spell, and it can tie you to them. I read that."

"That doesn't mean it's true," Marvin said.

"I know that, kid. I know how I sound. And when it's midday I think thinking like that is so much dog shit, but it gets night, or it's early morning and the light's just starting to creep in, I believe it. And I guess I always believed it. I think she's got me in a spell. Ain't nothing else would explain why I would want that cheating, conniving, pigeon-killing, house-burning, baby-murdering bitch back. It don't make no sense, does it?"

"No, sir," Marvin said, and then after a moment he added, "She's pretty old now, isn't she?"

"'Course she is. You think time stood still? She ain't the same. But neither am I. Neither is Jesus. But it's me and him, and one of us gets the girl, and so far he always gets her. What I want is to have her back, die quick, and have one of those Greek funerals. That way I get the prize, but I don't have to put up with it."

"What's a Greek funeral?"

"Heroes like Hercules had them. When he died, they put him on a pile of sticks and such and burned up the body, let his smoke rise to the heavens. Beats being buried in the ground or cooked up in some oven, your ashes scraped into a sack. Or having to spend your last days out with that woman, though that's exactly what I'm trying to do."

"Do Jesus and Felina live here in the city?" Marvin asked.

"They don't live nowhere. They got a motor trailer. And they got some retirement money. Like me. Jesus and me worked other jobs as well as wrestled. You couldn't make it just on the wrestling circuit, especially the underground circuit, so we got some of that social security money coming, thank goodness. They drive around to different places. He trains, and he comes back every five years. Each time I see him, it's like there's this look in his eyes that says 'Beat me this time and take this bitch off my hands.' Only he always fights like a bear and I can't beat him."

"You win, sure she'll go with you?"

"It's me or him, and that's all there is to it. Ain't nobody else now. Me or him. It's us she's decided to suck dry and make miserable."

"Can't you let it go?" Marvin asked.

X-Man laughed. It was a dark laugh, like a dying man that suddenly understands an old joke. "Wish I could, kid, 'cause if I could, I would."

They trained for the fight.

X-Man would say: "This is what Jesus the Bomb does. He comes at you, and next thing you know, you're on your ass, 'cause he grabs you like this, or like this. And he can switch from this to this." And so on.

Marvin did what he was told. He tried Jesus' moves. Every time he did, he'd lose. The old man would twist him, throw him, lock him, punch him (lightly), and even when Marvin felt he was getting good at it, X-Man would outsmart him in the end and come out of something Marvin thought an oiled weasel couldn't slither out of. When it was over, it was Marvin panting in the corner, X-Man wiping sweat off his face with a towel.

"That how Jesus does it?" Marvin asked, after trying all of the moves he had been taught.

"Yeah," said the old man, "except he does it better."

This went on for months, getting closer and closer to the day when the X-Man and Jesus the Bomb were to go at it. Got so Marvin was so focused on the training, he forgot all about the bullies.

Until one day Marvin was by himself, coming out of the store two blocks from the old man's place, carrying a sack with milk and vanilla cookies in it, and there's Hard Belly. He spotted Marvin and started across the street, pulling his hands out of his pockets, smiling.

"Well, now," Hard Belly said when he was near Marvin. "I bet you forgot about me, didn't you? Like I wasn't gonna get even. This time you ain't got your fossil to protect you."

Marvin put the sack on the sidewalk. "I'm not asking for trouble."

"That don't mean you ain't gonna get some," Hard Belly said, standing right in front of Marvin. Marvin didn't really plan on anything—he wasn't thinking about it—but when Hard Belly moved closer, his left jab popped out and hit him in the nose. Down went Hard Belly like he had been hit with a baseball bat. Marvin couldn't believe it, couldn't believe how hard his punch was, how good it was. He knew right then and there it was over between him and Hard Belly, because he wasn't scared anymore. He picked up the sack and walked back to the old man's place, left Hard Belly napping.

One night, during the time school was out for the Thanksgiving holiday, Marvin woke up. He was sleeping in the boxing ring, a blanket over him, and he saw there was a light on by the old man's bed. The old man was sitting on the edge of it, bent over, pulling boxes out from beneath. He reached in one and pulled out a magazine, then another. He spread the magazines on the bed and looked at them.

Marvin got up and climbed out of the ring and went over to him. The old man looked up. "Damn, kid. I wake you?"

"Woke up on my own. What you doing?"

"Looking at these old magazines. They're underground fight magazines. Had to order them through the mail. Couldn't buy them off the stands."

Marvin looked at the open magazines on the bed. They had a lot of photographs in them. From the poster on the wall, he recognized photographs of X-Man.

"You were famous," Marvin said.

"In a way, I suppose," X-Man said. "I look at these, I got to hate getting old. I wasn't no peach to look at, but I was strong then, looked better than now. Ain't much of the young me left."

"Is Jesus in them?"

X-Man flipped a page on one of the open magazines, and there was a photograph of a squatty man with a black mop of hair. The man's chest was almost as hairy. He had legs like a tree trunks.

X-Man grinned. "I know what you're thinking: Couple mugs like me and Jesus, what kind of love magnets are we? Maybe Felina ain't the prime beaver I say she is?"

The old man went around to the head of the bed and dragged a small cardboard box out from under it. He sat it on the bed between them, popped the lid, and scrounged around in a pile of yellowed photographs. He pulled one out. It was slightly faded, but it was clear enough. The woman in it looked maybe mid-twenties. It was a full shot, and she was indeed a knockout. Black hair, high cheekbones, full lips, and black as the Pit eyes that jumped out of the photo and landed somewhere in the back of Marvin's head.

There were other photos of her, and he showed Marvin all of them. There were close shots and far shots, and sneaky camera shots that rested on her ass. She was indeed fabulous to look at.

"She ain't that way now, but she's still got it somehow. What I was gonna do, kid, was gather up all these photos and pile them and burn them, then I was gonna send word to Jesus he could forget the match. That Felina was his until the end of time. But I think that every few years or so, and then I don't do it. You know what Jesus told me once? He said she liked to catch flies. Use a drinking glass and trap them, then stick a needle through them, string them on thread. Bunches of them. She'd knot one end, fasten the other to a wall with a thumbtack, watch them try to fly. Swat a fly, that's one thing. But something like that, I don't get it, kid. And knowing that, I ought to not get her. But it don't work that way. . . . Tell you what, you go on to bed. Me, I'm gonna turn off the light and turn in."

Marvin went and crawled under his blanket, adjusted the pillow under his head. When he looked at the old man, he still had the light on and had the cardboard box with the pictures in his lap. He was holding up a photograph, looking at it like it was a hand-engraved invitation to the Second Coming.

As Marvin drifted off, all he could think about were those flies on the thread.

———

Next day the old man didn't wake him for the morning workout, and when Marvin finally opened his eyes it was nearly noon. The old man was nowhere to be seen. He got up and went to the refrigerator to have some milk. There was a note on the door.

DON'T EAT HEAVY. I'M BRINGING THANKSGIVING.

Marvin hadn't wanted to spend Thanksgiving with his mother and the painter, so he hadn't really thought about it at all. Once his mother dropped him out of her mind, he had dropped the holidays out of his. But right then he thought about them, and hoped the painter would choke on a turkey bone.

He poured a glass of milk and sat in a chair by the ring and sipped it.

Not long after, the old man came back with a sack of groceries. Marvin got up and went over to him. "I'm sorry. I missed the workout."

"You didn't miss nothing. It's a fucking holiday. Even someone needs as much training as you ought to have a day off."

The old man pulled things out of the sack. Turkey lunch meat, some cheese slices, and a loaf of good bread, the kind you had to cut with a knife. And there was a can of cranberry sauce.

"It ain't exactly a big carving turkey, but it'll be all right," the old man said.

They made sandwiches and sat in the TV chairs with a little table between them. They placed their plates there, the old man put a video in his aging machine, and they watched a movie. An old black-and-white one. Marvin liked color, and he was sure he would hate it. It was called Night and the City. It was about wrestling. Marvin didn't hate it. He loved it. He ate his sandwich. He looked at the old man, chewing without his dentures. Right then he knew he loved him as dearly as if he were his father.

Next day they trained hard. Marvin had gotten so he was more of a challenge for the old man, but he still couldn't beat him.

On the morning of the bout with Jesus, Marvin got up and went out to the store. He had some money X-Man gave him now and then for being a training partner, and he bought a few items and took them home.

One of them was a bottle of liniment, and when he got back he used it to give the old man a rubdown.

When that was done, the old man stretched out on the floor on an old mattress and fell asleep as easily as a kitten. While he slept, Marvin took the rest of the stuff he had bought into the bathroom and made a few arrangements. He brought the bag out and wadded it up and shoved it in the trash.

Then he did what the old man had instructed him to do. He got folding chairs out of the closet, twenty-five of them, and set them up near the ring. He put one of them in front of the others, close to the ring.

At four-fifteen, he gently spoke to the old man, called him awake.

The old man got up and showered and put on red tights and a T-shirt with a photograph of his younger self on it. The words under the photograph read: X-MAN.

It was Christmas Eve.

About seven that evening they began to arrive. On sticks, in wheelchairs, and on walkers, supported by each other and, in a couple of cases, walking unassisted. They came to the place in dribbles, and Marvin helped them locate a chair. The old man had stored away some cheap wine and beer, and had even gone all out for a few boxes of crackers and a suspicious-looking cheese ball. These he arranged on a long foldout table to the left of the chairs. The old people, mostly men, descended on it like vultures alighting on fresh roadkill. Marvin had to help some of them who were so old and decrepit they couldn't hold a paper plate and walk at the same time.

Marvin didn't see anyone that he thought looked like Jesus and Felina. If one of the four women was Felina, she was certainly way past any sex appeal, and if any one of them was Jesus, X-Man had it in the bag. But, of course, none of them were either.

About eight o'clock Marvin answered a hard knocking on the door. When he opened it, there was Jesus. He was wearing a dark robe with red trim. It was open in front, and Marvin could see he had on black tights and no shirt. He was gray-haired where he had hair left on his head, and there was a thick thatch of gray hair on his chest, nestled there like a carefully constructed bird's nest. He had the same simian build as in the photograph. The Bomb looked easily ten years younger than his age; he moved easily and well.

With him was a tall woman and it was easy to recognize her, even from ancient photos. Her hair was still black, though certainly it came out of a bottle now, and she had aged well, looked firm of face and high of bone. Marvin thought maybe she'd had some work. She looked like a movie star in her fifties that still gets work for her beauty. Her eyes were like wells, and Marvin had to be careful not to fall into them. She had on a long black dress with a black coat hanging off her shoulders in a sophisticated way. It had a fur collar that at first glance looked pretty good and at second glance showed signs of decay, like a sleeping animal with mange.

"I'm here to wrestle," Jesus said.

"Yes, sir," Marvin said.

The woman smiled at Marvin, and her teeth were white and magnificent, and looked as real as his own. Nothing was said, but in some way or another he knew he was to take her coat, and he did. He followed after her and Jesus, and, watching Felina walk, Marvin realized he was sexually aroused. She was pretty damn amazing, considering her age, and he was reminded of an old story he had read about a succubus, a female spirit that preyed on men, sexually depleted them, and took their souls.

When Felina sashayed in and the old man saw her, there was a change in his appearance. His face flushed and he stood erect. She owned him.

Marvin put Felina's coat away, and when he hung it in the closet, a smell came off it that was sweet and tantalizing. He thought some of it was perfume, but knew most of it was her.

Jesus and X-Man shook hands and smiled at each other, but X-Man couldn't take his eyes off of Felina. She moved past them both as if unaware of their presence, and without being told took the chair that had been placed in front of the others.

The old man called Marvin over and introduced him to Jesus. "This kid is my protégé, Jesus. He's pretty good. Like me, maybe, when I started out, if I'd had a broke leg."

They both laughed. Marvin even laughed. He had begun to understand this was wrestling humor and that he had in fact been given a great compliment.

"You think you're gonna beat me this year?" Jesus said. "I sometimes don't think you're really trying."

"Oh, I'm trying all right," X-Man said.

Jesus was still smiling, but now the smile look pinned there when he spoke. "You win, you know she'll go with you?"

The old man nodded.

"Why do we keep doing this?" Jesus said.

X-Man shook his head.

"Well," Jesus said. "Good luck. And I mean it. But you're in for a fight."

"I know that," X-Man said.

It was nine o'clock when X-Man and Jesus took out their teeth and climbed into the ring, took some time to stretch. The chairs in the audience were near half empty and those that were seated were spread apart like Dalmatian spots. Marvin stood on the outside of the ropes at the old man's corner.

The old man came and leaned on the ropes. One of the elders in the audience, wearing red pants pulled up nearly to his armpits, dragged his chair next to the side of the ring, scraping it across the floor as he went. He had a cowbell in his free hand. He wheezed himself into the seat, placed the bell on his knee. He produced a large watch from his pants pocket and placed it on his other knee. He looked sleepy.

"We do this five years from now," X-Man said to Marvin, "it'll be in hell somewhere, and the devil will be our timekeeper."

"All right," said the timekeeper. "Geezer rules. Two minutes rounds. Three minutes rests. Goes until it's best two out of three or someone quits. Everybody ready?"

Both parties said they were.

Marvin looked at Felina. She was sitting with her hands in her lap. She appeared confident and smug, like a spider waiting patiently on a fly.

The timekeeper hit the watch with his left thumb and rang the bell with his right hand. X-Man and Jesus came together with a smacking sound, grabbing at each other's knees for a throw, bobbing and weaving. And then X-Man came up from a bob and threw a quick left. To Marvin's amazement, Jesus slipped it over his shoulder and hooked X-Man in the ribs. It was a solid shot, and Marvin could tell X-Man felt it. X-man danced back, and one elderly man in the small crowd booed.

"Go fuck yourself," X-Man yelled out.

X-Man and the Bomb came together again. There was a clenching of hands on shoulders, and Jesus attempted to knee X-Man in the balls. X-man was able to turn enough to take it on the side of the leg, but not in the charley horse point. They whirled around and around like angry lovers at a dance.

Finally X-Man faked, dove for Jesus' knee, and got hold of it, but Jesus twisted on him, brought one leg over X-Man's head, hooked the leg under his neck and rolled, grabbed X-Man's arm, stretched it out, and lifted his pelvis against it. There was a sound like someone snapping a stick over their knee, and X-Man tapped out. That ended the round. It had gone less than forty-five seconds.

X-Man waddled over to his corner, nursing his arm a little. He leaned on the ropes. Marvin brought out the stool.

"Put it back," the old man said. "I don't want them to think I'm hurt."

Marvin put it back, said, "Are you hurt?"

"Yeah, but that cracking you heard was just air bubbles in my arm. I'm fine. Fuck it. Put the stool back."

Marvin put the stool back. X-Man sat down. Across the way, Jesus was seated on his stool, his head hung. He and X-Man looked like two men who wouldn't have minded being shot.

"I know this," X-Man said. "This is my last match. After this, I ain't got no more in me. I can feel what's left of me running out of my feet."

Marvin glanced at Felina. One of the lights overhead was wearing out. It popped and went from light to dark and back to light again. Marvin thought for a moment, there in the shadow, Felina had looked older, and fouler, and her thick hair had resembled a bundle of snakes. But as he looked more closely, it was just the light.

The cowbell clattered. They had gotten some of their juice back. They moved around each other, hands outstretched. They finally clinched their fingers together, both hands. X-Man suddenly jutted his fingers forward in a way that allowed him to clench down on the back of Jesus' fingers, snap him to the floor in pain. It was a simple move, but it put the Bomb's face in front of X-Man's knee. X-man kneed him in the face so hard, blood spewed all over the matting, all over X-Man.

Still clutching Jesus's fingers, X-Man stepped back and squatted, pulled Jesus to his face. X-Man pulled free of the fingers, and as Jesus tried to rise, X-Man kicked him in the face. It was a hard kick. Jesus went unconscious.

The cowbell clattered. The timekeeper put the cowbell down and made his way to the ring. He climbed through and hitch-legged it over to Jesus. It took almost as much time as it would take for a blind man to find a needle in a haystack.

The timekeeper got down on one knee. Jesus groaned and sat up slowly. His face was a bloody mess.

The timekeeper looked him over. "You up for it?" he said.

"Hell, yeah," Jesus said.

"One to one!" yelled the timekeeper, and he made his slow pilgrimage back to his chair.

Jesus got up slowly, went back to his corner, trying to hold his head up high. X-Man was sitting on his stool, breathing heavily. "I hope I didn't break something inside the old cocksucker," he said.

X-Man closed his eyes and sat resting on his stool. Marvin was quiet. He thought the old man was asleep. Three minutes later, the cowbell clattered.

Jesus huffed loudly, creaked bones off the stool, stuttered-stepped to the center of the ring. X-Man came out in a slow shuffle.

They exchanged a few punches, none of which landed particularly well. Surprisingly, both seemed to have gotten a second wind. They tossed one another, and rolled, and jabbed, and gouged, and the bell rang again.

When X-Man was on his stool, he said, "My heart feels like a bird fluttering."

"You ought to quit," Marvin said. "It's not worth a heart attack."

"It ain't fluttering from the fight, but from seeing Felina."

Marvin looked. Felina was looking at X-Man the way a puppy looks at a dog treat.

"Don't fall for it," Marvin said. "She's evil. Goddamn evil."

"So you believe me?"

"I do. You think maybe she has those pipe cleaners with your hair with her?"

"How would I know?"

"In her coat, maybe?"

"Again, how would I know." And then it hit the old man. He knew what Marvin was getting at. "You mean if she did have, and you got them . . ."

"Yeah," Marvin said.

Marvin left X-Man sitting there, made a beeline for the closet. He opened the door and moved his hands around in there, trying to look like he was about natural business. He glanced back at X-Man, who had turned on his stool to look.

The cowbell rang. The two old gentlemen went at it again.

It was furious. Slamming punches to the head and ribs, the breadbasket. Clutching one another, kneeing in the balls. Jesus even bit the lobe off X-Man's ear. Blood was everywhere. It was a fight that would have been amazing if the two men in the ring were in their twenties, in top shape. At their age it was phenomenal.

Marvin was standing in the old man's corner now, trying to catch X-Man's eye, but not in a real obvious way. He didn't want him to lose focus, didn't want Jesus to come under him and lift him up and drive the old man's head into the ground like a lawn dart.

Finally the two clenched. The went around and around like that, breathing heavy as steam engines. Marvin caught X-Man's eye. Marvin lifted up two knotted pipe cleaners, dark hair in the middle of the knot. Marvin untwisted the pipe cleaners and the hair floated out like a puff of dark dandruff, drifted to the floor.

X-Man let out his breath, seemed to relax.

Jesus dove for him. It was like a hawk swooping down on a mouse. Next thing Marvin knew, Jesus had X-Man low on the hips in a two-arm clench, and was lifting him up, bending back at the same time so he could drive X-Man over his head, straight into the mat.

But as X-Man went over, he ducked his head under Jesus' buttocks, grasped the inside of Jesus' legs. Jesus flipped backwards, but X-Man came up on his back, not his head. Instead, his head was poking between Jesus' legs, and his toothless gums were buried in Jesus' tights, clamping down on his balls like a clutched fist. A cry went up from the crowd.

Jesus screamed. It was the kind of scream that went down your back and got hold of your tailbone and pulled at it. X-Man maintained the clamp. Jesus writhed and twisted and kicked and punched. The punches hit X-Man in the top of the head, but still he clung. When Jesus tried to roll out, X-Man rolled with him, his gums still buried deep in Jesus' balls.

Some of the oldsters were standing up from their seats, yelling with excitement. Felina hadn't moved or changed her expression.

Then it happened.

Jesus slapped out both hands on the mat, called, "Time." And it was over.

The elders left. Except Jesus and Felina.

Jesus stayed in the bathroom for a long time. When he came out, he was limping. The front of his tights were plumped out and dark with blood.

X-Man was standing, one hand on the back of a chair, breathing heavy.

Jesus said, "You about took my nuts, X-Man. I took one of your towels, shoved it down my pants to stop the blood. Them's some gums you got, X-man. Gums like that, you don't need teeth."

"All's fair in love and war," X-Man said. "Besides, old as you are, what you using your nuts for?"

"I hear that," Jesus said, and his whole demeanor was different. He was like a bird in a cage with the door left open. He was ready to fly out.

"She's all yours," Jesus said.

We all looked at Felina. She smiled slightly. She took X-Man's hand.

X-man turned and looked at her. He said, "I don't want her," and let go of her hand. "Hell, I done outlived my dick anyhow."

The look on Felina's face was one of amazement.

"You won her," Jesus said. "That's the rule."

"Naw," X-Man said. "Ain't no rule."

"No?" Jesus said, and you could almost see that cage door slam and lock.

"No," said X-Man, looking at Felina. "That hoodoo you done with the pipe cleaners. My boy here undid it."

"What the fuck are you talking about?" Felina said.

They just stared at each other for a long moment.

"Get out," X-Man said. "And Jesus. We ain't doing this no more."

"You don't want her?" Jesus said.

"No. Get out. Take the bitch with you. Get on out."

Out they went. When Felina turned the corner into the hallway, she paused and looked back. It was a look that said: You had me, and you let me go, and you'll have regrets.

X-Man just grinned at her. "Hit the road, you old bitch."

When they were gone, the old man stretched out on his bed, breathing heavily. Marvin pulled a chair nearby and sat. The old man looked at him and laughed.

"That pipe cleaner and hair wasn't in her coat, was it?"

"What do you mean?" Marvin said.

"That look on her face when I mentioned it. She didn't know what I was talking about. Look at me, boy. Tell me true."

Marvin took a moment, said, "I bought the pipe cleaners and some shoe polish. I cut a piece of my hair, made it dark with the shoe polish, twisted it up in the pipe cleaners."

X-Man let out a hoot. "You sneaky son of a bitch."

"I'm sorry," Marvin said.

"I'm not."

"You're not?"

"Nope. I learned something important. I'm a fucking dope. She didn't never have no power over me I didn't give her. Them pipe cleaners and the hair, hell, she forgot about that fast as she did it. Just some way to pass time for her, and I made it something special. It was just me giving myself an excuse to be in love with someone wasn't worth the gunpowder it would take to blow her ass up. She just liked having power over the both of us. Maybe Jesus will figure that out too. Maybe me and him figured a lot of things out today. It's all right, kid. You done good. Hell, it wasn't nothing I didn't know deep down, and now I'm out of excuses, and I'm done with her. It's like someone just let go of my throat and I can breathe again. All these years, and this thing with Felina, it wasn't nothing but me and my own bullshit."

About seven in the morning X-Man woke up Marvin.

"What's the matter?" Marvin asked.

X-Man was standing over him. Giving him a dentureless grin. "Nothing. It's Christmas. Merry Christmas."

"You too," Marvin said.

The old man had a T-shirt. He held it out with both hands. It said X-Man and had his photograph on it, just like the one he was wearing. "I want you to have it. I want you to be X-Man."

"I can't be X-Man. No one can."

"I know that. But I want you to try."

Marvin was sitting up now. He took the shirt.

"Put it on," said X-Man.

Marvin slipped off his shirt and, still sitting on the floor, pulled the X-Man shirt over his head. It fit good. He stood up. "But I didn't get you nothing."

"Yeah you did. You got me free."

Marvin nodded. "How do I look?"

"Like X-Man. You know, if I had had a son, I'd have been damn lucky if he'd been like you. Hell, if he'd *been* you. 'Course, that gets into me fucking your mother, and we don't want to talk about that. Now I'm going back to sleep. Maybe later we'll have something for Christmas dinner."

Later in the day Marvin got up, fixed coffee, made a couple of sandwiches, went to wake X-Man.

He didn't wake up. He was cold. He was gone. There were wrestling magazines lying on the bed with him.

"Damn," Marvin said, and sat down in the chair by the bed. He took the old man's hand to hold. There was something in it. A wadded-up photo of Felina. Marvin took it and tossed it on the floor and held the old man's hand for a long time.

After a while Marvin tore a page out of one of the wrestling magazines, got up, and put it to the hot plate. It blazed. He went over and held it burning in one hand while he used the other to pull out one of the boxes of magazines. He set fire to it and pushed it back under the bed. Flames licked around the edges of the bed. Other boxes beneath the bed caught fire. The bedclothes caught. After a moment the old man caught too. He smelled like pork cooking.

Like Hercules, Marvin thought. He's rising up to the gods.

Marvin, still wearing his X-Man shirt, got his coat out of the closet. The room was filling with smoke and the smell of burning flesh. He put his coat on and strolled around the corner, into the hallway. Just before he went outside, he could feel the heat of the fire warming his back.

Megan Lindholm

Books by Megan Lindholm include the fantasy novels *Wizard of the Pigeons*, *Harpy's Flight*, *The Windsingers*, *The Limbreth Gate*, *The Luck of the Wheels*, *The Reindeer People*, *Wolf's Brother*, and *Cloven Hooves*, the science fiction novel *Alien Earth*, and, with Steven Brust, the collaborative novel *The Gypsy*. Lindholm also writes as *New York Times* bestseller Robin Hobb, one of the most popular writers in fantasy today, having sold over one million copies of her work in paperback. As Robin Hobb, she's perhaps best-known for her epic fantasy Farseer series, including *Assassin's Apprentice*, *Royal Assassin*, and *Assassin's Quest*, as well as the two fantasy series related to it, the Liveship Traders series, consisting of *Ship of Magic*, *Mad Ship*, and *Ship of Destiny*, and the Tawny Man series, made up of *Fool's Errand*, *Golden Fool*, and *Fool's Fate*. She's also the author of the Soldier Son series, composed of *Shaman's Crossing*, *Forest Mage*, and *Renegade's Magic*. Most recently, as Robin Hobb, she's started a new series, the Rain Wilds Chronicles, consisting of *Dragon Keeper*, *Dragon Haven*, *City of Dragons*, and *Blood of Dragons*. As Megan Lindholm, her most recent book is a "collaborative" collection with Robin Hobb, *The Inheritance and Other Stories*.

In the autumnal and beautifully crafted story that follows, she shows us that even the oldest of dogs, white of muzzle and slow of step, may have one last bite left in them.

NEIGHBORS

Linda Mason was loose again.

It was three in the morning, and sleep had fled. Sarah had wandered to the kitchen in her robe, put on the kettle, and rummaged the cupboards until she found a box of Celestial Seasonings Tension Tamer tea bags. She had set out a teacup on a saucer and put the tea bag in her "tea for one" teapot when she heard someone outside in the dark, shouting her name. "Sarah! Sarah Wilkins! You'd better hurry! It's time to go!"

Her heart jumped high in her chest and hung there, pounding. Sarah didn't recognize the shrill voice, but the triumphantly defiant tone was alarming. She didn't want to look out the window. For a moment, she was eight years old again. Don't look under the bed, don't open the closet at night. As long as you don't look, there might be nothing there. Schrödinger's boogeyman. She reminded herself that she was much closer to sixty-eight than eight and drew back the curtain.

Low billows of fog cloaked the street, a precursor to fall in the Pacific Northwest. Her eyes adjusted and she saw crazy old Linda standing in the street outside the iron fence that surrounded Sarah's backyard. She wore pink sweats and flappy bedroom slippers. She had an aluminum baseball bat in her hands and a Hello Kitty backpack on her shoulders. The latter two items, Sarah was fairly certain, actually belonged to Linda's granddaughter. Linda's son and his wife lived with the old woman. Sarah pitied the daughter-in-law, shoved into the role of caretaker for Robbie's oddball mother. Alzheimer's was what most people said about Linda, but "just plain nuts" seemed as apt.

Sarah had known Linda for twenty-two years. They had carpooled their sons to YMCA soccer games. They'd talked over coffee, exchanged homemade jam and too many zucchini, fed each other's pets during vacation getaways, greeted each other in Safeway, and gossiped about the other neighbors. Not best friends, but neighborhood mom friends, in a fifties sort of way. Linda was one of the few older residents still in the neighborhood. The other parents she had known were long gone, had moved into condos or migrated as snowbirds or been packed off by their kids to senior homes. The houses would empty, and the next flock of young families would move in. Other than Linda, of her old friends, only Maureen and her husband, Hugh, still lived on the other end of the block, but they spent most days in Seattle for Hugh's treatments.

"Sarah! You'd better hurry!" Linda shouted again. Two houses down, a bedroom light came on. The kettle began to whistle. Sarah snatched it off the burner, seized her coat off the hook, and opened the back door. The darn porch light didn't work; the bulb had burned out last week, but it was too much trouble to get a step stool and a lightbulb and fix it. She edged down the steps carefully and headed to the fence, hoping that Sarge hadn't done his business where she would step in it.

"Linda, are you all right? What's going on?" She tried to speak to her as her old friend, but the truth was, Linda scared her now. Sometimes she was Linda, but abruptly she might say something wild and strange or mean. She did even stranger things. A few days ago, in the early morning, she had escaped into her front yard, picked all the ripe apples off her neighbor's tree, and thrown them into the street. "Better than letting them fall and rot like last year!" she shouted when they caught her at it. "You'll just waste them. Feed the future, I say! Give them to the ones who appreciate them!" When Robbie's wife had seized her by the arm and tried to drag her back into their house, Linda had slapped her. Linda's little granddaughter and her playmate had seen the whole thing. The child had started crying, but Sarah hadn't know if it was from distress, fear, or simple humiliation, for half the neighborhood had turned out for the drama, including the neighbor who owned the apple tree. That woman was furious and telling anyone who would listen that it was time to "put that crazy old woman in a home." She'd lived in the neighborhood a couple of years but Sarah didn't even know her name.

"I am in my home!" Linda had shrieked back at her. "Why are you living in Marilyn's home? What gives you more right to the apples off her tree than me? I helped her plant the damn thing!"

"Don't you think we'd put her in a home if we could afford one? Do you think I like living like this?" Robbie's wife had shouted at the neighbor.

Then she had burst into tears and finally managed to tow Linda back inside.

And now Linda was out in the foggy night, staring at Sarah with round wild eyes. The wind was blowing through her white hair, and leaves rustled past her on the pavement. She wore a pink running suit and her bedroom slippers. She had something on her head, something fastened to a wool cap. She advanced on the fence and tapped the baseball bat on top of it, making it ring.

"Don't dent my fence!" Sarah cried, and then, "Stay right there, Linda. Stay right there, I'm going to get help."

"*You* need help, not me!" Linda shouted. She laughed wildly, and quoted, "'Little child, come out to play, the moon doth shine as bright as day!' Except it doesn't! So that's what I take with me. Moonlight!"

"Linda, it's cold out here. Come inside and tell me there." The phone. She should be calling 911 right now. Alex had told her to get a cell phone, but she just couldn't budget one more payment a month. She couldn't even afford to replace her old cordless phone with the faulty ringer. "We'll have a cup of tea and talk. Just like old times when the kids were small." She remembered it clearly, suddenly. She and Maureen and Linda sitting up together, waiting for the kids to come home from a football game. Talking and laughing. Then the kids grew up and they'd gone separate ways. They hadn't had coffee together in years.

"No, Sarah. You come with me! Magic is better than crazy. And time is the only difference between magic and crazy. Stay in there, you're crazy. Come with me, you're magic. Watch!"

She did something, her hand fumbling at her breast. Then she lit up. "Solar power!" she shouted. "That's my ticket to the future!" By the many tiny LEDs, Sarah recognized what Linda was wearing. She'd draped herself in strings of Christmas lights. The little solar panels that had charged them were fastened to her hat.

"Linda, come inside and show me. I'm freezing out here!" They were shouting. Why was the neighborhood staying dark? Someone should be getting annoyed by their loud conversation; someone's dog should be barking.

"Time and tide wait for no man, Sarah! I'm off to seek my fortune. Last chance! Will you come with me?"

———

Inside the house, Sarah had to look up Linda's number in the phone book, and when she called it, no one answered. After ten rings it went to recording. She hung up, took the phone to the window and dialed again. No Linda out there now. The windows in her house were dark. What to do now? Go bang on the door? Maybe Robbie had already come outside and found his mom and taken her in. Call the police? She went back into the yard, carrying the receiver in one hand. "Linda?" she called into the foggy darkness. "Linda, where are you?"

No one answered. The fog had thickened and the neighborhood was dark now. Even the streetlight on the corner, the hateful one that shone into her bedroom window, had chosen this moment to be dark. She dialed Linda's number again, listened to it ring.

Back in the house, Sarah phoned her own son. She heard Alex's sleepy "What?" on the seventh ring. She poured out her story. He wasn't impressed. "Oh, Mom. It's not our business. Go back to bed. I bet she went right back home and she's probably asleep right now. Like I wish I was."

"But what if she's wandered off into the night? You know she's not in her right mind."

"She's not the only one," Alex muttered, and then said, "Look, Mom. It's four in the morning. Go back to bed. I'll drop by on my way to work, and we'll knock on their door together. I'm sure she's okay. Go back to bed."

So she did. To toss and turn and worry.

She woke up at seven to his key in the lock. Good heavens! She'd made him detour from his Seattle commute to come by, and she wasn't even up and ready to go knock on Linda's door. "Be right down!" she shouted down the stairs, and began pulling on clothes. It took her longer than it should have, especially tying her shoes. "Floor just keeps getting farther away every day," she muttered. It was her old joke with Russ. But Russ wasn't around any longer to agree with her. Sarge was sleeping across her bedroom door. She nudged the beagle and he trailed after her.

She opened the kitchen door to a wave of heat. "What are you doing?" she demanded. Alex had the back door open and was fanning it back and forth. "What's that smell?"

He glared at her. "The stove was on when I came in! You're damn lucky you didn't burn the house down. Why didn't your smoke detector go off?"

"Batteries must be dead," she lied. She had gotten tired of them going off for every bagel the old toaster scorched and had loosened the battery in the kitchen unit. "I must have left the burner on last night when Linda was outside. So it wasn't on all night, only three or four hours." The stove top still simmered with heat and the white ceramic around the abused burner was a creamy brown now. She started to touch it, and then drew her hand back. "A little scouring powder should clean that up. No harm done, thank goodness."

"No harm done? Only three or four hours? Shit, Mom, do you not understand how lucky you were?" To her dismay, he unfolded her kitchen step stool and climbed up to the smoke detector. He tugged the cover open and the battery fell to the floor.

"Well! There's the problem," she observed. "It must have come loose in there."

He eyed her. "Must have," he said in a tight voice. Before she could stoop down, he hopped off the stool, scooped it up, and snapped it back into place. He closed the cover.

"Want some coffee?" she asked as she turned on the pot. She'd preset the coffeepot just as she had for the last twenty years so she wouldn't have to fill it up every morning. Just push the button, and then sit at the table and read the paper in her pajamas until the first cup was ready when Russ would come down.

Or not, as was now the case.

"No. Thanks. I need to get on my way. Mom, you've got to be more careful."

"I *am* careful. It wouldn't have happened if the night hadn't been so weird."

"And you wouldn't have forgotten your card in the ATM last week, except that the fire truck went by, so you didn't hear the machine beeping at you as you walked away. But what about locking your keys in the car? And leaving the sprinkler running all night?"

"That was months ago!"

"That's my point! This 'forgetfulness' started months ago! It's only getting worse. And more expensive. We had that water bill. And the locksmith. Luckily, the ATM sucked your card back in and the bank called you. You didn't even realize it was gone! And now we're going to have a little spike in the power bill this month. You need to go to the doctor and get checked out. Maybe there's a pill for it."

"I'll handle it," she said. Now her voice was getting tight. She hated being lectured like this. "You'd better get on the road before the traffic builds up. You want some coffee in your commuter mug?"

He stared at her for a time, wanting to continue the argument, to reach some sort of imaginary resolution. Luckily, Alex didn't have the time. "Yeah. I'll get my mug. Looks like everything's okay at the Masons'. There goes Robbie to work. I don't think he'd be doing that if his mom were missing."

There was nothing to reply that wouldn't make her sound even more like a crackpot. When he came back in with his mug, she reached for the coffeepot and saw it was full of pale brown water. She'd forgotten to put the grounds in the filter. She didn't miss a beat as she took out the instant coffee. "I've stopped making a full pot just for myself," she said as she spooned powdered coffee into his commuter mug and poured the hot water over it. He took it with a sigh. Once he was gone, she fixed the coffee properly and sat down with her paper.

It was eleven o'clock before the police arrived, and one in the afternoon before an officer tapped on her door. She felt terrible as he carefully jotted down her account of what she had seen at 4 a.m. "And you didn't call the police?" the young man asked her, his brown eyes full of sorrow for her stupidity.

"I called her house twice, and then called my son. But I didn't see her outside, so I thought she'd gone home."

He folded his notebook with a sigh and tucked it into his pocket. "Well. She didn't," he said heavily. "Poor old lady, out there in her slippers and Christmas lights. Well, I doubt she went far. We'll find her."

"She was wearing a hot-pink workout suit. And bedroom slippers." She rummaged through her recall. "And she had a baseball bat. And a Hello Kitty backpack. Like she was going somewhere."

He took out his notebook, sighed again, and added the details. "I wish you had called," he said as he pocketed it again.

"So do I. But my son said she had probably gone home, and at my age it's pretty easy to doubt your own judgment on things."

"I imagine so. Good afternoon, ma'am."

It was Thursday. She went to see Richard in the nursing home. She took, as she always did, one of the photo albums from when they were children. She parked in the parking lot, crossed the street to the coffee shop, and bought a large vanilla latte. She carried it into the permanent pee smell of

Caring Manor, through the "parlor" with its floral sofa and dusty plastic flower arrangements, and went down the hall, past the inhabited wheelchairs parked along the walls. The hunched backs and wrinkly necks of the residents reminded her of turtles peering out of their shells. A few of the patients nodded at her as she passed, but most simply stared. Blue eyes faded to pale linen, brown eyes bleeding pigment into their whites, eyes with no one behind them anymore. There were familiar faces, residents who had been there at least as long as the three years that Richard had been here. She remembered their names, but they no longer did. They slumped in their chairs, waiting for nothing, their wheels a mockery to people who had no place to go.

There was a new nurse at the desk. Again. At first, Sarah had tried to greet every nurse and aide by name each time she visited Richard. It had proven a hopeless task. The nurses changed too often, and the lower echelon of aides who actually tended the residents changed even more frequently, as did the languages they spoke. Some of them were nice, chatting to Richard as they cleared away his lunch tray or changed his bedding. But others reminded her of prison guards, their eyes empty and resentful of their duties and the residents. She often brought them small gifts, jars of jam, squash from her garden, fresh tomatoes and peppers. She hoped those small bribes spoke even if they didn't understand all her words as she thanked them for taking such good care of her brother. Sometimes, when she was wakeful in the night, she prayed that they would be patient and kind, or at least not vindictive. Be kind when wiping feces from his legs, be kind when holding him up for his shower. Be kind while doing a task you hate for a wage that doesn't support you. Can anyone be that kind? she wondered.

Richard wasn't there that Thursday. She sat with the man who lived in his body, showing him pictures of when they went camping, of their first days of school, and of their parents. He nodded and smiled and said they were lovely photos. That was the worst, that even in his confusion, his gentle courtesy remained. She stayed the one hour she always stayed with him, no matter how heart-wrenching it was. When no one was looking, she gave him sips of her coffee. Richard wasn't allowed liquids anymore. Everything he ate was pureed and all his drinks, even his water, were thickened to a slime so that he wouldn't aspirate them. That was one of the problems with Alzheimer's. The swallowing muscles at the back of the throat weakened or people just forgot how to use them. So doctor's orders for Richard were that he could no longer have coffee. She defied that. He'd lost his books and his pipe smoking and walking by himself. His coffee was his last small pleasure in life, and she clung to it on his behalf. Every week she brought him a cup and helped him surreptitiously to drink it while it was still hot. He loved it. The coffee always won her a smile from the creature who had been her big, strong brother.

Cup empty, she went home.

Linda's disappearance was in the *Tacoma News Tribune* the next day. Sarah read the article. They had used an older photo, a calm and competent woman in a power suit. She wondered if it was because they had no snapshots of a wild-haired old woman. But then, no one had pictures of the grin she had worn when she'd turned her garden hose on the ten-year-old Thompson twins for squirting her cat with Super Soakers. It could not capture her smothered giggles when she had called Sarah at two in the morning and they'd both crept out to let the air out of all the tires of the cars parked outside Marty Sobin's place when her teenager had the drunken party while Marty was out of town. "Now they can't drive drunk," Linda had whispered with satisfaction. Linda from the old days. Sarah remembered how she had stood in the street, flat-footed, her teeth gritted, and forced Marsha Bates to screech to a halt to avoid hitting her with her dad's Jeep. "You're driving too fast for this neighborhood. Next time I tell your parents *and* the cops."

That Linda had hosted neighborhood Fourth of July barbecues and her house had been the one where the teenagers voluntarily gathered. Her Christmas lights were always first up and last down, and her Halloween jack-o'-lanterns were the largest on the street. That Linda had known how to start up a generator for the outdoor lights at the soccer picnic. After the big ice storm twelve years ago, she had taken her chain saw and cut up the tree that had fallen across the street when the city said no one could come for three days. Russ had opened the window and shouted, "Heads up, people! Crazy Norwegian lady with a chain saw!" and they had all laughed proudly. So proud that they could take care of themselves. But that Linda, and the cranky old woman she had become, were both gone now.

Her family put up posters. The police brought in a bloodhound. Robbie came by to visit and ask what she had seen that night. It was hard to meet his eyes and explain why she hadn't called the police. "I called your house. Twice. I let the phone ring twenty times."

"We turn the ringer off at night," he said dully. He'd been a heavy boy when he played goalie for the soccer team, and now he was just plain fat. A fat, tired man with a problem parent who had turned into a missing parent. It had to be something of a relief, Sarah thought, and then bit her lip to keep from saying it aloud.

As the days went by, the nights got cooler and rainier. There were no reported sightings. She couldn't have gotten far on foot. Could she? Had someone picked her up? What would someone want with a demented old woman with a baseball bat? Was she dead in the blackberries in some overgrown lot? Hitchhiking down Highway 99? Hungry and cold somewhere?

Now when Sarah awoke at two or three or four fifteen, guilt would keep her awake until true morning. It was horrid to be awake before the paper was delivered and before it was time to brew coffee. She sat at her table and stared at the harvest moon. "Boys and girls, come out to play," she whispered to herself. Her strange hours bothered Sarge. The pudgy beagle would sit beside her chair and watch her with his mournful hound eyes. He missed Russ. He'd been Russ's dog, and since Russ had died, his dog had become morose. She felt like he was just waiting to die now.

Well, wasn't she, too?

No. Of course not! She had her life, her schedule. She had her morning paper and her garden to tend, and her grocery shopping and her TV shows at night. She had Alex and Sandy, even if Sandy lived on the other side of the mountains. She had her house, her yard, and her dog, and other important things.

At four fifteen on a dark September morning, it was hard to remember what those important things were. Steady pattering rain had given way to silence and rising mist. She was working the sudoku in yesterday's paper, a stupid sort of puzzle, all logic and no cleverness, when Sarge turned to stare silently at the back door.

She turned off the light in the kitchen and peered out the back door window. The street was so dark! Not a house light showing anywhere. She clicked the switch on her porch light; the bulb was still burned out. Someone was out there; she heard voices. She cupped her hands around her face and pressed closer to the glass. Still couldn't see. She opened her back door softly and stepped quietly out.

Five young men, three abreast and two following. She didn't recognize any of them, but they didn't look like they came from her neighborhood. The teenagers hunched along in heavy coats and unlaced work boots, moving like a pack of dogs, their eyes roving from side to side. They carried sacks. The leader pointed at an old pickup truck parked across the street. They moved toward it, looked into the bed of it, and tried the locked doors. One peered through the side window and said something. Another one picked up a fallen tree branch and bashed it against the windshield. The rotted limb gave way in chunks and fell in the littered street. The others laughed at him and moved on. But the young vandal was stubborn. As he clambered into the bed of the truck to try to kick out the back window, Hello Kitty looked back at her.

Her heart leaped into her chest. A coincidence, she told herself. He was just a macho youngster wearing a Hello Kitty backpack to be ironic. It meant nothing, no more than that.

Yes. It did.

She was grateful that her porch light was out and her kitchen dark. She eased quietly inside, pushed the door almost closed, picked up her phone, and dialed 911, wincing at the beeps. Would he hear them? It rang three times before the operator picked up. "Police or fire?" the woman demanded.

"Police. Some men are trying to break into a truck parked in front of my house. And one is wearing a pink backpack like my friend was wearing the night—"

"Slow down, ma'am. Name and address."

She rattled them off.

"Can you describe the men?"

"It's dark and my porch light is out. I'm alone here. I don't want them to know I'm watching them and making this call."

"How many men? Can you give a general description?"

"Are the police coming?" she demanded, suddenly angry at all the useless questions.

"Yes. I've dispatched someone. Now. Please tell me as much as you can about the men."

Piss on it. She went to the door and looked out. He was gone. She looked up and down the street, but the night was hazy with fog. "They're gone."

"Are you the owner of the vehicle they were attempting to break into?"

"No. But the important thing is that one of them was wearing a pink backpack, just like the one my friend was wearing when she disappeared."

"I see." Sarah was sure the dispatcher didn't see at all. "Ma'am, as this is not an immediate emergency, we will still send an officer, but he may not arrive immediately. . . ."

"Fine." She hung up. Stupid. She went to the door and looked out again. Upstairs in the dresser drawer under Russ's work shirts there was a pistol, a little black .22 that she hadn't shot in years. Instead she took her long, heavy flashlight from the bottom drawer and stepped out into the backyard. Sarge followed her. She walked quietly to the fence, snapped on the flashlight, and shone it on the old truck. The beam barely reached it. Up the street and down, baffled by the fog, the light showed her nothing. She went back in the house with Sarge, locked the door, but left the kitchen light on and went back to bed. She didn't sleep.

The officer didn't come by until ten thirty. She understood. Tacoma was a violent little town; they had to roll first on the calls where people were actually in danger. He came, he took her report, and he gave her an incident number. The pickup truck was gone. No, she didn't know who it belonged to. Five young men, mid- to late teens, dressed in rough clothes, and the one with a pink backpack. She refused to guess their heights or their races. It had been dark. "But you saw the backpack clearly?"

She had. And she was certain it was identical to the one that Linda had been carrying.

The officer nodded and noted it down. He leaned on her kitchen table to look out the window. He frowned. "Ma'am, you said he hit the window with a fallen branch and it broke into pieces?"

"That's right. But I don't think the window broke."

"Ma'am, there are no tree branches out there. Or pieces in the street." He looked at her pityingly. "Is it possible you dreamed this? Because you were worried about your friend?"

She wanted to spit at him. "There's the flashlight I used. Still on the counter where I left it."

His eyebrows collided. "But you said it was dark and you couldn't see anything."

"I went out with the flashlight *after* I hung up with 911. To see if I could see where they had gone."

"I see. Well, thank you for calling us on this."

After he left, she went outside herself. She crossed the street to where the pickup had been parked. No pieces of branch on the ground. Not even a handful of leaves in the gutter. Her new neighbor had a lawn fetish. It was as groomed as Astroturf on a playfield, the gutters as clean as if vacuumed. She scowled to herself. Last night there had been dry leaves whispering as the wind blew, and there had definitely been a large, heavy rotten branch in the street. But the young apple trees in his planting strip were scarcely bigger around than a rake handle. Too small to have grown such a branch, let alone dropped one.

Sarah went back in her house. She wept for a time, then made a cup of tea and felt relieved that she hadn't called Alex about it. She catalogued the work she could do: laundry, deadheading the roses, taking in the last of the green tomatoes and making chutney of them. She went upstairs and took a nap.

After three weeks the neighborhood quit gossiping about Linda. Her face still smiled from a "missing" poster at Safeway next to the pharmacy counter. Sarah ran into Maureen there, picking up pills for Hugh, and they got Starbucks and wondered what had become of Linda. They talked about the old days, soccer games and tux rentals for proms and the time Linda had hot-wired Hugh's truck when no one could find the keys and Alex had needed stitches right away. They laughed a lot and wept a little, and worked their way back to the present. Maureen shared her news. Hugh was "holding his own" and Maureen said it as if being able to sit up in bed was all he really wanted to do. Maureen invited her to come pick the apples off their backyard tree. "I don't have time to do anything with them, and there are more than we can eat. I hate to see them just fall and rot."

It had felt good to have coffee and a conversation, and it made Sarah realize how long it had been since she had socialized. She thought about it the next morning as she sorted the mail on her table. A power bill, a brochure on long-term-care insurance, an AARP paper, and two brochures from retirement homes. She set the bill to one side and stacked the rest to recycle with the morning paper. She found a basket and was just leaving to raid Maureen's apple tree when Alex came in. He sat down at her table and she microwaved the leftover morning coffee for them.

"I had to come into Tacoma for a seminar, so I thought I'd drop by. And I wanted to remind you that the second half of property taxes is due the end of this month. You pay it yet?"

"No. But it's on my desk." That, at least, was true. It was on her desk. Somewhere.

She saw him eying the retirement home brochures. "Junk mail," she told him. "Ever since your dad signed us up for AARP, we get those things."

"Do you?" He looked abashed. "I thought it was because I asked them to send them. I thought maybe you'd look at them and then we could talk."

"About what? Recycling?" Her joke came out harder-edged than she had intended. Alex got his stubborn look. He would never eat broccoli—never. And he was going to have this conversation with her no matter what. She put a spoonful of sugar in her coffee and stirred it, resigned to an unpleasant half hour.

"Mom, we have to face facts." He folded his hands on the edge of the table. "Taxes are coming due; the second half of them is seven hundred bucks. House insurance comes due in November. And oil prices are going up, with winter heating bills ahead of us, and this place isn't exactly energy efficient." He spoke as if she were a bit stupid as well as old.

"I'll put on a sweater and move the little heater from room to room. Like I did last year. Zonal heating. Most efficient way to heat a home." She sipped her coffee.

He opened his hands on the table. "That's fine. Until we start to get mold in the house from damp in the unheated basement. Mom, this is a three-bedroom, two-bath house, and you live in maybe four rooms of it. The only bathtub is upstairs and the laundry is in the basement. That's a lot of stairs for you each day. The electrical box should have been replaced years ago. The refrigerator needs a new seal. The living room carpeting is fraying where it meets the tile."

All things she knew. She tried to make light of it. "And the bulb is burned out in the back porch light. Don't forget that!"

He narrowed his eyes at her. "When the beech tree dumps its leaves, we'll need to rake them off the lawn and get them out of the rain gutters. And next year the house is going to need paint."

She folded her lips. True, all true. "I'll cross those bridges as I come to them," she said, instead of telling him to mind his own damn business.

He leaned his elbows on the table and put his forehead in his hands.

He didn't look up at her as he said, "Mom, that just means you'll call me when you can't get the leaves into the lawn recycling bin. Or when the gutters are overflowing down the side of the house. You can't maintain this place by yourself. I want to help you. But it always seems that you call me when I'm prepping a presentation or raking my own leaves."

She stared at Alex, stricken. "I . . . Don't come, if you're that busy! No one dies from clogged gutters or leaves on the lawn." She felt ashamed, then angry. How dare he make himself a martyr to her needs? How dare he behave as if she were a burden? She'd asked if he had time to help her, not demanded that he come.

"You're my mom," he said, as if that created some irrevocable duty that no one could erase. "What will people think if I let the house start falling apart around you? Besides, your house is your major asset. It has to be maintained. Or, if we can't maintain it, we need to liquidate it and get you into something you can manage. A senior apartment. Or assisted living."

"Alex, I'll have you know this is my *home,* not my 'major—'"

Alex held up a commanding hand. "Mom. Let me finish. I don't have a lot of time today. So let me just say this. I'm not talking about a nursing home. I know how you hate visiting Uncle Richard. I'm talking about a place of your own with a lot of amenities, without the work of owning a home. This one, here?" He put his finger on a brochure, coaxed it out of the junk mail pile. "It's in Olympia. On the water. They have their own little dock, and boats that residents can use. You can make friends and go fishing."

She put a stiff smile on her face and tried to make a joke of it. "I can't rake leaves but you think I can row a boat?"

"You don't have to go fishing." She had annoyed him, popping his dream of his mom in a happy little waterfront terrarium. "I'm just saying that you *could,* that this place has all sorts of amenities. A pool. An exercise studio. Daily shuttles to the grocery store. You could enjoy life again."

He was so earnest. "The bathroom has this safety feature. If you fall, you pull a cord and it connects you, 24-7, to help. There's a dining hall so if you don't feel like cooking that day, you don't have to. There's an activity center with a movie room. They schedule game nights and barbecues and—"

"Sounds like summer camp for old farts," she interrupted him.

He was wordless for a moment. "I just want you to know the possibilities," he said stiffly. "You don't like this, fine. There are other places that are just apartments suited to older people. All the rooms on one level, grab bars in the bathrooms, halls wide enough for walkers. I just thought you might like something nicer."

"I have something nicer. My own home. And I couldn't afford those places."

"If you sold this house—"

"In this market? Ha!"

"Or rented it out, then."

She glared at him.

"It would work. A rental agency would manage it for a percentage. Lots of people do it. Look. I don't have time to argue today. Hell, I don't have time to argue any day! And that's really what we are discussing. I just don't have time to be running over here every day. I love you, but you have to make it possible for me to take care of you and still have a life of my own! I've got a wife and kids; they need my time just as much as you do. I can't work a job and take care of two households. I just can't."

He was angry now, and that showed how close he was to breaking. She looked at the floor. Sarge was under the table. He lifted sad brown eyes to her. "And Sarge?" she asked quietly.

He sighed. "Mom, he's getting old. You should think about what is best for him."

That afternoon, she got out the step stool and changed the bulb in the porch light. She dragged the aluminum ladder out of the garage, set it up, pulled the hose out, climbed the damn thing, and hosed out the gutters along the front of the garage. She raked the wet leaves and debris into a pile on a tarp and then wrestled it over to the edge of her vegetable plot and dumped them. Compost. Easier than fighting with a leaf bin.

She woke up at ten the next morning instead of six, aching all over, to an overcast day. Sarge's whining woke her. He had to go. Getting out of bed was a cautious process. She put on her wrapper and leaned on the handrail going down the stairs. She let Sarge out into the foggy backyard, found the Advil, and pushed the button on the coffeemaker. "I'm going to do it until I can't do it anymore," she said savagely. "I'm not leaving my house."

The newspaper was on the front doormat. As she straightened up, she looked at her neighborhood and was jolted by the change. When she and Russ had moved in, it had been an upwardly mobile neighborhood where lawns stayed green and mowed all summer, houses were repainted with clockwork regularity, and flower beds were meticulously tended.

Now her eyes snagged on a sagging gutter on the corner of the old McPherson house. And down the way, the weeping willow that had been Alice Carter's pride had a broken branch that dangled down, covered in dead leaves. Her lawn was dead, too. And the paint was peeling on the sunny side of the house. When had it all become so run-down? Her breath came faster. This was not how she recalled her street. Was this what Alex was talking about? Had her forgetfulness become so encompassing? She clutched the newspaper to her breast and retreated into the house.

Sarge was scratching at the back door. She opened it for the beagle and then stood staring out past her fence. The pickup truck was there again. Red and rusting, one tire flat, algae on the windows. The pieces of broken tree branch still littered the street, and the wind had heaped the fallen leaves against them. Slowly, her heart hammering, she lifted her eyes to the gnarled apple trees that had replaced her memory of broomstick saplings. "This cannot be," she said to the dog.

She lurched stiffly down the steps, Sarge trailing at her heels. She walked past her roses to the fence, peering through the tattered fog. Nothing changed. The more she studied her familiar neighborhood, the more foreign it became. Broken windows. Chimneys missing bricks, dead lawns, a collapsed carport. A rhythmic noise turned her head. The man came striding down the street, boots slapping through the wet leaves, the pink pack high on his shoulders. He carried the aluminum baseball bat across the front of his body, right hand gripping it, left hand cradling the barrel. Sarge growled low in his throat. Sarah couldn't make a sound.

He didn't even glance at them. When he reached the truck, he set his feet, measured the distance, and then hit the driver's-side window. The glass held. He hit it again, and then again, until it was a spiderwebbed, crinkling curtain of safety glass. Then he reversed the bat and rammed the glass out of his way. He reached in, unlocked the door, and jerked it open.

"Where's Linda? What did you do to her?"

Surely it was someone else who shouted the brave words. The man froze in the act of rummaging inside the cab. He straightened and spun around, the bat ready. Sarah's knees weakened and she grabbed the top rail of her fence to keep from sagging. The man who glared at her was in his late teens. The unlaced work boots looked too big for him, as did the bulky canvas jacket he wore. His hair was unkempt and his spotty beard an accident. He scanned the street in all directions. His eyes swept right past her and her growling dog without a pause as he looked for witnesses. She saw his chest rise and fall; his muscles were bunched in readiness.

She stared at him, waiting for the confrontation. *Should have grabbed the phone. Should have dialed 911 from inside the house. Stupid old woman. They'll find me dead in the yard and never know what happened.*

But he didn't advance. His shoulders slowly lowered. She remained standing where she was but he didn't even look at her. Not worth his attention. He turned back to the cab of the truck and leaned in.

"Sarge. Come, boy. Come." She moved quietly away from the fence. The dog remained where he was, tail up, legs stiff, intent on the intruder in his street. The sun must have wandered behind a thicker bank of clouds. The day grayed and the fog thickened until she could scarcely see the fence. "Sarge!" she called more urgently. In response to the worry in her voice, his growl deepened.

In the street, the thief stepped back from the truck, a canvas tool tote in his hands. He rummaged in it and a wrench fell. It rang metallic on the pavement and Sarge suddenly bayed. On his back, short, stiff hair stood up in a bristle. Out in the street, the man spun and stared directly at the dog. He knit his brows, leaning forward and peering. The fat beagle bayed again, and as the man lifted his bat, Sarge sprang forward, snarling.

The fence didn't stop him.

Sarah stared as Sarge vanished into the rolling fog and then reappeared in the street outside her fence, baying. The man stooped, picked up a chunk of the rotten branch, and threw it at Sarge. She didn't think it hit him, but the beagle yelped and dodged. "Leave my dog alone!" she shouted at him. "I've called the cops! They're on the way!"

He kept his eyes on the dog. Sarge bayed again, noisily proclaiming his territory. The thief snatched a wrench from the tool pouch and threw it. This time she heard a meaty thunk as it hit her dog, and Sarge's yipping as he fled was that of an injured dog. "Sarge! Sarge, come back! You bastard! You bastard, leave my dog alone!" For the man was pursuing him, bat held ready.

Sarah ran into the house, grabbed her phone, dialed it, and ran outside again. Ringing, ringing . . . "Sarge!" she shouted, fumbled the catch on the gate, and ran out into an empty street.

Empty.

No truck. No fallen branches or dead leaves. A mist under the greenbelt trees at the end of the street vanished as the sun broke through the overcast. She stood in a tidy urban neighborhood of mowed lawns and swept sidewalks. No shattered windshield, no shabby thief. Hastily, she pushed the "off" button on her phone. No beagle. "Sarge!" she called, her voice breaking on his name. But he was gone, just as gone as everything else she had glimpsed.

The phone in her hand rang.

Her voice shook as she assured 911 that everything was all right, that she had dropped the phone and accidentally pushed buttons as she picked it up. No, no one needed to come by, she was fine.

She sat at her kitchen table, stared at the street, and cried for two hours. Cried for her mind that was slipping away, cried for Sarge being gone, cried for a life spinning out of her control. Cried for being alone in a foreign world. She took the assisted living brochures out of the recycling bin, read them, and wept over the Alzheimer's wing with alarms on the doors. "Anything but this, God," she begged Him, and then thought of the sleeping pills the doctor had offered when Russ had died. She'd never filled the prescription. She looked for it in her purse. It wasn't there.

She went upstairs and opened the drawer and looked in at the handgun. She remembered Russ showing her how the catch worked, and how she had loaded the magazine with ammunition. They'd gone plinking at tin cans in a gravel pit. Years ago. But the gun was still there, and when she worked the catch, the magazine dropped into her hand. There was an amber plastic box of ammunition next to it, surprisingly heavy. Fifty rounds. She looked at it and thought of Russ and how gone he was.

Then she put it back, got her basket, and went to pick Maureen's apples. She and Hugh weren't home, probably up at the Seattle hospital. Sarah filled her basket with heavy apples and lugged it home, planning what she would make. Jars of applesauce, jars of apple rings spiced and reddened with Red Hots candy. Empty jars waited, glass shoulder to shoulder, next to the enamel canner and the old pressure cooker. She stood in the kitchen, staring up at them and then at the apples on the counter. Put them in jars for whom? Who could trust anything she canned? She should drag them all down and donate them.

She shut the cupboard. Done and over. Canning was as done and over as dancing or embroidery or sex. No use mooning over it.

She washed and polished half a dozen apples, put them in a pretty basket with a late dahlia, and went to visit Richard. She left the basket at the desk with a thank-you note for the nurses and went in with the cup of coffee. She gave him sips of it and told him everything, about the fog and Linda disappearing and the man with her backpack. He watched her face and listened to the story she couldn't tell anyone else. A shadow of life came back into his face as he offered a brother's best advice. "Shoot the son of a bitch." He shook his head, coughed, and added, "Poor old dog. But at least he probably went fast, eh? Better than a slow death." He gestured around him with a bony, age-spotted hand. "Better than this, Sal. Better than this."

She stayed an extra hour with him that day. Then she rode the bus home and went directly to bed. When she woke up at 2 a.m., she swept the floor and cleaned the bathroom and baked herself a lonely apple in the oven. The cinnamon-apple-brown-sugar smell made her weep. She ate it with tears on her cheeks.

That was the day she became completely unhooked from time. Without Sarge asking her to get up at six and feed him, what did it matter what time she got up, or when she cooked or ate or raked leaves? The newspaper would always wait for her, Safeway never closed, and she never knew which days would show her a pleasant fall afternoon in a quiet neighborhood and which ones would reveal a foggy world of derelict houses and rusting cars. Why not shop for groceries at one in the morning, or read the day's news at eight o'clock at night while eating a microwaved dinner? Time didn't matter anymore.

That, she decided, was the secret of it. She wondered if it happened to all old people, once they realized that time no longer applied to them. She began to deliberately go out into the yard on the foggy days to stare by choice into that dismal other world. Three days after Sarge had vanished, she saw a ragged little girl shaking the lower branches of an overgrown apple tree, hoping that the last wormy apples would fall for her. Nothing fell, but she kept trying. Sarah went back into the house and brought out the basket of apples from Maureen's tree. She stood in her backyard and pitched them over the fence, one at a time. She threw them underhand, just as she had used to pitch softballs for her children. The first three simply vanished in the fog. Then, as the mist thickened, one thunked to the weedy brown lawn by the child. The girl jumped on the apple, believing she had shaken it down herself. Sarah lobbed half a dozen more fat red apples, sprayed and watered and ripe. With each succeeding apple, the child's delight grew. She sat down under the tree, hunched her legs to her chest for warmth, and hungrily ate apple after apple. Sarah bit into an apple herself and ate it while she watched. When she was finished, it became a game for Sarah, to stand ready to lob an apple when the child shook the tree. When the girl couldn't eat any more, she stuffed them into her ragged backpack. When all the apples had been thrown, Sarah went back into the house, made herself tea, and thought about it until the mist burned away and she saw the first apples she had tossed lying in the street. She laughed, brushed her hair, put on her shoes, and went shopping.

For three days the mist came, but no child appeared. Sarah wasn't discouraged. The next time the mist swept through, she was ready. She had bagged the pink socks in plastic, taped securely shut. No telling how long they would lie there before the child came back. There were two sweatshirts, pink with sequins, and warm woolly tights and a sturdy blue backpack full of granola bars. One after another, she flung them over the fence and into the mist. She heard them land even though she couldn't see them. When the mist cleared and only one pair of socks remained in the street, she rejoiced. She hoped she would see the little girl come back and find her gifts. She didn't, but the next time the mist swirled, she could clearly see that the treasures were gone. "She found them," she congratulated herself, and planned more surprises.

Simple things. A bag of dried apricots. Oatmeal cookies with chocolate chips in a sturdy plastic tub. Over the fence and into the mist. Those she saw the girl find, and the look on her face as she opened the box was priceless. The nights got colder and snow threatened. Was it as cold in that other world? Where did the child sleep? Did she den in some bushes or lair in one of the abandoned houses? Sarah found her knitting needles and ferreted out a stash of yarn. She had forgotten these colors, heather purple and acorn-cap brown and moss green. They wrapped her needles and slid through her stiff fingers with the memories of days when she could hike the autumn hillsides. She took her knitting with her in a bag when she visited Richard, and even if he didn't know her, he remembered how their mother would never watch television without her knitting. They laughed at that, and cried a bit, too. His cough was worse. She gave him sips of coffee to clear his throat, and when he asked, in a boy's voice, if he could keep the green wool hat, she left it with him.

Sarah packaged together heathery woolen mittens, a matching hat, and a pair of pink rubber boots. On impulse, she added a picture dictionary. She put the things in ziplock bags and when the mist swirled in the winter winds, she grinned as she Frisbeed them over the fence and into the fog. Early in November, she threw a sack of orange and black Halloween crème candies, pumpkins and cats and ears of corn left over after a very disappointing turnout of trick-or-treaters at her door.

When she visited Richard, he was wearing his green hat in bed. She told him about the little girl, about the apples and the mittens. He laughed his old laugh, then coughed himself red in the face. The nurse came, and when she eyed his coffee suspiciously, Sarah smiled and drank the rest of it. "You're a nice lady," Richard told her as she was leaving. "You remind me of my sister."

Several nights later, in the middle of the night, a storm woke her and she came down the stairs to the kitchen. Outside, the wind blew past her chimney and brushed the tree branches against the roof. It would bring the last of the leaves down; she'd have to rake tomorrow. Through the wind, she heard a child's voice, perhaps the girl's. She opened her back door and stepped onto her porch. Overhead, the branches of the beech swayed and leaves rained, but in the street, a thick bank of mist rolled slowly past. She crossed her lawn and groped for the top of her fence. She strained her eyes and ears, trying to penetrate the fog and the darkness.

She almost stayed too long. The fence faded from her grip. She stepped back as it melted into fog. The porch light seemed distant. Mist roiled between her and her steps. Behind her, she heard heavier footfalls in the street. Men, not a child. She moved through the fog as if she were breasting deep water. Her breath was sobbing in and out of her as she stumbled up the steps. The men's footfalls rang clear behind her. Reaching around the door, into her house, she snapped off the porch light and stood frozen on the steps, peering through mist and dark.

They had the girl. One held her firmly by the wrist. She pointed and spoke to them. She touched her hat and spoke again. The man gripping her wrist shook his head. The girl pointed again, insistently, at the apple tree across the street. The man advanced on it. Sarah watched them as they methodically searched the tree, the area under the tree, and then the planting strip and the yard across the street. One of them dragged open the sagging door and vanished into the house. He emerged a short time later shaking his head. When they looked in her direction, she wondered what they saw. What was her house in their world and time? A deserted place with broken windows like the house across the street? A burned-out hulk like the Masons' home halfway down the block?

What would happen if the fog engulfed her house?

The man with Linda's backpack and the baseball bat stared intently at her porch. A swirl of mist followed her as she retreated into her kitchen, not daring to shut her door lest it make a noise. Noise, she knew, could reach from her world to theirs. She pushed a chair out of the way, hating how it scraped on the floor, and hunched low to peer out over the windowsill. She reached for the light switch and snapped the lights off. There. She could see more clearly.

Backpack Man was staring at her window as he crossed the street, lightly slapping the bat against his palm as he came. The mist had coalesced in her yard. She saw him come into her yard, unhampered by an iron fence that didn't exist in his world. He stood in her roses just below her kitchen window and stared up at her, his pale eyes focused past her. He studied her window, then threw back his head and shouted, "Sarah!" The word reached her, faint but clear. He stepped back, searching her window for her. She remained frozen. *He can't see me. I'm not in his world. Even if he knows my name, he can't see me.* He looked at the upper windows of her house and shook his head in frustration. "Sarah!" he shouted again. "You are there. You hear me! Come out!" Behind him, his cohorts took it up. "Sarah!" they chorused to the night. "Come out, Sarah!" The others drifted closer to flank Backpack Man.

They knew her name. Before they killed Linda, they had learned her name. And what else? The little girl took up the cry, her voice a thin echo. She stood close by the man who held her hand. Not his captive. Her protector.

Sarah slipped from her chair, folding down on the floor, her heart racing so she could scarcely breathe. Tears came and she huddled under her table, shaking, terrified that at any moment the window would shatter to his bat or he would step in through the open doorway. What a fool she was! Of course the child was part of their group. They would have a foraging territory, just like any group of primates. The gifts she had thrown intending only kindness to a hungry child had lured them here. The man out there wasn't a fool. He'd seen Sarge come out of nowhere, the dog he had probably hunted down for meat. He'd know there was something mysterious about her house. Had Linda told him something before they killed her and took her things? How much had she told? Had she been pursued by them, had she led them here when she tried to cross back to this world?

Too many questions. She was shaking with terror. She clenched her teeth to keep them from chattering, tried not to breathe lest they hear her panting. She squeezed her eyes shut and tried to be utterly still. She heard the door creak on its hinges. The rising wind pushing cold air into the room, or the man with the baseball bat? She curled tighter, put her hands over her head, and closed her eyes. *Don't move,* she told herself. *Stay still until the danger is gone.*

"Mom, what the hell! Are you all right? Did you fall? Why didn't you call me?"

Alex, face white, on his knees by the kitchen table, peering at her. "Can you move? Can you speak? Was it a stroke?"

She blinked and tried to make sense of what she saw. Alex had his coat on. Snowflakes on his shoulders. A wool watch cap pulled down over his ears. Cold air flowing in from the open back door. "I think I just fell asleep here," she said, and as his eyes widened, she tried to make repairs by saying, "Fell asleep reading at the table. I must have slid right down here without waking up."

"Reading what?" he demanded wearily.

She tried to hide how much it hurt to roll to her hands and knees and crawl out from under the table. She had to grab hold of the chair seat to lever herself up and then onto it. The kitchen table was bare. "Well, how odd!" she exclaimed, and forced a smile onto her face. "And what brings you by here today?"

"Your neighbors," he said heavily. "Maureen called. She was on her way up to Emergency with Hugh. She couldn't stop, but she saw that your back door was open but your lights weren't on. She didn't see any footprints in the snow and she was worried about you. So I came."

"How's Hugh?"

"I didn't ask. I came here instead."

She looked at the kitchen floor. A delta of melting snow showed where the storm had blown into her kitchen. She'd slept curled on the floor with the door open during a snowstorm. She creaked past him to the coffeepot without a word. She went to turn it on and saw the burned crust of dried coffee in the bottom of the pot. She moved methodically as she washed out the pot, measured water, and put grounds into a clean filter. She pushed the button. No light came on.

"I think you probably burned it out," Alex said heavily. He reached past her to unplug it. He didn't look at her as he took off the pot, threw away the grounds, and dumped the water down the sink. "I think you must have left it turned on for a long time to evaporate that much coffee." He pulled her small garbage can from under the sink. It was full. He tried unsuccessfully to stuff the coffeemaker into it and then left it perched crookedly on top.

He was quiet as he put water into two mugs and set them both in the microwave. She went and got the broom and swept the snow out the door, and then wiped up the water that remained. It hurt to bend; she was so stiff but didn't dare groan. Alex made instant coffee for both of them and then sat down heavily at her table. He gestured at the chair opposite, and she reluctantly joined him.

"Do you know who I am?" he asked her.

She stared at him. "You're my son, Alex. You're forty-two and your birthday was last month. Your wife has two children. I'm not losing my mind."

He opened his mouth, and then shut it. "What year is this?" He demanded.

"Two thousand and eleven. And Barack Obama is president. And I don't like him or the Tea Party. Are you going to give me a handful of change now and ask me how much more I need to make a dollar? Because I saw the same stupid 'Does Your Aging Parent Have Alzheimer's?' quiz in last week's Sunday paper."

"It wasn't a quiz. It was a series of simple tests to check mental acuity. Mom, maybe you can make change and tell me who I am, but you can't explain why you were sleeping on the floor under the table with the back door open. Or why you let the coffeepot boil dry." He looked around abruptly. "Where's Sarge?"

She told the truth. "He ran away. I haven't seen him for days."

The silence grew long. He looked at the floor guiltily and spoke in a gruff voice. "You should have called me. I would have done that for you."

"I didn't have him put down! He got out of the yard and ran off when a stranger shouted at him." She looked away from him. "He was only five. That's not that old for a dog."

"Bobbie called me a couple of nights ago. He said he came home from working late and saw you carrying groceries into the house at midnight."

"So?"

"So why were you buying groceries in the middle of the night?"

"Because I ran out of hot chocolate. And I wanted some for watching a late show, so I ran to the store for it, and while I was there, I thought I might as well pick up some other things I needed." Lie upon lie upon lie. She wouldn't tell him that the clock no longer mattered to her. Wouldn't say that time no longer controlled her. The heater cycled off. She heard it give a final tick and realized that it had been running constantly since she'd awakened. Probably it had run all night long.

Alex didn't believe her. "Mom, you can't live alone anymore. You're doing crazy things. And the crazy things are getting to be dangerous."

She stared into her mug. There was something final in his voice. Something more threatening than a stranger with a baseball bat.

"I don't want to drag you to the doctor and get a statement that you are no longer competent. I'd like us both to keep our dignity and avoid all that." He stopped and swallowed and she suddenly knew he was close to tears. She turned her head and stared out the window. An ordinary winter day, gray skies, wet streets. Alex sniffed and cleared his throat. "I'm going to call Sandy and see if she can get a few days off and come stay with you. We have to get a handle on how to proceed. I wish you'd let me get started on this months ago." He rubbed his cheeks and she heard the bristle of unshaven whiskers against his palms. He'd left his house in a panic. Maureen's call had scared him. "Mom, we need to clear out the house and put it on the market. You can come stay with me, or maybe Sandy can make room for you. Until we can find an assisted living placement for you."

Placement. Not until we can find an apartment or condo. Placement. Like putting something on a shelf. "No," she said quietly.

"Yes," he said. He sighed as if he were breathing his life out. "I can't give in to you again, Mom. I've let things go by too many times." He stood up. "When I came in here and saw you, I thought you were dead. And what flashed into my mind was that I was going to have to tell Sandy that I let you die on the floor alone. Because I didn't have the strength to stand up to you." He heaved another sigh. "I need to put you into a safe place so I can stop worrying about you."

"I'm sorry that I frightened you." Sincere words. She held back the other words, the ones that would tell him she would go down fighting, that neither he nor Sandy was going to keep her in a guest room like a guinea pig in a glass tank, nor board her out to a kennel for the elderly.

She only listened after that. He told her that he would call Sandy, that he'd be back tomorrow or Thursday at the latest. Would she be all right? Yes. Would she please stay in the house? Yes. He would call her every few hours today, and tonight he'd call her at bedtime. So would she please keep the phone near her, because if she didn't answer, he was coming back here. Yes. Yes to everything he said, not because she agreed or promised but because "yes" was the word that would make him feel safe enough to go away.

Then she asked, "But what about Richard? Tomorrow is Thursday. I always go see Richard on Thursdays."

For a moment he was silent. Then he said, "He doesn't know what day you come. He doesn't even know it's you. You could never go again, and he wouldn't miss you."

"*I* would miss *him*," she said fiercely. "I always go on Thursday mornings. Tomorrow I'm going to see him."

He stood up. "Mom. Yesterday was Thursday."

After Alex finally drove away, she made herself hot tea, found the ibuprofen, and sat down to think. She recalled the men standing in the street last night, the backpack man right outside her window, and a river of chill ran down her spine. She was in danger. And there was absolutely no one she would turn to for advice without running herself into even greater danger. Backpack Man might kill her with an aluminum baseball bat, but her family was contemplating something much worse. Death by bat would only happen once. If her children put her somewhere "safe," she'd wake up there day after day and night after night. To a woman who had broken free of time, that meant an eternity of cafeteria meals and time spent in a Spartan room. Alone. Because soon Alex would decide that it didn't matter if he ever visited her. She knew that now.

For the next few days she answered promptly whenever Alex called. She was bright and chipper on the phone, pretending enthusiasm for television movies that she cribbed from the TV guide. Twice she walked down to Maureen's, and twice she wasn't home. Sarah moved the accumulating newspapers off her doorstep and suspected Hugh was dying.

Sarah set the clocks to remind her when to go to bed and remained there, head on the pillow, blankets over her, until another clock rang to tell her to rise. She did not look out of the kitchen windows before ten or after five. The day that a flash of motion caught her eye and she looked out the window to see the girl run past in her hat the colors of freshly fallen acorns, she rose from the kitchen table and went to her bedroom and lay on the bed and watched *The Jerry Springer Show*.

The nursing home called to tell her that Richard had pneumonia. She sneaked out that day, caught the bus, and spent the whole morning with him. He didn't know her. They had taped an oxygen tube under his nose and the pink hissing sound reminded her of a balloon endlessly going flat. She tried to talk over it, couldn't, and just sat holding his hand. He stared at the wall. Waiting.

The next evening Sandy arrived. It startled Sarah when she walked in the front door without knocking, but she was glad to see her. She had driven over the mountains with her friend, a gaunt, morose woman who smoked cigarettes in the house and fountained apologies for "forgetting" that she shouldn't. Sandy had bought Safeway deli Chinese food and they ate at Sarah's table out of Styrofoam clamshells. The friend and Sandy talked of the friend's divorce from That Bastard and of Sandy's upcoming divorce from That Idiot. Sarah hadn't known a divorce was in Sandy's future. When she gently asked why, Sandy suddenly gulped, gasped that it was too complicated to explain, and fled the room with her friend trailing after her. Sarah numbly tidied up the kitchen and waited for her to come back down. When neither of them did, she eventually went to bed.

That was the first day. The next morning Sandy and the friend arose and began stripping the unused bedrooms that had been Alex's and Sandy's when they were teens. Sarah felt a mixture of relief and regret as she watched them finally emptying the closets and drawers of the "precious mementoes" that Sarah and Russ had longed to discard for years. "Lightening the load," Sandy called it, as they discarded old clothing and high school sports gear and required-reading paperbacks and ancient magazines and binders. One by one they carried the bulging black garbage sacks down the stairs and mounded them by the back porch. "Time to simplify!" Sandy's friend chortled cheerily each time she toted out another sack.

They ate sandwiches at lunch and then brought back pizza and beer for dinner. After dinner, they went right back to work. Sandy's friend had a laugh like a donkey's bray. Sarah escaped her cigarette smoke by going out into the dusky backyard. The evening was rainy, but when she stood under the copper beech, little of the water reached her. She stared out at the street. Empty. Empty and fog free. A calm neighborhood of mowed lawns and well-tended houses and shiny cars. Sandy came out with another bulging garbage bag. Sarah gave her daughter a rueful smile. "Better tie them shut, dear. The rain will ruin the clothing."

"The dump won't care, Mom."

"The dump? You're not taking them to Goodwill?"

Sandy gave a martyred sigh. "Secondhand stores have gotten really picky. They won't take a lot of this stuff and I don't have time to sort it. If I take all these bags there, they'll refuse half of them and I'll just have to go to the dump anyway. So I'll save myself a trip by going straight to the dump."

Sarah was drawing breath to protest, but Sandy had already turned and gone back for more. She shook her head. Tomorrow she would sort them herself and then call one of the charities for a pickup. She simply couldn't allow all that useful clothing and all those paperbacks to go to a dump. As the friend plopped down another sack, a seam split and a shirt Sarah recognized popped from it. Sandy came behind her friend with another bag.

"Wait a minute! That's your father's shirt, one of his good Pendletons. Was that in your room?" Sarah was almost amused at the idea that a shirt Sandy must have "borrowed" so many years ago would still have been in her room. But as she came smiling to the bag, she saw another familiar plaid behind it. "What's this?" she demanded as she drew out the sleeve of Russ's shirt.

"Oh, Mom." Sandy had been caught but she wasn't repentant. "We've started on Dad's closet. But relax. It's all men's clothing, nothing you can use. And it has to go."

"Has to go? What are you talking about?"

Sandy sighed again. She dropped the bag she carried and explained carefully, "The house has to be emptied so it can be staged by a realtor. I promise, there's nothing in these bags that you can take with you." She shook her head at the shock on her mother's face and added in a gentler voice, "Let it go, Mom. There's no reason to hang on to his clothing anymore. It's not Dad. It's just his old shit."

If she had used any other word, perhaps Sarah would have felt sorrow rather than anger. Any other word, and perhaps she could have responded rationally. But "shit"?

"Shit? His 'shit'? No, Sandy, it's not his 'shit.' Those are his clothes, the clothes and possessions of a man I loved. Do what you want with your old things. But those are mine, and I am not throwing them away. When the time comes for me to part with them, I'll know it. And then they will go somewhere where they can do someone some good. Not to the dump."

Sandy squeezed her eyes shut and shook her head. "Can't put this off any longer, Mom. You know it's why I came. I've only got this weekend to get all this stuff cleared out. I know it's hard, but you have to let us do it. We don't have time for you to be picky about it."

Sarah couldn't breathe. Had she agreed to this? When Alex had been there, talking and nagging, she had said, "Yes, yes," but that didn't mean she'd agreed to this, this destruction of her life. No. Not this fast, not like this! "No. No, Sandy." She spoke as firmly as if Sandy were still a teenager. "You are going to take all my things back upstairs. Do you hear me? This stops now!"

The friend spoke in a low voice. "Your brother warned you about this. Now you've upset her." She dropped her cigarette and ground it out on the porch step. She left the butt there. "Maybe you should call your bro. She looks really confused."

Sarah spun to confront the friend. "I'm standing here!" she shouted. "And you and your stinking cigarettes can get out of my house right now. I am not 'confused'; I am furious! Sandy, you should be ashamed of yourself, going through other people's things. You were taught better. What is the matter with you?"

Sandy's face went white, then scarlet. Anger flashed across it, to be caged by dignity. "Mom. I hate to see you like this. I have to be honest. Your mind is slipping. Alex has been updating me. He told me he'd talked to you about this, and that you'd looked at the brochures together and chosen a couple of places you'd like. Don't you remember at all?"

"We talked. That was all. Nothing was decided! Nothing."

Sandy shook her head sadly. "That's not what Alex said. He said you'd agreed, but he was taking it slow. But since that last incident, we have to act right away. Do you remember how he found you? Crouching under your table with the door open in a snowstorm?"

The friend was shaking her head, pityingly. Sarah was horrified. Alex had told Sandy, and Sandy had spread it to her friends. "That is none of your business," she said stiffly.

Sandy threw up her hands and rolled her eyes. "Really, Mom? Really? Do you think we can just walk off and say, 'Not my problem'? Because we can't. We love you. We want to do what is right. Alex has been talking to several very nice senior communities with lovely amenities. He's got it all figured out. If we use your social security and Dad's pension, Alex and I can probably scrape together enough extra to get you into a nice place until the house sells. After that—"

"No." Sarah said it flatly. She stared at Sandy, appalled. Who was this woman? How could she think she could just walk in and begin making decisions about Sarah's life? "Get out," she said.

Sandy glanced at her friend, who hadn't budged. She was watching both of them, her mouth slightly ajar, like a *Jerry Springer* spectator. Sandy spoke to her apologetically. "You'd better go for now, Heidi. I need to calm my mom down. Why don't you take the car and—"

"*You*, Sandy. I'm talking to you. Get. *Out.*"

Sandy's face went slack with shock. Her eyes came back to life first, and for a moment she looked eleven and Sarah would have done anything to take back her words. Then her friend spoke knowingly. "I *told* you that you should have called your bro."

Sandy huffed a breath. "You were right. We should have gotten the guardianship done and moved her out first. You were right."

Cold rushed through Sarah's body. "You just try it, missy. You just try it!"

Tears were leaking from Sandy's eyes now. The friend rushed to put a protective arm around her. "Come on, Sandy, let's go. We'll get some coffee and call your bro."

Even after the door had slammed behind them, and she had rushed over to lock it, Sarah couldn't calm down. She paced. Her hands trembled as she put on the kettle for tea. She climbed the stairs and looked at the chaos they had created.

In the kids' bedrooms, there were boxes neatly taped shut and labeled with their names. And across the hall, in the bedroom she and Russ had once shared, there were more boxes and half-filled garbage sacks. With a lurch of her heart, she recognized her old hiking jacket poking out of one. She pulled it out slowly and looked at it. It was still fine; there was nothing wrong with it. She put it on and zipped it. Tighter around her middle than it had been, but it still fit. It was still hers, not theirs. Her gaze traveled slowly from the sprawled bags to neatly stacked FedEx cardboard boxes. Each was labeled either "Sandy" or "Alex," but one was labeled "Heidi." Sarah tore the tape from it and dumped it out on the bed. Russ's ski parka. Two of his heavy leather belts. His Meerschaum pipe. His silver Zippo lighter. His tobacco humidor. She picked up the little wooden barrel and opened it. The aroma of Old Hickory tobacco drifted out to her and tears stung her eyes.

Anger suddenly fired her. She dumped out all the boxes and bags on the floor. Alex's box held Russ's sheath knife from his hunting days. Some wool winter socks, still with the labels on. The little .22 and its ammunition were in one of Sandy's boxes, along with Russ's 35mm camera, in its case. The extra lenses and the little tripod was in there, too. His Texas Instruments calculator, the first one he'd ever owned and so expensive when she got it for his Christmas gift. A couple of his ties, and his old Timex watch. She sank down to the floor, holding the watch in her hand. She lifted it to her ear, shook it, and listened again. Silence. As still as his heart. She got to her feet slowly, looked around the ransacked room, and then left it, closing the door softly behind her. She'd clean it up later. Put it all back where it belonged.

Halfway down the stairs, she knew that she wouldn't. There was no sense to it. Sandy had been right about that, at least. What did all the trappings mean if there was no man to go with them?

The kettle was whistling, and when she picked it up, it was almost dry.

The phone began to ring. She wanted to ignore it. Caller ID said it was Alex. She spoke before he could. "They were ransacking the house. Putting all your father's things into sacks to take to the dump. If that's how you're going to help me, how you're going to 'keep me safe,' then I'd rather be . . ." Abruptly she could think of nothing to say. She hung up the phone.

It rang again, and she let it, counting the rings until her answering machine picked up. She listened to Russ's voice answering the phone and waited for Alex's angry shout. Instead, an apologetic voice said that they hated to leave this sort of message on the phone but they had been trying to reach her all day without success. Richard had died that morning. They'd notified the funeral home listed on his Purple Cross card and his body had been picked up. His personal possessions had been boxed for her and could be claimed at the front desk. The voice offered his deepest condolences.

She stood frozen, unable to move toward the phone. Silence flowed in after that call. When the phone rang again, she took the receiver off the hook, opened the back, and jerked out the batteries. The box on the wall kept ringing. She tugged it off the wall mount and unplugged it. Silence came back, filling her ears with a different sort of ringing. What to do, what to do? One or both of her children would be on the way back by now. Richard was dead. His body was gone, all his possessions taped up in a box. Russ was gone. She had no allies left, no one who remembered who she had been. The people who loved her most were the ones who presented the gravest danger to her. They were coming. She was nearly out of time. Out of time.

She made a mug of black tea and carried it outside with her. The rain had stopped and the night was chill. Abruptly she was glad of the coat she wore. She watched the mist form; it wove itself among the wet tree branches and then detached to drop and mingle with the grayness rising from the trickling street gutters. They met in the middle, swirled together, and the streetlight at the end of the street suddenly went out. The traffic sounds died with it. Sarah sipped bitter black tea and waited for that other world to form beyond the mist.

It took shape slowly. Illuminated windows faded to black as the gray rolled down the street toward her. The silhouettes of the houses across the street shifted slightly, roofs sagging, chimneys crumpling as saplings hulked up into cracked and aging trees. The fog thickened into a fat mounded bank and rolled toward her. She waited, one decision suddenly clear. When it reached the fence, she picked up a garbage sack full of discarded possessions, whirled it twice, and tossed it. It flew into the mist and reappeared in that other place, landing in the littered street. Another bag. Another. By the fourth bag she was dizzy from whirling, but they were too heavy to toss any other way. She forced herself to go on, bag after bag, until her lawn was emptied of them. Better than the dump, she told herself. Better than a landfill.

Dizzy and breathless, she staggered up the porch steps and went to her bedroom. She opened the blind on the upstairs bedroom window and looked out. The fog had rolled into her yard. It billowed around her house like waves against a dock. Good. She opened the window. Bag after bag, box after box she shoved out. Sandy and Alex would find nothing left of her here. Nothing for them to throw out or tidy away. Until only the gun and the plastic box of ammunition remained on the floor.

She picked it up. Black metal, cold to the touch. She pushed the catch and the empty clip fell into her hand. She sat down on the bed and opened the plastic box of ammo. One little bullet after another she fed into the clip until it was full. The magazine snapped into place with a sound like a door shutting.

No. That was the front door shutting.

She jammed the ammunition box into her jacket pocket. She held the gun as Russ had taught her, pointing it down as she went down the stairs. They were in the living room. She heard Alex ask something in an impatient voice. Sandy whined an excuse. The friend interrupted, "Well, you weren't here! Sandy was doing the best she could."

Sarah hurried down the hall and into the kitchen. Her heart was pounding so that she could barely hear them now, but she knew they were coming. She opened the kitchen door and stepped out.

The fog lapped at the bottom steps. Out in the street, the voices of Backpack Man and his scavengers were clearer than she had ever heard them. They had found the things she had thrown out there. "Boots!" one man shouted in excitement. Two of the others were quarreling over Russ's old coat. Backpack Man was striding purposefully toward them, perhaps to claim it for himself. One of them took off running. He shouted something about "the others."

"Mom?" Alex's voice, calling her from inside the house.

"Mom?" Sandy's light footsteps in the kitchen. "Mom, where are you? Please. We're not angry. We just need to talk to you."

The fog had lapped over another step. Her porch light was dimming.

Backpack Man would likely kill her. Her children would put her away.

The little .22 handgun was cold and heavy in her hand.

She stepped off the porch. The concrete step she had swept a few days ago was squishy with moss under her foot.

"Mom? Mom?"

"Alex, we should call the police." Sandy's voice was rising to hysteria. "The phone's been torn off the wall!"

"Let's not be" something, something, something—his voice went fuzzy, like a bad radio signal. Their worried conversation became distant buzzing static.

She tottered into the dark garden. The ground was uneven. She waded through tall wet weeds. The copper beech was still there and she hid in its deep shade. In the street, the silhouettes of the men intently rooted through the bags and boxes. They spoke in low excited voices as they investigated their find. Others were coming to join them. In the distance there was an odd creaking, like a strange bird cry. Sarah braced her hands on the tree and blended her shadow with the trunk, watching them. Some of the new-comers were probably females in bulky clothes. The girl was there, and another, smaller child. They were rummaging in a box, peering at paper-back titles in the moonlight.

Two of the men closed in on the same garbage bag. One seized hold of a shirt sticking out of a tear and jerked on it, but the other man already had hold of its sleeve. An angry exclamation, a fierce tug, and then as one man possessed it, the other leaped on him. Fists flew, a man went down with a hoarse cry, and Backpack Man cursed them, brandishing his aluminum bat as he ran at them.

Sarah cringed behind the tree and measured her distance to the kitchen door. The house windows still gleamed but the light was grayish-blue, like the fading light from a dying Coleman lantern. Inside the room, her children passed as indistinct shadows. It wasn't too late. She could still go back. The friend lit a cigarette; she saw the flare of the match, the glow as she drew on it. The friend waved a hand, commiserating with Sandy and Alex.

Sarah turned away from the window. She took a breath; the air was cool and damp, rich with the smells of humus and rot. Out in the street, Backpack Man stood between the quarreling men. He held the shirt high in one hand and the bat in the other. "Daddy!" the little girl cried, and ran toward them. One of the men was sprawled in the street. The other man stood, still gripping a sleeve, hunched and defiant. The girl ran to him, wrapped herself around him.

"Let go!" Backpack Man warned them both. A hush had fallen over the tribe as they stared, awaiting Backpack Man's judgment. The distant creaking grew louder. Backpack Man raised his bat threateningly.

Sarah gripped the gun in both hands, stepped from the tree's shadow and thumbed off the safety. She had not known that she remembered how to do that. She'd never been a great shot; his chest was the largest target, and she couldn't afford a warning shot. "You!" she shouted as she waded through the low fogbank and out into that world. "Drop the bat or I'll shoot! What did you do to Linda? Did you kill her? Where is she?"

Backpack Man spun toward her, bat held high. Don't think. She pointed and fired, terror and resolve indistinguishable from one another. The bullet spanged the bat and whined away, hitting the Murphys' house with a solid thwack. Backpack Man dropped the bat and clutched his hand to his chest. "Where's Linda?" she screamed at him. She advanced on him, both hands on the gun, trying to hold it steady on his chest. The others had dropped their loot and faded back.

"I'm here! Dammit, Sarah, you took your sweet time. But looks like you thought to bring a lot more than I did!" Linda cackled wildly. "Bring any good socks in there?"

The creaking was a garden cart festooned with a string of LEDs. A halo of light illuminated it as Linda pushed it before her. The cart held two jerry cans, a loop of transparent tubing, and the tool roll from the truck. Three more battered carts, similarly lit, followed her in a solemn procession. As Sarah's mind scrambled to put it all in context, she heard the rattle of toenails on pavement and a much skinnier Sarge raced up to her, wriggling and wagging in excitement. They weren't dead. She wasn't alone. Sarah stooped and hugged the excited dog, letting him lap the tears off her cheeks.

Linda gave her time to recover as she barked her orders at the tribe.

"Benny, you come here and take this. Crank this fifty times and then it will light up. Hector, you know how to siphon gas. Check that old truck. We need every drop we can get to keep the Generac running. Carol, you pop the hood and salvage the battery."

The scavengers came to her, accepting the jerry cans and the siphon tube. Backpack Man bobbed a bow to her before accepting the crank light. As he turned away, Linda smiled at her. "They're good kids. A bit rough around the edges, but they're learning fast. You should have seen their faces the first time I fired up the generator. I know where to look for stuff like that. It was in the basement of that clinic on Thirtieth."

Sarah was speechless. Her eyes roved over Linda. Like the dog, she had lost weight and gained vitality. She hobbled toward Linda on the ragged remnants of her bedroom slippers. She gave a caw of laughter when she saw Sarah staring at her feet.

"Yes, I know. Dotty old woman. Thought of so many things—solar lights and a crank flashlight, aspirin, and sugar cubes and so on . . . and then walked out the door in my slippers. Robbie was right, my trolley was definitely off the tracks. But it doesn't matter so much over here. Not when the tracks are torn up for everyone."

"Russ's hiking boots are in one of those bags," Sarah heard herself say.

"Damn, you thought of everything. Cold-weather gear, books . . . and a pistol! I'd never have thought it of you. You pack any food?"

Sarah shook her head wordlessly. Linda looked at the gun she still held, muzzle down at her side, and nodded knowingly. "Didn't plan to stay long, did you?"

"I could go back and get some," Sarah said, but as she looked back at her house, the last lights of the past faded. Her home was a wreck, broken windows and tumbledown chimney. Her grapevines cloaked the ruins of the collapsed porch.

"Can't go back," Linda confirmed for her. She shook her head and then clarified: "For one, I don't want to." She looked around at her tribe. "Petey, pick up that bat. Remind everyone, we carry everything back and divvy up at the clinic. Not here in the street in the dark. Don't tear the bags and boxes; put the stuff back in them and let's hump it on home."

"Yes, Linda." Backpack Man bobbed another bow to her. Around her in the darkness, the others were moving to obey her. The girl stood, staring at both of them, her mittened hands clasped together. Linda shook a bony finger at her. "You get busy, missy." Then she motioned to Sarah to come closer. "What do you think?" she asked her. "Do you think Maureen will be ready soon?"

Lawrence Block

Here's a chiller about a dangerous woman with a dangerous plan in mind and the worst of intentions who maybe should have given the whole matter a little more thought. . . .

New York Times bestseller Lawrence Block, one of the kings of the modern mystery genre, is a Grand Master of Mystery Writers of America, the winner of four Edgar Awards and six Shamus Awards, and the recipient of the Nero Award, the Philip Marlowe Award, a Lifetime Achievement Award from the Private Eye Writers of America, and a Cartier Diamond Dagger for Life Achievement from the Crime Writers' Association. He's written more than fifty books and numerous short stories. Block is perhaps best known for his long-running series about alcoholic ex-cop/private investigator Matthew Scudder, the protagonist of novels such as *The Sins of the Fathers, In the Midst of Death, A Stab in the Dark,* and fifteen others, but he's also the author of the bestselling four-book series about the assassin Keller, including *Hit Man, Hit List, Hit Parade,* and *Hit and Run;* the eight-book series about globe-trotting insomniac Evan Tanner, including *The Thief Who Couldn't Sleep* and *The Canceled Czech;* and the eleven-book series about burglar and antiquarian book dealer Bernie Rhodenbarr, including *Burglars Can't Be Choosers, The Burglar in the Closet,* and *The Burglar Who Liked to Quote Kipling.* He's also written stand-alone novels such as *Small Town, Death Pulls a Doublecross,* and sixteen others, as well as novels under the names Chip Harrison, Jill Emerson, and Paul Kavanagh. His many short stories have been collected in *Sometimes They Bite, Like a Lamb to Slaughter, Some Days You Get the Bear, By the Dawn's Early Light, The Collected Mystery Stories, Death Wish and Other Stories, Enough Rope,* and *One Night Stands and Lost Weekends.* He's also edited thirteen mystery anthologies, including *Murder on the Run, Blood on Their Hands, Speaking of Wrath,* and, with Otto Penzler, *The*

Best American Mystery Stories 2001, and produced seven books of writing advice and nonfiction, including *Telling Lies for Fun & Profit.* His most recent books are the new Matt Scudder novel, *A Drop of the Hard Stuff,* the new Bernie Rhodenbarr novel, *Like a Thief in the Night,* and, writing as Jill Emerson, the novel *Getting Off.* He lives in New York City.

I KNOW HOW TO PICK 'EM

I sure know how to pick 'em.

Except I don't know as I've got any credit coming for this one, because it's hard to make the case that it was me that picked her. She walked into that edge-of-town roadhouse with the script all worked out in her mind, and all that was left to do was cast the lead.

The male lead, that is. Far as the true leading role was concerned, well, that belonged to her. That much went without saying. Woman like her, she'd have to be the star in all of her productions.

They had a jukebox, of course. Loud one. Be nice if I recalled what was playing when she crossed the threshold, but I wasn't paying attention—to the music, or to who came through the door. I had a beer in front of me, surprise surprise, and I was looking into it like any minute now it would tell me a secret.

Yeah, right. All any beer ever said to me was *Drink me down, horse. I might make things better and I sure can't make 'em worse.*

It was a country jukebox, which you could have guessed from the parking lot, where the pickups outnumbered the Harleys by four or five to one. So if I can't say what was playing when she came in, or even when I looked up from my PBR and got a look at her, I can tell you what wasn't playing. "I Only Have Eyes for You."

That wasn't coming out of that jukebox. But it should have been.

She was the beauty. Her face was all high cheekbones and sharp angles, and a girl who was just plain pretty would get all washed out standing next to her. She wasn't pretty herself, and a quick first glance might lead you to think that she wasn't attractive at all, but you'd look again and that first thought would get so far lost you'd forget you ever had it. There are fashion models with that kind of face. Film actresses, too, and they're the ones who keep on getting the good parts in their forties and fifties, when the pretty girls start looking like soccer moms and nosy neighbors.

And she only had eyes for me. Large, well-spaced eyes, a rich brown in color, and I swear I felt them on me before I was otherwise aware of her presence. Looked up, caught her looking at me, and she saw me looking and didn't look away.

I suppose I was lost right there.

She was a blonde, with her hair cut to frame and flatter her face. She was tall, say five-ten, five-eleven. Slender but curvy. Her blouse was silk, with a bold geometric print. It was buttoned too high to show a lot of cleavage, but when she moved it would cling to her and let you know what it wasn't showing.

The way her jeans fit, well, you all at once understood why people paid big money for designer jeans.

The joint wasn't crowded, it was early, but there were people between her and me. She flowed through them and they melted away. The bartender, a hard-faced old girl with snake tattoos, came over to take a drink order.

The blonde had to think it over. "I don't know," she said to me. "What should I have?"

"Whatever you want."

She put her hand on my arm. I was wearing a long-sleeved shirt, so her skin and mine never touched, but they might as well.

"Pick a drink for me," she said.

I was looking down at her hand, resting there on my forearm. Her fingernails were medium-long, their polish the bright color of arterial bleeding.

Pick a drink for her? The ones that came quickest to mind were too fancy for the surroundings. Be insulting to order her a shot and a beer. Had to be a cocktail, but one that the snake lady would know how to make.

I said, "Lady'll have a Cuervo margarita." Her hand was on my right arm, so rather than move it I used my left hand to poke the change I'd left on the bar top, indicating that the margarita was on me.

"And the same for you? Or another Blue Ribbon?"

I shook my head. "But you could give me a Joey C. twice to keep it company."

"Thank you," my blonde said, while the bartender went to work. "That's a perfect choice, a margarita."

The drinks came, hers in a glass with a salted rim, my double Cuervo in an oversize shot glass. She let go of my arm and picked up her drink, raised the glass in a wordless toast. I left my Cuervo where it was and returned the toast with my beer.

She didn't throw her drink back like a sailor, but didn't take a little baby-bird sip, either. She drank some and put the glass on the bar and her hand on my arm.

Nice.

No wedding ring. I'd noticed that right away, and hadn't needed a second glance to see that there'd been a ring on that finger, that it had come off recently enough to show not only the untanned band where the ring had been but the depression it had caused in the flesh. It said a lot, that finger. That she was married, and that she'd deliberately taken off her ring before entering the bar.

Hey, didn't I say? I know how to pick 'em.

But didn't I also say she picked me?

And picked that low-down roadhouse for the same reason. If my type was what she was looking for, that was the place to find it.

My type: well, big. Built like a middle linebacker, or maybe a tight end. Six-five, 230, big in the shoulders, narrow in the waist. More muscles than a man needs, unless he's planning to lift a car out of a rut.

Which I don't make a habit of. Not that good at lifting my poor self out of a rut, let alone an automobile.

Clean-shaven, when I shave; I was a day away from a razor when she came in and put her hand on my arm. But no beard, no mustache. Hair's dark and straight, and I haven't lost any of it yet. But I haven't hit forty yet, either, so who's to say I'll get to keep it?

My type: a big outdoorsy galoot, more brawn than brains, more street smarts than book smarts. Someone who probably won't notice you were wearing a wedding ring until a few minutes ago.

Or, if he does, won't likely care.

———

"Like to dance, little lady?"

I'd spotted him earlier out of the corner of my eye, a cowboy type, my height or an inch or two more, but packing less weight. Long and lean, built to play wide receiver to my tight end.

And no, I never played football myself. Only watch it when a TV's showing it in a room I'm in. Never cared about sports, even as a boy. Had the size, had the quickness, and I got tired of hearing I should go out for this team, go out for that one.

It was a game. Why waste my time on a game?

And here was this wide receiver, hitting on a woman who'd declared herself to be mine. She tightened her grip on my arm, and I guessed she was liking the way this was shaping up. Two studs taking it to the lot out back, squaring off, then doing their best to kill each other. And she'd stand there watching, the blood singing in her veins, until it was settled and she went home with the winner.

No question he was ready to play. He'd sized me up half an hour ago, before she was in the picture. There's a type of guy who'll do that: check out a room, work out who he might wind up fighting and how he'd handle it. Could be I'd done some of that myself, getting the measure of him, guessing what moves he'd make, guessing what would work against him.

Or I could walk away from it. Turn my back on both of 'em, head out of the bar, take my act on down the road. Not that hard to find a place that'd sell you a shot of Cuervo and a beer to back it up.

Except, you know, I never do walk away from things. Just knowing I could don't mean I can.

"Oh, that's very kind of you," she said. "But we were just leaving. Perhaps another time."

Getting to her feet as she said it, using just the right tone of voice, so as to leave no doubt that she meant it. Not cold, not putting him down, but nowhere near warm enough to encourage the son of a bitch.

Handled it just right, really.

I left my beer where it was, left my change there to keep it company. She took hold of my arm on the way out. There were some eyes on us as we left, but I guess we were both used to that.

When we hit the parking lot I was still planning the fight. It wasn't going to happen, but my mind was working it out just the same.

Funny how you'll do that.

You want to win that kind of a fight; what you want to do is get the first punch in. Before he sees it coming. First you bomb Pearl Harbor, then you declare war.

Let him think you're backing out of it, even. *Hey, I don't want to fight you!* And when he's afraid you're gonna chicken out, you give him your best shot. Time it right, take him by surprise, and one punch is all you need.

Wouldn't have done that with old Lash LaRue, though. Oh, not because it wouldn't have done the job. Would have worked just fine, put him facedown on the gravel, Wranglers and snap-fastened dude shirt and silly pompadour and all.

But that'd cheat her out of the fight she was hoping to see.

So what I'd have done, once we're outside and good to go, was spread my hands in a can't-we-work-this-out gesture, leaving it for him to sucker punch me. But I'd be ready, even though I wouldn't look ready, and I'd duck when he swung. They're always headhunters, dudes like him, and I'd be ducking almost before he was swinging, and I'd bury a fist midway between his navel and his nuts.

I'd do the whole deal with body shots. Why hurt your hands bouncing 'em off jawbone? Tall as he was, there was a whole lot of middle to him, and that's where I'd hammer him, and the first shot would take the fight out of him, and the starch out of his punches, if he even got to throw a second one.

I'd be aiming lefts at his liver. That's on the right, pretty much on the beltline. It's a legal punch in a boxing ring, never mind a parking lot, and if you find the spot it's a one-punch finisher. I haven't done it, or seen it done, but I believe it would be possible to kill a man with a liver shot.

But I was running the script for a fight that wasn't gonna happen, because my blonde had already written her own script and it turned out there wasn't a fight scene in it. Sort of a pity, in a way, because there'd have been a certain satisfaction in taking that cowboy apart, but his liver would live to fight another day. Any damage it sustained would be from the shots and beers he threw at it, not from any fists of mine.

And, you know, that would have been too easy, if all she was after was getting two roughnecks to duke it out over her. She had something a lot worse in mind.

"I hope I wasn't out of line," she said. "Getting us out of there. But I was afraid."

She hadn't seemed afraid.

"That you'd hurt him," she explained. "Kill him, even."

Her car was a Ford, the model the rental outfits were apt to give you. It was tucked between a pair of pickups, both of them showing dinged fenders and a lot of rust. She pressed a button to unlock the doors and the headlights winked.

I played the gentleman, tagging along at her side, reaching to open the driver's-side door for her. She hesitated, turned toward me, and it would have been a hard cue to miss.

I took hold of her and kissed her.

And yes, it was there, the chemistry, the biology, whatever you want to call it. She kissed back, and started to push her hips forward, then stopped herself, then couldn't stop herself. I felt the warmth of her through her jeans and mine, and I thought of doing her right there, just throwing her down and doing her on the gravel, with the two pickups screening us from view. Throw her a fast hard one, pull out and stand up while she's still quivering, and be out of there before she can get her game up and running.

Good-bye, little lady, because we just did what we came here to do, so whatever you've got to say, well, why do I have to listen to it?

I let go of her. She slipped behind the wheel, and I walked around the car and got in next to her. She started the engine but paused before putting the Ford in gear.

She said, "My name's Claudia."

Maybe it was and maybe it wasn't.

"Gary," I said.

"I don't live around here."

Neither did I. Don't live anywhere, really. Or, looking at it from another way, I live everywhere.

"My motel is just up the road. Maybe half a mile."

She waited for me to say something. What? *Are the sheets clean? Do they get HBO?*

I didn't say anything.

"Should we pick up something to drink? Because I don't have anything in the room."

I said I was fine. She nodded, waited for a break in the traffic, pulled onto the road.

I paid attention to the passing scenery, so I'd be able to come back for my car. A quarter mile down the road she took her right hand off the wheel and put it on my crotch. Her eyes never left the road. Another quarter mile and her hand returned to the wheel.

Had to wonder what was the point of that. Making sure I had something for her? Keeping me from forgetting why we were going to the motel?

Maybe just trying to show me she was every inch a lady.

I suppose I just keep on getting what I keep on looking for.

Because, face it, you don't go prospecting for Susie Homemaker in a low-down joint with a lot full of pickups and hogs. Walk into a room where you hear Kitty Wells singing how it wasn't God who made honky-tonk angels, well, what are you gonna find but a honky-tonk angel yourself?

You want a one-man woman, you want someone who'll keep house and buy into the whole white-picket-fence trip, there's other places you can go hunting.

And I wasn't showing up at Methodist socials, or meetings of Parents Without Partners, or taking poetry workshops at a continuing education program. I was—another song—looking for love in all the wrong places, so why blame fate for sending me a woman like Claudia?

Or whatever her name was.

The motel was a one-story non-chain number, presentable enough, but not where a woman like her would stay if all she wanted was a place to sleep. She'd pick a Ramada or a Hampton Inn, but what we had here was your basic no-tell motel. Clean enough, and reasonably well maintained, and set back from the road for privacy. Her unit was around the back, where the little Ford couldn't be seen from the road. If it wasn't a rental, if it was her own car, well, no one driving by could spot the plate.

Like it mattered.

Inside, with the door shut and the lock set, she turned to me and for the first time looked the least bit uncertain. Like she was trying to think what to say, or waiting for me to say something.

Well, the hell with that. She'd already groped my crotch in the car, and that ought to be enough to break the ice. I reached for her and kissed her, and I got one hand on her ass and drew her in close.

I could have peeled those jeans off of her, could have ripped that fine silk blouse. I had the impulse.

More, I wanted to do some damage. Soften her up with a fist in her belly, see what a liver shot would do to her.

Fact: I have thoughts like that. They'll come to me, and when they do I always get a quick flash of my mother's face. Just the quickest flash, like the flash of green you'll sometimes get when you watch the sun go down over water. It's gone almost before it registers, and afterward you can't quite swear that you really saw it.

Like that.

I was gentle with her. Well, gentle enough. She didn't pick me out of the crowd because she wanted tender words and butterfly kisses. I gave her what I sensed she wanted, but I didn't take her any further than she wanted to go. It wasn't hard to find her rhythm, wasn't hard to build her up and hold her back and then let it all happen for her, staying with her all the way, coaxing the last little quiver out of the sweet machinery of her body.

Nothing to it, really. I'd been taught young. I knew what to do and how to do it.

"I knew it would be good."

I was lying there, eyes closed. I don't know what I'd been thinking about. Sometimes my mind just wanders, goes off by itself somewhere and thinks its own thoughts, and then a car backfires or something changes the energy in the room, and I'm back where I was, and whatever I was thinking about is gone without a trace.

Must be like that for everybody, I suppose. Can't be that I'm that special, me and my private thoughts.

This time it was her voice, bringing the present back as sure as a thunderclap. I rolled over and saw she was half sitting in the bed beside me.

She'd taken the pillow from under her ass and had it supporting her head and shoulders.

She had the air of a woman smoking a cigarette, but she wasn't a smoker and there weren't any cigarettes around. But it was like that, the cigarette afterward, whether or not there was a cigarette in the picture.

"All I wanted," she said, "was to come in here and close a door and shut the world out, and then make everything in the world go away."

"Did it work?"

"Like magic," she said. "You didn't come."

"No."

"Was there something—"

"Sometimes I hold back."

"Oh."

"It makes the second time better. More intense."

"I can see how it would. But doesn't it take remarkable control?"

I hadn't been trying to hold back. I'd been trying to throw her a fuck she wouldn't quickly forget, that's all. But I didn't need to tell her all that.

"We'll be able to have a second time, won't we? You don't have to leave?"

"I'll be here all night," she said. "We can even have breakfast in the morning, if you'd like."

"I thought you might have to get home to your husband."

Her hands moved, and the fingers of her right hand fastened on the base of her ring finger, assuring themselves there was no ring there.

"Not the ring," I said. "The mark of the ring. A depression in the skin, because you must have taken it off just before you came into the road-house. And the thin white line, showing where the sun don't shine."

"Sherlock Holmes," she said.

She paused so that I could say something, but why help her out? I waited, and she said, "You're not married."

"No."

"Have you ever been?"

"Same answer."

She held her hand up, palm out, as if to examine her ring. I guess she was studying the mark where it had been.

She said, "I thought I'd get married right after high school. Where I grew up, if you were pretty, that's what happened. Or if you weren't pretty, but if somebody got you pregnant anyway."

"You were pretty."

She nodded. Why pretend she didn't know it? "But I wasn't pregnant, and this girlfriend got this idea, let's get out of this town, let's go to Chicago and see what happens. So just like that I packed a bag and we went, and it took her three weeks to get homesick and go right back."

"But not you."

"No, I liked Chicago. Or I thought I did. What I liked was the person I got to be in Chicago, not because it was Chicago but because it wasn't home."

"So you stayed."

"Until I went someplace else. Another city. And I had jobs, and I had boyfriends, and I spent some time between boyfriends, and it was all fine. And I thought, well, some women have husbands and children, and some don't, and it looks like I'll be one of the ones who don't."

I let her talk but didn't listen too closely. She met this man, he wanted to marry her, she thought it was her last chance, she knew it was a mistake, she went ahead and did it anyway. It was her story, but hardly hers alone. I'd heard it often enough before.

Sometimes I suppose it was true. Maybe it was true this time, far as that goes.

Maybe not.

When I got tired of hearing her I put a hand on her belly and stroked her. Her sudden intake of breath showed she wasn't expecting it. I ran my hand down, and her legs parted in anticipation, and I put my hand on her and fingered her. Just that, just lay beside her and worked her with my fingers. She'd closed her eyes, and I watched her face while my fingers did what they did.

"Oh! Oh! *Oh!*"

I got hard doing this, but didn't feel the need to do anything about it. After she came I just lay where I was. I closed my eyes and got soft again and lay there listening to all the silence in the room.

My father moved away when I was still in diapers. At least, that was what I was told. I don't remember him, and I'm not convinced he was there. Somebody got her pregnant, it wasn't the Holy Ghost, but did he ever know it? Did she even know his last name?

So I was raised by a single mother, though I don't recall hearing the term back then. Early on she brought men home, and then she stopped doing that. She might come home smelling of where she'd been and what she'd been doing, but she'd come home alone.

Then she stopped that, too, and spent her evenings in front of the TV.

One night we were watching some program, I forget what, and she said, "You're old enough now. I suppose you touch yourself."

I knew what she meant. What I didn't know was how to respond.

She said, "Don't be ashamed. Everybody does it, it's part of growing up. Let me see it." And, when confusion paralyzed me, "Take off your pajama bottoms and show me your dick."

I didn't want to. I did want to. I was embarrassed, I was excited, I was . . .

"It's getting bigger," she said. "You'll be a man soon. Show me how you touch yourself. Look how it grows! This is better than television. What do you think about when you touch it?"

Did I say anything? I don't believe I did.

"Titties?" She opened her robe. "You sucked on them when you were a baby. Do you remember?"

Wanting to look away. Wanting to stop touching myself.

"I'll tell you a secret. Touching your dick is nice, but it's nicer when someone else touches it for you. See? You can touch my titties while I do this for you. Doesn't that feel good? Doesn't it?"

I shot all over her hand. Thought she'd be angry. She put her hand to her face, licked it clean. Smiled at me.

"I don't know," she said.

Claudia, my blonde. I'd wondered, without much caring, just how natural that blondness might be. Still an open question, because the hair on her head was the only hair she had.

Had to wonder what my mother would have made of that. Shaving her legs was her concession to femininity, and one she accepted grudgingly.

Got so she'd have me do it. Come out of the bath, all warm from the tub, and I'd spread lather and wield the safety razor. I'd be growing whiskers in a couple of years, she told me. Might as well get in some practice for a lifetime of shaving.

I asked Claudia what she didn't know.

"I just wanted an adventure," she said.

"Shut the world out. Keep it on the other side of that door."

"But you've got a power," she said. "The same thing that drew me to you, pulled me right across the room to where you were standing—it scares me."

"Why's that?"

She closed her eyes, chose her words carefully. "What happens here stays here. Isn't that how it works?"

"Like Las Vegas?"

She opened her eyes, looked into mine. "I've done this sort of thing before," she said.

"I'm shocked."

"Not as often as you might think, but now and then."

"When the moon's full?"

"And left it behind me when I drove away. Like a massage, like a spa treatment."

"Then home to hubby."

"How was it hurting him? He never knew. And I was a better wife to him for having an outlet."

Taking her time getting to it. It was like watching a baseball pitcher going through an elaborate windup. Kind of interesting when you already knew what kind of curveball to expect.

"But this feels like more than that, doesn't it?"

She gave me a long look, like she wanted to say yes but was reluctant to speak the words.

Oh, she was good.

"You've thought of leaving him."

"Of course. But I have . . . oh, how to say this? He gives me a very comfortable life."

"That generally means money."

"His parents were wealthy," she said, "and he was an only child, and they're gone, and it's all come to him."

"I guess the Ford's a rental."

"The Ford? Oh, the car I'm driving. Yes, I picked it up at the airport. Why would you—oh, because I probably have a nicer car than that. Is that what you meant?"

"Something like that."

"We have several cars. There's a Lexus that I usually drive, and he bought me a vintage sports car as a present. An Aston Martin."

"Very nice."

"I suppose. I enjoyed driving it at first: the power, the responsiveness. Now I rarely take it out of the garage. It's an expensive toy. As am I."

"His toy. Does he take you out and play with you much?"

She didn't say anything.

I put my hand where she didn't have any hair. Not stroking her, just resting it there. Staking a claim.

I said, "If you divorced him—"

"I signed one of those things."

"A prenup."

"Yes."

"You'd probably get to keep the toys."

"Maybe."

"But the lush life would be over."

A nod.

"I suppose he's a lot older than you."

"Just a few years. He seems older, he's one of those men who act older than their years, but he's not that old."

"How's his health?"

"It's good. He doesn't exercise, he's substantially overweight, but he gets excellent reports at his annual physical."

"Still, anybody can stroke out or have a heart attack. Or a drunk driver runs a red light, hits him broadside."

"I don't even like to talk about something like that."

"Because it's almost like wishing for it."

"Yes."

"Still," I said, "it'd be convenient, wouldn't it?"

It wasn't like that with my mother. A stroke, a heart attack, a drunk driver. There one day and gone the next.

Not like that at all.

Two, three years after she showed me how much nicer it was to have someone else touch me. Two, three years when I went to school in the morning and came straight home in the afternoon and closed the door on the whole world.

She showed me all the things she knew. Plus things she'd heard or read about but never done.

And told me how to be with girls. "Like it's a sport and I'm your coach," she said. What to say, how to act, and how to get them to do things, or let me do things.

Then I'd come home and tell her about it. In bed, acting it out, fooling around.

Two, three years. And she started losing weight, and lost color in her face, and I must have noticed but it was day by day, and I was never conscious of it. And then I came home one day and she wasn't there, but there was a note, she'd be home soon. And an hour later she came in and I saw something in her face and I knew, but I didn't know what until she told me.

Ovarian cancer, and it had spread all through her, and they couldn't do anything. Nothing that would work.

Because of where it started, she wondered if it was punishment. For what we did.

"Except that's crap and I know it's crap. I was brought up believing in God, but I grew out of it, and I never raised you that way. And even if there was a God, he wouldn't work it that way. And what's wrong with what we did? Did it hurt anybody?"

And a little later, "All they can give me is chemo and all it'll do is hurt like fury and make my hair fall out and maybe stretch my life a few months longer. My sweet baby boy, I don't want you remembering a jaundiced old lady dying by inches and going crazy with the pain. I don't want to hang around that long, and you have to help me get out."

School. I didn't play sports, I didn't join clubs, I didn't have friends. But I knew who sold drugs; everybody knew that much. Anything you wanted, and what I wanted was downs, and that was easy.

She wanted to take them when I left for school, so that I'd be gone when it happened, but I talked her out of that. She took them at night, and I lay beside her and held her hand while sleep took her. And I stayed there, so I could tell when her breathing stopped, but I couldn't stay awake, I fell asleep myself, and when I woke up around dawn she was gone.

I straightened the house, went into my room and made the bed look as though it had been slept in. Went to school and kept myself from thinking about anything. Went home and, turning my key in the lock I had this flash, expecting her to be walking around when I opened the door.

Yeah, right. I found her where I'd left her, and I called the doctor, said I'd left in the morning without wanting to disturb her. He could tell it was pills, I could tell he could tell, but he wanted to spare me, said it was her heart giving out suddenly, said it happened a lot in cases like hers.

If she was alive, if she'd never gotten sick, I'd still be living there. With the two of us in that house, and the whole rest of the world locked out of it.

She said, "I can't pretend I never thought about it. But I never wished for it. He's not a bad man. He's been good to me."

"Takes good care of you."

"He cleans his golf clubs after he plays a round. Has this piece of flannel he uses to wipe the faces of the irons. Takes the cars in for their scheduled maintenance. And yes, he takes good care of me."

"Maybe that's all you want."

"I was willing to settle for it," she said.

"And now you're not?"

"I don't know," she said, and put her hand on me. For just a moment it was another hand, a firm but gentle hand, and I was a boy again. Just for an instant, and then that passed.

And she went on holding me, and she didn't say anything, but I could hear her voice in my head as clearly as if she'd spoken. *Willing to settle? Not anymore, my darling, because I've met you, and my world has changed forever. If only something could happen to him and we could be together forever. If only—*

"You want me to kill him," I said.

"Oh my God!"

"Isn't that where you were headed?"

She didn't answer, breathed deeply in and out, in and out. Then she said, "Have you ever—"

"Government puts you in a uniform, gives you a rifle, sends you halfway around the world. Man winds up doing a whole lot of things he might never do otherwise."

All of which was true, I suppose, but it had nothing much to do with me. I was never in the service.

Went to sign up once. You drift around, different things start looking good to you. Army shrink asked me a batch of questions, heard something he didn't like in my answers, and they thanked me for my time and sent me on my way.

Have to say that man was good at his job. I wouldn't have liked it there, and they wouldn't have liked me much, either.

She found something else to talk about, some rambling story about some neighbor of hers. I lay there and watched her lips move without taking in what she was saying.

Why bother? What she wasn't saying was more to the point.

Pleased with herself, I had to figure. Because she'd managed to get where she wanted to go without saying the words herself. Played it so neatly that I brought it up for her.

Like, I'm two steps ahead of you, missy. Knew where you were going, saw what a roundabout route you had mapped out for yourself, figured I'd save us some time.

Better now, looking without listening. And it was like I couldn't hear her if I wanted to, all I could hear was her voice speaking in my head, telling me what I knew she was thinking. How we could be together for the rest of our lives, how I was all she wanted and all she needed, how we'd have a life of luxury and glamour and travel. Her voice in my head, drawing pictures of her idea of my idea of paradise.

Voices.

She moved, lay on her side. Stopped talking, and I stopped hearing that other voice, and she ran a hand the length of my body. And kissed my face and my neck, and worked her way south.

Yeah, right. To give me a hint of the crazy pleasures on offer once her husband was dead and buried. Because every man loves that, right?

Thing is, I don't. Not since another woman took the pills I'd bought her and didn't wake up.

One time, I had this date with a girl in my class. And she was coaching me.

You can get her to suck it. She'll still be a virgin, she can't get pregnant from it, and she'll be making you happy. Plus deep down she's plain dying to do it.

But what you want to do is help her out, tell her when she's doing something wrong. Like you'll be her *coach, you know?*

Then she was gone, and since then I don't like having anybody doing that to me.

That army shrink? I guess he knew his business.

Still, she got it hard.

It plays by its own rules, doesn't it? The blood flows there or it doesn't, and you can't make it happen or keep it from happening. Didn't mean I enjoyed it, didn't mean I wanted her to keep it up. More she did it, less I liked it.

Took hold of her head, moved her away.

"Is something wrong?"

"My turn," I said, and spread her out on the bed, and tucked a pillow under her ass, and stuck a finger in to make sure she was wet. Stuck the finger in her mouth, gave her a taste of herself.

Got on her, rode her long and hard, long and hard. She had one of those rolling orgasms that won't quit, on and on and on, the gift that keeps on giving.

I don't know where my mind was while this was going on. Off somewhere, tuned in to something else. Watching HBO while she was getting fucked on Showtime.

When she was done I just stayed where I was, on her and in her. Looked down at her face, jaw slack, eyes shut, and saw what I hadn't seen earlier.

That she looked like a pig. Just had a real piggish quality to her features. Never saw it before.

Funny.

Her eyes opened. And her mouth started running, telling me it had never been like this before.

"Did you—"

"Not yet."

"My God, you're still hard! Is there anything—"

"Not just yet," I said. "Something I'd like to know first. When you walked into the bar?"

"A lifetime ago," she said. And relaxed into what she thought was going to be a stroll down memory lane. How we met, how we fell in love without a word being spoken.

I said, "What I wondered. How did you know?"

"How did I—"

"How'd you know I was the one man in there who'd be willing to kill your husband for you?"

Eyes wide. Speechless.

"What did you see? What did you think you saw?"

And my hips started working, slowly, short strokes.

"Had it all worked out in your mind," I said. I moved my elbows so they were on her shoulders, pinning her to the bed, and my hands found her neck, circled it.

"So you'd be out of town, maybe pick up some other lucky guy to make sure you'd have an alibi. Get off good with him, because all the while you're thinking about how I'm doing it, killing your husband. Wondering exactly how I'm doing it: Am I using a gun, a knife, a club? And you think of me doing him with my bare hands and that's what really gets you off, isn't it? Isn't it?"

She was saying something, but I couldn't hear it. Couldn't have heard a thunderclap, couldn't have heard the world ending.

"Filling my head with happily ever after, but once he's gone you don't need me anymore, do you? Maybe you'd find another sucker, get him to take me off the board."

Thrusting harder now. And my hands tightening on her throat. The terror in her eyes, Jesus, you could taste it.

Then the light went out of her eyes, and just like that she was gone.

Three, four more strokes and I got where I was going. What's funny is I didn't really feel it. The machinery worked, and I emptied myself into her, but you couldn't call it sensational, because, see, there wasn't a whole lot of sensation involved. There was a release, and that felt good, the way a piss does when you've been walking around with a full bladder.

Fact is, it's like that more often than not. I'd say the army shrink could explain it, but let's not make him into a genius. All he knew was the army was better off without me.

Most anybody's better off without me.

Claudia, for sure. Lying there now with her throat crushed and her eyes glassy. Minute I laid eyes on her, I knew she had the whole script worked out in her mind.

How'd she know? How'd she pick me?

And if I knew all that, if I could read her script and figure out a different ending than the one she had in mind, why'd I buy her a drink? All's said and done, how much real choice did I have in the matter once she'd gone and laid her hand on my arm?

Time to leave this town now, but who was I kidding? I'd find the same thing in the next town, or the town after that. Another roadhouse, where I might have to fight a guy or might not, but either way I'd walk out with a woman. She might not look as fine as this one, and she might have more hair besides what she had on her head, but she'd have the same plans for me.

And if I stayed out of the bars? If I went to some church socials, or Parents Without Partners, or some such?

Might work, but I wouldn't count on it. My luck, I'd wind up in the same damn place.

Like I said, I really know how to pick 'em.

Brandon Sanderson

Another of the fastest-rising stars in the fantasy genre, along with writers such as Joe Abercrombie, Patrick Rothfuss, Scott Lynch, Lev Grossman, and K. J. Parker, *New York Times* bestseller Brandon Sanderson was chosen to finish Robert Jordan's famous Wheel of Time sequence, left uncompleted on Jordan's death, an immense task that Sanderson tackled with volumes such as *The Gathering Storm, Towers of Midnight,* and *A Memory of Light.* He is also well-known for another fantasy series, the Mistborn sequence, which consists of *The Final Empire, The Well of Ascension, The Hero of Ages,* and *The Alloy of Law,* as well as the young adult fantasy series Alcatraz, consisting of *Alcatraz Versus the Evil Librarians, Alcatraz Versus the Scrivener's Bones, Alcatraz Versus the Knights of Crystallia,* and *Alcatraz Versus the Shattered Lens.* His other books include the novels *Elantris, Warbreaker,* and *Firstborn,* and the start of the new Stormlight Archive series, *The Way of Kings.* He lives in American Fork, Utah, and maintains a website at brandonsanderson.com.

Here he takes us deep into the sinister silence of the Forests for the tale of a desperate and dangerous woman who will risk anything, *do* anything, to save her family, even in a place where hungry ghosts wait unseen behind every tree, and one false move means instant death. . . .

SHADOWS FOR SILENCE
IN THE FORESTS OF HELL

"The one you have to watch for is the White Fox," Daggon said, sipping his beer. "They say he shook hands with the Evil itself, that he visited the Fallen World and came back with strange powers. He can kindle fire on even the deepest of nights, and no shade will dare come for his soul. Yes, the White Fox. Meanest bastard in these parts for sure. Pray he doesn't set his eyes on you, friend. If he does, you're dead."

Daggon's drinking companion had a neck like a slender wine bottle and a head like a potato stuck sideways on the top. He squeaked as he spoke, a Lastport accent, voice echoing in the eaves of the waystop's common room. "Why . . . why would he set his eyes on me?"

"That depends, friend," Daggon said, looking about as a few overdressed merchants sauntered in. They wore black coats, ruffled lace poking out the front, and the tall-topped, wide-brimmed hats of fortfolk. They wouldn't last two weeks out here, in the Forests.

"It depends?" Daggon's dining companion prompted. "It depends on what?"

"On a lot of things, friend. The White Fox is a bounty hunter, you know. What crimes have you committed? What have you done?"

"Nothing." That squeak was like a rusty wheel.

"Nothing? Men don't come out into the Forests to do 'nothing,' friend."

His companion glanced from side to side. He'd given his name as Earnest. But then, Daggon had given his name as Amity. Names didn't mean a whole lot in the Forests. Or maybe they meant everything. The right ones, that was.

Earnest leaned back, scrunching down that fishing-pole neck of his as if trying to disappear into his beer. He'd bite. People liked hearing about the White Fox, and Daggon considered himself an expert. At least, he was an expert at telling stories to get ratty men like Earnest to pay for his drinks.

I'll give him some time to stew, Daggon thought, smiling to himself. *Let him worry.* Earnest would pry him for more information in a bit.

While he waited, Daggon leaned back, surveying the room. The merchants were making a nuisance of themselves, calling for food, saying they meant to be on their way in an hour. That *proved* them to be fools. Traveling at night in the Forests? Good homesteader stock would do it. Men like these, though . . . they'd probably take less than an hour to violate one of the Simple Rules and bring the shades upon them. Daggon put the idiots out of his mind.

That fellow in the corner, though . . . dressed all in brown, still wearing his hat despite being indoors. That fellow looked truly dangerous. *I wonder if it's him,* Daggon thought. So far as he knew, nobody had ever seen the White Fox and lived. Ten years, over a hundred bounties turned in. Surely someone knew his name. The authorities in the forts paid him the bounties, after all.

The waystop's owner, Madam Silence, passed by the table and deposited Daggon's meal with an unceremonious thump. Scowling, she topped off his beer, spilling a sudsy dribble onto his hand, before limping off. She was a stout woman. Tough. Everyone in the Forests was tough. The ones that survived, at least.

He'd learned that a scowl from Silence was just her way of saying hello. She'd given him an extra helping of venison; she often did that. He liked to think that she had a fondness for him. Maybe someday . . .

Don't be a fool, he thought to himself as he dug into the heavily gravied food. Better to marry a stone than Silence Montane. A stone showed more affection. Likely, she gave him the extra slice because she recognized the value of a repeat customer. Fewer and fewer people came this way lately. Too many shades. And then there was Chesterton. Nasty business, that.

"So . . . he's a bounty hunter, this Fox?" The man who called himself Earnest seemed to be sweating.

Daggon smiled. Hooked right good, this one was. "He's not just a bounty hunter. He's *the* bounty hunter. Though, the White Fox doesn't go for the small-timers—and no offense, friend, but you seem pretty small-time."

His friend grew more nervous. What *had* he done? "But," the man stammered, "he wouldn't come for me—er, pretending I'd done something, of course—anyway, he wouldn't come in here, would he? I mean, Madam Silence's waystop, it's protected. Everyone knows that. Shade of her dead husband lurks here. I had a cousin who saw it, I did."

"The White Fox doesn't fear shades," Daggon said, leaning in. "Now, mind you, I don't *think* he'd risk coming in here—but not because of some shade. Everyone knows this is neutral ground. You've got to have some safe places, even in the Forests. But . . ."

Daggon smiled at Silence as she passed him by, on the way to the kitchens again. This time she didn't scowl at him. He was getting through to her for certain.

"But?" Earnest squeaked.

"Well . . ." Daggon said. "I could tell you a few things about how the White Fox takes men, but you see, my beer is nearly empty. A shame. I think you'd be very interested in how the White Fox caught Makepeace Hapshire. Great story, that."

Earnest squeaked for Silence to bring another beer, though she bustled into the kitchen and didn't hear. Daggon frowned, but Earnest put a coin on the side of the table, indicating he'd like a refill when Silence or her daughter returned. That would do. Daggon smiled to himself and launched into the story.

Silence Montane closed the door to the common room, then turned and pressed her back against it. She tried to still her racing heart by breathing in and out. Had she made any obvious signs? Did they know she'd recognized them?

William Ann passed by, wiping her hands on a cloth. "Mother?" the young woman asked, pausing. "Mother, are you—"

"Fetch the book. Quickly, child!"

William Ann's face went pale, then she hurried into the back pantry. Silence clutched her apron to still her nerves, then joined William Ann as the girl came out of the pantry with a thick, leather satchel. White flour dusted its cover and spine from the hiding place.

Silence took the satchel and opened it on the high kitchen counter, revealing a collection of loose-leaf papers. Most had faces drawn on them. As Silence rifled through the pages, William Ann moved to look through the peephole back into the common room.

For a few moments, the only sound to accompany Silence's thumping heart was that of hastily turned pages.

"It's the man with the long neck, isn't it?" William Ann asked. "I remember his face from one of the bounties."

"That's just Lamentation Winebare, a petty horse thief. He's barely worth two measures of silver."

"Who, then? The man in the back, with the hat?"

Silence shook her head, finding a sequence of pages at the bottom of her pile. She inspected the drawings. *God Beyond,* she thought. *I can't decide if I want it to be them or not.* At least her hands had stopped shaking.

William Ann scurried back and craned her neck over Silence's shoulder. At fourteen, the girl was already taller than her mother. A fine thing to suffer, a child taller than you. Though William Ann grumbled about being awkward and lanky, her slender build foreshadowed a beauty to come. She took after her father.

"Oh, God *Beyond,*" William Ann said, raising a hand to her mouth. "You mean—"

"Chesterton Divide," Silence said. The shape of the chin, the look in the eyes . . . they were the same. "He walked right into our hands, with four of his men." The bounty on those five would be enough to pay her supply needs for a year. Maybe two.

Her eyes flickered to the words below the pictures, printed in harsh, bold letters. **Extremely dangerous. Wanted for murder, rape, extortion.** And, of course, there was the big one at the end: **And assassination.**

Silence had always wondered if Chesterton and his men had intended to kill the governor of the most powerful city on this continent, or if it had it been an accident. A simple robbery gone wrong. Either way, Chesterton understood what he'd done. Before the incident, he had been a common—if accomplished—highway bandit.

Now he was something greater, something far more dangerous. Chesterton knew that if he were captured, there would be no mercy, no quarter. Lastport had painted Chesterton as an anarchist, a menace, and a psychopath.

Chesterton had no reason to hold back. So he didn't.

Oh, God Beyond, Silence thought, looking at the continuing list of his crimes on the next page.

Beside her, William Ann whispered the words to herself. "He's out there?" she asked. "But where?"

"The merchants," Silence said.

"What?" William Ann rushed back to the peephole. The wood there—indeed, all around the kitchen—had been scrubbed so hard that it had been bleached white. Sebruki had been cleaning again.

"I can't see it," William Ann said.

"Look closer." Silence hadn't seen it at first either, even though she spent each night with the book, memorizing its faces.

A few moments later William Ann gasped, raising her hand to her mouth. "That seems so *foolish* of him. Why is he going about perfectly visible like this? Even in disguise."

"Everyone will remember just another band of fool merchants from the fort who thought they could brave the Forests. It's a clever disguise. When they vanish from the paths in a few days, it will be assumed—if anyone cares to wonder—that the shades got them. Besides, this way Chesterton can travel quickly and in the open, visiting waystops and listening for information."

Was this how Chesterton discovered good targets to hit? Had they come through her waystop before? The thought made her stomach turn. She had fed criminals many times; some were regulars. Every man was probably a criminal out in the Forests, if only for ignoring taxes imposed by the fortfolk.

Chesterton and his men were different. She didn't need the list of crimes to know what they were capable of doing.

"Where's Sebruki?" Silence said.

William Ann shook herself, as if coming out of a stupor. "She's feeding the pigs. Shadows! You don't think they'd recognize her, do you?"

"No," Silence said. "I'm worried she'll recognize them." Sebruki might only be eight, but she could be shockingly—disturbingly—observant.

Silence closed the book of bounties. She rested her fingers on its leather.

"We're going to kill them, aren't we?" William Ann asked.

"Yes."

"How much are they worth?"

"Sometimes, child, it's not about what a man is worth." Silence heard the faint lie in her voice. Times were increasingly tight, with the price of silver from both Bastion Hill and Lastport on the rise.

Sometimes it wasn't about what a man was worth. But this wasn't one of those times.

"I'll get the poison." William Ann left the peephole and crossed the room.

"Something light, child," Silence cautioned. "These are dangerous men. They'll notice if things are out of the ordinary."

"I'm not a fool, Mother," William Ann said dryly. "I'll use fenweed. They won't taste it in the beer."

"Half dose. I don't want them collapsing at the table."

William Ann nodded, entering the old storage room, where she closed the door and began prying up floorboards to get to the poisons. Fenweed would leave the men cloudy-headed and dizzy, but wouldn't kill them.

Silence didn't dare risk something more deadly. If suspicion ever came back to her waystop, her career—and likely her life—would end. She needed to remain, in the minds of travelers, the crotchety but fair innkeeper who didn't ask too many questions. Her waystop was a place of perceived safety, even for the roughest of criminals. She bedded down each night with a heart full of fear that someone would realize a suspicious number of the White Fox's bounties stayed at Silence's waystop in the days preceding their demise.

She went into the pantry to put away the bounty book. Here, too, the walls had been scrubbed clean, the shelves freshly sanded and dusted. That child. Who had heard of a child who would rather clean than play? Of course, given what Sebruki had been through . . .

Silence could not help reaching onto the top shelf and feeling the crossbow she kept there. Silver boltheads. She kept it for shades, and hadn't yet turned it against a man. Drawing blood was too dangerous in the Forests. It still comforted her to know that in a true emergency she had the weapon at hand.

Bounty book stowed, she went to check on Sebruki. The child was indeed caring for the pigs. Silence liked to keep a healthy stock, though of course not for eating. Pigs were said to ward away shades. She used any tool she could to make the waystop seem more safe.

Sebruki knelt inside the pig shack. The short girl had dark skin and long, black hair. Nobody would have taken her for Silence's daughter, even if they hadn't heard of Sebruki's unfortunate history. The child hummed to herself, scrubbing at the wall of the enclosure.

"Child?" Silence asked.

Sebruki turned to her and smiled. What a difference one year could make. Once, Silence would have sworn that this child would never smile again. Sebruki had spent her first three months at the waystop staring at walls. No matter where Silence had put her, the child had moved to the nearest wall, sat down, and stared at it all day. Never speaking a word. Eyes dead as those of a shade. . . .

"Aunt Silence?" Sebruki asked. "Are you well?"

"I'm fine, child. Just plagued by memories. You're . . . cleaning the *pig shack* now?"

"The walls need a good scrubbing," Sebruki said. "The pigs do so like it to be clean. Well, Jarom and Ezekiel prefer it that way. The others don't seem to care."

"You don't need to clean so hard, child."

"I like doing it," Sebruki said. "It feels good. It's something I can do. To help."

Well, it was better to clean the walls than stare blankly at them all day. Today, Silence was happy for anything that kept the child busy. Anything, so long as she didn't enter the common room.

"I think the pigs will like it," Silence said. "Why don't you keep at it in here for a while?"

Sebruki eyed her. "What's wrong?"

Shadows. She was so observant. "There are some men with rough tongues in the common room," Silence said. "I won't have you picking up their cussing."

"I'm not a child, Aunt Silence."

"Yes you are," Silence said firmly. "And you'll obey. Don't think I won't take a switch to your backside."

Sebruki rolled her eyes, but went back to work and began humming to herself. Silence let a little of her grandmother's ways out when she spoke with Sebruki. The child responded well to sternness. She seemed to crave it, perhaps as a symbol that someone was in control.

Silence wished she actually were in control. But she was a Forescout—the

surname taken by her grandparents and the others who had left Homeland first and explored this continent. Yes, she was a Forescout, and she'd
be damned before she'd let anyone know how absolutely powerless she felt
much of the time.

Silence crossed the backyard of the large inn, noting William Ann
inside the kitchen mixing a paste to dissolve in the beer. Silence passed
her by and looked in on the stable. Unsurprisingly, Chesterton had said
they'd be leaving after their meal. While a lot of folk sought the relative
safety of a waystop at night, Chesterton and his men would be accustomed to sleeping in the Forests. Even with the shades about, they would
feel more comfortable in a camp of their own devising than they would in
a waystop bed.

Inside the stable, Dob, the old stable hand, had just finished brushing
down the horses. He wouldn't have watered them. Silence had a standing
order to not do that until last.

"This is well done, Dob," Silence said. "Why don't you take your break
now?"

He nodded to her with a mumbled, "Thank'ya, mam." He'd find the
front porch and his pipe, as always. Dob hadn't two wits to rub together,
and he hadn't a clue about what she really did at the waystop, but he'd
been with her since before William's death. He was as loyal a man as she'd
ever found.

Silence shut the door after him, then fetched some pouches from the
locked cabinet at the back of the stable. She checked each one in the dim
light, then set them on the grooming table and heaved the first saddle back
onto its owner's back.

She was near finished with the saddling when the door eased open. She
froze, immediately thinking of the pouches on the table. Why hadn't she
stuffed them in her apron? Sloppy!

"Silence Forescout," a smooth voice said from the doorway.

Silence stifled a groan and turned to confront her visitor. "Theopolis,"
she said. "It's not polite to sneak about on a woman's property. I should have
you thrown out for trespassing."

"Now, now. That would be rather like . . . the horse kicking at the man
who feeds him, hmmm?" Theopolis leaned his gangly frame against the
doorway, folding his arms. He wore simple clothing, no markings of his
station. A fort tax collector often didn't want random passers to know of

his profession. Clean-shaven, his face always had that same patronizing smile on it. His clothing was too clean, too new to be that of one who lived out in the Forests. Not that he was a dandy, nor was he a fool. Theopolis was dangerous, just a different kind of dangerous from most.

"Why are you here, Theopolis?" she said, hefting the last saddle onto the back of a snorting roan gelding.

"Why do I always come to you, Silence? It's not because of your cheerful countenance, hmmm?"

"I'm paid up on taxes."

"That's because you're mostly exempt from taxes," Theopolis said. "But you haven't paid me for last month's shipment of silver."

"Things have been a little dry lately. It's coming."

"And the bolts for your crossbow?" Theopolis asked. "One wonders if you're trying to forget about the price of those silver boltheads, hmmm? And the shipment of replacement sections for your protection rings?"

His whining accent made her wince as she buckled the saddle on. Theopolis. Shadows, what a day!

"Oh my," Theopolis said, walking over to the grooming tale. He picked up one of the pouches. "What are these, now? That looks like wetleek sap. I've heard that it glows at night if you shine the right kind of light upon it. Is this one of the White Fox's mysterious secrets?"

She snatched the pouch away. "Don't say that name," she hissed.

He grinned. "You have a bounty! Delightful. I have always wondered how you tracked them. Poke a pinhole in that, attach it to the underside of the saddle, then follow the dripping trail it leaves? Hmmm? You could probably track them a long way, kill them far from here. Keep suspicion off the little waystop?"

Yes, Theopolis was dangerous, but she needed *someone* to turn in her bounties for her. Theopolis was a rat, and like all rats he knew the best holes, troughs, and crannies. He had connections in Lastport, and had managed to get her the money in the name of the White Fox without revealing her.

"I've been tempted to turn you in lately, you know," Theopolis said. "Many a group keeps a betting pool on the identity of the infamous Fox. I could be a rich man with this knowledge, hmmm?"

"You're already a rich man," she snapped. "And though you're many things, you are not an idiot. This has worked just fine for a decade. Don't tell me you'd trade wealth for a little notoriety?"

He smiled, but did not contradict her. He kept half of what she earned from each bounty. It was a fine arrangement for Theopolis. No danger to him, which was how she knew he liked it. He was a civil servant, not a bounty hunter. The only time she'd seen him kill, the man he'd murdered couldn't fight back.

"You know me too well, Silence," Theopolis said with a laugh. "Too well indeed. My, my. A bounty! I wonder who it is. I'll have to go look in the common room."

"You'll do nothing of the sort. Shadows! You think the face of a tax collector won't spook them? Don't you go walking in and spoiling things."

"Peace, Silence," he said, still grinning. "I obey your rules. I am careful not to show myself around here often, and I don't bring suspicion to you. I couldn't stay today anyway; I merely came to give you an offer. Only, now you probably won't need it! Ah, such a pity. After all the trouble I went to in your name, hmmm?"

She felt cold. "What help could you possibly give me?"

He took a sheet of paper from his satchel, then carefully unfolded it with too-long fingers. He moved to hold it up, but she snatched it from him.

"What is this?"

"A way to relieve you of your debt, Silence! A way to prevent you from ever having to worry again."

The paper was a writ of seizure, an authorization for Silence's creditors—Theopolis—to claim her property as payment. The forts claimed jurisdiction over the roadways and the land to either side of them. They did send soldiers out to patrol them. Occasionally.

"I take it back, Theopolis," she spat. "You most certainly *are* a fool. You'd give up everything we have for a greedy land snatch?"

"Of course not, Silence. This wouldn't be giving up anything at all! Why, I *do* so feel bad seeing you constantly in my debt. Wouldn't it be more efficient if I took over the finances of the waystop? You would remain working here, and hunting bounties, as you always have. Only, you would no longer have to worry about your debts, hmmm?"

She crumpled the paper in her hand. "You'd turn me and mine into slaves, Theopolis."

"Oh, don't be so dramatic. Those in Lastport have begun to worry that such an important waypoint as this is owned by an unknown element.

You are drawing attention, Silence. I should think that is the last thing you want."

Silence crumpled the paper further in her hand, fist tight. Horses shuffled in their stalls. Theopolis grinned.

"Well," he said. "Perhaps it won't be needed. Perhaps this bounty of yours is a big one, hmmm? Any clues to give me, so I don't sit wondering all day?"

"Get out," she whispered.

"Dear Silence," he said. "Forescout blood, stubborn to the last breath. They say your grandparents were the first of the first. The first people to come scout this continent, the first to homestead the Forests . . . first to stake a claim on hell itself."

"Don't call the Forests that. This is my home."

"But it is how men saw this land, before the Evil. Doesn't that make you curious? Hell, land of the damned, where the shadows of the dead made their home. I keep wondering: Is there really a shade of your departed husband guarding this place, or is it just another story you tell people? To make them feel safe, hmmm? You spend a fortune in silver. That offers the real protection, and I never *have* been able to find record of your marriage. Of course, if there wasn't one, that would make dear William Ann a—"

"*Go.*"

He grinned, but tipped his hat to her and stepped out. She heard him climb into the saddle, then ride off. Night would come before too long; it was probably too much to hope that the shades would take Theopolis. She'd long suspected that he had a hiding hole somewhere near, probably a cavern he kept lined with silver.

She breathed in and out, trying to calm herself. Theopolis was frustrating, but he didn't know everything. She forced her attention back to the horses and got out a bucket of water. She dumped the contents of the pouches into it, then gave a hearty dose to the horses, who each drank thirstily.

Pouches that dripped sap in the way Theopolis indicated would be too easy to spot. What would happen when her bounties removed their saddles at night and found the sap packets? They'd know someone was coming for them. No, she needed something less obvious.

"How am I going to manage this?" she whispered as a horse drank from her bucket. "Shadows. They're reaching for me on all sides."

Kill Theopolis. That was probably what Grandmother would have done. She considered it.

No, she thought. *I won't become that. I won't become her.* Theopolis was a thug and a scoundrel, but he had not broken any laws, nor had he done anyone direct harm that she knew. There had to be rules, even out here. There had to be lines. Perhaps, in that respect, she wasn't so different from the fortfolk.

She'd find another way. Theopolis only had a writ of debt; he had been required to show it to her. That meant she had a day or two to come up with his money. All neat and orderly. In the Fortress Towns, they claimed to have civilization. Those rules gave her a chance.

She left the stable. A glance through the window into the common room showed her William Ann delivering drinks to the "merchants" of Chesterton's gang. Silence stopped to watch.

Behind her, the Forests shivered in the wind.

Silence listened, then turned to face them. You could tell fortfolk by the way they refused to face the Forests. They averted their eyes, never looking into the depths. Those solemn trees covered almost every inch of this continent, those leaves shading the ground. Still. Silent. Animals lived out there, but fort surveyors declared that there were no predators. The shades had gotten those long ago, drawn by the shedding of blood.

Staring into the Forests seemed to make them . . . retreat. The darkness of their depths withdrew, the stillness give way to the sound of rodents picking through fallen leaves. A Forescout knew to look the Forests straight on. A Forescout knew that the surveyors were wrong. There *was* a predator out there. The Forest itself was one.

Silence turned and walked to the door into the kitchen. Keeping the waystop had to be her first goal, so she was committed to collecting Chesterton's bounty now. If she couldn't pay Theopolis, she had little faith that everything would stay the same. He'd have a hand around her throat, as she couldn't leave the waystop. She had no fort citizenship, and times were too tight for the local homesteaders to take her in. No, she'd *have* to stay and work the waystop for Theopolis, and he would squeeze her dry, taking larger and larger percentages of the bounties.

She pushed open the door to the kitchen. It—

Sebruki sat at the kitchen table holding the crossbow in her lap.

"God Beyond!" Silence gasped, pulling the door closed as she stepped inside. "Child, what are you—"

Sebruki looked up at her. Those haunted eyes were back, eyes void of life and emotion. Eyes like a shade.

"We have visitors, Aunt Silence," Sebruki said in a cold, monotone voice. The crossbow's winding crank sat next to her. She had managed to load the thing and cock it, all on her own. "I coated the bolt's tip with black blood. I did that right, didn't I? That way, the poison will kill him for sure."

"Child . . ." Silence stepped forward.

Sebruki turned the crossbow in her lap, holding it at an angle to support it, one small hand holding the trigger. The point turned toward Silence.

Sebruki stared ahead, eyes blank.

"This won't work, Sebruki," Silence said, stern. "Even if you were able to lift that thing into the common room, you wouldn't hit him—and even if you did, his men would kill us all in retribution!"

"I wouldn't mind," Sebruki said softly. "So long as I got to kill him. So long as I pulled the trigger."

"You care nothing for us?" Silence snapped. "I take you in, give you a home, and this is your payment? You steal a weapon? You *threaten* me?"

Sebruki blinked.

"What is wrong with you?" Silence said. "You'd shed blood in this place of sanctuary? Bring the shades down upon us, beating at our protections? If they got through, they'd kill everyone under my roof! People I've promised safety. How *dare* you!"

Sebruki shook, as if coming awake. Her mask broke and she dropped the crossbow. Silence heard a snap, and the catch released. She felt the bolt pass within an inch of her cheek, then break the window behind.

Shadows! Had the bolt grazed Silence? Had Sebruki *drawn blood*? Silence reached up with a shaking hand, but blessedly felt no blood. The bolt hadn't hit her.

A moment later Sebruki was in her arms, sobbing. Silence knelt down, holding the child close. "Hush, dear one. It's all right. It's all right."

"I heard it all," Sebruki whispered. "Mother never cried out. She knew I was there. She was strong, Aunt Silence. That was why I could be strong, even when the blood came down. Soaking my hair. I heard it. *I heard it all.*"

Silence closed her eyes, holding Sebruki tight. She herself had been the only one willing to investigate the smoking homestead. Sebruki's father had stayed at the waystop on occasion. A good man. As good a man as was left after the Evil took Homeland, that was.

In the smoldering remains of the homestead, Silence had found the corpses of a dozen people. Each family member had been slaughtered by Chesterton and his men, right down to the children. The only one left had been Sebruki, the youngest, who had been shoved into the crawl space under the floorboards in the bedroom.

She'd lain there, soaked in her mother's blood, soundless even as Silence found her. She'd only found the girl because Chesterton had been careful, lining the room with silver dust to protect against shades as he prepared to kill. Silence had tried to recover some of the dust that had trickled between the floorboards, and had run across eyes staring up at her through the slits.

Chesterton had burned thirteen different homesteads over the last year. Over fifty people murdered. Sebruki was the only one who had escaped him.

The girl trembled as she heaved with sobs. "Why . . . Why?"

"There is no reason. I'm sorry." What else could she do? Offer some foolish platitude or comfort about the God Beyond? These were the Forests. You didn't survive on platitudes.

Silence did hold the girl until her crying began to subside. William Ann entered, then stilled beside the kitchen table, holding a tray of empty mugs. Her eyes flickered toward the fallen crossbow, then at the broken window.

"You'll kill him?" Sebruki whispered. "You'll bring him to justice?"

"Justice died in Homeland," Silence said. "But yes, I'll kill him. I promise it to you, child."

Stepping timidly, William Ann picked up the crossbow, then turned it, displaying its now broken bow. Silence breathed out. She should never have left the thing where Sebruki could get to it.

"Care for the patrons, William Ann," Silence said. "I'll take Sebruki upstairs."

William Ann nodded, glancing at the broken window.

"No blood was shed," Silence said. "We will be fine. Though if you get a moment, see if you can find the bolt. The head is silver. . . ." This was hardly a time when they could afford to waste money.

William Ann stowed the crossbow in the pantry as Silence carefully set Sebruki on a kitchen stool. The girl clung to her, refusing to let go, so Silence relented and held her for a time longer.

William Ann took a few deep breaths, as if to calm herself, then pushed back out into the common room to distribute drinks.

Eventually, Sebruki let go long enough for Silence to mix a draught. She carried the girl up the stairs to the loft above the common room, where the three of them made their beds. Dob slept in the stable and the guests in the nicer rooms on the second floor.

"You're going to make me sleep," Sebruki said, regarding the cup with reddened eyes.

"The world will seem a brighter place in the morning," Silence said. *And I can't risk you sneaking out after me tonight.*

The girl reluctantly took the draught, then drank it down. "I'm sorry. About the crossbow."

"We will find a way for you to work off the cost of fixing it."

That seemed to comfort Sebruki. She was a homesteader, Forests born. "You used to sing to me at night," Sebruki said softly, closing her eyes, laying back. "When you first brought me here. After . . . after . . ." She swallowed.

"I wasn't certain you noticed." Silence hadn't been certain Sebruki noticed anything, during those times.

"I did."

Silence sat down on the stool beside Sebruki's cot. She didn't feel like singing, so she began humming. It was the lullaby she'd sung to William Ann during the hard times right after her birth.

Before long, the words came out, unbidden:

"Hush now, my dear one . . . be not afraid. Night comes upon us, but sunlight will break. Sleep now, my dear one . . . let your tears fade. Darkness surrounds us, but someday we'll wake. . . ."

She held Sebruki's hand until the child fell asleep. The window by the bed overlooked the courtyard, so Silence could see as Dob brought out Chesterton's horses. The five men in their fancy merchant clothing stomped down off the porch and climbed into their saddles.

They rode in a file out onto the roadway; then the Forests enveloped them.

One hour after nightfall, Silence packed her rucksack by the light of the hearth.

Her grandmother had kindled that hearth's flame, and it had been burning ever since. She'd nearly lost her life lighting the fire, but she hadn't been willing to pay any of the fire merchants for a start. Silence shook her head. Grandmother always had bucked convention. But then, was Silence any better?

Don't kindle flame, don't shed the blood of another, don't run at night. These things draw shades. The Simple Rules, by which every homesteader lived. She'd broken all three on more than on occasion. It was a wonder she hadn't been withered away into a shade by now.

The fire's warmth seemed a distant thing as she prepared to kill. Silence glanced at the old shrine, really just a closet, she kept locked. The flames reminded her of her grandmother. At times, she thought of the fire *as* her grandmother. Defiant of both the shades and the forts, right until the end. She'd purged the waystop of other reminders of Grandmother, all save the shrine to the God Beyond. That was set behind a locked door beside the pantry, and next to the door had once hung her grandmother's silver dagger, symbol of the old religion.

That dagger was etched with the symbols of divinity as a warding. Silence carried it, not for its wardings, but because it was silver. One could never have too much silver in the Forests.

She packed the sack carefully, first putting in her medicine kit and then a good-sized pouch of silver dust to heal withering. She followed that with ten empty sacks of thick burlap, tarred on the inside to prevent their contents from leaking. Finally, she added an oil lamp. She wouldn't want to use it, as she didn't trust fire. Fire could draw shades. However, she'd found it useful to have on prior outings, so she brought it. She'd only light it if she ran across someone who already had a fire started.

Once done, she hesitated, then went to the old storage room. She removed the floorboards and took out the small, dry-packed keg that lay beside the poisons.

Gunpowder.

"Mother?" William Ann asked, causing her to jump. She hadn't heard the girl enter the kitchen.

Silence nearly dropped the keg in her startlement, and that nearly stopped her heart. She cursed herself for a fool, tucking the keg under her arm. It couldn't explode without fire. She knew that much.

"Mother!" William Ann said, looking at the keg.

"I probably won't need it."

"But—"

"I know. Hush." She walked over and placed the keg into her sack. Attached to the side of the keg, with cloth stuffed between the metal arms, was her grandmother's firestarter. Igniting gunpowder counted as kindling flames, at least in the eyes of the shades. It drew them almost as quickly as blood did, day or night. The early refugees from Homeland had discovered that in short order.

In some ways, blood was easier to avoid. A simple nosebleed or issue of blood wouldn't draw the shades; they wouldn't even notice. It had to be the blood of another, shed by your hands—and they would go for the one who shed the blood first. Of course, after that person was dead, they often didn't care who they killed next. Once enraged, shades were dangerous to all nearby.

Only after Silence had the gunpowder packed did she notice that William Ann was dressed for traveling in trousers and boots. She carried a sack like Silence's.

"What do you think you're about, William Ann?" Silence asked.

"You intend to kill five men who had only half a dose of fenweed by yourself, Mother?"

"I've done similar before. I've learned to work on my own."

"Only because you didn't have anyone else to help." William Ann slung her sack onto her shoulder. "That's no longer the case."

"You're too young. Go back to bed; watch the waystop until I return."

William Ann remained firm.

"Child, I told you—"

"Mother," William Ann said, taking her arm firmly, "you aren't a *youth* anymore! You think I don't see your limp getting worse? You can't do everything by yourself! You're going to have to start letting me help you sometime, dammit!"

Silence regarded her daughter. Where had that fierceness come from?

It was hard to remember that William Ann, too, was Forescout stock. Grandmother would have been disgusted by her, and that made Silence proud. William Ann had actually had a childhood. She wasn't weak, she was just . . . normal. A woman could be strong without having the emotions of a brick.

"Don't you cuss at your mother," Silence finally told the girl.

William Ann raised an eyebrow.

"You may come," Silence said, prying her arm out of her daughter's grip. "But you *will* do as you are told."

William Ann let out a deep breath, then nodded eagerly. "I'll warn Dob we're going." She walked out, adopting the natural slow step of a Homesteader as she entered the darkness. Even though she was within the protection of the waystop's silver rings, she knew to follow the Simple Rules. Ignoring them when you were safe led to lapses when you weren't.

Silence got out two bowls, then mixed two different types of glowpaste. When finished, she poured them into separate jars, which she packed into her sack.

She stepped outside into the night. The air was crisp, chill. The Forests had gone silent.

The shades were out, of course.

A few of them moved across the grassy ground, visible by their own soft glow. Ethereal, translucent, the ones nearby right now were old shades; they barely had the forms of men any longer. The heads rippled, faces shifting like smoke rings. They trailed waves of whiteness about an arm's length behind them. Silence had always imagined that as tattered remains of their clothing.

No woman, not even a Forescout, looked upon shades without feeling a coldness inside of her. The shades were about during the day, of course; you just couldn't see them. Kindle fire, draw blood, and they'd come for you even then. At night, though, they were different. Quicker to respond to infractions. At night they also responded to quick motions, which they never did during the day.

Silence took out one of the glowpaste jars, bathing the area around her in a pale green light. The light was dim, but even and steady, unlike torchlight. Torches were unreliable, since you couldn't relight them if they went out.

William Ann waited at the front with the lantern poles. "We will need to move quietly," Silence told her while affixing the jars to the poles. "You may speak, but do so in a whisper. I said you will obey me. You will, in all things, immediately. These men we're after . . . they will kill you, or worse, without giving the deed a passing thought."

William Ann nodded.

"You're not scared enough," Silence said, slipping a black covering around the jar with the brighter glowpaste. That plunged them into darkness, but the Starbelt was high in the sky today. Some of that light would filter down through the leaves, particularly if they stayed near the road.

"I—" William Ann began.

"You remember when Harold's hound went mad last spring?" Silence asked. "Do you remember that look in the hound's eyes? No recognition? Eyes that lusted for the kill? Well, that's what these men are, William Ann. Rabid. They need to be put down, same as that hound. They won't see you as a person. They'll see you as meat. Do you understand?"

William Ann nodded. Silence could see that she was still more excited than afraid, but there was no helping that. Silence handed William Ann the pole with the darker glowpaste. It had a faintly blue light to it but didn't illuminate much. Silence put the other pole to her shoulder, sack over the other, then nodded toward the roadway.

Nearby, a shade drifted toward the boundary of the waystop. When it touched the thin barrier of silver on the ground, it crackled like sparks and drove the thing backward with a sudden jerk. The shade floated the other way.

Each touch like that cost Silence money. The touch of a shade ruined silver. That was what her patrons paid for: a waystop whose boundary had not been broke for over a hundred years, with a long-standing tradition that no unwanted shades were trapped within. Peace, of a sort. The best the Forests offered.

William Ann stepped across the boundary, which was marked by the curve of the large silver hoops jutting from the ground. They were anchored below by concrete so you couldn't just pull one up. Replacing an overlapping section from one of the rings—she had three concentric ones surrounding her waystop—required digging down and unchaining the section. It was a lot of work, which Silence knew intimately. A week didn't pass that they didn't rotate or replace one section or another.

The shade nearby drifted away. It didn't acknowledge them. Silence didn't know if regular people were invisible to them unless the rules were broken, or if the people just weren't worthy of attention until then.

She and William Ann moved out onto the dark roadway, which was somewhat overgrown. No road in the Forests was well maintained. Perhaps if the forts ever made good on their promises, that would change. Still, there was travel. Homesteaders traveling to one fort or another to trade food. The grains grown out in Forest clearings were richer, tastier than what could be produced up in the mountains. Rabbits and turkeys caught in snares or raised in hutches could be sold for good silver.

Not hogs. Only someone in one of the Forts would be so crass as to eat a pig.

Anyway, there *was* trade, and that kept the roadway worn, even if the trees around did have a tendency to reach down their boughs—like grasping arms—to try to cover up the pathway. Reclaim it. The Forests did not like that men had infested them.

The two women walked carefully and deliberately. No quick motions. Walking so, it seemed an eternity before something appeared on the road in front of them.

"There!" William Ann whispered.

Silence released her tension in a breath. Something glowing blue marked the roadway in the light of the glowpaste. Theopolis's guess at how she tracked her quarries had been a good one, but incomplete. Yes, the light of the paste known as Abraham's Fire did make drops of wetleek sap glow. By coincidence, wetleek sap *also* caused a horse's bladder to loosen.

Silence inspected the line of glowing sap and urine on the ground. She'd been worried that Chesterton and his men would cut into the Forests soon after leaving the waystop. That hadn't been likely, but still, she'd worried.

Now she was sure she had the trail. If Chesterton cut into the Forests, he'd do it a few hours after leaving the waystop, to be more certain their cover was safe. She closed her eyes and breathed a sigh of relief, then found herself offering a prayer of thanks by rote. She hesitated. Where had that come from? It had been a long time.

She shook her head, rising and continuing down the road. By drugging all five horses, she got a steady sequence of markings to follow.

The Forests felt . . . dark this night. The light of the Starbelt above didn't seem to filter through the branches as well as it should. And there seemed to be more shades than normal, prowling between the trunks of trees, glowing just faintly.

William Ann clung to her lantern pole. The child had been out in the night before, of course. No Homesteader looked forward to doing so, but none shied away from it, either. You couldn't spend your life trapped inside, frozen by fear of the darkness. Live like that, and . . . well, you were no better off than the people in the forts. Life in the Forests was hard, often deadly. But it was also free.

"Mother," William Ann whispered as they walked. "Why don't you believe in God anymore?"

"Is this really the time, girl?"

William Ann looked down as they passed another line of urine, glowing blue on the roadway. "You always say something like that."

"And I'm usually trying to avoid the question when you ask it," Silence said. "But I'm also not usually walking the Forests at night."

"It just seems important to me now. You're wrong about me not being afraid enough. I can hardly breathe, but I do know how much trouble the waystop is in. You're always so angry after Master Theopolis visits. You don't change our border silver as often as you used to. One out of two days, you don't eat anything but bread."

"And you think this has to do with God, why?"

William Ann kept looking down.

Oh, shadows, Silence thought. *She thinks we're being punished.* Fool girl. Foolish as her father.

They passed the Old Bridge, walking its rickety wooden planks. When the light was better, you could still pick out timbers from the New Bridge down in the chasm below, representing the promises of the forts and their gifts, which always looked pretty but frayed before long. Sebruki's father had been one of those who had come put the Old Bridge back up.

"I believe in the God Beyond," Silence said, after they reached the other side.

"But—"

"I don't worship," Silence said, "but that doesn't mean I don't believe. The old books, they called this land the home of the damned. I doubt that worshiping does any good if you're already damned. That's all."

William Ann didn't reply.

They walked another good two hours. Silence considered taking a short-cut thorough the woods, but the risk of losing the trail and having to double back felt too dangerous. Besides. Those markings, glowing a soft blue-white in the unseen light of the glowpaste . . . those were something *real*. A life-line of light in the shadows all around. Those lines represented safety for her and her children.

With both of them counting the moments between urine markings, they didn't miss the turnoff by much. A few minutes walking without see-ing a mark, and they turned back without a word, searching the sides of the path. Silence had worried this would be the most difficult part of the hunt, but they easily found where the men had turned into the Forests. A glowing hoofprint formed the sign; one of the horses had stepped in an-other's urine on the roadway, then tracked it into the Forests.

Silence set down her pack and opened it to retrieve her garrote, then held a finger to her lips and motioned for William Ann to wait by the road. The girl nodded. Silence couldn't make out much of her features in the darkness, but she did hear the girl's breathing grow more rapid. Being a Homesteader and accustomed to going out at night was one thing. Being alone in the Forests . . .

Silence took the blue glowpaste jar and covered it with her handkerchief. Then she took off her shoes and stockings and crept out into the night. Each time she did this, she felt like a child again, going into the Forests with her grandfather. Toes in the dirt, testing for crackling leaves or twigs that would snap and give her away.

She could almost hear his voice giving instructions, telling her how to judge the wind and use the sound of rustling leaves to mask her as she crossed noisy patches. He'd loved the Forests until the day they'd claimed him. *Never call this land hell,* he had said. *Respect the land as you would a dangerous beast, but do not hate it.*

Shades slid through the trees nearby, almost invisible with nothing to illuminate them. She kept her distance, but even so, she occasionally turned to see one of the things drifting past her. Stumbling into a shade could kill a man, but that kind of accident was uncommon. Unless enraged, shades moved away from men who got too close, as if blown by a soft breeze. So long as you were moving slowly—and you *should* be—you would be all right.

She kept the handkerchief around the jar except when she wanted to check specifically the markings nearby. Glowpaste illuminated shades, and shades that glowed too brightly might give warning of her approach.

A groan sounded nearby. Silence froze, heart practically bursting from her chest. Shades made no sound; that had been a man. Tense, silent, she searched until she caught sight of him, well hidden in the hollow of a tree. He moved, massaging his temples. The headaches from William Ann's poison were upon him.

Silence considered, then crept around the back of the tree. She crouched down, then waited a painful five minutes for him to move. He reached up again, rustling the leaves.

Silence snapped forward and looped her garrote around his neck, then pulled tight. Strangling wasn't the best way to kill a man in the Forests. It was so slow.

The guard started to thrash, clawing at his throat. Shades nearby halted.

Silence pulled tighter. The guard, weakened by the poison, tried to push back at her with his legs. She shuffled backward, still holding tightly, watching those shades. They looked around like animals sniffing the air. A few of them started to dim, their own faint natural luminescence fading, their forms bleeding from white to black.

Not a good sign. Silence felt her heartbeat like thunder inside. *Die, damn you!*

The man finally stopped jerking, motions growing more lethargic. After he trembled a last time and fell still, Silence waited there for a painful eternity, holding her breath. Finally, the shades nearby faded back to white, then drifted off in their meandering directions.

She unwound the garrote, breathing out in relief. After a moment to get her bearings, she left the corpse and crept back to William Ann.

The girl did her proud; she'd hidden herself so well that Silence didn't see her until she whispered, "Mother?"

"Yes," Silence said.

"Thank the God Beyond," William Ann said, crawling out of the hollow where she'd covered herself in leaves. She took Silence by the arm, trembling. "You found them?"

"Killed the man on watch," Silence said with a nod. "The other four should be sleeping. This is where I'll need you."

"I'm ready."

"Follow."

They moved back along the path Silence had taken. They passed the heap of the scout's corpse and William Ann inspected it, showing no pity. "It's one of them," she whispered. "I recognize him."

"Of course it's one of them."

"I just wanted to be sure. Since we're . . . you know."

Not far beyond the guard post, they found the camp. Four men in bedrolls slept amid the shades as only true Forestborn would ever try. They had set a small jar of glowpaste at the center of the camp, inside a pit so it wouldn't glow too brightly and give them away, but it was enough light to show the horses tethered a few feet away on the other side of the camp. The green light also showed William Ann's face, and Silence was shocked to see not fear but intense anger in the girl's expression. She had taken quickly to being a protective older sister to Sebruki. She was ready to kill after all.

Silence gestured toward the rightmost man, and William Ann nodded. This was the dangerous part. On only a half dose, any of these men could still wake to the noise of their partners dying.

Silence took one of the burlap sacks from her pack and handed it to William Ann, then removed her hammer. It wasn't some war weapon, like her grandfather had spoken of. Just a simple tool for pounding nails. Or other things.

Silence stooped over the first man. Seeing his sleeping face sent a shiver through her. A primal piece of her waited, tense, for those eyes to snap open.

She held up three fingers to William Ann, then lowered them one at a time. When the third finger went down, William Ann shoved the sack down over the man's head. As he jerked, Silence pounded him hard on the side of the temple with the hammer. The skull cracked and the head sank in a little. The man thrashed once, then grew limp.

Silence looked up, tense, watching the other men as William Ann pulled the sack tight. The shades nearby paused, but this didn't draw their attention as much as the strangling had. So long as the sack's lining of tar kept the blood from leaking out, they should be safe. Silence hit the man's head twice more, then checked for a pulse. There was none.

They carefully did the next man in the row. It was brutal work, like slaughtering animals. It helped to think of these men as rabid, as she'd told

William Ann earlier. It did not help to think of what the men had done to Sebruki. That would make her angry, and she couldn't afford to be angry. She needed to be cold, quiet, and efficient.

The second man took a few more knocks to the head to kill, but he woke more slowly than his friend. Fenweed made men groggy. It was an excellent drug for her purposes. She just needed them sleepy, a little disoriented. And—

The next man sat up in his bedroll. "What . . . ?" he asked in a slurred voice.

Silence leaped for him, grabbing him by the shoulders and slamming him to the ground. Nearby shades spun about as if at a loud noise. Silence pulled her garrote out as the man heaved at her, trying to push her aside, and William Ann gasped in shock.

Silence rolled around, wrapping the man's neck. She pulled tight, straining while the man thrashed, agitating the shades. She almost had him dead when the last man leaped from his bedroll. In his dazed alarm, he chose to dash away.

Shadows! That last one was Chesterton himself. If he drew the shades upon himself . . .

Silence left the third man gasping and threw caution aside, racing after Chesterton. If the shades withered him to dust, she'd have *nothing*. No corpse to turn in meant no bounty.

The shades around the campsite faded from view as Silence reached Chesterton, catching him at the perimeter of the camp by the horses. She desperately tackled him by the legs, throwing the groggy man to the ground.

"You bitch," he said in a slurred voice, kicking at her. "You're the inn-keeper. You poisoned me, you *bitch*!"

In the forest, the shades had gone completely black. Green eyes burst alight as they opened their earthsight. The eyes trailed a misty light.

Silence battered aside Chesterton's hands as he struggled.

"I'll pay you," he said, clawing at her. "I'll pay you—"

Silence slammed her hammer into his arm, causing him to scream. Then she brought it down on his face with a crunch. She ripped off her sweater as he groaned and thrashed, somehow wrapping it around his head and the hammer.

"William Ann!" she screamed. "I need a bag. A bag, girl! Give me—"

William Ann knelt beside her, pulling a sack over Chesterton's head as the blood soaked through the sweater. Silence reached to the side with a frantic hand and grabbed a stone, then smashed it into the sack-covered head. The sweater muffled Chesterton's screams but also muffled the rock. She had to beat again and again.

He finally fell still. William Ann held the sack against his neck to keep the blood from flowing out, her breath coming in in quick gasps. "Oh, God Beyond. Oh, *God* . . ."

Silence dared look up. Dozens of green eyes hung in the forest, glowing like little fires in the blackness. William Ann squeezed her eyes shut and whispered a prayer, tears leaking down her cheeks.

Silence reached slowly to her side and took out her silver dagger. She remembered another night, another sea of glowing green eyes. Her grandmother's last night. *Run, girl! RUN!*

That night, running had been an option. They'd been close to safety. Even then, Grandmother hadn't made it. She might have, but she hadn't.

That night horrified Silence. What Grandmother had done. What Silence had done. . . . Well, tonight, she had one only hope. Running would not save them. Safety was too far away.

Slowly, blessedly, the eyes started to fade away. Silence sat back and let the silver knife slip out of her fingers to the ground.

William Ann opened her eyes. "Oh, God Beyond!" she said as the shades faded back into view. "A miracle!"

"Not a miracle," Silence said. "Just luck. We killed him in time. Another second and they'd have enraged."

William Ann wrapped her arms around herself. "Oh, shadows. Oh, shadows. I thought we were dead. Oh, shadows."

Suddenly, Silence remembered something. The third man. She hadn't finished strangling him before Chesterton ran. She stumbled to her feet, turning.

He lay there, immobile.

"I finished him off," William Ann said. "Had to strangle him with my hands. My hands . . ."

Silence glanced back at her. "You did well, girl. You probably saved our lives. If you hadn't been here, I'd never have killed Chesterton without enraging the shades."

The girl still stared out into the woods, watching the placid shades.

"What would it take?" she asked. "For you to see a miracle instead of a coincidence?"

"It would take a miracle, obviously," Silence said. "Instead of just a coincidence. Come on. Let's put a second sack on these fellows."

William Ann joined her, lethargic as she helped put sacks on the heads of the bandits. Two sacks each, just in case. Blood was the most dangerous. Running drew shades, but slowly. Fire enraged them immediately, but it also blinded and confused them.

Blood, though . . . blood shed in anger, exposed to the open air . . . a single drop could make the shades slaughter you, and then everything else within their sight.

Silence checked each man for a heartbeat, just in case, and found none. They saddled the horses and heaved the corpses, including the scout, into the saddles and tied them in place. They took the bedrolls and other equipment, too. Hopefully, the men would have some silver on them. Bounty laws let Silence keep what she found unless there was specific mention of something stolen. In this case, the forts just wanted Chesterton dead. Pretty much everyone did.

Silence pulled a rope tight, then paused.

"Mother!" William Ann said, noticing the same thing. Leaves rustling out in the Forests. They'd uncovered their jar of green glowpaste to join that of the bandits, so the small campsite was well illuminated as a gang of eight men and women on horseback rode in through the Forests.

They were from the forts. The nice clothing, the way they kept looking into the Forests at the shades . . . City people for certain. Silence stepped forward, wishing she had her hammer to look at least a little threatening. That was still tied in the sack around Chesterton's head. It would have blood on it, so she couldn't get it out until that dried or she was in someplace very, *very* safe.

"Now, look at this," said the man at the front of the newcomers. "I couldn't believe what Tobias told me when he came back from scouting, but it appears to be true. All five men in Chesterton's gang, killed by a couple of Forest Homesteaders?"

"Who are you?" Silence asked.

"Red Young," the man said with a tip of the hat. "I've been tracking this lot for the last four months. I can't thank you enough for taking care of them for me." He waved to a few of his people, who dismounted.

"Mother!" William Ann hissed.

Silence studied Red's eyes. He was armed with a cudgel, and one of the women behind him had one of those new crossbows with the blunt tips. They cranked fast and hit hard but didn't draw blood.

"Step away from the horses, child," Silence said.

"But—"

"Step away." Silence dropped the rope of the horse she was leading. Three fort people gathered up the ropes, one of the men leering at William Ann.

"You're a smart one," Red said, leaning down and studying Silence. One of his women walked past, towing Chesterton's horse with the man's corpse slumped over the saddle.

Silence stepped up, resting a hand on Chesterton's saddle. The woman towing it paused, then looked at her boss. Silence slipped her knife from its sheath.

"You'll give us something," Silence said to Red, knife hand hidden. "After what we did. One quarter, and I don't say a word."

"Sure," he said, tipping his hat to her. He had a fake kind of grin, like one in a painting. "One quarter it is."

Silence nodded. She slipped the knife against one of the thin ropes that held Chesterton in the saddle. That gave her a good cut on it as the woman pulled the horse away. Silence stepped back, resting her hand on William Ann's shoulder while covertly moving the knife back into its sheath.

Red tipped his hat to her again. In moments, the bounty hunters had retreated back through the trees toward the roadway.

"One quarter?" William Ann hissed. "You think he'll pay it?"

"Hardly," Silence said, picking up her pack. "We're lucky he didn't just kill us. Come on." She moved out into the Forests. William Ann walked with her, both moving with the careful steps the Forests demanded. "It might be time for you to return to the waystop, William Ann."

"And what are you going to do?"

"Get our bounty back." She was a Forescout, dammit. No prim fort man was going to steal from her.

"You mean to cut them off at the white span, I assume. But what will you do? We can't fight so many, Mother."

"I'll find a way." That corpse meant freedom—*life*—for her daughters.

She would not let it slip away, like smoke between the fingers. They entered the darkness, passing shades that had, just a short time before, been almost ready to wither them. Now the spirits drifted away, completely ambivalent toward the flesh that passed them.

Think, Silence. Something is very wrong here. How had those men found the camp? The light? Had they heard her and William Ann talking? They'd claimed to have been chasing Chesterton for months. Shouldn't she have heard of them before now? These men and women looked too crisp, too new to have been out in the Forests for months trailing killers.

It led to a conclusion she did not want to admit. One man had known she was hunting a bounty today and had seen how she was planning to track that bounty. One man had cause to see that bounty stolen from her.

Theopolis, I hope I'm wrong, she thought. *Because if you're behind this . . .*

Silence and William Ann trudged through the guts of the Forest, a place where the gluttonous canopy above drank in all of the light, leaving the ground below barren. Shades patrolled these wooden halls like blind sentries. Red and his bounty hunters were of the forts. They would keep to the roadways; that was her advantage. The Forests were no friend to a Homesteader, no more than a familiar chasm was any less dangerous a drop.

But Silence was a sailor on this abyss. She could ride its winds better than any fort dweller. Perhaps it was time to make a storm.

What Homesteaders called the "white span" was a section of roadway lined by mushroom fields. It took about an hour through the Forests to reach the span, and Silence was feeling the price of a night without sleep by the time she arrived. She ignored the fatigue, tromping through the field of mushrooms, holding her jar of green light and giving an ill cast to trees and furrows in the land.

The roadway bent around through the Forests, then came back this way. If the men were heading toward Lastport or any of the other nearby forts, they would come this direction. "You continue on," Silence said to William Ann. "It's only another hour's hike back to the waystop. Check on things there."

"I'm not leaving you, Mother."

"You promised to obey. Would you break your word?"

"And you promised to let me help you. Would you break yours?"

"I don't need you for this," Silence said. "And it will be dangerous."

"What are you going to do?"

Silence stopped beside the roadway, then knelt, fishing in her pack. She came out with the small keg of gunpowder. William Ann went as white as the mushrooms.

"Mother!"

Silence untied her grandmother's firestarter. She didn't know for certain if it still worked. She'd never dared compress the two metal arms, which looked like tongs. Squeezing them together would grind the ends against one another, making sparks, and a spring at the joint would make them come back apart.

Silence looked up at her daughter, then held the firestarter up beside her head. William Ann stepped back, then glanced to the sides, toward nearby shades.

"Are things really that bad?" the girl whispered. "For us, I mean?"

Silence nodded.

"All right, then."

Fool girl. Well, Silence wouldn't send her away. The truth was, she probably *would* need help. She intended to get that corpse. Bodies were heavy, and there wasn't any way she'd be able to cut off just the head. Not out in the Forests, with shades about.

She dug into her pack, pulling out her medical supplies. They were tied between two small boards, intended to be used as splints. It was not difficult to tie the two boards to either side of the firestarter. With her hand trowel, she dug a small hole in the roadway's soft earth, about the size of the powder keg.

She then opened the plug to the keg and set it into the hole. She soaked her handkerchief in the lamp oil, stuck one end in the keg, then positioned the firestarter boards on the road with the end of the kerchief next to the spark-making heads. After covering the contraption with some leaves, she had a rudimentary trap. If someone stepped on the top board, that would press it down and grind out sparks to light the kerchief. Hopefully.

She couldn't afford to light the fire herself. The shades would come first for the one who made the fire.

"What happens if they don't step on it?" William Ann asked.

"Then we move it to another place on the road and try again," Silence said.

"That could shed blood, you realize."

Silence didn't reply. If the trap was triggered by a footfall, the shades wouldn't see Silence as the one causing it. They'd come first for the one who triggered the trap. But if blood was drawn, they would enrage. Soon after, it wouldn't matter who had caused it. All would be in danger.

"We have hours of darkness left," Silence said. "Cover your glowpaste."

William Ann nodded, hastily putting the cover on her jar. Silence inspected her trap again, then took William Ann by the shoulder and pulled her to the side of the roadway. The underbrush was thicker there, as the road tended to wind through breaks in the canopy. Men sought out places in the Forests where they could see the sky.

The men came along eventually. Silent, illuminated by a jar of glowpaste each. Fortfolk didn't talk at night. They passed the trap, which Silence had placed on the narrowest section of roadway. She held her breath, watching the horses pass, step after step missing the lump that marked the board. William Ann covered her ears, hunkering down.

A hoof hit the trap. Nothing happened. Silence released an annoyed breath. What would she do if the firestarter was broken? Could she find another way to—

The explosion struck her, the wave of force shaking her body. Shades vanished in a blink, green eyes snapping open. Horses reared and whinnied, men yelling.

Silence shook off her stupefaction, grabbing William Ann by the shoulder and pulling her out of hiding. Her trap had worked better than she'd assumed; the burning rag had allowed the horse who had triggered the trap to take a few steps before the blast hit. No blood, just a lot of surprised horses and confused men. The little keg of gunpowder hadn't done as much damage as she'd anticipated—the stories of what gunpowder could do were often as fanciful as stories of the Homeland—but the sound had been incredible.

Silence's ears rang as she fought through the confused men, finding what she'd hoped to see. Chesterton's corpse lay on the ground, dumped from his saddleback by a bucking horse and a frayed rope. She grabbed the corpse under the arms and William Ann took the legs. They moved sideways into the Forests.

"Idiots!" Red bellowed from amid the confusion. "Stop her! It—"

He cut off as shades swarmed the roadway, descending upon the men. Red had managed to keep his horse under control, but now he had to dance it back from the shades. Enraged, they had turned pure black, though the blast of light and fire had obviously left them dazed. They fluttered about, like moths around a flame. Green eyes. A small blessing. If those turned red . . .

One bounty hunter, standing on the road and spinning about, was struck. His back arched, black-veined tendrils crisscrossing his skin. He dropped to his knees, screaming as the flesh of his face shrank around his skull.

Silence turned away. William Ann watched the fallen man with a horrified expression.

"Slowly, child," Silence said in what she hoped was a comforting voice. She hardly felt comforting. "Carefully. We can move away from them. William Ann. Look at me."

The girl turned to look at her.

"Hold my eyes. Move. That's right. Remember, the shades will go to the source of the fire first. They are confused, stunned. They can't smell fire like they do blood, and they'll look from it to the nearest sources of quick motion. Slowly, easily. Let the scrambling city men distract them."

The two of them eased into the Forests with excruciating deliberateness. In the face of so much chaos, so much danger, their pace felt like a crawl. Red organized a resistance. Fire-crazed shades could be fought, destroyed, with silver. More and more would come, but if the men were clever and lucky, they'd be able to destroy those nearby and then move slowly away from the source of the fire. They could hide, survive. Maybe.

Unless one of them accidentally drew blood.

Silence and William Ann stepped through a field of mushrooms that glowed like the skulls of rats and broke silently beneath their feet. Luck was not completely with them, for as the shades shook off their disorientation from the explosion, a pair of them on the outskirts turned and struck out toward the fleeing women.

William Ann gasped. Silence deliberately set down Chesterton's shoulders, then took out her knife. "Keep going," she whispered. "Pull him away. Slowly, girl. *Slowly*."

"I won't leave you!"

"I will catch up," Silence said. "You aren't ready for this."

She didn't look to see if William Ann obeyed, for the shades—figures of jet black streaking across the white-knobbed ground—were upon her. Strength was meaningless against shades. They had no real substance.

Only two things mattered: moving quickly and not letting yourself be frightened.

Shades *were* dangerous, but so long as you had silver, you could fight. Many a man died because he ran, drawing even more shades, rather than standing his ground.

Silence swung at the shades as they reached her. *You want my daughter, hellbound?* she thought with a snarl. *You should have tried for the city men instead.*

She swept her knife through the first shade, as Grandmother had taught. *Never creep back and cower before shades. You're Forescout blood. You claim the Forests. You are their creature as much as any other. As am I. . . .*

Her knife passed through the shade with a slight tugging feeling, creating a shower of bright white sparks that sprayed out of the shade. The shade pulled back, its black tendrils writhing about one another.

Silence spun on the other. The pitch sky let her see only the thing's eyes, a horrid green, as it reached for her. She lunged.

Its spectral hands were upon her, the icy cold of its fingers gripping her arm below the elbow. She could feel it. Shade fingers had substance; they could grab you, hold you back. Only silver warded them away. Only with silver could you fight.

She rammed her arm in farther. Sparks shot out its back, spraying like a bucket of wash water. Silence gasped at the horrid, icy pain. Her knife slipped from fingers she could no longer feel. She lurched forward, falling to her knees as the second shade fell backward, then began spinning about in a mad spiral. The first one flopped on the ground like a dying fish, trying to rise, but its top half fell over.

The cold of her arm was so *bitter*. She stared at the wounded arm, watching the flesh of her hand wither upon itself, pulling in toward the bone.

She heard weeping.

You stand there, Silence. Grandmother's voice. Memories of the first time she'd killed a shade. *You do as I say. No tears! Forescouts don't cry. Forescouts DON'T CRY.*

She had learned to hate her that day. Ten years old, with her little knife, shivering and weeping in the night as her grandmother had enclosed her and a drifting shade in a ring of silver dust.

Grandmother had run around the perimeter, enraging it with motion. While Silence was trapped in there. With death.

The only way to learn is to do, Silence. And you'll learn, one way or another!

"Mother!" William Ann said.

Silence blinked, coming out of the memory as her daughter dumped silver dust on the exposed arm. The withering stopped as William Ann, choking against her thick tears, dumped the entire pouch of emergency silver over the hand. The metal reversed the withering, and the skin turned pink again, the blackness melting away in sparks of white.

Too much, Silence thought. William Ann had used all of the silver dust in her haste, far more than one wound needed. It was difficult to summon any anger, for feeling flooded back into her hand and the icy cold retreated.

"Mother?" William Ann asked. "I left you, as you said. But he was so heavy, I didn't get far. I came back for you. I'm sorry. I came back for you!"

"Thank you," Silence said, breathing in. "You did well." She reached up and took her daughter by the shoulder, then used the once-withered hand to search in the grass for Grandmother's knife. When she brought it up, the blade was blackened in several places but still good.

Back on the road, the city men had made a circle and were holding off the shades with silver-tipped spears. The horses had all fled or been consumed. Silence fished on the ground, coming up with a small handful of silver dust. The rest had been expended in the healing. Too much.

No use worrying about that now, she thought, stuffing the handful of dust in her pocket. "Come," she said, hauling herself to her feet. "I'm sorry I never taught you to fight them."

"Yes you did," William Ann said, wiping her tears. "You've told me all about it."

Told. Never shown. *Shadows, Grandmother. I know I disappoint you, but I won't do it to her. I can't. But I am a good mother. I will protect them.*

The two left the mushrooms, taking up their grisly prize again and tromping through the Forests. They passed more darkened shades floating toward the fight. All of those sparks would draw them. The city men were dead. Too much attention, too much struggle. They'd have a thousand shades upon them before the hour was out.

Silence and William Ann moved slowly. Though the cold had mostly retreated from Silence's hand, there was a lingering . . . something. A deep shiver. A limb touched by the shades wouldn't feel right for months.

That was far better than what could have happened. Without William Ann's quick thinking, Silence could have become a cripple. Once the withering settled in—that took a little time, though it varied—it was irreversible.

Something rustled in the woods. Silence froze, causing William Ann to stop and glance about.

"Mother?" William Ann whispered.

Silence frowned. The night was so black, and they'd been forced to leave their lights. *Something's out there*, she thought, trying to pierce the darkness. *What are you?* God Beyond, protect them if the fighting had drawn one of the Deepest Ones.

The sound did not repeat. Reluctantly, Silence continued on. They walked for a good hour, and in the darkness Silence hadn't realized they'd neared the roadway again until they stepped onto it.

Silence heaved out a breath, setting down their burden and rolling her tired arms in their joints. Some light from the Starbelt filtered down upon them, illuminating something like a large jawbone to their left. The Old Bridge. They were almost home. The shades here weren't even agitated; they moved with their lazy, almost butterfly, gaits.

Her arms felt so sore. That body felt as if it were getting heavier every moment. Men often didn't realize how heavy a corpse was. Silence sat down. They'd rest for a time before continuing on. "William Ann, do you have any water left in your canteen?"

William Ann whimpered.

Silence started, then scrambled to her feet. Her daughter stood beside the bridge, and something dark stood behind her. A green glow suddenly illuminated the night as the figure took out a small vial of glowpaste. By that sickly light, Silence could see that the figure was Red.

He held a dagger to William Ann's neck. The city man had not fared well in the fighting. One eye was now a milky white, half his face blackened, his lips pulled back from his teeth. A shade had gotten him across the face. He was lucky to be alive.

"I figured you'd come back this way," he said, the words slurred by his shriveled lips. Spittle dripped from his chin. "Silver. Give me your silver."

His knife . . . it was common steel.

"*Now!*" he roared, pulling the knife closer to William Ann's neck. If he so much as nicked her, the shades would be upon them in heartbeats.

"I only have the knife," William Ann lied, taking it out and tossing it to the ground before him. "It's too late for your face, Red. That withering has set in."

"I don't care," he hissed. "Now the body. Step away from it, woman. Away!"

Silence stepped to the side. Could she get to him before he killed William Ann? He'd have to grab that knife. If she sprang just right . . .

"You killed my men," Red growled. "They're dead, all of them. God, if I hadn't rolled into the hollow . . . I had to *listen* to it. Listen to them being slaughtered!"

"You were the only smart one," she said. "You couldn't have saved them, Red."

"Bitch! You killed them."

"They killed themselves," she whispered. "You come to my Forests, take what is mine? It was your men or my children, Red."

"Well, if you want your child to live through this, you'll stay very still. Girl, pick up that knife."

Whimpering, William Ann knelt. Red mimicked her, staying just behind her, watching Silence, holding the knife steady. William Ann picked up the knife in trembling hands.

Red pulled the silver knife from William Ann, then held it in one hand, the common knife at her neck in the other. "Now the girl is going to carry the corpse, and you're going to wait right there. I don't want you coming near."

"Of course," Silence said, already planning. She couldn't afford to strike right now. He was too careful. She would follow through the Forests, along the road, and wait for a moment of weakness. Then she'd strike.

Red spat to the side.

Then a padded crossbow bolt shot from the night and took him in the shoulder, jolting him. His blade slid across William Ann's neck and a dribble of blood ran down it. The girl's eyes widened in horror, though it was little more than a nick. The danger to her throat wasn't important.

The blood was.

Red tumbled back, gasping, hand to his shoulder. A few drops of blood glistened on his knife. The shades in the Forests around them went black. Glowing green eyes burst alight, then deepened to crimson.

Red eyes in the night. Blood in the air.

"Oh, hell!" Red screamed. "Oh, *hell*." Red eyes swarmed around him.

There was no hesitation here, no confusion. They went straight for the one who had drawn blood.

Silence reached for William Ann as the shades descended. Red grabbed the girl around and shoved her through a shade, trying to stop it. He spun and dashed the other direction.

William Ann passed through the shade, her face withering, skin pulling in at the chin and around the eyes. She stumbled through the shade and into Silence's arms.

Silence felt an immediate, overwhelming panic.

"No! Child, no. No. *No* . . ."

William Ann worked her mouth, making a choking sound, her lips pulling back toward her teeth, her eyes open wide as her skin pulled back and her eyelids shriveled.

Silver. I need silver. I can save her. Silence snapped her head up, clutching William Ann. Red ran down the roadway, slashing the silver dagger all about, spraying light and sparks. Shades surrounded him. Hundreds, like ravens flocking to a roost.

Not that way. The shades would finish with him soon and would look for flesh—any flesh. William Ann still had blood on her neck. They'd come for her next. Even without that, the girl was withering fast.

The dagger wouldn't be enough to save William Ann. Silence needed dust, silver dust, to force down her daughter's throat. Silence fumbled in her pocket, coming out with the small bit of silver dust there.

Too little. She *knew* that would be too little. Her grandmother's training calmed her mind, and everything became immediately clear.

The waystop was close. She had more silver there.

"M . . . Mother . . ."

Silence heaved William Ann into her arms. Too light, the flesh drying. Then she turned and ran with everything she had across the bridge.

Her arms stung, weakened from having hauled the corpse so far. The corpse . . . she couldn't lose it!

No. She couldn't think on that. The shades would have it, as warm enough flesh, soon after Red was gone. There would be no bounty. She had to focus on William Ann.

Silence's tears felt cold on her face as she ran, wind blowing her. Her daughter trembled and shook in her arms, spasming as she died. She'd become a shade if she died like this.

"I won't lose you!" Silence said into the night. "Please. I won't lose you. . . ."

Behind her, Red screamed a long, wailing screech of agony that cut off at the end as the shades feasted. Near her, other shades stopped, eyes deepening to red.

Blood in the air. Eyes of crimson.

"I hate you," Silence whispered into the air as she ran. Each step was agony. She *was* growing old. "I hate you! What you did to me. What you did to us."

She didn't know if she was speaking to Grandmother or the God Beyond. So often, they were the same in her mind. Had she ever realized that before?

Branches lashed at her as she pushed forward. Was that light ahead? The waystop?

Hundreds upon hundreds of red eyes opened in front of her. She stumbled to the ground, spent, William Ann like a heavy bundle of branches in her arms. The girl trembled, her eyes rolled back in her head.

Silence held out the small bit of silver dust she'd recovered earlier. She longed to pour it on William Ann, save her a little pain, but she knew with clarity that was a waste. She looked down, crying, then took the pinch and made a small circle around the two of them. What else could she do?

William Ann shook with a seizure as she rasped, drawing in breaths and clawing at Silence's arms. The shades came by the dozens, huddling around the two of them, smelling the blood. The flesh.

Silence pulled her daughter close. She should have gone for the knife after all; it wouldn't heal William Ann, but she could have at least fought with it.

Without that, without anything, she failed. Grandmother had been right all along.

"Hush now, my dear one . . ." Silence whispered, squeezing her eyes shut. "Be not afraid."

Shades came at her frail barrier, throwing up sparks, making Silence open her eyes. They backed away, then others came, beating against the silver, their red eyes illuminating writhing black forms.

"Night comes upon us," Silence whispered, choking at the words, "but sunlight will break."

William Ann arched her back, then fell still.

"Sleep now . . . my . . . my dear one. . . . Let your tears fade. Darkness surrounds us, but someday . . . we'll wake. . . ."

So tired. *I shouldn't have let her come.*

If she hadn't, Chesterton would have gotten away from her, and she'd have probably died to the shades then. William Ann and Sebruki would have become slaves to Theopolis, or worse.

No choices. No way out.

"Why did you send us here?" she screamed, looking up past hundreds of glowing red eyes. "What is the point?"

There was no answer. There was never an answer.

Yes, that *was* light ahead; she could see it through the low tree branches in front of her. She was only a few yards from the waystop. She would die, like Grandmother had, mere paces from her home.

She blinked, cradling William Ann as the tiny silver barrier failed.

That . . . that branch just in front of her. It had such a very odd shape. Long, thin, no leaves. Not like a branch at all. Instead, like . . .

Like a crossbow bolt.

It had lodged into the tree after being fired from the waystop earlier in the day. She remembered facing down that bolt earlier, staring at its reflective end.

Silver.

Silence Montane crashed through the back door of the waystop, hauling a desiccated body behind her. She stumbled into the kitchen, barely able to walk, and dropped the silver-tipped bolt from a withered hand.

Her skin continued to pull tight, her body shriveling. She had not been able to avoid withering, not when fighting so many Shades. The crossbow bolt had merely cleared a path, allowing her to push forward in a last, frantic charge.

She could barely see. Tears streamed from her clouded eyes. Even with the tears, her eyes felt as dry as if she had been standing in the wind for an hour while holding them wide open. Her lids refused to blink, and she couldn't move her lips.

She had . . . powder. Didn't she?

Thought. Mind. What?

She moved without thought. Jar on the windowsill. In case of broken circle. She unscrewed the lid with fingers like sticks. Seeing them horrified a distant part of her mind.

Dying. I'm dying.

She dunked the jar of silver powder in the water cistern and pulled it out, then stumbled to William Ann. She felt to her knees beside the girl, spilling much of the water. The rest she dumped on her daughter's face with a shaking arm.

Please. Please.

Darkness.

"We were sent here to be strong," Grandmother said, standing on the cliff edge overlooking the waters. Her whited hair curled in the wind, writhing, like the wisps of a shade.

She turned back to Silence, and her weathered face was covered in droplets of water from the crashing surf below. "The God Beyond sent us. It's part of the plan."

"It's so easy for you to say that, isn't it?" Silence spat. "You can fit anything into that nebulous *plan*. Even the destruction of the world itself."

"I won't hear blasphemy from you, child." A voice like boots stepping in gravel. She walked toward Silence. "You can rail against the God Beyond, but it will change nothing. William was a fool and an idiot. You are better off. We are *Forescouts*. We *survive*. We will be the ones to defeat the Evil, someday." She passed Silence by.

Silence had never seen a smile from Grandmother, not since her husband's death. Smiling was wasted energy. And love . . . love was for the people back in Homeland. The people who'd died to the Evil.

"I'm with child," Silence said.

Grandmother stopped. "William?"

"Who else?"

Grandmother continued on.

"No condemnations?" Silence asked, turning, folding her arms.

"It's done," Grandmother said. "We are Forescouts. If this is how we must continue, so be it. I'm more worried about the waystop, and meeting our payments to those damn forts."

I have an idea for that, Silence thought, considering the lists of bounties she'd begun collecting. *Something even you wouldn't dare. Something dangerous. Something unthinkable.*

Grandmother reached the woods and looked at Silence, scowled, then pulled on her hat and stepped into the trees.

"I will not have you interfering with my child," Silence called after her. "I will raise my own as I will!"

Grandmother vanished into the shadows.

Please. Please.

"*I will!*"

I won't lose you. I won't. . . .

Silence gasped, coming awake and clawing at the floorboards, staring upward.

Alive. She was alive!

Dob the stableman knelt beside her, holding the jar of powdered silver. She coughed, lifting fingers—plump, the flesh restored—to her neck. It was hale though ragged from the flakes of silver that had been forced down her throat. Her skin was dusted with black bits of ruined silver.

"William Ann!" she said, turning.

The child lay on the floor beside the door. William Ann's left side, where she'd first touched the shade, was blackened. Her face wasn't too bad, but her hand was a withered skeleton. They'd have to cut that off. Her leg looked bad, too. Silence couldn't tell how bad without tending the wounds.

"Oh, child . . ." Silence knelt beside her.

But the girl breathed in and out. That was enough, all things considered.

"I tried," Dob said. "But you'd already done what could be done."

"Thank you," Silence said. She turned to the aged man, with his high forehead and dull eyes.

"Did you get him?" Dob asked.

"Who?"

"The bounty."

"I . . . yes, I did. But I had to leave him."

"You'll find another," Dob said in his monotone, climbing to his feet. "The Fox always does."

"How long have you known?"

"I'm an idiot, mam," he said. "Not a fool." He bowed his head to her, then walked away, slump-backed as always.

Silence climbed to her feet, then groaned, picking up William Ann. She lifted her daughter to the rooms above and saw to her.

The leg wasn't as bad as Silence had feared. A few of the toes would be lost, but the foot itself was hale enough. The entire left side of William Ann's body was blackened, as if burned. That would fade, with time, to grey.

Everyone who saw her would know exactly what had happened. Many men would never touch her, fearing her taint. This might just doom her to a life alone.

I know a little about such a life, Silence thought, dipping a cloth into the water bin and washing William Ann's face. The youth would sleep through the day. She had come very close to death, to becoming a shade herself. The body did not recover quickly from that.

Of course, Silence had been close to that, too. She, however, had been there before. Another of Grandmother's preparations. Oh, how she hated that woman. Silence owed who she was to how that training toughened her. Could she be thankful for Grandmother and hateful, both at once?

Silence finished washing William Ann, then dressed her in a soft nightgown and left her in her bunk. Sebruki still slept off the draught William Ann had given her.

So she went downstairs to the kitchen to think difficult thoughts. She'd lost the bounty. The shades would have had at that body; the skin would be dust, the skull blackened and ruined. She had no way to prove that she'd taken Chesterton.

She settled against the kitchen table and laced her hands before her. She wanted to have at the whiskey instead, to dull the horror of the night.

She thought for hours. Could she pay Theopolis off some way? Borrow from someone else? Who? Maybe find another bounty. But so few people came through the waystop these days. Theopolis had already given her warning with his writ. He wouldn't wait more than a day or two for payment before claiming the waystop as his own.

Had she really gone through so much, still to lose?

Sunlight fell on her face and a breeze from the broken window tickled her cheek, waking her from her slumber at the table. Silence blinked, stretching, limbs complaining. Then she sighed, moving to the kitchen counter. She'd left out all of the materials from the preparations last night, her clay bowls thick with glowpaste that still shone faintly. The silver-tipped crossbow bolt still lay by the back door. She'd need to clean up and get breakfast ready for her few guests. Then, think of *some* way to . . .

The back door opened and someone stepped in.

. . . to deal with Theopolis. She exhaled softly, looking at him in his clean clothing and condescending smile. He tracked mud onto her floor as he entered. "Silence Montane. Nice morning, hmmm?"

Shadows, she thought. *I don't have the mental strength to deal with him right now.*

He moved to close the window shutters.

"What are you doing?" she demanded.

"Hmmm? Haven't you warned me before that you loathe that people might see us together? That they might get a hint that you are turning in bounties to me? I'm just trying to protect you. Has something happened? You look awful, hmmm?"

"I know what you did."

"You do? But, see, I do many things. About what do you speak?"

Oh, how she'd like to cut that grin from his lips and cut out his throat, stomp out that annoying Lastport accent. She couldn't. He was just so blasted *good* at acting. She had guesses, probably good ones. But no proof.

Grandmother would have killed him right then. Was she so desperate to prove him wrong that she'd lose everything?

"You were in the Forests," Silence said. "When Red surprised me at the bridge, I assumed that the thing I'd heard—rustling in the darkness—had been him. It wasn't. He implied he'd been waiting for us at the bridge. That thing in the darkness, it was you. *You* shot him with the crossbow to jostle him, make him draw blood. Why, Theopolis?"

"Blood?" Theopolis said. "In the night? And you *survived*? You're quite fortunate, I should say. Remarkable. What else happened?"

She said nothing.

"I have come for payment of debt," Theopolis said. "You have no bounty to turn in, then, hmmm? Perhaps we will need my document after all. So kind of me to bring another copy. This really will be wonderful for us both. Do you not agree?"

"Your feet are glowing."

Theopolis hesitated, then looked down. There the mud he'd tracked in shone very faintly blue in the light of the glowpaste remnants.

"You followed me," she said. "You *were* there last night."

He looked up at her with a slow, unconcerned expression. "And?" He took a step forward.

Silence backed away, her heel hitting the wall behind her. She reached around, taking out the key and unlocking the door behind her. Theopolis grabbed her arm, yanking her away as she pulled open the door.

"Going for one of your hidden weapons?" he asked with a sneer. "The crossbow you keep hidden on the pantry shelf? Yes, I know of that. I'm disappointed, Silence. Can't we be civil?"

"I will never sign your document, Theopolis," she said, then spat at his feet. "I would sooner die, I would sooner be put out of house and home. You can take the waystop by force, but I will *not* serve you. You can be damned, for all I care, you bastard. You—"

He slapped her across the face. A quick but unemotional gesture. "Oh, do shut up."

She stumbled back.

"Such dramatics, Silence. I can't be the only one to wish you lived up to your name, hmmm?"

She licked her lip, feeling the pain of his slap. She lifted her hand to her face. A single drop of blood colored her fingertip when she pulled it away.

"You expect me to be frightened?" Theopolis asked. "I know we are safe in here."

"City fool," she whispered, then flipped the drop of blood at him. It hit him on the cheek. "Always follow the Simple Rules. Even when you think you don't have to. And I wasn't opening the pantry, as you thought."

Theopolis frowned, then glanced over at the door she had opened. The door into the small old shrine. Her grandmother's shrine to the God Beyond.

The bottom of the door was rimmed in silver.

Red eyes opened in the air behind Theopolis, a jet-black form coalescing in the shadowed room. Theopolis hesitated, then turned.

He didn't get to scream as the shade took his head in its hands and drew his life away. It was a newer shade, its form still strong despite the writhing blackness of its clothing. A tall woman, hard of features, with curling hair. Theopolis opened his mouth, then his face withered away, eyes sinking into his head.

"You should have run, Theopolis," Silence said.

His head began to crumble. His body collapsed to the floor.

"Hide from the green eyes, run from the red," Silence said, taking out her silver dagger. "Your rules, Grandmother."

The shade turned to her. Silence shivered, looking into those dead, glassy eyes of a matriarch she loathed and loved.

"I hate you," Silence said. "Thank you for making me hate you." She retrieved the silver-tipped crossbow bolt and held it before her, but the shade did not strike. Silence edged around, forcing the shade back. It floated away from her, back into the shrine lined with silver at the bottom of its three walls, where Silence had trapped it years ago.

Her heart pounding, Silence closed the door, completing the barrier, and locked it again. No matter what happened, that shade left Silence alone. Almost, she thought it remembered. And almost, Silence felt guilty for trapping that soul inside the small closet for all these years.

Silence found Theopolis's hidden cave after six hours of hunting.

It was about where she'd expected it to be, in the hills not far from the Old Bridge. It included a silver barrier. She could harvest that. Good money there.

Inside the small cavern, she found Chesterton's corpse, which Theopolis had dragged to the cave while the Shades killed Red and then hunted Silence. *I'm so glad, for once, you were a greedy man, Theopolis.*

She would have to find someone else to start turning in bounties for her. That would be difficult, particularly on short notice. She dragged the corpse out and threw it over the back of Theopolis's horse. A short hike took her back to the road, where she paused, then walked up and located Red's fallen corpse, withered down to just bones and clothing.

She fished out her grandmother's dagger, scored and blackened from the fight. It fit back into the sheath at her side. She trudged, exhausted, back to the waystop and hid Chesterton's corpse in the cold cellar out back of the stable, beside where she'd put Theopolis's remains. She hiked back into the kitchen. Beside the shrine's door where her grandmother's dagger had once hung, she had placed the silver crossbow bolt that Sebruki had unknowingly sent her.

What would the fort authorities say when she explained Theopolis's death to them? Perhaps she could claim to have found him like that. . . .

She paused, then smiled.

———

"Looks like you're lucky, friend," Daggon said, sipping at his beer. "The White Fox won't be looking for you anytime soon."

The spindly man, who still insisted his name was Earnest, hunkered down a little farther in his seat.

"How is it you're still here?" Daggon asked. "I traveled all the way to Lastport. I hardly expected to find you here on my path back."

"I hired on at a homestead nearby," said the slender-necked man. "Good work, mind you. Solid work."

"And you pay each night to stay here?"

"I like it. It feels peaceful. The Homesteads don't have good silver protection. They just . . . let the shades move about. Even inside." The man shuddered.

Daggon shrugged, lifting his drink as Silence Montane limped by. Yes, she was a healthy-looking woman. He really *should* court her, one of these days. She scowled at his smile and dumped his plate in front of him.

"I think I'm wearing her down," Daggon said, mostly to himself, as she left.

"You will have to work hard," Earnest said. "Seven men have proposed to her during the last month."

"What!"

"The reward!" the spindly man said. "The one for bringing in Chesterton and his men. Lucky woman, Silence Montane, finding the White Fox's lair like that."

Daggon dug into his meal. He didn't much like how things had turned out. Theopolis, that dandy, had been the White Fox all along? Poor Silence. How had it been, stumbling upon his cave and finding him inside, all withered away?

"They say that this Theopolis spent his last strength killing Chesterton," Earnest said, "then dragging him into the hole. Theopolis withered before he could get to his silver powder. Very like the White Fox, always determined to get the bounty, no matter what. We won't soon see a hunter like him again."

"I suppose not," Daggon said, though he'd much rather that the man had kept his skin. Now who would Daggon tell his tales about? He didn't fancy paying for his own beer.

Nearby, a greasy-looking fellow rose from his meal and shuffled out of the front door, looking half-drunk already, though it was only noon.

Some people. Daggon shook his head. "To the White Fox," he said, raising his drink.

Earnest clinked his mug to Daggon's. "The White Fox, meanest bastard the Forests have ever known."

"May his soul know peace," Daggon said, "and may the God Beyond be thanked that he never decided we were worth his time."

"Amen," Earnest said.

"Of course," Daggon said, "there *is* still Bloody Kent. Now, *he's* a right nasty fellow. You'd better hope he doesn't get your number, friend. And don't you give me that innocent look. These are the Forests. Everybody here has done something, now and then, that you don't want others to know about. . . ."

Sharon Kay Penman

New York Times bestseller Sharon Kay Penman has been acclaimed by *Publishers Weekly* as "an historical novelist of the first water." Her debut novel, *The Sunne in Splendour,* about Richard III, was a worldwide hit, and her acclaimed Welsh Princes trilogy—*Here Be Dragons, Falls the Shadow,* and *The Reckoning*—was similarly successful. Her other books include a sequence about Eleanor of Aquitaine—*When Christ and His Saints Slept, Time and Chance,* and *Devil's Brood*—and the Justin de Quincy series of historical mysteries, which include *The Queen's Man, Cruel as the Grave, Dragon's Lair,* and *Prince of Darkness.* Her most recent book is a novel about Richard, Coeur de Lion, *Lionheart.* She lives in Mays Landing, New Jersey, and maintains a website at sharonkaypenman.com.

Here she takes us back to twelfth-century Sicily to show us that a queen in exile is still a queen—and a very dangerous woman indeed.

A QUEEN IN EXILE

Constance de Hauteville was shivering although she was standing as close to the hearth as she could get without scorching her skirts. Her fourth wedding anniversary was a month away, but she was still not acclimated to German winters. She did not often let herself dwell upon memories of her Sicilian homeland; why salt unhealed wounds? But on nights when sleet and ice-edged winds chilled her to the very marrow of her bones, she could not deny her yearning for the palm trees, olive groves, and sun-splashed warmth of Palermo, for the royal palaces that ringed the city like a necklace of gleaming pearls, with their marble floors, vivid mosaics, cascading fountains, lush gardens, and silver reflecting pools.

"My lady?" One of her women was holding out a cup of hot mulled wine and Constance accepted it with a smile. But her unruly mind insisted upon slipping back in time, calling up the lavish entertainments of Christmas courts past, presided over by her nephew, William, and Joanna, his young English queen. Royal marriages were not love matches, of course, but dictated by matters of state. If a couple were lucky, though, they might develop a genuine respect and fondness for each other. William and Joanna's marriage had seemed an affectionate one to Constance, and when she'd been wed to Heinrich von Hohenstaufen, King of Germany and heir to the Holy Roman Empire, she'd hoped to find some contentment in their union. It was true that he'd already earned a reputation at twenty-one for ruthlessness and inflexibility. But he was also an accomplished poet, fluent in several languages, and she'd sought to convince herself that he had a softer side he showed only to family. Instead, she'd found a man as cold and unyielding as the lands he ruled, a man utterly lacking in the passion and exuberance and joie de vivre that made Sicily such an earthly paradise.

Finishing the wine, she turned reluctantly away from the fire. "I am ready for bed," she said, shivering again when they unlaced her gown, exposing her skin to the cool chamber air. She sat on a stool, still in her chemise, a robe draped across her shoulders as they removed her wimple and veil and unpinned her hair. It reached to her waist, the moonlit pale gold so prized by troubadours. She'd been proud of it once, proud of her de Hauteville good looks and fair coloring. But as she gazed into an ivory hand mirror, the woman looking back at her was a wary stranger, too thin and too tired, showing every one of her thirty-five years.

After brushing out her hair, one of her women began to braid it into a night plait. It was then that the door slammed open and Constance's husband strode into the chamber. As her ladies sank down in submissive curtseys, Constance rose hastily. She'd not been expecting him, for he'd paid a visit to her bedchamber just two nights ago, for what he referred to as the "marital debt," one of his rare jests, for if he had a sense of humor, he'd kept it well hidden so far. When they were first married, she'd been touched that he always came to her, rather than summoning her to his bedchamber, thinking it showed an unexpected sensitivity. Now she knew better. If they lay together in her bed, he could then return to his own chamber afterward, as he always did; she could count on one hand the times they'd awakened in the same bed.

Heinrich did not even glance at her ladies. "Leave us," he said, and they hastened to obey, so swiftly that their withdrawal seemed almost like flight.

"My lord husband," Constance murmured as the door closed behind the last of her attendants. She could read nothing in his face; he'd long ago mastered the royal skill of concealing his inner thoughts behind an impassive court mask. As she studied him more closely, though, she saw subtle indicators of mood—the faintest curve at the corner of his mouth, his usual pallor warmed by a faint flush. He had the oddest eye color she'd ever seen, as grey and pale as a frigid winter sky, but they seemed to catch the candlelight now, shining with unusual brightness.

"There has been word from Sicily. Their king is dead."

Constance stared at him, suddenly doubting her command of German.

Surely she could not have heard correctly? "William?" she whispered, her voice husky with disbelief.

Heinrich arched a brow. "Is there another King of Sicily that I do not know about? Of course I mean William."

"What . . . what happened? How . . . ?"

His shoulders twitched in a half shrug. "Some vile Sicilian pestilence, I suppose. God knows, the island is rife with enough fevers, plagues, and maladies to strike down half of Christendom. I know only that he died in November, a week after Martinmas, so his crown is ours for the taking."

Constance's knees threatened to give way and she stumbled toward the bed. How could William be dead? There was just a year between them; they'd been more like brother and sister than nephew and aunt. Theirs had been an idyllic childhood, and later she'd taken his little bride under her wing, a homesick eleven-year-old not yet old enough to be a wife. Now Joanna was a widow at twenty-four. What would happen to her? What would happen to Sicily without William?

Becoming aware of Heinrich's presence, she looked up to find him standing by the bed, staring down at her. She drew a bracing breath and got to her feet; she was tall for a woman, as tall as Heinrich, and drew confidence from the fact that she could look directly into his eyes. His appearance was not regal. His blond hair was thin, his beard scanty, and his physique slight; in an unkind moment, she'd once decided he put her in mind of a mushroom that had never seen the light of day. He could not have been more unlike his charismatic, expansive, robust father, the emperor Frederick Barbarossa, who swaggered through the imperial court like a colossus. And yet it was Heinrich who inspired fear in their subjects, not Frederick; those ice-color eyes could impale men as surely as any sword thrust. Even Constance was not immune to their piercing power, although she'd have moved heaven and earth to keep him from finding that out.

"You do realize what this means, Constance? William's queen was barren, so that makes you the legitimate and only heir to the Sicilian throne. Yet there you sit as if I'd brought you news of some calamity."

Constance flinched, for she knew that was what people whispered of her behind her back. To Heinrich's credit, he'd never called her "barren," at least not yet. He must think it, though, for they'd been wed nigh on four years and she'd not conceived. So far she'd failed in a queen's paramount duty. She wondered sometimes what Heinrich had thought of the marriage his father had arranged for him—a foreign wife eleven years his elder. Had he been as reluctant to make the match as she'd been? Or had he been willing to gamble that his flawed new wife might one day bring him Sicily, the richest kingdom in Christendom?

"Joanna was not barren," she said tautly. "She gave birth to a son."

"Who did not live. And she never got with child again. Why do you think William made his lords swear to recognize your right to the crown if he died without an heir of his body? He wanted to assure the succession."

Constance knew better. William had never doubted that he and Joanna would one day have another child; they were young and he was an optimist by nature. And because he was so confident of this, he'd been unfazed by the uproar her marriage had stirred. What did it matter that his subjects were horrified at the prospect of a German ruling over them when it would never come to pass? But now he was dead at thirty-six and the fears of his people were suddenly very real, indeed.

"It may not be as easy as you think, Heinrich," she said, choosing her words with care. "Our marriage was very unpopular. The Sicilians will not welcome a German king."

He showed himself to be as indifferent to the wishes of the Sicilian people as William had been, saying coolly, "They do not have a choice."

"I am not so sure of that. They might well turn to William's cousin Tancred." She was about to identify Tancred further, but there was no need. Heinrich never forgot anything that involved his self-interest.

"The Count of Lecce? He is baseborn!"

She opened her mouth, shut it again. It would not do to argue that the Sicilians would even prefer a man born out of wedlock to Heinrich. She knew it was true, though. They'd embrace her bastard cousin before they'd accept her German husband.

Heinrich was regarding her thoughtfully. "You do want the crown, Constance?" he said at last. She felt a flare of indignation that it had not even occurred to him she might mourn William, the last of her family, and she merely nodded. But he seemed satisfied by that muted response. "I'll send your women back in," he said. "Sleep well, for you'll soon have another crown to add to your collection."

As soon as the door closed, Constance sank down on the bed, and after a moment she kicked off her shoes and burrowed under the covers. She was shivering again. Cherishing this rare moment of privacy before her attendants returned, she closed her eyes and said a prayer for William's immortal soul. She would have Masses said for him on the morrow, she decided, and that gave her a small measure of comfort. She would pray for Joanna, too, in her time of need. Propping herself up with feather-filled pillows, then, she sought to make sense of the conflicting, confused emotions unleashed by William's untimely death.

She'd not expected this, had thought William would have a long, prosperous reign and would indeed have a son to succeed him. They'd been arrogant, she and William, assuming they knew the Will of the Almighty. They ought to have remembered their Scriptures: *A man's heart deviseth his way, but the Lord directeth his steps.* But Heinrich was right. She was the lawful heir to the Sicilian throne. Not Tancred. And she did want it. It was her birthright. Sicily was hers by blood, the land she loved. So why did she feel such ambivalence? As she shifted against the pillows, her gaze fell upon the only jewelry she wore, a band of beaten gold encrusted with emeralds—her wedding ring. As much as she wanted Sicily, she did not want to turn it over to Heinrich. She did not want to be the one to let the snake loose in Eden.

Constance's forebodings about Tancred of Lecce would prove to be justified. The Sicilians rallied around him and he was crowned King of Sicily in January of 1190. Constance dutifully echoed Heinrich's outrage, although she'd seen this coming. She was not even surprised to learn that Tancred had seized Joanna's dower lands, for they had strategic importance, and Tancred well knew that a German army would be contesting his claim to the crown. But she was utterly taken aback when Tancred took Joanna prisoner, holding her captive in Palermo, apparently fearing Joanna would use her personal popularity on Constance's behalf. Heinrich wanted to strike hard and fast at the man who'd usurped his wife's throne. Vengeance would have to wait, though, for his father had taken the cross and was planning to join the crusade to free Jerusalem from the Sultan of Egypt, the Saracen Salah al-Din, known to the crusaders as Saladin, and he needed Heinrich to govern Germany in his absence.

Frederick Barbarossa departed for the Holy Land that spring. The German force dispatched by Heinrich was routed by Tancred, who continued

to consolidate his power and had some success at the papal court, for the
Pope considered the Holy Roman Empire to be a greater threat than Tancred's illegitimacy. In September, Joanna's captivity was ended by the arrival in Sicily of the new English king, her brother Richard, known to
friends and foes alike as Lionheart. Like Frederick, he was on his way
to the Holy Land, and was accompanied by a large army. He was enraged to
learn of his sister's plight and demanded she be set free at once, her dower
lands restored. Tancred wisely agreed, for Richard knew war the way a
priest knew his Paternoster. For Constance, that was the only flare of light
in a dark, drear year. And then in December they learned that Heinrich's
father was dead. Never reaching the Holy Land, Frederick had drowned
fording a river in Armenia. Heinrich wasted no time. Daring a January
crossing of the Alps, he and Constance led an army into Italy. They halted
in Rome to be crowned by the Pope, and then rode south. The war for the
Sicilian crown had begun.

Salerno sweltered in the August sun. Usually sea breezes made the heat
tolerable, but this has been one of the hottest, driest summers in recent
memory. The sky was barren of clouds, a faded, bleached blue that seemed
bone white by midday. Courtyards and gardens offered little shade and
the normal city noise was muted, the streets all but deserted. Standing
on the balcony of the royal palace, Constance wished she could believe that
the citizens had been driven indoors by the heat. But she knew a more
potent force was at work—fear.

The Kingdom of Sicily encompassed the mainland south of Rome as well
as the island itself, and as the German army swept down the peninsula,
town after town opened their gates to Heinrich. The citizens of Salerno
even sought him out. Although their archbishop was firmly in Tancred's
camp, the Salernitans pledged their loyalty to Heinrich and invited Constance to stay in their city while he laid siege to Naples.

At first Constance had enjoyed her sojourn in Salerno. It was wonderful to be back on her native soil. She was delighted with her luxurious
residence—the royal palace that had been built by her father, the great King
Roger. She savored the delicious meals that graced her table, delicacies
rarely available beyond the Alps—melons, pomegranates, oranges, sugar-
coated almonds, rice, shrimp, oysters, fish that were swimming in the blue

Mediterranean that morning and sizzling in the palace kitchen pans that afternoon. Best of all, she was able to consult with some of the best doctors in Christendom about her failure to conceive. She could never have discussed so intimate a matter with a male physician. But women were allowed to attend Salerno's famed medical school and licensed to practice medicine. She'd soon found Dame Martina, whose consultation was a revelation.

Constance had taken all the blame upon herself for her barren marriage; common wisdom held that it was always the woman's fault. That was not so, Martina said briskly. Just as a woman may have a defect of her womb, so might a man have a defect in his seed. Moreover, there were ways to find out which one had the problem. A small pot should be filled with the woman's urine and another with her husband's. Wheat bran was then added to both pots, which were to be left alone for nine days. If worms appeared in the urine of the man, he was the one at fault, and the same was true for the woman.

"I doubt that my lord husband would agree to such a test," Constance had said wryly, imagining Heinrich's incredulous, outraged reaction should she even hint that the fault might be his. But she took the test herself, and when her urine was found to be worm-free on the ninth day, her spirits had soared. Even if no one else knew it, she knew now that she did not have a defective womb; she was not doomed to be that saddest of all creatures, a barren queen.

Martina offered hope, too, explaining that sometimes neither husband nor wife was at fault and yet his seed would not take root in her womb. But this could be remedied, she assured Constance. She must dry the male parts of a boar and then make a powder of them, which she was then to drink with a good wine. And to assure the birth of a male child, Constance and Heinrich must dry and powder the womb of a hare, then drink it in wine. Constance grimaced at that, glad she'd be spared such an unappetizing concoction until she and Heinrich were reunited. How would she get him to cooperate, though? She'd have to find a way to mix the powder into his wine undetected on one of his nocturnal visits to her bedchamber. She was so grateful to Martina that she offered the older woman a vast sum to become her personal physician, and Martina gladly accepted, tempted as much by the prestige of serving an empress as by the material benefits.

But then reports began to reach Salerno from the siege of Naples. For the first time, Heinrich was encountering fierce resistance, led by Tancred's brother-in-law, the Count of Acerra, and Salerno's own archbishop. Heinrich had hired ships from Pisa, but they were not numerous enough to blockade the harbor, and so he would be unable to starve the Neapolitans into surrender. Tancred had chosen to make his stand on the island of Sicily knowing that his most dangerous weapon was the hot, humid, Italian summer. Heinrich's German troops were unaccustomed to such stifling heat and they soon began to sicken. Army camps were particularly vulnerable to deadly contagions like the bloody flux; Constance had been told that more crusaders died from disease than from Saracen swords in the Holy Land.

She'd hoped that the Salernitans would remain in ignorance of the setbacks Heinrich was experiencing, but that was an unrealistic hope, for Naples was less than thirty miles to the north of Salerno. She could tell as soon as word began to trickle into the city, for the people she encountered in the piazza were subdued or sullen, and the palace servants could not hide their dismay. Even Martina had anxiously asked her if she was sure Heinrich would prevail and did not seem completely convinced by Constance's assurances. Salerno had assumed that Tancred would be no match for the large German army and self-preservation had won out over loyalty to the Sicilian king. Now they began to fear that they'd wagered on the wrong horse.

When almost a fortnight passed without any word from Heinrich, Constance dispatched Sir Baldwin, the head of her household knights, to Naples to find out how bad things really were. Standing now on the palace balcony, she shaded her eyes against the glare of the noonday sun and wondered if this would be the day Baldwin would return. She would never admit it aloud, but she wanted him to stay away as long as possible, so sure was she that he would be bringing bad news.

"Madame?" Hildegund was standing by the door. Most of Constance's attendants were Sicilians, including Dame Adela, who'd been with her since childhood, and Michael, the Saracen eunuch who attracted so much attention at Heinrich's court; the Germans were shocked that Saracens were allowed to live freely in a Christian country and horrified that William had relied upon the men called "the palace eunuchs" in the governance of his kingdom. Constance had taken care not to reveal that William had spoken Arabic or that it was one of the official languages of Sicily, and she'd insisted that Michael had embraced the True Faith, even though she knew that many eunuchs' conversion to Christianity was often pretense. How could she ever make Heinrich or his subjects understand the complex mosaic that was Sicilian society? Hildegund was one of her few German ladies-in-waiting, a self-possessed, sedate widow who'd been a great asset in Constance's struggles to learn German, and Constance gave her a fond smile, nodding when the other woman reminded her it was time for the day's main meal.

Dinners were very different now than they'd been at the outset of her stay in Salerno. Then the local lords and their ladies had competed eagerly for an invitation from the empress, and the great hall had usually been crowded with finely garbed guests showing off their silks and jewels as they sought to curry favor with Constance. For over a week, though, her invitations to dine had been declined with transparent excuses, and on this Sunday noon, the only ones sharing her table were the members of her own household.

The palace cooks had prepared a variety of tasty dishes, but Constance merely picked at the roast capon on her trencher. Glancing around, she saw that few of the others had much appetite, either. Reminding herself that she should be setting an example for her household, she began an animated conversation with Martina and her chaplain just as shouting drifted through the open windows. Riders were coming in. Constance set her wine cup down and got slowly to her feet as Baldwin was admitted to the hall. One look at his face told her all she needed or wanted to know, but she made herself reach out and take the proffered letter as he knelt before her.

Gesturing for him to rise, she broke her husband's seal and quickly scanned the contents. It was not written in Heinrich's hand, of course; he always dictated his letters to a scribe, for he never sent her a message that was not meant for other eyes. A low murmur swept the hall as those watching saw her color fade, leaving her skin so pale it seemed almost translucent. When she glanced up, though, her voice was even, revealing none of her inner distress. "I will not mislead you," she said. "The news is not good. Many have died of the bloody flux and the emperor himself has been stricken with this vile malady. He has decided that it would be best to end the siege and yesterday his army began a retreat from Naples."

There were gasps, smothered cries, a few muttered obscenities from some of her knights. "What of us, my lady?" a young girl blurted out. "What will become of us?"

"The emperor wants us to remain in Salerno. He says that my presence here will be proof that he intends to return and the war is not over."

There was an appalled silence. Taking advantage of it, she beckoned to Baldwin and led the way out into the courtyard. The sun was blinding, and when she sank down on the edge of the marble fountain, she could feel the heat through the silk of her gown. "How ill is he, Baldwin?" she asked, so softly that she felt the need to repeat herself, swallowing until she had enough saliva for speech.

He knelt beside her, gazing up intently into her face. "Very ill, my lady. His doctors said he was sure to die if he stayed. I fear that his wits have been addled by his fever, for he did not seem to realize the danger you are in now that he is gone."

Constance did not think it was the fever, but rather Heinrich's supreme self-confidence. He did not understand that the Salernitans' fear of him was dependent upon his presence. When word got out that his army was retreating, the people would see it as a defeat, and they'd begin to fear Tancred more than Heinrich, for they'd betrayed him by inviting her into their city. She could feel a headache coming on, and rubbed her temples in a vain attempt to head it off. The wrath of a king was indeed to be feared. Heinrich's father had razed Milan to the ground as punishment for past treachery, and her brother, William's father, had destroyed the town of Bari as a brutal warning to would-be rebels. Was Tancred capable of such ruthless vengeance? She did not think so, but how were the frightened citizens of Salerno to know that?

"My lady . . . I think we ought to leave this place today. A healthy army travels less than ten miles a day and this army is battered and bleeding. If we make haste, we can overtake them."

Constance bit her lip. She agreed with Baldwin; she was not safe here, not now. But her pride rebelled at the thought of fleeing like a thief in the night. How would the Sicilians consider her worthy to rule over them if she gave in to her fears like a foolish, timid woman? Her father would not have run away. And Heinrich would never forgive her if she disobeyed him and fled Salerno, for his letter had clearly stated that her presence was important as a pledge to his supporters, a warning to his enemies—proof that he would be back. She'd not wanted Heinrich as her husband; still less did she want him as her enemy. How could she live with a man who hated her . . . and he would, for her flight would make it impossible for him to pretend he'd not suffered a humiliating defeat.

"I cannot, Baldwin," she said. "It is my husband's wish that I await him here in Salerno. Even if the worst happens and Tancred comes to lay siege to the city, Heinrich will send troops to defend it . . . and us."

"Of course, madame," Baldwin said, mustering up all the certainty he could. "All will be well." But he did not believe it and he doubted that Constance did, either.

It took only two days for word to reach Salerno of the German army's retreat. The streets were soon crowded with frantic men and women trying to convince themselves that they'd not made a fatal mistake. Constance sent out public criers to assure them that Heinrich would soon return. But as dusk descended, a new and terrifying rumor swept the city—that the German emperor had died of the bloody flux. And that was the spark thrown into a hayrick, setting off a conflagration.

Constance and her household had just finished their evening meal when they heard a strange noise, almost like the roaring of the sea, a distant, dull rumble that grew ever louder. She sent several of her knights to investigate and they soon returned with alarming news. A huge mob was gathering outside the gates of the palace, many of them drunk, all of them scared witless by what they'd brought upon themselves.

Baldwin and her knights assured Constance and the women that the mob would not be able to force an entry into the palace grounds, and departed then to join the men guarding the walls. But soon afterward, they came running back into the great hall. "We've been betrayed," Baldwin gasped. "Those cowardly whoresons opened the gates to them!" Bolting the thick oaken doors, they hastened to latch the shutters as Baldwin dispatched men to make sure all of the other entrances to the palace were secure. Constance's women gathered around her, in the way she'd seen chicks flock to the mother hen when a hawk's shadow darkened the sun. The awareness that they were all looking to her for answers stiffened her spine, giving her the courage she needed to face this unexpected crisis. She'd feared that Salerno would soon be under siege by the army Tancred had sent to defend Naples. She'd not realized that the greatest danger would come from within.

She reassured them as best she could, insisting that the townspeople would disperse once they realized that they could not gain entry to the palace itself. Her words rang hollow even to herself, for the fury of the mob showed no signs of abating. Theirs had been a spontaneous act of panic, and they'd been ill prepared for an assault. But now those in the hall could hear cries for axes, for a battering ram. When Constance heard men also shouting for kindling and torches, she knew they dared not wait for cooler heads to prevail or for the craven city officials to intervene.

Calling to Baldwin, she drew him toward the dais. "I must talk to them," she said softly. "Mayhap I can make them see reason."

He was horrified. "My lady, they are mad with fear. There is no reasoning with them."

She suspected that he was right, but what else could she do? "Nevertheless, I have to try," she said, with a steadfastness she was far from feeling. "Come with me to the solar above the hall. I can speak to them from the balcony."

He continued to argue halfheartedly, for he did not know what else to do, either, and when she turned toward the stairwell, he trailed at her heels. The solar was dark, for no oil lamps had been lit, and the heat was suffocating. Constance waited while Baldwin unlatched the door leading out onto the small balcony; she could feel perspiration trickling along her ribs and her heart was beating so rapidly that she felt light-headed.

The scene below her was an eerie one. The darkness was stabbed with flaring torches, illuminating faces contorted with anger and fear. She saw women in the surging throng and, incredibly, even a few children darting about on the edges of the crowd as if this were a holy day festival. Some were passing wineskins back and forth, but most drew their courage from their desperation. They were still calling for firewood, urging those closest to the street to find anything that would burn. It took a few moments for them to notice the woman standing motionless above them, gripping the balcony railing as if it were her only lifeline.

"Good people of Salerno!" Constance swallowed with difficulty, worried that they'd not hear her. Before she could continue, they began to point and shout. She heard her name, heard cries of "Bitch!" and "Sorceress!" and then "German slut!"

"I am not German!" There was no worry of being heard now; her voice resonated across the courtyard, infused with anger. "I am Sicilian born and bred, as you all are. I am the daughter of King Roger of blessed memory. This is my homeland as much as it is yours."

She wasn't sure if it was the mention of her revered father's name, but the crowd quieted for the moment. "I know you are confused and fearful. But you've heeded false rumors. The Emperor Heinrich is not dead! Indeed, he is already on the mend. I had a letter from him just this morn, saying he expects to return very soon."

She paused for breath. "You know my lord husband. He remembers those who do him a good service. When he leads his army back to Salerno, he will be grateful to you for keeping his wife safe. You will be rewarded for your loyalty." Another pause, this one deliberate. "But this you must know, too. The Emperor Heinrich never forgets a wrong done him. If you betray his faith, if you do harm to me or mine, he will not forgive. He will leave a smoldering ruin where your city once stood. Dare any of you deny it? You know in your hearts that I speak true. You have far more to fear from the emperor if you bring his wrath down upon you than ever you do from that usurper in Palermo."

She thought she had them, could see some heads nodding, see men lowering clubs and bows as she spoke. But her mention of Tancred was a tactical error, reminding them that his supporters were just thirty miles away at Naples, while Heinrich's army was decimated by the bloody flux, fleeing with their tales tucked between their legs. The spell broken, the crowd began to mutter among themselves, and then one well-dressed youth with a sword at his hip shouted out, "She lies! That German swine breathed his last the day after he fled the siege camp! Send her to join him in Hell!"

The words were no sooner out of his mouth than one of his allies brought up his bow, aimed, and sent an arrow winging through the dark toward the balcony. His aim was true, but Baldwin had been watching those with weapons, and as soon as the bowman moved, he dove from the shadows, shoving Constance to the ground. There was a shocked silence and then a woman cried, "Holy Mother Mary, you killed her!" Someone else retorted that they had nothing left to lose then and more arrows were loosed. Crawling on their hands and knees, Constance and Baldwin scrambled back into the solar and she sat on the floor, gasping for breath as he fumbled with the door. Several thuds told them that arrows had found their mark.

Once she could draw enough air into her lungs again, Constance held out her hand, let him help her to her feet. "Thank you," she said, and tears stung her eyes when he swore that he'd defend her as long as he had breath in his body, for that was no empty boast. He would die here in the palace at Salerno. They all would die unless the Almighty worked a miracle expressly on their behalf. She insisted that he escort her back to the hall, for at least she could do that much for her household. She would stand with them to the last.

She expected hysteria, but her women seemed stunned. Constance ordered wine to be brought out, for what else was there to do? They could hear the sounds of the assault, knew it was only a matter of time until the mob would break down the doors. As the noise intensified, Martina drew Constance aside, surreptitiously showing her a handful of herbs clutched in the palm of her hand. "They work quickly," she murmured, and would have dropped them into Constance's wine cup had she not recoiled.

"Jesu, Martina! Self-slaughter is a mortal sin!"

"It is a better fate than what awaits us, my lady. They are sore crazed and there are none in command. What do you think they will do to you once they get inside? On the morrow, they'll be horrified by what they did this night. But their remorse and guilt will change nothing."

Constance could not repress a shudder, but she continued to shake her head. "I cannot," she whispered, "nor can you, Martina. We'd burn for aye in Hell if we did."

Martina said nothing, merely slipped the herbs back into a pouch swinging from her belt. She stayed by Constance's side, occasionally giving the younger woman a significant look, as if reminding her there was still time to change her mind. Constance mounted the steps of the dais, holding up her hand for silence. "We must pray to Almighty God that His will be done," she said, surprised that her voice sounded so steady. There were a few stifled sobs from her women, but when she knelt, they knelt, too. So did the men, after carefully placing their weapons within reach. Those who'd not been shriven of their sins sought out Constance's chaplain, following him behind the decorated wooden screen that he was using as a makeshift confessional.

Michael had not joined the others to confess, confirming Constance's suspicions that his Christian faith was camouflage. He was a good man, though, and she hoped the Almighty would be merciful with him. The eunuch had stayed in a window recess, monitoring the progress of the assault by the sounds filtering into the hall. "My lady!" he called out suddenly. "Something is happening!" Before anyone could stop him, he unlatched the shutters, peering out into the dark. And then he flung the shutters wide.

By now they all could hear the screams. Baldwin hastened to the window. "The mob is being dispersed by men on horseback, madame! God has heard our prayers!"

The crowd scattered as knights rode into their midst. The courtyard was soon cleared of all but the riders and the crumpled bodies of those who'd been too slow or too stubborn. Having come so close to death, Constance was hesitant to believe deliverance was at hand, not until she saw for herself. Kneeling on the window seat, she watched as the last of the rioters fled. But she had no time to savor her reprieve, for it was then that she recognized the man in command of the knights. As if feeling her eyes upon him, he glanced her way, and at once acknowledged her with a gallant gesture only slightly spoiled by the bloodied sword in his hand.

"Dear God," Constance whispered, sitting back in the window seat. Martina was beside her now and when she asked who he was, Constance managed a faint, mirthless smile. "His name is Elias of Gesualdo, and he is both my salvation and my downfall. He arrived just in time to spare our lives, but on the morrow, he will deliver me into the hands of his uncle— Tancred of Lecce."

The following four months were difficult ones for Constance. She knew Tancred well enough to be sure she'd be treated kindly, and she was. Tancred and his queen, Sybilla, acted as if she were an honored guest rather than a prisoner, albeit one under constant discreet surveillance. But she found it humiliating to be utterly dependent upon the mercy of the man who'd usurped her throne, and she could not help contrasting her barrenness with Sybilla's fecundity, mother to two sons and three daughters. She was even more mortified when Heinrich adamantly refused to make any concessions in order to gain her freedom. It was not to be her husband who eventually pried open the door of her gilded prison. Pope Celestine agreed to give Tancred what he most wanted—papal recognition of his kingship—but in return he wanted Constance transferred to his custody. Tancred reluctantly agreed, and on a January day in 1192, Constance found herself riding toward Rome in the company of three cardinals and an armed escort.

She'd not find freedom in Rome, for the Pope saw her as a valuable hostage in his dealings with Heinrich, but at least she'd not be living in the same palace with Tancred and his queen. And a prolonged stay in Rome was not entirely unwelcome, for she was not eager to be reunited with the man who'd put her in such peril and then done nothing to rescue her from a predicament of his own making.

The cardinals seemed uncomfortable with their role as gaolers and set a pace that would be easy for Constance and her ladies. There were only three now, Adela, Hildegund, and Dame Martina, for her Sicilian attendants had chosen to remain in their homeland, and after the horror of Salerno, Constance could not blame them. They'd been on the road for several hours when Constance saw their scout galloping back toward their party, his expression grim. Nudging her mare forward, she joined the cardinals as they conferred with him. As she reined in beside them, they forced smiles, explaining that there was a band of suspicious-looking men up ahead who might well be bandits. They thought it best to turn aside and avoid a confrontation.

Constance agreed blandly that it was indeed best, her face giving away nothing. They had forgotten that Latin was one of the official languages of Sicily, and while she was not as fluent as Heinrich, she'd caught two words in the conversation that had ended abruptly as she came within earshot—*praesidium imperatoris*. It was not bandits they feared. The men up ahead were members of Heinrich's elite imperial guard.

Constance did not know how they happened to be here, but it did not matter. Dropping back beside her women, she told them softly to be ready to act when she did. She could see the riders for herself now in the distance. When the cardinals and their men veered off the main road onto a dirt lane that led away from the Liri River, Constance followed. Waiting until the guard riding at her side moved ahead of her mare, she suddenly brought her whip down upon the horse's haunches. The startled animal shot forward as if launched by a crossbow, and she was already yards away before the cardinals and their escort realized what had happened. She heard shouting and glanced back to see that several of the cardinals' men were in pursuit, their stallions swift enough to outrun her mare. But by then the imperial guards were riding toward her. Pulling back the hood of her mantle so there'd be no doubt, she cried out, "I am your empress. I put myself under your protection."

The cardinals did their best, angrily warning the Germans that they'd bring the wrath of the Holy Father down upon their heads if they interfered, insisting that the empress was in the custody of the Pope. The imperial guards merely laughed at them. Constance and her ladies were soon riding away with their new protectors, the knights thrilled to have recovered such a prize, knowing that their fortunes were made. Constance's women were elated, too. But while Constance felt a grim sense of satisfaction, she did not share their jubilation. She was still a hostage. Even an imperial crown did not change that.

Two years after Constance's fortuitous encounter with Heinrich's imperial guards, Tancred was dying in his palace at Palermo. His was a bitter end, for his nineteen-year-old son had died suddenly in December, leaving a four-year-old boy as his heir, and he knew fear of the Holy Roman emperor would prevail over loyalty to a child. Upon learning of Tancred's death, Heinrich led an army across the Alps into Italy once again.

Upon their May arrival in Milan, Constance had gone to bed, saying she must rest before the evening's feast given in their honor by the Bishop of Milan. Adela had been concerned about her mistress for some weeks, but this open acknowledgment of fatigue, so unlike Constance, sent her searching for Dame Martina. Once they'd found a private corner safe from eavesdroppers, she confessed that she feared the empress was ailing. Martina was not surprised, for she, too, had noticed Constance's flagging appetite, exhaustion, and pallor.

"I've spoken to her," she admitted, "but she insists she is well. I fear that her downcast spirits are affecting her health . . . ." She let her words trail off, sure that Adela would understand. They both knew Constance was troubled by what the future held for Sicily and its people. She'd not said as much, but there was no need to put her unspoken fears into words, for they knew the man she'd married. "I will speak with her again after the revelries tonight," she promised, and Adela had to be content with that.

When Adela returned to Constance's chamber, she was relieved to find the empress up and dressing, for that made it easier to believe she was not ill, merely tired. Once she was ready to descend to the great hall where Heinrich and the Bishop of Milan awaited her, her ladies exclaimed over the beauty of her gown, brocaded silk the color of a Sicilian sunrise, and the jewelry that was worth a king's ransom, but Constance felt like a richly wrapped gift that was empty inside.

Heinrich was waiting impatiently. "You're late," he murmured as she slipped her arm through his. They'd had one of the worst quarrels of their marriage a fortnight ago and the strain still showed. They'd patched up a peace, were civil both in public and private, but nothing had changed. They were still at odds over Salerno. Constance agreed that the Salernitans deserved punishment. She'd have been satisfied with razing the town walls and imposing a heavy fine upon its inhabitants, for they'd acted out of terror, not treachery. Heinrich saw it differently, saying they owed him a blood debt and he meant to collect it. Constance thought that his implacable hatred toward the men and women of Salerno was a fire fed by his awareness that he'd made a great mistake, a mistake he would never acknowledge. But despite her anger, she'd not reached for that weapon, knowing it would rebound back upon her. Glancing at him now from the corner of her eye, she felt a flicker of weary resentment, and then summoned up a smile for the man approaching them.

She'd met Bishop Milo two years ago at Lodi and it was easy enough to draw upon those memories for polite conversation. She was accustomed to making such social small talk. This time it would be different, though. She'd barely had a chance to acknowledge his flowery greeting when the ground seemed to shift under her feet, as if she were suddenly on the deck of a ship. She started to say she needed to sit, but it was too late. She was already spiraling down into the dark.

Constance settled back against the pillows, watching as Martina inspected a glass vial of her urine. She'd asked no questions during the doctor's examination, not sure she wanted the answers, for she'd suspected for some time that she might be seriously ill. She was about to ask for wine when the door opened and her husband entered, followed by a second man whose appearance, uninvited, in the empress's quarters shocked her ladies.

"I want my physician to examine you," Heinrich announced without preamble. "You are obviously ill and need care that this woman cannot provide."

Constance sat up in bed. "'This woman' is a licensed physician, Heinrich. I want her to attend me." Unable to resist a small jab, she added, "She studied in Salerno and was with me during the assault upon the palace, where she showed both courage and loyalty. I trust her judgment."

He mustered up a smile that never reached his eyes. "I am sure she is competent for womanly ailments. Nonetheless, I want Master Conrad to take over your treatment. I must insist, my dear, for your health is very important to me."

That, Constance did not doubt; it would be awkward for him if she were to die before he could be crowned King of Sicily, for then he'd have no claim to the throne other than right of conquest. "No," she said flatly, and saw a muscle twitch in his cheek as his eyes narrowed. But Martina chose that moment to intervene.

"Whilst I am gratified by the empress's faith in my abilities," she said smoothly, "I am sure Master Conrad is a physician of renown. But there is no need for another opinion. I already know what caused the empress to faint."

Heinrich did not bother to mask his skepticism. "Do you, indeed?"

Martina regarded him calmly. "I do. The empress is with child."

Constance gasped, her eyes widening. Heinrich was no less stunned. Reaching out, he grasped Martina's arm. "Are you sure? God save you if you lie!"

"Heinrich!" Constance's protest went unheeded. Martina met Heinrich's eyes without flinching, and after a moment he released his hold.

"I am very sure," Martina said confidently, and this time she directed her words at Constance. "By my reckoning, you will be a mother ere the year is out."

Constance lay back, closing her eyes. When she opened them again, Heinrich was leaning over the bed. "You must rest now," he said. "You can do nothing that might put the baby at risk."

"You will have to continue on without me, Heinrich, for I must travel very slowly." He agreed so readily that she realized that she had leverage now, for the first time in their marriage. He leaned over still farther, his lips brushing her cheek, and when he straightened, he told Martina that his wife was to have whatever she wanted and her commands were to be obeyed straightaway, as if they came from his own mouth. Beckoning to Master Conrad, who'd been shifting awkwardly from foot to foot, he started toward the door. There he paused and, looking back at Constance, he laughed, a sound so rare that the women all started, as if hearing thunder in a clear, cloudless sky.

"God has indeed blessed me," he said exultantly. "Who can doubt now that my victory in Sicily is ordained?"

As soon as the door closed behind him, Constance reached out her hand to Martina, their fingers entwining. "Are you sure?" She was echoing Heinrich's words, but his had been a threat; hers were both a plea and a prayer.

"I am indeed sure, my lady. You told me your last flux was in March. Did you never think . . . ?"

"No . . . my fluxes have been irregular the last year or two. I thought . . . I feared I might be reaching that age when a woman could no longer conceive." It was more than that, though. She'd not thought she might be pregnant because she no longer had hope.

Adela was weeping, calling her "my lamb" as if she were back in the nursery. Hildegund had dropped to her knees, giving thanks to the Almighty, and Katerina, the youngest of her ladies, was dancing around the chamber, as light on her feet as a windblown leaf. Constance wanted to weep and pray and dance, too. Instead, she laughed, the laughter of the carefree girl she'd once been, back in the days of her youth when her world had been filled with tropical sunlight and she'd never imagined the fate that was to be hers—exile in a frigid foreign land and a marriage that was as barren as her womb.

Dismissing the others to return to the festivities, for she wanted only Adela and Martina with her now, she placed her hand upon her belly, trying to envision the tiny entity that now shared her body. So great was her joy that she could at last speak the truth. "I'd not celebrated Tancred's death," she confided. "I could not, for I knew what it meant for Sicily. It would become merely another appendage of the Holy Roman Empire, its riches plundered, its independence gone, and its very identity lost. But now . . . now it will pass to my son. He will rule Sicily as my father and nephew did. He will be more than its king. He will be its savior."

At that, Adela began to weep in earnest and Martina found herself smiling through tears. "You ought to at least consider, madame, that you may have a daughter."

Constance laughed again. "And I would have welcomed one, Martina. But this child will be a boy. The Almighty has blessed us with a miracle. How else could I become pregnant in my forty-first year after a marriage of eight barren years? It is God's Will that I give birth to a son."

Despite her euphoria, Constance was well aware that the odds were not in her favor; at her age, having a first child posed considerable risks, with miscarriage and stillbirth very real dangers. She chose to pass the most perilous months of her pregnancy at a Benedictine nunnery in Meda, north of Milan, and when she did resume her travels, it was done in easy stages. She had selected the Italian town of Jesi for her lying-in. Located on the crest of a hill overlooking the Esino River, it had fortified walls and was friendly to the Holy Roman Empire; Heinrich had provided her with his imperial guards, but Constance was taking no chances of another Salerno.

Although she'd been spared much of the early morning nausea that so many women endured, her pregnancy was not an easy one. Her ankles and feet were badly swollen, her breasts very sore and tender, and she was exhausted all the time, suffering backaches, heartburn, breathlessness, and sudden mood swings. But some of her anxiety eased upon her arrival in Jesi, for Martina assured her she was less likely to miscarry in the last months. She was heartened, too, by the friendliness of Jesi's citizens, who seemed genuinely pleased that she'd chosen to have her baby in their town, and as November slid into December, she was calmer than at any time in her pregnancy.

Heinrich's army had encountered little resistance, and the surrender of Naples in August caused a widespread defection from Tancred's embattled queen and young son. Constance was troubled to learn of the bloody vengeance Heinrich had wreaked upon Salerno in September, but she heeded Martina's admonition that too much distress might harm her baby and tried to put from her mind images of burning houses, bodies, grieving widows, and terrified children. In November, she was delighted by the arrival of Baldwin, Michael, and several of her household knights. When Heinrich took Salerno, they'd been freed from captivity and he sent them on to Jesi. Constance joked to Martina that her marriage would have been much happier had she only been pregnant the entire time; by now they were far more than physician and patient, sharing the rigors of her pregnancy as they'd shared the dangers in Salerno.

In December, Constance learned that Heinrich had been admitted into Palermo and Sybilla had yielded upon his promise that her family would be safe and her son allowed to inherit Tancred's lands in Lecce. Constance could not help feeling some sympathy for Sybilla and she was gladdened by the surprising leniency of Heinrich's terms. She was staying in the Bishop of Jesi's palace, and they celebrated Heinrich's upcoming coronation with as lavish a feast as Advent allowed. Later that day, she was tempted by the mild weather to venture out into the gardens.

Accompanied by Hildegund and Katerina, she was seated in a trellised arbor when there was a commotion at the end of the garden and several young men trooped in, tossing a pig's-bladder ball back and forth. Constance recognized them—one of the bishop's clerks and two of Heinrich's household knights, who'd been entrusted to bring her word of his triumph. Setting down her embroidery, she smiled at their tomfoolery, thinking that one day it would be her son playing camp ball with his friends.

"The emperor has been truly blessed by God this year." Constance could no longer see them, but she knew their voices. This speaker was Pietro, the clerk, who went on to ask rhetorically how many men gained a crown and an heir in one year. "God grant," he added piously, "that the empress will birth a son." There was a burst of laughter from Heinrich's knights, and when Pietro spoke again, he sounded puzzled. "Why do you laugh? It is in the Almighty's Hands, after all."

"You truly are an innocent." This voice was Johann's, the older of the knights. "Do you really think that the emperor would go to so much trouble to secure an heir and then present the world with a girl? When pigs fly!"

Constance's head came up sharply, and she raised a hand for silence when Katerina would have spoken. "I do not understand your meaning," Pietro said, and now there was a note of wariness in his voice.

"Yes, you do. You are just loath to say it aloud. After eight years, Lord Heinrich well knew he was accursed with a barren wife. Then, lo and behold, this miraculous pregnancy. Why do you think the empress chose this godforsaken town, truly at the back of beyond, for her lying-in? It would have been much harder in Naples or Palermo, too many suspicious eyes. Here it will be easy. Word will spread that her labor pangs have begun, and under cover of night the babe will be smuggled in—mayhap one of Heinrich's by-blows—and then the church bells will peal out joyfully the news that the emperor has a robust, healthy son."

Constance caught her breath, her hand clenching around the embroidery; she never even felt the needle jabbing into her palm. Katerina half rose, but subsided when Hildegund put a restraining hand on her arm.

"Clearly you had too much wine at dinner," Pietro said coldly, which set off more laughter from the young knights. By now Constance was on her feet. As she emerged from the arbor, Pietro saw her first and made a deep obeisance. "Madame!"

The blood drained from Johann's face, leaving him whiter than a corpse candle. "Ma-madame," he stuttered, "I—I am so very sorry! It was but a jest. As—as Pietro said, I'd quaffed too much wine." His words were slurring in his haste to get them said, his voice high-pitched and tremulous. "Truly, I had to be in my cups to make such a vile joke. . . ."

Constance's own voice was like ice, if ice could burn. "I wonder if my lord husband will find your jest as amusing as you do."

Johann made a strangled sound, then fell to his knees. "Madame . . . please," he entreated, "please . . . I beg of you, do not tell him. . . ."

Constance stared down at him until he began to sob, and then turned and walked away. Johann crumpled to the ground, Pietro and the other knight still frozen where they stood. Hildegund glared at the weeping knight, then hurried after Constance, with Katerina right behind her. "Will she tell the emperor?" she whispered, feeling a twinge of unwelcome pity for Johann's stark terror.

Hildegund shook her head. "I think not," she said, very low, and then spat, "Damn that misbegotten, callow lackwit to eternal damnation for this! Of all things for our lady to hear as her time grows nigh . . ."

"My lamb, what does it matter what a fool like that thinks?"

Constance paid no heed. She'd been pacing back and forth, seething, showing a command of curses that her women did not know she'd possessed. But when she lost color and began to pant, Martina put an arm around her shoulders and steered her toward a chair. Coming back a few moments later with a wine cup, she put it in Constance's hand. "Drink this, my lady. It will calm your nerves. Adela is right: you are upsetting yourself for naught. Surely you knew there would be mean-spirited talk like this, men eager to believe the worst of the emperor?"

Constance set the cup down so abruptly that wine splashed onto her sleeve. "Of course I knew that, Martina! Heinrich has more enemies than Rome has priests. But do you not see? These were his own knights, men sworn to die for him if need be. If even *they* doubt my pregnancy . . ."

Adela knelt by the chair, wincing as her old bones protested. "It does not matter," she repeated stoutly. "The chattering of magpies, no more than that."

Constance's outrage had given way now to despair. "It does matter! My son will come into this world under a shadow, under suspicion. People will not believe he is truly the flesh of my flesh, the rightful heir to the Sicilian crown. He will have to fight his entire life against calumnies and slander. Rebels can claim it as a pretext for rising up against him. A hostile Pope might well declare him illegitimate. He will never be free of the whispers, the doubts . . ." She closed her eyes, tears beginning to seep through her lashes. "What if he comes to believe it himself . . . .?"

Adela began to weep, too. Martina reached for Constance's arm and gently but firmly propelled her to her feet. "As I said, this serves for naught. Even if you are right and your fears are justified, there is nothing you can do to disprove the gossip. Now I want you to lie down and get some rest. You must think of your baby's welfare whilst he is in your womb, not what he might face in years to come."

Constance did not argue; let them put her to bed. But she did not sleep, lying awake as the sky darkened and then slowly began to streak with light again, hearing Johann's voice as he mocked the very idea that Heinrich's aging, barren wife could conceive.

Baldwin was uneasy, for it was not fitting that he be summoned to his lady's private chamber; he was sure Heinrich would not approve. "You sent for me, Madame?" he asked, trying to conceal his dismay at his empress's haggard, ashen appearance.

"I have a task for you, Sir Baldwin." Constance was sitting in a chair, her hands so tightly clasped that her ring was digging into her flesh. "I want you to set up a pavilion in the piazza. And then I want you to send men into the streets, telling the people that I shall have my lying-in there, in that tent, and the matrons and maidens of Jesi are invited to attend the birth of my child."

Baldwin's jaw dropped; for the life of him, he could think of nothing to say. But Constance's women were not speechless and they burst into scandalized protest. She heard them out and then told Baldwin to see that her command was obeyed. He'd seen this expression on her face once before, as she was about to step out onto that Salerno balcony, and he knelt, kissing her hand. "It will be done, madame."

Adela, Hildegund, and Katerina had subsided, staring at her in shocked silence. Martina leaned over the chair, murmuring, "Are you sure you want to do this?"

Constance's breath hissed through her teeth. "Christ on the Cross, Martina! Of course I do not want to do this!" Raising her head then, she said, "But I *will* do it! I will do it for my son."

On the day after Christmas, the piazza was as crowded as if it were a market day. There was a festive atmosphere, for the townsmen knew they were witnessing something extraordinary—at least their wives were. Occasionally one of them would emerge from the tent to report that all was going as it ought and then disappear back inside. The men joked and gossiped and wagered upon the sex of the child struggling to be born. Within the tent, the mood was quite different. At first, the women of Jesi had been excited, whispering among themselves, feeling like spectators at a Christmas play. But almost all of them had their own experiences in the birthing chamber, had endured what Constance was suffering now, and as they watched her writhe on the birthing stool, her skin damp with perspiration, her face contorted with pain, they began to identify with her, to forget that she was an empress, highborn and wealthy and privileged beyond their wildest dreams. They'd been honored to bear witness to such a historic event. Now they found themselves cheering her on as if she were one of them, for they were all daughters of Eve and, when it came to childbirth, sisters under the skin.

Martina was consulting with two of the town's midwives, their voices low, their faces intent. Adela was coaxing Constance to swallow a spoonful of honey, saying it would give her strength, and she forced herself to take it upon her tongue. She knew why they were so concerned. When her waters had broken, they told her it meant the birth was nigh, yet her pains continued, growing more severe, and it did not seem to her that any progress was being made. "I want Martina," she mumbled, and when the physician hastened back to her side, she caught the other woman's wrist. "Remember . . . if you cannot save us both, save the child. . . ." Her words were faint and fading, but her eyes blazed so fiercely that Martina could not look away. "Promise . . ." she insisted, ". . . promise," and the other woman nodded, not trusting her voice.

Time had no meaning anymore for Constance; there was no world beyond the stifling confines of this tent. They gave her wine mixed with bark of cassia fistula, lifted her stained chemise to massage her belly, anointed her female parts with hot thyme oil, and when she continued to struggle, some of the women slipped away to pray for her in the church close by the piazza. But Martina kept insisting that it would be soon now, that her womb was dilating, holding out hope like a candle to banish the dark, and after an eternity Constance heard her cry out that she could see the baby's head. She bore down one more time and her child's shoulders were free. "Again," Martina urged, and then a little body, skin red and puckered, slid out in a gush of blood and mucus, into the midwife's waiting hands.

Constance sagged back, holding her breath until she heard it, the soft mewing sound that proved her baby lived. Martina's smile was as radiant as a sunrise. "A man-child, Madame! You have a son!"

"Let me have him . . ." Constance said feebly. There was so much still to be done. The naval cord must be tied and cut. The baby must be cleaned and rubbed with salt before being swaddled. The afterbirth must be expelled and then buried so as not to attract demons. But Martina knew that all could wait. Taking the baby, she placed him in his mother's arms, and as they watched Constance hold her son for the first time, few of the women had dry eyes.

When word spread six days later that the empress would be displaying her son in public, the piazza was thronged hours before she was to make her appearance. The men had heard their women's stories of the birth and were eager to see the miracle infant for themselves; he was a native of Jesi, after all, they joked, one of their own. The crowd parted as Constance's litter entered the square, and they applauded politely as she was assisted to the ground, moved slowly toward the waiting chair. Once she was seated, she signaled and Martina handed her a small, bundled form. Constance drew back the blanket, revealing a head of feathery, reddish hair. As the infant waved his tiny fists, she held him up for all to see. "My son, Frederick," she said, loudly and clearly, "who will one day be King of Sicily."

They applauded again and smiled when Frederick let out a sudden, lusty cry. Constance smiled, too. "I think he is hungry," she said, and the mothers in the crowd nodded knowingly, looking around for the wet nurse; highborn ladies like Constance did not suckle their own babies. They were taken aback by what happened next. The empress's ladies came forward, temporarily blocking the crowd's view. When they stepped aside, a gasp swept the crowd, for Constance had opened her mantle, adjusted her bodice, and begun to nurse her son. When the townspeople realized what she was doing—offering final, indisputable, public proof that this was a child of her body, her flesh and blood—they began to cheer loudly. Even those who were hostile to Constance's German husband joined in, for courage deserved to be acknowledged, to be honored, and they all knew they were watching an act of defiant bravery, the ultimate expression of a mother's love.

Author's Note:

Constance was obviously a courageous woman, but was she also a dangerous one? The events following Frederick's birth give us our answer. Heinrich's generous peace terms had been bait for a trap. He'd shown his hand during his Christmas coronation by having the bodies of Tancred and his son dragged from their royal tombs. Four days later, he claimed to discover a plot against him and ordered that Sybilla, her children, and the leading Sicilian lords be arrested and taken to Germany. Sybilla and her daughters eventually escaped, but her five-year-old son died soon after being sent to a monastery, said to have been blinded and castrated before his death. Heinrich's heavy-handed rule provoked a genuine rebellion in 1197, and there is some evidence that Constance was involved in the conspiracy. Heinrich certainly thought so, for he forced her to watch as he executed the ringleader by having a red-hot crown nailed to his head. But in September 1197, Heinrich died unexpectedly at Messina. Constance at once took control of the government, surrounded herself with Sicilian advisers, and expelled all the Germans. But she would survive Heinrich by barely a year, in which she worked feverishly to protect her son. She had him crowned and then formed an alliance with the new Pope, Innocent III, naming him as Frederick's guardian before her death in November 1198 at age forty-four. Frederick would prove to be one of the most brilliant, controversial, and remarkable rulers of the Middle Ages—King of Sicily, Holy Roman Emperor, even King of Jerusalem. And Constance? Dante placed her in Paradise.

Lev Grossman

A novelist and journalist, Lev Grossman is a senior writer and book critic for *Time* and coauthor of the TIME.com blog TechLand. His quirky 2009 fantasy novel *The Magicians* was a phenomenal international sensation, and landed on the *New York Times* Best Seller list as well as being named a *New Yorker* Best Book of 2009, and its sequel, *The Magician King*, published in 2011, has enjoyed similar acclaim. Grossman's other books include the novels *Warp* and *Codex*. He lives in Brooklyn, New York, and maintains a website at levgrossman.com.

Here he takes us to an ancient, venerable school for wizards, one haunted by a thousand age-old traditions as well as spirits of a different kind, to show us that even the most innocent of pranks can end up having dangerous and even deadly consequences.

THE GIRL IN THE MIRROR

You could say it all started out as an innocent prank, but that wouldn't strictly be true. It wasn't *that* innocent. It was just that Wharton was behaving badly, and in the judgment of the League he had to be punished for it. Then maybe he would cut it out, or behave a little less badly, or at the very least the League would have the satisfaction of having caused Wharton to suffer, and that counted for something. A lot really.

You couldn't call it innocent. But you had to admit it was pretty understandable. And anyway, is there really any such thing as an innocent prank?

Plum was president of the League—unelected but undisputed—and also its founder. In enlisting the others she had presented the League as a glorious old Brakebills tradition, which it actually wasn't, probably, though since the college had been around for something like four hundred years it seemed very likely to Plum that there must have been, at some point in the past, another League or at any rate something along the same lines, which you could count as a historical precedent. You couldn't rule out the possibility. Though in fact she'd gotten the idea from a P. G. Wodehouse story.

They met after hours in a funny little trapezoidal study off the West Tower that as far as they could tell had fallen off the faculty's magical security grid, so it was safe to break curfew there. Plum was lying full length on the floor, which was the position from which she usually conducted League business. The rest of the girls were scattered limply around the room on couches and chairs, like confetti from a successful but rather exhausting party that was thankfully now all but over.

Plum made the room go silent—it was a little spell that ate sound in about a ten-yard radius—and all the attention immediately focused on her. When Plum did a magic trick, everybody noticed.

"Let's put it to a vote," she said solemnly. "All those in favor of prank-ing Wharton, say aye."

The ayes came back in a range of tones from righteous zeal to ironic detachment to sleepy acquiescence. This business of clandestine after-hours scheming could certainly take a whack at your sleep schedule, Plum had to admit. It was a little unfair on the others, because Plum was a quick study who went through homework like a hot knife through butter, and she knew it wasn't that easy for all of them. From her vantage point on the floor, with her eyes closed, her long brown hair splayed out in a fan on the carpet, which had once been soft and woolly but which had been trodden down into a shiny, hard-packed grey, the vote sounded more or less unanimous.

Anyway, there was fairly evidently a plurality in the room. She dispensed with a show of nays.

"It's maddening," Emma said in the silence that followed, by way of spiking the football. "Absolutely *maddening*."

That was an exaggeration, but the room let it go. It's not like Wharton's crime was a matter of life and death. But a stop would be put to it. This the League swore.

Darcy sat on the couch opposite the long mirror with the scarred white frame that leaned against one wall. She toyed with her reflection—with both of her long, elegant hands she was working a spell that stretched it and then squished it, stretched, then squished. The technicalities were beyond Plum, but then, mirror-magic was Darcy's specialty. It was a bit show-offy of her, but you couldn't blame her. Darcy didn't have a lot of opportunities to use it.

The facts of the Wharton case were as follows. At Brakebills, most serving duties at dinner were carried out by First Years, who then ate separately afterwards. But, by tradition, one favored Fourth Year was cho-sen every year to serve as wine steward, in charge of pairings and pourings and whatnot. Wharton had had this honor bestowed upon him, and not for no reason. He did know a lot about wine, or at any rate he seemed to be able to remember the names of a whole lot of different regions and appellations and whatever else. (In fact, another Fourth Year with the unintentionally hilarious name of Claire Bear had been tipped for wine steward this year. Wharton showed her up, coolly and publicly, by distinguishing between a Gigondas and a Vacqueyras in a blind tasting.)

But in the judgment of the League, Wharton had sinned against the honor of his office, sinned most grievously, by systematically short-pouring the wine, especially for the Fifth Years, who were allowed two glasses with dinner. Seriously, these were like three-quarter pours. Everybody agreed. For such a crime, there could be no forgiveness.

"What do you suppose he does with it all?" Emma said.

"Does with what?"

"The extra wine. He must be saving it. I bet he ends up with an extra bottle every night."

There were eight girls in the League, of whom six were present, and Emma was the youngest and the only Second Year, but she wasn't cowed by her elders. In fact, she was, in Plum's opinion, even a bit too keen on the League and her role in same. She could have made just a little show of being intimidated once in a while. Plum was just saying.

"I dunno," Plum said. "I guess he drinks it."

"He couldn't get through a bottle a night," Darcy said. She had a big poofy 1970s Afro; it even had an Afro pick sticking out of it.

"He and his boyfriend, then. What's his name. It's Greek."

"Epifanio." Darcy and Chelsea said it together.

Chelsea lay on the couch at the opposite end from Darcy, her honey-blond head on the armrest, knees drawn up, lazily trying to mess up Darcy's mirror tricks. Darcy's spells were marvels of intricacy and precision, but it was much easier to screw up somebody else's spell than it was to cast one yourself. That was one of the many small unfairnesses of magic.

Darcy frowned and concentrated harder, pushing back. The interference caused an audible buzz, and, under the stress, Darcy's reflection in the mirror twisted and spiraled in on itself in weird ways.

"Stop," she said. "You're going to break it."

"He's probably got some set spell running that eats it up," Emma said. "Has to feed it wine once a day. Like a virility thing."

"Of course that's where your mind would go," Plum said.

"Well," Emma said, flushing mauve—gotcha!—"you know. He's so buff."

Chelsea saw her moment and caused Darcy's reflection to collapse in on itself, creepily, like it had gotten sucked into a black hole, and then vanish altogether. In the mirror it looked like she wasn't even there—her end of the couch was empty, though the cushion was slightly depressed.

"Ha," said Chelsea.

"Buff does *not* mean virile."

That was Lucy, an intensely earnest, philosophical Fifth Year; her tone betrayed a touch of what might have been the bitterness of personal experience. Plump and wan and Korean, Lucy floated cross-legged in one of the room's irregular upper corners. Her dark straight hair was loose and so long that it hung down past her bum.

"I bet he gives it to the ghost," Lucy went on.

"There is no ghost," Darcy said.

Somebody was always saying that Brakebills had a ghost. It was like Plum saying there was a League: you could never prove it either way.

"Come to that," said Chelsea, who had consolidated her victory over Darcy in the mirror game by plopping her feet in Darcy's lap, "what *does* 'virile' mean?"

"Means he's got spunk in his junk," Darcy said.

"Girls, please," Plum said, by way of getting things back on track. "Neither Wharton's spunk nor his junk are germane here. The question is, what to do about the missing wine? Who's got a plan?"

"*You've* got a plan," Darcy and Chelsea said at the same time, again. The two of them were like stage twins.

"I do have plan."

"*Plum has a plan,*" intoned tiny, cheery Holly from the one good armchair.

Plum always had a plan; she couldn't help it. Her brain seemed to secrete them naturally. Plum's plan was to take advantage of what she perceived to be Wharton's Achilles' heel, which was his pencils. He didn't use the school-issued ones, which as far as Plum was concerned were entirely functional and sufficient unto the day: deep Brakebills blue in color, with "Brakebills" in gold letters down the side. But Wharton didn't like them—he said they were too fat, he didn't like their "hand-feel," and the lead was soft and mushy. Wharton brought his own from home instead.

In truth, Wharton's pencils were remarkable pencils: olive green in color and made from some oily, aromatic wood that released a waxy aroma reminiscent of distant exotic rain forest trees. God knows where he got them from. The erasers were bound in rings of a dull grey brushed steel that looked too industrial and high-carbon for the task of merely containing the erasers, which were, instead of the usual fleshy pink, a light-devouring black. Wharton kept his pencils in a flat silver case, which also contained (in its own crushed-velvet nest) a sharp little knife that he used to keep them sharpened to wicked points.

Moreover, whatever life Wharton had led before becoming a magician-in-training at Brakebills, it must have included academic decathlon or debating or something, because he had a whole arsenal of spinning-pencil tricks of the kind that people commonly used to intimidate rival math-letes. He performed them constantly and unconsciously and seemingly involuntarily. It was annoying, even over and above the wine thing.

Plum planned to steal the pencils and hold them for ransom, the ransom being an explanation of what the hell Wharton did with all that wine, along with a pledge to stop doing same. By 11:30 p.m. that night, the League was yawning, and Darcy and Chelsea had restored Darcy's reflection and then begun wrangling with it all over again, but Plum's plan had been fully explained, fleshed out, approved, improved, and then made needlessly complex. Cruel, curly little barbs had been added to it, and all roles had been assigned.

It was rough justice, but someone had to enforce order at Brakebills, and if the faculty didn't, then the League's many hands were forced. The faculty might turn a blind eye, if it chose, but the League's many eyes were sharp and unblinking.

Darcy's image in the mirror shivered and blurred.

"Stop it!" Darcy said, really annoyed now. "I told you—"

She had told her, and now it did. The mirror broke: there was a loud sharp *tick,* and a white star appeared in the glass in the lower right-hand corner, with thin cracks branching out from it, as if some tiny invisible projectile had struck it there. Plum thought of Tennyson: *The mirror cracked from side to side . . .*

"Oh, shit!" Chelsea said. Her hands flew to her mouth. "I hope that wasn't, like, super expensive."

The instant it happened, the mirror's face went dark, and it stopped reflecting anything in the room at all. It must not have been a real mirror at all but a magical device designed to behave like one. At first Plum thought it had gone completely black, but then she saw that there were soft shadowy shapes there: a sofa and chairs. The mirror, or whatever it was, was showing them the same room they were in, but empty, and in darkness. Was it the past? The future? There was something uncanny about it—it was as if someone had been there moments ago and had only just left, turning out the lights on their way out.

Plum got up at 8:00 the next morning, late by her standards, but instead of rejuvenating her brain, the extra sleep had just made it all muzzy. She'd counted on feeling all sparkly with excitement and anticipation at the prospect of the impending prank, but instead she just drifted vaguely into the shower and then out of it and into her clothes and downstairs in the direction of her first class. Her mind, she had often noticed, was a lens that alternated between states of lethally sharp focus and useless, strengthless blurriness, apparently without her having any say in the matter. Her mind had a mind of its own. This morning it was in its strengthless blur mode.

As a Fifth Year who'd finished all her required coursework, Plum was taking all seminars that semester, and her first class was a small colloquium on period magic, fifteenth-century German, to be specific—lots of elemental stuff and weird divination techniques and Johannes Hartlieb. Tiny Holly sat opposite her across the table, and such was Plum's strengthless, blurry state that Holly had touched her sharp little nose meaningfully, twice, before Plum remembered that that was the signal that Stages One and Two of the plan had already been completed successfully. She snapped into focused mode.

Stage One: "Crude but Effective." A few hours earlier Chelsea's boyfriend would have smuggled her into the Boys' Tower under pretense of a predawn snog, not out of character for either of them. Nature having taken its course, Chelsea would have torn herself from the arms of her beloved and gone and stood outside of Wharton's door, her back pressed against it, smoothed back her honeyed locks from her forehead in an automatic gesture, rolled her eyes back into her head, and entered his room in a wispy, silvery, astral state. She tossed his room for the pencil case, found it, and grasped it with both of her barely substantial hands. She couldn't get the pencil case out of the room that way, but she didn't have to. All she had to do was lift it up against the window.

Wharton himself might or might not have observed this, depending on whether or not he was asleep in his blameless couch, but it mattered not. *Let him see.*

Once Chelsea got the case over by the window, earnest Lucy would have line of sight from a window in an empty lecture hall opposite Wharton's room, which meant she could teleport the pencil case in that direction, from inside Wharton's room to midair outside it. Three feet was about as far as she could jump it, but that was plenty.

The pencil case would then fall forty feet to where keen Emma waited shivering in the bushes in the cold February predawn to catch it in a blanket. No magic required.

Effective? Undeniably. Needlessly complex? Perhaps. But needless complexity was the signature of the League. That was how the League rolled.

All this accomplished, it was on to Stage Two: "Breakfast of Champions." Wharton would descend late, having spent the morning searching his room frantically for his pencils and not finding them. Through a fog of anxiety, he would barely notice that his morning oatmeal had been plunked down in front of him not by some anonymous First Year but by tiny Holly in guise of same. The first mouthful would not sit right with him. He would stop and examine his morning oatmeal more closely.

It would be garnished, not with the usual generous pinch of brown sugar, but with a light dusting of aromatic, olive-green pencil shavings. Compliments of the League.

As the day wore on, Plum got into the spirit of the prank. She knew she would. It was mostly just her mornings that were bad.

Her schedule ground forward, ingesting the day in gulps like an anaconda swallowing a wildebeest. Accelerated Advanced Kinetics; Quantum Gramarye; Joined-Hands Tandem Magicks; Cellular-Level Plant Manipulation. All good clean American fun. Plum's course load would have been daunting for a doctoral candidate, possibly several doctoral candidates, but Plum had arrived at Brakebills with a head full of more magical theory and practice than most people left with. She wasn't one of these standing starters, the cold openers, who reeled through their first year with aching hands and eyes full of stars. Plum had come prepared.

Brakebills was an extremely secret and highly exclusive institution—as the only accredited college for magic on the North American continent, it had a very large applicant pool to draw from, and it drank that pool dry. Though, technically, nobody actually applied there: Fogg simply skimmed the cream of eligible high school seniors, the cream of the cream really—the outliers, the extreme cases of precocious genius and obsessive motivation, who had the brains and the high pain tolerance necessary to cope with the intellectual and physical rigors that the study of magic would demand from them.

Needless to say, that meant that the Brakebills student body was quite the psychological menagerie. Carrying that much onboard cognitive processing power had a way of distorting your personality. Moreover, in order to actually want to work that hard, you had to be at least a little bit fucked up.

Plum was a little bit fucked up, but not the kind of fucked up that *looked* fucked up on the outside. She presented as funny and self-assured. When she got to Brakebills, she rolled up her sleeves and cracked her knuckles and did other appropriately confident body language, then she waded right in. Until they saw her in class, a lot of the First Years mistook her for an upperclasswoman.

But Plum made sure not to do so well that, for example, she was graduated early. She was in no hurry. She liked Brakebills. Loved it, really. Needed it, even. She felt safe here. She wasn't so funny and self-assured that she never soothed herself to sleep by imagining she was Padma Patil (because sorry, Hermione, but Ravenclaw FTW). Plum was a closet Romantic, as were most of the students, and Brakebills was a Romantic's dream. Because what were magicians if not Romantics—dreamers who dreamed so passionately and urgently and brokenheartedly that reality itself couldn't take it, and cracked under the strain like an old mirror?

Plum had arrived at Brakebills cocked, locked, sound checked, and ready to rock. When people asked her what the hell kind of an adolescence she'd had that she arrived here in such a cocked, locked, and rock-ready state, she told them the truth, which is that she'd grown up in Seattle, the only daughter of a mixed couple—one magician, one Nintendo lifer who was fully briefed on the existence of magic but had never shown much talent at it himself. They'd homeschooled her, and given her her head, and quite a head it was. Basically, she knew a lot of magic because she'd had an early start and she was really good at it and nobody got in her way.

That was the truth. But when she got to the end of the true part, she told them lies in order to skip over the part she didn't like to talk about, or even think about. Plum was a woman of mystery, and she liked it that way. She felt safe. No one was ever going to know the whole truth about Plum. Preferably not even Plum.

But not-thinking about the truth required a certain amount of distraction. Hence the Accelerated Advanced Kinetics and Quantum Gramarye and all her other hard-core magical academics. And hence the League.

Plum wound up having a pretty good day; at any rate, it was a lot better than Wharton's day. In his first-period class, he found more pencil shavings on the seat of his chair. Walking to lunch, he found his pockets stuffed full of jet-black pencil eraser rubbings. It was like a horror movie—his precious pencils were slowly dying, minute by minute, and he was powerless to save them! He would rue his short-pouring ways, so he would.

Passing Wharton by chance in a courtyard, Plum let her eyes slide past his with a slow, satisfied smile. He looked like a haunted man—a ghost of his former self. The thought balloon over his head said, per Milton: What fresh hell is this?

Finally—and this was Plum's touch, and she privately thought it was the deftest one—in his fourth-period class, a practicum on diagramming magical energies, Wharton found that the Brakebills pencil he was using, on top of its bad hand feel and whatever else, wouldn't draw what he wanted it to. Whatever spell he tried to diagram, whatever points and rays and vectors he tried to sketch, they inevitably formed a series of letters.

The letters spelled out: *COMPLIMENTS OF THE LEAGUE.*

Plum wasn't a bad person, and she supposed that at heart Wharton probably wasn't a bad person either. Truth be told, the sight of him in the courtyard gave her a pang. She'd actually had a bit of a crush on buff, clever, presumably virile Wharton in her Second Year, before he came out; in fact, in all psychoanalytic fairness, she couldn't rule out the possibility that this whole prank was in part a passive-aggressive expression of said former crush. Either way, she was relieved that the final stage—Stage Nine (too many?)—was tonight at dinner, and that the whole thing wouldn't be drawn out any further. They'd only had to destroy two of Wharton's precious special pencils. And really, the second one wasn't all the way destroyed.

Dinners at Brakebills had a nice formal pomp about them; when one was cornered at alumni functions by sad, nostalgic Brakebills graduates who peaked in college, sooner or later they always got around to reminiscing about evenings in the ol' dining hall. The hall was long and dark and narrow and paneled in dark wood and lined with murky oil paintings of past deans in various states of period dress (though Plum thought that the mid-twentieth-century portraits, aggressively Cubist and then Pop, rather subtracted from the gravitas of the overall effect). Light came from hideous, lumpy, lopsided old silver candelabras placed along the table every ten feet, and the candle flames were always flaring up or snuffing out or changing color under the influence of some stray spell or other. Everybody wore identical Brakebills uniforms. Students' names were inscribed on the table at their assigned places, which changed nightly according to, apparently, the whim of the table. Talk was kept to a low murmur. A few people—never Plum—always showed up late, whereupon their chairs were taken away and they had to eat standing up.

Plum ate her first course as usual, two rather uninspired crab cakes, but then excused herself to go to the ladies'. As Plum passed behind her, Darcy discreetly held out the silver pencil case behind her back, and Plum pocketed it. She wasn't going to the ladies', of course. Well, she was, but only because she had to. She wasn't going back after.

Plum walked briskly down the hall toward the Senior Common Room, which the faculty rarely bothered to lock, so confident were they that no student would dare to cross its threshold. But Plum dared.

She closed the door quietly behind her. All was as she had envisioned it. The Senior Common Room was a cavernous, silent, L-shaped chamber with high ceilings, lined with bookcases and littered with shiny red-leather couches and sturdy reclaimed-wood worktables that looked like their wood had been reclaimed from the True Cross. It was empty, or almost. The only person there was Professor Coldwater, and he hardly counted.

She figured he might be there; most of the faculty were at dinner right now, but according to the roster, it was Professor Coldwater's turn to eat late, with the First Years. But that was all right, because Professor Coldwater was notoriously, shall we say, out of it.

Or not exactly out of it, but he was preoccupied. His attention, except when he was teaching, always seemed to be somewhere else. He was always walking around frowning and running his fingers through his weird shock of white hair and executing little fizz-poppy spells with one hand, and muttering and mumbling to himself like he was doing math problems in his head, which he probably was, because when he wasn't doing them in his head he was doing them on blackboards and whiteboards and napkins and in the air in front of his face with his fingers.

The students could never quite decide whether he was romantic and mysterious or just unintentionally hilarious. His actual students, the ones in his Physical Magic seminar, had a kind of cultish reverence for him, but the other faculty seemed to look down on him. He was young for a professor, thirty maybe—it was hard to tell with the hair—and technically he was the most junior faculty at the school, so he was constantly getting handed the jobs nobody else wanted, such as eating with the First Years. He didn't seem to mind. Or maybe it was just that he didn't notice.

Right now, Professor Coldwater was standing at the far end of the room with his back to her. He was tall and skinny and stood bolt upright, staring at the bookcase in front of him but not actually taking down a book. Plum breathed a silent prayer to whatever saint it was who watched over absentminded professors and made sure their minds stayed absent. She glided noiselessly across the thick overlapping oriental carpets, cutting swiftly through the right angle of the L into its shorter arm where Professor Coldwater couldn't see her. Even if he did see her, she doubted he would bother to report her; worst case, he would just kick her out of the Senior Common Room. Either way, it was totally worth it.

Because it was time for the grand reveal. Wharton would open the wine closet, which was actually a whole room the size of a studio apartment, to find Plum already in position, having entered it on the sly through a secret back passage. Then she would present the League's demands, and she would the learn the truth of the matter.

It was the chanciest bit of the plan, because the existence of this secret back passage was a matter of speculation, but whatever, if it didn't work, she'd just make her entrance the normal, less dramatic way. And it was reasonably confident speculation. Plum was almost positive that the passage was there. It ran, or it once had run, between the Senior Common Room and the wine closet, so the faculty could cherry-pick the best bottles for their private use. Its location had been divulged to her by the elderly Professor Desante, her erstwhile undergraduate advisor, when she was in her cups, which was usually—Professor Desante was a woman who liked a drink, and she preferred harder stuff than wine. Plum had filed the information away for just such an eventuality.

Professor Desante had also said that nobody used the passage much anymore, though why nobody would use such an obviously useful passage was not obvious to Plum. But Plum figured that even if it had been sealed up, she could and would unseal it. She was on League business, and the League stopped at nothing.

Plum looked quickly over her shoulder—Coldwater still out of view and/or otherwise engaged—then knelt down by the wainscoting. Third panel from the left. Hm—the one on the end was half a panel, not sure whether she should count it. Well, she'd try it both ways. She traced a word with her finger, spelling it out in a runic alphabet—the Elder Futhark—and meanwhile clearing her mind of everything but the taste of a really oaky chardonnay paired with a hot buttered toast point.

Lemon squeezy. She felt the locking spell release even before the panel swung outward on a set of previously invisible hinges. It was a door, albeit a humble, hobbitlike door, about two-thirds height. Any professors who used it would have to stoop and duck their august heads. But presumably such an indignity was worth it for some good free wine.

Annoyingly, though, the passage *had* been sealed. It had been bricked up, only about three feet in, and the bricks had been bricked in such a way as to form a design that Plum recognized as an absolutely brutal hardening charm—just a charm, yes, but a massively powerful one. Not undergraduate stuff. Some professor had bothered to put this here, and they'd spent some time on it too. Plum pursed her lips and snorted out through her nose.

She stared at the pattern for five minutes, in the dimness of the little passageway, lost to the world. In her mind, the pattern in the bricks floated free of the wall and hung before her all on its own, pure and abstract and shining. Her world shrank and focused. Mentally, she entered the pattern, inhabited it, pushed at it from the inside, feeling for any sloppy joins or subtle imbalances.

There must be something. Come on, Plum: it's easier to screw magic up than it is to make it. You know this. Chaos is easier than order. Whoever drew this seal was smart. But was she smarter than Plum?

There was something odd about the angles. The essence of a glyph like this wasn't the angles, it was the topology—you could deform it a good deal and not lose the power as long as its essential geometric properties were intact. The angles of the joins were, up to a point, arbitrary. But the funny thing about the angles of these joins was that they were funny. They were sharper than they needed to be. They were nonarbitrary. There was a pattern to them, a pattern within the pattern.

17 degrees. 3 degrees. 17 and 3. Two of them here, two of them there, the only angles that appeared twice. She snorted again when she saw it. A simple alphabetical code. A moronically simple alphabetical code. 17 and 3. Q and C. Quentin Coldwater.

It was a signature of sorts. A watermark. A Coldwatermark. Professor Coldwater had set this seal. And when she saw that, she saw it all. Maybe it was on purpose—maybe he'd wanted a weak spot, a key, in case he needed to undo it later. Either way, his little vanity signature was the flaw in the pattern. She extracted the little knife from Wharton's pencil case and worked it into the crumbly mortar around one specific brick. She ran it all the way around the edge, then she stressed the pattern—she couldn't unpick it, but she could push at it, pluck its taught strings, so that it resonated. It resonated so hard that that one brick vibrated itself clean out of the wall, on the other side. Clunk.

Deprived of that one brick, and hence the integrity of its pattern, the rest of the wall gave up the ghost and fell apart. Funny that it should have been him—everybody knew Coldwater was a wine lush. Plum ducked her head, stepped over the threshold, and drew the panel closed behind her. It was dark in the passageway, and chilly, much chillier than in the cozy Senior Common Room. The walls were old, unfinished boards over stone.

Dead reckoning, it was about one hundred yards from the Senior Common Room to the back of the wine closet, but she'd only gone twenty before she got to a door, this one unlocked and unsealed. She closed it behind her. More passage, then another door. Odd. You could never tell what you were going to find in this place, even after living here for four and a half years. Brakebills was old, really old. It had been built and rebuilt a lot of times by a lot of different people.

More doors, until the fourth or fifth one opened onto open air—a little square courtyard she'd never seen before. Mostly grass, with one tree, a fruit tree of some kind, espaliered against a high stone wall. She'd always found espaliers a little creepy. It was like somebody had crucified the poor thing.

Also, not that it mattered, but there shouldn't have been a moon out, not tonight. She hurried across the courtyard to the next door, but it was locked.

She fingered the doorknob gently, inquiringly. She checked it for magical seals, and wow. Somebody smarter than her and Professor Coldwater put together had shut it up tight.

"Well, blow me down," she said.

Her internal GPS told her that she ought to be going straight ahead, but there was another door off the courtyard, a heavy wooden one on a different wall. She went for door number two, which was heavy but which opened easily.

She had suspected before, but now she was sure, that she was traversing some magically noncontiguous spaces here, because this door opened directly onto one of the upper floors of the library. It wasn't impossible—or it was, obviously, but it was one of the possible impossibles, as Donald Rumsfeld would have said if he'd secretly been a magician. (Which fat chance. Now there was an impossible impossible.) It was preposterous, and a bit creepy, but it wasn't magically impossible.

The Brakebills library was arranged around the interior walls of a tower that narrowed toward the top, and this must have been one of the teensy tiny uppermost floors, which Plum had only ever glimpsed from far below, and which, to be honest, she'd always assumed were just there for show. She never thought there were any actual books in them. What the hell would they shelve up here?

It looked tiny from below, and it was tiny—in fact, now she realized that these upper floors must be built to false perspective, to make the tower look taller than it was, because it was very tiny indeed, barely a balcony, like one of those medieval folly houses that mad kings built for their royal dwarfs. She had to navigate it on her hands and knees. The books looked real, though, their brown leather spines flaking like pastry, with letters stamped on them in gold—some interminable many-volume reference work about ghosts.

And like a few of the books in the Brakebills library, they weren't quiet or inanimate. They poked themselves out at her from the shelves as she crawled past, as if they were inviting her to open them and read, or daring her to, or begging her. A couple of them actually jabbed her in the ribs. They must not get a lot of visitors, she thought. Probably this was like when you visit the puppies at the shelter and they all jump up and want to be petted.

No, thank you. She liked her books to wait, decorously and patiently, until she chose to read them herself. It was a relief to crawl through the miniature door at the end of the balcony—it was practically a cat door—and back into a normal corridor. This was taking a long time, but it wasn't too late. The main course would be half over, but there was still dessert, and she thought there was cheese tonight too. She could still make it if she hurried.

This corridor was tight, almost a crawl space. In fact, it was one—as near as she could tell, she was actually inside one of the walls of Brakebills. It was a wall of the dining hall: she could hear the warm hum of talk and the clatter of silverware, and she could actually look out through a couple of the paintings—there were peepholes in the eyes, like in old movies about haunted houses. They were just serving the main, a nice rare lamb spiked with spears of rosemary. The sight of it made her hungry. She felt a million miles away, even though she was standing right there. She almost felt nostalgic, like one of those teary alums, for the time when she was sitting at the table with her bland crab cakes, half an hour ago, back when she knew exactly where she was.

And there was Wharton, showily pouring his mingy glasses of red, totally unrepentant. The sight emboldened her. That was why she was here. For the League.

Though, God, how long was this going to take? The next door opened out onto the roof. The night air was bone cold. She hadn't been up here since the time Professor Sunderland had turned them into geese, and they'd flown down to Antarctica. It was lonely and quiet up here after the dining hall—she was very high up, higher than the leafless tops of all but the tallest trees. She had to stay on her hands and knees because the roof was so sharply raked, and the shingles were gritty under her palms. She could see the Hudson River, a long, sinuous silver squiggle. She shivered just looking at it.

Which way to go? There was no obvious path. She was losing the thread. Finally Plum just jimmied the lock on the nearest dormer window and let herself in.

She was in a student's room. Actually, if she had to guess, she'd guess it was Wharton's room, though obviously she'd never seen it, because her crush had remained in a theoretical state. What were the odds? These spaces were beyond noncontiguous. She began to suspect that somebody at Brakebills, possibly Brakebills itself, was fucking with her.

"OMG," she said out loud. "The irony."

Well, fuck away, she thought, and we shall see who fucks last. She half suspected that she had stumbled into a magical duel with Wharton himself, except no way could he pull off something like this. Maybe he had help—maybe he was part of a shadowy Anti-League, committed to frustrating the goals of the League! Actually, that would be kind of cool.

The room was messy as hell, which was somehow endearing, since she thought of Wharton as a control freak. And it had a nice smell. She decided that she wasn't going to fight against the dream logic of what was happening; she was going to play it out. Steer into the skid. To leave by the front door would have been to break the dream spell, so instead she opened Wharton's closet door, somehow confident that—yes, look, there was a little door at the back of it.

She couldn't help but notice, by the by, that his closet was full, practically packed solid, with boxes of those pencils. Why, exactly, had they thought he was going to freak out at the loss of two pencils? There were like 5,000 of them in here. The aroma of tropical wood oil was suffocating. She opened the door and stooped through.

From here on out, her travels ran entirely on dream rails. The door in the back of Wharton's closet took her into another courtyard, but now it was daytime. They were losing temporal, uh, contiguousness—contiguity?—as well as spatial. It was earlier today, because there she was, Plum herself, crossing the lightly frosted grass, and passing Wharton, and there was the eye sliding. It was a strange sight. But Plum's tolerance for strange had been on the rise, lo this past half hour.

She watched herself leave the courtyard. That was her in a nutshell, Plum thought: standing there and watching her own life go by. She wondered whether, if she shouted and waved her arms, she would hear herself, or if this was more of a two-way-mirror deal. She frowned. The causality of it became tangled. This much at least was clear: if that's what her ass looked like from behind, well, not bad. She would take it.

The next door was even more temporally noncontiguous, because it put her in a different Brakebills entirely, a curiously reduced Brakebills. It was a smaller and darker and somehow denser Brakebills. The ceilings were lower, the corridors were narrower, and the air smelled like wood smoke. She passed an open doorway and saw a group of girls huddled together on a huge bed. They wore white nightgowns and had long, straight hair and bad teeth.

Plum understood what she was seeing. This was Brakebills of long ago. The Ghost of Brakebills Past. The girls looked up only momentarily, incuriously, as she passed. No question what they were up to.

"Another League," she said to herself. "I *knew* there must have been one."

Then the next door opened on a room that she thought she knew—no, she *knew* she knew it, she just didn't want to think about it. She had been here before, a long time ago. The room was empty now, but something was coming, it was on its way, and when it got here, all hell was going to break loose. It was the thing: the thing that she could not and would not think about. She had seen this all happen before, and she hadn't been able to stop it. Now she knew it was coming, and it was going to happen anyway.

She had to get out, get out now, before the horror started all over again. "No!" Plum said. "No, no, no, no, *no*."

She ran. She tried to go back, the first time she'd tried that, but the door was locked behind her, so she ran ahead blindly and crashed through the next door. When she opened her eyes again she was in the little trapezoidal lounge where the League held its meetings.

Oh. Oh, thank God. She was breathing hard, and she sobbed once. It wasn't real. It wasn't real. Or it was real, but it was over. She didn't care, either way she was safe. This whole fucked-up magical mystery tour was over. She wasn't going back, and she wasn't going to go forward either. She was safe right here. She wasn't going to think about it. Nobody had to know.

Plum sank down on the ragged couch, boneless. It was so saggy it almost swallowed her up. She felt like she could fall asleep right here. She almost wondered if she had when she opened her eyes again and looked at the reflection in the long mirror that Darcy and Chelsea had cracked earlier. Of course she wasn't in it: magic mirror. Right. Plum was relieved not to have to look at her own face right now. Then her relief went away.

Another girl stood there in the mirror instead of her. Or at least it was shaped like a girl. It was blue and naked, and its skin gave off an unearthly light. Even its teeth were blue. Its eyes were utterly mad.

This was horror of a different kind. New horror.

"You," the ghost whispered to Plum.

It was her: the ghost of Brakebills. She was real. Jesus Christ, that's who was fucking with her. She was the spider at the center of the web.

Plum stood up, but after that, she didn't move; all moving was over with. If she moved, she wouldn't live long. She'd spent enough time around magic to know instinctively that she was in the presence of something so raw and powerful that if she touched it, it would snuff her out in a second. That blue girl was like a downed power line. The insulation had come off the world, and pure naked magical current was arcing in front of her.

It was beyond horror: Plum felt calm, detached. She was caught in the gears of something much bigger than her, and they would grind her up if they wanted to. They were already in motion. There was nothing she could do. Part of her wanted them to. She had been waiting so long for her doom to catch up to her.

But then: bump. The sound came from the wall to her left—it sounded like something had run into it from the other side. A little plaster fell. The bump was followed by a man's voice saying something like "Oof." Plum looked.

The ghost in the mirror didn't.

"I know," it whispered. "I saw."

The wall exploded, throwing plaster in all directions, and a man crashed through it covered with white dust. It was Professor Coldwater. He shook himself like a wet dog to get some of the dust off. White witchery sparked around both his hands like Roman candles, so bright it made purple flares in her vision.

Always keeping one hand pointed at the blue ghost, he walked toward Plum till he stood between her and the mirror.

"Careful," he said over his shoulder, relatively calmly given the circumstances.

He reared back one of his long legs and kicked in the mirror. It took him three kicks—the first two times the glass just starred and sagged, but the third time his foot went right through it. It got a little stuck when he tried to pull it out.

It was a measure of how shocked she was that Plum's first reaction was: *I must tell Chelsea that she doesn't have to worry about paying for it.*

Breaking the mirror didn't dispel the ghost—it was still watching them, though it had to peer around the edge of the hole. Professor Cold-water turned around to face the wall behind Plum and joined his hands together.

"Get down," he said.

The air shimmered and rippled around them. Then she had to throw her forearm over her eyes, and her hair crackled with so much static electricity, it made her scalp hurt. The entire world was shot through with light. She didn't see but she heard and felt the door behind her explode out of its frame.

"Run," Professor Coldwater said. "Go on, I'm right behind you."

She did. She hurdled the couch like a champion and felt a shock wave as Professor Coldwater threw some final spell at the ghost. It lifted Plum off her feet and made her stagger, but she kept on running.

Going back was faster than going forward had been. She seemed to be bounding ahead seven-league-boots-style, which at first she thought was adrenaline till she realized, no, it was just magic. One stride took her through the hell room, another and she was in colonial Brakebills, then she was in Wharton's room, on the roof, in the crawl space, the library, the creepy-pear-tree courtyard, the passage. The sound of doors slamming behind her was like a string of firecrackers going off.

They stopped just short of the Senior Common Room, breathing hard. He was right behind her, just as he'd said. She wondered if he'd just saved her life; at any rate, she definitely felt bad about having made fun of him behind his back. He resealed the passageway behind him. She watched him work, dazed but fascinated: moving in fast-motion, his arms flying crazily, like a time-lapse movie, he assembled an entire intricately patterned brick wall in about five seconds.

She couldn't help but notice that this time he caught the resonance pattern, the one she'd used to break the last seal, and corrected it.

Then they were alone in the Senior Common Room. It could all have been a dream except for the plaster dust on the shoulders of Professor Cold-water's blazer.

"What did she say to you?" he said.

"She?" Plum said. "Oh, the ghost. Nothing. She said 'You,' and then she didn't say anything else.

"'You,'" he repeated. He was staring over her shoulder—he'd already gone absentminded again. One of his fingers was still crackling with a bit of white fire; he shook it and it went out. "Hm. Do you still want to go to the wine closet? That's what you were looking for, wasn't it?"

Plum laughed in spite of herself. The wine closet. She'd completely forgotten about it. She still had Wharton's stupid pencil case in her stupid pocket. It seemed too pointless to go through with it. Everything was too sad and too strange now.

But somehow, she thought, it would be even sadder not to go through with it.

"Sure," she said, aiming for jaunty and almost getting there. "Why not. So there really is a secret passage?"

"Of course. I steal bottles all the time."

He drew the rune word on the next panel over from the one she'd used.

"You don't count the half panel," he said.

Aha. The door opened. It was just what she thought: a doddle, not even one hundred yards, more like seventy-five.

She squared her shoulders and checked her look in a pier glass. The hair was a little wild, but she supposed that would be part of the effect. She was surprised, and almost a tiny bit disappointed, to see her own face looking back at her. She wondered whose ghost the ghost was, and how she died, and why she was still here. Probably she wasn't here for the fun of it. Probably she wasn't a nostalgic alumna haunting Brakebills out of school spirit. Probably she needed something. Hopefully, that thing wasn't, you know, to kill Plum.

But if it was, she would have done it—wouldn't she?—and she hadn't. Plum wasn't a ghost. It was actually worth telling herself that: Having seen a real one—and she hadn't even thought they were real, but live and learn—she knew the difference now, really knew it. I didn't die just then, she thought, and I didn't die in that room. It felt like I did, I wanted to die, but I didn't, because if I had died then, I would have *died*. And I don't want to be a ghost. I don't want to haunt my own life.

She'd just closed the secret door to the wine closet behind her—it was concealed behind a trick wine rack—when Wharton came bustling through the front door with the rumble and glow of the cheese course subsiding behind him. Her timing was perfect. It was all very "League."

Wharton froze, with a freshly recorked bottle in one hand and two inverted wineglasses dangling from the fingers of the other. Plum regarded him calmly.

"You've been short-pouring the Fifth Years," she said.

"Yes," he said. "You have my pencils."

She watched him. Part of the charm of Wharton's face was its asymmetry. He'd had a harelip corrected at some point, and the surgery had gone well, so that all that was left was a tiny tough-guy scar, as if he'd taken one straight in the face at some point but just kept on trucking.

Also, he had an incredibly precious widow's peak. Some guys had all the luck.

"It's not the pencils I mind," he said, "so much as the case. And the knife. They're vintage silver, Smith and Sharp. You can't find those anywhere anymore."

She took the case out of her pocket.

"Why have you been short-pouring the Fifth Years?"

"Because I need the extra wine."

"Okay, but what do you need it *for*?" Plum said. "I'll give you back the pencils and all that. I just want to know."

"What do you think I need it for?" Wharton said. "I give it to that fucking ghost. That thing scares the shit out of me."

"You're an idiot," Plum said. "The ghost doesn't care about wine." For some reason, she now felt like an authority on the subject of what the ghost did or did not care about. "The ghost doesn't care about *you*. And if it did, there'd be nothing you could do about it. Certainly not placate it by giving it wine."

She handed him the case.

"The pencils are inside. Knife, too."

"Thank you."

He dropped it in the pocket of his apron and set the two empty wineglasses down on a shelf.

"Wine?" he said.

"Thank you," Plum said. "I'd love some."

Nancy Kress

Nancy Kress began selling her elegant and incisive stories in the mid-seventies, and has since become a frequent contributor to *Asimov's Science Fiction*, *The Magazine of Fantasy & Science Fiction*, *Omni*, *Sci Fiction*, and elsewhere. Her books include the novel version of her Hugo- and Nebula-winning story, *Beggars in Spain*, and a sequel, *Beggars and Choosers*, as well as *The Prince of Morning Bells*, *The Golden Grove*, *The White Pipes*, *An Alien Light*, *Brainrose*, *Oaths and Miracles*, *Stinger*, *Maximum Light*, *Crossfire*, *Nothing Human*, *Crucible*, *Dogs*, *Steal Across the Sky*, and the Probability Trilogy, comprised of *Probability Moon*, *Probability Sun, and Probability Space*. Her short work has been collected in *Trinity and Other Stories*, *The Aliens of Earth*, *Beaker's Dozen*, and *Nano Comes to Clifford Falls and Other Stories*. Her most recent books are a new novel, *After the Fall, Before the Fall, During the Fall*, and two new collections, *Fountain of Age* and *Five Stories*. In addition to the awards for "Beggars in Spain," she has also won Nebula Awards for her stories "Out of All Them Bright Stars" and "The Flowers of Aulit Prison," the John W. Campbell Memorial Award in 2003 for her novel *Probability Space*, and another Hugo in 2009 for "The Erdmann Nexus." She lives in Seattle, Washington, with her husband, writer Jack Skillingstead.

Here she takes us to a ruined future America to ask the question, in a world where only basic brute survival counts, is there any room left for beauty? And would you be willing to kill for it if you found it?

SECOND ARABESQUE, VERY SLOWLY

When we came to the new place it was already night and I couldn't see anything. It wasn't like Mike to move us after dark. But our pack had taken longer than he'd expected, or longer than the scouts had said, to travel south. That was partly my fault. I can't walk as fast or long as I once could. And neither could Pretty, because that day turned out to be her Beginning.

"My belly hurts, it does," the girl moaned.

"Just a little farther," I said, hoping that was true. Hoping, too, that I wouldn't have to threaten her. Pretty turned ugly when she felt bad and whined when she didn't, although never in Mike's presence. "A little farther, and tomorrow you'll have your ceremony."

"With candy?"

"With candy."

So Pretty trudged through the dark, broken, rubble-choked streets with me and the other six girls, behind a swinging lantern. The night was cold for July. The men closest to us—although I don't call fifteen-year-olds men, even if Mike does—walked bent over with the weight of our belongings. The men on the perimeter carried weapons. The danger was partly from other packs wanting foraging territory, although there are fewer territorial firefights than when I was young. Still, we have desirable assets: seven young women, at least two of them fertile, plus three children and me. And then there are the dogs. Cities are full of wild dogs.

I could hear them, howling in the distance. As that distance grew smaller and Mike still had us stumbling along by patchy moonlight and one lantern, I left the girls in Bonnie's charge and walked double time to find Mike.

"What be you doing here?" he demanded, gaze and rifle both focused outward. "Get back to them girls!"

"It's the girls I'm concerned about. How much farther?"

"Get back there, Nurse!"

"I'm asking because Pretty is in some pain. She's at her Beginning."

That took his attention from any dangers in the darkness. "Yeah? You sure?"

"Yes," I said, although I wasn't.

Mike gave his slow, rare smile. He wasn't a bad pack leader. Huge, strong, illiterate—well, they all were, and I needed them to be—he cared about his people, and wasn't any more brutal to us than discipline required. A big improvement on Lew, our previous leader. Sometimes Mike could even lurch into moments of grace, as he did now. "She be okay?"

"Yes." Nothing that the start of her monthlies and a little candy wouldn't cure.

And then, even more surprising, "You be okay, Nurse?"

"Yes."

"How old you be now?"

"Sixty," I said, shaving off four years. I was under no illusions what Mike would do once I could no longer keep up with the pack. Already Bonnie had learned half of what I had to teach her. Not even a Nurse would be allowed to slow down the nomadic moving that meant food.

We had kept walking as we talked. Mike said, "I be first, with Pretty."

"She knows that."

He grunted, not asking her thoughts about it. If Pretty were fertile, she must be mated with a fertile male, and no one knew which of the pack men that might be. Nor did we have any idea how to find out. So Pretty, like Junie and Lula before her, would be mated with all of them in turn. Already Pretty, a natural flirt when she wasn't a natural whiner, tossed her long blond hair and flashed her shapely legs at all of them.

The dogs were closer now, and I had lost Mike's attention. I stood still, waiting for the center of the pack to reach me, and rejoined my charges.

By the time we reached our new building, the moon had vanished behind the clouds, a drizzle had started, and I could see nothing. The men led us past some large structures—the city was full of large structures, most ruined but mostly on the insides—and through a metal door. Steps downward. Cold, damp. A featureless corridor. Still, this place would be easy to defend, since it was underground and nearly windowless. The scouts had prepared the women's room, which did have a small window, to which they'd vented our propane stove. The room was warm and blanketed. Junie and Lula bedded down their children, who were already half-asleep. So were the girls. I stayed awake long enough to prepare Pretty a hot tisane—only herbs, not drugs—to ease her cramps, and then fell into sleep.

In the morning I woke first and made my way outside to pee. The guard, a gentle sixteen-year-old named Guy, nodded at me. "Morning, Nurse."

"Good morrow to you, sir," I said, and Guy grinned. He was one of the few that was interested in the learning—history, literature—I sometimes tossed out. He could even read; I was teaching him. "Where is the piss pit?"

He told me. I continued outside, blinking a little in the bright sunshine, along the side of the building and around a corner, where I stopped dead.

I knew this place. I had never been here before, but I knew it.

Three large buildings set around a vast square of now broken and weedy stone, with steps at the far end leading down to a deserted street. On the tallest building, five wide, immensely tall arches looked down on a sea of smashed glass. The other two buildings, glass fronts also smashed, bristled with balconies, with marble, with stone sculptures too large to break or carry away. Inside, still visible, were remnants of ancient, tattered carpet.

I said aloud, "This is Lincoln Center." But the perimeter guard, sitting with his rifle on the edge of what had once been a fountain, was too far away to hear. I wasn't talking to him, anyway. I was talking to my grandmother.

"My best job, Susan," she'd said to me, "was when I was on the cleaning crew at Lincoln Center."

"Tell me," I said, although I'd heard all this so many times before that I could recite it. I never tired of it.

"I was young, before I went to nursing school. We deep-cleaned the Metropolitan Opera House the last two weeks in August and the first two weeks in September, when there were no performances," she always began. "It was way before the Infertility Plague, you know."

I knew. My grandmother was very old then, older than I am now, and dying. I was twelve. Grandmother was frantically teaching me to Nurse, in case I should prove infertile, which the following year, I did. Packs not desperate for bedmates have no use for infertile women unless a girl can prove herself as a fighter. I was no fighter.

"We lowered all twenty-one electric chandeliers at the Met—think of that, Susan, *twenty-one*—and cleaned each crystal drop individually. Every other year all the red carpet was completely replaced, at a cost of $700,000. In 1990s dollars! Every five years the seats were replaced in the New York State Theater—that's what it was called then, although later they changed the name, I forget to what. Five window washers worked every day of the year, constantly keeping the windows bright. At night, when all the buildings were lit up, they shone out on the plaza like liquid gold. People laughed and talked and lined up by the hundreds to hear opera and see ballet and watch plays and listen to concerts. And such rich performances as I saw . . . you can't imagine!"

No liquid gold now. No performances, no electricity, no opera nor ballet nor plays nor concerts. Grandmother had been talking about a time gone when I was born, and I am old.

I went back inside. Pretty was awake, her huge blue eyes filled with awe at herself. "Nurse! It started—my blood! I'm at my Beginning!"

"Congratulations," I said. "We'll have your ceremony today."

"I am a woman now," she said, with pride. I looked at her round, childish, simple face; at her skinny arms and legs; at her concave belly, not even distended with fluid retention. She was thirteen, early for our girls to Begin. Kara was a year older, with no sign of her monthlies. I said gently, "Yes, Pretty. You're a woman now. You can bear the pack a child."

"You other childless," Pretty said importantly, "you have to obey me now!"

The younger girls, Seela and Tiny, scowled ferociously.

My grandmother taught me a great deal more than nursing. And I read. Books might have survived the destruction and stupid rioting when the world realized that 99 percent of its women had contracted a virus that destroyed their eggs. Most books had not, however, survived time and damp and rats and insects. But some did.

How many other people are left in the world? There is no way to tell.

Census organizations, radio and TV stations, central governments—all that vanished decades ago. Too few people left to sustain them. The world now—or at least this part of it—consists of the communities and the packs. The communities live outside the city, and they farm. I have never seen one. I was born to a pack—although not this one—my mother and grandmother captive to it. The packs prefer to be hunter-gatherers in urban environments. We hunt meat—rabbits, deer, dogs—and gather canned goods. Not exactly what happened during the Stone Age, but we manage. Every once in a while rumors come of places that have preserved more of civilization, usually small cities north and west—"Endicott," "Bath," "Ithaca"—but I have no knowledge of them.

However, it turned out that among the others that *were* left in the world was a pack based just blocks away, in an old hotel on a street called "Central Park South," and Mike was furious with his scouts. "You don't *find this out?*"

The men hung their heads.

"You put us in danger 'cause you don't find this out? I deal with you later. Now we gotta parley."

I was startled. Parley, not move? But later Guy, off duty and cleaning his guns, explained it to me. "There be a big forest here, Nurse, with lotsa game. Mike wants to stay."

So Mike left with half his pack, all heavily armed, to parley for hunt-gather rights with the other pack. Meanwhile, guarded by Guy and his friend Jemmy, Bonnie and I looked for a good place to hold Pretty's ceremony.

Bonnie, my apprentice, might or might not make a good Nurse when I can no longer keep up with the pack. Smart and strong, she already knew more than I let Mike realize. She could use our dwindling supplies of pre-plague medicines, those miracles whose making is lost to us. More important, she could find, prepare, and administer the plant drugs we relied on: bilberry for diarrhea, horsetail to stop bleeding, elderberry for fever, primrose for rashes. She could set a bone, dig out a bullet, use maggots to clean a wound.

But Bonnie had neither warmth nor that brisk reassurance that, as much as drugs, brings men to healing. Bonnie was like stone. I'd never seen her smile, seldom heard her speak except in answer to a question, never surprised interest or delight on her face. Big, ungainly, painfully homely, she had colorless hair and almost no chin. I think she had a bad time when she Began, which was before I was taken into this pack. Her thighs and breasts bore permanent scars. Lew might have had her shot when she was declared infertile except it was about that time he was killed in a pack war. I persuaded Mike to let Bonnie become my apprentice. That also rescued her from the sex list, since Nurses—even apprentice Nurses—were the only women who got to invite men to bed. Bonnie never did.

She said nothing as she and I, Guy and Jemmy, went into all the ruined buildings of what had been Lincoln Center. From Grandmother's descriptions I recognized them all. Above us, in the New York State Theater, broken seats once supported the asses of people watching dancers. Our housing below had probably been practice rooms. In the Metropolitan Opera House, the building with five tall arches, the caved-in stage had once held opera singers. Here, in Somebody Hall (my memory wasn't what it had been), orchestras had played music. All the musicians wore black, with the women in long and sparkly dresses. Grandmother told me. In the Vivian Beaumont Theater, off to the side of the Met, the collapsed roof sheltered actors performing plays. The small library beside the Met had been burned and was now overgrown with weeds, wildflowers, and saplings.

But it was underneath the Vivian Beaumont, below street level and behind two locked doors that Guy shot open with his rifle, that we found it. I had brought a lantern, and now I lit it, although we'd left both doors open for light. The first door led to a downward-sloping ramp of concrete, the second to another small theater, eight rows of seats in a half circle, windowless and untouched except for time and rats. No looters had taken or destroyed the seats; no rain had rotted the wooden, uncurtained stage; no wild dogs nested in the tiny rooms beyond.

Jemmy let out a whoop and swung himself up to a booth on the back wall. Probably he hoped for undestroyed machinery, and his second whoop said he'd found it. A faint glow appeared in the booth.

"Jemmy!" I shouted up. "If you waste candles like that, Mike will flog you himself!"

No answer, and the light did not go off. Guy shrugged and laughed. "You know Jemmy."

"Help me up onto that stage," I said.

He did, leaping up gracefully to stand beside me, the lantern at our feet. I looked out over the darkened seats. What must it have been like, to stand here as an actor, a musician, a dancer? To perform in front of people who watched you with delight? To control an audience?

"Such rich performances as I saw . . . you can't imagine."

Boots on the corridor, and then a voice in the darkness: "Nurse? Get your ass back to them girls! Pretty waiting!"

"Is that you, Karl?"

"Yeah."

"Don't you ever again talk to me in that tone of voice, young man, or I will tell Mike that you're disrespecting a Nurse and you will go to the bottom of the sex list, if you even stay on it at all!"

Silence, then a sullen, "Yes'm."

"In fact, you bring all the girls here. This is where we'll have Pretty's ceremony, and we'll have it now."

"Here? Now?"

"You heard me."

"Yes'm." And then: "You tell Mike I disrespected you?"

"Not if you get those girls here right away."

Karl galloped off, his boots loud on the concrete ramp. Guy grinned at me. Then he gazed out into the darkness and I saw that he had been doing just what I had: imagining himself a performer in a vanished time. All at once he grabbed me around the waist and swung me into a dance.

I was never a dancer, and I am old. I stumbled, and Guy let me go. He danced alone, as he never would have done had anybody been present except me and his trusted friend Jemmy, who probably wasn't even looking away from his precious machinery. I watched Guy move gracefully through the two-step that packs danced at the rare gatherings, and sadness washed over me that Guy could never be anything but a low-level pack soldier. He was too kind and too dreamy to ever become a leader like Mike, too male to ever be as important as a fertile girl.

Bonnie watched, wooden-faced, before she turned away.

Pretty's ceremony was lit by thirteen candles, one for each year of her age, as was customary. No men present, of course, not even the two male children, year-old Davey and eight-year-old Rick, whose mother, Emma, died last year giving birth to a stillborn girl. Nothing I did saved either one of them, and if Lew had still been pack chief, I think I would have been shot then and there.

The two mothers, Junie and Lula, sat on chairs, with Lula's baby, Jaden, on her lap. Jaden started to fuss and Lula gave her the breast. Bonnie, as my apprentice but also as an infertile female, stood behind the mothers. The girls who had not yet had their Beginnings sat to one side on the floor, their hands full of wildflowers. Seela and Tiny, ten and nine, looked interested. Kara, her own Beginning only a few months off, judging from her buds of breasts, wore an expression I could not interpret.

Pretty, now neither child nor mother, sat in the center of the circle, on a sort of throne made of a chair covered with a blanket, which in turn was spread with towels. Old, as faded as everything else we take from abandoned buildings, the towels had once been sun-yellow. Pretty's legs were spread wide, the thighs smeared with the new blood she was so proud of. One by one, the unBegun girls laid flowers between Pretty's legs.

"May you be blessed with children," said Tiny, looking excited.

"May you be blessed with children." Seela, jealousy on her thin little face.

"May you be . . . blessed with . . . children." Kara could barely get the words out. Her face creased with anguish. Her fingers trembled.

Pretty looked at her in astonishment. "What be wrong with *you*?"

Bonnie pushed forward. "Be you sick, Kara? What be your symptoms?"

"I'm not sick! Leave me alone!"

"Come here, Kara," I said in the tone that all of the girls, and most of the younger men, obeyed instantly. I had been in charge of these girls since the pack acquired them, of Kara since she was four. Kara came to me. She had always been complicated, sweet-natured and hardworking (unlike lazy Pretty), but too excitable. Death distressed her too much, happiness elated her too much, beauty transported her too much. I have seen her in tears over a sunset.

"Do not spoil Pretty's ceremony," I said to her in a low voice, and she subsided.

Afterward, however, while the two mothers took Pretty aside for the traditional sex instruction that was hardly ever needed and the unBegun girls played with Jaden, I led Kara off the stage, to the back of the theater. "Sit."

"Yes, Nurse. What is this place?"

"It was a theater. Kara, what troubles you?"

She looked away, looked down, looked everywhere but at me until I took her chin in my hand and made her face me. Then she blurted, "I don't want to!"

"Don't want to what?"

"Any of it! Begin, have a ceremony, bed with Mike and all them. Have a baby—I don't want to!"

"Many girls are frightened at first." I remembered my own first bedding, with a pack leader much less gentle than I suspected Mike would be. So long ago. Yet I had come to like sex, and right up until a few years ago, I had sometimes gone with Buddy off-list, until he was killed by that wild dog.

"I be frightened, yes. But I also don't want to!"

"Is there something you want to do instead?" I was afraid she would say "nurse." I already had Bonnie, and anyway, even if she proved infertile, Kara would not make a Nurse. No amount of hard work would make up for her lack of stability and brains.

"No."

"What, then?" For girls there was only mother, nurse, or infertile bed-mate, and the last became camp drudges with little respect, when packs kept infertile women at all. Our last such, Daisy, had run away. I didn't like to imagine what had happened to her. Kara knew all this.

"I don't know!" It was a wail of pure anguish. I had no time for this: a self-indulgent girl with no aim, merely obstruction of what was necessary. A woman did what she had to do, just as men did. I left her sitting in the tattered velvet chair and went back to Pretty. It was her day, not Kara's.

Bonnie still stood, stony, beside Pretty's flower-strewn chair.

Mike returned from the parley looking pleased, a rare look for him. The other pack, smaller than ours, was not only unwilling to go to war over the urban forest but was interested in trading, even in possible joint hunting and foraging trips. I knew without being told that Mike hoped to eventually unite the two packs and become chief of both. The men brought back gifts from the other pack. Evidently their base had heaps of things so sealed in plastic—blankets, pillows, even clothing—that no rats had gotten into them and they looked almost new. Each of the girls got a fluffy white robe stitched with "St. Regis Hotel."

"Can't we move to a hotel?" Lula cried, twirling around in hers.

"Too hard to defend," Karl said. He reached up to catch Lula and pull her onto his lap. She giggled. Lula has always liked Karl; she maintained that she "knows" he fathered Jaden. Jaden did have his bright blue eyes.

We were all at Pretty's ceremony feast in the common room, an underground room in what Grandmother remembered as the New York State Theater. The common room had a wooden floor, a curious wooden rail on three sides, and a smashed, unusable piano in one corner. The boys had swept up the huge amount of mirror glass that yesterday lay all around. Junie had spread blankets on the floor for the feast, which tasted wonderful. Rabbit shot that morning and roasted with wild onions over open fires built on the stone terrace in front of the Vivian Beaumont. Cans of beans that Eric had brought back from foraging. A salad of dandelion greens and the candy that Pretty so loved and I had been hoarding since winter: maple sap mixed with nuts. Every lantern we owned was lit, giving the room a romantic glow.

Mike eyed Pretty, who blushed and cast eyes at him. The younger men watched enviously. I didn't have much sympathy for them. They were at the bottom of the sex list, of course, and, they didn't get much. Too bad—they should have treated Bonnie better when they had her.

Besides Bonnie, two of the young men seemed unaware of the heavy scent of sex filling the common room. Guy and Jemmy kept giving me significant looks, and eventually I got up from my dinner and went to them. "Do you need me?"

"I have a pain," Jemmy said, loud enough for Mike to hear. Jemmy was a terrible actor. His eyes shone, and every muscle in his body tensed with excitement. I had never seen anybody less in pain.

I went to Mike. "Jemmy is ill. I'm taking him to the sickroom to examine, in case it's contagious."

Mike nodded, too absorbed by Pretty to pay much attention.

Jemmy and I slipped out. Guy followed with a lantern. As soon as we were beyond earshot of the sullen guard—he was missing the feast—I said to Jemmy, "Well?"

"We want to show you something. Please come, Nurse!"

The pack had raised Jemmy since he was six and his mother died. He had a lively curiosity but, unlike Guy, Jemmy had never learned to read, although not because he shared the men's usual scorn for reading as useless and feminine. Jemmy said that the letters jumped places in front of his eyes, which made no sense but seemed to be true, since otherwise he was intelligent. Too delicately built to ever be of much use to Mike, he could make any mechanical equipment function again. It was Jemmy who figured out how to get the generators we sometimes found to run on the fuel we also sometimes found. The generators never lasted long, and most of the machinery they were supposed to power had decayed or rusted beyond use, but every once in a while we got lucky. Until the fuel ran out.

"Is it another generator?" I asked.

"Half be that!" Jemmy said.

Guy added mysteriously, "No, one-third."

But this arithmetic was too much for Jemmy, whose instincts about machinery were just that: instincts. He ignored Guy and pulled me along.

We went outside the building, across the square to the Vivian Beaumont, and to the rear of the building. It was dark out and there was a light drizzle, but the boys ignored it. I didn't get much choice. In the little underground theater our single lantern cast a forlorn glow.

"You climb up there," Jemmy said, pointing to the booth halfway up the wall. "The steps be gone, but I found a ladder."

"I'm not going up a ladder," I said, but of course I did. Their excitement was contagious. Also worrying: This was not the way Mike wanted his pack men to behave. In Mike's mind, fighters spoke little and showed less.

I was no longer young nor agile, and the ladder was a trial. But, lit from above by the lantern Guy carried, I heaved myself into the small space. The first thing I saw was a pile of books. "Oh!"

"That's not first," Guy said gleefully, preventing me from snatching at one. "The other things first!"

I said, "Let go of those books!"

Jemmy, scampering up the ladder like a skinny squirrel, echoed, "The other things first!"

I demanded of Guy, "Where did you find the books?"

"Here."

A noise filled the small space: another of Jemmy's generators. I was far more interested in the books.

Jemmy said, "I can't believe this still works! It be already connected or I don't know how to do. Look!"

A flat window standing on a table flickered and glowed. A moment of surprise, and then the word came to me: *teevee*. Grandmother had told me

about them. I never saw one work before, and when I was a child I confused *teevee* and *teepee*, so that I thought tiny people must live in the window, as we sometimes lived in teepees on summer forages.

They did.

She started out alone on the stage, except for words that appeared briefly
below her:

Pas De Deux from The Four Temperaments
Music by Paul Hindemith
Choreography by George Balanchine

The girl wore tight, clinging clothes that Mike would never have per-
mitted on his women: too inflaming for men far down the sex list. On her
feet were flimsy pink shoes with pink ribbons and square toes. The girl
raised one arm in a curve above her head and then raised her body up onto
the ends of those pink shoes—how could she do that? Music started. She
began to dance.

I heard myself gasp.

A man came onto the screen and they moved toward each other. She
turned away from him, turned back, moved toward him. He lifted her then,
waist-high, and carried her so that she seemed to float, legs stretched in a
beautiful arch, across the stage. They danced together, all their movements
light and precise and swift—so swift! It was achingly beautiful. Coiling
around each other, the girl lifting her leg as high as her head, standing on her
other on the ends of her toes. They flowed from one graceful pose to another,
defying gravity. I had never seen anything so fragile, so moving. Never.

It lasted only a short time. Then the teevee went black.

"I can't believe the cube still works!" Jemmy said gleefully. "Want to see
the other one?"

But Guy said nothing. In the shadows cast upward from the lantern, his
face looked much older, and almost in pain. He said, "What is it? What is
it called?"

"Ballet," I said.

Silently he handed me the pile of books. Three, four, five of them. The
top one read in large gold letters: *The Story of Giselle.* The others were *A
Ballet Companion: The Joy of Classical Dance, Basic Ballet Positions, Dancing
for Mr. B.,* and a very small *2016 Tour Schedule.*

Guy shivered. Jemmy, oblivious to all but his mechanical miracle, said, "The other one be longer. See, these cubes fit into this slot. Only two cubes still work, though."

White words on a black screen: TAKING CLASS ON VIDEO. Then a whole roomful of women and men standing—oh! at wooden railings before mirrors; the place might be our common room, long ago. Music from a piano and then a woman's voice said, "Plié . . . and *one* two three four. Martine, less tense in your hand. Carolyn, breathe with the movement. . . ."

They were not on the ends of their toes, not until partway through "class." Before that came strange commands from the unseen woman: *battement tendu, rondes de jambs a terre, porte de bras.* After they rose on the ends of their toes—but only the women, I noticed—came more commands: "Jorge, your hand looks like a dead chicken—hold the fingers loosely!" "No, no, Terry—you are doing *this,* and you should be doing *this.*" Then the woman herself appeared, and she looked as old or older than I, although much slimmer.

"Now center work. . . . No, that is too slow, John, and one and one and one . . . good. Now an *arabesque penchée.* . . . Breathe with it, softly, softly . . ."

On the teevee, dancers doing impossible, bewitching things with their bodies.

"Again. . . . Timon, please start just before the arabesque. . . ."

A roomful of dancers, each with one leg rising slowly behind, arms curved forward, to balance on one foot and make a body line so exquisite that my eyes blurred.

The teevee again went black. Jemmy said, "Let's not play it again—I want to save fuel." Guy, to my astonishment, knelt before me, as if he were doing atonement to Mike.

"Nurse, I need your help," he said.

"Get up, you young idiot!"

"I need your help," he repeated. "I want to bring Kara here, and I can't without you."

Kara. All at once, certain speculative looks he has given her sprang into my mind. I pushed him away, scandalized. "Guy! You can't bed Kara! Why, she hasn't Begun, and even if she had, Mike would kill you!"

"I don't want to bed her!" He rose, looking no less desperate but much more determined. "I want to dance with her."

"Dance with her!"

"Like that." He gestured toward the blank teevee and tried out his new word, with reverence. "Ballet."

Even Jemmy looked shocked. "Guy—you can't do that!"

"I can learn. So can Kara."

I said the first thing that came into my mind, which, like most first things, was idiotic. "The Nurse on the teevee said it takes years of work to become a dancer!"

"I know," Guy said, "years to be like them be. But we could learn *some*, Kara and me, and maybe dance for the pack. Mike might like that."

"Mike like a girl who has not yet Begun to be handled by you? You're crazy, Guy!"

"I have to dance," he said doggedly. "Ballet. With Kara. She be the only one possible!"

He was right about that. Pretty, spoiled and conventional, would never learn the hard things which that dance Nurse had demanded. Tiny and Seela were too young, Lula and Junie busy with children, Bonnie big and ungainly—what was I thinking? The whole thing was not only ridiculous, but dangerous.

"Put ballet out of your mind," I said severely. "If you don't, I will tell Mike."

I climbed ponderously down the ladder and made my way alone through the dark little theater to the door. But I carried the five books, and in my bare room in the underground of the David H. Koch Theater (I had finally found a faded sign with the correct name), I used an entire precious candle, reading them for most of the night.

Two days later, the chief of the St. Regis pack returned Mike's visit. This was a risk for him, since he arrived with only two lieutenants. It was a clear gesture of cooperation, not war, and it put everyone in a good mood. We ate at noon under a bright summer sky on a not-too-cracked terrace, beside a long shallow pool filled with both debris and two huge jutting pieces of stone that, looked at from certain directions, might be a person lying down. A sentence from my grandmother floated into my troubled mind: "Every autumn they had trouble with leaves in the Vivian Beaumont reflecting pool."

My girls built fires at first light and cooked all morning. None of the girls were present at the meal, of course; Mike would not let anyone but sworn pack men see how many women the pack possessed, nor which ones might be fertile. But I was there, serving the dishes, and the only one not cheerful.

Mike had made a bad mistake.

I knew it as soon as the chief of the other pack, Keither, began to talk. No, before—when I watched him as he studied Mike, studied our pack, studied the way the guards were set, studied everything he could see. Keither had a long, intelligent face and continuously darting eyes. He spoke well; I would bet my medicine box that this man could, and did, read. More, he had the ability to say whatever would be well received, without slipping into outright flattery. Mike, of much simpler mind, saw none of this. He had a leader's nose for treachery but not for subtlety. He could not see that Keither, with a smaller and more lightly armed pack than Mike's, aspired to the leadership of ours. There would be trouble. Not yet, maybe not even soon, but eventually.

It would do no good to tell Mike this, of course. He would not listen. I was Nurse, but I was a woman.

"I brought you a gift," Keither said, when the food had been consumed and praised. From his sack he pulled out a bottle of Jack Daniel's. Mike already knew it was there, of course—no sack could be brought unexamined beyond our perimeter. But if the men were not surprised, they were enormously pleased. Cups were passed around, toasts made, jokes exchanged. The younger men drank too much. Neither Mike nor Keither took more than a courtesy sip.

Still, the liquor prolonged the meeting. Talk grew louder. The men agreed to a joint hunting expedition, to leave the next morning. Both chiefs would go—a much greater risk on their part than on ours, since their pack was so much smaller. We would also send twice as many men as they did, further lessening our risk. Keither had been based in Manhattan for months and offered to show Mike good and bad foraging areas, boundaries of other packs' territories, and other useful information.

"We have no Nurse," Keither said. "Is yours up for trade? Or does she have an apprentice who is?"

"No," Mike said, with courtesy but without explanation. Keither didn't mention it again.

I was tired. Serving sixteen men, sitting cross-legged for hours on the concrete terrace, is hard on a body of my age. When the first tinges of sunset touched the sky, I caught Mike's eye. He nodded and let me go.

In the women's room, the girls crowded around me. "What be they like?" "Did they bring any more gifts?" "Did you find out how many women they have?" The girls sounded too insistent, crowded too close; they were hiding something. And: "Be you tired, Nurse? Maybe you go to your room and rest?"

I pushed off the wave of white robes. "Where's Kara?"

She sat alone in a corner. But the minute she raised her face, shining with exaltation, I knew. Or maybe I had known all along. After all, I could have left the feast hours earlier, and had not.

This way, I was innocent. So far.

My false innocence did not last past the next afternoon. Mike and nine other men departed on the hunting trip, leaving his first lieutenant, Joe, in command. Joe sent me with a guard of three men to the ruins of a nearby drugstore to see if there were any medicines I could use. There weren't; the place had been picked over long ago. Most of my medicines came from homes, left in ruined bathrooms, stored in drawers beside beds crawling with vermin. The expiration dates on the drugs have long since passed. However, a surprising number of them were still effective, and scalpels, scissors, gauze, and alcohol swabs don't decay.

By the time we got back, it was mid-afternoon of a gorgeous July day. Men sat in the sunshine, weapons on their knees, talking and laughing. Lula and Junie had the babies on blankets to kick their fat little legs. Pretty sat combing her hair in full view of the lounging men. She had taken to sex like a squirrel to trees, and with Mike gone her list was due for variety.

I didn't ask anyone where the other girls were. Tiny and Seela would be playing together, under guard. Bonnie would be preparing medicinal plants, pounding leaves and boiling bark and drying berries. I slipped around the back of the Vivian Beaumont, pushed open the door to the underground corridor, and made my way in the dark to the theater. That door was locked. I pounded on it, and eventually Jemmy opened it.

"Nurse—"

I slapped him across the face and strode down the aisle.

They were onstage and had not even heard me over the music. Over their intense concentration. Over their wonder, visible on both faces.

Guy noticed me first. "Nurse!"

Kara turned ashen and clutched what I now knew was called a barre. The boys must have brought it from the base building: a heavy-looking length of wood fastened not to a wall, as in the common room, but to heavy metal poles on either end. They had lugged the generator and the teevee down from the booth—I couldn't imagine how—and installed both onstage. On the teevee the music abruptly stopped and the older woman said, "No, no—drop your right shoulder, Alicia!"

Kara dropped her right shoulder.

Guy's face turned stony, such a good imitation of Mike that I was startled. I said, "What are you doing?"

"We're taking class."

Taking class. Following the movements of the dancers on the screen. All at once my anger was swamped by pity. They were so young. Growing up in such a barren world (my grandmother saying, "*Such rich performances as I saw!*"), but they hadn't know how barren it was. Now they did, and they thought things could be changed.

"Children, you *can't.* If Mike ever finds out that you put your hands on a girl who hasn't Begun—"

"I didn't touch her!" Guy said.

"—you know you'd be shot. Instantly. Guy, *think!*"

He came to the edge of the stage and knelt, looking down at me. "Nurse, I have to do this. I *have* to. And I can't dance alone. 'Ballet is woman.'"

I had read that just last night. Some famous ballet maker whose name I had never heard. I said, "You stole my books."

"I borrowed one. It has pictures that— Nurse, I have to."

"So do I," Kara said.

"Kara, come with me this minute."

"No," she said. Her defiance shocked me even more than their stupid notion that they could teach themselves to dance. I turned on Jemmy.

"And what about *you*? Is this insane love of machinery worth getting yourself shot?"

I saw from his face that Jemmy hadn't even considered this. He looked from me to Guy, back again, then at the ground. I had him.

"Go, Jemmy. Now. None of us will ever tell anyone you were here."

He scuttled down the aisle like a rabbit pursued by dogs. One misguided idiot down.

"If Mike ever finds out you were alone with her—"

"We're not alone!" Kara said. "We have a chaperone!"

"Who? If you mean Jemmy—"

"Me," Bonnie said, stepping from the shadows at the side of the stage.

If Kara had been a shock, Bonnie was an earthquake. Bonnie, who did not break rules and who had always treated Kara with faint disdain: for her high-strung emotion, for her fragile beauty. Bonnie had no command over Guy, but she had a borrowed—from me—authority over Kara.

"Bonnie? You *allowed* this?"

Bonnie said nothing. In the dimness onstage I couldn't see her face.

"Nurse," Guy said again, "we *have* to."

"No, you don't. Kara, come with me."

"No." And then, in a rush, "I won't be like Pretty! I won't let men touch me and sex with me and stick themselves up me until I get swollen and pregnant and maybe die like Emma did! I won't, I won't, *I won't!*" Her voice rose to a shriek, surprising Guy. Kara had just broken the strongest rule among the pack: loyalty. You followed the chief, you obeyed those above you, you did not cause trouble. And you kept your fear to yourself.

I made my voice soothing. "Kara, you heard what the woman on the teevee said. It takes years to become a real dancer. *Years.* This isn't possible, dear heart."

"We know that," Guy said. "We don't be stupid enough to think we can do everything they do. But we can do *some.*"

"And that's worth dying for?"

"Nobody will die if you tell Joe that you give us reading lessons here. Everybody knows Kara and me are learning to read off you!"

"No," I repeated. "It's too great a risk, for nothing."

And then Bonnie—Bonnie!—spoke up. "Not for nothing. Nurse, first watch the dancing."

Guy seized on this. "Yes! Watch just once! It's so beautiful!"

It wasn't beautiful. Kara and Guy took their places beside the railing, and he turned on Jemmy's teevee. The woman said, *"Battement tendu,"* and Guy and Kara swung their legs forward, down, to the side, down, to the back down. Their legs reached neither the height nor the purity of line of the dancers on-screen, but they were not without grace. Guy showed a flexibility and power I had not expected, and Kara a flowing delicacy. None of it made any difference.

They went through a few more steps and Guy turned off the screen. "We have to learn all we can before the generator fuel runs out. But we have the books, too. And later on in class there be combinations of steps!"

Five window washers worked every day of the year, constantly keeping the windows bright. At night, when all the buildings were lit up, they shone out on the plaza like liquid gold. So little in this hard life was bright, and nothing was liquid gold. But not at risk of our lives.

"No," I said.

Two days later, I fell in the forest—which I had learned from an old map was called "Central Park"—and tore my knee open on a pointed rock.

"Oh!" The pain was immediate and sharp, but not as sharp as my fear. I was old; if I couldn't walk when the pack moved on, I would be finished.

Bonnie was instantly beside me. "Nurse?"

I tried to rise, could not, was caught in her strong arms. I blinked back tears as we both stared at the white bone below my leathery flesh.

Then I fainted.

The sickroom under the New York State Theater, bare and dark, was no larger than a big closet. Lula sat beside me nursing Jaden, Madonna and child by a single smoky candle. "Grandmother . . ." I whispered, or maybe it was another word, I couldn't be sure. Everything felt blurry, as if I'd opened my eyes underwater.

"Nurse?" Lula said. She put down the baby, who immediately began to scream, and picked up a cup. "Here, drink this now, you be needing to sleep—"

A smell of mint, a bitter taste beneath the sweetness of honey. I slept.

The sickroom still, and I lay alone. Complete darkness. I groped for my leg and felt the hump of bandages, the wooden splint over the knee. Pain, muted. How long had I lain here?

Hours went by until Bonnie came with breakfast, with hot tea, with her wooden, unrevealing face.

"How bad is it, Bonnie? Will I walk again?"

"Can't say until you can stand."

"Is Mike back?"

"Not yet. Drink this."

"What is—"

"Just tea."

I needed more than just tea. I needed to be able to walk.

"Nurse? Nurse, you hear me?"

I did, dragging myself back from far away, or maybe it was Pretty who was far away. Only she was not. She crouched beside me, except that now there were two of her, and then three. How could that be? One Pretty was enough. Unless she was fertile and had given birth to herself again and yet again. . . .

"I be pregnant!" one of the Prettys shouted triumphantly. And then: "Can she hear me?"

"I don't know," Bonnie said.

"It be Mike's! I know! Bonnie, can she hear me?"

"I don't know."

And then, all of a sudden, I couldn't.

I was Grandmother, walking through Lincoln Center, watching the light spill from high arched windows, liquid gold. I took down twenty-one chandeliers and polished each crystal so bright that it burned my hand. The burning spread to the Library for the Performing Arts and charred it to the ground. Windows shattered and pieces of glass pierced me. "Lincoln Kirstein won't like that!" my grandmother cried. "He spent a fortune to build this place!" I laughed and kept on tacking down red carpet.

Finally, clarity returned. I knew who I was and where I was, and it was not Bonnie standing beside my bedroll but Joe, Mike's lieutenant, who'd been left in charge for—how long now?

"How be you, Nurse?" Joe said awkwardly.

I had known Joe since he was ten. A ferocious fighter, loyal, careful about guarding our camps but easygoing about what happened within the perimeter. However, he didn't look easy now.

I said, "My head is clear."

It wasn't my head he was interested in. "Can you walk?"

"I don't know."

"Find out." He left, abrupt and unsmiling. Cold slid down my spine.

Junie arrived a few minutes later, breathless with running, carrying Davey. "Oh, Nurse, be you better?"

"Yes. Send Bonnie to me."

"I don't know where she be! I wanted her a while ago to give Jaden something for that teething, she fusses so, Lula said maybe Bonnie give her something to calm her down but—"

Junie prattled on while I put one palm flat against the wall and tried to stand. I could do so, but only barely.

"Junie, how long have I been here?"

"Be . . . let me think . . . be a month? More?"

More than a month. Drugged for more than a month for the pain of a torn kneecap.

I said, "Find Bonnie and send her to me."

"I will. But, Nurse, Joe says—no, Tony, he be back and he—"

"Tony?" Tony had gone on the joint hunting trip with Mike and Keither's pack. I looked more closely at Junie, and now I saw the fear on her face. Davey felt it, too; his fat little hands clutched her body. I said, "Is Mike dead?"

"Tony says not when he ran off. Tony, he escaped. They got ambushed two days out—Nurse, Keither's pack be big, he lied, most of them not at the hotel when our men went there. They going to trade Mike for somebody, I forget who or why, and Tony escaped and Joe says we move out tomorrow morning! It ain't safe here no more. Oh, Nurse, can you walk?"

"Find Jemmy. Tell him to cut me a stick—*this* long—to lean on. Tell him I want it this minute."

"But you told me to find Bonnie and—"

"Not Bonnie. Jemmy. Now."

By the time Jemmy arrived with the stick, I'd eased my weight onto my leg, fallen, discovered the splint would hold, and gotten up again. Bonnie's splint was heavy; the cane balanced it. Leaning on Jemmy's shoulder, I got myself into the corridor without injuring anything further. In the women's room, the girls worked frantically even though the pack would not move until dawn and there was little enough to gather up. Anything taken must be carried. Each girl had her backpack, and the mothers had baby slings. The pockets of winter coats were stuffed with food. The coats themselves must be worn, no matter how hot the day, because we couldn't afford to lose them. In the morning, blankets would be rolled up with cooking utensils and strapped to Rick, eight years old and not ready to fight, and to whichever of the other men Joe chose.

Outside the building, the first stars shone faintly in a deep blue sky, although on the western horizon clouds mounted high. The air smelled of rain to come and the trees swayed. The Met loomed dark against the cobalt sky. *At night, when all the buildings were lit up, they shone out on the plaza like liquid gold. People laughed and talked and lined up by the hundreds to hear opera and see ballet and watch plays and listen to concerts.*

Somewhere a dog bayed, then another. A pack, hunting.

I said to Jemmy, "Take me to them."

Shadows beside the Vivian Beaumont, shadows in the sloping underground corridor. Jemmy wedged open the door with a rock so that I could hear if the guards started shooting. Inside the theater, more shadows.

They didn't see me. The barre had been pushed to the back of the stage, out of the way. Guy, barefoot, was stripped to the waist. Kara, also barefoot, wore white tights and something filmy and clinging and dotted with holes, unearthed from who knows what ancient storage area. Music played. It wasn't the thin, slightly tinny music of the piano that played for "class." This was the full, glorious sound of the music from the other recording, *The Four Temperaments*. And I realized what Guy had done.

While he arranged steps and combinations for him and Kara, he had held Paul Hindemith's music in his mind. Their dancing perfectly matched the music, blended with it, *was* it. In that blending, Guy's and Kara's inexperience became less important, in part because he had chosen so well movements that they could perform with grace. From studying the ballet books, I could even name some of them: *bourrées, pas de chat, battements.*

The names were unimportant. What mattered was the dancing. They never touched, but Kara's young body, on demi-pointe, bent toward his with sorrow, with loss, with longing, without ever reaching him. He yearned toward her but I knew it was not her he yearned for, nor she for him. The sorrow was for the dancing itself, so briefly embraced, lost tomorrow. The loss was of all the beauty they once might have had, were the world different. Guy raised his leg, extended his arm, and balanced in a perfect arabesque. In the soft glow of lantern light, the dancing figures were liquid gold, and they lit up the bare stage with heartbreaking regret for vanished beauty.

But it was Bonnie who stunned me.

She stood to one side of the stage: chaperone, guard, and something more. Never had I imagined that her homely face could look like that. She was not just alive; she shone with the ferocity of the angel guarding the gate to Eden. I had not known, not even suspected.

"Bonnie," I said. It came out a whisper, heard only by Jemmy. Before I could find a louder voice, the door behind me jerked open and a man roared, "What the fuck!"

Mike.

I turned. Blood caked the left side of his face, matted his beard. His left arm was in a crude sling. Behind him crowded three or four men. Mike pushed past me and ran toward the stage.

I lurched after him as fast as I could, pushing through the pain in my knee. "Wait! Wait! Don't—"

The men rammed past me. Mike stood below the stage, on which Kara and Guy had frozen.

"—do anything!" I yelled. "Bonnie was here the whole time, they were never alone!"

One of the other men—his back to me, I couldn't see who—raised a second lantern high in the air beside Mike, and I saw what Mike saw: the blood on Kara's thighs, brilliant red on the white tights. She had Begun.

I grabbed Mike's good arm. "Never alone! Do you understand, they were never alone! He never touched her!"

If it had been Joe, he might have shot Guy right there on the stage. If it had been Lew, he might have shot them both. Mike gave Guy a look of profound disgust: at his bare chest, at the arabesque Mike had interrupted, at everything about Guy that Mike would never understand. To me, apparently not even noticing my leg, Mike growled, "Take them girls to where they belong."

Someone fired a rifle at the teevee screen, and the music stopped.

Bonnie would answer none of my questions. She sat, silent and wooden, in the sickroom until Mike had time to send for her. "What did you give me?" I demanded. "In what dosage? And, Bonnie—*why?*"

She said nothing.

Lincoln Kirstein, Grandmother once told me, *got this place built. He used his own money and made others donate money and founded a great ballet company. He wasn't a dancer or a choreographer or a musician. He didn't make ballets, but he made ballet happen.*

Kara was not with us. She had been sent to the women's room. In a week or so, when she stopped bleeding, she would be sent to Mike's bed, to Joe's, to Karl's, to every man who might prove her fertile. Even shrieking, she would be sent.

A few hours later, Mike sent for me. Two men carried me between them to a room at the end of the corridor. Small, with concrete walls, it still held the twisted and rusted remains of those big machines that once gave out food and drink in exchange for coins. There was an ancient sofa nested by rats, a sagging table, a few chairs. I could picture dancers coming here from the practice rooms, throwing themselves across the sofa, resting for a moment with a candy bar or soda.

Mike's men sat me in a mostly intact chair and he said, "Why, Nurse?"

The same question I had asked Bonnie. My concern now was to shield her as much as I could. "They wanted to dance, Mike, that's all. They were never alone and he never—"

"You don't know that. You be unconscious the whole time." He eyed my leg. Someone had cleaned up the blood from his eye and beard.

"Yes, that's true, but if Bonnie says she was always with them, then she was. She obeys orders, Mike. I told her that I'd given Kara and Guy permission to dance and that she must stay with them."

"You? *You* gave permission?"

"Yes, me. I mean, you know Bonnie—does she seem the type of person interested in dancing?"

Mike frowned; he was not used to considering what "type of person" a woman might be. "You did this, Nurse? Not Bonnie?"

"Not Bonnie. And she's a good Nurse, Mike. She can make medicines just as well as I did. And do everything else, too."

Finally his gaze lifted from my bandaged knee to my face. He said simply, "Do you want to be shot or left behind?"

Shooting would be kinder. But I said, "Left behind."

He shrugged, losing interest. He still had a Nurse; Kara had not been touched; there were fighting tactics to occupy his mind. Into that indifference I dared to ask, "Guy?"

Mike scowled. To his men he said, "Take her wherever she wants to be left, and bring me the new Nurse." He strode from the room, having already forgotten me.

Mike's men left me under the Vivian Beaumont, just inside the first door, at the top of the sloping corridor. In the dark I groped in my pocket for the candle and matches. It wasn't easy to keep one hand on the wall, hold the candle and my cane in the other, and hobble my painful way down the corridor and through the second door. By the time I reached the shallow steps at the far side of the stage, I was crawling.

My five ballet books lay neatly stacked in a corner, where Guy had studied them who knew how many nights while I lay drugged and Kara, locked in the women's room, flexed and pointed her toes and dreamed of pointe shoes. I opened *The Story of Giselle* and turned the pages by candlelight until I found a photograph of a dancer in a long, filmy skirt held impossibly high by her partner, soaring in an exquisite arc above him. There are worse ways to die than gazing at beauty. From my pocket, I drew my packet of distilled monkshood leaves. Fairly quick, and not as painful as most.

Something moaned somewhere behind me.

They had beaten him bloody and chained him to a concrete column in one of the tiny dressing rooms behind the stage. Guy breathed as if in pain, but I could find no broken bones. Mike had not wanted him to die too quickly. He would either starve or be found by Keither's pack when they came looking for revenge, or for our women, or just for war.

"Guy?"

He moaned again. I searched the room but found no key to his chains. Sitting beside him, I held in one hand that packet of monkshood that did not contain enough for both of us, and in the other *The Story of Giselle*. And then, because I am old and had broken my knee and had lain inactive for over a month while Guy and Kara reinvented the dangers of ballet, I fell asleep.

"Nurse? Nurse?" And then: "Susan!"

The candle had gone out. But the dressing room was lit by a lantern—two lanterns. Bonnie and Kara stood there, dressed in men's clothing and backpacks, and both carried semiautomatic machine guns. On Kara, it looked like a butterfly equipped with a machete. In the sudden light, Guy's eyelids fluttered open.

"Oh!" Kara said, one hand flying to her mouth. The gun wobbled.

Bonnie snapped, "Don't you dare fuss!" and I was startled at her tone, which was my own. Had been my own. "Nurse, can you—"

"No," I said.

Bonnie didn't argue. She dropped to her knees and ran her hands impersonally over Guy.

"I already did that," I said. "Nothing broken."

"Then he can walk. Kara, pull Nurse out of here, back to the stage. Guy, pull yourself as far from the post as you can."

He did, closing his swollen and blood-crusted eyes. Kara tugged me away. Even from the stage, the sound of Bonnie's gun—not the semiautomatic—was loud as she shot at the chain. Even the ricochets—surely dangerous!—made my ears ring. After a few moments Guy and Bonnie emerged, he leaning on her and dragging lengths of chain on both ankles. But he was able to bend and scoop them off the floor. I caught at Bonnie's knee.

"Bonnie—how—"

"In their stew. Kara and I were serving."

"Dead?"

"I don't know. Some, maybe."

"What did you use? Pokeweed? Cowbane? Snakeroot?"

"Skyweed. The seeds."

Kara said suddenly, "Not the other girls, though. We wouldn't do that." And then: "But I won't bed anybody!"

Bonnie said, "And you have to dance."

I gaped at her. Kara wanted to dance, Guy wanted to dance, but it was *Bonnie* who was determined that they would dance. Slowly I said, "Where will you go?"

"North. Away from the city. It's going to rain hard, and that will cover our tracks before the pack revives."

"Try to find a farm community. Or, if you can, places called 'Ithaca' or 'Endicott' or 'Bath.' I'm not sure they exist, but they might. Have you got that map I found? And my medicine sack?"

"Yes. Do you have—"

"Yes."

"We have to go now, Nurse. Jemmy is with us, too."

Jemmy. Perhaps they would find a generator. Bonnie extracted the two recording cubes, *The Four Temperaments* and *Taking Class on Video,* from the blasted teevee. Kara was helping Guy dress in warm coat, boots, a rain poncho. He swayed on his feet but remained upright. She handed him her rifle, which actually seemed to steady him. Kara turned to me and her lips trembled.

"Don't," I said in my harshest tone. Kara, not understanding, looked hurt. But Bonnie knew.

"Good-bye, Nurse," she said, without painful sentiment, and grasped the other two to lead them away.

I waited until the sound of their boots crossed the stage, until the door to the theater closed, until they had had enough time to leave camp. Then I crawled out of the Vivian Beaumont. The rain had just started, sweet on the summer night air. The cookfires on the plaza sputtered and hissed. Beside them lay the men. Farther out would be the perimeter, and then the guards who had gone from their hearty dinner to the outposts on nearby streets or rooftops.

Two of the men by the fire were already dead. I thought most of the others, including Mike, might recover, but skyweed seeds are tricky. So much depends on how they are dried, pounded, leached, and stored. Bonnie knew a lot, but not as much as I did. I gathered up the men's guns, made a pile of them under a rain poncho, and sat beside it under another poncho, a loaded semiautomatic beside me.

This could happen several ways. If Keither's pack showed up soon, the kindest thing would be to shoot Mike and the others before they revived.

Keither's pack would claim the girls, who would be no better nor worse off than they were now. Fertile women were precious.

If Mike and the others revived after I judged Bonnie to be far enough away, I would swallow my packet of monkshood and let Mike take on Keither.

But . . . with skyweed, more of these men should have vomited before their paralysis. If Bonnie had misjudged her preparation or dosages, and the pack regained their senses and strength soon enough to follow her, I would do what was necessary.

We lowered all twenty-one electric chandeliers at the Met—think of that, Susan, twenty-one—and cleaned each crystal drop individually. Every other year all the red carpet was completely replaced, at a cost of $700,000. Every five years the seats were replaced. Five window washers worked every day of the year, constantly keeping the windows bright. At night, when all the buildings were lit up, they shone out on the plaza like liquid gold. People laughed and talked and lined up by the hundreds to hear opera and see ballet and watch plays and listen to concerts. And such rich performances as I saw . . . you can't imagine!

No, I can't. No more than I can imagine what will happen to Guy, and Kara, and ballet. No more than I could have imagined Bonnie caught in an enchantment she had never expected: the enchantment of the lost past, rising from ruin like a dancer rising into arabesque. Had that storm lain in her all along, needing only something to passionately love?

There are all kinds of storms, and all kinds of performances. Under the poncho, I hold my gun, and listen to the rain falling on Lincoln Center, and wait.

Diana Rowland

Hell hath no fury like a woman whose city has been scorned. . . .

Diana Rowland has worked as a bartender, a blackjack dealer, a pit boss, a street cop, a detective, a computer forensics specialist, a crime scene investigator, and a morgue assistant. She won the marksmanship award in her police academy class, has a black belt in hapkido, and has handled numerous dead bodies in various states of decomposition. A graduate of Clarion West, her novels include *Mark of the Demon, Blood of the Demon, Secrets of the Demon, Sins of the Demon,* and *My Life as a White Trash Zombie.* Her most recent books are *Touch of the Demon* and *Even White Trash Zombies Get the Blues.* She has lived her entire life below the Mason-Dixon Line and is deeply grateful for the existence of air-conditioning.

CITY LAZARUS

A grey dawn and low tide revealed the body at the water's edge, facedown and partially buried in the silt. One arm drifted in the sluggish current as the river plucked at it. A fetid scent drifted to the people standing on the levee, though the odor likely had more to do with illegal sewage than the corpse.

Rain plopped onto the mud in scattered drops as the flatboat inched out to the body, a thick rope dragging in its wake and doled out by workers on firmer ground. Captain Danny Faciane watched from his vantage on the levee and scowled beneath the hood of his raincoat. He fully understood the necessity for the slow progress across the silt, but he still chafed at it. The tide wouldn't wait for them to complete their business, though at the moment it was more the early hour and the lack of coffee in his system that frustrated him. Yet it paid to be cautious with this river. Since the collapse of the Old River Control Structure, she might not have the teeth she once had, but she still had a few tricks left in her.

Danny's attention drifted to his right, toward the two bridges that spanned the river. The headlights of cars only crossed along one of them. Not enough traffic anymore to warrant having both. Across the river, a grounded ship leaned drunkenly in the mud. Light flickered from a dozen places, the cutting torches of workers fighting to salvage what they could of the trapped heap. Danny wondered if the salvage workers would attack the unused bridge next, like termites drawn to wood.

"I need to learn how to weld," a detective grumbled from behind him. Danny glanced back to see that Farber's attention had also been caught by the crawling lights on the defunct ship.

Danny shook his head. "They'll be gone as soon as they finish. Only a few ships left to cut up. Probably not even a year's worth of work left."

"Maybe so, but in that year those fuckers'll make three times what we do. Besides, I still think the city'll have work for 'em. New Orleans has a way of taking care of itself."

Danny let out a snort. He had little doubt that the welders made more than Farber, but he knew damn well that they didn't come close to matching his own take. And he sure as hell didn't share Farber's bright-eyed optimism about the future of the city. "Filthy work," he said instead. "And dangerous."

"What *we* do is dangerous," Farber protested. Danny cocked an eyebrow at him, let out a low bark of laughter.

"Only if you're doing it wrong," he said, then hunched his shoulders against the gust of wind that sought to drive the sluggish rain into his face. "Like this. Fuck this early morning shit."

The muttered commands and curses of the men in the flatboat drifted to him as they reached the corpse. They fought the pull of the tenacious mud as the river held on to her prize, but finally managed to get the corpse free of its partial grave. It flopped into the bottom of the boat, one mud-covered foot still on the edge as the workers onshore pulled the flatboat back.

Danny walked over as the men pulled the body from the boat and set it on the ground. "Can you wash his face off?" he asked nobody in particular, waited as someone found a bottle of water and dumped it over the victim's face. Danny scowled as he crouched by the body, and only part of it was because of the rank smell of the mud. "It's Jimmy Ernst."

"Jesus," one of the men from the flatboat muttered. "We crawled across the stinking mud for that piece of shit?"

Danny's mouth twisted in sour agreement as he cast a practiced eye over the body. The crime scene tech pulled a pair of gloves out of the side pocket of her pants and held them out for Danny, but he shook his head. He had no intention of touching the corpse and risking getting dirty. Coroner would take care of cleaning the fucking muck off before they did the autopsy.

"Well, that's damn interesting," he said, tilting his head.

"Whatcha got?" Farber asked, crouching beside him.

"He was murdered." Danny pointed to the two scorch marks on the dead guy's neck. Maybe there were more, hiding beneath the filth, but those alone would've been enough. Latest generation of Tasers left that sort of mark, delivering enough punch to paralyze for about half a minute.

Long enough to get cuffs on a perp. Or a few licks in. Whichever they deserved more.

Danny straightened, let his gaze drift over what was left of the Mississippi River. This wasn't the first body to be pulled from the sucking muck and it wouldn't be the last. The banks were a morass of sinkholes and unpredictable currents. Easy enough to die, especially after a couple of jolts from a Taser.

"I've seen enough," he told the crime scene tech as she snapped her pictures in an aimless, desultory fashion. She didn't give a shit about Jimmy Ernst any more than he did.

"See you back at the precinct," Farber said.

Danny nodded, turned away, walked back over the rocks of the now-pointless levee, over the weed-covered train tracks, and up to the street. The rain had paused, and a glance at the sky told him that he had time enough to grab some coffee and finish waking up before the skies opened up again. No pressing need to get back to the precinct station. There sure as hell wasn't any rush to close *this* case. He'd give it a week or so and then suspend it for lack of evidence.

Café Du Monde was open and already catering to a few persistent tourists, but he continued past and up North Peters, his footsteps echoing back at him from the many silent storefronts. Three years ago, before the river changed course, the Quarter would already have been bustling at this hour, with vendors making deliveries and shop owners hosing off sidewalks and garbage men calling out to each other as the trucks rumbled their way through the narrow streets.

Near the French Market, he crossed over to Decatur Street, made his way to the coffee shop on the corner of St. Peters. He flashed his badge to get his coffee and croissant for free, then returned outside to sit at a table under the green-and-white-striped awning.

A scrawny dog reeking of wet and sewage and despair slunk along the sidewalk toward him. Grey with one black ear, hope flickered in its eyes that Danny would throw a piece of the croissant its way, drop a crumb. It had probably been a pet at one time. Lots of animals had been left behind after the Switch, when their owners had abandoned their houses and all ties to the area and rushed away in a desperate flight to find new opportunities elsewhere, as any industry in New Orleans that depended on the river dried up.

The dog whined and sat about a foot from Danny. "Go away," he muttered, shoving the dog carefully away with his foot. To his annoyance, that contact only seemed to encourage the mutt. It came back, and this time put a paw on Danny's knee. He swore and pulled his leg away, pissed to see a broad smear of who-the-fuck-knew-what left behind. "You fucking mutt!" He shot his foot out again. It wasn't a savage blow, but he made sure there was enough force behind it to get his message across. The mutt let out a high-pitched yelp and went sprawling back, then crouched, eyes on Danny. For a brief instant, Danny wondered if the dog would attack him. There were plenty of desperate animals in the city, and a smart person stayed alert. His hand twitched to his gun, more than ready to shoot the thing if it came at him, but after a few seconds, it lowered its head and loped unevenly away, taking its stink with it.

Danny let out a sigh of relief as he snatched up napkins and wiped at the grime on his pants. Shooting the dog here would have drawn all sorts of fucked-up attention. Wouldn't have mattered if the dog had been attacking him; there'd be plenty of people ready to Monday-morning-quarterback the decision, explaining how he should have used less force or found a way to be absolutely certain that the dog intended to cause him harm. There'd even be those who'd insist that, as an officer of the law, he ought to have been willing to suffer a bite or two, and had progressed to lethal force too quickly.

Fuck that, Danny thought grimly. You did what you had to do to survive, especially in this city. You looked out for yourself, because no one else was going to do it for you.

He dropped the soiled napkins onto the table and stood, scowling down at the remaining stain. He picked up his coffee and croissant, began to cross the street, but paused at the sight of a woman on the opposite corner who was holding a folded red umbrella in one hand.

She was beautiful, with dark hair and lighter eyes, and skin a pale brown that made him wonder if she had a touch of Creole blood somewhere down the line. She had on shorts and sandals, paired with a black sleeveless T-shirt that hugged a sleek and toned figure that still held curves in all the right places. Young—early twenties, perhaps. Not rich. That was easy enough to tell. The rich who'd stayed behind were *obscenely* rich, had found ways to make even more profit from the shift in the river, and were far from subtle about flaunting that wealth and influence. A waitress maybe? A stripper? She sure as hell had the body for it.

But it wasn't just her looks that caused her to stand out to Danny. It was more that she didn't have the familiar beat-down look about her, the desperate shift of the eyes, as if seeking any possible escape from this fucked-up shell of a city. She seemed calm, perhaps a touch of worry or sadness in her eyes as they met his. Then she smiled, and he knew it was for him. Daring and coy at the same time, with a whisper of amusement skimming across her features before she broke the gaze, turned away, and continued down the street away from him.

He took a step to follow, then stopped as his phone buzzed in a familiar cadence. He breathed out a curse as he snatched it off his belt, skimmed the text.

Replacing the phone in its holder, he watched the girl continue down the street until she turned a corner. Then he spun and walked the other way to answer the summons.

"You and me, Danny," Peter Bennett said as he looked out over the dregs of the river. Rain pattered against the broad window of the condo, streaking the view of the deserted Riverwalk and the empty wharves. "We're a lot alike." He flicked a glance back at the cop. "We know how to go along with change, find the ways to make it work for us."

Danny leaned up against the back of the black leather couch, hands stuffed into his pockets as he gave the lanky man an agreeable smile. "I'm cool with doing what needs to be done," he replied. After the Old River Control Structure crumbled beneath the weight of spring flooding and insufficient funding, Peter was one of those very rich who'd not only stayed in the city but managed to get even richer. Judicious investments in the Atchafalaya Basin had paid off handsomely when the river changed course, but the real money had come from Peter's uncanny ability to land cleanup contracts. A threefold increase in the amount of water flowing down the Atchafalaya River had, of course, caused a fair amount of destruction, and the man knew there was much to be gained during times of disaster. There'd been plenty of men like Peter who'd made their fortunes after Katrina.

"And that's the key to it all," Peter said with a firm nod. "Too many other people want to clutch their chests and worry about rebuilding, get everything back to how it *used* to be." He let out a snort. "Did you know the city council is still whining to the governor about having the river dredged so that shipping traffic can resume?" He didn't wait for an answer. "Waste of time. Time to let the old New Orleans die. That river is a toothless whore compared to the badass bitch it used to be, but there's still a lot that can be done with this city. Gotta change with the times."

"That's right," Danny replied. He didn't say the first thing that leaped to mind, that even a toothless whore could still shove a knife into you. Jimmy Ernst could testify to that. But Peter didn't want to hear that sort of thing, and Danny was damn good at knowing when to keep his mouth shut. "So, you got something that needs doing?" That's what the text had said. *Got something I need you to do.*

Peter turned away from the dismal view, picked up the cup of coffee from the table by the window, and took a gulp. "Cold." He grimaced. "Get me a new one, will you, Danny? Get one for yourself too." He smiled, magnanimous.

Danny nodded and pushed off the couch, headed to the sleek black and chrome of the kitchen. "Glad to. Your coffee's damn good." He knew where the mugs were, knew how the man took his coffee.

"It's a free enterprise thing, see?" Peter said while Danny poured and stirred. "There's a shop down on Dumaine Street in the Quarter. I bought it about a year ago and rented it out to a guy who sells old books and shit. Dunno how he makes a fucking living with that, but he pays his rent." He scowled at that last bit, took the mug that Danny handed him.

"You want him out?"

Peter took a sip. Smiled down at the coffee. "That's damn good." Looked back up at Danny. "I have plans for that space. Council's going to vote my way about the poker room. I've made sure of that." His smile widened. "*You* made sure of that."

Danny chuckled. Easiest drunk-driving arrest he'd ever made. Helped that he'd been tipped off by Peter that Councilman Walker was leaving the wine tasting to drive the one and a half blocks to his house.

"But there's a little thing in the guy's lease that says I can evict him *if* there's evidence of criminal activity," Peter continued.

Danny nodded, took a sip from his own mug. It was bitter, too dark a roast for his liking, and he preferred it with a lot of cream in it. But Peter took his black and Danny didn't want to nitpick. "I'm sure I can do something about that," he said.

The bedroom door opened. A young woman with sleep-tousled blond hair, wearing only underwear and a tank top, peered out. Her gaze took in Danny and dismissed him, then settled on Peter. A pout formed on her full lips, or at least that's the expression Danny thought that she was trying for. There was a little too much uncertainty and not enough confidence, if any, for her to be able to pull it off, and he couldn't help but think that the girl on the corner would've been able to do it and make it alluring and amusing at the same time.

"Hey, babe," she said to Peter, leaning against the doorframe in what she tried to make a sexy position. "Come back to bed. I need a morning workout."

Danny took a sip of coffee to hide his grin at the sad display. He'd seen it a dozen times before, watched Peter's girl-of-the-month pitch a desperate bid to win back his interest, and seen it fail every time. Peter liked the new and shiny, and got rid of anything with too much wear and tear on it. Didn't matter that he was the one who fucked it up. He was a good-looking man—blue eyed, dark haired, athletic build—as well as being one of the richest men in the city. There was always more new and shiny to be had, more girls convinced that they might become the next Mrs. Peter Bennett.

Peter waved a dismissing hand, eyes on the rain-streaked view. "I'm busy."

Her pout deepened. "But I'm ready now, sweetie. Come give me some."

Now Peter looked her way. He took in her expression and her state of partial undress. Annoyance crawled briefly over his face instead of the lust she was surely hoping for, but then it shifted to amusement as Peter jerked his head toward Danny.

"Let him," he said, eyes on her.

Shock flashed across her face, but only for an instant. Eyes dead, she turned her pouty smile onto Danny. She had nothing to lose, even if it meant buying just a few more days in Peter's care, such as it was. It was worth it to her, Danny knew.

Danny set his mug down, moved to her, gave her a mild push to precede him into the bedroom.

———

When he came back out, he closed the door behind him. She wasn't sniv-eling, at least. Still, she'd probably be gone by the next day and Peter would be on the prowl for some other chick he could use up and throw away.

"That didn't take long," Peter said, without looking up from his laptop.

"I wasn't trying to make her happy," Danny replied. He looped his tie back around his neck, knotted it quickly.

A smile twitched across Peter's mouth as he tapped an envelope on the table. Danny scooped it up and tucked it into his jacket. He didn't bother counting it.

"I think I'll go visit a bookstore now," he said with a grin.

"Tell me if you find anything dirty."

The aroma of sweat and stale coffee greeted Danny as he entered the sta-tion with his arrestee. He kept a hand on the upper arm of the handcuffed man, guided him around the other dregs and the other cops.

"You can't do this!" his guy kept saying, as if hoping that if he said it enough, it would be true, that a cop couldn't simply walk into his book-store and find drugs that were never there before. "Please. Please! I have a family. You can't do this. Those drugs weren't mine. You—"

Danny gave him a hard yank, pulled him off-balance. His guy let out a yelp as he struggled for footing and went down on one knee. Danny crouched, making a show of helping him back to his feet while he leaned in close to the guy's ear.

"You need to settle the fuck down and be a good boy," he said in a calm, low voice. "This is going to happen whether you behave or not. You want it to be worse?" He met the guy's eyes. "It can be worse."

Sweat tracked down the side of the man's face. Danny watched as a spark of rebellion struggled for life within his eyes.

"There's a lot of paperwork in an arrest like this," Danny continued smoothly. "Some of it might get lost. Maybe it's the part that describes the evidence and the chain of custody. Or maybe it's the part that says you were booked into jail and need to have a bond set. Which one you want lost? You want to have the case thrown out before it goes to trial? Or you want to spend an extra week or so in central lockup?"

The spark of rebellion died. His head dropped.

"That's right," Danny said, helping the unresisting man back up to his feet. "You be a good boy and this'll all be over soon."

Danny booked him in, filed the initial paperwork, and was on his way down the hall to his office when he saw her sitting in an interview room. The girl from the corner. She'd changed into jeans and a deep maroon blouse, but he'd have known her no matter what she was wearing. She looked small and scared in the metal chair, her hands clasped around a paper cup of coffee and her eyes on Detective Farber in the opposite chair.

He stepped into the open doorway, knocked on the jamb. She jerked her eyes up to his. A whisper of a smile touched her mouth and he thought that maybe now she didn't look so scared. "Whatcha got?" he asked Farber without taking his eyes from her.

"She talked to Jimmy Ernst late last night," the detective explained. "Might've been the last one to see him alive. We're just getting started."

"I'll take over," Danny said, moving into the room. He shifted his gaze, caught Farber's eye. The other man hesitated, then flicked a glance back at the girl, hid a grin.

"Yeah, sure thing." He stood and picked up his things. "By the way, Ernst had a gun on him. It's been sent to the lab." Ballistics testing was routine. Maybe they could pin some cold cases on Ernst and improve their stats. Farber's eyes flicked toward the girl, then back to Danny. "Lemme know if you get anything," he added, the double meaning hanging in the air.

Danny waited for him to leave, closed the door, and took a seat in the empty chair. "I'm Captain Danny Faciane," he told her. "I'd like to ask you a few questions."

"Okay." She paused. "I'm Delia," she said, releasing her grip on the paper cup.

"Last name?"

She sat back. "Rochon. Delia Rochon. I talked to Jimmy last night. About midnight or so, I guess. He used to come by the club a lot." Distaste skimmed across her features.

He wrote her name on the pad. "Club?"

"Freddy-Z's." Her eyes dropped to the hands in her lap. "I'm a dancer."

A stripper. Freddy-Z's was one of the best in what was left of the city. Danny jotted the info down. Not because it was important to the case, but because he wanted her to think it was, that it wasn't simply important to him that he knew where to find her again.

He went ahead and asked her about her conversation with Jimmy Ernst, went through the motions the same way they did with most other cases like this. She gave him a clear but sparse tale of the encounter. Jimmy had asked her about a girl who'd used to work at the club, wanted to know where she was now. Delia hadn't told him anything. Nothing too exciting.

She didn't like the victim. She never came out and said so, but it was clear in her manner, the hardening of her eyes when she spoke of him. Then again, Danny knew that he'd be hard pressed to find anyone who did. Jimmy was a pimp, specializing in girls who looked *really* young.

Danny finally set the pen down on the pad. She looked at the pen, then to him. "Am I under arrest?" she asked, voice small but steady.

He let out a snort. "For Jimmy? Nah. We don't give a fuck about him." No one would ever go to jail for that murder. Not unless they came to the station and made a full confession—and that's how it was for most of the murders in this city, not only for scum like Ernst. Danny, and everyone else, did just enough to keep from being indicted for malfeasance.

The cops in this city knew how to survive. And a few smart ones, like him, knew how to prosper.

He walked her out, offered to have an officer drive her home, but she merely smiled and shook her head. It was raining again, a steady downpour that would wash all the trash into the streets and clog the drains, but she simply opened her umbrella and walked out into it without a hitch in her stride. He watched the red umbrella grow smaller in the distance until it was lost in the grey haze of the rain.

Danny talked to the bartender at Freddy-Z's later that day, found out that Delia had started there about a month ago. No one knew much about her. Then again, no one really cared, according to the bartender. They didn't give a shit about the girls' personal lives as long as they showed up on time and kept any trouble they were in away from the club. Delia did both.

She was working that night. He made sure he was there to see her. He didn't even try to convince himself he was checking out a possible witness. He knew damn well that he wanted to see more of her, and not simply the more that happened when she pulled her clothing off.

Neon flashed in tempo to the bass thump of the music. The mingled scents of sweat and sex, money and misery, swirled around the dancers and the men gazing up at them. Delia worked the pole with a lithe grace and sureness that spoke of years of training, and Danny wondered if, in some distant past, she'd been a far different sort of dancer. Yet, despite her obvious strength and control, she exuded a sensuousness, a base sexuality, that he doubted she'd learned in a ballet class.

She only looked at him once, a lingering caress of attention paired with a shy smile, at odds with the sultry glances she bestowed on the other patrons. And because it would have seemed odd or rude for him not to, he held up a fiver and slipped it under her G-string when she paused before him, then felt dirty for doing so with this girl.

"She's a fucking hot piece," said a familiar voice. Danny turned his head, forced a smile for Peter. The other man's eyes were on Delia. Appreciative. Admiring. Hungry.

"She's a witness in one of my cases," Danny found himself saying. Maybe Peter would be scared off by that. He was usually pretty careful about not associating with criminal types. After all, that's what he had Danny for.

But Peter merely smiled, kept his gaze on Delia.

Danny knew what would happen next. Peter would get a lap dance, then pay for a private room. It was possible that he'd invite Danny to come with him, and with any other girl he'd have gone and enjoyed himself.

Danny stood, moved to the bar on a pretense of getting another drink. The envelope crinkled within his jacket and he frowned. He'd been so caught up in thoughts of her that he'd forgotten to take it out and put it someplace safe. But now he felt only relief. He didn't even think before calling the manager over, paying the money for a private room with Delia and another one for Peter with a different dancer. Part of him knew that there was every chance that this wouldn't work. Peter had money and influence and was used to getting what he wanted. But Danny had his own sort of influence. He slid the manager a hundred, along with an agreement to help the man out if he ever got into the sort of trouble that Danny could help with. A few minutes later, the club's second-prettiest dancer made her way over to where Peter sat.

Peter raised an eyebrow as the blonde draped herself around his shoulders, chuckled under his breath as she rubbed her breasts on the back of his neck. He scanned the room for Delia, then asked the blond girl a question. She shrugged and nodded in Danny's direction; he fixed a smile on his face and lifted his drink as Peter looked his way, tried to make it look as if he'd bought the girl for Peter simply because it was a cool thing for one guy to do for another.

The two men locked eyes, gaze broken when the blond dancer took Peter's hand to lead him to the back room. He stood and followed, paused as they neared the bar.

He leaned in to Danny. "I saw what you did there," Peter said, mouth showing amusement that his eyes didn't share. "I think it's cute that you like that girl enough to pull a stunt like that." He paused. "Don't you ever fucking cockblock me like that again."

He turned without waiting for a response and continued through the curtains to the private rooms.

Danny stayed where he was, hands clenched into fists in the pockets of his jacket, telling himself he was controlling himself from going after Peter and beating that smug, superior smile from his face, but knowing that he was actually fighting down the sick knowledge that he and Peter might be cut from the same cloth, but they sure as shit weren't *equals*, weren't partners of any sort. And as much as he hated Peter at this moment, he knew that when the man summoned him he'd go and do what he was told, like a goddamned trained dog. Too much to lose if he didn't.

He also knew that he didn't want to go to a private room with Delia. He turned back to the bartender. "The redheaded kid down by the left stage. Is he a dick to the girls?"

Bartender shook his head. "Nah. Comes in with twenty bucks a coupla times a week. Never caused trouble."

"Give him my room. Tell him happy fucking birthday." He peeled off another hundred to cover a tip. "And tell him if he gets out of line with Delia, I'll break his fucking neck."

He left the club, waited in the bar across the street for her to finish her shift. When he finally saw her step out of the back door, he dropped a twenty to cover his tab and went out to meet her.

She was with two other women. A petite, mousy thing who tried and failed to do "sexy librarian" and a curvy Hispanic with big tits and long legs. As he approached they paused their low conversation. Delia's eyes held a whisper of uncertainty, but the other two watched him with the naked wariness of a rabbit watching a fox.

He wanted to growl to the two rabbits to get lost, watch them skitter off, but instead he merely asked Delia, "Can I buy you a cup of coffee?"

As if she hadn't heard his question, she turned to the other girls. "I'll see y'all tomorrow night," she told them, exchanged quick hugs. Not until the two were halfway down the block did she return her attention to Danny. Her mouth pressed into a tight, thin line.

"I'm not a whore," she said flatly.

Danny found himself smiling. "I know. I promise, I just want to buy you a cup of coffee."

The look she gave him was measuring, doubtful. He wondered if she knew what he'd done in the club and, if so, whether she could possibly understand why. Then again, he didn't completely understand it himself.

"There's a café over on Decatur," she finally said. "It's really good, but I don't like walking there by myself at night."

"I'll protect you," he replied.

She liked her coffee sweet and rich, added enough cream to where it matched the pale mocha color of her skin. Her croissant she tore into small bits before eating it in dainty bites between sips of coffee and conversation.

Like anyone else in the city, they talked first about why they were still there after the Switch, why they hadn't abandoned the city the way that the river had. After all, anyone who could had left, leaving only the very poor, the rich who knew how to profit from disaster, and the few people those rich needed to get richer and stay comfortable.

"Lots of cops left and went over to Morgan City," he told her. "Plenty of work there. But . . . I dunno. I didn't want to leave, and I had enough seniority to avoid the layoffs." And plenty of stroke, too, he added silently. He'd called in a lot of favors to make sure that not only would he stay but those in line ahead of him for promotion would get the ax instead. He'd made captain less than six months later.

"This is my home" was all she said to explain why she stayed. "I love this city."

"Even now?" he asked her, eyebrow cocked in disbelief.

"Especially now," she replied, a soft smile on her lips.

He thought about that for a moment while he drank his café au lait. The night breeze brought the stagnant scent of the river, mingled with the aroma of beer and piss in the street. Even hours before dawn, the muggy air wrapped around them with warm tendrils, promising a brutal summer to come. But this city suited him, suited his personality. The Switch had been the best goddamn thing that had ever happened to him.

"Me too," he finally said, because he knew she expected it, and pushed aside the strange twinge of sadness that came from realizing that he loved it for far different reasons than she did.

Though he never went back inside the club, he waited for her each night and walked her to the café. On the third night, she tucked her arm through his as they walked. On the fifth, she greeted him with a kiss and a smile.

On the seventh, she asked, "Do you have a coffeemaker at home?"

He had an apartment south of the Quarter, a more than decent place where he lived for free, thanks to a desperate landlord who agreed that it was better to have a cop live there than have squatters take up residence. With so many vacant homes and apartments in the city, it was rare for any cop to pay rent.

It was almost a mile from the café, but she insisted that she didn't mind walking.

His place wasn't overly messy, but it sure as hell wasn't set up as a nice place to have company. The curtains had been left behind by the previous tenants, and had likely been old back then. Décor was limited to a pile of magazines with scantily clad women on the covers, a cluster of empty beer bottles on the coffee table, and, by the door, a framed newspaper article from several years back with the headline: *Witness recants testimony. NOPD officers cleared in wrongdoing.*

He never brought girls back here, had never thought what it would look like through a woman's eyes. Oddly ashamed, he started to apologize, but she stopped him with a smile. "It's all right. It's good. You're a good person." Which only made his shame increase, because he knew that he *wasn't*, though it had never mattered to him before.

He snaked his arms around her waist and pulled her tightly to him. She let out a small squeak of surprise. "Nah, I'm a bad boy," he said, trying to be flip, yet feeling it like a confession. He instantly felt silly for saying it and sorry for being rough. He didn't want this girl to think of him like that. He didn't want her to be the kind who was only attracted to the assholes and pricks.

But she simply smiled and laid her hand on his cheek. "You're not fooling me," she said, voice low and husky. "You're my good boy."

Danny knew how to fuck, how to get what he wanted, how not to care. He'd lost count of the number of prostitution "arrests" he'd made—girls who'd paid their fine directly to him with their mouth or cunt. It had been a long time since he'd had any sort of concern for the pleasure of his partner, and he felt like a fumbling virgin as he touched Delia, shamed and horrified when his uncertainty translated into a betrayal of his own physical response.

Yet she neither mocked nor took insult. Lowering her head, she gently coaxed him back, easing him, exciting him. And before he could squander her efforts, he shifted her to her back and returned the attention. She tasted sweet and wild, and as she tightened her hands in the sheet and cried out, he couldn't help but feel a pleasure that nearly matched her own. When she finally lay spent and shaking, only then did he move up and find his own release, thrilled beyond measure when she clasped her arms and legs around him and cried out his name.

He held her close after, stroking her hair as her breath warmed his chest, savoring the almost foreign sensation of feeling whole, secure. Happy.

The next night they walked out to what was left of the Mississippi, made their way upriver, and stood on a dock where, only three years earlier, the Canal Street Ferry had loaded and unloaded thousands of cars and people. The river had a bit more temper here due to the bend in it and the way the silt had settled. The current roiled beyond the mud, but to Danny it felt like an older woman trying to prove she was young and attractive. *Look at me,* he imagined the river saying. *I still got it. I'm still a bad girl.* In a few more years, the silt would build up more and the river would subside, muttering, disgruntled, and hurt to be so unappreciated.

"When I was a kid, my mom would take me out to the levee nearly every Sunday afternoon," Danny told Delia. "We'd sit and watch the ships and barges go up and down the river and we'd make up stories about what they carried and where they were going."

"That sounds nice," she said, tilting her head to look at him.

"Yeah. It was cool. She'd pack sandwiches and chips and we'd make a picnic of it."

She leaned up against him. "Do your parents still live here?"

"Dad left when I was about six," he said. "Mom died about ten years ago. Cancer." He shrugged to show her how much it didn't affect him anymore. He wanted to tell her that he'd scattered his mother's ashes in the river or on the levee or somewhere that would have been meaningful in some way, but the truth was that he'd never even picked them up from the funeral home. He didn't care what happened to the ashes—not because he hadn't loved his mother, but because he felt it was just one more stupid, sentimental detail that people wanted to believe was important.

He looked out toward the bones of a ship that had been stripped nearly clean by the welders. That's what it's like, he thought. No one cared where that metal would end up. That ship would never be rebuilt.

"Do you remember where you were when it happened?" she asked him, and for an instant he thought she was talking about his mother's death.

"You mean the Switch?" he asked, to be certain. She nodded. "Sure," he said, thinking quickly. The truth was he didn't remember exactly. Probably working. Maybe at home. It wasn't until about a week later that it started to sink in to everyone that nothing was ever going to be the same, but even then he didn't remember being upset or worked up over it. The fickle bitch of a river had run off, it wasn't ever coming back, and that's all there was to it. "I was on a domestic violence call," he decided to say. "I'd just put handcuffs on a guy for slapping his wife when my partner told me the spillway had collapsed and the river was changing course."

She looked at him as if expecting him to say more. He wondered if maybe he should make some more crap up, add some details and tell her that the guy worked on a ship and had come home to find out that his wife had been screwing another guy. Maybe tell her that he'd slapped his wife in front of their six-year-old son, and that as soon as he was bailed out, he hopped on another ship and never returned.

No, Danny decided. Best to leave it as it was. One thing he'd learned from the perps he arrested was that most of them tripped themselves up by making their lies too complicated. Keep it simple and short. Less to keep straight that way. "So, where were you?" he asked her.

Delia blinked, pursed her lips. "I was at the emergency room with a neighbor of mine. She . . . fell and broke her wrist. I was playing with her daughter in the waiting room when it came on the TV."

She turned back to the water, rubbing her arms against the light breeze. "I wonder what they'll name it?"

He slipped an arm around her, pulled her close, smiled as she nestled against him. "Seems wrong not to call it the Mississippi."

She shook her head. "But she's gone. Left us behind. Atchafalaya has her now."

"You think the city needs to get over it and move on?" he asked her with an indulgent smile.

A grin touched her mouth. "It's never going to get her back. New Orleans needs to stop being the mopey boyfriend. It needs to take a shower and start dating again. It can be better than it was before."

He chuckled and gave her a squeeze, but his thoughts were on men like Peter and their plans for the city. It wasn't going to be cleaned up. It wouldn't get better, at least not for the people who weren't running the show. The only thing the city had left was tourism, and they had no intention of making the city "family friendly" or any of that shit.

The city council would eventually cave in to pressure. New Orleans would sell itself out, fill up with casinos and even more bars and prostitutes. It made him sad, which surprised him. That kind of place would suit him and his temperament.

"New Orleans will become the whore," he said, more to himself than to her.

"Not if I have anything to say about it," she murmured, then sighed and leaned her head against him. Danny wondered if she knew that there was nothing she could do about it, nothing that could stop the city's slide into total debauchery and corruption. There were too many players lined up against her. His gut twisted with the knowledge that, not only was he was one of them, he wasn't sure that he was capable of doing anything else.

A week later, he met her as usual, but her kiss of greeting seemed distracted and her smile forced. He asked her if something was wrong, but she only shook her head. "It's nothing," she insisted. "Just a guy asking for stuff I don't do." Before he could puff up in righteous defense of his woman, she put her hand on his chest and gave him the smile that always touched the place deep inside him that told him that, to this woman even if no one else, he was special and strong.

"It's all right," she assured him, though a shimmer of doubt touched the corners of her mouth.

The doubt stayed, darkening her eyes and hunching her shoulders. At times he thought she was on the verge of tears. It took several more days for him to coax it out of her, patiently weathering the denials, the false smiles, and the protestations that everything was fine. He wasn't the most honest cop on the beat, but he still knew how to ferret out the truth.

"It's this one guy," she finally confessed while they lay tangled in the sheets of his bed and she rested her head on his chest. A shudder passed through her. "He's rich and powerful, which is why the owners don't toss him out." She lifted her head, met his eyes. "It's not that he's mean or a jerk. But he *wants* me." She swallowed, then managed a chuckle. "Doesn't that sound ridiculously egotistical?"

He smiled, stroked her hair back from her face. "Not to me. I can perfectly understand wanting you."

Delia dropped her head back to his chest, nestled closer to him. "He wants me to be his girlfriend. I told him I wasn't interested." She sighed. "I'm sure it'll all blow over, but right now he's awfully insistent. And, he's . . . ugh."

"Skeevy?"

"No, not that. He's clean-cut, decent looking. But it's . . . it's the way he sees other people. As things to be used. He's not nice."

He wrapped his arms around her, pulled her close, kissed the top of her head while tension curdled his gut. "Who is this guy?" he asked, even though he had a feeling he already knew. "I'll take care of it."

She lifted her head again, a frown puckering her forehead. "I don't want you hurting anyone for me."

"I won't," he lied. He knew damn well how to cover his tracks. As long as it wasn't Peter. Please don't let it be Peter. "Give me his name. I'll make sure that he knows you're off-limits. Nice and friendly."

Peter opened the door of his condo at the knock, an amused smile curving his mouth at the sight of Danny on the doorstep. "What a nice surprise. Come on in."

Danny gave the man a short nod, entered. "Need to talk to you."

"I'm always here for a friend," Peter said, closing the door. "By the way, I never did get to thank you for taking care of that business with the bookstore owner." He moved to the kitchen, pulled down two mugs from the cabinet. "I don't know what you said to him, but he took the eviction with nary a whimper." He poured coffee for himself, then slid a look toward Danny. "So nice when people do as they're told. Makes everyone's life so much more pleasant. Coffee?"

Danny jerked his head in a nod. Peter knew why he was there, Danny realized. He'd been expecting him. He took the mug from the man, forced himself to sip at the bitter liquid.

"I've done a lot of stuff for you," he began, then stopped. None of that made a difference in this situation. He had a speech ready, a chest-pounding "get away from my woman" rant, but one look at Peter's eyes told him that it was the wrong tack, that it would be pointless. He swallowed to try to clear the bitter taste from his mouth, took a deep breath. "Look, there's this girl I really like. Delia. She, uh, says that you've asked her out, and I wanted to talk to you, man-to-man, ask you to leave her be." As soon as the words were out of his mouth, he hated himself. This wasn't man-to-man. This was the dog groveling to his master.

Peter frowned over his mug. "Delia? Is that the stripper chick you've been mooning over?"

"We've been seeing each other," Danny said, jaw tight.

The other man cocked an eyebrow at him. "Is that so? She sure has been friendly with me at the club." The he chuckled, shook his head. "But that's her job, isn't it? I have to say, she's quite good. I could almost believe she really is glad to see me each night."

"Yeah," Danny managed. "She's good. We're good . . . together. I'm asking you to, uh, please back off." He didn't know that Peter had been going to the club so often. How many times had he been in a private room with Delia while Danny waited like an eager puppy in the bar across the street?

"For you, of course," Peter said with a magnanimous nod. "I wish you both the best." Took a sip of coffee, walked over to the window to gaze out at the muddy swath that was more bayou than river now. "Of course, for your sake, I hope she doesn't get a better offer." He glanced back at Danny. "Or rather, if she does get a better offer, that she doesn't take it."

"Right," Danny said. "Appreciate you understanding."

Peter set the mug down on the table by the window. "By the way, the final vote on the poker room is day after tomorrow. I need you to lean on Councilman Nagle. Catch him doing something." His smile widened. "Maybe your Delia can help you out with that." Then he shrugged. "Or not. Best to keep business and pleasure separate, right?"

"Right," Danny repeated. It was a challenge, a power play. Peter wanted to know how much he could trust him. Wanted to know how far Danny would go to keep the influence that had protected him for so long.

Yet Danny knew that it didn't matter. It was already too late. Danny had tried to bare his teeth. From now on, Peter would be watching his back, waiting for the moment when he could throw Danny to the wolves and keep his own hands clean.

Danny simply had to find a way to do the same to Peter first.

He jerked his head in a nod. "Got it. I'll take care of it."

Peter's smile widened. "You're a good friend. Give my best to Delia."

The next week was quiet and calm. Danny readied himself for the next time Peter called on him, ready to record the exchange or whatever else he could do, but his phone remained silent. Delia spent every night at his apartment, only returning to her own place to change clothes and water her plants. She told him that Peter had stopped coming to the club and wanted to know what Danny had done. He merely smiled and said, "Better that you don't know." He couldn't tell her that he'd done nothing except grovel, that the only reason Peter left her alone was because it suited Peter to do so.

And, as Danny had feared, it didn't last.

"He came to my apartment!" she told him after he opened his door to see her standing on his front step. Her lower lip trembled and her eyes were red from weeping. He quickly pulled her inside, took her to the couch, and held her while she poured it all out to him.

Peter had given her an ultimatum—go with him or he'd not only have her evicted but he'd make sure she never found work in this city again.

"I don't know what to do," she told him, looking more defeated and beaten down than he'd ever imagined she could be. "I can't . . . I *won't* leave New Orleans. It's too special to me." Delia's eyes lifted to his. "People like him are destroying this city. I hate it. I hate them all!" Her voice broke on the last word.

Sweat pricked Danny's palms. He could kill Peter. There were a hundred different ways he could do it and stage it like an accident or suicide. Or maybe Danny could go to the feds, tell them everything he knew about Peter's dealings.

"I'll take care of it," he said, kissing her. He stood up, but she caught at his hand.

"I don't want you getting into trouble," she said, eyes wide and frightened.

"It'll be fine. I promise." He gently pulled free of her grasp. "You can count on me."

Danny walked along Chartres Street to Dumaine, headed to Jackson Square and watched pigeons swarm around a bum with a bag of stale bread. A handful of street artists gamely displayed their wares, casting desperate smiles to the sparse trickle of tourists wandering by, and ignoring him, since he was obviously a local and not worth wasting the energy of false friendliness on.

He would kill Peter Bennett, he told himself. That was the only way out. Going to the feds wasn't an option. Anything Danny told them would sink him just as thoroughly as it would Peter, and he didn't have any evidence other than his own testimony.

Late afternoon turned to dusk as he sat on a bench in the park and considered his options, planned out his steps. When full dark came, he headed down Decatur, stopped in a sleazy T-shirt shop full of tourist

crap, and bought a cap. After that, he cut over to the Riverwalk, entered
Peter's building, and took the elevator to his floor, keeping the cap pulled
low over his face to avoid being caught by any cameras.

Peter answered the door, eyebrow lifting in mild surprise at Danny's
presence. His gaze flicked to the cap and then back to Danny's face. "You
okay? You look upset."

"Yeah," he replied. "A bit. Can I come in?"

"Absolutely." Peter stepped aside, closed the door behind him. Danny
swept his gaze around the condo. No one else here. No one else on this
floor, for that matter. No one had seen him come in. He had it all planned.
Collapsible baton in his pocket to take Peter down, then make it look like
an accidental fall in the shower. Doubtful it would be found out as murder
even if there was a proper investigation.

Peter leaned up against the counter, watched Danny impassively.
Maybe he knew why the cop was here. Probably did, in fact. He had to
have known it would come to this.

"I almost forgot," Peter said abruptly, pushing off the counter and moving to his desk. "Forgot to give you that, ah, loan money you asked for."

Sweat prickled Danny's back and his hand eased toward his gun. This
was perfect. Peter was going to pull a gun from that drawer and then
Danny could shoot him in self-defense.

But it was a thick envelope that Peter retrieved from the drawer.
Danny dropped his hand before Peter could see, heart thudding unevenly. The man was paying him for busting Councilman Nagle with a
prostitute earlier in the week. Nagle had agreed to vote Peter's way rather
than face a humiliating arrest, and the poker room had been approved,
no doubt the first of many.

Peter held out the envelope to him. "I think you'll be happy with this.
I know I am. Good work with that, by the way."

He didn't move for several seconds, then finally stepped forward and
took the envelope. Opened it to see that it held at least ten grand.

Danny closed the envelope and tucked it into the pocket in his jacket.
"Appreciate this," he said, voice sounding odd and rough in his ears. He
didn't have to kill Peter. He had other options. He could take Delia away
from here. He'd convince her to leave. They could start over somewhere
else. Away from this fucked-up city. Away from Peter.

"Come by next week," Peter said. "We'll talk." He paused. "You should bring Delia by sometime. Unless you two broke up already?" He lifted a bottle of water, drank without ever taking his eyes from Danny.

"No," Danny replied, feeling the weight of the question, responding to the statements.

The man grinned. "That's real cute. How long you think that'll last?"

He wasn't talking about Delia, Danny knew. Peter was toying with him, wanting to know how long this little flare of defiance would go on before Danny settled down and behaved again.

Like the dog at the café, who'd slunk off instead of attacking. That dog was probably dead now, Danny thought, or at the very least still hungry, slinking through the city, willing to brave a few kicks to get a scrap or two.

No more slinking. No more scraps.

"Forever," he replied. With a practiced move, he pulled the baton from his pocket and snapped it open. Baring his teeth as he stepped toward Peter. Reveling in the shock and fear on the man's face as the dog finally turned on his master.

He called her in the elevator, asked her to meet him at the Canal Street Ferry. He figured he'd beat her there, but when he arrived at the dock, he saw her leaning on the rail down at the end, looking out over the wallowing river and the blinking lights of cars crossing the bridge.

A tension he hadn't even been aware of leached away. A part of him hadn't been sure she'd come, afraid that she'd cut her losses and leave him behind. Yet now he realized that she'd known where he'd gone, had been waiting nearby for him.

She turned at the sound of his hurrying footsteps, watched him as he approached.

"Danny . . . ?" she said, reaching up to touch his face. "What's going on?"

He caught her hand in his, kissed it. "I love you, baby. I'll keep you safe forever, I swear it."

Her breath caught. "Oh God. What did you do?"

"It's cool," he said. "I swear. I . . . I'm good."

She bit her lip, then closed her eyes, wrapped her arms around him. "Yes, you are."

He lowered his head and breathed in the scent of her, feeling all the shit and the muck of his life slipping away. "Let's go," he said. "Let's leave this place forever and start over somewhere else." He didn't want to stay, but he also knew he couldn't leave her behind. She'd end up as beaten and broken as those other girls . . . yet, even as he thought it, he knew that it was an excuse, knew that he wasn't strong enough to leave without her. But maybe if they *both* left, started over . . . maybe *he* could get unbroken.

She pulled back, shock and disappointment flashing across her features. "You want me to leave? I can't!"

"It's just a city, baby," he said, holding her face in his hands. "Nothing but a bunch of buildings and streets and crap and assholes."

"No. It's so much *more* than that." She tried to shake her head. "There's a *soul* to this place, rich and wonderful. We survived Katrina and we'll survive this. We . . . *I* . . . have to stay. Why can't you see it?" She reached up, pulled his hands from her face, but continued to hold them. "Oh, Danny," she breathed. "Peter's gone now. You don't have to be who you were anymore."

She knew, he realized, as the last of his tension dissipated. She *knew* he'd killed Peter, understood the lengths he'd go to for her . . . and didn't hate him for it. "No. I can be better," he insisted. "I *can* be . . . if I'm with you." He squeezed her hands. "But not here. It can't work here. New Orleans died when the river left. There's always gonna be guys like Peter here, looking to cash in on the wreckage. They'll tear this city up and salvage every scrap they can from it, and they won't give a shit who gets crushed in the process."

He couldn't see her expression in the gloom, but he heard a sigh of what sounded like resignation come from her. Maybe she was starting to see things his way? "I have money," he told her. "We can go to Lafayette. Start over. We'll be together." His phone rang and he cursed, pulled it out to see it was Detective Farber. Ice knotted his stomach. Had Peter been found already?

"Think about it," he mouthed to Delia before he stepped back and answered the phone.

"Get this," Farber said without preamble. "Ernst's gun matched the slugs found in Jack-D's body." Jack-D, a pimp even sleazier than Jimmy Ernst, who specialized in girls who didn't just *look* very young but really *were*. He'd been found down on Basin Street the day before Ernst took a swim in the mud. "Betcha one of Jack-D's boys capped Ernst as a get back," the detective continued. "At any rate, we got enough to close both cases."

"Yeah," Danny said. "That's good. Do it." He hung up, looked out at the river and frowned. Didn't make sense that a pussy like Jimmy would go after Jack-D. Didn't make sense that anyone would give enough of a shit to take out Jimmy in revenge. A whisper of unease lifted the hairs on the back of his neck. Delia had known Peter was dead. Had she *wanted* Danny to kill him?

He began to turn back to Delia, felt two prongs of cold metal against his throat an instant before hot lightning flashed through his body. He dropped to the concrete of the dock as pain danced through his nerve endings and he fought for control of his muscles.

She stooped and slipped the Taser back into her purse, pulled him upright, and leaned him against the railing. She was strong—those dancer muscles served her well as she toppled him over the side to the waiting muck below.

He landed flat on his back. The impact knocked his breath from him, but the mud quickly gave way beneath his weight. She leaned over the railing, met his eyes as he sank.

Delia checked her watch, waited as the river slid along its banks with a contented, relieved sigh. In the distance, metal groaned as a ship heeled over with the change in the tide. Moonlight painted the river in a sheet of soft grey, an elegant lady settling into comfortable retirement.

She looked down at the silt below. Barely a ripple to show that anything had disturbed it. A sigh of regret slipped from her. "You were a good boy, Danny," she murmured, a sad smile touching her mouth. "The best one yet."

Delia touched her fingers to her lips, blew a tender good-bye kiss toward the silt below, then turned and headed back to the heart of her city.

Diana Gabaldon

New York Times bestselling author Diana Gabaldon is a winner of the Quill Award and of the RITA Award given by the Romance Writers of America. She's the author of the hugely popular Outlander series of time-travel romances, international bestsellers that include *Cross Stitch, Dragonfly in Amber, Voyager, Drums of Autumn, The Fiery Cross, A Breath of Snow and Ashes,* and *An Echo in the Bone.* Her historical series about the strange adventures of Lord John include the novels *Lord John and the Private Matter; Lord John and the Brotherhood of the Blade;* a chapbook novella, *Lord John and the Hell-Fire Club;* and a collection of Lord John stories, *Lord John and the Hand of Devils.* Her most recent novels are two new Lord John books, *The Scottish Prisoner* and *Red Ant's Head,* and a novel omnibus, *A Trail of Fire.* She's also written a contemporary mystery, *White Knight.* A guidebook to and appreciation of her work is *The Outlandish Companion.*

In the fast-paced story that follows, the young Jamie Fraser, one day to be one of the protagonists of the Outlander books, is forced out of his Scottish home and set to wandering in the world, with many new experiences waiting ahead of him, some pleasant, some decidedly not—and some dangerous and dark.

VIRGINS

OCTOBER, 1740

NEAR BORDEAUX, FRANCE

Ian Murray knew from the moment he saw his best friend's face that something terrible had happened. The fact that he was seeing Jamie Fraser's face at all was evidence enough of that, never mind the look of the man.

Jamie was standing by the armorer's wagon, his arms full of the bits and pieces Armand had just given him, white as milk and swaying back and forth like a reed on Loch Awe. Ian reached him in three paces and took him by the arm before he could fall over.

"Ian." Jamie looked so relieved at seeing him that Ian thought he might break into tears. "God, Ian."

Ian seized Jamie in embrace, and felt him stiffen and draw in his breath at the same instant he felt the bandages beneath Jamie's shirt.

"Jesus!" he began, startled, but then coughed and said, "Jesus, man, it's good to see ye." He patted Jamie's back gently and let go. "Ye'll need a bit to eat, aye? Come on, then."

Plainly they couldn't talk now, but he gave Jamie a quick private nod, took half the equipment from him, and then led him to the fire, to be introduced to the others.

Jamie'd picked a good time of day to turn up, Ian thought. Everyone was tired, but happy to sit down, looking forward to their supper and the daily ration of whatever was going in the way of drink. Ready for the possibilities a new fish offered for entertainment, but without the energy to include the more physical sorts of entertainment.

"That's Big Georges over there," Ian said, dropping Jamie's gear and gesturing toward the far side of the fire. "Next to him, the wee fellow wi' the warts is Juanito; doesna speak much French and nay English at all."

"Do any of them speak English?" Jamie likewise dropped his gear, and sat heavily on his bedroll, tucking his kilt absently down between his knees. His eyes flicked round the circle, and he nodded, half-smiling in a shy sort of way.

"I do." The captain leaned past the man next to him, extending a hand to Jamie. "I'm *le capitaine*—Richard D'Eglise. You'll call me Captain. You look big enough to be useful—your friend says your name is Fraser?"

"Jamie Fraser, aye." Ian was pleased to see that Jamie knew to meet the Captain's eye square, and had summoned the strength to return the handshake with due force.

"Know what to do with a sword?"

"I do. And a bow, forbye." Jamie glanced at the unstrung bow by his feet, and the short-handled ax beside it. "Havena had much to do wi' an ax before, save chopping wood."

"That's good," one of the other men put in, in French. "That's what you'll use it for." Several of the others laughed, indicating that they at least understood English, whether they chose to speak it or not.

"Did I join a troop of soldiers, then, or charcoal-burners?" Jamie asked, raising one brow. He said that in French—very good French, with a faint Parisian accent—and a number of eyes widened. Ian bent his head to hide a smile, in spite of his anxiety. The wean might be about to fall face-first into the fire, but nobody—save maybe Ian—was going to know it, if it killed him.

Ian *did* know it, though, and kept a covert eye on Jamie, pushing bread into his hand so the others wouldn't see it shake, sitting close enough to catch him if he should in fact pass out. The light was fading into gray now, and the clouds hung low and soft, pink-bellied. Going to rain, likely, by the morning. He saw Jamie close his eyes just for an instant, saw his throat move as he swallowed, and felt the trembling of Jamie's thigh near his own.

What the devil's happened? he thought in anguish. *Why are ye here?*

It wasn't until everyone had settled for the night that Ian got an answer.

"I'll lay out your gear," he whispered to Jamie, rising. "You stay by the fire that wee bit longer—rest a bit, aye?" The firelight cast a ruddy glow on Jamie's face, but he thought his friend was likely still white as a sheet; he hadn't eaten much.

Coming back, he saw the dark spots on the back of Jamie's shirt, blotches where fresh blood had seeped through the bandages. The sight filled him with fury as well as fear. He'd seen such things; the wean had been flogged. Badly, and recently. *Who? How?*

"Come on, then," he said roughly, and, bending, got an arm under Jamie's and got him to his feet and away from the fire and the other men. He was alarmed to feel the clamminess of Jamie's hand and hear his shallow breath.

"What?" he demanded, the moment they were out of earshot. "What happened?"

Jamie sat down abruptly.

"I thought one joined a band of mercenaries because they didna ask ye questions."

Ian gave him the snort this statement deserved, and was relieved to hear a breath of laughter in return.

"Eejit," he said. "D'ye need a dram? I've got a bottle in my sack."

"Wouldna come amiss," Jamie murmured. They were camped at the edge of a wee village, and D'Eglise had arranged for the use of a byre or two, but it wasn't cold out, and most of the men had chosen to sleep by the fire or in the field. Ian had put their gear down a little distance away, and with the possibility of rain in mind, under the shelter of a plane tree that stood at the side of a field.

Ian uncorked the bottle of whisky—it wasn't good, but it *was* whisky— and held it under his friend's nose. When Jamie reached for it, though, he pulled it away.

"Not a sip do ye get until ye tell me," he said. "And ye tell me *now, a charaid.*"

Jamie sat hunched, a pale blur on the ground, silent. When the words came at last, they were spoken so softly that Ian thought for an instant he hadn't really heard them.

"My faither's dead."

He tried to believe he *hadn't* heard, but his heart had; it froze in his chest.

"Oh, Jesus," he whispered. "Oh, God, Jamie." He was on his knees then, holding Jamie's head fierce against his shoulder, trying not to touch his hurt back. His thoughts were in confusion, but one thing was clear to him—Brian Fraser's death hadn't been a natural one. If it had, Jamie would be at Lallybroch. Not here, and not in this state.

"Who?" he said hoarsely, relaxing his grip a little. "Who killed him?"

More silence, then Jamie gulped air with a sound like fabric being ripped.

"I did," he said, and began to cry, shaking with silent, tearing sobs.

It took some time to winkle the details out of Jamie—and no wonder, Ian thought. He wouldn't want to talk about such things, either, or to remember them. The English dragoons who'd come to Lallybroch to loot and plunder, who'd taken Jamie away with them when he'd fought them. And what they'd done to him then, at Fort William.

"A hundred lashes?" he said in disbelief and horror. "For protecting your *home*?"

"Only sixty, the first time." Jamie wiped his nose on his sleeve. "For escaping."

"The *first* ti—Jesus, God, man! What . . . how . . ."

"Would ye let go my arm, Ian? I've got enough bruises, I dinna need any more." Jamie gave a small, shaky laugh, and Ian hastily let go, but wasn't about to let himself be distracted.

"Why?" he said, low and angry. Jamie wiped his nose again, sniffing, but his voice was steadier.

"It was my fault," he said. "It—what I said before. About my . . ." He had to stop and swallow, but went on, hurrying to get the words out before they could bite him in a tender place. "I spoke chough to the commander. At the garrison, ken. He—well, it's nay matter. It was what I said to him made him flog me again, and Da—he—he'd come. To Fort William, to try to get me released, but he couldn't, and he—he was there, when they . . . did it."

Ian could tell from the thicker sound of his voice that Jamie was weeping again but trying not to, and he put a hand on the wean's knee and gripped it, not too hard, just so as Jamie would ken he was there, listening.

Jamie took a deep, deep breath and got the rest out.

"It was . . . hard. I didna call out, or let them see I was scairt, but I couldna keep my feet. Halfway through it, I fell into the post, just—just hangin' from the ropes, ken, wi' the blood . . runnin' down my legs. They thought for a bit that I'd died—and Da must ha' thought so, too. They told me he put his hand to his head just then, and made a wee noise and then . . . he fell down. An apoplexy, they said."

"Mary, Mother o' God, have mercy on us," Ian said. "He—died right there?"

"I dinna ken was he dead when they picked him up or if he lived a bit after that." Jamie's voice was desolate. "I didna ken a thing about it; no one told me until days later, when Uncle Dougal got me away." He coughed, and wiped the sleeve across his face again. "Ian . . . would ye let go my knee?"

"No," Ian said softly, though he did indeed take his hand away. Only so he could gather Jamie gently into his arms, though. "No. I willna let go, Jamie. Bide. Just . . . bide."

Jamie woke dry-mouthed, thickheaded, and with his eyes half swollen shut by midgie bites. It was also raining, a fine, wet mist coming down through the leaves above him. For all that, he felt better than he had in the last two weeks, though he didn't at once recall why that was—or where he was.

"Here." A piece of half-charred bread rubbed with garlic was shoved under his nose. He sat up and grabbed it.

Ian. The sight of his friend gave him an anchor, and the food in his belly another. He chewed slower now, looking about. Men were rising, stumbling off for a piss, making low rumbling noises, rubbing their heads and yawning.

"Where are we?" he asked. Ian gave him a look.

"How the devil did ye find us if ye dinna ken where ye are?"

"Murtagh brought me," he muttered. The bread turned to glue in his mouth as memory came back; he couldn't swallow, and spat out the half-chewed bit. Now he remembered it all, and wished he didn't. "He found the band, but then left; said it would look better if I came in on my own."

His godfather had said, in fact, *"The Murray lad will take care of ye now. Stay wi' him, mind—dinna come back to Scotland. Dinna come back, d'ye hear me?"* He'd heard. Didn't mean he meant to listen.

"Oh, aye. I wondered how ye'd managed to walk this far." Ian cast a worried look at the far side of the camp, where a pair of sturdy horses was being brought to the traces of a canvas-covered wagon. "*Can* ye walk, d'ye think?"

"Of course. I'm fine." Jamie spoke crossly, and Ian gave him the look again, even more slit-eyed than the last.

"Aye, right," he said, in tones of rank disbelief. "Well. We're maybe twenty miles from Bordeaux; that's where we're going. We're takin' the wagon yon to a Jewish moneylender there."

"Is it full of money, then?" Jamie glanced at the heavy wagon, interested.

"No," Ian said. "There's a wee chest, verra heavy so it's maybe gold, and there are a few bags that clink and might be silver, but most of it's rugs."

"Rugs?" He looked at Ian in amazement. "What sort of rugs?"

Ian shrugged.

"Couldna say. Juanito says they're Turkey rugs and verra valuable, but I dinna ken that he knows. He's Jewish, too," Ian added, as an afterthought. "Jews are—" He made an equivocal gesture, palm flattened. "But they dinna really hunt them in France, or exile them anymore, and the Captain says they dinna even arrest them, so long as they keep quiet."

"And go on lending money to men in the government," Jamie said cynically. Ian looked at him, surprised, and Jamie gave him the *I went to the Université in Paris and ken more than you do* smart-arse look, fairly sure that Ian wouldn't thump him, seeing he was hurt.

Ian looked tempted, but had learned enough merely to give Jamie back the *I'm older than you and ye ken well ye havena sense enough to come in out of the rain, so dinna be trying it on* look instead. Jamie laughed, feeling better.

"Aye, right," he said, bending forward. "Is my shirt verra bloody?"

Ian nodded, buckling his sword belt. Jamie sighed and picked up the leather jerkin the armorer had given him. It would rub, but he wasn't wanting to attract attention.

He managed. The troop kept up a decent pace, but it wasn't anything to trouble a Highlander accustomed to hill-walking and running down the odd deer. True, he grew a bit light-headed now and then, and sometimes his heart raced and waves of heat ran over him—but he didn't stagger any more than a few of the men who'd drunk too much for breakfast.

He barely noticed the countryside, but was conscious of Ian striding along beside him, and took pains now and then to glance at his friend and nod, in order to relieve Ian's worried expression. The two of them were close to the wagon, mostly because he didn't want to draw attention by lagging at the back of the troop, but also because he and Ian were taller than the rest by a head or more, with a stride that eclipsed the others, and he felt a small bit of pride in that. It didn't occur to him that possibly the others didn't *want* to be near the wagon.

The first inkling of trouble was a shout from the driver. Jamie had been trudging along, eyes half-closed, concentrating on putting one foot ahead of the other, but a bellow of alarm and a sudden loud *bang!* jerked him to attention. A horseman charged out of the trees near the road, slewed to a halt and fired his second pistol at the driver.

"What—" Jamie reached for the sword at his belt, half-fuddled but starting forward; the horses were neighing and flinging themselves against the traces, the driver cursing and on his feet, hauling on the reins. Several of the mercenaries ran toward the horseman, who drew his own sword and rode through them, slashing recklessly from side to side. Ian seized Jamie's arm, though, and jerked him round.

"Not there! The back!" He followed Ian at a run, and sure enough, there was the Captain on his horse at the back of the troop, in the middle of a melee, a dozen strangers laying about with clubs and blades, all shouting.

"*Caisteal DHOON!*" Ian bellowed, and swung his sword over his head and flat down on the head of an attacker. It hit the man a glancing blow, but he staggered and fell to his knees, where Big Georges seized him by the hair and kneed him viciously in the face.

"*Caisteal DHOON!*" Jamie shouted as loud as he could, and Ian turned his head for an instant, a big grin flashing.

It was a bit like a cattle raid, but lasting longer. Not a matter of hit hard and get away; he'd never been a defender before and found it heavy going. Still, the attackers were outnumbered, and began to give way, some glancing over their shoulders, plainly thinking of running back into the wood.

They began to do just that, and Jamie stood panting, dripping sweat, his sword a hundredweight in his hand. He straightened, though, and caught the flash of movement from the corner of his eye.

"*Dhooon!*" he shouted, and broke into a lumbering, gasping run. Another group of men had appeared near the wagon and were pulling the driver's body quietly down from its seat, while one of their number grabbed at the lunging horses' bridles, pulling their heads down. Two more had got the canvas loose and were dragging out a long rolled cylinder, one of the rugs, he supposed.

He reached them in time to grab another man trying to mount the wagon, yanking him clumsily back onto the road. The man twisted, falling, and came to his feet like a cat, knife in hand. The blade flashed, bounced off the leather of his jerkin and cut upward, an inch from his face. Jamie squirmed back, off balance, narrowly keeping his feet, and two more of the bastards charged him.

"On your right, man!" Ian's voice came sudden at his shoulder, and without a moment's hesitation he turned to take care of the man to his left, hearing Ian's grunt of effort as he laid about himself.

Then something changed; he couldn't tell what, but the fight was suddenly over. The attackers melted away, leaving one or two of their number lying in the road.

The driver wasn't dead; Jamie saw him roll half over, an arm across his face. Then he himself was sitting in the dust, black spots dancing before his eyes. Ian bent over him, panting, hands braced on his knees. Sweat dripped from his chin, making dark spots in the dust that mingled with the buzzing spots that darkened Jamie's vision.

"All . . . right?" Ian asked.

He opened his mouth to say yes, but the roaring in his ears drowned it out, and the spots merged suddenly into a solid sheet of black.

He woke to find a priest kneeling over him, intoning the Lord's Prayer in Latin. Not stopping, the priest took up a little bottle and poured oil into the palm of one hand, then dipped his thumb into the puddle and made a swift sign of the Cross on Jamie's forehead.

"I'm no dead, aye?" Jamie said, then repeated this information in French. The priest leaned closer, squinting nearsightedly.

"Dying?" he asked.

"Not that, either." The priest made a small disgusted sound, but went ahead and made crosses on the palms of Jamie's hands, his eyelids and his lips.

"*Ego te absolvo,*" he said, making a final quick sign of the Cross over

Jamie's supine form. "Just in case you've killed anyone." Then he rose swiftly to his feet and disappeared behind the wagon in a flurry of dark robes.

"All right, are ye?" Ian reached down a hand and hauled him into a sitting position.

"Aye, more or less. Who was that?" He nodded in the direction of the recent priest.

"Père Renault. This is a verra well-equipped outfit," Ian said, boosting him to his feet. "We've got our own priest, to shrive us before battle and give us extreme unction after."

"I noticed. A bit overeager, is he no?"

"He's blind as a bat," Ian said, glancing over his shoulder to be sure the priest wasn't close enough to hear. "Likely thinks better safe than sorry, aye?"

"D'ye have a surgeon, too?" Jamie asked, glancing at the two attackers who had fallen. The bodies had been pulled to the side of the road; one was clearly dead, but the other was beginning to stir and moan.

"Ah," Ian said thoughtfully. "That would be the priest, as well."

"So if I'm wounded in battle, I'd best try to die of it, is that what ye're sayin'?"

"I am. Come on, let's find some water."

They found a rock-lined irrigation ditch running between two fields, a little way off the road. Ian pulled Jamie into the shade of a tree and, rummaging in his rucksack, found a spare shirt, which he shoved into his friend's hands.

"Put it on," he said, low voiced. "Ye can wash yours out; they'll think the blood on it's from the fightin'." Jamie looked surprised but grateful and, with a nod, skimmed out of the leather jerkin and peeled the sweaty, stained shirt gingerly off his back. Ian grimaced; the bandages were filthy and coming loose, save where they stuck to Jamie's skin, crusted black with old blood and dried pus.

"Shall I pull them off?" he muttered in Jamie's ear. "I'll do it fast."

Jamie arched his back in refusal, shaking his head.

"Nay, it'll bleed more if ye do." There wasn't time to argue; several more of the men were coming. Jamie ducked hurriedly into the clean shirt and knelt to splash water on his face.

"Hey, Scotsman!" Alexandre called to Jamie. "What's that you two were shouting at each other?" He put his hands to his mouth and hooted, "Goooooon!" in a deep, echoing voice that made the others laugh.

"Have ye never heard a war cry before?" Jamie asked, shaking his head at such ignorance. "Ye shout it in battle, to call your kin and your clan to your side."

"Does it mean anything?" Petit Phillipe asked, interested.

"Aye, more or less," Ian said. "Castle Dhuni's the dwelling place of the chieftain of the Frasers of Lovat. *Caisteal Dhuin* is what ye call it in the *Gàidhlig*—that's our own tongue."

"And that's our clan," Jamie clarified. "Clan Fraser, but there's more than one branch, and each one will have its own war cry, and its own motto." He pulled his shirt out of the cold water and wrang it out; the bloodstains were still visible, but faint brown marks now, Ian saw with approval. Then he saw Jamie's mouth opening to say more.

Don't say it! he thought, but as usual, Jamie wasn't reading his mind, and Ian closed his eyes in resignation, knowing what was coming.

"Our clan motto's in French, though," Jamie said, with a small air of pride. *"Je suis prest."*

It meant "I am ready," and was, as Ian had foreseen, greeted with gales of laughter, and a number of crude speculations as to just what the young Scots might be ready for. The men were in good humor from the fight, and it went on for a bit. Ian shrugged and smiled, but he could see Jamie's ears turning red.

"Where's the rest of your queue, Georges?" Petit Phillipe demanded, seeing Big Georges shaking off after a piss. "Someone trim it for you?"

"Your wife bit it off," Georges replied, in a tranquil tone indicating that this was common badinage. "Mouth like a sucking pig, that one. And a *cramouille* like a—"

This resulted in a further scatter of abuse, but it was clear from the sidelong glances that it was mostly performance for the benefit of the two Scots. Ian ignored it. Jamie had gone squiggle-eyed; Ian wasn't sure his friend had ever heard the word *cramouille* before, but he likely figured what it meant.

Before he could get them in more trouble, though, the conversation by the stream was stopped dead by a strangled scream beyond the scrim of trees that hid them from the roadside.

"The prisoner," Alexandre murmured, after a moment.

Ian knelt by Jamie, water dripping from his cupped hands. He knew what was happening; it curdled his wame. He let the water fall and wiped his hands on his thighs.

"The Captain," he said softly to Jamie. "He'll . . . need to know who they were. Where they came from."

"Aye." Jamie's lips pressed tight at the sound of muted voices, the sudden meaty smack of flesh and a loud grunt. "I know." He splashed water fiercely onto his face.

The jokes had stopped. There was little conversation now, though Alexandre and Josef-from-Alsace began a random argument, speaking loudly, trying to drown out the noises from the road. Most of the men finished their washing and drinking in silence and sat hunched in the shade, shoulders pulled in.

"Père Renault!" The Captain's voice rose, calling for the priest. Père Renault had been performing his own ablutions a discreet distance from the men, but rose at this summons, wiping his face on the hem of his robe. He crossed himself and headed for the road but, on the way, paused by Ian and motioned toward his drinking cup.

"May I borrow this from you, my son? Only for a moment."

"Aye, of course, Father," Ian said, baffled. The priest nodded, bent to scoop up a cup of water, and went on his way. Jamie looked after him, then at Ian, brows raised.

"They saw he's a Jew," Juanito said nearby, very quietly. "They want to baptize him first." He knelt by the water, fists curled tight against his thighs.

Hot as the air was, Ian felt a spear of ice run right through his chest. He stood up fast, and made as though to follow the priest, but Big Georges snaked out a hand and caught him by the shoulder.

"Leave it," he said. He spoke quietly, too, but his fingers dug hard into Ian's flesh. He didn't pull away, but stayed standing, holding Georges's eyes. He felt Jamie make a brief, convulsive movement, but said, "No!" under his breath, and Jamie stopped.

They could hear French cursing from the road, mingled with Père Renault's voice. *"In nomine Patris, et Filii . . ."* Then struggling, spluttering and shouting, the prisoner, the Captain and Mathieu, and even the priest all using such language as made Jamie blink. Ian might have laughed, if not for the sense of dread that froze every man by the water.

"No!" shouted the prisoner, his voice rising above the others, anger lost in terror. "No, please! I told you all I—" There was a small sound, a hollow noise like a melon being kicked in, and the voice stopped.

"Thrifty, our Captain," Big Georges said, under his breath. "Why waste a bullet?" He took his hand off Ian's shoulder, shook his head, and knelt down to wash his hands.

There was a ghastly silence under the trees. From the road, they could hear low voices—the Captain and big Mathieu speaking to each other and, over that, Père Renault repeating *"In nomine Patris, et Filii . . ."* but in a very different tone. Ian saw the hairs on Jamie's arms rise and he rubbed the palms of his hands against his kilt, maybe feeling a slick from the chrism oil still there.

Jamie plainly couldn't stand to listen, and turned to Big Georges at random.

"Queue?" he said with a raised brow. "That what ye call it in these parts, is it?"

Big Georges managed a crooked smile.

"And what do you call it? In your tongue?"

"Bot," Ian said, shrugging. There were other words, but he wasn't about to try one like *clipeachd* on them.

"Mostly just cock," Jamie said, shrugging, too.

"Or 'penis,' if ye want to be all English about it," Ian chimed in.

Several of the men were listening now, willing to join in any sort of conversation to get away from the echo of the last scream, still hanging in the air like fog.

"Ha," Jamie said. "Penis isna even an English word, ye wee ignoramus. It's Latin. And even in Latin, it doesna mean a man's closest companion—it means 'tail.'"

Ian gave him a long, slow look.

"Tail, is it? So ye canna even tell the difference between your cock and your arse, and ye're preachin' to me about *Latin*?"

The men roared. Jamie's face flamed up instantly, and Ian laughed and gave him a good nudge with his shoulder. Jamie snorted, but elbowed Ian back, and laughed, too, reluctantly.

"Aye, all right, then." He looked abashed; he didn't usually throw his education in Ian's face. Ian didn't hold it against him; he'd floundered for a bit, too, his first days with the company, and that was the sort of thing you did, trying to get your feet under you by making a point of what you were good at. But if Jamie tried rubbing Mathieu's or Big Georges's face in his Latin and Greek, he'd be proving himself with his fists, and fast, too. Right this minute, he didn't look as though he could fight a rabbit and win.

The renewed murmur of conversation, subdued as it was, dried up at once with the appearance of Mathieu through the trees. Mathieu was a big man, though broad rather than tall, with a face like a mad boar and a character to match. Nobody called him "Pig-face" *to* his face.

"You, cheese-rind—go bury that turd," he said to Jamie, adding with a narrowing of red-rimmed eyes, "Far back in the wood. And go before I put a boot in your arse. Move!"

Jamie got up—slowly—eyes fixed on Mathieu with a look Ian didn't care for. He came up quick beside Jamie and gripped him by the arm.

"I'll help," he said. "Come on."

"Why do they want this one buried?" Jamie muttered to Ian. "Giving him a *Christian* burial?" He drove one of the trenching spades Armand had lent them into the soft leaf mold with a violence that would have told Ian just how churned up his friend was, if he hadn't known already.

"Ye kent it's no a verra civilized life, *a charaid*," Ian said. He didn't feel any better about it himself, after all, and spoke sharp. "Not like the *Université*."

The blood flamed up Jamie's neck like tinder taking fire, and Ian held out a palm in hopes of quelling him. He didn't want a fight, and Jamie couldn't stand one.

"We're burying him because D'Eglise thinks his friends might come back to look for him, and it's better they don't see what was done to him, aye? Ye can see by looking that the other fellow was just killed fightin'. Business is one thing; revenge is another."

Jamie's jaw worked for a bit, but gradually the hot flush faded and his clench on the shovel loosened.

"Aye," he muttered, and resumed digging. The sweat was running down his neck in minutes, and he was breathing hard. Ian nudged him out of the way with an elbow and finished the digging. Silent, they took the dead man by the oxters and ankles and dragged him into the shallow pit.

"D'ye think D'Eglise found out anything?" Jamie asked as they scattered matted chunks of old leaves over the raw earth.

"I hope so," Ian replied, eyes on his work. "I wouldna like to think they did that for nothing."

He straightened up and they stood awkwardly for a moment, not quite looking at each other. It seemed wrong to leave a grave, even that of a stranger and a Jew, without a word of prayer. But it seemed worse to say a Christian prayer over the man—more insult than blessing, in the circumstances.

At last Jamie grimaced and bending, dug about under the leaves, coming out with two small stones. He gave one to Ian, and one after the other, they squatted and placed the stones together atop the grave. It wasn't much of a cairn, but it was something.

It wasn't the Captain's way to make explanations, or to give more than brief, explicit orders to his men. He had come back into camp at evening, his face dark and his lips pressed tight. But three other men had heard the interrogation of the Jewish stranger, and by the usual metaphysical processes that happen around campfires, everyone in the troop knew by the next morning what he had said.

"Ephraim bar-Sefer," Ian said to Jamie, who had come back late to the fire after going off quietly to wash his shirt out again. "That was his name." Ian was a bit worrit about the wean. His wounds weren't healing as they should, and the way he'd passed out . . . He'd a fever now; Ian could feel the heat coming off his skin, but he shivered now and then, though the night wasn't bitter.

"Is it better to know that?" Jamie asked bleakly.

"We can pray for him by name," Ian pointed out. "That's better, is it not?"

Jamie wrinkled up his brow, but after a moment nodded.

"Aye, it is. What else did he say, then?"

Ian rolled his eyes. Ephraim bar-Sefer had confessed that the band of attackers were professional thieves, mostly Jews, who—

"Jews?" Jamie interrupted. "Jewish *bandits*?" For some reason, the thought struck him as funny, but Ian didn't laugh.

"Why not?" he asked briefly, and went on without waiting for an answer. The men gained advance knowledge of valuable shipments and made a practice of lying in wait, to ambush and rob.

"It's mostly other Jews they rob, so there's nay much danger of being pursued by the French army or a local judge."

"Oh. And the advance knowledge—that's easier come by, too, I suppose, if the folk they rob are Jews. Jews live close by each other in groups," he explained, seeing the look of surprise on Ian's face. "They all read and write, though, and they write letters all the time; there's a good bit of information passed to and fro between the groups. Wouldna be that hard to learn who the moneylenders and merchants are and intercept their correspondence, would it?"

"Maybe not," Ian said, giving Jamie a look of respect. "Bar-Sefer said they got notice from someone—he didna ken who it was, himself—who kent a great deal about valuables comin' and goin'. The person who knew wasna one of their group, though; it was someone outside, who got a percentage o' the proceeds."

That, however, was the total of the information bar-Sefer had divulged. He wouldn't give up the names of any of his associates—D'Eglise didn't care so much about that—and had died stubbornly insisting that he knew nothing of future robberies planned.

"D'ye think it might ha' been one of ours?" Jamie asked, low voiced.

"One of—oh, our Jews, ye mean?" Ian frowned at the thought. There were three Spanish Jews in D'Eglise's band: Juanito, Big Georges, and Raoul, but all three were good men, and fairly popular with their fellows. "I doubt it. All three o' them fought like fiends. When I noticed," he added fairly.

"What I want to know is how the thieves got away wi' that rug," Jamie said reflectively. "Must have weighed, what, ten stone?"

"At least that," Ian assured him, flexing his shoulders at the memory. "I helped load the wretched things. I supposed they must have had a wagon somewhere nearby, for their booty. Why?"

"Well, but . . . *rugs*? Who steals rugs? Even valuable ones. And if they kent ahead of time that we were comin', presumably they kent what we carried."

"Ye're forgettin' the gold and silver," Ian reminded him. "It was in the front of the wagon, under the rugs. They had to pull the rugs out to get at it."

"Mmphm." Jamie looked vaguely dissatisfied—and it was true that the bandits had gone to the trouble to carry the rug away with them. But there was nothing to be gained by more discussion and when Ian said he was for bed, he came along without argument.

They settled down in a nest of long yellow grass, wrapped in their plaids, but Ian didn't sleep at once. He was bruised and tired, but the excitements of the day were still with him, and he lay looking up at the stars for some time, remembering some things and trying hard to forget others— like the look of Ephraim bar-Sefer's head. Maybe Jamie was right and it was better not to have kent his right name.

He forced his mind into other paths, succeeding to the extent that he was surprised when Jamie moved suddenly, cursing under his breath as the movement hurt him.

"Have ye ever done it?" Ian asked suddenly.

There was a small rustle as Jamie hitched himself into a more comfortable position.

"Have I ever done what?" he asked. His voice sounded that wee bit hoarse, but none so bad. "Killed anyone? No."

"Nay, lain wi' a lass."

"Oh, that."

"Aye, *that*. Gowk." Ian rolled toward Jamie and aimed a feint toward his middle. Despite the darkness, Jamie caught his wrist before the blow landed.

"Have you?"

"Oh, ye haven't, then." Ian detached the grip without difficulty. "I thought ye'd be up to your ears in whores and poetesses in Paris."

"Poetesses?" Jamie was beginning to sound amused. "What makes ye think women write poetry? Or that a woman that writes poetry would be wanton?"

"Well, o' course they are. Everybody kens that. The words get into their heads and drive them mad, and they go looking for the first man who—"

"Ye've bedded a poetess?" Jamie's fist struck him lightly in the middle of the chest. "Does your mam ken that?"

"Dinna be telling my mam anything about poetesses," Ian said firmly.

"No, but Big Georges did, and he told everyone about her. A woman he met in Marseilles. He has a book of her poetry, and read some out."

"Any good?"

"How would I ken? There was a good bit o' swoonin' and swellin' and burstin' goin' on, but it seemed to be to do wi' flowers, mostly. There was a good wee bit about a bumblebee, though, doin' the business wi' a sunflower. Pokin' it, I mean. With its snout."

There was a momentary silence as Jamie absorbed the mental picture.

"Maybe it sounds better in French," he said.

"I'll help ye," Ian said suddenly, in a tone that was serious to the bone.

"Help me . . . ?"

"Help ye kill this Captain Randall."

He lay silent for a moment, feeling his chest go tight.

"Jesus, Ian," he said, very softly. He lay for several minutes, eyes fixed on the shadowy tree roots that lay near his face.

"No," he said at last. "Ye can't. I need ye to do something else for me, Ian. I need ye to go home."

"Home? What—"

"I need ye to go home and take care of Lallybroch—and my sister. I—I canna go. Not yet." He bit his lower lip hard.

"Ye've got tenants and friends enough there," Ian protested. "Ye need me here, man. I'm no leavin' ye alone, aye? When ye go back, we'll go together." And he turned over in his plaid with an air of finality.

Jamie lay with his eyes tight closed, ignoring the singing and conversation near the fire, the beauty of the night sky over him, and the nagging pain in his back. He should perhaps be praying for the soul of the dead Jew, but he had no time for that just now. He was trying to find his father.

Brian Fraser's soul must still exist, and he was positive that his father was in heaven. But surely there must be some way to reach him, to sense him. When first Jamie had left home, to foster with Dougal at Beannachd, he'd been lonely and homesick, but Da had told him he would be, and not to trouble overmuch about it.

"Ye think of me, Jamie, and Jenny and Lallybroch. Ye'll not see us, but we'll be here nonetheless, and thinking of you. Look up at night, and see the stars, and ken we see them, too."

He opened his eyes a slit, but the stars swam, their brightness blurred. He squeezed his eyes shut again and felt the warm glide of a single tear down his temple. He couldn't think about Jenny. Or Lallybroch. The homesickness at Dougal's had stopped. The strangeness when he went to Paris had eased. This wouldn't stop, but he'd have to go on living anyway.

Where are ye, Da? he thought in anguish. *Da, I'm sorry!*

He prayed as he walked next day, making his way doggedly from one Hail Mary to the next, using his fingers to count the Rosary. For a time, it kept him from thinking and gave him a little peace. But eventually the slippery thoughts came stealing back, memories in small flashes, quick as sun on water. Some he fought off—Captain Randall's voice, playful as he took the cat in hand—the fearful prickle of the hairs on his body in the cold wind when he took his shirt off—the surgeon's *"I see he's made a mess of you, boy. . . ."*

But some memories he seized, no matter how painful they were. The feel of his da's hands, hard on his arms, holding him steady. The guards had been taking him somewhere, he didn't recall and it didn't matter, just suddenly his da was there before him, in the yard of the prison, and he'd stepped forward fast when he saw Jamie, a look of joy and eagerness on his face, this blasted into shock the next moment, when he saw what they'd done to him.

"Are ye bad hurt, Jamie?"

"No, Da, I'll be all right."

For a minute, he had been. So heartened by seeing his father, sure it would all come right—and then he'd remembered Jenny, taking that bastard into the house, sacrificing herself for—

He cut that one off short, too, saying, "Hail Mary, full of grace, the Lord is with thee!" savagely out loud, to the startlement of Petit Phillipe, who was scuttling along beside him on his short bandy legs. "Blessed art thou amongst women," Phillipe chimed in obligingly. "Pray for us sinners, now and at the hour of our death, amen!"

"Hail Mary," said Père Renault's deep voice behind him, taking it up, and within seconds seven or eight of them were saying it, marching solemnly to the rhythm, and then a few more. . . . Jamie himself fell silent, unnoticed. But he felt the wall of prayer a barricade between himself and the wicked sly thoughts and, closing his eyes briefly, felt his father walk beside him, and Brian Fraser's last kiss soft as the wind on his cheek.

They reached Bordeaux just before sunset, and D'Eglise took the wagon off with a small guard, leaving the other men free to explore the delights of the city—though such exploration was somewhat constrained by the fact that they hadn't yet been paid. They'd get their money after the goods were delivered next day.

Ian, who'd been in Bordeaux before, led the way to a large, noisy tavern with drinkable wine and large portions.

"The barmaids are pretty, too," he observed, watching one of these creatures wend her way deftly through a crowd of groping hands.

"Is it a brothel upstairs?" Jamie asked, out of curiosity, having heard a few stories.

"I dinna ken," Ian said, with a certain regret, though in fact he'd never been to a brothel, out of a mixture of penury and fear of catching the pox. His heart beat a little faster at the thought, though. "D'ye want to go and find out, later?"

Jamie hesitated.

"I—well. No, I dinna think so." He turned his face toward Ian and spoke very quietly. "I promised Da I wouldna go wi' whores, when I went to Paris. And now . . . I couldna do it without . . . thinkin' of him, ken?"

Ian nodded, feeling as much relief as disappointment.

"Time enough another day," he said philosophically, and signaled for another jug. The barmaid didn't see him, though, and Jamie snaked out a long arm and tugged at her apron. She whirled, scowling, but seeing Jamie's face, wearing its best blue-eyed smile, chose to smile back and take the order.

Several other men from D'Eglise's band were in the tavern, and this byplay didn't pass unnoticed.

Juanito, at a nearby table, glanced at Jamie, raised a derisive eyebrow, then said something to Raoul in the Jewish sort of Spanish they called Ladino; both men laughed.

"You know what causes warts, friend?" Jamie said pleasantly—in Biblical Hebrew. "Demons inside a man, trying to emerge through the skin." He spoke slowly enough that Ian could follow this, and Ian in turn broke out laughing—as much at the looks on the two Jews' faces as at Jamie's remark.

Juanito's lumpy face darkened, but Raoul looked sharply at Ian, first at his face, then, deliberately, at his crotch. Ian shook his head, still grinning, and Raoul shrugged but returned the smile, then took Juanito by the arm, tugging him off in the direction of the back room, where dicing was to be found.

"What did you say to him?" the barmaid asked, glancing after the departing pair, then looking back wide-eyed at Jamie. "And what tongue did you say it in?"

Jamie was glad to have the wide brown eyes to gaze into; it was causing his neck considerable strain to keep his head from tilting farther down in order to gaze into her décolletage. The charming hollow between her breasts drew the eye . . .

"Oh, nothing but a little bonhomie," he said, grinning down at her. "I said it in Hebrew." He wanted to impress her, and he did, but not the way he'd meant to. Her half-smile vanished, and she edged back a little.

"Oh," she said. "Your pardon, sir, I'm needed . . ." and with a vaguely apologetic flip of the hand, she vanished into the throng of customers, pitcher in hand.

"Eejit," Ian said, coming up beside him. "What did ye tell her that for? Now she thinks ye're a Jew."

Jamie's mouth fell open in shock. "What, me? How, then?" he demanded, looking down at himself. He'd meant his Highland dress, but Ian looked critically at him and shook his head.

"Ye've got the lang neb and the red hair," he pointed out. "Half the Spanish Jews I've seen look like that, and some of them are a good size, too. For all yon lass kens, ye stole the plaid off somebody ye killed."

Jamie felt more nonplussed than affronted. Rather hurt, too.

"Well, what if I was a Jew?" he demanded. "Why should it matter? I wasna askin' for her hand in marriage, was I? I was only talkin' to her, for God's sake!"

Ian gave him that annoyingly tolerant look. He shouldn't mind, he knew; he'd lorded it over Ian often enough about things he kent and Ian didn't. He did mind, though; the borrowed shirt was too small and chafed him under the arms and his wrists stuck out, bony and raw-looking. He didn't look like a Jew, but he looked like a gowk and he knew it. It made him cross-grained.

"Most o' the Frenchwomen—the Christian ones, I mean—dinna like to go wi' Jews. Not because they're Christ-killers, but because of their . . . um . . ." He glanced down, with a discreet gesture at Jamie's crotch. "They think it looks funny."

"It doesna look *that* different."

"It does."

"Well, aye, when it's . . . but when it's—I mean, if it's in a state that a lassie would be lookin' at it, it isna . . ." He saw Ian opening his mouth to ask just how he happened to know what an erect, circumcised cock looked like. "Forget it," he said brusquely, and pushed past his friend. "Let's be goin' down the street."

At dawn, the band gathered at the inn where D'Eglise and the wagon waited, ready to escort it through the streets to its destination—a warehouse on the banks of the Garonne. Jamie saw that the Captain had changed into his finest clothes, plumed hat and all, and so had the four men—among the biggest in the band—who had guarded the wagon during the night. They were all armed to the teeth, and Jamie wondered whether this was only to make a good show, or whether D'Eglise intended to have them stand behind him while he explained why the shipment was one rug short, to discourage complaint from the merchant receiving the shipment.

He was enjoying the walk through the city, though keeping a sharp eye out as he'd been instructed, against the possibility of ambush from alleys, or thieves dropping from a roof or balcony onto the wagon. He thought the latter possibility remote, but dutifully looked up now and then. Upon lowering his eyes from one of these inspections, he found that the Captain had dropped back, and was now pacing beside him on his big gray gelding.

"Juanito says you speak Hebrew," D'Eglise said, looking down at him as though he'd suddenly sprouted horns. "Is this true?"

"Aye," he said cautiously. "Though it's more I can read the Bible in Hebrew—a bit—there not bein' so many Jews in the Highlands to converse with." There had been a few in Paris, but he knew better than to talk about the *Université* and the study of philosophers like Maimonides. They'd scrag him before supper.

The Captain grunted, but didn't look displeased. He rode for a time in silence, but kept his horse to a walk, pacing at Jamie's side. This made Jamie nervous, and after a few moments, impulse made him jerk his head to the rear and say, "Ian can, too. Read Hebrew, I mean."

D'Eglise looked down at him, startled, and glanced back. Ian was clearly visible, as he stood a head taller than the three men with whom he was conversing as he walked.

"Will wonders never cease?" the Captain said, as though to himself. But he nudged his horse into a trot and left Jamie in the dust.

It wasn't until the next afternoon that this conversation returned to bite Jamie in the arse. They'd delivered the rugs and the gold and silver to the warehouse on the river, D'Eglise had received his payment, and consequently the men were scattered down the length of an *alle* that boasted cheap eating and drinking establishments, many of these with a room above or behind where a man could spend his money in other ways.

Neither Jamie nor Ian said anything further regarding the subject of brothels, but Jamie found his mind returning to the pretty barmaid. He had his own shirt on now, and had half a mind to find his way back and tell her he wasn't a Jew.

He had no idea what she might do with that information, though, and the tavern was clear on the other side of the city.

"Think we'll have another job soon?" he asked idly, as much to break Ian's silence as to escape from his own thoughts. There had been talk around the fire about the prospects; evidently there were no good wars at the moment, though it was rumored that the King of Prussia was beginning to gather men in Silesia.

"I hope so," Ian muttered. "Canna bear hangin' about." He drummed long fingers on the tabletop. "I need to be movin'."

"That why ye left Scotland, is it?" He was only making conversation, and was surprised to see Ian dart him a wary glance.

"Didna want to farm, wasna much else to do. I make good money here. *And* I mostly send it home."

"Still, I dinna imagine your da was pleased." Ian was the only son;

Auld John was probably still livid, though he hadn't said much in Jamie's hearing during the brief time he'd been home, before the redcoats—

"My sister's marrit. Her husband can manage, if . . ." Ian lapsed into a moody silence.

Before Jamie could decide whether to prod Ian or not, the Captain appeared beside their table, surprising them both.

D'Eglise stood for a moment, considering them. Finally he sighed and said, "All right. The two of you, come with me."

Ian shoved the rest of his bread and cheese into his mouth and rose, chewing. Jamie was about to do likewise when the Captain frowned at him.

"Is your shirt clean?"

He felt the blood rise in his cheeks. It was the closest anyone had come to mentioning his back, and it was too close. Most of the wounds had crusted over long since, but the worst ones were still infected; they broke open with the chafing of the bandages or if he bent too suddenly. He'd had to rinse his shirt almost every night—it was constantly damp and that didn't help—and he knew fine that the whole band knew, but nobody'd spoken of it.

"It is," he replied shortly, and drew himself up to his full height, staring down at D'Eglise, who merely said, "Good, then. Come on."

The new potential client was a physician named Dr. Hasdi, reputed to be a person of great influence among the Jews of Bordeaux. The last client had made the introduction, so apparently D'Eglise had managed to smooth over the matter of the missing rug.

Dr. Hasdi's house was discreetly tucked away in a decent but modest side street, behind a stuccoed wall and locked gates. Ian rang the bell, and a man dressed like a gardener promptly appeared to let them in, gesturing them up the walk to the front door. Evidently, they were expected.

"They don't flaunt their wealth, the Jews," D'Eglise murmured out of the side of his mouth to Jamie. "But they have it."

Well, these did, Jamie thought. A manservant greeted them in a plain tiled foyer, but then opened the door into a room that made the senses swim. It was lined with books in dark wood cases, carpeted thickly underfoot, and what little of the walls was not covered with books was

adorned with small tapestries and framed tiles that he thought might be
Moorish. But above all, the scent! He breathed it in to the bottom of his
lungs, feeling slightly intoxicated, and looking for the source of it, finally
spotted the owner of this earthly paradise, sitting behind a desk and staring . . . at him. Or maybe him and Ian both; the man's eyes flicked back
and forth between them, round as sucked toffees.

He straightened up instinctively, and bowed.

"We greet thee, Lord," he said, in carefully rehearsed Hebrew. "Peace
be on your house." The man's mouth fell open. Noticeably so; he had a
large, bushy dark beard, going white near the mouth. An indefinable
expression—surely it wasn't amusement?—ran over what could be seen of
his face.

A small sound that certainly *was* amusement drew his attention to one
side. A small brass bowl sat on a round, tile-topped table, with smoke
wandering lazily up from it through a bar of late afternoon sun. Between
the sun and the smoke, he could just make out the form of a woman
standing in the shadows. She stepped forward, materializing out of the
gloom, and his heart jumped.

She inclined her head gravely to the soldiers, addressing them impar-
tially.

"I am Rebekah bat-Leah Hauberger. My grandfather bids me make
you welcome to our home, gentlemen," she said, in perfect French, though
the old gentleman hadn't spoken. Jamie drew in a great breath of relief;
he wouldn't have to try to explain their business in Hebrew, after all. The
breath was so deep, though, that it made him cough, the perfumed smoke
tickling his chest.

He could feel his face going red as he tried to strangle the cough, and
Ian glanced at him out of the sides of his eyes. The girl—yes, she was
young, maybe his own age—swiftly took up a cover and clapped it on the
bowl, then rang a bell and told the servant something in what sounded
like Spanish. *Ladino?* he thought.

"Do please sit, sirs," she said, waving gracefully toward a chair in front
of the desk, then turning to fetch another standing by the wall.

"Allow me, Mademoiselle!" Ian leapt forward to assist her. Jamie, still
choking as quietly as possible, followed suit.

She had dark hair, very wavy, bound back from her brow with a
rose-colored ribbon, but falling loose down her back, nearly to her waist.

He had actually raised a hand to stroke it before catching hold of himself. Then she turned round. Pale skin, big, dark eyes, and an oddly knowing look in those eyes when she met his own—which she did, very directly, when he set the third chair down before her.

Annalise. He swallowed, hard, and cleared his throat. A wave of dizzy heat washed over him, and he wished suddenly that they'd open a window.

D'Eglise, too, was visibly relieved at having a more reliable interpreter than Jamie, and launched into a gallant speech of introduction, much decorated with French flowers, bowing repeatedly to the girl and her grandfather in turn.

Jamie wasn't paying attention to the talk; he was still watching Rebekah. It was her passing resemblance to Annalise de Marillac, the girl he'd loved in Paris, that had drawn his attention—but now he came to look, she was quite different.

Quite different. Annalise had been tiny and fluffy as a kitten. This girl was small—he'd seen that she came no higher than his elbow; her soft hair had brushed his wrist when she sat down—but there was nothing either fluffy or helpless about her. She'd noticed him watching her, and was now watching *him,* with a faint curve to her red mouth that made the blood rise in his cheeks. He coughed and looked down.

"What's amiss?" Ian muttered out of the side of his mouth. "Ye look like ye've got a cocklebur stuck betwixt your hurdies."

Jamie gave an irritable twitch, then stiffened as he felt one of the rawer wounds on his back break open. He could feel the fast-cooling spot, the slow seep of pus or blood, and sat very straight, trying not to breathe deep, in hopes that the bandages would absorb the liquid before it got onto his shirt.

This niggling concern had at least distracted his mind from Rebekah bat-Leah Hauberger, and to distract himself from the aggravation of his back, he returned to the three-way conversation between D'Eglise and the Jews.

The Captain was sweating freely, whether from the hot tea or the strain of persuasion, but he talked easily, gesturing now and then toward his matched pair of tall, Hebrew-speaking Scots, now and then toward the window and the outer world, where vast legions of similar warriors awaited, ready and eager to do Dr. Hasdi's bidding.

The Doctor watched D'Eglise intently, occasionally addressing a soft rumble of incomprehensible words to his granddaughter. It did sound like the Ladino Juanito spoke, more than anything else; certainly it sounded nothing like the Hebrew Jamie had been taught in Paris.

Finally the old Jew glanced among the three mercenaries, pursed his lips thoughtfully, and nodded. He rose and went to a large blanket chest that stood under the window, where he knelt and carefully gathered up a long, heavy cylinder wrapped in oiled cloth. Jamie could see that it was remarkably heavy for its size from the slow way the old man rose with it, and his first thought was that it must be a gold statue of some sort. His second thought was that Rebekah smelled like rose petals and vanilla pods. He breathed in, very gently, feeling his shirt stick to his back.

The thing, whatever it was, jingled and chimed softly as it moved. Some sort of Jewish clock? Dr. Hasdi carried the cylinder to the desk and set it down, then curled a finger to invite the soldiers to step near.

Unwrapped with a slow and solemn sense of ceremony, the object emerged from its layers of linen, canvas, and oilcloth. It *was* gold, in part, and not unlike statuary, but made of wood and shaped like a prism, with a sort of crown at one end. While Jamie was still wondering what the devil it might be, the Doctor's arthritic fingers touched a small clasp and the box opened, revealing yet more layers of cloth, from which yet another delicate, spicy scent emerged. All three soldiers breathed deep, in unison, and Rebekah made that small sound of amusement again.

"The case is cedarwood," she said. "From Lebanon."

"Oh," D'Eglise said respectfully. "Of course!"

The bundle inside was dressed—there was no other word for it; it was wearing a sort of caped mantle and a belt—with a miniature buckle—in velvet and embroidered silk. From one end, two massive golden finials protruded like twin heads. They were pierced work, and looked like towers, adorned in the windows and along their lower edges with a number of tiny bells.

"This is a *very* old Torah scroll," Rebekah said, keeping a respectful distance. "From Spain."

"A priceless object, to be sure," D'Eglise said, bending to peer closer.

Dr. Hasdi grunted and said something to Rebekah, who translated:

"Only to those whose Book it is. To anyone else, it has a very obvious and attractive price. If this were not so, I would not stand in need of your services." The Doctor looked pointedly at Jamie and Ian. "A respectable man—a Jew—will carry the Torah. It may not be touched. But you will safeguard it—and my granddaughter."

"Quite so, Your Honor." D'Eglise flushed slightly, but was too pleased to look abashed. "I am deeply honored by your trust, sir, and I assure you . . ." But Rebekah had rung her bell again, and the manservant came in with wine.

The job offered was simple. Rebekah was to be married to the son of the chief rabbi of the Paris synagogue. The ancient Torah was part of her dowry, as was a sum of money that made D'Eglise's eyes glisten. The Doctor wished to engage D'Eglise to deliver all three items—the girl, the scroll, and the money—safely to Paris; the Doctor himself would travel there for the wedding, but later in the month, as his business in Bordeaux detained him. The only things to be decided were the price for D'Eglise's services, the time in which they were to be accomplished, and the guarantees D'Eglise was prepared to offer.

The Doctor's lips pursed over this last; his friend Ackerman, who had referred D'Eglise to him, had not been entirely pleased at having one of his valuable rugs stolen en route, and the Doctor wished to be assured that none of *his* valuable property—Jamie saw Rebekah's soft mouth twitch as she translated this—would go missing between Bordeaux and Paris. The Captain gave Ian and Jamie a stern look, then altered this to earnest sincerity as he assured the Doctor that there would be no difficulty; his best men would take on the job, and he would offer whatever assurances the Doctor required. Small drops of sweat stood out on his upper lip.

Between the warmth of the fire and the hot tea, Jamie was sweating, too, and could have used a glass of wine. But the old gentleman stood up abruptly and, with a courteous bow to D'Eglise, came out from behind his desk and took Jamie by the arm, pulling him up and tugging him gently toward a doorway.

He ducked, just in time to avoid braining himself on a low archway, and found himself in a small, plain room with bunches of drying herbs hung from its beams. What—

But before he could formulate any sort of question, the old man had got hold of his shirt and was pulling it free of his plaid. He tried to step back, but there was no room, and willy-nilly, he found himself set down on a stool, the old man's horny fingers pulling loose the bandages. The Doctor made a deep sound of disapproval, then shouted something in which the words *agua caliente* were clearly discernible, back through the archway.

He daren't stand up and flee—not and risk D'Eglises's new arrangement. And so he sat, burning with embarrassment, while the physician probed, prodded, and—a bowl of hot water having appeared—scrubbed at his back with something painfully rough. None of this bothered Jamie nearly as much as the appearance of Rebekah in the doorway, her dark eyebrows raised.

"My grandfather says your back is a mess," she told him, translating a remark from the old man.

"Thank ye. I didna ken that," he muttered in English, but then repeated the remark more politely in French. His cheeks burned with mortification, but a small, cold echo sounded in his heart. *"He's made a mess of you, boy."*

The surgeon at Fort William had said it, when the soldiers had dragged Jamie to him after the flogging, legs too wabbly to stand by himself. The surgeon had been right, and so was Dr. Hasdi, but it didn't mean Jamie wanted to hear it again.

Rebekah, evidently interested to see what her grandfather meant, came round behind Jamie. He stiffened, and the Doctor poked him sharply in the back of the neck, making him bend forward again. The two Jews were discussing the spectacle in tones of detachment; he felt the girl's small, soft fingers trace a line between his ribs and nearly shot off the stool, his flesh erupting in goose bumps.

"Jamie?" Ian's voice came from the hallway, sounding worried. "Are ye all right?"

"Aye!" he managed, half-strangled. "Don't—ye needn't come in."

"Your name is Jamie?" Rebekah was now in front of him, leaning down to look into his face. Her own was alive with interest and concern. "James?"

"Aye. James." He clenched his teeth as the Doctor dug a little harder, clicking his tongue.

"Diego," she said, smiling at him. "That's what it would be in Spanish— or Ladino. And your friend?"

"He's called Ian. That's—" He groped for a moment and found the English equivalent. "John. That would be . . ."

"Juan. Diego and Juan." She touched him gently on the bare shoulder.

"You're friends? Brothers? I can see you come from the same place—where is that?"

"Friends. From . . . Scotland. The—the—Highlands. A place called Lallybroch." He'd spoken unwarily, and a pang shot through him at the name, sharper than whatever the Doctor was scraping his back with. He looked away; the girl's face was too close; he didn't want her to see.

She didn't move away. Instead, she crouched gracefully beside him and took his hand. Hers was very warm, and the hairs on his wrist rose in response, in spite of what the Doctor was doing to his back.

"It will be done soon," she promised. "He's cleaning the infected parts; he says they will scab over cleanly now and stop draining." A gruff question from the Doctor. "He asks, do you have fever at night? Bad dreams?"

Startled, he looked back at her, but her face showed only compassion. Her hand tightened on his in reassurance.

"I . . . yes. Sometimes."

A grunt from the Doctor, more words, and Rebekah let go his hand with a little pat, and went out, skirts a-rustle. He closed his eyes and tried to keep the scent of her in his mind—he couldn't keep it in his nose, as the Doctor was now anointing him with something vile smelling. He could smell himself, too, and his jaw prickled with embarrassment; he reeked of stale sweat, campfire smoke, and fresh blood.

He could hear D'Eglise and Ian talking in the parlor, low voiced, discussing whether to come and rescue him. He would have called out to them, save that he couldn't bear the Captain to see . . . He pressed his lips together tight. Aye, well, it was nearly done; he could tell from the Doctor's slower movements, almost gentle now.

"Rebekah!" the Doctor called, impatient, and the girl appeared an instant later, a small cloth bundle in one hand. The Doctor let off a short burst of words, then pressed a thin cloth of some sort over Jamie's back; it stuck to the nasty ointment.

"Grandfather says the cloth will protect your shirt until the ointment is absorbed," she told him. "By the time it falls off—don't peel it off, let it come off by itself—the wounds will be scabbed, but the scabs should be soft and not crack."

The Doctor took his hand off Jamie's shoulder, and Jamie shot to his feet, looking round for his shirt. Rebekah handed it to him. Her eyes were fastened on his naked chest, and he was—for the first time in his life—embarrassed by the fact that he possessed nipples. An extraordinary but not unpleasant tingle made the curly hairs on his body stand up.

"Thank you—ah, I mean . . . *gracias, Señor*." His face was flaming, but he bowed to the Doctor with as much grace as he could muster. *"Muchas gracias."*

"De nada," the old man said gruffly, with a dismissive wave of one hand. He pointed at the small bundle in his granddaughter's hand. "Drink. No fever. No dream." And then, surprisingly, he smiled.

"Shalom," he said, and made a shooing gesture.

D'Eglise, looking pleased with the new job, left Ian and Jamie at a large tavern called Le Poulet Gai, where some of the other mercenaries were enjoying themselves—in various ways. The Cheerful Chicken most assuredly did boast a brothel on the upper floor, and slatternly women in various degrees of undress wandered freely through the lower rooms, picking up new customers with whom they vanished upstairs.

The two tall young Scots provoked a certain amount of interest from the women, but when Ian solemnly turned his empty purse inside out in front of them—having put his money inside his shirt for safety—they left the lads alone.

"Couldna look at one of those," Ian said, turning his back on the whores and devoting himself to his ale. "Not after seein' the wee Jewess up close. Did ye ever seen anything like?"

Jamie shook his head, deep in his own drink. It was sour and fresh and went down a treat, parched as he was from the ordeal in Dr. Hasdi's surgery. He could still smell the ghost of Rebekah's scent, vanilla and roses, a fugitive fragrance among the reeks of the tavern. He fumbled in his sporran, bringing out the little cloth bundle Rebekah had given him.

"She said—well, the Doctor said—I was to drink this. How, d'ye think?" The bundle held a mixture of broken leaves, small sticks, and a coarse powder, and smelled strongly of something he'd never smelled before. Not bad; just odd. Ian frowned at it.

"Well . . . ye'd brew a tea of it, I suppose," he said. "How else?"

"I havena got anything to brew it in," Jamie said. "I was thinkin' . . . maybe put it in the ale?"

"Why not?"

Ian wasn't paying much attention; he was watching Mathieu Pig-face, who was standing against a wall, summoning whores as they passed by, looking them up and down and occasionally fingering the merchandise before sending each one on with a smack on the rear.

He wasn't really tempted—the women scairt him, to be honest—but he was curious. If he ever *should* . . . how did ye start? Just grab, like Mathieu was doing, or did ye need to ask about the price first, to be sure you could afford it? And was it proper to bargain, like ye did for a loaf of bread or a flitch of bacon, or would the woman kick ye in the privates and find someone less mean?

He shot a glance at Jamie, who, after a bit of choking, had got his herbed ale down all right and was looking a little glazed. He didn't think Jamie knew, either, but he didn't want to ask, just in case he did.

"I'm goin' to the privy," Jamie said abruptly and stood up. He looked pale.

"Have ye got the shits?"

"Not yet." With this ominous remark, he was off, bumping into tables in his haste, and Ian followed, pausing long enough to thriftily drain the last of Jamie's ale as well as his own.

Mathieu had found one he liked; he leered at Ian and said something obnoxious as he ushered his choice toward the stairs. Ian smiled cordially and said something much worse in *Gàidhlig*.

By the time he got to the yard at the back of the tavern, Jamie had disappeared. Figuring he'd be back as soon as he rid himself of his trouble, Ian leaned tranquilly against the back wall of the building, enjoying the cool night air and watching the folk in the yard.

There were a couple of torches burning, stuck in the ground, and it looked a bit like a painting he'd seen of the Last Judgement, with angels on the one side blowing trumpets and sinners on the other, going down to Hell in a tangle of naked limbs and bad behavior. It was mostly sinners out here, though now and then he thought he saw an angel floating past the corner of his eye. He licked his lips thoughtfully, wondering what was in the stuff Dr. Hasdi had given Jamie.

Jamie himself emerged from the privy at the far side of the yard, looking a little more settled in himself, and, spotting Ian, made his way through the little knots of drinkers sitting on the ground singing, and the others wandering to and fro, smiling vaguely as they looked for something, not knowing what they were looking for.

Ian was seized by a sudden sense of revulsion, almost terror; a fear that he would never see Scotland again, would die here, among strangers.

"We should go home," he said abruptly, as soon as Jamie was in earshot. "As soon as we've finished this job."

"Home?" Jamie looked strangely at Ian, as though he were speaking some incomprehensible language.

"Ye've business there, and so have I. We—"

A skelloch and the thud and clatter of a falling table with its burden of dishes interrupted them. The back door of the tavern burst open and a woman ran out, yelling in a sort of French that Ian didn't understand but knew fine was bad words from the tone of it. Similar words in a loud male voice, and big Mathieu charged out after her.

He caught her by the shoulder, spun her round, and cracked her across the face with the back of one meaty hand. Ian flinched at the sound, and Jamie's hand tightened on his wrist.

"What—" Jamie began, but then stopped dead.

"*Putain de . . . merde . . . tu fais . . . chier,*" Mathieu panted, slapping her with each word. She shrieked some more, trying to get away, but he had her by the arm, and now jerked her round and pushed her hard in the back, knocking her to her knees.

Jamie's hand loosened, and Ian grabbed his arm, tight.

"Don't," he said tersely, and yanked Jamie back into the shadow.

"I wasn't," Jamie said, but under his breath and not noticing much what he was saying, because his eyes were fixed on what was happening, as much as Ian's were.

The light from the door spilled over the woman, glowing off her hanging breasts, bared in the ripped neck of her shift. Glowing off her wide round buttocks, too; Mathieu had shoved her skirts up to her waist and was behind her, jerking at his flies one-handed, the other hand twisted in her hair so her head pulled back, throat straining and her face white-eyed as a panicked horse.

"*Pute!*" he said, and gave her arse a loud smack, open-handed. "Nobody says no to me!" He'd got his cock out now, in his hand, and shoved it into the woman with a violence that made her hurdies wobble and knotted Ian from knees to neck.

"*Merde*," Jamie said, still under his breath. Other men and a couple of women had come out into the yard and were gathered round with the others, enjoying the spectacle as Mathieu set to work in a businesslike manner. He let go of the woman's hair in order to grasp her by the hips and her head hung down, hair hiding her face. She grunted with each thrust, panting bad words that made the onlookers laugh.

Ian was shocked—and shocked as much at his own arousal as at what Mathieu was doing. He'd not seen open coupling before, only the heaving and giggling of things happening under a blanket, now and then a wee flash of pale flesh. This . . . He ought to look away, he knew that fine. But he didn't.

Jamie took in a breath, but no telling whether he meant to say something. Mathieu threw back his big head and howled like a wolf and the watchers all cheered. Then his face convulsed, gapped teeth showing in a grin like a skull's, and he made a noise like a pig gives out when you knock it clean on the head, and collapsed on top of the whore.

The whore squirmed out from under his bulk, abusing him roundly. Ian understood what she was saying now, and would have been shocked anew if he'd had any capacity for being shocked left. She hopped up, evidently not hurt, and kicked Mathieu in the ribs once, then twice, but having no shoes on, didn't hurt him. She reached for the purse still tied at his waist, stuck her hand in and grabbed a handful of coins, then kicked him once more for luck and stomped off into the house, holding up the neck of her shift. Mathieu lay sprawled on the ground, his breeks around his thighs, laughing and wheezing.

Ian heard Jamie swallow and realized he was still gripping Jamie's arm. Jamie didn't seem to have noticed. Ian let go. His face was burning all the way down to the middle of his chest, and he didn't think it was just torchlight on Jamie's face, either.

"Let's . . . go someplace else," he said.

"I wish we'd . . . done something," Jamie blurted. They hadn't spoken at all after leaving Le Poulet Gai. They'd walked clear to the other end of the street and down a side alley, eventually coming to rest in a small tavern, fairly quiet. Juanito and Raoul were there, dicing with some locals, but gave Ian and Jamie no more than a glance.

"I dinna see what we *could* have done," Ian said reasonably. "I mean, we could maybe have taken on Mathieu together and got off with only bein' maimed. But ye ken it would ha' started a kebbie-lebbie, wi' all the others there." He hesitated, and gave Jamie a quick glance before returning his gaze to his cup. "And . . . she *was* a whore. I mean, she wasna a—"

"I ken what ye mean." Jamie cut him off. "Aye, ye're right. And she did go with the man, to start. God knows what he did to make her take against him, but there's likely plenty to choose from. I wish—ah, feckit. D'ye want something to eat?"

Ian shook his head. The barmaid brought them a jug of wine, glanced at them, and dismissed them as negligible. It was rough wine that took the skin off the insides of your mouth, but it had a decent taste to it, under the resin fumes, and wasn't too much watered. Jamie drank deep, and faster than he generally did; he was uneasy in his skin, prickling and irritable, and wanted the feeling to go away.

There were a few women in the place, not many. Jamie had to think that whoring maybe wasn't a profitable business, wretched as most of the poor creatures looked, raddled and half-toothless. Maybe it wore them down, having to . . . He turned away from the thought and finding the jug empty, waved to the barmaid for another.

Juanito gave a joyful whoop and said something in Ladino. Looking in that direction, Jamie saw one of the whores who'd been lurking in the shadows come gliding purposefully in, bending down to give Juanito a congratulatory kiss as he scooped in his winnings. Jamie snorted a little, trying to blow the smell of her out of his neb—she'd passed by close enough that he'd got a good whiff of her: a stink of rancid sweat and dead fish. Alexandre had told him that was from unclean privates, and he believed it.

He went back to the wine. Ian was matching him, cup for cup, and likely for the same reason. His friend wasn't usually irritable or crankit, but if he was well put out, he'd often stay that way until the next dawn—a good sleep erased his bad temper, but 'til then you didn't want to rile him.

He shot a sidelong glance at Ian. He couldn't tell Ian about Jenny. He just . . . couldn't. But neither could he think about her, left alone at Lallybroch . . . maybe with ch—

"Oh, God," he said, under his breath. "No. Please. No."

"Dinna come back," Murtagh had said, and plainly meant it. Well, he *would* go back—but not yet awhile. It wouldn't help his sister, him going

back just now and bringing Randall and the redcoats straight to her like flies to a fresh-killed deer. . . . He shoved that analogy hastily out of sight, horrified. The truth was, it made him sick with shame to think about Jenny, and he tried not to—and was the more ashamed because he mostly succeeded.

Ian's gaze was fixed on another of the harlots. She was old, in her thirties at least, but had most of her teeth and was cleaner than most. She was flirting with Juanito and Raoul, too, and Jamie wondered whether she'd mind if she found out they were Jews. Maybe a whore couldn't afford to be choosy.

His treacherous mind at once presented him with a picture of his sister, obliged to follow that walk of life to feed herself, made to take any man who . . . Blessed Mother, what would the folk, the tenants, the servants, do to her if they found out what had happened? The talk . . . He shut his eyes tight, hoping to block the vision.

"That one's none sae bad," Ian said meditatively, and Jamie opened his eyes. The better-looking whore had bent over Juanito, deliberately rubbing her breast against his warty ear. "If she doesna mislike a Jew, maybe she'd . . ."

The blood flamed up in Jamie's face.

"If ye've got any thought to my sister, ye're no going to—to—pollute yourself wi' a French whore!"

Ian's face went blank, but then flooded with color in turn.

"Oh, aye? And if I said your sister wasna worth it?"

Jamie's fist caught him in the eye and he flew backward, overturning the bench and crashing into the next table. Jamie scarcely noticed, the agony in his hand shooting fire and brimstone from his crushed knuckles up his forearm. He rocked to and fro, injured hand clutched between his thighs, cursing freely in three languages.

Ian sat on the floor, bent over, holding his eye and breathing through his mouth in short gasps. After a minute, he straightened up. His eye was puffing already, leaking tears down his lean cheek. He got up, shaking his head slowly, and put the bench back in place. Then he sat down, picked up his cup and took a deep gulp, put it down and blew out his breath. He took the snot-rag Jamie was holding out to him and dabbed at his eye.

"Sorry," Jamie managed. The agony in his hand was beginning to subside, but the anguish in his heart wasn't.

"Aye," Ian said quietly, not meeting his eye. "I wish we'd done something, too. Ye want to share a bowl o' stew?"

Two days later, they set off for Paris. After some thought, D'Eglise had decided that Rebekah and her maid would travel by coach, escorted by Jamie and Ian. D'Eglise and the rest of the troop would take the money, with some men sent ahead in small groups to wait, both to check the road ahead, and so that they could ride in shifts, not stopping anywhere along the way. The women obviously would have to stop, but if they had nothing valuable with them, they'd be in no danger.

It was only when they went to collect the women at Dr. Hasdi's residence that they learned the Torah scroll and its custodian, a sober-looking man of middle age introduced to them as Monsieur Peretz, would be traveling with Rebekah. "I trust my greatest treasures to you, gentlemen," the Doctor told them, through his granddaughter, and gave them a formal little bow

"May you find us worthy of trust, Lord," Jamie managed in halting Hebrew, and Ian bowed with great solemnity, hand on his heart. Dr. Hasdi looked from one to the other, gave a small nod, and then stepped forward to kiss Rebekah on the forehead.

"Go with God, child," he whispered, in something close enough to Spanish that Jamie understood it.

All went well for the first day, and the first night. The autumn weather held fine, with no more than a pleasant tang of chill in the air, and the horses were sound. Dr. Hasdi had provided Jamie with a purse to cover the expenses of the journey, and they all ate decently and slept at a very respectable inn—Ian being sent in first to inspect the premises and insure against any nasty surprises.

The next day dawned cloudy, but the wind came up and blew the clouds away before noon, leaving the sky clean and brilliant as a sapphire overhead. Jamie was riding in the van, Ian post, and the coach was making good time, in spite of a rutted, winding road. As they reached the top of a small rise, though, Jamie saw that a small stream had run through the roadbed in the dip below, making a bog some ten feet across. He brought his horse to a sudden stop, raising a hand to halt the coach, and Ian reined up alongside him.

"What—" he began, but was interrupted. The driver had pulled his team up for an instant but, at a peremptory shout from inside the coach, now snapped the reins over the horses' backs and the coach lunged forward, narrowly missing Jamie's horse, which shied violently, flinging its rider off into the bushes.

"Jamie! Are ye all right?" Torn between concern for his friend and for his duty, Ian held his horse, glancing to and fro.

"Stop them! Get them! *Ifrinn!*" Jamie scuttled crabwise out of the weeds, face scratched and bright red with fury. Ian didn't wait, but kicked his horse and lit out in pursuit of the heavy coach, this now lurching from side to side as it ran down into the boggy bottom. Shrill feminine cries of protest from inside were drowned by the driver's exclamation of *"Ladrones!"*

That was one word he kent in Spanish—"thieves." One of the *ladrones* was already skittering up the side of the coach like an eight-legged cob, and the driver promptly dived off the box, hit the ground and ran for it.

"Coward!" Ian bellowed, and gave out with a Hieland screech that set the coach-horses dancing, flinging their heads to and fro, and giving the would-be kidnapper fits with the reins. He forced his own horse—who hadn't liked the screeching any better than the coach-horses—through the narrow gap between the brush and the coach, and as he came even with the driver, had his pistol out. He drew down on the fellow—a young chap with long yellow hair—and shouted at him to pull up.

The man glanced at him, crouched low, and slapped the reins on the horses' backs, shouting at them in a voice like iron. Ian fired, and missed— but the delay had let Jamie catch them up; he saw Jamie's red head poke up as he climbed the back of the coach, and there were more screams from inside as Jamie pounded across the roof and launched himself at the yellow-haired driver.

Leaving that bit of trouble to Jamie to deal with, Ian kicked his horse forward, meaning to get ahead and seize the reins, but another of the thieves had beat him to it and was hauling down on one horse's head. Aye, well, it worked once. Ian inflated his lungs as far as they'd go and let rip.

The coach-horses bolted in a spray of mud. Jamie and the yellow-haired driver fell off the box, and the whoreson in the road disappeared, possibly trampled into the mire. Ian hoped so. Blood in his eye, he reined up his own agitated mount, drew his broadsword, and charged across the road, shrieking like a *ban-sidhe* and slashing wildly. Two thieves stared up at him openmouthed, then broke and ran for it.

He chased them a wee bit into the brush, but the going was too thick for his horse, and he turned back to find Jamie rolling about in the road, earnestly hammering the yellow-haired laddie. Ian hesitated—help him, or see to the coach? A loud crash and horrible screams decided him at once and he charged down the road.

The coach, driverless, had run off the road, hit the bog, and fallen sideways into a ditch. From the clishmaclaver coming from inside, he thought the women were likely all right, and, swinging off his horse, wrapped the reins hastily round a tree and went to take care of the coach-horses before they killed themselves.

It took no little while to disentangle the mess single-handed—luckily the horses had not managed to damage themselves significantly—and his efforts were not aided by the emergence from the coach of two agitated and very disheveled women carrying on in an incomprehensible mix of French and Ladino.

Just as well, he thought, giving them a vague wave of a hand he could ill-spare at the moment. *It wouldna help to hear what they're saying.* Then he picked up the word "dead," and changed his mind. Monsieur Peretz was normally so silent that Ian had in fact forgotten his presence in the confusion of the moment. He was even more silent now, Ian learned, having broken his neck when the coach overturned.

"Oh, Jesus," he said, running to look. But the man was undeniably dead, and the horses were still creating a ruckus, slipping and stamping in the mud of the ditch. He was too busy for a bit to worry about how Jamie was faring, but as he got the second horse detached from the coach and safely tethered to a tree, he did begin to wonder where the wean was.

He didn't think it safe to leave the women; the banditti might come back, and a right numpty he'd look if they did. There was no sign of their driver, who had evidently abandoned them out of fright. He told the ladies to sit down under a sycamore tree and gave them his canteen to drink from, and after a bit, they stopped talking quite so fast.

"Where is Diego?" Rebekah said, quite intelligibly.

"Och, he'll be along presently," Ian said, hoping it was true. He was beginning to be worrit himself.

"Perhaps he's been killed, too," said the maidservant, who shot an ill-tempered glare at her mistress. "How would you feel then?"

"I'm sure he wouldn't—I mean, he's not. I'm sure," Rebekah repeated, not sounding all that sure.

She was right, though; no sooner had Ian decided to march the women back along the road to have a keek, when Jamie came shambling around the bend himself, and sank down in the dry grass, closing his eyes.

"Are you all right?" Rebekah asked, bending down anxiously to look at him from under the brim of her straw traveling hat. He didn't look very peart, Ian thought.

"Aye, fine." He touched the back of his head, wincing slightly. "Just a wee dunt on the heid. The fellow who fell down in the road," he explained to Ian, closing his eyes again. "He got up again, and hit me from behind. Didna knock me clean out, but it distracted me for a wee bit, and when I got my wits back, they'd both gone—the fellow that hit me, and the one I was hittin'."

"Mmphm," said Ian, and, squatting in front of his friend, thumbed up one of Jamie's eyelids and peered intently into the bloodshot blue eye behind it. He had no idea what to look for, but he'd seen Père Renault do that, after which he usually applied leeches somewhere. As it was, both that eye and the other one looked fine to him; just as well, as he hadn't any leeches. He handed Jamie the canteen and went to look the horses over.

"Two of them are sound enough," he reported, coming back. "The light bay's lame. Did the bandits take your horse? And what about the driver?"

Jamie looked surprised.

"I forgot I had a horse," he confessed. "I dinna ken about the driver— didna see him lyin' in the road, at least." He glanced vaguely round. "Where's Monsieur Pickle?"

"Dead. Stay there, aye?"

Ian sighed, got up, and loped back down the road, where he found no sign of the driver, though he walked to and fro calling for a while. Fortunately he did find Jamie's horse, peaceably cropping grass by the verge. He rode it back and found the women on their feet, discussing something in low voices, now and then looking down the road, or standing on their toes in a vain attempt to see through the trees.

Jamie was still sitting on the ground, eyes closed—but at least upright.

"Can ye ride, man?" Ian asked softly, squatting down by his friend. To his relief, Jamie opened his eyes at once.

"Oh, aye. Ye're thinkin' we should ride into Saint-Aubaye, and send someone back to do something about the coach and Peretz?"

"What else is there to do?"

"Nothing I can think of. I dinna suppose we can take him with us." Jamie got to his feet, swaying a little, but without needing to hold on to the tree. "Can the women ride, d'ye think?"

Marie could, it turned out—at least a little. Rebekah had never been on a horse. After more discussion than Ian would have believed possible on the subject, he got the late M. Peretz decently laid out on the coach's seat with a handkerchief over his face against the flies, and the rest of them finally mounted: Jamie on his horse with the Torah scroll in its canvas wrappings bound behind his saddle—between the profanation of its being touched by a Gentile and the prospect of its being left in the coach for anyone happening by to find, the women had reluctantly allowed the former—the maid on one of the coach horses, with a makeshift pair of saddlebags made from the covers of the coach's seats, these filled with as much of the women's luggage as they could cram into them, and Ian with Rebekah on the saddle before him.

Rebekah looked like a wee dolly, but she was surprisingly solid, as he found when she put her foot in his hands and he tossed her up into the saddle. She didn't manage to swing her leg over, and instead lay across the saddle like a dead deer, waving her arms and legs in agitation. Wrestling her into an upright position, and getting himself set behind her, left him red-faced and sweating far more than dealing with the horses had.

Jamie gave him a raised eyebrow, as much jealousy as amusement in it, and he gave Jamie a squinted eye in return and put his arm round Rebekah's waist to settle her against him, hoping that he didn't stink too badly.

It was dark by the time they made it into Saint-Aubaye and found an inn that could provide them with two rooms. Ian talked to the landlord, and arranged that someone should go in the morning to retrieve

M. Peretz's body and bury it; the women weren't happy about the lack of proper preparation of the body, but as they insisted he must be buried before the next sundown, there wasn't much else to be done. Then he inspected the women's room, looked under the beds, rattled the shutters in a confident manner, and bade them good night. They looked that wee bit frazzled.

Going back to the other room, he heard a sweet chiming sound, and found Jamie on his knees, pushing the bundle that contained the Torah scroll under the single bed.

"That'll do," he said, sitting back on his heels with a sigh. He looked nearly as done up as the women, Ian thought, but didn't say so.

"I'll go and have some supper sent up," he said. "I smelled a joint roasting. Some of that, and maybe—"

"Whatever they've got," Jamie said fervently. "Bring it all."

They ate heartily, and separately, in their rooms. Jamie was beginning to feel that the second helping of tarte tatin with clotted cream had been a mistake when Rebekah came into the men's room, followed by her maid carrying a small tray with a jug on it, wisping aromatic steam. Jamie sat up straight, restraining a small cry as pain flashed through his head. Rebekah frowned at him, gull-winged brows lowering in concern.

"Your head hurts very much, Diego?"

"No, it's fine. No but a wee bang on the heid." He was sweating and his wame was wobbly, but he pressed his hands flat on the wee table and was sure he looked steady. She appeared not to think so, and came close, bending down to look searchingly into his eyes.

"I don't think so," she said. "You look . . . clammy."

"Oh. Aye?" he said, rather feebly.

"If she means ye look like a fresh-shucked clam, then aye, ye do," Ian informed him. "Shocked, ken? All pale and wet and—"

"I ken what 'clammy' means, aye?" He glowered at Ian, who gave him half a grin—damn, he must look awful; Ian was actually worried. He swallowed, looking for something witty to say in reassurance, but his gorge rose suddenly and he was obliged to shut both mouth and eyes tightly, concentrating fiercely to make it go back down.

"Tea," Rebekah was saying firmly. She took the jug from her maid and poured a cup, then folded Jamie's hands about it and, holding his hands with her own, guided the cup to his mouth. "Drink. It will help."

He drank, and it did. At least he felt less queasy at once. He recognized the taste of the tea, though he thought this cup had a few other things in it, too.

"Again." Another cup was presented; he managed to drink this one alone and, by the time it was down, felt a good bit better. His head still throbbed with his heartbeat, but the pain seemed be standing a little apart from him, somehow.

"You shouldn't be left alone for a little while," Rebekah informed him, and sat down, sweeping her skirts elegantly around her ankles. He opened his mouth to say that he wasn't alone, Ian was there—but caught Ian's eye in time and stopped.

"The bandits," she was saying to Ian, her pretty brow creased, "who do you think that they were?"

"Ah . . . well, depends. If they kent who ye were, and wanted to abduct ye, that's one thing. But could be they were no but random thieves, and saw the coach and thought they'd chance it for what they might get. Ye didna recognize any of them, did ye?"

Her eyes sprang wide. They weren't quite the color of Annalise's, Jamie thought hazily. A softer brown . . . like the breast feathers on a grouse.

"Know who I was?" she whispered. "Wanted to abduct me?" She swallowed. "You . . . think that's possible?" She gave a little shudder.

"Well, I dinna ken, of course. Here, *a nighean,* ye ought to have a wee nip of that tea, I'm thinkin'." Ian stretched out a long arm for the jug, but she moved it back, shaking her head.

"No, it's medicine—and Diego needs it. Don't you?" she said, leaning a little forward to peer earnestly into Jamie's eyes. She'd taken off the hat, but had her hair tucked up—mostly—in a lacy white cap with pink ribbon. He nodded obediently.

"Marie—bring some brandy, please. The shock . . ." She swallowed again, and wrapped her arms briefly around herself. Jamie noticed the way it pushed her breasts up, so they swelled just a little above her stays. There was a little tea left in his cup; he drank it automatically.

Marie came with the brandy, and poured a glass for Rebekah—then one for Ian, at Rebekah's gesture, and when Jamie made a small polite noise in his throat, half-filled his cup, pouring in more tea on top of it.

The taste was peculiar, but he didn't really mind. The pain had gone off to the far side of the room; he could see it sitting over there, a wee glowering sort of purple thing with a bad-tempered expression on its face. He laughed at it, and Ian frowned at him.

"What are ye giggling at?"

Jamie couldn't think how to describe the pain-beastie, so just shook his head, which proved a mistake—the pain looked suddenly gleeful and shot back into his head with a noise like tearing cloth. The room spun and he clutched the table with both hands.

"Diego!" Chairs scraped and there was a good bit of clishmaclaver that he paid no attention to. Next thing he knew, he was lying on the bed looking at the ceiling beams. One of them seemed to be twining slowly, like a vine growing.

". . . and he told the Captain that there was someone among the Jews who kent about . . ." Ian's voice was soothing, earnest and slow so Rebekah would understand him—though Jamie thought she maybe understood more than she said. The twining beam was slowly sprouting small green leaves, and he had the faint thought that this was unusual, but a great sense of tranquility had come over him and he didn't mind it a bit.

Rebekah was saying something now, her voice soft and worried, and with some effort, he turned his head to look. She was leaning over the table toward Ian, and he had both big hands wrapped round hers, reassuring her that he and Jamie would let no harm come to her.

A different face came suddenly into his view; the maid, Marie, frowning down at him. She rudely pulled back his eyelid and peered into his eye, so close he could smell the garlic on her breath. He blinked hard, and she let go with a small "Hmph!" then turned to say something to Rebekah, who replied in quick Ladino. The maid shook her head dubiously, but left the room.

Her face didn't leave with her, though. He could still see it, frowning down at him from above. It had become attached to the leafy beam, and he now realized that there was a snake up there, a serpent with a woman's head, and an apple in its mouth—that couldn't be right, surely it should be a pig?—and it came slithering down the wall and right over his chest, pressing the apple close to his face. It smelled wonderful, and he wanted to bite it, but before he could, he felt the weight of the snake change, going soft and heavy, and he arched his back a little, feeling the distinct imprint of big round breasts squashing against him. The snake's tail—she was mostly a woman now, but her backend seemed still to be snakeish—was delicately stroking the inside of his thigh.

He made a very high-pitched noise, and Ian came hurriedly to the bed.

"Are ye all right, man?"

"I—oh. Oh! Oh, Jesus, do that again."

"Do *what*—" Ian was beginning, when Rebekah appeared, putting a hand on Ian's arm.

"Don't worry," she said, looking intently at Jamie. "He's all right. The medicine—it gives men strange dreams."

"He doesna look like he's asleep," Ian said dubiously. In fact, Jamie was squirming—or thought he was squirming—on the bed, trying to persuade the lower half of the snake-woman to change, too. He *was* panting; he could hear himself.

"It's a waking dream," Rebekah said reassuringly. "Come, leave him. He'll fall quite asleep in a bit, you'll see."

Jamie didn't think he'd fallen asleep, but it was evidently some time later that he emerged from a remarkable tryst with the snake-demon—he didn't know how he knew she was a demon, but clearly she was—who had not changed her lower half, but had a very womanly mouth about her—and a number of her friends, these being small female demons who licked his ears—and other things—with great enthusiasm.

He turned his head on the pillow to allow one of these better access and saw, with no sense of surprise, Ian kissing Rebekah. The brandy bottle had fallen over, empty, and he seemed to see the wraith of its perfume rise swirling through the air like smoke, wrapping the two of them in a mist shot with rainbows.

He closed his eyes again, the better to attend to the snake-lady, who now had a number of new and interesting acquaintances. When he opened them sometime later, Ian and Rebekah were gone.

At some point, he heard Ian give a sort of strangled cry and wondered dimly what had happened, but it didn't seem important, and the thought drifted away. He slept.

He woke sometime later, feeling limp as a frostbitten cabbage leaf, but the pain in his head was gone. He just lay there for a bit, enjoying the feeling.

It was dark in the room, and it was some time before he realized from the smell of brandy that Ian was lying beside him.

Memory came back to him. It took a little time to disentangle the real memories from the memory of dreams, but he was quite sure he'd seen Ian embracing Rebekah—and her, him. What the devil had happened *then*?

Ian wasn't asleep; he could tell. His friend lay rigid as one of the tomb-figures in the crypt at St. Denis, and his breathing was rapid and shaky, as though he'd just run a mile uphill. Jamie cleared his throat, and Ian jerked as though stabbed with a brooch-pin.

"Aye, so?" he whispered, and Ian's breathing stopped abruptly. He swallowed, audibly.

"If ye breathe a word of this to your sister," he said in an impassioned whisper, "I'll stab ye in your sleep, cut off your heid, and kick it to Arles and back."

Jamie didn't want to think about his sister, and he did want to hear about Rebekah, so he merely said, "Aye. So?"

Ian made a small grunting noise, indicative of thinking how best to begin, and turned over in his plaid, facing Jamie.

"Aye, well. Ye raved a bit about the naked she-devils ye were havin' it away with, and I didna think the lass should have to be hearing that manner o' thing, so I said we should go into the other room, and—"

"Was this before or after ye started kissing her?" Jamie asked. Ian inhaled strongly through his nose.

"After," he said tersely. "And she was kissin' me back, aye?"

"Aye, I noticed that. So then . . . ?" He could feel Ian squirming slowly, like a worm on a hook, but waited. It often took Ian a moment to find words, but it was usually worth waiting for. Certainly in this instance.

He was a little shocked—and frankly envious—and he did wonder what might happen when the lass's affianced discovered she wasn't a virgin, but he supposed the man might not find out; she seemed a clever lass. It might be wise to leave D'Eglise's troop, though, and head south, just in case. . . .

"D'ye think it hurts a lot to be circumcised?" Ian asked suddenly.

"I do. How could it not?" His hand sought out his own member, protectively rubbing a thumb over the bit in question. True, it wasn't a very big bit, but . . .

"Well, they do it to wee bairns," Ian pointed out. "Canna be that bad, can it?"

"Mmphm," Jamie said, unconvinced, though fairness made him add, "Aye, well, and they did it to Christ, too."

"Aye?" Ian sounded startled. "Aye, I suppose so—I hadna thought o' that."

"Well, ye dinna think of Him bein' a Jew, do ye? But He was, to start."

There was a momentary, meditative silence before Ian spoke again.

"D'ye think Jesus ever did it? Wi' a lass, I mean, before he went to preachin'?"

"I think Père Renault's goin' to have ye for blasphemy, next thing."

Ian twitched, as though worried that the priest might be lurking in the shadows.

"Père Renault's nowhere near here, thank God."

"Aye, but ye'll need to confess yourself to him, won't ye?"

Ian shot upright, clutching his plaid around him.

"What?"

"Ye'll go to hell, else, if ye get killed," Jamie pointed out, feeling rather smug. There was moonlight through the window and he could see Ian's face, drawn in anxious thought, his deep-set eyes darting right and left from Scylla to Charybdis. Suddenly Ian turned his head toward Jamie, having spotted the possibility of an open channel between the threats of hell and Père Renault.

"I'd only go to hell if it was a mortal sin," he said. "If it's no but venial, I'd only have to spend a thousand years or so in Purgatory. That wouldna be so bad."

"Of course it's a mortal sin," Jamie said, cross. "Anybody kens fornication's a mortal sin, ye numpty."

"Aye, but . . ." Ian made a "wait a bit" gesture with one hand, deep in thought. "To be a *mortal* sin, though, ye've got the three things. Requirements, like." He put up an index finger. "It's got to be seriously wrong." Middle finger. "Ye've got to *know* it's seriously wrong." Ring finger. "And ye've got to give full consent to it. That's the way of it, aye?" He put his hand down and looked at Jamie, brows raised.

"Aye, and which part of that did ye not do? The full consent? Did she rape ye?" He was chaffing, but Ian turned his face away in a manner that gave him a sudden doubt. "Ian?"

"Noo . . ." his friend said, but it sounded doubtful, too. "It wasna like that—exactly. I meant more the seriously wrong part. I dinna think it was . . ." his voice trailed off.

Jamie flung himself over, raised on one elbow.

"Ian," he said, steel in his voice. "What did ye *do* to the lass? If ye took her maidenheid, it's seriously wrong. Especially with her betrothed. Oh—" a thought occurred to him, and he leaned a little closer, lowering his voice. "Was she no a virgin? Maybe that's different." If the lass was an out-and-out wanton, perhaps . . . She probably *did* write poetry, come to think . . .

Ian had now folded his arms on his knees and was resting his forehead on them, his voice muffled in the folds of his plaid. ". . . dinna ken . . ." emerged in a strangled croak.

Jamie reached out and dug his fingers hard into Ian's calf, making his friend unfold with a startled cry that made someone in a distant chamber shift and grunt in their sleep.

"What d'ye mean ye dinna ken? How could ye not notice?" he hissed.

"Ah . . . well . . . she . . . erm . . . she did me wi' her hand," Ian blurted. "Before I could . . . well."

"Oh." Jamie rolled onto his back, somewhat deflated in spirit, if not in flesh. His cock seemed still to want to hear the details.

"Is that seriously wrong?" Ian asked, turning his face toward Jamie again. "Or—well, I canna say I really gave full *consent* to it, because that wasna what I had in mind doing at all, but . . ."

"I think ye're headed for the Bad Place," Jamie assured him. "Ye meant to do it, whether ye managed or not. And how did it happen, come to that? Did she just . . . take hold?"

Ian let out a long, long sigh, and sank his head in his hands. He looked as though it hurt.

"Well, we kissed for a bit, and there was more brandy—lots more. She . . . er . . . she'd take a mouthful and kiss me and, er . . . put it into my mouth, and . . ."

"*Ifrinn!*"

"Will ye not say 'Hell!' like that, please? I dinna want to think about it."

"Sorry. Go on. Did she let ye feel her breasts?"

"Just a bit. She wouldna take her stays off, but I could feel her nipples through her shift—did ye say something?"

"No," Jamie said with an effort. "What then?"

"Well, she put her hand under my kilt and then pulled it out again like she'd touched a snake."

"And had she?"

"She had, aye. She was shocked. Will ye no snort like that?" he said, annoyed. "Ye'll wake the whole house. It was because it wasna circumcised."

"Oh. Is that why she wouldna . . . er . . . the regular way?"

"She didna say so, but maybe. After a bit, though, she wanted to look at it, and that's when . . . well."

"Mmphm." Naked demons versus the chance of damnation or not, Jamie thought Ian had had well the best of it this evening. A thought occurred to him. "Why did ye ask if being circumcised hurts? Ye werena thinking of doing it, were ye? For her, I mean?"

"I wouldna say the thought hadna occurred to me," Ian admitted. "I mean . . . I thought I should maybe marry her, under the circumstances. But I suppose I couldna become a Jew, even if I got up the nerve to be circumcised—my mam would tear my heid off if I did."

"No, ye're right," Jamie agreed. "She would. *And* ye'd go to Hell." The thought of the rare and delicate Rebekah churning butter in the yard of a Highland croft or waulking urine-soaked wool with her bare feet was slightly more ludicrous than the vision of Ian in a skullcap and whiskers— but not by much. "Besides, ye havena got any money, have ye?"

"A bit," Ian said thoughtfully. "Not enough to go and live in Timbuktoo, though, and I'd have to go at least that far."

Jamie sighed and stretched, easing himself. A meditative silence fell, Ian no doubt contemplating perdition, Jamie reliving the better bits of his opium dreams, but with Rebekah's face on the snake-lady. Finally he broke the silence, turning to his friend.

"So . . . was it worth the chance of goin' to Hell?"

Ian sighed long and deep once more, but it was the sigh of a man at peace with himself.

"Oh, aye."

Jamie woke at dawn, feeling altogether well, and in a much better frame of mind. Some kindly soul had brought a jug of sour ale and some bread and cheese. He refreshed himself with these as he dressed, pondering the day's work.

He'd have to collect a few men to go back and deal with the coach. He supposed the best thing to do with M. Peretz was to fetch him here *in* the coach, and then see if there were any Jews in the vicinity who might be prevailed upon to bury him—the women insisted that he ought to be buried before sundown. If not . . . well, he'd cross that road when he came to it.

He thought the coach wasn't badly damaged; they might get it back upon the road again by noon. . . . How far might it be to Bonnes? That was the next town with an inn. If it was too far, or the coach too badly hurt, or he couldn't dispose decently of M. Peretz, they'd need to stay the night here again. He fingered his purse, but thought he had enough for another night and the hire of men; the Doctor had been generous.

He was beginning to wonder what was keeping Ian and the women. Though he kent women took more time to do anything than a man would, let alone getting dressed—well, they had stays and the like to fret with, after all. . . . He sipped ale, contemplating a vision of Rebekah's stays, and the very vivid images his mind had been conjuring ever since Ian's description of his encounter with the lass. He could all but see her nipples through the thin fabric of her shift, smooth and round as pebbles. . . .

Ian burst through the door, wild-eyed, his hair standing on end.

"They're gone!"

Jamie choked on his ale.

"What? How?"

Ian understood what he meant, and was already heading for the bed.

"No one took them. There's nay sign of a struggle, and their things are gone. The window's open, and the shutters aren't broken."

Jamie was on his knees alongside Ian, thrusting first his hands and then his head and shoulders under the bed. There was a canvas-wrapped bundle there, and he was flooded with a momentary relief—which disappeared the instant Ian dragged it into the light. It made a noise, but not the gentle chime of golden bells. It rattled, and when Jamie seized the corner of the canvas and unrolled it, the contents were shown to be nought but sticks and stones, these hastily wrapped in a woman's petticoat to give the bundle the appropriate bulk.

"*Cramouille!*" he said, this being the worst word he could think of on short notice. And very appropriate, too, if what he thought had happened really had. He turned on Ian.

"She drugged me and seduced you, and her bloody maid stole in here and took the thing whilst ye had your fat heid buried in her . . . er . . ."

"Charms," Ian said succinctly, and flashed him a brief, evil grin. "Ye're only jealous. Where d'ye think they've gone?"

It was the truth, and Jamie abandoned any further recriminations, rising and strapping on his belt, hastily arranging dirk, sword, and ax in the process.

"Not to Paris, would be my guess. Come on, we'll ask the ostler."

The ostler confessed himself at a loss; he'd been the worse for drink in the hay shed, he said, and if someone had taken two horses from the shelter, he hadn't waked to see it.

"Aye, right," said Jamie, impatient, and, grabbing the man's shirtfront, lifted him off his feet and slammed him into the inn's stone wall. The man's head bounced once off the stones and he sagged in Jamie's grip, still conscious but dazed. Jamie drew his dirk left-handed and pressed the edge of it against the man's weathered throat.

"Try again," he suggested pleasantly. "I dinna care about the money they gave ye—keep it. I want to know which way they went, and when they left."

The man tried to swallow, and abandoned the attempt when his Adam's apple hit the edge of the dirk.

"About three hours past moonrise," he croaked. "They went toward Bonnes. There's a crossroads no more than three miles from here," he added, now trying urgently to be helpful.

Jamie dropped him with a grunt.

"Aye, fine," he said in disgust. "Ian—oh, ye've got them." For Ian had gone straight for their own horses while he dealt with the ostler, and was already leading one out, bridled, the saddle over his arm. "I'll settle the bill, then."

The women hadn't made off with his purse, that was something. Either Rebekah bat-Leah Hauberger had some vestige of conscience—which he doubted very much—or she just hadn't thought of it.

It was just past dawn; the women had perhaps six hours' lead.

"Do we believe the ostler?" Ian asked, settling himself in the saddle.

Jamie dug in his purse, pulled out a copper penny and flipped it, catching it on the back of his hand.

"Tails we do, heads we don't?" He took his hand away and peered at the coin. "Heads."

"Aye, but the road back is straight all the way through Yvrac," Ian pointed out. "And it's nay more than three miles to the crossroads, he said. Whatever ye want to say about the lass, she's no a fool."

Jamie considered that one for a moment, then nodded. Rebekah couldn't have been sure how much lead she'd have—and unless she'd been lying about her ability to ride (which he wouldn't put past her, but such things weren't easy to fake and she was gey clumsy in the saddle), she'd want to reach a place where the trail could be lost before her pursuers could catch up with her. Besides, the ground was still damp with dew; there might be a chance. . . .

"Aye, come on, then."

Luck was with them. No one had passed the inn during the late night watches, and while the roadbed was trampled with hoof marks, the recent prints of the women's horses showed clear, edges still crumbling in the damp earth. Once sure they'd got upon the track, the men galloped for the crossroads, hoping to reach it before other travelers obscured the marks.

No such luck. Farm wagons were already on the move, loaded with produce headed for Parcoul or La Roche-Chalais, and the crossroads was a maze of ruts and hoofprints. But Jamie had the bright thought of sending Ian down the road that lay toward Parcoul, while he took the one toward La Roche-Chalais, catching up the incoming wagons and questioning the drivers. Within an hour, Ian came pelting back with the news that the women had been seen, riding slowly and cursing volubly at each other, toward Parcoul.

"And *that*," he said, panting for breath, "is not all."

"Aye? Well, tell me while we ride."

Ian did. He'd been hurrying back to find Jamie, when he'd met Josef-from-Alsace just short of the crossroads, come in search of them.

"D'Eglise was held up near Poitiers," Ian reported in a shout. "The same band of men that attacked us at Marmande—Alexandre and Raoul both recognized some of them. Jewish bandits."

Jamie was shocked, and slowed for a moment to let Ian catch him up.

"Did they get the dowry money?"

"No, but they had a hard fight. Three men wounded badly enough to need a surgeon, and Paul Martan lost two fingers of his left hand. D'Eglise pulled them into Poitiers, and sent Josef to see if all was well wi' us."

Jamie's heart bounced into his throat. "Jesus. Did ye tell him what happened?"

"I did not," Ian said tersely. "I told him we'd had an accident wi' the coach, and ye'd gone ahead with the women; I was comin' back to fetch something left behind."

"Aye, good." Jamie's heart dropped back into his chest. The last thing he wanted was to have to tell the Captain that they'd lost the girl and the Torah scroll. And he'd be damned if he would.

They traveled fast, stopping only to ask questions now and then, and by the time they pounded into the village of Aubeterre-sur-Dronne, were sure that their quarry lay no more than an hour ahead of them—if the women had passed on through the village.

"Oh, those two?" said a woman, pausing in the act of scrubbing her steps. She stood up slowly, stretching her back. "I saw them, yes. They rode right by me, and went down the lane there." She pointed.

"I thank you, madame," Jamie said, in his best Parisian French. "What lies down that lane, please?"

She looked surprised that they didn't know, and frowned a little at such ignorance.

"Why, the chateau of the Vicomte Beaumont, to be sure!"

"To be sure," Jamie repeated, smiling at her, and Ian saw a dimple appear in her cheek in reply. *Merci beaucoup, madame!*

"What the devil . . . ?" Ian murmured. Jamie reined up beside him, pausing to look at the place. It was a small manor house, somewhat run-down, but pretty in its bones. And the last place anyone would think to look for a runaway Jewess, he'd say that for it.

"What shall we do now, d'ye think?" he asked, and Jamie shrugged and kicked his horse.

"Go knock on the door and ask, I suppose."

Ian followed his friend up to the door, feeling intensely conscious of his grubby clothes, sprouting beard, and general state of uncouthness. Such concerns vanished, though, when Jamie's forceful knock was answered.

"Good day, gentlemen!" said the yellow-haired bugger he'd last seen locked in combat in the roadbed with Jamie the day before. The man smiled broadly at them, cheerful despite an obvious black eye and a freshly split lip. He was dressed in the height of fashion, in a plum velvet suit, his hair was curled and powdered, and his yellow beard was neatly trimmed. "I hoped we would see you again. Welcome to my home!" he said, stepping back and raising his hand in a gesture of invitation.

"I thank you, Monsieur . . . ?" Jamie said slowly, giving Ian a sidelong glance. Ian lifted one shoulder in the ghost of a shrug. Did they have a choice?

The yellow-haired bugger bowed. "Pierre Robert Heriveaux d'Anton, Vicomte Beaumont, by the grace of the Almighty, for one more day. And you, gentlemen?"

"James Alexander Malcolm MacKenzie Fraser," Jamie said, with a good attempt at matching the other's grand manner. Only Ian would have noticed the faint hesitation, or the slight tremor in his voice when he added, "Laird of Broch Tuarach."

"Ian Alastair Robert MacLeod Murray," Ian said, with a curt nod, and straightened his shoulders. "His . . . er . . . the laird's . . . tacksman."

"Come in, please, gentlemen." The yellow-haired bugger's eyes shifted just a little, and Ian heard the crunch of gravel behind them, an instant before he felt the prick of a dagger in the small of his back. No, they didn't have a choice.

Inside, they were relieved of their weapons, then escorted down a wide hallway and into a commodious parlor. The wallpaper was faded, and the furniture was good but shabby. By contrast, the big Turkey carpet on the floor glowed like it was woven from jewels. A big roundish thing in the middle was green and gold and red, and concentric circles with wiggly edges surrounded it in waves of blue and red and cream, bordered in a soft, deep red, and the whole of it so ornamented with unusual shapes it would take you a day to look at them all. He'd been so taken with it the first time he saw it he'd spent a quarter of an hour looking at the shapes before Big Georges caught him at it and shouted at him to roll the thing up, they hadn't all day.

"Where did ye get this?" Ian asked abruptly, interrupting something the Vicomte was saying to the two rough-clad men who'd taken their weapons.

"What? Oh, the carpet! Yes, isn't it wonderful?" The Vicomte beamed at him, quite unself-conscious, and gestured the two roughs away toward the wall. "It's part of my wife's dowry."

"Your wife," Jamie repeated carefully. He darted a sideways glance at Ian, who took the cue.

"That would be Mademoiselle Hauberger, would it?" he asked. The Vicomte blushed—actually blushed—and Ian realized that the man was no older than he and Jamie were.

"Well. It—we—we have been betrothed for some time, and in Jewish custom, that is almost like being married."

"Betrothed," Jamie echoed again. "Since . . . when, exactly?"

The Vicomte sucked in his lower lip, contemplating them. But whatever caution he might have had was overwhelmed in what were plainly very high spirits.

"Four years," he said. And unable to contain himself, he beckoned them to a table near the window, and proudly showed them a fancy document, covered with colored scrolly sorts of things and written in some very odd language that was all slashes and tilted lines.

"This is our ketubah," he said, pronouncing the word very carefully. "Our marriage contract."

Jamie bent over to peer closely at it.

"Aye, verra nice," he said politely. "I see it's no been signed yet. The marriage hasna taken place, then?" Ian saw Jamie's eyes flick over the desk, and could see him passing the possibilities through his mind: Grab the letter opener off the desk and take the Vicomte hostage? Then find the sly wee bitch, roll her up in one of the smaller rugs, and carry her to Paris? That would doubtless be Ian's job, he thought.

A slight movement as one of the roughs shifted his weight caught Ian's eye and he thought, *Don't do it, eejit!* at Jamie, as hard as he could. For once, the message seemed to get through; Jamie's shoulders relaxed a little and he straightened up.

"Ye do ken the lass is meant to be marrying someone else?" he asked baldly. "I wouldna put it past her not to tell ye."

The Vicomte's color became higher.

"Certainly I know!" he snapped. "She was promised to me first, by her father!"

"How long have ye been a Jew?" Jamie asked carefully, edging round the table. "I dinna think ye were born to it. I mean—ye *are* a Jew, now, aye? For I kent one or two, in Paris, and it's my understanding that they dinna marry people who aren't Jewish." His eyes flicked round the solid, handsome room. "It's my understanding that they mostly aren't aristocrats, either."

The Vicomte was quite red in the face by now. With a sharp word, he sent the roughs out—though they were disposed to argue. While the brief discussion was going on, Ian edged closer to Jamie and whispered rapidly to him about the rug in *Gàidhlig*.

"Holy God," Jamie muttered in the same language. "I didna see him or either of those two at Marmande, did you?"

Ian had no time to reply and merely shook his head, as the roughs reluctantly acquiesced to Vicomte Pierre's imperious orders and shuffled out with narrowed eyes aimed at Ian and Jamie. One of them had Jamie's dirk in his hand, and drew this slowly across his neck in a meaningful gesture as he left.

Aye, they might manage in a fight, he thought, returning the slit-eyed glare, *but not that wee velvet gomerel.* Captain D'Eglise wouldn't have taken on the Vicomte, and neither would a band of professional highwaymen, Jewish or not.

"All right," the Vicomte said abruptly, leaning his fists on the desk. "I'll tell you."

And he did. Rebekah's mother, the daughter of Dr. Hasdi, had fallen in love with a Christian man, and run away with him. The Doctor had declared his daughter dead, as was the usual way in such a situation, and done formal mourning for her. But she was his only child, and he had not been able to forget her. He had arranged to have information brought to him, and knew about Rebekah's birth.

"Then her mother died. That's when I met her—about that time, I mean. Her father was a judge, and my father knew him. She was fourteen and I sixteen; I fell in love with her. And she with me," he added, giving the Scots a hard eye, as though daring them to disbelieve it. "We were betrothed, with her father's blessing. But then her father caught a flux and died in two days. And—"

"And her grandfather took her back," Jamie finished. "And she became a Jew?"

"By Jewish belief, she was born Jewish; it descends through the mother's line. And . . . her mother had told her, privately, about her lost heritage. She embraced it, once she went to live with her grandfather."

Ian stirred, and cocked a cynical eyebrow. "Aye? Why did ye not convert then, if ye're willing to do it now?"

"I said I would!" The Vicomte had one fist curled round his letter opener as though he would strangle it. "The miserable old wretch said he did not believe me. He thought I would not give up my—my—this life." He waved a hand dismissively around the room, encompassing, presumably, his title and property, both of which would be confiscated by the government the moment his conversion became known.

"He said it would be a sham conversion and the moment I had her, I would become a Christian again, and force Rebekah to be Christian, too. Like her father," he added darkly.

Despite the situation, Ian was beginning to have some sympathy for the wee popinjay. It was a very romantic tale, and he was partial to those. Jamie, however, was still reserving judgment. He gestured at the rug beneath their feet.

"Her dowry, ye said?"

"Yes," said the Vicomte, but sounded much less certain. "She says it belonged to her mother. She had some men bring it here last week, along with a chest and a few other things. Anyway," he said, resuming his self-confidence and glowering at them, "when the old beast arranged her marriage to that fellow in Paris, I made up my mind to—to—"

"To abduct her. By arrangement, aye? Mmphm," Jamie said, making a noise indicating his opinion of the Vicomte's skills as a highwayman. He raised one red brow at Pierre's black eye, but forbore to make any more remarks, thank God. It hadn't escaped Ian that they were prisoners, though it maybe had Jamie.

"May we speak with Mademoiselle Hauberger?" Ian asked politely. "Just to make sure she's come of her own free will, aye?"

"Rather plainly, she did, since you followed her here." The Vicomte hadn't liked Jamie's noise. "No, you may not. She's busy." He raised his hands and clapped them sharply, and the rough fellows came back in, along with a half-dozen or so male servants as reinforcement, led by a tall, severe-looking butler, armed with a stout walking-stick.

"Go with Ecrivisse, gentlemen. He'll see to your comfort."

"Comfort" proved to be the chateau's wine cellar, which was fragrant, but cold. Also dark. The Vicomte's hospitality did not extend so far as a candle.

"If he meant to kill us, he'd have done it already," Ian reasoned.

"Mmphm." Jamie sat on the stairs, the fold of his plaid pulled up around his shoulders against the chill. There was music coming from somewhere outside: the faint sound of a fiddle and the tap of a little hand drum. It started, then stopped, then started again.

Ian wandered restlessly to and fro; it wasn't a very large cellar. If he didn't mean to kill them, what did the Vicomte mean to do with them?

"He's waiting for something to happen," Jamie said suddenly, answering the thought. "Something to do wi' the lass, I expect."

"Aye, reckon." Ian sat down on the stairs, nudging Jamie over. "*A Dhia,* that's cold!"

"Mm," said Jamie absently. "Maybe they mean to run. If so, I hope he leaves someone behind to let us out, and doesna mean to leave us here to starve."

"We wouldna starve," Ian pointed out logically. "We could live on wine for a good long time. Someone would come, before it ran out." He paused a moment, trying to imagine what it would be like to stay drunk for several weeks.

"That's a thought." Jamie got up, a little stiff from the cold, and went off to rummage the racks. There was no light to speak of, save what seeped through the crack at the bottom of the door to the cellar, but Ian could hear Jamie pulling out bottles and sniffing the corks.

He came back in a bit with a bottle and, sitting down again, drew the cork with his teeth and spat it to one side. He took a sip, then another, then tilted back the bottle for a generous swig, and handed it to Ian.

"No bad," he said.

It wasn't, and there wasn't much conversation for the next little while.

Eventually, though, Jamie set the empty bottle down, belched gently, and said, "It's her."

"What's her? Rebekah, ye mean. I daresay." Then after a moment, "What's her?"

"It's her," Jamie repeated. "Ken what the Jew said—Ephraim bar-Sefer? About how his gang knew where to strike, because they got information from some outside source? It's her. She told them."

Jamie spoke with such certainty that Ian was staggered for a moment, but then marshaled his wits.

"That wee lass? Granted, she put one over on us—and I suppose she at least kent about Pierre's abduction, but . . ."

Jamie snorted.

"Aye, Pierre. Does the mannie strike ye either as a criminal or a great schemer?"

"No, but—"

"Does she?"

"Well . . ."

"Exactly."

Jamie got up and wandered off into the racks again, this time returning with what smelled to Ian like one of the very good local red wines. It was like drinking his mam's strawberry preserves on toast with a cup of strong tea, he thought approvingly.

"Besides," Jamie went on, as though there'd been no interruption in his train of thought, "d'ye recall what the maid said to her? When I got my heid half-stove in? 'Perhaps he's been killed. How would you feel then?' Nay, she'd planned the whole thing—to have Pierre and his lads stop the coach and make away with the women and the scroll, and doubtless Monsieur Pickle, too. *But*—" he added, sticking up a finger in front of Ian's face to stop him interrupting, "then Josef-from-Alsace tells ye that thieves—and the *same* thieves as before, or some of them—attacked the band wi' the dowry money. Ye ken well, that canna have been Pierre. It had to be her who told them."

Ian was forced to admit the logic of this. Pierre had enthusiasm, but couldn't possibly be considered a professional highwayman.

"But a lass . . ." he said, helplessly. "How could she—"

Jamie grunted.

"D'Eglise said Doctor Hasdi's a man much respected among the Jews of Bordeaux. And plainly he's kent as far as Paris, or how else did he make the match for his granddaughter? But he doesna speak French. Want to bet me that she didna manage his correspondence?"

"No," Ian said, and took another swallow. "Mmphm."

Some minutes later, he said, "That rug. And the other things Monsieur le Vicomte mentioned—her *dowry*."

Jamie made an approving noise.

"Aye. Her percentage of the take, more like. Ye can see our lad Pierre hasna got much money, and he'd lose all his property when he converted. She was feathering their nest, like—makin' sure they'd have enough to live on. Enough to live *well* on."

"Well, then," Ian said, after a moment's silence. "There ye are."

The afternoon dragged on. After the second bottle, they agreed to drink no more for the time being, in case a clear head should be necessary if or when the door at last opened, and aside from going off now and then to have a pee behind the farthest wine racks, they stayed huddled on the stairs.

Jamie was singing softly along to the fiddle's distant tune when the door finally *did* open. He stopped abruptly, and lunged awkwardly to his feet, nearly falling, his knees stiff with cold.

"Monsieurs?" said the butler, peering down at them. "If you will be so kind as to follow me, please?"

To their surprise, the butler led them straight out of the house, and down a small path, in the direction of the distant music. The air outside was fresh and wonderful after the must of the cellar, and Jamie filled his lungs with it, wondering what the devil . . . ?

Then they rounded a bend in the path and saw a garden court before them, lit by torches driven into the ground. Somewhat overgrown, but with a fountain tinkling away in the center—and just by the fountain, a sort of canopy, its cloth glimmering pale in the dusk. There was a little knot of people standing near it, talking, and as the butler paused, holding them back with one hand, Vicomte Pierre broke away from the group and came toward them, smiling.

"My apologies for the inconvenience, gentlemen," he said, a huge smile splitting his face. He looked drunk, but Jamie thought he wasn't—no smell of spirits. "Rebekah had to prepare herself. And we wanted to wait for nightfall."

"To do what?" Ian asked suspiciously, and the Vicomte giggled. Jamie didn't mean to wrong the man, but it was a giggle. He gave Ian an eye and Ian gave it back. Aye, it was a giggle.

"To be married," Pierre said, and while his voice was still full of joie de vivre, he said the words with a sense of deep reverence that struck Jamie somewhere in the chest. Pierre turned and waved a hand toward the darkening sky, where the stars were beginning to prick and sparkle. "For luck, you know—that our descendants may be as numerous as the stars."

"Mmphm," Jamie said politely.

"But come with me, if you will." Pierre was already striding back to the knot of . . . well, Jamie supposed they must be wedding guests . . . beckoning to the Scots to follow.

Marie the maid was there, along with a few other women; she gave Jamie and Ian a wary look. But it was the men with whom the Vicomte was concerned. He spoke a few words to his guests, and three men came back with him, all dressed formally, if somewhat oddly, with little velvet skullcaps decorated with beads, and enormous beards.

"May I present Monsieur Gershom Ackerman, and Monsieur Levi Champfleur. Our witnesses. And Reb Cohen, who will officiate."

The men shook hands, murmuring politeness. Jamie and Ian exchanged looks. Why were *they* here?

The Vicomte caught the look and interpreted it correctly.

"I wish you to return to Doctor Hasdi," he said, the effervescence in his voice momentarily supplanted by a note of steel. "And tell him that everything—everything!—was done in accordance with proper custom and according to the Law. This marriage will not be undone. By anyone."

"Mmphm," said Ian, less politely.

And so it was that a few minutes later they found themselves standing among the male wedding guests—the women stood on the other side of the canopy—watching as Rebekah came down the path, jingling faintly. She wore a dress of deep red silk; Jamie could see the torchlight shift and shimmer through its folds as she moved. There were gold bracelets on both wrists, and she had a veil over her head and face, with a little headdress sort of thing made of gold chains that dipped across her forehead, strung with little medallions and bells—it was this that made the jingling sound. It reminded him of the Torah scroll, and he stiffened a little at the thought.

Pierre stood with the rabbi under the canopy; as she approached, he stepped apart, and she came to him. She didn't touch him, though, but proceeded to walk round him. And round him, and round him. Seven times she circled him, and the hairs rose a little on the back of Jamie's neck; it had the faint sense of magic about it—or witchcraft. Something she did, binding the man.

She came face-to-face with Jamie as she made each turn and plainly could see him in the light of the torches, but her eyes were fixed straight ahead; she made no acknowledgment of anyone—not even Pierre.

But then the circling was done and she came to stand by his side. The rabbi said a few words of welcome to the guests, and then, turning to the bride and groom, poured out a cup of wine and said what appeared to be a Hebrew blessing over it. Jamie made out the beginning, "Blessed are you, Adonai our God . . ." but then lost the thread.

Pierre reached into his pocket when Reb Cohen stopped speaking, took out a small object—clearly a ring—and, taking Rebekah's hand in his, put it on the forefinger of her right hand, smiling down into her face with a tenderness that, despite everything, rather caught at Jamie's heart. Then Pierre lifted her veil, and he caught a glimpse of the answering tenderness on Rebekah's face in the instant before her husband kissed her.

The congregation sighed as one.

The rabbi picked up a sheet of parchment from a little table nearby. The thing Pierre had called a ketubah, Jamie saw—the wedding contract.

The rabbi read the thing out, first in a language Jamie didn't recognize, and then again in French. It wasn't so different from the few marriage contracts he'd seen, laying out the disposition of property and what was due to the bride and all . . . though he noted with disapproval that it provided for the possibility of divorce. His attention wandered a bit then; Rebekah's face glowed in the torchlight like pearl and ivory, and the roundness of her bosom showed clearly as she breathed. In spite of everything he thought he now knew about her, he experienced a brief wave of envy toward Pierre.

The contract read and carefully laid aside, the rabbi recited a string of blessings; he kent it was blessings because he caught the words "Blessed are you, Adonai . . ." over and over, though the subject of the blessings seemed to be everything from the congregation to Jerusalem, so far as he could tell. The bride and groom had another sip of wine.

A pause then, and Jamie expected some official word from the rabbi, uniting husband and wife, but it didn't come. Instead, one of the witnesses took the wineglass, wrapped it in a linen napkin, and placed it on the ground in front of Pierre. To the Scots' astonishment, he promptly stamped on the thing—and the crowd burst into applause.

For a few moments, everything seemed quite like a country wedding, with everyone crowding round, wanting to congratulate the happy couple. But within moments, the happy couple was moving off toward the house, while the guests all streamed toward tables that had been set up at the far side of the garden, laden with food and drink.

"Come on," Jamie muttered, and caught Ian by the arm. They hastened after the newly wedded pair, Ian demanding to know what the devil Jamie thought he was doing.

"I want to talk to her—alone. You stop him, keep him talking for as long as ye can."

"I—how?"

"How would I know? Ye'll think of something." They had reached the house and, ducking in close upon Pierre's heels, Jamie saw that, by good luck, the man had stopped to say something to a servant. Rebekah was just vanishing down a long hallway; he saw her put her hand to a door.

"The best of luck to ye, man!" he said, clapping Pierre so heartily on the shoulder that the groom staggered. Before he could recover, Ian, very obviously commending his soul to God, stepped up and seized him by the hand, which he wrang vigorously, meanwhile giving Jamie a private *Hurry the bloody hell* up! sort of look.

Grinning, Jamie ran down the short hallway to the door where he'd seen Rebekah disappear. The grin disappeared as his hand touched the doorknob, though, and the face he presented to her as he entered was as grim as he could make it.

Her eyes widened in shock and indignation at sight of him.

"What are you doing here? No one is supposed to come in here but me and my husband!"

"He's on his way," Jamie assured her. "The question is—will he get here?"

Her little fist curled up in a way that would have been comical, if he didn't know as much about her as he did.

"Is that a threat?" she said, in a tone as incredulous as it was menacing. "Here? You dare threaten me *here*?"

"Aye, I do. I want that scroll."

"Well, you're not getting it," she snapped. He saw her glance flicker over the table, probably in search either of a bell to summon help, or something to bash him on the head with, but the table held nothing but a platter of stuffed rolls and exotic sweeties. There *was* a bottle of wine, and he saw her eyes light on that with calculation, but he stretched out a long arm and got hold of it before she could.

"I dinna want it for myself," he said. "I mean to take it back to your grandfather."

"Him?" Her face hardened. "No. It's worth more to him than *I* am," she added bitterly, "but at least that means I can use it for protection. As long as I have it, he won't try to hurt Pierre or drag me back, for fear I might damage it. I'm keeping it."

"I think he'd be a great deal better off without ye, and doubtless he kens that fine," Jamie informed her, and had to harden himself against the sudden look of hurt in her eyes. He supposed even spiders might have feelings, but that was neither here nor there.

"Where's Pierre?" she demanded, rising to her feet. "If you've harmed a hair on his head, I'll—"

"I wouldna touch the poor gomerel and neither would Ian—Juan, I mean. When I said the question was whether he got to ye or not, I meant whether he thinks better of his bargain."

"What?" He thought she paled a little, but it was hard to tell.

"You give me the scroll to take back to your grandfather—a wee letter of apology to go with it wouldna come amiss, but I willna insist on that—or Ian and I take Pierre out back and have a frank word regarding his new wife."

"Tell him what you like!" she snapped. "He wouldn't believe any of your made-up tales!"

"Oh, aye? And if I tell him exactly what happened to Ephraim bar-Sefer? And why?"

"Who?" she said, but now she really had gone pale to the lips, and put out a hand to the table to steady herself.

"Do ye ken yourself what happened to him? No? Well, I'll tell ye, lass." And he did so, with a terse brutality that made her sit down suddenly, tiny pearls of sweat appearing round the gold medallions that hung across her forehead.

"Pierre already kens at least a bit about your wee gang, I think—but maybe not what a ruthless, grasping wee besom ye really are."

"It wasn't me! I didn't kill him!"

"If not for you, he'd no be dead, and I reckon Pierre would see that. I can tell him where the body is," he added, more delicately. "I buried the man myself."

Her lips were pressed so hard together that nothing showed but a straight white line.

"Ye havena got long," he said, quietly now, but keeping his eyes on hers. "Ian canna hold him off much longer, and if he comes in—then I tell him everything, in front of you, and ye do what ye can then to persuade him I'm a liar."

She stood up abruptly, her chains and bracelets all a-jangle, and stamped to the door of the inner room. She flung it open, and Marie jerked back, shocked.

Rebekah said something to her in Ladino, sharp, and with a small gasp, the maid scurried off.

"All *right*," Rebekah said through gritted teeth, turning back to him. "Take it and be damned, you *dog*."

"Indeed I will, ye bloody wee bitch," he replied with great politeness. Her hand closed round a stuffed roll, but instead of throwing it at him, she merely squeezed it into paste and crumbs, slapping the remains back on the tray with a small exclamation of fury.

The sweet chiming of the Torah scroll presaged Marie's hasty arrival, the precious thing clasped in her arms. She glanced at her mistress and, at Rebekah's curt nod, delivered it with great reluctance into the arms of the Christian dog.

Jamie bowed, first to maid and then mistress, and backed toward the door.

"Shalom," he said, and closed the door an instant before the silver platter hit it with a ringing thud.

———

"Did it hurt a lot?" Ian was asking Pierre with interest when Jamie came up to them.

"My God, you have no idea," Pierre replied fervently. "But it was worth it." He divided a beaming smile between Ian and Jamie and bowed to them, not even noticing the canvas-wrapped bundle in Jamie's arms. "You must excuse me, gentlemen; my bride awaits me!"

"Did what hurt a lot?" Jamie inquired, leading the way hastily out through a side door. No point in attracting attention, after all.

"Ye ken he was born a Christian, but converted in order to marry the wee besom," Ian said. "So he had to be circumcised." He crossed himself at the thought, and Jamie laughed.

"What is it they call the stick-insect things where the female one bites off the head of the male one after he's got the business started?" he asked, nudging the door open with his bum.

Ian's brow creased for an instant.

"Praying mantis, I think. Why?"

"I think our wee friend Pierre may have a more interesting wedding night than he expects. Come on."

Bordeaux

It wasn't the worst thing he'd ever had to do, but he wasn't looking forward to it. Jamie paused outside the gate of Dr. Hasdi's house, the Torah scroll in its wrappings in his arms. Ian was looking a bit worm-eaten, and Jamie reckoned he kent why. Having to tell the Doctor what had happened to his granddaughter was one thing; telling him to his face with the knowledge of what said granddaughter's nipples felt like fresh in the mind . . . or the hand . . .

"Ye dinna have to come in, man," he said to Ian. "I can do it alone."

Ian's mouth twitched, but he shook his head and stepped up next to Jamie.

"On your right, man," he said, simply. Jamie smiled. When he'd been five years old, Ian's da, Auld John, had persuaded his own da to let Jamie handle a sword cack-handed, as he was wont to do. "And you, lad," he'd said to Ian, very serious, "it's your duty to stand on your laird's right hand, and guard his weak side."

"Aye," Jamie said. "Right, then." And rang the bell.

Afterward, they wandered slowly through the streets of Bordeaux, making their way toward nothing in particular, not speaking much.

Dr. Hasdi had received them courteously, though with a look of mingled horror and apprehension on his face when he saw the scroll. This look had faded to one of relief at hearing—the manservant had had enough French to interpret for them—that his granddaughter was safe, then to shock, and finally to a set expression that Jamie couldn't read. Was it anger, sadness, resignation?

When Jamie had finished the story, they sat uneasily, not sure what to do next. Dr. Hasdi sat at his desk, head bowed, his hands resting gently on the scroll. Finally, he raised his head, and nodded to them both, one and then the other. His face was calm now, giving nothing away.

"Thank you," he said in heavily accented French. "Shalom."

"Are ye hungry?" Ian motioned toward a small *boulangerie* whose trays bore filled rolls and big, fragrant round loaves. He was starving himself, though half an hour ago, his wame had been in knots.

"Aye, maybe." Jamie kept walking, though, and Ian shrugged and followed.

"What d'ye think the Captain will do when we tell him?" Ian wasn't all that bothered. There was always work for a good-sized man who kent what to do with a sword. And he owned his own weapons. They'd have to buy Jamie a sword, though. Everything he was wearing, from pistols to ax, belonged to D'Eglise.

He was busy enough calculating the cost of a decent sword against what remained of their pay that he didn't notice Jamie not answering him. He did notice that his friend was walking faster, though, and, hurrying to catch up, he saw what they were heading for. The tavern where the pretty brown-haired barmaid had taken Jamie for a Jew.

Oh, like that, is it? he thought, and hid a grin. Aye, well, there was one sure way the lad could prove to the lass that he wasn't a Jew.

The place was moiling when they walked in, and not in a good way; Ian sensed it instantly. There were soldiers there, army soldiers and other fighting-men, mercenaries like themselves, and no love wasted between them. You could cut the air with a knife, and judging from a splotch of half-dried blood on the floor, somebody had already tried.

There were women, but fewer than before, and the barmaids kept their eyes on their trays, not flirting tonight.

Jamie wasn't taking heed of the atmosphere; Ian could see him looking round for her; the brown-haired lass wasn't on the floor. They might have asked after her—if they'd known her name.

"Upstairs, maybe?" Ian said, leaning in to half-shout into Jamie's ear over the noise. Jamie nodded and began forging through the crowd, Ian bobbing in his wake, hoping they found the lass quickly so he could eat whilst Jamie got on with it.

The stairs were crowded—with men coming down. Something was amiss up there, and Jamie shoved someone into the wall with a thump, pushing past. Some nameless anxiety shot jolted down his spine, and he was half-prepared before he pushed through a little knot of onlookers at the head of the stairs and saw them.

Big Mathieu, and the brown-haired girl. There was a big open room here, with a hallway lined with tiny cubicles leading back from it; Mathieu had the girl by the arm and was boosting her toward the hallway with a hand on her bum, despite her protests.

"Let go of her!" Jamie said, not shouting, but raising his voice well enough to be heard easily. Mathieu paid not the least attention, though everyone else turned to look at Jamie, startled.

He heard Ian mutter, "Joseph, Mary and Bride preserve us," behind him, but paid no heed. He covered the distance to Mathieu in three strides, and kicked him in the arse.

He ducked, by reflex, but Mathieu merely turned and gave him a hot eye, ignoring the whoops and guffaws from the spectators.

"Later, little boy," he said. "I'm busy now."

He scooped the young woman into one big arm and kissed her sloppily, rubbing his stubbled face hard over hers, so she squealed and pushed at him to get away.

Jamie drew the pistol from his belt.

"I said, let her go." The noise dropped suddenly, but he barely noticed for the roaring of blood in his ears.

Mathieu turned his head, incredulous. Then he snorted with contempt, grinned unpleasantly and shoved the girl into the wall so her head struck with a thump, pinning her there with his bulk.

The pistol was primed.

"*Salop!*" Jamie roared. "Don't touch her! Let her go!" He clenched his teeth and aimed with both hands, rage and fright making his hands tremble.

Mathieu didn't even look at him. The big man half turned away, a casual hand on her breast. She squealed as he twisted it, and Jamie fired. Mathieu whirled, the pistol he'd had concealed in his own belt now in hand, and the air shattered in an explosion of sound and white smoke.

There were shouts of alarm, excitement—and another pistol went off, somewhere behind Jamie. *Ian?* he thought dimly, but no, Ian was running toward Mathieu, leaping for the massive arm rising, the second pistol's barrel making circles as Mathieu struggled to fix it on Jamie. It discharged, and the ball hit one of the lanterns that stood on the tables, which exploded with a *whuff* and a bloom of flame.

Jamie had reversed his pistol and was hammering at Mathieu's head with the butt before he was conscious of having crossed the room. Mathieu's mad-boar eyes were almost invisible, slitted with the glee of fighting, and the sudden curtain of blood that fell over his face did nothing but enhance his grin, blood running down between his teeth. He shook Ian off with a shove that sent him crashing into the wall, then wrapped one big arm almost casually around Jamie's body and, with a snap of his head, butted him in the face.

Jamie had turned his head reflexively and thus avoided a broken nose, but the impact crushed the flesh of his jaw into his teeth and his mouth filled with blood. His head was spinning with the force of the blow, but he got a hand under Mathieu's jaw and shoved upward with all his strength, trying to break the man's neck. His hand slipped off the sweat-greased flesh, though, and Mathieu let go his grip in order to try to knee Jamie in the stones. A knee like a cannonball struck him a numbing blow in the thigh as he squirmed free, and he staggered, grabbing Mathieu's arm just as Ian came dodging in from the side, seizing the other. Without a moment's hesitation, Mathieu's huge forearms twisted; he seized the Scots by the scruffs of their necks and cracked their heads together.

Jamie couldn't see and could barely move, but kept moving anyway, groping blindly. He was on the floor, could feel boards, wetness . . . His pawing hand struck flesh and he lunged forward and bit Mathieu as hard as he could in the calf of the leg. Fresh blood filled his mouth, hotter than his own, and he gagged but kept his teeth locked in the hairy flesh, clinging stubbornly as the leg he clung to kicked in frenzy. His ears were ringing, he was vaguely aware of screaming and shouting, but it didn't matter.

Something had come upon him and nothing mattered. Some small remnant of his consciousness registered surprise, and then that was gone, too. No pain, no thought. He was a red thing and while he saw things, faces, blood, bits of room, they didn't matter. Blood took him, and when some sense of himself came back, he was kneeling astride the man, hands locked around the big man's neck, hands throbbing with a pounding pulse, his or his victim's, he couldn't tell.

Him. Him. He'd lost the man's name. His eyes were bulging, the ragged mouth slobbered and gaped, and there was a small, sweet *crack* as something broke under Jamie's thumbs. He squeezed with all he had, squeezed and squeezed and felt the huge body beneath him go strangely limp.

He went on squeezing, couldn't stop, until a hand seized him by the arm and shook him, hard.

"Stop," a voice croaked, hot in his ear. "Jamie. Stop."

He blinked up at the white, bony face, unable to put a name to it. Then drew breath—the first he could remember drawing for some time—and with it came a thick stink, blood and shit and reeking sweat, and he became suddenly aware of the horrible spongy feeling of the body he was sitting on. He scrambled awkwardly off, sprawling on the floor as his muscles spasmed and trembled.

Then he saw her.

She was lying crumpled against the wall, curled into herself, her brown hair spilling across the boards. He got to his knees, crawling to her.

He was making a small whimpering noise, trying to talk, having no words. Got to the wall and gathered her into his arms, limp, her head lolling, striking his shoulder, her hair soft against his face, smelling of smoke and her own sweet musk.

"A nighean," he managed. "Christ, *a nighean*. Are ye . . ."

"Jesus," said a voice by his side, and he felt the vibration as Ian—thank God, the name had come back, of course it was Ian—collapsed next to him. His friend had a bloodstained dirk still clutched in his hand. "Oh, Jesus, Jamie."

He looked up, puzzled, desperate, and then looked down as the girl's body slipped from his grasp and fell back across his knees with impossible boneless grace, the small dark hole in her white breast stained with only a little blood. Not much at all.

He'd made Jamie come with him to the cathedral of St. Andre, and insisted he go to confession. Jamie had balked—no great surprise.

"No. I can't."

"We'll go together." Ian had taken him firmly by the arm and very literally dragged him over the threshold. Once inside, he was counting on the atmosphere of the place to keep Jamie there.

His friend stopped dead, the whites of his eyes showing as he glanced warily around.

The stone vault of the ceiling soared into shadow overhead, but pools of colored light from the stained-glass windows lay soft on the worn slates of the aisle.

"I shouldna be here," Jamie muttered under his breath.

"Where better, eejit? Come on," Ian muttered back, and pulled Jamie down the side aisle to the chapel of Saint Estephe. Most of the side chapels were lavishly furnished, monuments to the importance of wealthy families. This one was a tiny, undecorated stone alcove, containing little more than an altar, a faded tapestry of a faceless saint, and a small stand where candles could be placed.

"Stay here." Ian planted Jamie dead in front of the altar and ducked out, going to buy a candle from the old woman who sold them near the main door. He'd changed his mind about trying to make Jamie go to confession; he knew fine when ye could get a Fraser to do something, and when ye couldn't.

He worried a bit that Jamie would leave, and hurried back to the chapel, but Jamie was still there, standing in the middle of the tiny space, head down, staring at the floor.

"Here, then," Ian said, pulling him toward the altar. He plunked the candle—an expensive one, beeswax and large—on the stand, and pulled the paper spill the old lady had given him out of his sleeve, offering it to Jamie. "Light it. We'll say a prayer for your da. And . . . and for her."

He could see tears trembling on Jamie's lashes, glittering in the red glow of the sanctuary lamp that hung above the altar, but Jamie blinked them back and firmed his jaw.

"All right," he said, low voiced, but he hesitated. Ian sighed, took the spill out of his hand and, standing on tiptoe, lit it from the sanctuary lamp.

"Do it," he whispered, handing it to Jamie, "or I'll gie ye a good one in the kidney, right here."

Jamie made a sound that might have been the breath of a laugh, and lowered the lit spill to the candle's wick. The fire rose up, a pure high flame with blue at its heart, then settled as Jamie pulled the spill away and shook it out in a plume of smoke.

They stood for some time, hands clasped loosely in front of them, watching the candle burn. Ian prayed for his mam and da, his sister and her bairns . . . with some hesitation (was it proper to pray for a Jew?), for Rebekah bat-Leah, and with a sidelong glance at Jamie, to be sure he wasn't looking, for Jenny Fraser. Then the soul of Brian Fraser . . . and then, eyes tight shut, for the friend beside him.

The sounds of the church faded, the whispering stones and echoes of wood, the shuffle of feet and the rolling gabble of the pigeons on the roof. Ian stopped saying words, but was still praying. And then that stopped, too, and there was only peace, and the soft beating of his heart.

He heard Jamie sigh, from somewhere deep inside, and opened his eyes. Without speaking, they went out, leaving the candle to keep watch.

"Did ye not mean to go to confession yourself?" Jamie asked, stopping near the church's main door. There was a priest in the confessional; two or three people stood a discreet distance away from the carved wooden stall, out of earshot, waiting.

"It'll bide," Ian said, with a shrug. "If ye're goin' to Hell, I might as well go, too. God knows, ye'll never manage alone."

Jamie smiled—a wee bit of a smile, but still—and pushed the door open into sunlight.

They strolled aimlessly for a bit, not talking, and found themselves eventually on the river's edge, watching the Garonne's dark waters flow past, carrying debris from a recent storm.

"It means 'peace,'" Jamie said at last. "What he said to me. The Doctor. 'Shalom.'" Ian kent that fine.

"Aye," he said. "But peace is no our business now, is it? We're soldiers." He jerked his chin toward the nearby pier, where a packet-boat rode at anchor. "I hear the King of Prussia needs a few good men."

"So he does," said Jamie, and squared his shoulders. "Come on, then."

Author's note: I would like to acknowledge the help of several people in researching aspects of Jewish history, law, and custom for this story: Elle Druskin (author of *To Catch a Cop*), Sarah Meyer (registered midwife), Carol Krenz, Celia K. and her Reb Mom, and especially Darlene Marshall (author of *Castaway Dreams*). I'm indebted also to Rabbi Joseph Telushkin's very helpful book *Jewish Literacy*. Any errors are mine.

Sherrilyn Kenyon

Be careful what you search for—because you just might *find* it.

New York Times bestseller Sherrilyn Kenyon is one of the superstars of the paranormal romance field. She's probably best-known for the twenty-two-volume Dark-Hunter series, including such titles as *Night Embrace, Dance with the Devil, Kiss of the Night,* and *Bad Moon Rising,* and extending to manga and short stories as well as novels, but she also writes the League series, including *Born of Night, Born of Fire, Born of Ice,* and *Born of Shadows,* and the Chronicles of Nick series, which includes *Infinity* and *Invincible.* She's also produced the four-volume B.A.D. (Bureau of American Defense) sequence, three of those written with Dianna Love, including *Silent Truth, Whispered Lies, Phantom in the Night,* and the collection *Born to be BAD,* and the three-volume Belador Code sequence, again written with Dianna Love. Her most recent novels are *Born of Silence,* a League novel, and *Infamous,* part of the Chronicles of Nick series. There's a compendium to the Dark-Hunter series, *The Dark-Hunter Companion,* written by Kenyon and Alethea Kontis, and Kenyon has also written non-fiction such as *The Writer's Guide to Everyday Life in the Middle Ages* and *The Writer's Digest Character Naming Sourcebook.* She lives in Spring Hill, Tennessee, and maintains a website at sherrilynkenyon.com.

HELL HATH NO FURY

Based on a true legend

"I don't think we should be here."

"Oh, c'mon, Cait, calm down. Everything's fine. We have the equipment set up and—"

"I feel like someone's watching me." Cait Irwin turned around slowly, scanning the thick woods, which appeared to be even more sinister now that the sun was setting. The trees spread out in every direction, so thick and numerous that she couldn't even see where they'd parked her car, never mind the highway that was so far back that nothing could be heard from it.

We could die here and no one would know . . .

Anne, her best friend from childhood, cocked her hip as she lowered her thermal-imaging camera to smirk at Cait. "I hope something *is* watching you . . . Which direction should I be shooting?"

Cait shook her head at her friend's joy. There was nothing Anne loved more than a good ghost sighting. "Anne, I'm not joking. There's something here." She pinned her with a caustic glower. "You brought me along because I'm psychic, right?"

"Yeah."

"Then trust me. This"—Cait rubbed the chills from her arms—"isn't right."

"What's going on?" Brandon set his large camera crate down next to Anne's feet as he rejoined them. He and Jamie had gone out to set their DVRs and cameras for the night.

While she and Anne were slight of frame, Brandon and Jamie were well bulked, Brandon more from beer and channel surfing, but Jamie from hours spent in the gym. Even so, with his blond hair and blue eyes,

Brandon was good-looking in a Boy Scout kind of way. But Jamie had that whole dark, brooding, sexy scowl thing that made most women melt and giggle whenever he glanced their way.

Anne indicated her with a jerk of her chin. "Wunderkind over there is already picking up something."

Brandon's eyes widened. "I hope you mean spiritwise and not some backwoods bug we have no immunity to. I left my vitamin C at home."

Cait shivered as another wave of trepidation went through her. This one was even stronger than the previous one. "Whose bright idea was this anyway?"

Anne pointed to Brandon, who grinned proudly.

He winked at her. "C'mon, Cait. It's a ghost town. We don't get to investigate one of these every day. Surely ye of the unflappable constitution isn't wigging out like a little girl at a horror movie."

"Boo!"

Cait shrieked as Jamie grabbed her from behind.

Laughing, he stepped around her, then shrugged his Alienware backpack off his shoulder and set it next to the camera case.

She glared at the walking mountain. "Damn it, Jamie! You're not funny!"

"No, but *you* are. I didn't know you could jump that high. I'm impressed."

Hissing at him like a feral cat, she flicked her nails in his direction. "If I didn't think it'd come back on me, I'd hex you."

He flashed that devilish grin that was flanked by dimples so deep, they cut moons into both of his cheeks. "Ah, baby, you can hex me up any time you want!"

Cait suppressed a need to strangle him. All aggravation aside, a martial arts instructor who was built like Rambo might come in handy one day. And still her Spidey senses tingled, warning her that that day might not be too far in the future.

"We're not supposed to be here." She bit her lip as she glanced around, trying to find what had her so rattled.

"No one is," Brandon said in a spooky tone. "This ground is cursed. Oooo-eeee-oooo . . ."

She ignored him. But he was right. At one time, Randolph County had been the richest in all of Alabama. Until the locals had forced a Native

American business owner to leave her store behind and walk the Trail of Tears.

"Louina . . ."

Cait jerked around as she heard the faint whisper of the woman's name; it was the same name as the ghost town they were standing in. Rather cruel to name the town after the woman who'd been run out of it for no real reason.

"Louina," the voice repeated, even more insistent than before.

"Did you hear that?" she asked the others.

"Hear what?" Jamie checked his DVR. "I'm not picking up anything."

Something struck her hard in the chest, forcing her to take a step back. Her friends and the forest vanished. She suddenly found herself inside an old trading post. The scent of the pine-board walls and floor mixed with that of spices and flour. But it was the soaps on the counter in front of her that smelled the strongest.

An older Native American woman, who wore her hair braided and coiled around her head, straightened the jars on the countertop while a younger, pregnant woman who had similar features, leaned against the opposite end.

But what shocked Cait was how much she looked like the older woman. Right down to the black hair and high eyebrows.

The younger woman—Elizabeth; Cait didn't know how she knew that, but she did—reached into one of the glass jars and pulled out a piece of licorice. "They're going to make you leave, Lou. I overheard them talking about it."

Louina scoffed at her sister's warning before she replaced the lid and pulled the jar away from her. "Our people were here long before them, and we'll be here long after they're gone. Mark my words, Lizzie."

Elizabeth swallowed her piece of licorice. "Have you not heard what they've done to the Cherokee in Georgia?"

"I heard. But the Cherokee aren't the Creek. Our nation is strong."

Elizabeth jerked, then placed her hand over her distended stomach where her baby kicked. "He gets upset every time I think about you being forced to leave."

"Then don't think about it. It won't happen. Not as long as I've been here."

"Cait!"

Cait jumped as Jamie shouted in her face. "W-what?"

"Are you with us? You blanked out for a second."

Blinking, she shook her head to clear it of the images that had seemed so real that she could taste Elizabeth's licorice. "Where was that original trading post you guys mentioned being here?"

Brandon shrugged. "No idea. We couldn't find any information about it, other than it was owned by the Native American woman the town was named for. Why?"

Because she had a bad feeling that they were standing on it. But there was nothing to corroborate that. Nothing other than a bad feeling in the pit of her stomach.

In fact, there was nothing left of this once-thriving town other than rows of crosses in a forgotten cemetery, and a marker that proclaimed it Louina, Alabama.

That thought had barely finished before she saw Louina again in her mind. She was standing a few feet away, to Cait's left, with a wagon filled with as much money and supplies as she could carry. Furious, she spat on the ground and then spoke in Creek to the men who'd come to confiscate her home and store, and force her to leave.

Cait knew it was Creek, a language she knew not at all, and yet the words were as clear to her as if they'd been spoken in English.

"I curse this ground and all who dwell here. For what you've done to me . . . for the cruelty you have shown others, no one will make my business prosper, and when my sister passes from this existence to the next, within ten years of that date, there will be nothing left of this town except gravestones."

The sheriff and his deputies who'd been sent to escort her from her home laughed in her face. "Now, don't be like that, Louina. This ain't personal against you."

"No, but it is personal against *you*." She cast a scathing glare at all of them. "No one will remember any of you as ever having breathed, but they will remember my name, Louina, and the atrocity that you have committed against me."

One of the deputies came from behind the wagon with a stern frown. "Louina? This can't be all you own."

A cruel smile twisted her lips. "I couldn't carry all of my gold."

That piqued the deputies' interest.

"Where'd you leave it?" the sheriff asked.

"The safest place I know. In the arms of my beloved husband."

The sheriff rubbed his thumb along the edge of his lips. "Yeah, but no one knows where you buried him."

"I know and I won't forget . . ." She swept a chilling gaze over all of them. "Anything." And with that, she climbed onto her wagon and started forward without looking back. But there was no missing the smug satisfaction in her eyes.

She was leaving more than her store behind.

Cait could hear Louina's malice as if they were her own thoughts. *They will tear each other apart, questing for the gold my husband will never release . . .*

It was Louina's final revenge.

One paid tribute to by the eerie rows of cross-marked graves in the old Liberty Missionary Baptist Church Cemetery.

The weakness of our enemy is our strength.

Make my enemy brave, smart, and strong, so that if defeated, I will not be ashamed.

Cait felt Louina with her like her own shadow. A part of her that she could only see if the light hit it just right.

Louina whispered in her ear, but this time Cait didn't understand the words. Yet what was unmistakable was the feeling of all-consuming dread that wouldn't go away, no matter what she tried.

She sighed before she implored her group one more time. "We need to leave."

All three of them balked.

"We just got the equipment set out."

"What? Now? We've been here all day!"

"Really, Cait? What are you thinking?"

They spoke at once, but each voice was as clear as Louina's. "We should *not* be here," she insisted. "The land itself is telling me that we need to go. Screw the equipment, it's insured."

"No!" Brandon adamantly refused.

It was then that she understood why they were being stubborn, when Brandon had spent his entire life saying that if you ran into a malevolent haunting, you abandoned that place because nothing was worth the chance of being possessed.

Only one thing would make him and Jamie forget about their own beliefs.

Greed.

"You're not here for the ghosts. You're here for the *treasure*."

Jamie and Brandon exchanged a nervous glance.

"She *is* psychic," Anne reminded them.

Brandon cursed. "Who told you about the treasure?"

"Louina."

"Can she tell you where it is?" Jamie asked hopefully.

Cait screwed her face up at him. "Is that really all you're concerned with?"

"Well . . . not *all*. We *are* here for the science. Natural curiosity being what it is. But let's face it, the equipment's not cheap and a little payback wouldn't be bad."

His choice of words only worsened her apprehension.

"Can you really not feel the anger here?" She gestured in the direction of the cemetery; that had been the first place they'd set up the equipment and it was there that her bad feelings had started. "It's so thick, I can smell it."

"I feel humidity."

Jamie raised his hand. "Sign me up for hunger."

"Annoyed," Brandon chimed in. "Look, it's for one night. Me and Jamie are going to dowse a little and try to find a place to dig."

How could he appear so chipper about what they were planning? "You'll be digging up a grave."

They froze.

"What?" Brandon asked.

Cait nodded. "The treasure is buried with Louina's husband, William, who was one of the Creek leaders during the Red Stick War."

Jamie narrowed his gaze suspiciously. "How do you know all of this?"

"I told you. Louina. She keeps speaking to me."

Brandon snorted. "I'm laying money on Google. Nice try, C. You probably know where the money is and you're trying to scare us off. No deal, sister. I want a cut."

Laughing, Jamie chucked him on the back, then headed to the cooler to grab a beer.

Anne stepped closer to her. "Are you serious about this?"

Cait nodded. "I wish they'd believe me. But yeah. We shouldn't be here. This land is saturated with malevolence. It's like a flowing river under the soil."

And with those words, she lost Anne's support. "Land can't be evil or cursed. You know that." She walked over to the men.

Cait knew better. Part Creek herself, she'd been raised on her mother's belief that if someone hated *enough,* they could transfer that hatred into objects and into the soil. Both were like sponges—they could carry hatred for generations.

Louina was out there, and she was angry.

Most of all, she was vengeful.

And she's coming for us . . .

Cait felt like a leper as she sat alone by the fire, eating her protein bar. The others were off in the woods, trying to summon the very entity that she knew was with her.

"Louina?" Jamie called, his deep voice resonating through the woods. "If you can hear me, give me a sign."

While it was a common phrase, for some reason tonight it bothered her. She mocked him silently as she pulled the protein bar's wrapper down lower.

Suddenly, a scream rang out.

Cait shot to her feet and listened carefully. Who was it, and where were they? Her heart pounded in her ears.

"Brandon!" Anne shouted, her voice echoing through the woods.

Cait ran toward them as fast as she could.

By the time she found them, Brandon was on his back with a twig poking all the way through his arm.

"He said he wanted a cut . . ."

She jerked around, trying to pinpoint the voice that had spoken loud and clear. "Did you hear that?" she asked the others.

"All I hear is Brandon whining like a bitch. Suck it up already, dude. Damn. You keep that up and I'm buying you a bra."

"Fuck you!" he snarled at Jamie. "Let me stab you with a stick and see how you feel. You the bitch. Asshole!"

"Boys!" Cait moved to stand between them. "What happened?"

"I don't know," Brandon hissed as Anne tried to see the wound. "I was walking, going over the thermal scan, when all of a sudden I stumbled and fell into a tree. Next thing I knew . . . this!" He held it up for her to see.

Cringing, Cait averted her eyes from the grisly wound. "We need to get him to the hospital."

"Not on your life," Brandon snarled. "I'll be all right."

"I take it back. You're not a bitch. You're insane. Look at that wound. I hate to agree with Cait, 'cause I doubt there's a hospital anywhere near here, but you need help."

"It's a flesh wound."

Cait shook her head. "Anne, you should have never let him watch Monty Python."

"I should have never left him alone to go to the bathroom," Anne growled at him. "They're right. You need to see a doctor. You could get rabies or something."

Yeah, 'cause rabid trees were a *huge* problem here in Alabama. Cait barely caught herself before she laughed. Anne hated to be laughed at.

"I'm not leaving till I find that treasure!"

Greed, pride, and stupidity. The three most fatal traits any human could possess.

A sudden wind swept around them. This time she wasn't the only one who heard the laughter it carried.

"What was that?" Jamie asked.

"Louina."

"Would you *stop* with that shit?" Brandon snapped through gritted teeth. "You're really getting on my nerves."

And they were getting on hers.

Fine. Whatever. She wasn't going to argue anymore. It was their lives. His wound. Who was she to keep him safe when he obviously had no interest in it?

Arms akimbo, Jamie sighed. "What do you think are the odds that, assuming Cait's right, and Louina's husband has the gold in his grave, that it's in the cemetery? Didn't most of the Native Americans in this area convert over to Baptist?"

Cait shook her head. "He won't be there."

"What makes you say that?"

"If it was that easy to find, it would have been found long ago."

"Yeah, good point. Square one sucks." Jamie glanced back at Brandon. "You sure about the doctor?"

"Positive."

"All right. I'm heading back out. Cait? You coming?"

"You can't go alone." She followed as he switched his flashlight on and went back to his EMF detector and air ion counter.

"You want to take this?" He held his full-spectrum camcorder out to her.

"Sure." She opened it and turned it back on so that she could see the world through the scope of the small screen.

After few minutes, he paused. "Do you really believe any of the bullshit you've been spewing?"

"You know me, James. Have I ever spewed bullshit on site?"

"Nah. That's what has me worried." He narrowed his gaze at her. "Did I ever tell you that my great-grandmother was Cherokee?"

"No, you didn't."

He nodded. "She died when I was six, but I still remember her, and something she'd always say keeps echoing in my head."

"What?"

"'Listen, or your tongue will keep you deaf.'"

Cait was about to compliment her wisdom when she glanced down at the screen.

Holy Mother . . .

Gasping, she dropped the camera and jumped back.

"What?" Jamie turned around to see if there was something near.

Terrified and shaking, Cait couldn't speak. She couldn't get the image out of her mind. She gestured to the camera.

With a stern frown, Jamie picked it up and ran it back. Even in the darkness, she knew the moment he saw what had stolen her tongue. He turned stark white.

Right before he'd spoken about his Cherokee great-grandmother, a huge . . . something with fangs had been about to pounce on him. Soulless eyes of black had stared down as its mouth opened to devour him. Then the moment he'd repeated the quote, it had pulled back and vanished.

Eyes wide, he gulped. "We have to leave."

She nodded, because she still couldn't speak. Jamie took her arm gently and led her through the woods back to where they'd left Anne and Brandon.

They were already gone. Jamie growled in frustration. "Brandon!" he called out. "Anne?"

Only silence answered them.

"All who dwell here will pay . . ." Louina's voice was more insistent now. *"But I hurt those I should not have cursed."*

Cait flinched as she saw an image of Elizabeth as an old woman in a stark hand-built cabin. Her gray hair was pulled back into a bun as she lit a candle and placed it in the window while she whispered a Creek prayer.

Oh, Great Father Spirit, whose voice I hear in the wind–

Whose breath gives life to all the world and with whom I have tried to walk beside throughout my days.

Hear me. I need your strength and wisdom.

Let me walk in beauty, and make my eyes ever behold the glorious sunset you have provided.

Make my hands respect the things you have made and my ears sharp to hear your voice even when it's nothing more than a faint whisper.

Make me wise so that I may understand the things you have taught my people. And why you have taken things from me that have given me pain.

Help me to remain calm and strong in the face of all that comes at me. Against my enemies and those out to do me harm.

Let me learn the lessons you have hidden in every leaf and rock. In the joy of the stream. In the light of the moon and sun.

Help me seek pure thoughts and act with the intention of helping others and never myself.

Help me find compassion without empathy overwhelming me.

I seek strength, not to be greater than my brother, but to fight my greatest enemy . . .

Myself.

Make me always ready to come to you with clean hands and straight eyes. So that when my life fades, as the fading sunset, my spirit may come to you without shame.

And most of all, Great-Grandfather, keep my sons safe and warm wherever they may be.

Elizabeth leaned over and kissed the old photographs of two young men in cavalry uniforms that she had sitting in the window beside the candle she lit every night—just in case they finally found their way home. It was a ritual she'd practiced every single night for the last fifty-two years. Since the war had ended and her boys had failed to return home to tend their crops.

She refused to believe them dead. Just as she refused to die and let her sister's curse harm the town where they had both been born.

Her heart aching, she pulled two brittle letters from her pocket, the last that her boys had written to her, and sat down at the table. Old age had taken her sight so that she could no longer read the words, not even with her spectacles. But it didn't matter. She'd long ago committed their words to her heart.

> *I dream only of returning home to marry Anabelle. Give her my best, Mother. Soon I will see you both again.*
>
> *Robert*

He'd only been nineteen when he'd left her home with his older brother John, when they'd been conscripted to fight a war that had nothing to do with them. Eighteen months older, John had sworn that he would watch over Robert and return him home.

"On my life, Ecke. I'll bring him back whole and hale."

And I will watch for you every day, and every night I will light a candle to help guide you both to my door.

Tears swam in her eyes, but they didn't fall. She was stronger than that. Instead, she reached for the old hand-carved horn her father had given to her when she'd been a child. "Take this, Lizzie. Should anyone come to our door while your brothers and I are in the field, sound it loud to let us know and then hide with your mother and sisters until we can get to you."

So much had changed. To this day, she didn't regret marrying her husband. She had loved her John more than anything. But he had left her far too soon. She'd laid him to rest on a cold February morning when Robert was barely seven. Since her brothers had been forced to leave along with her sister, Lou, she'd raised the boys on her own, along with her daughter, Mary.

There is no death, only a change of worlds . . .

Soon she would change. She could feel the Great Spirit with her more and more.

Do not grieve for that which is past or for that which you cannot prevent.

"I will see you again soon, my sons." And she would be with her John . . .

Cait flinched as she felt Louina's pain.

You must live your life from beginning to end. No one can do it for you. But be careful when you seek to destroy another. For it is your soul that will be consumed and you are the one who will cry. Never allow anger and hatred to poison you.

"I am poison . . ."

Those words echoed in Cait's head as she followed Jamie in his quest to locate their friends.

"Maybe they went to the hospital, after all." That was her hope until they reached the tents they'd pitched earlier.

Tents that were now shredded and lying strewn across the ground. Jamie ran ahead, then pulled up short. With a curse, he turned and caught her before she could get too close.

"You don't want to know."

"W-what?"

His gaze haunted, he tightened his arms around her. "Trust me, Cait. You don't want to see them. We have to call the authorities."

Tears welled in her eyes. "Anne?"

He shook his head. "It looks like an animal attack of some kind."

"Why!"

"I don't know."

But her question wasn't for Jamie. It was for Louina.

Words spoken in anger have strong power and they cannot be undone. For those who are lucky, they can be forgiven in time. But for others . . .

It is always our own words and deeds than condemn us. Never the ill intent or wishes of our enemies.

Do not dabble with what you don't understand. There are some doors that are blown from their hinges when they are opened. Doors that will never again be sealed.

"Welcome to my hell."

They both jerked at the voice beside them.

There in the darkness stood Louina. Her gray hair fanned out around her shoulders. Her old calico dress was faded against her white apron.

"My sister protects you. For that you should give thanks. Now go and never come here again."

But it wasn't that simple.

"I will not leave and allow you to continue hurting others."

Louina laughed. "You can't stop me."

For the first time in her life, Cait understood the part of her bloodline that had always been mysterious and undefined. She was the great-great-granddaughter of Elizabeth.

It all came together in her mind at once. Her grandmother had told her the story of Elizabeth, who'd died when her cabin caught fire while she was sleeping. Something had knocked the candle that she lit for her sons from her window.

"*You* killed her!" Cait accused.

"She wanted to die. She was tired."

But that wasn't true and she knew it. Yes, Elizabeth had been tired. She'd been almost a hundred and ten years old. Yet she'd been so determined to keep her sister's curse at bay that she'd refused Death every time it tried to claim her.

Until Louina had intervened.

In that moment, Cait felt a connection to Elizabeth. One she embraced.

Jamie released her. "What are you doing?"

Cait looked down to see the glow that enveloped her. Warm and sweet, it smelled like sunshine. It was Elizabeth.

"This ends, Louina. As you said, you are the poison that must be purged."

Shrieking, Louina ran at her.

True to her warrior heritage, Cait stood her ground. She would not back down. Not in this.

Louina's spirit slammed into Cait with enough force to knock her down. She groaned as pain filled her. Still, she stood up again, and closed her eyes. "You will not defeat me. It is time for you to rest. You have not shown respect to those who dwell on this earth."

"They didn't show it to me!"

"And you allowed them to turn you away from the Great Spirit, who loves us all. To do things you knew weren't right!"

"They spat in my face!"

"You returned their hatred with more hatred." Cait reached her hand out to Louina. "Like Elizabeth, you're tired. Nothing is more draining than to keep the fires of hatred burning."

"Nothing is more draining."

"You will not fight me?"

Cait shook her head. "I want to comfort you. It's time to let go, Louina. Release the hatred." And then she heard Elizabeth in her ear, telling her what to say. "Remember the words of Crazy Horse. Upon suffering beyond suffering, the Red Nation shall rise again and it shall be a blessing for a sick world. A world filled with broken promises, selfishness, and separations. A world longing for light again. I see a time of Seven Generations when all the colors of mankind will gather under the Sacred Tree of Life and the whole Earth will become one circle again. In that day, there will be those among the Lakota who will carry knowledge and understanding of unity among all living things and the young white ones will come to those of my people and ask for this wisdom. I salute the light within your eyes where the whole Universe dwells. For when you are at that center within you and I am that place within me, we shall be one."

Louina pulled back as she heard those words. "We are one," she repeated.

Elizabeth pulled away from Cait and held her hand out to Louina. "I have missed my sister."

"I have missed mine."

Jamie placed his hands on Cait's shoulders. "Are you all right?"

She wasn't sure. "Did you see any of that?"

"Yes, but I'm going to deny it if you ever ask me that in public."

Tears filled her eyes as she remembered Anne and Brandon. "Why did we come this weekend?"

"*We* came for greed. You came to help a friend."

Suddenly, a low moan sounded.

"Call for help!" Jamie said. He released her and ran back to their camp. She dialed 911, hoping it would pick up.

"Anne's still breathing." Jamie pulled his jacket off to drape it over her. "What about Brandon?"

He went to check while the phone rang.

"It's faint, but yeah . . . I think he's alive too."

Cait prayed for a miracle that she hoped would be granted.

Epilogue

Cait sat next to Anne's bed while the nurse finished checking her vitals. She didn't speak until after the woman had left them alone.

"Sorry we didn't have any readings to show you guys."

Anne shook her head. "Who cares? I'm just glad I'm alive. But . . ."

"But what?"

"Are you and Jamie ever going to tell us what really happened?"

Cait reached up to touch the small gold ring that she'd found on her car seat when she'd gone out to the road to help direct the medics to where Brandon and Anne had been. Inside the band were the names John and Elizabeth. It was the only gold to be found in Louina.

The treasure so many had sought had been used to fund a school and church over a century ago.

Years after her sister had given her the gold to support herself and her children, Elizabeth had taken the last of it and had it melted into this ring.

Smiling, Cait met Anne's gaze. "Maybe one day."

"And what about the treasure?"

"Anne, haven't you learned yet that it's not gold that is precious? It's people. And you are the greatest treasure of my life. I'm glad I still have my best friend."

Anne took her hand and held it. "I'm grateful to be here and I'm truly grateful for you. But—"

"There are no buts."

She nodded. "You're right, Cait. I'd lost sight of what my grandfather used to say."

"And that was?"

" 'When all the trees have been cut down and all the animals have been hunted to extinction, when all the waters are polluted and the air is unsafe to breathe, only then will you discover you cannot eat money.' "

Jamie laughed, drawing their attention to the door where he stood with a balloon bouquet for Anne.

"What's so funny?" Cait asked.

"I think we all came away from the weekend with a different lesson."

Cait arched her brow. "And that is?"

"Anne just said hers. You learned that revenge is a path best left alone. Brandon learned to shut up and get help when he's wounded."

"And you?" Anne asked.

"I learned two things. One, the most dangerous place for a man to be is between two fighting women. And two, no matter the species, the deadliest gender is always the female. Men will fight until they die. Women will take it to the grave and then find a way *back*."

S. M. Stirling

When all that's left between you and the total collapse of civilization is the law, you need somebody tough enough to enforce it—no matter what the cost.

Considered by many to be the natural heir to Harry Turtledove's title of King of the Alternate History Novel, fast-rising science fiction star S. M. Stirling is the bestselling author of the Island in the Sea of Time series (*Island in the Sea of Time, Against the Tide of Years, On the Oceans of Eternity*), in which Nantucket comes unstuck in time and is cast back to the year 1250 B.C., and the Draka series (including *Marching Through Georgia, Under the Yoke, The Stone Dogs,* and *Drakon,* plus an anthology of Draka stories by other hands edited by Stirling, *Drakas!*), in which Tories fleeing the American Revolution set up a militant society in South Africa and eventually end up conquering most of the Earth. He's also produced the Dies the Fire series (*Dies the Fire, The Protector's War, A Meeting at Corvallis*), plus the five-volume Fifth Millennium series, and the seven-volume series The General (with David Drake), as well as stand-alone novels such as *Conquistador* and *The Peshawar Lancers*. Stirling has also written novels in collaboration with Raymond E. Feist, Jerry Pournelle, Holly Lisle, Shirley Meier, Karen Wehrstein, and *Star Trek* actor James Doohan, as well as contributed to the Babylon 5, T2, Brainship, War World, and the Man-Kzin Wars series. His short fiction has been collected in *Ice, Iron and Gold*. Stirling's newest series include the Change series, consisting of *The Sunrise Lands, The Scourge of God, The Sword of the Lady, The High King of Montival,* and *The Tears of the Sun,* and the Lords of Creation series, consisting of *The Sky People* and *In the Courts of the Crimson Kings*. Most recently, he started a new series, Shadowspawn, which consists so far of *A Taint in the Blood* and *The*

Council of Shadows. His most recent novel is a new volume in the Change series, *Lord of Mountains*. Born in France and raised in Europe, Africa, and Canada, he now lives with his family in Santa Fe, New Mexico.

PRONOUNCING DOOM

DUN CARSON
(EAST-CENTRAL WILLAMETTE VALLEY)
DÙTHCHAS OF THE CLAN MACKENZIE
(FORMERLY WESTERN OREGON)
5TH AUGUST, CHANGE YEAR I/1999 AD

I am riding to pass sentence on an evildoer, Juniper Mackenzie thought. *It's part of being Chief, but I liked being a folk musician a lot better! The old tales were less stressful as songs than real life.*

"Water soon, Riona," she said to her horse, and the mare twitched her ears backward.

The smell of horse sweat from the dozen mounts of her party was strong, though she'd been used to that even before the Change; a horse-drawn Traveler wagon had been part of her persona, as well as fun. It was a hot day after a dry week, perfect harvest weather, which was more important than comfort. It didn't *usually* rain in summertime here, but that didn't mean it absolutely couldn't happen.

In the old world before the machines stopped, rain would have been a nuisance. Now, in the new world—where food came from within walking distance or didn't come at all—it would be a disaster. So the heat and the sun that threatened her freckled redhead's skin was a good thing, and the sweat and prickling be damned. At least there was less smoke in the air than there had been last summer, in the first Change Year.

Her mouth thinned a little at the memory; it had been burning cities then, and forest fires raging through woods where deadwood had accumulated through generations of humans trying to suppress the burn cycle. The pall had lain like smog all over the Willamette country, caught in the great valley between the Cascades and the Coast Range until the autumn rains washed it out.

Always a little bitter on the lips, the taste of a world going down in flame and horror. Always reminding you of what was happening away from your refuge.

With a practiced effort of will she started to force herself back into the moment, to the slow clop of hooves on the asphalt, the moving creak of leather between her thighs and the sleeping face of her son in the light carrying-cradle across the saddlebow before her. Strips of shadow from the roadside trees fell across her face, like a slow flicker as the horses walked.

You had to learn to do that, or the memories would drive you mad. Many *had* gone mad with what they'd seen and done and endured after the machines stopped, in screaming fits or rocking and weeping or just an apathy that killed as certainly as knife or rope or *Yersinia pestis* in the lungs. Many of them people who might have lived, otherwise. Even now there was still very little to spare for those not functional enough to pull their weight, though the definition of *sane* had gotten much more elastic.

What surplus there was had to go to the children; they'd rescued as many orphans as they could. When a youngster learned to laugh again, it gave you heart that the world would go on.

So you're not smelling fire all the time this year. Enjoy that. Think about the children growing up in a world you have to make worth it; your *children, and all the others. Don't think of the rest.* Especially *don't think of what those mass graves in the refugee camps around Salem smelled like, where the Black Death hit.* She hadn't gotten very close, on that scouting trip. But close enough—

No.

Scents of dust, the subtly varied baked-green smells of grass and trees and crops, the slight musty sweetness of cut stems. The lands around Dun Carson were mostly harvested now, flat squares of dun stubble alternating with pasture, clumps of lushly green Douglas fir and Garry oak at intervals or along creeks running low and slow with summer.

A reaper pulled by two of those priceless quarter horses traded from the ranching country east of the Cascades was finishing its work as they passed. The crude wire-and-wood machine had been built over the winter from a model salvaged from a museum. Its revolving creel pushed through the last of a rippling yellow-blond field and the rattling belt behind the cutting bar left a swath of cut grain in its wake. The driver looked up long enough to wave, then went back to her work.

Last year they'd used scythes from garden-supply stores and from walls where they'd been souvenirs for lifetimes, and improvised sickles and bread-knives and the bare hands of desperately unskilled refugees working until they dropped. Farming like this was grinding hard work even if you knew what you were doing, and so few did. Fortunately they had a few to direct and teach the rest, some real farmers, some hobbyists, and a few utterly priceless Amish fled from settlements overrun by the waves of starving refugees or the kidnap squads of Norman Arminger, the northern warlord.

We've mostly harvested what we planted last year; now we need to get on to the volunteer fields.

Much—most—of the land planted to grain before the Change had just stood until the kernels fell out of the ear. Chaos and fighting as people spilled out of cities instantly uninhabitable when electricity and engines failed, plague and bandits and sheer lack of tools and skill. A field left like that self-seeded enough to produce a second crop, thin and patchy and weedy but a thousand times more valuable than gold.

Sunlight flashed off the spears of the binders following along behind the reaper. They moved the weapons up each time they advanced to tie a new double armful of cut wheat into sheaves and stand them in neat tripods. She blinked at the way the honed metal cast the light back, remembering . . .

. . . the little girl the Eaters used as decoy giggling and bringing out the knife and cutting for her throat, and the smell so much like roast pork from the shuttered buildings behind her . . .

"Focus," Judy Barstow Mackenzie said from her other side.

And we help each other to . . . not exactly forget . . . put it aside. Are any of us still completely sane? Are there any of us who aren't suffering from . . . post-traumatic stress disorder, wasn't it called? Certainly it's the ones who were least anchored in the world-as-it-was who've done best since the Change. The rest cling to us.

"Thanks," Juniper said.

"What's a Maiden for?" Judy said stoutly. "If not to keep her High Priestess on track?"

The tone was light, but Juniper leaned over and touched her shoulder.

"And friends," she said. "Friends do that."

They'd known each other since their early teens—a decade and a half ago, now, and they'd discovered the Craft together. They were very unlike: Juniper short and slight and with eyes of willow-leaf green, Judy bold-featured, big-boned, and olive-skinned, raven-haired and inclined to be a little stout in the old days.

"That too, sure and it is, arra!" Judy said in a mock-Irish accent plastered over her usual strong trace of New York, and winked. "I wouldn't be thinkin' otherwise."

Juniper winced slightly at the brogue. *She* could talk that way and sound like the real thing. Her mother had been genuine-article Irish when she met a young American airman on leave in the London pub where she was working. From Achill Island in the west of County Mayo at that, where she'd grown up speaking Gaelic. That burbling lilt had only tinged Juniper's General American, except when she let it out deliberately during performances—she'd been a singer before the Change, working the Renaissance Faires and pagan festivals and conventions.

Nowadays she used it more and more, especially on public occasions. If people were going to put it on anyway, at least she could give them something more to imitate than fading memories of bad movies on late-night TV.

"It's going to be unpleasant, but straightforward," Judy said seriously. "I did the examination and there's no doubt about it. He's guilty and he deserves it."

"I know." Juniper took a deep breath. "I don't know why I'm feeling so . . . out of control," she said. "And that's a fact. It's . . ."

She looked upward, into a sky with only a few high white wisps of cloud.

"It's as if there were a thunderstorm coming, and there isn't."

The Dun Juniper procession came around the bend and Juniper sighed to herself at the sight of the tarps strung by the crossroads between the roadside firs and oaks and Lombardy poplars. Partly that was sheer desire for shade. Partly it was . . .

Her daughter's fingers flew; Eilir had been deaf since birth:

Why the frustrated sighing, Great Mother? she asked. *They've done what you asked.*

Juniper sent her a quick, irritated glance. Eilir looked as tired as her mother felt, despite being fourteen and very fit. She was tall, already a few inches taller than her mother, strong and graceful as a deer; the splendid body was a legacy of her father, who'd been an athlete and football player.

And a thoughtless selfish bastard who got a teenager pregnant on her first time and in the backseat of his car at that. But then Eilir's wit and heart come from the Mackenzie side, I think!

Juniper filled her lungs and let the flash of temper out with the breath, a technique mastered long ago.

She signed: *Do you feel it? There's an* anger *in the air. In the ground, in the feel of things, like a louring threat.*

Eilir's pale blue eyes narrowed, then went a little distant.

I think so, Spooky-Mom, she replied after a moment. *Yes, a bit.*

They both looked at Judy, who shook her head and shrugged.

"Not me. You're the mystical one. I just made sure we had clean robes and plenty of candles for the Sabbats."

The Earth is the Mother's, Eilir signed, her face utterly stark for once. *Maybe it's Her anger we're feeling.*

They halted in the center where the roads met. Juniper handed down her nine-month-old son, Rudi, to Melissa Aylward Mackenzie, swelling with her own pregnancy.

"I feel it too," the younger woman said seriously.

She was new-come to the Old Religion, like so many others, but already High Priestess of Dun Fairfax, and here to help with organizing the rite.

"Let's hope we're doing the right thing in Her eyes, then," Juniper said. "Get the littles in order, would you, Mellie? This is going to be hard on them."

She nodded soberly, then smiled a little as she hefted Rudi expertly. Juniper shook her head and stretched in a creak of saddle leather; riding made your back ache. Some distant part of her noticed how casual people had already become about standing in the middle of roads, now that cars and trucks were a fading memory.

We've better things to do than this, she went on to her daughter. Her fingers and hands danced, as fluent as speaking aloud: *It's the harvest and nobody has time to spare. Spending most of yesterday and last night hammering out the ritual and the guidelines for this was hard, even with ten minds pooled together. I hate having to do things on the fly, especially when it's setting a precedent . . . but what else can we do?*

Eilir shrugged. *Lock him up like they used to, until it's convenient?*

Juniper didn't bother to dignify that with an answer; it wasn't meant to be taken seriously. Nor could they spare anyone to supervise a criminal's labor, even if they were willing to go down that road, which they weren't.

Sam Aylward, her chief armsman, held her stirrup as she dismounted. She stretched again as her boots touched the asphalt, settling the plaid pinned across her shoulder with a twitch. The Dun Juniper contingent were all wearing the same Highland costume, one that had started as half a joke and spread because it was so convenient. All in a sort of dark green–light brown–dull orange tartan that owed everything to a warehouse full of salvaged blankets and nothing whatsoever to Scotland.

About a third of the Dun Fairfax folk wore the kilt too, and the clothing of the rest showed in tears and patches and tatters why the pre-Change clothes were running out so shockingly fast. They just weren't designed to stand up under the sort of daily grind of hard outdoor labor that nearly everyone did these days. And salvaging more from the unburned parts of the cities was getting to be impossibly dangerous and labor-intensive now that the nearby towns had been stripped. Only big well-armed parties could do it at all, what with bandits and pint-sized warlords popping up everywhere and the crawling terror of the Eater bands lurking in the ruins amid their hideous game of stalking and feasting.

A note popped up from the vast sprawling mental file cabinet she had to lug around these days:

Check on the flax and wool and spinning-wheel projects after we've got the harvest out of the way. We don't need to make our own cloth yet, but we have to have the seeds and tools and skills built up for when we do.

She'd been a skilled amateur weaver herself before the Change, and they'd organized classes in it over the winter. Fortunately it was something you could put down and pick up later.

Melissa left her group and walked over to the stretched tarp shelter to the southwest of the crossroads where the children and nursing mothers sat. Rudi gurgled and waved chubby arms, his eyes and delighted toothless smile fixed on her face.

Thank the Lord and Lady he's a good baby. Eilir was a lot more trouble. Of course, I had less knowledge then, and a great deal less help. It really does *take a village, or at least that makes it a lot easier.*

"They're doing flags for all the Duns," Juniper observed to Chuck Barstow. "It's a good idea, sure. People need symbols."

"Dennie had it right when he insisted on the green flag, though," Chuck said. "We need a symbol for the whole Clan as well. Where do you want it?"

Juniper pursed her lips. She'd made the old sigil of the Singing Moon Coven into a flag: dark antlers and crescent silver moon on green silk. Embroidery was another skill that had turned from hobby to cherished lifeline. The still air of the late summer made it and all the others planted around the tarp shelters hang limp, as if waiting with indrawn breath. Fortunately hers was suspended from a crossbar on the staff, which meant you could see what was on it.

"Next to Dun Carson's, please."

Dun Carson's silver labrys on blood red was planted right in front of the northwest tarp, where the crossroads made a vaguely north–south, east–west cross. Chuck planted the point on the bottom of the Clan's into the earth with a shove and twist. Brian Carson stood with his brother's widow and his orphaned niece and nephew, next to the two tables she'd requested at the center. His wife, Rebekah, stood on his other side, looking a little stiff.

Melissa and her helpers took over the job of looking after the littles. The southeast quadrant held representatives from other duns within a fifteen-mile radius; volunteers came forward to take the horses, unsaddling and hobbling and watering them before turning them loose in a pasture.

How the Change has limited us, thought Juniper. *Fifteen miles is a long way again! This will be recorded and sent out in the* Sun Circle. *Some witnessing is a good idea, but turning it into a circus is not.*

There were better than fifty adults under the judgment tarp, probably ten or fifteen teenagers—

—eòghann, thought Juniper. *We'll call them* eòghann.

That meant *youth* or *helper* in her mother's language.

We need a name for the teenagers who are ready to begin to learn the adult needs and responsibilities, but not yet given a vote. Eóghann will do, since everyone seems determined to play at being Celts.

Juniper shook herself slightly. The profound silence was broken only by the occasional wail from one of the babies, the hoof-clop of a horse shifting its weight or a cough coming through clearly. No trace of the whine and murmur of machine noise in the background anymore, and that still startled her sometimes with a quietness unlike anything she'd ever experienced unless on a hiking trip in wilderness. It made familiar places unfamiliar.

She stood behind the large folding table. There was a tall chair for her . . .

A bar stool! she thought. *That's funny on more levels than I can cope with today.*

Most people were sitting on sturdy boxes and baskets in neat rows, very unlike the Clan's usual laissez-faire order. Front and center sat the man who was the focus of this day's process, set apart from them by the white tarp under him and a clear circle of aversion.

On either side of him stood men from the Dun. They had knives in their belts, but that was simply the tool everyone carried now. One also had a pickax handle in his hand, though, and the other a baseball bat.

And they're needed, Juniper thought as she took him in with a grimace. *Yes, with this one.*

He was a strong man, of medium height and well muscled, with striking chiseled features and curly black hair he wore fairly short. The sort who quivered with suppressed anger at the world, to whom everything that thwarted his will was an elemental affront.

He's not afraid, really, she thought; she'd always been good at reading people. *Which means he's not only wicked, he's very arrogant, very stupid, or both.*

As she watched, he shot a sudden glance over his shoulder, a flicker of something triumphant on his face, which he schooled at once as he looked forward again.

"Armsmen, take custody of the prisoner," she said coolly, and saw a moment's doubt on his face.

The men of the Dun moved aside for Sam and Chuck and went to sit with the rest. From their expressions, they were thankful to turn the task over to a uniformed authority, and they weren't the only ones.

Besides their kilts, the two men wore what had been chosen as the Mackenzie war kit, though there hadn't been time to craft enough for everyone yet: a brigandine of two layers of green leather (salvaged from upholstery) with little steel plates riveted between, quivers and yew longbows slung across their backs, shortswords and long dirks and soup-plate bucklers at their belts, a small wicked *sgian dub* knife tucked into one boot-top. The plain bowl helmets with the spray of raven feathers at the brow made them somehow seem less human and more like walking symbols.

Chuck Barstow had a spear as well as the war-harness. The prisoner would have been less surly if he knew what it portended, or that Chuck was High Priest of the Singing Moon Coven as well as second-in-command of their militia. The spear's polished six-foot shaft was *rudha-an*, the same sacred rowan wood used for wands. The head was a foot-long section cut from a car's leaf spring, ground down to a murderous double-edged blade and socketed onto the wood white-hot before it was plunged into a bath of brine and blood and certain herbs.

It had also been graven with ogham runes, the ones that had come again and again when she tossed the yew sticks of divination on the symbol-marked cloth of the *Bríatharogam*. Just two:

Úath, terror.

Whose kenning was *bánad gnúise*, the blanching of faces. For horror and fear and the Hounds of Anwyn.

Gétal, death.

Whose meaning was *tosach n-échto*, called the beginning of slaying. For the taking of life and for sacrifice.

Juniper took a deep breath, and closed her eyes for an instant to make herself believe she was truly here and not imagining it. The dull heat she had felt before came back, manyfold, as if the soil beneath her feet was throbbing with rage.

"Bring him before me."

Her own voice startled her, though casting her trained soprano to carry was second nature for a professional singer. Now it was somehow like the metal on the edge of a knife.

"You heard Lady Juniper, gobshite," Sam said, just barely loud enough for her to catch.

The hand he rested on the man's shoulder to move him forward might have looked friendly, from any distance. Juniper could see the wrist and scarred, corded forearm flex, and the prisoner's eyes went wide for an instant as it clamped with crushing precision. Sam had been born and raised on a small English farm; his trade had been a peculiar type of soldiering for half his forty-two years, before chance or the Weavers left him trapped and injured in the woods near her home just after the Change.

His hobby had been making and using the longbow of his ancestors. He was stocky and of middle height, but those thick spade-shaped hands could crack walnuts between thumb and two fingers. And she happened to know that he hated men like this with a pure and deadly passion.

Chuck Barstow looked grimmer; he'd been a Society fighter and a gardener besides a member of the Singing Moon, not a real warrior by trade, though everyone had seen death and battle in the last eighteen months. But he was equally determined as he paced forward to keep the prisoner bracketed. From the way his eyes were fixed and showed white around the blue, he was *feeling* something too, besides the gravity of the moment, and not enjoying it.

Judy Barstow was at the far right of the table next to a woman who sat tensely upright; her white face frightened and her eyes carefully not focused.

Our prime exhibit, thought Juniper. *Even if I just nursed Rudy, my breasts ache. But why is it so hard to breathe?*

Eilir had moved to sit at the smaller, shorter table, set in an L to the larger one. She turned and her fingers flew. *Shall I find some cold tea for you?*
Yes, thanks.

She drank the lukewarm chamomile thirstily as her daughter pulled a fresh book out of her saddlebags. Ice in summer was a memory, and a possibility someday when they had time for icehouses, but you could get a little coolness by using coarse porcelain.

The book was covered in black leather, carefully tooled with the words:
The Legal Proceedings of Clan Mackenzie, Second Year of the Change.
And below that:
Capital Crimes.

Eilir opened it to a fresh page, pulled out an ink bottle and a steel-nibbed pen that had come out of retirement in an antiques store in Sutterdown. Nobody thought it odd that a fourteen-year-old was acting as court clerk. Standards had changed.

The first pages of the book contained the rituals they had come up with last night, after they had hashed out the legal and moral basis for judging the case. The first pages of the book covered all that, written in Eilir's neat print.

Juniper looked over to the Dun Carson witnesses sitting in the southeast quadrant. Everybody was still, the sensation of their focused attention like and unlike a performance.

"I have been called here to listen to the Dun's judgment against Billy Peers Mackenzie . . ."

"Hey!" the man yelled. "I ain't never said nothing about Mackenzie. That was you-all. I'm William Robert Peers."

Juniper hesitated and then turned her head.

"I will only say this once, Mr. Peers. You will keep your mouth closed until I give you leave to speak. If you speak out of turn again, your guards will gag you. Gags are very uncomfortable. I advise you to be quiet."

"But you can't do that! It isn't legal!"

Sam's hand moved once, and the man stopped with his mouth gaping open. He reached into his sporran, pulled out the gag and shoved it into the man's mouth with matter-of-fact competence, checking carefully to make sure that his tongue lay flat and that it wasn't so large as to stop him from swallowing. The rags wrapped around the wooden core had been steeped in chamomile and fennel seed tea and dried so that it wouldn't taste too foul. Straps around the head held it in place without cutting at the corners of his mouth. He struggled, though it was as ineffectual as a puppy in a man's hands.

"I said I would speak only once. All of you, take heed. If I state a consequence will follow, it will follow. Second chances belong to the times before the Change, when we were rich enough to waste time arguing. You have one minute to stand quiet."

A glance at her watch.

She gazed dispassionately at the struggling man trying to spit the carefully constructed gag out of his mouth. Then she began to count the measured seconds out loud. After the tenth second passed, it caught Peers' attention. At the twentieth second, he stopped struggling.

"Better. If you cause any further disruption, you will be knocked unconscious. I have no time to waste now, in the midst of harvest."

Peers jerked, started to struggle again, saw a sudden movement out of the corner of his eye as Sam raised a hand stiffened into a blade, flinched and subsided. Juniper waited and then turned again to the north leg of the crossroads. She lifted her arms, and Judy placed her staff in her hands; it had the Triple Moon—waxing and full and waning—above two raven heads of silver, and the shaft was also of mountain rowan.

"I have been called here by the Óenach of Dun Carson and by the Ollam of Dun Carson; Sharon Carson, Hearthmistress, Cynthia Carson,

Priestess and First Armsman of Dun Carson, Ray Carson, Second Armsman and Herd Lord in Training, and Brian Carson, Herd and Harvest
Lord, pro-tem, and his wife, Rebekah Carson, the tanner.

"I am Juniper Mackenzie, Chief of the Clan Mackenzie. I am Ollam
Brithem, high judge over our people."

Juniper winced at the power she was claiming. *But I am needed as chief,
and so I must take this burden on. Threes; everything in threes. Continue, woman,
get this over.*

"I am called here, by Óenach, Ollam, and the Gods to hear, to judge,
and to speak. Does any deny my right, my obligation, or my calling? Speak
now or hold your tongue thereafter, for this place and time is consecrated
by our gathering. All we do here is holy—and legal."

Distantly, she was aware that Peers tried to struggle again and quickly
subsided as Sam gripped the back of his neck.

A long silence and she continued, face raised to the sun, eyes closed
against its burning light:

"Let us be blessed!"

"*Manawyddan*—Restless Sea, wash over me."

A green branch sprinkled salt water over her. She tasted the salt on her
lips like tears. Four Priestesses came with green branches, each trailed by a
child holding a bowl of salt water. Each cleansed the people in one of the
quarters; the last pair assiduously cleansed the empty northeastern quarter.

"*Manawyddan*—Restless Sea! Cleanse and purify me! I make myself a
vessel; to listen and to *hear*."

"*Rhiannon*—White Mare, stand by me, run with me, carry me! That
the land and I can be one, with Earth's wisdom."

She bent and took a pinch of the dry dust from the road and sprinkled
it in front of her. There was a long ripple as the Dun Carson people did
the same, and the witnesses.

"*Rhiannon—White Mare, ground me.*"

"*Arianrhod—Star-tressed Lady;* dance through our hearts, our minds, and
through our eyes, bring Your light to us."

She took a torch from Eilir and lit it; the resinous wood flared up. Eilir
took it to the four corners of the crossroads and lit each torch.

"*Arianrhod—Star-tressed Lady;* Bring Your light to me, to us, to the
world.

"*Sea and Land and Sky, I call on you:*

"Hear and hold and witness thus,
"All that we say
"All that we agree
"All that we together do.
"Honor to our Gods! May they hold
"Our oaths
"Our truths."

Then she spoke formally: "Let all here act with truth, with honor and with duty, that justice, safety and protection all be served for this our Clan, and may Ogma of the Honey Tongue lend us His eloquence in pursuit of Truth."

"This Dun's Óenach is begun! By what we decide, we are bound, each soul and our people together."

She turned in place, looking at all the people assembled, and rapped the butt of her staff on the ground.

"I am here, we are here, the Gods are here. So mote it be!"

"*So mote it be!*" the massed voices replied.

She noticed that Rebekah said the words and was glad. They weren't actually religious and it meant she was participating in the Clan's work, rather than standing back, claiming religious exemption. She moved over to the chair and hoisted herself up on it. She could feel Chuck move into place behind her, still holding the spear upright as a symbol of her justice.

The morning sun was pouring down on the tarps and she could feel the heat and sweat that started to trickle down her back and breasts. The kilt had been comfortable while riding down to the crossroads through the forest . . . now the soft wool was sticking to her legs and her kneesocks made her legs itch.

Well, I'm not the only one uncomfortable on all the levels possible.

Juniper tapped her fingers on the table and took up the gavel that Sam had crafted her yesterday evening as they hashed out procedure. She banged it once on the block of wood and spoke formally:

"We are gathered here to make a decision with regards to the matter of the sexual assault visited upon Debbie Meijer yesterday by William Robert Peers, know to us as Billy Peers Mackenzie, who denies that he has accepted the name or Clan of Mackenzie."

She frowned and moved her hand to stop another blow to the struggling Billy. "You will be given your time to talk at its proper place."

He shook his head, his eyes angry and desperate, and she pursed her lips and shook her head in her turn, pointing to the poised hand. He subsided, but his black scowl remained.

"First I am going to address the greater issue. What right have we to judge and sentence and carry out these sentences upon the members of our community and those who dwell upon our land? For more than a year, we have been hurrying from incident to incident, making it up as we go along . . ."

A crack of laughter interrupted her. That was a charge often leveled at pre-Change wiccans: *They just make up the ritual as they go along.*

"But all just law is based on need and precedents and the will of the people. Not much of it is from the legal system that covered the needs of a highly urban, complex society that numbered hundreds of millions and was rich enough to spare the time for slow careful perusals of accusations and defenses.

"We no longer live in the old world of cities and bureaucracies. We live in small, closed villages where the question of guilt is frequently easily established and we have no real need of the elaborate forensic apparatus used previously to establish the *beyond doubt* criteria used before."

She met Billy's angry eyes: "This is how we have been operating and how we will continue to operate in future, until we see a need for something different. Our methods and their success or failure were discussed and reviewed by myself and my advisors. We have reviewed the past seventeen months of work and dispute in the duns and codified the results."

She gestured to the book beneath Eilir's hand: "Clan Mackenzie is a conglomeration of independent settlements that have asked for and received membership in the Clan, that we may support each other and defend each other in a world where nobody can survive alone and no single family can survive alone. These are the means we have found to live together, and live decently. *And it has worked.* We are alive, where millions . . . hundreds of millions . . . almost certainly *billions* . . . have died."

A low murmur went through the group as she looked around, meeting their eyes. That was why so many had joined the group she'd started with a few friends and coven-members meeting at her country retreat, and taken up all its ways. It was what she'd meant that first day, when she'd told them . . .

"It's a Clan we will have to be, as it was in the old days, if we're to live at all."

A low approving rumble at that; the words were already folklore. Perhaps the trappings that had come along with that thought weren't necessary, were just the by-product of that group's obsessions and pastimes from before the Change . . . but the whole thing *worked,* and nobody was going to argue with that. Herself least of all.

Then she went on: "*Salus populi suprema lex*: The good of the people is the highest law. If a person lives in a Dun of the Clan, they are a member of that Dun and subject to the rules, benefits, and obligations of the group. No one compels them to remain, but if they do, it is on the group's chosen terms. This includes the reality of work, of mutual defense, and the obligation to respect others. The Ollam and Óenach of a Dun have every right to judge wrongdoing in their territories and by their people or towards their people.

"Who chooses the Ollam? The people of the Dun. Dun Carson was led by John and Sharon Carson Mackenzie until his death fighting the Protector's men when they tried to take Sutterdown last year. Dun Carson is led by an Ollam of five at this time. They have collectively requested that the Chief Ollam of the Clan deliver the doom in this matter, and that it be witnessed by as many sober and credible members of the other Duns as is possible. We are here today for this purpose."

Two more people were taking down her words in shorthand. Juniper paced her speech to make it easier on her own scribe-daughter to read her lips.

"I will hear first from Debbie Meijer, who also resides in Dun Carson, but has not accepted the name of Mackenzie."

She watched as the injured woman's eyes focused on her, as if she'd been jarred out of some inward prison that was protection as well. Everyone looked lean and fit these days, as well as weathered, but there was gentleness to her face, as well as pain; she had blue-green eyes, and brown hair caught beneath a kerchief. She shrank back for a minute and then rose at Judy's quiet urging and walked forward. Juniper watched her swallow and clench her teeth. She made a slight gesture and Debbie's face contracted. She shook for an instant and then faced the Dun's members.

"I am Debbie Meijer. I've lived with you at Dun Carson since . . . since the Protector's men stole us from Lebanon, and I, uh, escaped. I've not taken the Clan or the name; I've been waiting for my husband, Mark, to come back. Those of you here all know that the 'tinerants have been seeking news of the people stolen from Lebanon, but not much has been heard.

"I . . . I've done my best to fit in and be useful. It's been hard. I've learned and learned and learned for more than a year. I went from an independent, competent citizen to a dependent, stupid member of a farming community."

A wave of motion shook the Carson and Rebekah stepped forward, holding out a green branch.

"I recognize Rebekah Carson." Juniper smiled at Debbie and raised a hand with a gentle gesture to stay her words for a moment:

"Debbie is a good, hard worker who has struggled with the grief she feels for the loss of her husband and her family, who were all on the east coast. We have all liked and supported her."

Juniper hesitated, suppressing a stab of anger; that support had been sadly lacking in some respects. She'd said they were to be as a Clan, and that meant that each protected the other.

No, that needs to be said; but later. Now Debbie needs to finish.

She looked up. Peers was slouched, managing to look as insolent as a man could while gagged and standing under Sam Aylward's hand. He turned his head, caught Debbie's eyes, and moved his hips, slightly but unmistakably.

Juniper's finger pointed. Sam Aylward carefully did *not* smile.

Crack.

Sam's hand slapped across his face, with a sound like leather hitting a board and a speed that was deceptive because of the brisk unhurried casualness of the motion. The man's head whipped around and he staggered. Blood showed around his lips and nose, and his eyes widened with shock.

"You will be respectful," Juniper said flatly. Then: "Please continue, Debbie. Tell us what happened."

Debbie bit her lip and met Juniper's eyes. Her defensive posture straightened and her voice firmed up.

"Yesterday wasn't where it started. Yesterday was where it ended. I've been here since August, last year. Billy Bob came in March or April . . ."

"April!" somebody called from the assembly.

Debbie nodded. "It started right away. He stood in line next to me at suppertime and rubbed himself on me. Cynthia saw him do it and reamed him out in front of everybody. He said that he was only trying to be friendly, and I was a cold bitch and Cynthia a buttinsky kid."

Juniper felt her lips thin out; her eyes went to the Carson girl. Cynthia nodded, but didn't speak.

"After that," continued Debbie, "he was more careful about who'd see him. He followed me when he could, grabbed me, and would touch me every time he could. That hip thing he just did . . . he'd do it every time he could when we were all together. Ray caught him at it a couple of times and told him to stop and Brian backed him up . . . but it just made him a bit more careful.

"He tried to . . . He knocked on my door . . . I guess it was late April, late at night. I didn't even think about the danger; I just opened it and he shoved it open and tried to get in. It hit me in the face and breast and hurt and I screamed and everybody poured out. He tried to say that I had invited him in, but nobody believed him.

"After that, I had to keep my door locked. In May, he tried to climb in the window and I slammed it on his fingers . . . After *that* I had to keep my window closed and just put up with the heat. Ray and Brian were pissed because he said I had slammed his fingers in a door, not the window, and he hadn't done anything. But Tammy saw him fall that day and then they believed me. They kept him away from me by making sure he worked away from the house and I worked close. Sharon and Rebekah told me to be careful to not do anything more to excite him or provoke him. But I *wasn't* doing anything. It was all him.

"Yesterday, we were harvesting and after dinner I went up to my room to change my shirt. I'm glad for the kilt. Pants would be brutal in this heat and I don't like shorts, but I needed a lighter shirt; I was sweltering.

"He was hiding behind the door of my room and he punched me in the back and I stumbled—turned to scream and he punched me in the stomach, threw me on the floor, ripped off my panties . . ."

Juniper caught Judy's eyes and she moved closer to the woman, who'd gone rigid, her voice flat, her face expressionless.

". . . raped me . . . I couldn't breath from the punch. Then he flipped me over and half on the bed and did it from behind and through the behind. He gagged me with my shirt and bit my breasts all over and then punched me again and left me there. Cynthia found me later."

"Not much later," said Cynthia. "When she didn't come back down, I went upstairs. At most ten or fifteen minutes."

Juniper nodded and pointed at Brian. "How did he evade your watchfulness?"

The man looked chagrined. "Well, he didn't. He's just such a slacker, I never thought of it. I just thought he'd gone off somewhere to have a nap. Ray wanted to go look for him, but I told him we were too busy. I shouldn't have ignored him."

"Some nap!" exclaimed Debbie, tears suddenly rolling down her flaming cheeks.

Judy led her away, a careful arm around her shoulders.

Juniper nodded, feeling the anger on her face and knowing it scared Brian Carson.

"Judy?" she asked.

Judy Barstow came forward again: everyone knew she'd been a registered nurse and midwife before the Change, and in overall charge of the Clan's health care since. She wasn't as popular as Juniper—her brisk, no-nonsense personality was a little more abrasive—but nobody doubted her competence.

"I conducted the examination yesterday evening. Debbie has been hit. There is a bruise on her back, between the shoulder blades. There is a wound, made by a ring from the placement. She was, indeed, struck in her solar plexus. Soft belly tissue doesn't show bruises as easily, but there are two marks similar to the ring mark on her back. By tomorrow, I believe she'll have serious bruising on her front. I also believe there is internal damage, probably to her spleen. I hope it will heal, but for now, she's on light duty, mostly off her feet.

"She was clearly raped, vaginally and anally. There is considerable trauma and damage to the surrounding structures as well as rips and tears from fingernails. Sperm was present in both places."

Juniper nodded, her stomach roiling. *I wish Eilir didn't need to hear this! Or any of the Clan's children. Unfortunately they all need to hear it, loud and clear.*

"One last item, then, before I speak as Ollam and Brithem. Brian compiled a set of weregeld statements for Billy Bob and Debbie."

She looked down and made a moue at them.

"Billy Bob's will not surprise many people. He arrived empty-handed except for a belt knife and an ax, but not hungry, on a bicycle in late April of this year, claiming to have come from Hood River where the Portland

Protective Association, in the person of one Conrad Renfew... now calling himself *Count* Conrad Renfew... took over. He was accepted into Dun Carson. His record since then has been that of a slacker and troublemaker. Brian considers that he hasn't actually done enough work day to day to cover his room and board. He also shorted, cheated, or went absent on sentry go twice before being removed from the sentry rolls altogether.

"I am going to send out an advisory to all the Duns. We now have intelligence about Hood River. Though the Portland Protective Association took it over, for once the people of Hood River are actually *grateful* to them for this."

That brought another murmur, this time of surprise. The PPA's Lord Protector was, at the very least, a psychopath, though a very able and surprisingly farsighted one; his followers ranged from extremely hard men to outright thugs. But there were times when people would accept the hardest hand if it meant life and peace enough to sow and reap, and the Association was trying very hard indeed to get agriculture going again in its territories. Nor did they tolerate outlaw raiders...

If only because it's competition, she thought mordantly, and went on:

"They had a homegrown bandit problem, a very bad one. Any Dun that took in Hood River people over the period from March through late April will need to look carefully at them. They may be the bandits themselves, the ones Renfrew didn't hang or behead. I suspect that is the case here.

"To continue. Debbie's weregeld sheet states that she arrived with the titles to seventy acres outside of Lebanon and another hundred acres up by Silverton. This she handed over to the Clan in November when the Kyklos asked for free title to the lands they took possession of in September. We received a large consignment of goods in return for that and several other property titles. Debbie is credited with a proportional value of that shipment. Debbie is a hard worker, very community minded, and easy to get along with. She has been learning a number of skills for our Changed world, caring for dairy cattle, butter-making and cheese-making, and sewing and preserving food as well as the standard tasks."

Juniper folded her hands over the papers and looked into the insolent hazel eyes of the gagged man before her.

"Before I say anything about this particular case, I have something to say that will be sent to all the Clan territories. *Dun Carson failed to protect Debbie Meijer."*

She paused, to allow Eilir to catch up and to control herself. She caught Brian and then Rebekah's eyes. They dropped theirs and flushed with shame.

"Harassment, bullying, tormenting, destructive teasing . . . none of these are acceptable behaviors in a world where everybody depends on everybody else and nobody can move away. Children are taught by admonishment and example because they know no better. But adults are expected to listen and understand and conform. Chronic problems must not be allowed to fester. We of the Clan *must* be able to trust each other; our *lives* depend upon it."

Juniper drummed her fingers on the table and scowled into the sneering face of the gagged man. "Billy Bob brought up the legality of our actions. I will address this point first."

She felt an angry satisfaction to see how he hated that she spoke of him by the nicknames he'd used back when he'd arrived in Clan Mackenzie territory.

"Clan Mackenzie is a sovereign state. We are neither bound by nor follow the legal system of the old United States of America, which is utterly unsuited to this world we find ourselves in. Therefore, Mr. Peers, you are not in Kansas anymore, and we will not allow you to try legal quibbles or time-wasting efforts to negotiate yourself out of your just deserts, no, that we will not!

"Now is the time when you will speak. When I tell you to not speak anymore, you will close your mouth and not speak anymore. When I ask you a question, you will answer it directly. You will not speak other than to answer the questions I put to you until I give you leave to speak freely.

"Do you understand?"

She saw the sly look in his eyes as he nodded and nodded herself in turn.

"Do you agree to only answer the questions put to you and to be silent when ordered?"

The way his teeth showed reassured her that she was reading the situation well. He nodded, slowly, as if he were forcing his head to move against rigid sinews.

"The gag will be used, if necessary. Be warned that attempts to blame your victim will be met with gagging. Rape is an offense against the

Goddess Herself and an insult to the Horned Lord, Her consort and lover. It is a vile mockery of the Great Rite by which They made and maintain the world and to let it go unpunished would be to risk Their anger.

"We have religious freedom here; you are being punished for your crime against Debbie Meijer, not against the Powers who make and shape the world, whatever else we mean by it. However, insulting our morals is blasphemy and will be met with severe penalties. And you . . . well, you *are* a rapist."

She nodded to Alex, who unstrapped the gag device. Billy Bob spit out the tongue depressor and drew in a breath . . . and froze as his eyes met hers. She held them until he let go of the breath and slumped slightly.

"Better," she approved. "Did you rape Debbie Meijer?"

Once again he drew in a breath and met her eyes . . . and hesitated.

"You can't prove it!" he challenged.

"Why not? Are you sure nobody saw you?"

"Of course . . . nobody saw me. I wasn't there!" Juniper grimaced wryly. *Good recovery*, she thought. *Not going to get him on a* Perry Mason.

Juniper nodded. "We do not depend on people seeing you. Proof, as you call it, is a matter of belief. Everybody in the Dun's Óenach believes you did what you are accused of, based on observations and tracking of movements and knowledge of who and what you are. Your guilt has been established to the satisfaction of the Dun, and I have accepted it.

"Debbie's unsupported word and the state of her body are enough to prove to us she has been raped. Her struggle with your continual harassment is enough to condemn you in the eyes of the community. The mark of your ring on her body in three places is also very telling. Keep in mind that I was not asked to come and decide if you were guilty. That was established yesterday afternoon when you were locked up and Judy Barstow Mackenzie made her examination of Debbie. You are the man who raped her. My task is to determine what to do with you.

"In Clan Mackenzie our guiding principle is the weregeld principal, of compensation. For injury to property or failure to do your share you may be fined labor or goods for the waste you caused. For repeated offenses, expulsion by the vote of the community.

"For injury—which can cover malicious gossip, physical assault, and damage to a persons' property or animals—the only question is how dangerous the perpetrator is. We have a responsibility. We cannot turn a dangerous person out to the world if we reasonably believe that he or she will injure another person.

"For murder. The circumstances of the cause of death must be reviewed by a coroner appointed by the Dun's Ollam and the decision will rest upon those findings and the conclusion with the Ollam and the Óenach."

She could see that Billy Bob was relaxing. He shrugged. After a few seconds' thought, she nodded at him. "I have reached my decision. Do you have any final words to say?"

"Sure!" he said, sitting up again. "Gimme my bike, load the saddlebags with enough food, and I'll be gone north before the door hits the back wheel!"

The members of Dun Carson stirred, anger on many faces; a few shouted wordlessly in rage or denial. Juniper let them settle down; Billy Bob started to twist, but Sam was still holding his shoulder and he could no more break that hold than he could the steel grip of a vise.

"As far as the Dun is concerned, you have not managed to work enough to justify your keep in the four months you have been here. You came with nothing but an old bike, which has been, since, broken up for repair parts."

"Fuck!" yelled Billy Bob. "That was *my* bike and *you* owe *me*!"

"No," said Juniper. "You owe the Clan four months' room and board. Room is assessed at a pint of wheat a day and board at three pints of wheat a day. For one hundred and twenty-six days, total. This is a little more than five bushels of wheat."

"You're crazy!" he said, staring at her. "Where'm I going to get wheat?"

"From the sweat of your brow!" said Brian, anger clotting his voice.

Billy Bob swung around but Juniper spoke; her voice diamond edged. "Stop. That is moot; infliction of injury trumps all else."

There was silence before she went on: "Does anybody from the Óenach have anything to say about the potential of Billy Bob raping another woman if he is expelled?"

One of the older children—*eóghann*, she reminded herself—raised a hand. "May I speak?" he asked. Juniper frowned as the boy's mother reached out a hand and then drew it back.

"Yes. You have a voice, but not a vote."

"He . . . yesterday—early; and before, he used to work next to me. I tried to get changed around, but Brian said that it would hurt morale and I should be able to ignore him. But he always talked; he'd say really ugly things about

Debbie. He was always talking about her. Sometimes he talked about other women, not from here, and not all from Hood River. He'd laugh and chuckle . . . like it was as much . . . fun . . . to talk about it to me, yelling at him to shut up, as it was to do the gross things he told me about."

Juniper didn't put her head down on the table, or scream, or dance with rage. But the impulse was surely there.

"Does anybody else have a similar story?"

She winced, and so did the Óenach. All the raised hands were of the *eóghann* and a sprinkling went up in the children's section.

Brian's red face went white and his arm went around Rebekah. Their thirteen-year-old daughter's hand was waving in the air. Juniper counted.

"Failure to properly address the issue has left your children vulnerable to a rapist. And he took advantage of your carelessness. Nine *eóghann* and three children have been molested, physically or verbally.

"Before I proceed, Dun Carson Óenach, your Ollam have failed you. Do you wish to vote in a new Ollam?"

The Óenach seethed as people turned and spoke with each other. Cynthia and Ray stood close to their mother, all three crying. Rebekah and Brian had opened their arms for Sara, who came running to them, tears flying off her cheeks.

"You told Debbie to not make too many waves or provoke him . . ."

Eilir turned with her pen poised and her face grim.

What a can of worms, oh mother-mine. Juniper nodded. *I keep thinking we've understood the Change and all the little Changes. But it keeps biting us in the butt.*

A man stood up, looking around at the rest of the Óenach and twisting his cap in his hands. Nods and encouraging hand waves pushed him forward:

"I'm Josh Heathrow. I kind'a called myself a pagan before the Change. Accepting the Goddess was easy for me; but I haven't really wanted to go for the full priesthood. Still, the Óenach asked me to speak for all of them. And the bottom line is, we don't think any of us could have done better. And it sucks to kick somebody out to starve . . . or get taken by Eaters . . . and that's what it would be. But . . . things have changed. We've got to work with that, and it isn't easy getting our heads around it.

"Once something physical actually happened, Brian did something about it; quick too. I guess we all feel that this is one of those lessons and we need to make real sure we don't do it again. But, nobody seems to want the Carsons booted out. They're all good folk and pretty conscientious, and this *was* their land, for generations. Uh, maybe the fields, you know, wouldn't like it if we changed that."

He looked around and abruptly sat again. Juniper had been scanning the faces as he spoke.

"There is consensus, then?" she asked.

"*Aye!*"

"Very well. Brian, you and Rebekah will have to come to the Hall. I expect that I will come here, as well. We'll take time to examine different situations and possible strategies. Sharon, Cynthia, and Ray will spend extra hours with Judy, reviewing their soon-to-be responsibilities.

"Having done that, I pronounce the sentence."

"Hey! Wait! I ain't been found guilty yet . . . or convicted!"

Peer's eyes bulged with the sudden terror of illusions pierced at last.

"Didn't you hear me tell you I was not brought to judge your guilt? I am here to pronounce your doom."

Billy Bob started up, screaming obscenities and denials, and Sam forced the gag back in his mouth. A swift kick to the back of the leg put him on his knees, whooping air in and out through his nose, and the armsman gripped him by a handful of hair.

Juniper stood and raised her staff again: "Hear the word of the Ollam Brithem of Clan Mackenzie!"

Silence fell, except for the slobbering panting of the gagged man and the far-off nicker of a horse:

"Dun Carson will accept two trained priestesses and a priest into the Dun to help those wounded in their hearts by this man's deeds. These will not be members of the Dun, but will work, as we all do.

"Debbie has six months to decide if she wishes to stay with Dun Carson, join another Dun, or lead a group north to reclaim her land near Lebanon, becoming an Ollam chief in her turn. Should she leave Dun Carson, Dun Carson shall dower her with goods equivalent to her hard work as set forward by Brian Carson in this sheet. Dun Juniper will give her support against the amount her surrender of the title to the acres in Silverton has given the Clan. Dun Carson will add a weregeld of an extra one-fifth for allowing her to suffer sexual harassment for four months, and will make formal apology."

Juniper stood and took the spear from Chuck. She pointed it at the prone body of Billy Bob, and the light flashed off it, flickering in the graven Ogham characters.

"This man is a mad dog. He attacks the young, and destroys the reputation of his victims as well as their honor and integrity. Expelling him will not protect us from him. He could return at any moment, hide and attack us and ours by stealth, knowing our defenses. Or he would find and prey on others. We must remove him from the circle of the world, for we are responsible. We found him in our nest, on our land, despoiling our people. Last night I and my advisors discussed the possible permutations. We have established a ritual and will deliver death through it. Let the Guardians of the Northern Gate judge him; let him make amends and come to know himself in the Land of Summer.

"Death is a dread thing and all of us have found ourselves over the past year confronted by death and the fear of death. I killed a man scant hours after the Change, saving another. But we must not let ourselves become calloused by it, nor shut it away and out of our minds. And so Dun Carson will carry out the sentence. We will not hide from ourselves what we have decided to do, nor let another bear the burden."

Billy kicked and tried to spasm himself upright. His scream was blurred, but he struggled until the hair began to tear out by the roots.

Sam thoughtfully backheeled him in the stomach. "Oi'd give it a rest, if Oi was you, mate. It'll hurt more, else."

Chuck lifted up a pot.

"There are fifty-three marbles in this urn. Six green ones, four red ones, a black one, and forty-two blue ones. Each adult will take a marble. The six people who pick a green marble will dig the grave, six feet down, by six feet long by three feet wide."

He pointed to the unoccupied northeastern corner of the crossroads, where three shovels stood driven into the sod.

"The four red marbles are for the four people who will escort him to his place of execution and hold him there. The black marble is for the executioner. Everybody over sixteen will witness. Parents may allow children from fourteen to sixteen to be present.

"The youngsters are to return to the Dun, out of the sight and sound of the execution."

Billy Bob's body bucked, thrashing. A stink suddenly filled the air as his bowels loosed and he fainted. Judy gestured forward some of the witnesses from the other Duns. They stripped the unconscious man, wiped him down with rags, and put an old polyester bathrobe on him, grimacing in distaste.

Sam Aylward snorted. "Oi'd have made 'im dig it 'isself," he observed mildly.

The pot passed around the Óenach; some snatched at the marbles, some hesitated, some held theirs up, and others looked at it in their palm before opening their fingers. One or two sobbed with relief when their marble was blue. Gradually six people walked over to the shovels and began to lay out the grave and dig, using tarps to heap up the soil. Four people, three men and a woman, came to stand over the prone man. Then a sound burst across the pavilion and a woman Juniper did not know walked up to the man and opened her hand. The black marble fell on his shirt.

"Fitting," said Brian. "She's been trying to make us do something about the man. And threatening to do it herself."

Juniper grimaced. "Well, unless she's a stone-cold killer, she's going to learn precisely the lesson I want to teach the entire Dun and the moiety of Clan Mackenzie, about paying and punishment."

"Lady," said Brian. "Sarah's only thirteen, but she wants to stay . . . and Rebekah and I think she should."

Juniper was reaching for Rudy, shifting her blouse and plaid so that she could nurse the cranky baby. She hesitated, focused on getting Rudy latched on; not that that generally took much, but she usually didn't nurse him under a shawl.

What are we going to do when nursing bras fall apart? Stays . . . ugh!

As Rudy began to feed she met Sarah's eyes. "Why?" she asked simply.

The girl looked ready to cry and angry at the same time. "He . . . he threatened to kill me. Said . . . well, said he'd killed Bunny FooFoo and he'd do me just like that."

The girl looked sick and Juniper had to force herself to lift a brow at Brian. The heavyset man shook his head gloomily.

"You know, Lady. I wasn't one for your religion. But it seems like I've got an almighty clout upside the head for being careless.

"Yeah, the rabbit was killed. I tried to tell her it was a coyote, but even I didn't believe it and for sure she didn't; but she didn't fight me on it. And we really needed the rabbit; it was a French Angora and we were hoping to start a specialty wool stock with it. Sarah's trying to breed back the traits from the kits, but it'd be a lot easier if the male was still here.

"I'm babbling. Sara needs to see he really does die. And I do too. I just wish he could die ten times."

Juniper shook her head, rocking the baby. "It's easy and normal for you to feel you are punishing him. And warning others about it. But it doesn't work that way. Think of it as culling the herd. This is a protective measure and we're going to make it pretty much as quick as possible."

She shifted the baby to the other breast and looked at Sara. "I don't want you to watch. I understand why you do, but I don't think it is healthy."

She looked at Brian and then Rebekah.

"Do you have a better reason for her watching? There's going to be no doubt that he's dead."

Brian shook his head and hesitated. "You know, Lady. It says in the Bible, *the wages of sin is death*. But it's been a long, long time since we really meant those words. We all focus on the living gift of God. How many people are going to try to live by sacred works, like you Mackenzies do . . . and what's it going to mean to justice?"

Chuck was standing by them and he shook his head. "If you think we had true, pure, unadulterated justice in the old world . . ."

"No," said Rebekah. "It was flawed, and people got off scot-free . . . and we nearly let this man get off scot-free. But that doesn't mean that the old ways were any better. The law was cruel and harsh. Did it really need to be?"

She shook her head and then looked at her daughter. "Is that it? You're afraid we'll let him get off, like they let that teacher go free after Melly complained about him?"

Sara nodded, tears in her eyes. The four adults shook their heads. Rebekah turned her daughter to the group of children.

"Go. He is going to die. And if he escapes, in that ratty tatty bathrobe of your uncle's, I promise to tell you."

Sara resisted and then moved back towards the group of younger people. Rebekah was frowning and started when Brian placed a hand on her shoulder.

"What is it, love?" he asked.

She shook her head. "A thought. One we need to talk over, later."

The grave-diggers climbed out of the pit and pulled the ladder after themselves, wiping brows; one stopped and looked at the sweat on his palm, as if shocked that it was the same as any other work. The rest crowded together around the hole, far enough back that they didn't break down the fragile walls. The escorts slapped Billy Bob awake and heaved him up. He struggled, but the four held him tightly.

He was struggling too hard for them to get him down into the cool, loamy recess. Juniper walked forward to stand at the north end of the grave. When the escorts looked to her for ideas on what to do, she spread her hands.

"This is the burden the Powers have chosen for you, my friends," she said quietly, her voice cutting through the strangled grunts. "And it is yours."

They held him in the center and looked at each other. One gestured the ladder to be placed at the far end. The woman and one of the men let go and climbed down. With shocking suddenness the two men grabbed Peers by the arms and legs, swung him over the grave, and let his feet go. He dropped and the two down below grabbed him and shoved him down onto the ground; it was moist and brown-gray, with an earthworm crawling from a clod. The scent rose from the dark earth, loamy and rich. There was a sense of *rightness* to it.

Ropes and stakes bound his feet and arms and shoulders to the ground.

"Lady? Do we take off the gag?" asked one of them, just as Judy came bustling up with the soiled ground cloth, clothes, and rags.

"Ask him. And ask yourselves. Do you care if he goes silenced to his death, or would you rather hear his last screams? What are you willing to live with?"

They climbed out, all but one. "Well?" he asked. Juniper stood, her arms aching from holding the hefty weight of the nine-month-old . . . and refusing to give him back to Melissa. The Óenach murmured and shifted, whispered and rustled.

Josh Heathrow stepped forward again, carefully on the verge. He looked down and asked.

"What do you want? Gag out before you are killed or shall we leave it in?"

Juniper heard a thump. The man on the ladder gave an impatient exclamation and jumped down. "He wants it out, but it's clear he's going to be ugly about it," he called up.

"No class," said Chuck in a regretful sotto voice. "Nothing like the grand old tradition of English highwaymen proudly declaiming their prowess on the gibbets."

Juniper sighed and gently kicked him on the shin. Josh was consulting with the Óenach and Ollam again.

Finally he leaned over. "We don't need his curses, and we don't need to give him any further opportunity to work harm. And we don't need more fuel for nightmares. Leave the gag in."

Judy neatly dropped the bundle of dirty cloth in at the foot of the grave.

Brian stepped forward with Ray by his side, white, and shuddering, but gulping in a big breath of air as his uncle spoke.

"Óenach and Ollam have agreed that this man did"—he looked over at Juniper for a second—"profane the Great Rite and the precious mysteries of love by raping a woman of the Dun, yesterday. His offense against the Powers is his, but it is our right to judge him for his offense against our sister. We have since learned that he also attempted to corrupt some of our children. Mad dogs must die. There is no cure that is worth the price we'd pay.

"Mairead, are you ready?"

The woman who'd taken the black marble stepped forward. Like many, her face was white as she realized just what she was going to do.

This is not the heat of battle, when you strike out blindly in fury and in fear, Juniper thought. *This is not the hot blood of a quarrel. This we do with deliberation and with ceremony. We have our doubts, but we hide them. We call upon the Powers; we say, the Law; we say, we the People; we say, the State. But what we do, we still do as human souls.*

The Chief stepped forward; Chuck and she grasped the spear to hand it to the chosen one. Juniper gasped, and felt the High Priest's hand stiffen on the rowan wood beside hers. Eilir's head came around too, and more than one among the onlookers. The jolt she felt was still hot and angry, but it was the wound tension before the lightning strikes, and there was something else in it, a calling—

"This man was a child once," she said, as if the words welled up from the innermost part of her mind. "The Mother gave him being, and his mother loved him. He was given great gifts—a strong healthy body, a cunning mind, a nimble tongue, a great will to live, or he would not have survived this long. He was given a *life,* and such a sorry botch he has made of it for himself and for others."

All of them were looking at her, wire-tense and focused. Her voice rose:

"Can you not *feel* the anger of the Powers at what he has done, and what he has profaned? The slighting of the Mystery that They give us, for our joy and that we might join Them in bringing forth life?"

A sound like wind through trees as the people nodded.

"Yet now we help him make atonement; and so also we appease Them with this sacrifice. But even in the anger of the Dark Mother, there is love. The Keeper of Laws is stern, but just. Beyond the Gate in the Land of Summer, Truth stands naked and he will know himself. He himself will choose how to make himself whole, and be reborn through the cauldron of Her who is Mother-of-All into the life he chooses. So mote it be!"

"So mote it be!"

Mairead shook as the High Priestess and High Priest solemnly handed her the spear.

"This spear was made for this purpose alone," Juniper said. "It is blessed and consecrated for it."

The shaft wobbled dangerously and Sam jumped to the rescue.

"'Ere," said Sam. "Hold on, lass. Let me reverse it. Now, poke it over the edge. You, Danny, put it where Oi told you to. There. Now, both 'ands on the shaft . . . see, where I wrapped deer-hide around it so it won't slip. One hard shove. Don't let 'im suffer. It's at the right angle now. It'll go into his heart, neat and quick. *Now.*"

Juniper kept her face calm by main force of effort. *Have I asked too much? Should I start a tradition of black-masked executioners? No! This is our justice and we need to own it.*

Mairead trembled and Brian stepped to her left and Josh to her right. They set their hands on the shaft, above and below hers.

"Come," said Josh. "You must do it. But we'll add our strength to yours. It'll be quick."

Even as Mairead gulped and tightened her hands, Sharon and Rebekah stepped forward and put hands on her shoulders. Juniper watched her close her eyes . . . not to block out the sight, but to feel the position of the shaft, and then she pushed, sudden and hard.

The razor-sharp head sliced into Billy Bob's chest cavity and through his heart and the body bucked once more and was still. The man down in the grave, Sam, and Brian all thrust a little harder, getting the head fixed into the soil beneath.

And something *snapped*. The hot anger that had risen up from her feet was gone, with only a brief cool wind of sorrow. Then the day was merely a day once more, and there was work to be done.

Juniper thrust Rudy into Eilir's arms and turned, took up a shovel and filled it with the grave dirt.

"I cast you out," she said clearly, and carefully threw the dirt into the grave.

The last man climbed out, pulled by his friends. Willing hands grabbed the shovels and began to rain the dirt back into the grave.

"I cast you out."

"I protect the children."

"I reject your blasphemy."

"I protect myself."

Juniper stood back. Mairead was still trembling. People came to hug her, but the mood remained somber. Juniper nodded to herself as she took back Rudy. Her hands moved in sign, small ones, restrained by the child.

Yes. This is how we own our lives.

The grave filled quickly, the long shaft poking out above the ground. Red and black ribbons were tied around it and Juniper turned north again, the hot afternoon sunshine on her left, now. Eilir reached for Rudy and she let him go.

Sharon moved to stand at her left hand, and to her surprise, not Cynthia, but Rebekah, moved over to her right.

She lifted her arms:

"*Manawyddan—Restless Sea*, cleanse and purify us! We have taken our actions in defense of our people. They are not actions to take lightly. Restless Sea, cleanse us!

"*Rhiannon—White Mare*, hold him deep in the earth, that he may have time to learn and be reborn to try again."

"*Arianrhod—Star-tressed Lady;* bring Your light to us, light of reason. Protect us from the night fears; give us eyes that we may see protect those we love before harm befalls them."

"*This gathering of the Dun for justice is done. We have met in sorrow, debated in pain, and leave with resolution. So mote it be!*"

"So mote it be!" called the Óenach as they picked up their boxes and baskets, pulled down the tarps, and offered hospitality to the neighbors.

Juniper nodded in approval when the witnesses all made *namaste,* and refused quiet words of support and offers of help shared forth before they left to seek their own homes and the labor that would not, could not, wait.

"Lady, what should we do now?" asked Cynthia Carson.

"Keep a wake, I think," said Juniper. "You'll have to play this by ear. But I think the next day or two should be focusing on doing all the small tasks. You are all upset, and it's easier for you to make mistakes."

Brian and Ray and Sharon nodded. They picked up the bundles of tarps the others had left behind and trudged back to the Dun.

Juniper sighed. "And it's home for us, too, now. We may reach there before the sunset, we may indeed."

She rubbed her forehead fretfully. "I wish we hadn't needed to deal with something this grotesque for our first foray into a capital crime."

Sam shrugged, holding Melissa close. "If not this, then something else, Lady. Whatever it was, it would have felt loik the worst thing to us."

Juniper sighed and shrugged. *I want to be home and with my loved ones. I think we'll be waking the night too.*

Samuel Sykes

Sometimes you'd better *listen,* as hard as you can, if you want to survive . . .

Samuel Sykes is a relatively new author. His novels to date include *Tome of the Undergates, Black Halo,* and *The Skybound Sea,* which together make up the Aeons' Gate series. Born in Phoenix, Arizona, he now lives in Flagstaff, Arizona.

NAME THE BEAST

When the fires of the camp had died and the crows settled in the boughs of the forest, she could hear everything her husband said.

"And the child?" Rokuda had asked her. He spoke in the moment the water struck the flame. His words were in the steam: as airy, as empty.

They only spoke at night. They only spoke when the fires were doused.

"She's asleep," Kalindris had replied. Her words were heavier in the darkness.

"Good. She will need her rest." There had never been a darkness deep enough to smother the glimmer of his green eyes. *"You should, too. I want you bright and attentive."*

She had not looked up from sharpening her knife. Just as she had decided not to stab him with it for talking to her in such a way. Fair trade, she had reasoned. She ran her finger along the edge, felt it bite cleanly. She slid it into a scabbard before reaching for her boots, just where she had always left them.

"She can rest. She can stay resting. I'll leave before dawn. I'll be back before dusk. She never has to know."

"No."

For want of hackles, her ears rose up, sharp and pointed like her knife. They folded flat against her head. Rokuda had not seen it. Even if he had, she had reasoned, he wouldn't care. He was like that.

"I asked no question," she had replied.

"What am I to tell her, then?" Rokuda had asked.

"Whatever you wish. I left without her. The beast was too close. The tribe was in danger. I could not to wait for her." She had pulled on her boots. *"I don't need your words. You can give them to her."*

"No."

"Do not say that word to me."

"She has to learn. She has to learn to hunt the beast, to hate the beast, to kill it."

"Why?"

"Because we are shicts. Our tribes came to this world from the Dark Forest. Before humans, before tulwars, before any monkey learned to walk on two legs, we were here. And we will be here long after them. Because to protect this land, they all must die."

His speeches no longer inflamed her. She felt only chill in his words now.

"She has to learn to be like a shict," Rokuda had said. *"She has to learn our legacy."*

"Yours."

Kalindris felt him in the darkness as he settled beside her. She felt his hand even before he had touched her. In the prickle of gooseflesh upon her skin, in the cold weight in the pit of her belly. Her body froze, tensing for a tender blow. She felt each knucklebone of each finger as he pressed his hand against the skin of her flank.

Like it belonged there.

"Be reasonable about this . . ." Honey sliding down bark, his voice had come.

"Don't touch me."

"The other tribesmen won't look at her. They won't listen to her. They look at her and wonder what kind of creatures she came from. What her parents were to raise . . . her. You must take her to the forest. You will show her how it's done."

"I must do nothing. And you can't change everything you don't like."

"Yes I can."

Bark peeling off in strips, his voice came. He tightened his fingers. She felt every hair of every trace of skin rising up. She felt the knife at her belt. She heard it in its sheath. She heard her own voice.

Steam in darkness. Airy. Empty.

"Don't touch me."

Between the sunlight seeping through the branches overhead, she could hear the forest.

A deer's hoof scratching at the moss of a fallen log. A tree branch shaking as a bird took off into the sky. A line of ants so thick as to forget they were ever individuals marching across a dead root.

Sounds of life. Too far. Her ears rose. Kalindris listened closer.

A moth trying hard to remain motionless as a badger snuffed around the fallen branch it sat upon. A tree groaning as it waited for the rot creeping down its trunk to reach its roots. The crunch of dead leaves beneath a body as a boar, snout thick with disease and phlegm, settled down to die.

Closer. She drew in a breath, let it fill her, exhaled.

Air leaving dry mouths. Drops of salt falling on hard earth. A whining, noisy plea without words.

And she heard it.

The Howling told Kalindris who needed to die.

"This is taking forever."

Her ears lowered. Her brows furrowed. Her frown deepened.

The child.

Talking.

Again.

"You already *found* the tracks," the child complained. "Two *hours* ago. We could have found the beast by now. Instead I've spent half an hour waiting, half an hour searching for more tracks, half an hour shooting arrows through the gap between those branches over there and half an hour wondering how best to shoot myself with my own bow so I can deny boredom the pleasure of killing me."

The Howling left her, swift and easy as it had come. The shicts asked for nothing for their goddess, Riffid. To invite her attention was to invite her ire. She had given them nothing but life and the Howling and then left to the Dark Forest. They had spent generations honing it, the sense above all others, the voice of life and of death.

And somehow, the child's whining could send it away in an instant.

"When do we get to the *hunt*?"

It didn't matter. The Howling had shown Kalindris enough. The other noises of life and death weren't important. She held on only to that final one, that which teetered between the two. The sound of uncertainty. The sound that waited for her to tip the balance toward darkness.

Kalindris rose. The leaves fell from her hunting leathers as she slung the bow and quiver over her shoulder. The leather settled into a familiar furrow upon the bare skin of her neck's crook, the only other presence she had ever allowed that close to her throat. And the only one she ever would again, she thought as she rubbed a scar across her collarbone. She could still feel as she ran her hands across the scarred flesh. Every knucklebone of every finger, sinking into her skin.

Without a glance behind her, Kalindris hopped off the rock and set off after the noise. The forest rose up around her in aloof pillars, not like the familial closeness of the inner woods that left no room for sunlight. Too much light here on the border of the sea of trees; too much seeing, not enough listening. The Howling didn't speak clearly here. She had to keep her ears up and open.

They rose up like spears and she listened. Leaves crunching, an offended cry, hurried breath.

The child.

Following.

Still.

"*Hey!* Don't treat me like I'm an idiot!" the child protested, hurrying after her. "If you're going to try to abandon me, at least be a little less obvious about it. It might give me the opportunity to track you and get *something* done today."

Abandonment needed more than she had to give. That needed malice, anger, and she could spare none for the child. That was for someone else, along with her arrows, her knife and this day.

"Why won't you talk to me?" the child asked. "I did everything right. I followed the tracks like you showed me. I've done everything you told me to. What did I do wrong?"

The child spoke too much. That was why Kalindris didn't speak; the child used all the words. That was what she did wrong. She shouldn't need nearly as much as she used. She shouldn't need *any*. The Howling was the shict language, that which came with breath and wailing as they were born.

And the child couldn't hear it. The child couldn't use it. She could only breathe. She could only wail.

It hurt Kalindris' ears.

"Are we at least going the right way?" the child asked. "I can't come back until the beast is dead. If I do, I don't get my feathers. I won't be accepted." The child's voice dropped. "Father said."

She stopped and cringed.

Rokuda said. Rokuda said lots of things. Rokuda said things like they were fact, like his word was all that mattered. Anyone that disagreed saw those bright green eyes and wide, sharp smile and heard his honey when he told them they were wrong.

Before Kalindris knew it, her back hurt. Her spine was rigid like a spear and visible beneath her skin. She turned around, ears flat against the side of her head, teeth bared.

The child stood there. Her hair was too bright, cut like some golden shrubbery and the feathers in her locks stuck out at all strange angles. The bow around skinny shoulders was strung and strung wrong, the skinny arms were too small to pull back the arrow. And her ears stuck out awkwardly, one up and one down, long and smooth and without notches in them. They were always trying to listen for something they couldn't hear.

Her eyes were far too green.

"Your father," she said, "is not always right."

"If that were true, everyone wouldn't listen to him when he speaks," the child protested. She swelled with a rehearsed kind of pride, the kind she clearly felt she should have, rather than actually possessed. "When Father speaks, people listen. When he tells them to do something, they *do it.*"

Words. Heavy words coming from the child. Like she believed them.

An agonizing moment of concentration was needed for Kalindris to unclench every knucklebone of every finger from her fist. She had to turn away and tear her eyes and shut her ears to the child. She hefted her quiver, continued to follow the noise through the trees.

"We shouldn't have come here. We should have listened to it."

"We had no choice. Just keep moving. *Keep* moving."

Mother and Father were fighting again.

"It got Eadne. That *thing* got my Eadne. And we left her. And we ran. From our own land!"

"Gods, will you just *shut up* and let me think?"

Mother and Father were not scared because they were fighting. And so neither was Senny.

Whenever she would get scared, she would look to Mother and Father. Mother would look at Father and get mad. Father would look at Mother and start yelling. And they would fight too much to be scared. So she would hold onto the little knife tucked away in her belt and she would be ready to fight and she wouldn't be scared, either.

No matter how fast they were running. No matter how hard Mother was pulling on her arm.

"It *killed* her. It left her in a tree and painted the bark red with her. We should have stayed. We should have buried her. We shouldn't have run."

"We didn't have a choice, you *idiot*. It was going to come for us next. It's coming for us *now*. Think of her."

Senny knew who they were talking about. Father called them monsters. They had come to their little house and told him to leave. They said it was their forest. He told them he wouldn't. So they took Eadne.

Their name sounded like an angry word.

Father reached down and took Senny's other hand. He pulled on it, too. Maybe to show Mother he could pull harder, so he wasn't as scared. She pulled her hand back so she could grab the little knife and show Father she wasn't scared, either.

But he didn't notice.

He was looking forward. Mother was looking back. They said Eadne was back there, but Eadne wasn't coming with them. They weren't talking about Eadne. Maybe they didn't want her to feel scared. She already knew, though. She had seen Eadne up in the tree with the branches and the leaves and her legs all blowing the same way in the wind.

Mother wanted to go back, but she kept moving forward with Father. Through the trees, back to their little house by the brook.

It was a good house. She knew that even if Father hadn't said so when he told Mother they were going to live there. Bushes full of berries that were good to eat grew by the brook. And there were snares to set and rabbits to catch and Mother had showed her how to make stew. The forest was scary, but Father had given her the little knife. They told her never to go in there.

She looked past Mother's arm at the trees. When they had come here, they looked dark and scary. But she had gone in there with the little knife. She knew there were places there they could hide from the beast, from that *thing* that got Eadne.

"Father," she said.

"Keep moving," Father said.

"But, Father, the forest—"

"I know, I know, I know."

Senny held up the little knife. "There are places, and there are berries and we could go there and I'm not—"

"Gods damn it, not *now,* you little shit!"

He didn't say that word around her a lot. Because he thought she didn't know what it meant. But he said it before, when he told them they were coming to the forest, when he built the house, when the people with the feathers in their hair came and told him to go away. His name for them was that word. She knew what it meant.

And he used it a lot more when he was scared. It was what the monsters were named. What their name sounded like.

"I don't care if the shit's upset because we're in a lot more shit than we need to be because you won't shut the shit up about all the *shit!*"

Mother wasn't talking anymore.

Maybe Mother was scared, too.

She held on to her little knife. And she held on to Mother's hand.

When the moon began to sink over the sea of trees and the starving owls went to their holes hungry, she tried not to hear him.

"One more thing."

Only in darkness did Rokuda speak to her. Only when he could not see her trying to ignore him, when she could not go busy herself with some other task and pretend, for a while, he wasn't hers. Only when he couldn't see her run her fingers along the scar on her collarbone.

"I want you to bring back proof," he had said.

"Proof," Kalindris had echoed.

"A trophy. Something to show the tribe she has done it. I want you to make sure she had blood on her hands."

"You want me to bring it back to you."

"Yes. Take it and shove it in her hands, if you must. Tell her that it will make me proud. She will do it then."

"She can't shoot," Kalindris had said. *"She can't draw the bow back far enough and she can't stalk prey. She's loud. Like you."* Kalindris continued lacing up her boots. *"She can't do it."*

"She has to."

Kalindris froze as Rokuda sat on the furs next to her. The furs that had remained cold for years. She never slept in them unless the winter was too cold. But when she lay beside him, she didn't feel the biting chill of winter. She felt sweaty, cold, clammy. Sick.

As she did now.

"They look at her like she's not one of them. I can't have that. And so she has to know what it is to be shict."

He spoke that name too easily. Like it was a word. Shict was more than that. It should not have been uttered in the darkness, Kalindris had thought.

"She should know that already," Kalindris had replied, securing the laces tightly.

"No one taught her." Rokuda had edged closer.

"No one should have to. We are born knowing who we are. The Howling tells us."

"She wasn't. You have to teach her."

Kalindris had said nothing as she rose up and moved to her bow. It was never far from her, save those times when he moved it. In the darkness, she preferred to keep it close.

But when she rose, he reached out. He took her by her wrist and she felt herself freeze. It grew cold again, cold as their bed.

"You have to show her," Rokuda had insisted.

"I don't have to do anything," she had tried to speak. But her words were smothered in the darkness.

He tightened his fingers around her wrist and she felt cold all over. She felt every point he had ever touched her, a bead of cold sweat forming everywhere his fingerprint lingered on her skin. She grew silent, rigid. And when he spoke, his voice was an icicle snapping on a winter's day.

"You will."

She stared across the clearing and spoke softly, as to not stir the leaves before her.

"Do you know why?"

Kalindris' own voice.

Strange and uncomfortable in her own mouth.

But the child was looking up at her. The child had her bow in her hands, an arrow in the string.

Kalindris pointed out to the log. The deer scratched at the moss with a hoof, pulled green scraps from the wood, and slurped them up from the ground. It wasted many sounds as it ate: grinding its teeth, grunting in satisfaction, slurping the greenery down noisily. It couldn't hear her whispering to the child from the underbrush.

"Why it has to die?" Kalindris reiterated.

The child stared at the deer, squinting hard. She could almost hear the child's thoughts, imagined them as noisy, jumbled things. The Howling was not there to give them clarity and focus.

"Food?" the child asked.

"No."

"I don't know. Competition? We kill it or we are killed?"

"By a deer?"

"It has horns!" the child protested.

The deer looked up at the sudden noise. Kalindris and the child were still and quiet. The deer was too hungry to leave. It continued to gnaw and to make noise.

"Why does it have to die?" Kalindris asked.

The child thought carefully. She winced with the realization.

"Because we can only know who we are by who everyone else is. We can only know what it means to be us if we know that we are not the others. And so we kill them, to know that, to know who we are and why we are here and why Riffid gave us life and nothing else. We kill. And because we are the killers, we are who we are."

She felt her ears flatten against the side of her head. Her father's words. Her father's words repeated to a thousand people who would never speak against him, never tell him no. She hadn't told him no, either. Not when she first heard it. Not until it was too late.

"No," she said.

"But Father said—"

"No." She spoke more forcefully. "Look at it. Why does it have to die?"

And the child looked at the deer. And then the child looked at her.

"Does it have to?" she asked.

The sound of ears rising. The sound of eyelids opening wide. The sound of a breath going short. Realization. Acknowledgment. Resignation. Sorrow.

The child.

Listening.

Wordless.

"Why does it have to die?" she asked again.

"Because," the child said, "I have to kill it."

Kalindris nodded. No smiles. No approval. No sounds.

The child raised her bow, drew the arrow back and held it. She trusted only her eyes. She checked her aim once, then twice, then a third time. On the fourth, when her hands had started to quiver from the strain, she shot.

The arrow struck the deer in the tender part between the leg and the nethers. It quivered there, severing something that the deer needed. The beast let out a groan, its breath mist. It staggered on its hooves, turned to flee. But its legs didn't remember anything before the arrow. It shambled, bleeding, toward the forest.

The child drew an arrow and shot again. She trusted only her heart now. The arrow flew too wide. She shrieked, her voice panicked, and shot again. Words befouled the air and the arrow sank into the earth, heavy with her fear.

The deer took another step before it fell. The arrow stood quivering in the deer's neck and the beast lay on its side, breathing heavily, spilling breath and blood onto the earth.

Kalindris approached it, the child behind her. She reached behind and grabbed the child, shoving her forward. The child stared at the deer's eyes, at herself reflected in the great brown mirror of its gaze.

The child looked to her.

Kalindris reached into her belt and pulled the knife free. She held it out to the child. The child looked at it like it was something that shouldn't be there, something that she would only ever see hung upon the wall of her father's tent.

She thrust the handle toward the child.

"Why?" Kalindris asked the child.

The child looked up at her. The sight of eyes wide and pleading. The sight of resentment. The sight of fear and hate and betrayal for making the child do this.

But no words.

The child took the knife and knelt beside the deer. She pressed it to its throat. She winced and she cut through the fur and the hide and the sinew to the root of the beast's neck.

She opened it up and it spilled upon her. It spilled over her hands and onto her arms. And the child kept cutting silently.

As the brook babbled alongside them, she tried to keep up with her parents.

"Are you scared, darling?"

Senny wasn't. She was trying hard not to be, anyway. She shook her head and held up the little knife. Father didn't seem to notice.

"You don't need to be scared," he said. "Not when I'm here. We're going to get through this, all right?"

She nodded. She wasn't scared.

"I'm sorry for what I said earlier, darling. I was just irritated. Your mother was screaming so loud."

Mother didn't seem to notice that they were talking about her. Mother held on to her hand and kept pulling her toward the cottage. The brook was nearby, churning away. Vines of berries grew nearby, ripe and bright in the sunlight.

They could go to the forest to avoid the beast, maybe. They could run there and live together there. The cottage was nice and she would miss it and she would miss Eadne and she tried very hard not to think about Eadne because whenever she did she felt like she was going to throw up and then Mother would cry.

"Darling, everything's going to be all right," Father said. He wasn't looking at her, though. "Everything will be fine, don't worry."

"I'm not worried, Father," she said. "I'm not scared. I still have the knife you gave me. Look."

"It'll be all right, darling."

"Father, we could go deeper into the forest. We could escape the beast there and come back when it's gone. I've been there, Father. It's not as dark as it looks. There are berries and food and we could go there instead of the cottage."

"Yes, darling. The forest."

"Father, Mother is scared. She's holding on to my hand so hard that it hurts. Father?"

Father said the same thing again. Over and over. All "darling" and "mm-hm" and "fine, fine, all right." She soon stopped talking. Father wasn't listening. Because if Father listened, he would hear her voice starting to sound like it always did whenever her throat felt funny and she wanted to cry.

And then he'd be scared. And then Mother would be more scared.

He needed to say his words so he couldn't hear her. And she needed to stay quiet. And Mother needed to hold her hand until it hurt. And she needed not to throw up or cry or do any of those things that a scared little child would do.

Maybe when Eadne was around, she could do that.

Eadne was dead.

When the sun began to scowl over their tent and the first wolves rose to the hunt, she hated herself like she hated him.

"*I want to ask you something,*" Rokuda had said.

"*No.*" Kalindris had replied.

It was a noise Rokuda only heard from her. He had no idea what it meant. "*Why aren't you bothered by this?*" he had asked, undeterred.

"*By what?*"

"*By how they see her, by the fact that they think she's not one of us. Not a shict.*" He forced difficult words through a snarl. "*Not mine.*"

"*I don't pay attention to what she does.*"

"*Why not? Haven't you seen what they think of her? How they look at her?*"

"*No.*"

"*They look at her like . . . like she's . . . like she* isn't . . . "

His words had failed him and he had begun to snarl. He hated it when words would not work for him, because when his words would not work, neither would the Howling speak for him. And when he couldn't speak, he started snarling, because people couldn't agree with him. People could tell him "no."

And that was when he started making scars.

"*She reaches out to try to hold on to your hand when she's scared. She . . . she asks them things, instead of* knowing *what the Howling tells her.*" She heard his nails rake the fur and find that insufficient for his rage. She heard strands of his hair snap from his scalp as he pulled it. "*She cries when she gets hurt. She snarls when she gets angry.*"

"*Children do that.*"

"*Not my heir.*"

"Your heir is a child."

"Not one of our *children. Not one of our people. We don't . . . do that."*

"She does."

"And you don't even care*! You don't even look at her. Don't you know what they're saying about us? How they look at us?"*

"Don't care."

"You used to."

"Don't anymore."

And she had heard it. Silence before a crack of thunder. Grains of earth falling after a drop of rain kicks them up. Moan of wind over hillsides. The moment before he drew a breath, before he spoke with the intent of being heard.

"You used to stand with me in front of them, remember? You and your bow, the proud huntress next to me, so strong and brave. They looked up to us as I spoke. They listened to me and I cared only if you heard me."

Honey fermenting in a skein. Dandelions flying on the breeze. Steam after the fire had been doused. The words he spoke that had made her listen, the words he spoke that made him powerful, the words he spoke when he had been Rokuda and she had been Kalindris and they had no need for words.

"You used to listen to my words, you used to nod when they nodded and cheer when they cheered. And when I was done and I looked out over all of them smiling, I looked beside me and yours was always the biggest smile and the best."

The words he spoke when she thought those were all she ever needed.

"You had a lot of words," Kalindris had said.

"I still do. I still have everything. Everything except that proud huntress that stood beside me. Where did she go?"

Kalindris had waited at the flap of the tent. When she opened it to the cold dawn light, the world was silent. She looked briefly over her shoulder and saw his eyes, so vast and green. And out the corner of her eye, she saw only a glimpse of it. But the scar on her collarbone, the one he had given her, was still there.

"She fell in love with someone silent and gentle. They ran away and died somewhere far in the woods and left you and I behind."

She had spoken briefly. And then she had left.

———

"You're not doing it right. You're not *doing* it right." Teeth coming in through a cub's mouth. "You're supposed to talk to me. You're supposed to be able to do this." Claws digging for something in the earth that wasn't there. "Stop it. *Stop it*. Stop it and do it already." A leg in a snare, being gnawed off.

The child.

Talking to the earth.

Still.

She watched, arms folded, impassive as the child crawled through the riverbank, following a flayed line through the mud. The child followed it over the bank, through the ebb, around the trees, back to where it began. The child cursed at it, made demands of it, whined at it and now simply spewed words, to the tracks, to the earth, to herself.

The child's hands were thick with mud, belly smeared with it, face painted brown where she had clutched her head in frustration. And she crawled with her hands upon the ground, as though she could strangle answers out of the earth.

The earth wouldn't talk to her.

The child wanted everything. The child wanted the tracks to tell her without listening to them. The child wanted the land to yield to her because she wanted it to that badly. The child wanted. The child spoke. The child whined and demanded and she never listened.

Like her father.

Kalindris was surprised to find her hands clenched into fists at her side.

"He said it was supposed to be easy," the child whined. "It's supposed to be easy. Why didn't he—" She slammed the heel of her palm against her forehead. A muddy bruise was left behind. "*No, no*. It's you, not him. You're doing something wrong. It's you, *you're* the failure, *that's* why they hate you."

His legacy. In the mud. Striking herself in the head.

In some wordless part of herself, Kalindris tried to convince herself that the child deserved this. The child who couldn't listen, the child who always spoke, his child belonged in the mud.

Kalindris was surprised to hear her own voice.

"It's metaphor. The earth doesn't actually talk to you." The child continued to paw at it and plead to it. "Look. You've ruined the tracks. We can start—"

"Shut up!"

The child.

Baring teeth.

Snarling.

"I don't want to hear it or you or anything, I just want to find the beast and kill it and bring it back and show it to him and then he'll talk to me and I don't *need* you or anyone else to talk to me if Father will so I never have to see you again!"

The child was liquid. White flecks of spittle gathered at her mouth. Tears brimmed in the corners of her eyes. Viscous mucus dripped from her nostrils. The child was melting, trembling herself to death. The child turned away, looked back into the silent earth.

"I wasn't asleep."

And Kalindris had no words for the child. The child who had just spoken to her like it was *her* fault the child's ears couldn't hear. The child who presumed to dismiss *her*. The child who acted like it was *her* fault, *her* problem, *her* flaw that made this moment of mud and tears and spit.

Like her father. Every bit.

She was surprised to find tears in her eyes.

And she, too, turned. The earth spoke to her, though. Told her where the beast had gone. Told her how to deny the child and how that made sense that she should be angry and vengeful against a child.

The child.

Weeping.

And she shut her ears and walked away.

Mother was scared. And Father was scared.

Senny knew this because no one was yelling anymore.

Mother wrapped her hands tightly around her and held her close in the corner of their cottage. Father stood with his hatchet in his hand, peering through the windows. Mother had her. Father had his hatchet. And they were both still scared.

She wasn't, though. She had her little knife. Father had given it to her so she wouldn't be scared. She couldn't be scared with the little knife, even if Father was.

She thought about giving it to Father, to see if it would help. But she pulled it back when she heard a voice, even if it was Father's.

"I'm going out there."

"What? Why would you do that?"

"To look for that thing. It might not even be around. We didn't see it when we found—"

"No. Don't go out there," Mother said. "It already got Eadne. You can't let it get your daughter and me, you have to stay here, you have to, you *have* to."

"I have to protect you," Father said. "I have to keep you safe. We can't live like this. We can't let that beast chase us away. We have to . . ."

To not be scared, Senny wanted to say. We have to be brave.

"I'm going," Father said. "Not far. Not long. Just stay here. I'll be back."

Senny nodded. She held her little knife tightly. Mother held her tightly. So tightly it hurt. She leaned into it, though, let Mother hold on to her because Mother didn't have a little knife.

Father pushed the door open. Birds were singing outside. The sun was shining that orange way it got when it started going beneath the trees. The brook was babbling outside, talking loud and wondering where the little girl was that talked back to it. Father walked out two steps from the doorway and looked around with his hatchet in his hand.

The birds kept singing. The brook kept talking. The sun kept shining.

And Father was dead.

She knew it. She saw the arrow in his shoulder, pinning him to the cottage door. She saw another fly out and hit him in the wrist. He dropped his hatchet. Mother screamed. Father screamed. Father bled all over the door. And Senny held on to the little knife.

The beast came up. The beast was a lady. Her hair was long and wild and she wore dirty clothes and her ears were huge and she had big teeth and a scar on her neck. Her knife was big. Her knife was shiny. And she brought it up and against Father's neck and opened him up and his blood spilled all over her.

And the birds just kept on singing, even though Father was dead.

When the birds kept singing and the woman would not stop weeping, she looked at the Beast.

There were many names for them: intruder, human, monkey, *kou'ru*. It was Rokuda that had began calling them Beasts, to make them a threat instead of a people, a word instead of a thing that had children. It had made the tribe nod in approval and mutter how they were Beasts, these creatures that came and threatened the shict lands.

She had killed one already, left the body swinging in a tree as warning to these two. But she had known, even then, that she would have to kill them, too. She had killed many.

Even before Rokuda gave them a new name, she had killed them. They were the enemy, they were the disease. Killing defined a shict. And these kills were meant for the child. The blood that poured down Kalindris' hands should have been on the child's. She was supposed to have come back to the tribe with her hands red and her eyes shut and the tribe would know she was one of them and her father would be proud of his heir.

The child's kill. Rokuda's glory. Kalindris denied one through the other.

The little human girl stood in front of her cowering mother, holding up a little knife like it was a match for the broad red blade in Kalindris' hands. She looked up at Kalindris, trying her hardest not to show fear. Kalindris looked down at her, trying to decide how best to end this quickly. A clean blow through one, then the other, she thought, in the heart to end it quickly.

Clean and quick.

Just as soon as the child stopped staring at her.

Like she owed her an explanation.

"Do you know why?" Heavy, choked, weak. Kalindris' words.

The human child did not say a thing. Her mother wrapped her arms around the child's tiny form, tried to hold her back. The child would not lower her knife.

"Why I have to kill you?" she asked again.

The child said nothing. Kalindris opened her mouth to tell her. No words came.

"Your knife is too small," Kalindris said. She held up her own blade, thick and choked with red. "You can't do anything with it. You aren't meant to hold it. Put it down."

The child did not put it down. Kalindris raised her weapon, took a step forward, as if to step around the child. The child moved in front of her, thrust her little knife at Kalindris like it would do something. Like she could use it. Like she wasn't scared.

Kalindris hesitated. She looked over her shoulder, as though she expected the child—her child—to be there.

"You don't have to die here," she said, without looking at the child—the human child. "Your . . . your father isn't you. Your mother isn't you. I'll take them. You can run."

She looked at the child and her little knife.

"Go. Run away."

The child did not run. The child did not move.

"Why aren't you running?"

"I can't." The child spoke in a terrified voice.

"Why not?"

"Because she's my mother."

The pages of a book fallen from a shelf, turning. Ashes in a long-dead fireplace settling beneath charred logs. A mother weeping. Birds singing. Blood pattering onto the floor from a hole in a soft throat, drop by drop.

Slow sounds.

Quiet sounds.

Full of nothing.

Kalindris could hear the whisper of leather as she slid the blade back into its sheath. Kalindris could hear the sound of her boots on the floor as she turned around and walked out of the cabin. Kalindris could hear the sound of the human child drop to the floor and weep.

She could hear it all the way back to the forest.

And her child.

A river running. Wind blowing through the leaves. A wolf howling.

And birds singing.

No matter how hard she tried, how she angled her ears, how she strained to hear something else, something full of meaning, this was all she could hear. These sounds, common and pointless, the sort of thing any ugly creature could hear.

The Howling wasn't talking to her.

"Where were you?"

The child.

Asking.

Concerned.

She walked into the clearing with her bow on her back and her knife in her belt. The child was sitting down on her heels, looking up at her as she walked past.

"You washed," the child noted, looking at her clean, bloodless hands. "When? What did you do?"

She did not look back at the child as she sat down beside her. She let her legs hang over a small ledge, dangling over a dying brook whose babble had turned to poetic muttering as it sputtered into a thin stream. She looked to her right and saw the child's feet in their little boots, covered in mud, flecked with blood from the dead deer.

Only a few droplets of red. The rest mixed with the mud. It seemed like so much to look at it.

"Why do we kill, child?" she asked absently.

"You already asked me this."

"I know. Tell me again."

The child kicked her feet a little. A few flecks of mud came off. Not the blood.

"I guess I don't know," the child said.

She said nothing.

They stared, together, into the forest. Their ears pricked up, listening to the sounds. Birds kept singing, one more day they marked by noisy chatter. The wind kept blowing, same as it always had. Somewhere far away, one more deer loosed a long, guttural bugle into the sky.

"Did you kill the beast?" the child asked.

She said nothing.

"I was supposed to do it."

"I didn't."

The child looked at her. "I'm not an idiot."

"No."

She reached over, wrapped an arm around the child and drew her close. A heart beating; excited. A breath drawn in sharply; quivering. A shudder through the body; terrified. She drew the child closer.

"But let me pretend you are for a little while."

No more noises. No more sounds. No more distant cries and close Howling. Only words. Only the child's voice.

"I was supposed to kill it. Father said."

"Your father isn't always right."

"You are?"

"No."

"Then why should I believe you?"

"Because."

"That's not a good reason."

She looked down at the child and smiled. "I'll think of one later, all right?"

The child looked back at her. Her smile came more slowly, more nervous, like she was afraid it would be slapped out of her mouth at any moment. Kalindris blamed herself for that look, for these words that came heavy and slowly. She would learn how to use them better.

There would be time for that. Without so much blood and cold nights. Without so many thoughts of Rokuda and his words. She would learn them on her own. She would tell them to the child.

Her child.

Her daughter.

Smiling.

There would be time enough to look into her daughter's eyes, long from now, and know what it meant to need no words. There would be a time when she would look into her daughter's eyes and simply know.

For now, she had only the sound of her daughter's smile. And forever.

Pat Cadigan

Everyone knows what that road to hell is paved with, don't they?

Pat Cadigan was born in Schenectady, New York, and now lives in London with her family. She made her first professional sale in 1980, and has subsequently come to be regarded as one of the best new writers of her generation. Her story "Pretty Boy Crossover" has appeared on several critic's lists as among the best science fiction stories of the 1980s, and her story "Angel" was a finalist for the Hugo Award, the Nebula Award, *and* the World Fantasy Award (one of the few stories ever to earn that rather unusual distinction). Her short fiction—which has appeared in most of the major markets, including *Asimov's Science Fiction* and *The Magazine of Fantasy & Science Fiction*—has been gathered in the collections *Patterns* and *Dirty Work*. Her first novel, *Mindplayers*, was released in 1987 to excellent critical response, and her second novel, *Synners*, released in 1991, won the Arthur C. Clarke Award as the year's best science fiction novel, as did her third novel, *Fools*, making her the only writer ever to win the Clarke Award twice. Her other books include the novels *Dervish Is Digital*, *Tea from an Empty Cup*, and *Reality Used to Be a Friend of Mine*, and, as editor, the anthology *The Ultimate Cyberpunk*, as well as two making-of movie books and four media tie-in novels. Her most recent book was a novel, *Cellular*.

CARETAKERS

"Hey, Val," said my sister Gloria, "you ever wonder why there aren't any female serial killers?"

We were watching yet another documentary on the Prime Crime Network. We'd been watching a lot of those in the month since she had moved in. Along with two suitcases, one stuffed with products especially formulated for curly brown hair, and a trash bag containing two sets of expensive, high-thread-count bed linens, my little sister had also brought her fascination with the lurid and sensational disguised as an interest in current events—the inverse of expensive sheets in a trash bag, you might say.

"What about Aileen What's-Her-Name?" I said.

"One. And they executed her pretty fast. So fast you can't remember her last name."

"I can remember it," I said. "I just can't pronounce it. And it wasn't *that* fast—at least ten years after they caught her. They executed Bundy pretty quickly, too, didn't they? In Florida. Her, too, now that I think of it."

Gloria gave a surprised laugh. "I had no idea you were such an expert on serial killers."

"We've watched enough TV shows about them," I said as I went into the kitchen for more iced tea. "I could probably make one on my iPad." An exaggeration but not much; the shows were so formulaic that sometimes I wasn't sure which ones were repeats. But I didn't really mind indulging Gloria. She was fifteen years younger, so I was used to making allowances, and as vices went, true-crime TV was pretty minor. More to the point, Gloria had been visiting Mom in the care home every day without fail. I'd expected the frequency to drop after the first two weeks but she was still spending every afternoon playing cards with Mom or reading to her or just hanging (unquote). I had to give her credit for that, even though I was fairly sure she felt this made her exempt from having to look for paid employment.

When I returned, Gloria was busy with my iPad. "Don't tell me there's an app for serial killers?" I said, a little nervous.

"I Googled them and you're right—Aileen Wuornos and Ted Bundy both died in the Florida State Prison. Over twenty years apart—he got the chair, she got lethal injection. But still." She looked up at me. "Think it's something about Florida?"

"Dunno but I *really* wish you hadn't done that on my iPad," I said, relieving her of it. "Google can't keep anything to themselves. Now I'll probably get a flood of gory crime scene photo spam."

I could practically see her ears prick up, like a terrier's. "You can get that stuff?"

"*No.*" I moved the iPad out of her reach. "I forbid it. Make do with the crime porn on cable."

"Party pooper."

"I get that a lot." I chuckled. On TV, credits were scrolling upward too fast to read over a sepia photograph of a stiff-looking man, probably a serial killer. Abruptly, it changed to a different set of credits rolling even more quickly against a red background. At the bottom of the screen was the legend, *NEXT: Deadlier Than the Male—Killer Ladies.*

I grimaced at my sister, who brandished the remote control, grinning like a mad thing, or maybe a killer lady. "Come on, isn't one of the movie channels showing *Red Dawn*?" I pumped my fist. "Wolverines?"

Gloria rolled her eyes. "How about something we *haven't* seen a bajillion times already?"

"How much *is* a bajillion?" I asked.

"Like the exact size or the universe or how many times you've seen *Red Dawn*, nobody knows." She nodded at the iPad on my lap. "Not worried about crime scene spam anymore?"

My face grew warm. "I was surfing on automatic pilot," I said, which was either half-true or half a lie, depending.

"Yeah, *you're* not really interested in any of that gory stuff."

"The least you could do is microwave us some popcorn," I said. "There's at least one bag left in the cupboard."

She cringed in pretend horror. "This stuff *doesn't* kill your appetite?"

"If I pick up some pointers, I might kill *you.*"

As usual, the ad break was long enough that Gloria was back with a big bowl of movie-style buttered before the end of the opening credits.

According to the listings, this was a *Killer Ladies* marathon, back-to-back episodes into the wee hours. After a teleshopping break from 4 to 6 a.m., early risers could breakfast with *Deadly Duos—Killer Couples.*

Killer Ladies followed the usual formula but ratcheted up the melodrama. The Ladies in question were all abnormal, evil, twisted, unnatural, cold, devious, and unrepentant, while most of their victims were warm, easygoing, trusting, generous, open, honest, well-liked, down-to-earth, and the best friend anyone could ever ask for. Except for a few misfits who were uneducated, foolish, immature, troubled, reckless, self-destructive, or habitually unlucky, and the occasional ex-con with a long criminal record (no one ever had a short criminal record).

Between bursts of urgent narration and detectives who spoke only in monotone, there were some nuggets of real information, much of it new to me. Of course, I hadn't known a lot to begin with—the only other notorious Killer Lady I could think of besides Aileen Wuornos was Lizzie Borden. Killer Ladies were a hell of a lot more interesting than their male counterparts. Unlike men, who seemed mainly to gratify themselves by asserting power, Killer Ladies were all about getting away with it. They planned carefully, sizing up their victims and their situations, and waited for the right time.

They were also masters—or mistresses—of camouflage, with the unwitting help of a society that even in these parlous times still sees women as nurturers, not murderers. When not killing someone, many of the Killer Ladies were nurses, therapists, babysitters, assistants, even teachers (remembering some I'd had, I could believe it).

Eventually I dozed off and woke to see a repeat of the first episode we'd watched. Gloria was absolutely unrouseable, so I threw one of Mom's hand-crocheted afghans over her. Then the devil got into me—I tucked a pillow under her arm with a note saying, *This is the pillow I didn't smother you with. Good morning!* before I staggered off to bed.

The note I found on my own pillow when I woke later said, *Still alive? (One answer only) [__]Yes (we need more cereal) [__]No (we don't)*

The expression on Gloria's face as I sat down to breakfast made me wince. "Oh, no, not *another* bench warrant for parking tickets."

"No, of course not. I took care of that. *You* took care of that," she added quickly. "I didn't sleep very well."

"I tried to wake you so you could sleep in a real bed. You didn't stay up all night, did you?" Staying up all night and then sleeping all day was something Gloria was prone to when life handed her lemons without water, sugar, or glasses; I'd warned her that wouldn't fly with me.

"No. All those Killer Ladies gave me bad dreams."

For a moment I thought she was kidding, but she had the slightly haunted look of a person who had found something very unpleasant in her own head and hadn't quite stopped seeing it yet. "Jeez, Glow-bug, I'm sorry. I shouldn't have left that note."

"Oh, no, *that* was funny," Gloria said with a small laugh. "Did you find mine?"

"Yeah. Yours is funnier, because it's true."

"I'll remember you said that." She looked down at the bowl in front of her. "You can have this," she said, pushing it toward me. "I'm not hungry. All night, I kept dreaming about Angels of Death. You know, the sneaky ones."

"They were all sneaky," I said through a yawn. "Women are better at staying under the radar, remember?"

"Yeah, but the ones who took care of people, like nurses and aides, they were the sneakiest." Pause. "I can't stop thinking about Mom. How much do you know about that place she's in?"

I shook my head. "Trash TV's got you jumping at shadows. Better swear off the crime channels for a while."

"Come on, Val, didn't all that stuff about Angels of Death creep *you* out?"

"You're the crime buff," I said evenly. "*I* want my MTV. Or, failing that, wolverines."

"You didn't last night," she said with a short, humorless laugh.

"Touché. But enough is enough. Tonight is box-set DVD night. One of those bizarro things where even the cast didn't know what was happening—*Lost Heroes of Alcatraz* or *4400 Events in 24 Hours*. What do you say?"

My bad mash-ups didn't rate even an eye roll so I checked out the morning news on the iPad while I ate her cereal. Maybe getting her own iPad would put her in a better frame of mind, I thought. She'd love the games. Not to mention the camera—although I'd have to make her promise in writing not to upload any sneaky candids to the web.

"Val?" she said after a bit. "Even if I *am* jumping at shadows, humor me for a minute. How *did* you find that home?"

The only way to kill shadows was to turn on all the lights, I thought resignedly. That was what big sisters were for, although I'd never imagined I'd still be doing it at fifty-three. "It's a nice place, isn't it?" She nodded. "Doesn't have that institutional smell, residents aren't wandering around confused or tied to their beds, lying in their own—"

"*Val.*" She gave me the Eyebrow. "You're not answering the question."

"Okay, okay. I didn't find it—Mom did. She and Dad had an insurance plan through Stillman Saw and Steel—"

"But Stillman went under twenty years ago!"

"Lemme finish, will ya? Stillman went under, but the insurance company didn't. Mom and Dad maintained the policy and Mom kept it up after Dad died. She knew she didn't want us to have to go through what she did with Grandma, which was the same thing Grandma had been through with *her* mother. You were only a baby when Grandma died, so you missed it. But I didn't."

Gloria looked skeptical. "I have friends whose parents spent a fortune on policies that never paid them a nickel."

"Mom showed me everything some years back. Obviously it's all aboveboard and legit—otherwise, she wouldn't be able to afford that place." I decided not to mention that although Mom had seemed perfectly all right to me at the time, she had already felt herself starting to slip. "The policy pays about half the cost, her pension and the proceeds from the sale of her house cover the rest."

"And when the money from the house is gone?"

"We step up, little sister. What else?"

Her eyes got huge. "But I'm broke. I don't even have anything I can sell."

"Well, if you don't win the lottery, you'll have to go to Plan B and get a job," I said cheerfully. Gloria looked so dismayed, I wasn't sure whether I wanted to laugh or smack her one. "But we'll cross that bridge when we come to it. *If* we come to it."

"What do you mean by that?"

This was something I'd hoped to avoid until such time as it became moot. "Mom made a living will. She's DNR—Do Not Resuscitate. No defibrillator, no tubes, no ventilator, no extraordinary measures. Her body, minus useful organs or parts, goes to the local med school. *Her* decision," I added in response to Gloria's half-horrified, half-grossed-out expression. "You know Mom—waste not, someone else would be glad to have that liver."

Gloria gave a short laugh in spite of herself. "Okay, but *Mom's* liver? She's eighty-four. Do they take *anything* from people that old?"

I shrugged. "No idea. If they don't, that's more for the med students."

"It doesn't sound very respectful."

"On the contrary, Glow-bug—they actually hold memorial services twice a year for all the people who willed their remains to the school. They invite the families and they read out the names of all the deceased, thanking them for their contribution to the future of medicine."

She looked a little less grossed-out, but no happier. "What happens after, uh, you know, when they . . . when they're done?"

"They offer cremation. Although Mom said she'd prefer compost. There's an organization that plants trees and flowering bushes—"

"Stop it!"

"I'm sorry, Sis, maybe I shouldn't have told you about that part. But it *is* what Mom wants."

"Yeah, but she's got Alzheimer's."

"She was clear as a bell when she set this up."

We went back and forth. Gloria just couldn't seem to get her mind around our mother's rather alternative approach to death. A Viking funeral would probably have been easier for her to accept. From the various things she said, I wasn't sure whether she felt guilty for being the ever-absent daughter or hurt that no one had thought it necessary to consult her. Maybe it was a little of both.

Or a lot of both. The age difference had always made it hard for me to see things from her perspective. I'd thought it would get easier as we got older, but it hadn't, probably because Gloria was still where she'd been at twenty-five, trying to decide what she wanted to be when she grew up.

"Sorry, Glow-bug," I said finally, collecting the breakfast things. "This debate is called on account of my job."

"I don't know how you do it," she said, watching me rinse the bowls and put them in the dishwasher.

"Do what—make a living?"

"Stay awake looking at spreadsheets."

"It helps to see all the little numbers with dollar signs," I told her. "I'm sure you can find something to keep your eyes open." But probably not Plan B yet, I thought as I shut myself in my office and woke the computer.

Doing other people's taxes isn't the most exciting work I've ever done, but it's virtually recession-proof and less physically demanding than cleaning toilets. It's not even really that hard once you know how—although knowing how can be tricky. Every third change in regulations, I added another hard drive to back up my backups. There wasn't as much paper as there used to be, which was a relief. But I couldn't bring myself to rely completely on cloud storage—there's tempting Fate and then there's teasing it so unmercifully that Fate has to make an example of you. I stuck with CD-ROMs—not enough room on USB drives for sticky notes. One of my younger colleagues had a system using stickers with symbols—a clever idea but I thought I was a little too old for such an extreme administrative make-over. Especially after my recent lifestyle makeover.

In the ten years since Lee and I had come to our senses and called it quits, I'd discovered that living alone agreed with me. But that was over now. At first, Gloria had made vague noises about looking for a place of her own when she got back on her feet—whatever that meant—but I didn't kid myself. My sister was here for the duration. Even a boyfriend was unlikely to change things. The kind of men Gloria attracted invariably wanted to move in with *her* rather than vice versa, usually because they needed to.

I heard the car pull out of the driveway just as I stopped for lunch; the usual time Gloria headed out to see Mom. Mom's appetite was poor these days, but Gloria could usually get a few extra bites into her. It was one of the reasons the staff was so fond of her.

"I wish everyone's family was like her," a young nurse named Jill Franklyn had confided on my last visit. "She doesn't treat the staff like servants and she isn't texting or talking on the phone the whole time she's here. And even if most people had the time to come every day, they probably wouldn't."

I couldn't help feeling slightly defensive. Two visits a week was my self-imposed minimum, although I tried to make it three more often than not. I didn't always succeed, something I was usually too tired to feel guilty about. Which was what I felt guilty about instead. Meanwhile, Mom kept saying that I should think less about twice-weekly visits and more about a week or two in the Caribbean.

Tempting, but the web meant that my work could follow me and probably would. The last time I'd gone away, a five-day stay in a forest lodge had become half a day when I got a panicky text from a client whose house had burned to the ground just before he'd been called in for an audit. Well, I've since heard mosquitoes in the Maine woods grow to the size of eagles and sometimes carry off small children.

Of course, a mosquito with a seven-foot wing span might pale next to work that had been piling up for two weeks. Or not. There was only one way to find out.

Funny how I'd started thinking about taking time off again now that Gloria was here. So she didn't have a job and probably wouldn't get one except at gunpoint—she had lightened my load from the start. If she kept it up, I might even be able to revive my all-but-dormant social life—call friends, go shopping. Eat out. See a new movie in a theater. Just thinking about it gave me a lift.

Gloria was still out at five, so I spent another hour at my desk finishing work I'd have otherwise left for the next morning. When she hadn't come back by six, however, I started getting nervous. For all her faults, my sister was an excellent driver, but that didn't make her immune to bad drivers or, worse, bad intentions. Was there a fee to trace a LoJack, I wondered, or did the car have to be reported stolen first? Or could I do it myself? I vaguely remembered registering the navigation software; was there a Find My Car app, like Find My iPad?

Fortunately, I heard her pull into the driveway before I tried something stupid. "Anybody home?" Gloria called, coming in through the kitchen. "If you're a burglar, clear out."

"No burglars, just me," I called back.

She bustled in, curls bouncing with happy excitement, and held up a bag from Wok On the Wild Side. "You'll never guess what I did."

"You're right," I said, making room on the coffee table. "So you'd better just tell me."

"*I* got a *job*."

My jaw dropped; all hope of taking even a long weekend out of town evaporated as my social life rolled over and went back to sleep. "You . . . got . . . a job?"

She was busy taking little white cartons out of the bag and putting them on the table. "What, you didn't think that was possible?"

"No, it's just—I didn't know you were looking for a job."

"Relax, big sister," she laughed. "It's not a *real* job."

I blinked at her. "You got an *imaginary* job?"

"What? No, of course not. I am now an official volunteer aide at Mom's home!"

"Official—seriously?" I wasn't sure I'd heard her right. "Are you qualified?"

"As a matter of fact, big sister, I am."

This was probably the most startling thing she'd said in the last two minutes. Or maybe ever—*qualified* was not a word I associated with my sister. "How?" I asked weakly.

"Did you *actually* forget that I was a lifeguard almost every summer when I was in high school?" she said with a superior smile. I'd already been living away from home then, so I hadn't forgotten as much as I'd barely known in the first place. Mostly what I remembered was how Gloria practically lived in a swimsuit from May till September. And how even when I'd still looked good in one myself, I'd never looked *that* good. "After graduation, I taught swimming at the Y and for the Red Cross," she was saying, "and I've been lifeguarding and teaching swim classes on and off for years."

I still didn't get it. "The people at the care home go swimming a lot?"

She rolled her eyes. "I know CPR, you idiot."

Heat rushed into my face; I felt like *two* idiots.

Gloria laughed again. "Guess you won't faint after all. For a minute there, I wasn't too sure." She went into the kitchen for some plates while I sat on the couch feeling like a bad person as well as an idiot.

"I can also teach water aerobics," she said chattily, plopping a dish on my lap. "Well, actually, I'd have to update my aqua-aerobics certificate, but I've kept my CPR current. It's such a pain in the ass if a pool needs someone but can't hire you because your CPR's out-of-date." She served me from three different cartons and then held up a pair of chopsticks. "Want me to break these apart for you? Or would you like a fork?"

"I'm still *qualified* for sticks, thank you," I said. She handed them over, grinning; I wasn't quite there yet. "So . . . what? You got up this morning and decided to be an official volunteer? Or one of the nurses heard you talking about your summers as a lifeguard and said, 'Hey, you must know CPR, want to volunteer?'"

Her grin turned faintly sly as she served me and then herself. "Actually, I did the paperwork a couple of weeks ago."

Another surprise. "You never mentioned it to me," I said.

"There was no reason to, till now. I mean, if I ended up not volunteering, there'd be nothing to talk about anyway. Besides, do *you* tell *me* every single thought that crosses your mind?" Now her bright smile was so innocent that I actually wasn't sure whether that had been a jab or not. "Of course not," she went on. "Who would?"

I ate in silence, musing on the concept of my sister the qualified volunteer with the mad CPR skillz. I had none myself, which now that I thought of it was rather shortsighted. Even if none of my clients had ever had a heart attack after seeing what they owed the government, it wasn't impossible; many of them were already in heart-attack country. Meanwhile Gloria rattled on about recognizing the signs of a stroke, the right way to perform the Heimlich maneuver, and how CPR classes were good for meeting handsome firemen.

At last, the Gloria I knew and loved, I thought, relieved. "You know, I don't think you'll be meeting many handsome firemen at the home," I said when she paused for breath.

"Unless it burns down. *Kidding!*" she added, then sobered almost as quickly. "That's what I'm there to prevent."

I was baffled again. "Only you can prevent nursing home fires?"

"I'll make sure no Angel of Death tries anything."

I waited for her to laugh; she didn't. "You're serious."

"As a heart attack, sister." She impaled a shrimp that had been eluding her and popped it into her mouth.

Another reason to be glad she was qualified, I thought, feeling surreal. "I didn't realize you'd be there twenty-four hours a day."

She gave me the Eyebrow. "What are you talking about?"

"Most Angels of Death do their thing when everyone's asleep," I said. "Remember? Or did you sleep through that part of the *Killer Ladies* marathon?"

"No, I remember. Obviously I can't be there 24/7, but I'll make it obvious I'm watching closely. Every day as soon as I come in, I'll make the rounds, talk to everybody, see how they're doing. Make sure they're getting the right meds in the right amounts—"

"Don't the doctors and nurses do that?" I asked.

"I'll only double-check if something doesn't seem right," Gloria replied. "Volunteers don't give meds. We're not even supposed to have our own stuff when we're on duty. Like, not even an aspirin."

I barely heard her; something else occurred to me. "Doesn't being an official volunteer mean less time to visit with Mom?"

"She'll still know that I'm around."

This was going to be interesting, I thought, and probably not in a good way.

A fat lot I knew—it already was.

In the days that followed, my mother improved visibly. She was happier and more alert for longer; even her appetite was better. I was glad, but at the same time I knew from talking with her doctor that it wasn't permanent and the inevitable deterioration could be gradual or sudden. Not to mention cruel.

"Thanks to TV and movies, a lot of people think of dementia patients as daffy old folks who smile at things that aren't there and don't know what day it is," Dr. Li had told me, her normally friendly face a bit troubled. "People with dementia become frightened and angry and they lash out in unexpected and uncharacteristic ways. People who have never raised a hand in anger suddenly punch a nurse—or a relative. Or they bite—and unlike the old days, most still have enough teeth to draw blood. Or they get amorous and grabby. I treated a nun once, former professor of classical studies who spoke six languages. Swore like a biker in all of them and had a passion for—well, never mind."

There was a lot more that was even harder to listen to, but I came away feeling—well, not exactly prepared, because I didn't think I'd ever be truly prepared for certain behaviors no matter how realistic I tried to be, but maybe just a little less unprepared. So far, my mother was very much like herself, even when she couldn't remember why she wasn't in the old house or how old I was. And there had been fewer of those with Gloria around.

Mom's good streak held for about a month and a half. Every visit, she'd tell me to go on vacation; before long, I was looking at travel websites with real intent and work be damned. There was a nagging concern in the back of my mind, however, as to how a change like my absence would affect Mom's stability.

I decided to talk it over with her before I did anything, or didn't. She'd probably just tell me to fly to Jamaica for lunch—Jamaica was her latest idea of a dream destination—but what the hell, I thought as I arrived on my usual Thursday afternoon. My mother was outside on the patio, enjoying the lovely weather, an aide told me, and would I mind bringing her a glass of cranberry juice, thanks.

I found her parked at one of the umbrella tables in her wheelchair, away from the handful of other residents also outside. The lovely weather was lost on her. She sat glaring at a book of sudoku puzzles and holding a thick mechanical pencil in one fist like a dagger. The wheelchair meant that she was having dizzy spells, no doubt because she had swimmer's ear again. It could be chronic for people who needed two hearing aids. As I got closer, I saw that she was only wearing one today. Hence the sudoku, which she did only when she wanted to be alone.

"Well, *you* took your sweet time," she said as I sat down next to her and put the cranberry juice on the table. "I asked for that hours ago."

"Mom, it's me, Valerie," I said, hoping I didn't sound like my heart was sinking.

"Oh, for chrissakes, I *know* who you are." My mother looked as if she couldn't believe how stupid I was. "You *said* you'd bring me some cranberry juice and I've been waiting *forever*. S'matter, they make you pick the cranberries yourself?"

"I'm sorry you had to wait, Mom," I said gently, "but I just got here. This is Thursday. My last visit was Sunday."

She started to say something, then stopped. She set the pencil on the table and looked around—at the patio, at the umbrella overhead, at the aide and the elderly man in a bright blue sweat suit coming slowly up the path from the garden in front of us, at me, at herself—searching for what Dr. Li referred to as *mental true north*, some single thing that hasn't suddenly changed like the rest of the traitor world. Her face went from bewildered to fearful to suspicious, until finally she sat back heavily, covering her eyes with one hand.

"It's okay, Mom," I said, putting an arm around her. She was little more than skin and bones now, but in three days she seemed to have diminished even more.

"*There* you are!" Gloria materialized on Mom's other side. "Why didn't you tell me you were here?" Her too-bright smile vanished as Mom looked her over with a critical frown, tsk-ing at a food stain on her navy blue smock. "What's wrong? What did you say to her?"

"Nothing, I've only been here two minutes.

Gloria was about to answer when Mom put both hands up. "Don't *fight*," she said. "I can't *stand* when women fight. The hectoring—*hector, hector, hector*! Like crows arguing with seagulls. Is today Thursday?"

The fast change of subject was not, in fact, unusual; my mother thought segues were for politicians and game-show hosts. "All day," I said.

She pushed the book and pencil away. "I don't like writing outdoors. I told them that but they always forget. Maybe Alzheimer's is catching. Take me inside."

I moved to obey but Gloria beat me to it in a rush that seemed oddly desperate. "That's what I'm here for," she told me, as if it explained something, or everything.

My mother wanted a nap, so Gloria and I helped her into bed, fluffed her pillows, and promised not to *hector-hector-hector* even if she couldn't hear us. I settled into the chair by her bed, intending to dip into one of the novels on my iPad. But as soon as Mom fell asleep, Gloria insisted that I go back outside with her.

"Is this going to take long?" I said.

"It's *important.*"

I followed Gloria away from the now empty patio, down the walk to a bench under a large maple tree. "Make it fast," I said. "I'd like to be back before Mom wakes up."

"Not so loud." She leaned forward and spoke in a half whisper. "As an aide, I see and hear a lot more than when I was a visitor. I think there's something funny going on. And I don't mean funny ha-ha."

At last, the Gloria I knew and loved. "Why? Did something in particular happen?" When she didn't answer right away, I added, "Or did someone just give you a dirty look?"

She drew back, looking stony as she folded her arms. "I should have known you wouldn't take me seriously. You never have."

"That's not true," I said promptly, but I could hear the lie in my own voice.

"You think it's just my imagination, because I'm the little sister. *Baby* sister. I'll never be more than a child to you. You have no idea what it was like, growing up with you three adults. Dad, Mom, and Mom, Jr. You all knew better about everything. When you weren't all *tolerating* me—ho-hum, another Christmas, we have to do *Santa* again; you all acted like you didn't want me to grow up. Like Mom trying to make me sit on Santa's lap when I was *eight*."

"Just for the photo," I said, which was true. "I know, I was there. She wanted me to sit on his other knee but the guy said he'd quit if I tried it." Also true; the bastard.

Gloria almost smiled at the memory, then caught herself. "You're doing it *again*—trying to pacify me. Just listen to me for once, will you? Something's not right here."

"I'm only asking why you think that," I said, trying to sound utterly reasonable and not at all like I might be smarting (a *very* tiny bit) from certain (*very* minor) points she'd scored. "It's a fair question. If it was the other way round, you'd ask me the same thing. Especially if this was the first you'd heard about anything being the slightest bit wrong even though I'd been coming here every day for weeks."

"I *told* you, this isn't like just visiting," she said. "You don't know, you haven't done both." A movement behind Gloria caught my eye, an aide looking around the patio. She picked up my mother's forgotten sudoku book and dropped it in the large front pocket of her smock, then paused when she noticed us. I smiled and waved. Gloria twisted around to look; when she turned back to me, she was pissed off again.

"Fine. *Don't* believe me. I'll *prove* it. Then you can't say I'm *jumping at shadows*." She got up and walked off. Unbidden, the memory came to me of her doing the same thing as a toddler during what Mom called one of her bossy episodes. I suppressed a smile, just in case she looked back, but she didn't. She hadn't back then, either.

Things were strained between us after that. My tries at initiating a conversation fell flat; if she answered at all, it was usually just a wordless grunt that let me know she hadn't gone deaf. She thawed a bit by Monday, occasionally even speaking to me first. Encouraged, I suggested we go shopping and see a movie, in an actual movie theater, my treat, including popcorn dripping with artery-hardening butter-flavored goop. She declined politely, saying her feet hurt. Considering she always went straight into the tub as soon as she came home, they probably hurt all the way up to her hips.

Maybe finding a bath all ready and waiting when she got home would soften her up even more, I thought. The first time surprised the hell out of her; she sounded awkward when she thanked me, and spent the whole evening watching movies with me in the living room, even making a bowl of popcorn without being asked. She wasn't quite as surprised the second time; the third time, she asked me what I wanted.

"What do you think I want?" I said, holding half a pastrami on pumpernickel; I'd splurged at the deli counter that morning, a treat for the extra work I had to put in on a new account. "I want us to be friends again. I want us to be *sisters* again. You're acting like I owe you money *and* I slept with your boyfriend."

She stared down at me, expressionless. "You just don't take *anything* seriously, do you?"

"Oh, for chrissakes." I sighed. "I'm trying to break the ice between us before it turns into permafrost." Her mouth curled briefly and I felt a surge of irritation. "I'm sorry—still not serious enough?"

"Don't bother running any more baths," she told me. "I keep a swimsuit at the home so I can use the Jacuzzi. Sometimes Mom and I go in together."

I bit back a smart remark about being a lifeguard in a whirlpool and then felt ashamed for even thinking it. Maybe I *had* been making her feel small all her life and never realized it.

"I was just trying to do something nice for you," I said. "I've seen how much work you do—"

"How kind of you to notice," she said stiffly. "But, being a grown-up, I can run my own baths." She actually turned on her heel and walked out.

"Fine," I said at her back, my sympathy evaporating. If my sister wanted to be taken seriously—as a grown-up, no less—she could damned well act like one instead of a thirteen-year-old girl with her period.

Oh, no, you didn't, said my brain.

My face burned, even though I was alone. Okay, maybe Gloria did have her period. Back in the day, I hadn't exactly been a ray of sunshine during Shark Week. Now I was coping with the onset of menopause and doing fairly well thanks to hormones, but every day wasn't a picnic and neither was I.

My thoughts chased each other round and round. Had I really been horrible to Gloria all her life? Or were we just doomed to be permanently out of step no matter what? We were from different generations, after all; we practically spoke a different language. Still, if I had acted like that after she had run a bath for me, my conscience would have tortured me for *years*. Of course, that was me-the-older-sister. Could I see things as if I were the younger sister? Etc., etc., and so on, and so forth. When I finally remembered to eat the sandwich I'd been looking forward to all day, it sat in my stomach like a hockey puck.

My indigestion subsided later when I heard her go out again instead of putting her sore feet up. Gloria wasn't letting the problems between us affect her relationship with my car.

Gloria continued volunteering with a wholeheartedness she'd never shown for paid employment, or at least none that hadn't involved wearing a bathing suit. I did wonder occasionally if her apparent dedication might really be an unhealthy obsession with finding evidence that didn't exist to prove something that wasn't true.

Except that when I saw her during my visits, she didn't look obsessed. She looked cheerfully busy, the way people do when they're happy in their work. Maybe in trying to prove something to me, Gloria had found herself, discovered that caregiving was lifeguarding in street clothes— unlikely but not impossible. Her being too embarrassed to say so wasn't impossible, either, and even less unlikely.

Unless she still believed that something wasn't right and she was playing a role more Method than anything Brando had ever done while she watched and waited for something to happen. I really couldn't tell. While she wasn't openly hostile, she was still distant and had little to say beyond updates on Mom.

Maybe *I* was jumping at shadows now. After a lifetime as the grasshopper in a family of ants, Gloria was now up close and personal with the reality of Mom's decline. Coming to terms with that would shake anyone up. I wished like anything she'd talk about it with me, but if she really felt that I'd always patronized her, I could hardly be surprised that she was keeping her distance. Nor could I blame her.

Eventually, she warmed up enough that we occasionally saw a movie or went out to eat together, but the wall between us remained. Much as I wanted to, I didn't push her. Partly because I was afraid she'd get angry and shut me out again. But I'd also developed this rather weird, superstitious idea that looking too closely at her newfound self-discipline would somehow jinx it. She'd stop volunteering or even visiting more than once a month, if that. Eventually, despite rules I'd laid down, she'd drift into sleeping all day and staying up all night. I'd seen it happen before. Regardless of what had inspired her sense of purpose, I didn't want her to lose it. Even if it meant we'd never say anything deeper than *It's gonna rain* or *Guess what's on TV? Hint: wolverines!* to each other for the rest of our lives.

Gloria held still for *Red Dawn* and even made popcorn. But she never suggested any more true-crime programs. That was fine with me, although I wasn't sure what it meant, if it meant anything at all.

A month and a half after Gloria's initial blowup, Mr. Santos and his daughter Lola sought me out to tell me my sister was a hero. Mr. Santos was a wiry little man in his late seventies who shared my mother's fondness for puzzles and card games. I knew Lola to nod to, but she and her father had made Gloria's acquaintance in a big way.

"I've never seen anything like that in real life," Lola Santos said, looking at me through wide, dark eyes, as if my being Gloria's older sister was an accomplishment in itself. "I was in the bathroom for maybe two minutes. Gloria had brought him some juice—"

"And if she hadn't, I wouldn't be here right now." Mr. Santos thumped his chest twice with one bony fist before his daughter caught his hand.

"Don't, Popi, you're still bruised!"

"Good. The bruises remind me of the heroine with the curly brown hair and the dimple in her cheek who saved my life." He shook his index finger at me. "She's a wonderful girl, your sister. I don't know what we'd do without her. She's our heroine. She's *my* personal heroine."

"And mine," Lola added.

I had no idea what to say to that, so I just smiled and thanked them for telling me. I tried to talk to Gloria about it at home later, but she wasn't very forthcoming; when she started to look annoyed, I let it go. The next day I rearranged my work schedule and went back to see if I could find out anything else, but I might as well not have bothered. I couldn't get any more out of Mr. Santos than what he had already told me. My mother alternately claimed to have been taking a nap or sitting in the garden. The few other residents I spoke to had nothing new or useful to add. Even the usually chatty Jill Franklyn was reticent on the subject; after praising Gloria's mad CPR skillz and her ability to stay calm in a crisis, she made a very pointed comment about patient privacy and the confidentiality of medical records. I took the hint and spent the rest of the time with Mom, who was slightly confused by my consecutive visits.

I went back to three visits a week, on the grounds that it made Mom happy and not because I was still trying to find out more about Gloria's big heroic moment. Because that would have been pointless, considering that I'd gotten a full account from Mr. Santos and Lola themselves. Happy ending, smiles all round—what more could there possibly be to the story? If I were jumping at shadows now, they were shadows I couldn't even name. Maybe all the *she's a heroine* business was getting on my nerves; weeks after the fact, it had yet to die down.

Jealous much? said that still small voice in my brain.

I was pretty sure I hadn't become that neurotic. Practically certain. But if I *were*—I *wasn't*, but if I *were*—I told myself, there was still only one way to kill the shadows. Mom would benefit from the extra visits and so would I—no one knew how much longer she'd be herself. If good things sometimes got done for stupid reasons, it didn't make them any less good. Did it?

"Weren't you here yesterday?" my mother asked as I sat down next to her at the umbrella table. To my surprise, she seemed vaguely annoyed.

"No, I came on Thursday and today's Saturday. What's the matter, you sick of me hanging around?"

"I don't understand why you won't take advantage of Gloria's being here," she said, "and go away, even just for a long weekend. Instead, you come here more. What's the matter with you? Don't you have a life?"

"No," I said honestly.

"What about your friends?"

"They don't have lives, either. It's rough out there. I was thinking about moving in with you."

My mother gave a grim laugh. "You better win the lottery first. They don't let you split expenses." She looked around. "Where's that thing? You know, with all the books inside and the screen. I coulda sworn I had it. See if I left it in my room, will ya? Since you're here anyway."

My mother's door was open; inside, an aide stood with her back to me, doing something on the tray table next to the bed. On her left was a cart, both shelves crowded with water pitchers.

"Oh, hi," I said cheerfully, and she jumped. The pitcher she'd been holding sprang out of her hands, spilling water over the bed before it fell to the floor. "Oh, damn, I'm so sorry!" I rushed to help.

"Don't, it's okay, I can take care of this, it's fine—" The aide sounded almost desperate as she tried to wave me away, grab the pitcher, and pick up several small white pills all at once. "It's only water, not plutonium, I can manage, really, I can."

"I'm sure, but let me help anyway," I said guiltily as I got down on my knees. The pitcher had come apart and the lid had gone under the bed. I used it to sweep up several small white pills.

"I was just taking something for a headache," the aide said, grabbing up the pills and dumping them into the front pocket of her smock, ignoring the minor dust bunnies attached. "I have cluster headaches, they're murder."

"How awful." I had no idea what cluster headaches were, but judging by how stricken she looked, she wasn't exaggerating much. Her olive complexion had gone almost ashy. I made another sweep with the pitcher lid in case I'd missed any pills before I got to my feet. "I really am sorry, I didn't meant to sneak up on you. I should change the bed—"

"*No*, absolutely *not*, you don't come here to do the housekeeping, I'll take care of it." She spoke so quickly she was almost babbling. "I'll take care of this, you don't have to worry, *please* don't take any time away from your visit, but if—" she cut off suddenly. Her color had improved slightly but now she looked like she was going to cry.

"What's wrong? Is it your headache?" I asked.

I was about to suggest she sit down and drink some water when she said, "It's nothing. Please, just go on with your visit, I'll be all right."

"Look, you won't even let me help you change the bed, so *anything* I can do to make up for scaring the bejeebus out of you, just tell me."

She looked down, embarrassed. "It's kind of stupid."

"Kind of stupid—that's definitely in my wheelhouse," I said. That got me a smile.

"Okay, it's that—I just—" All at once, she was stripping the bed. "No, I can't. I *was* going to ask if you'd mind not mentioning this to your mother, but forget it." She dropped a bundle of wet linens on the floor and started to pull off the padded mattress cover. "It's only because I feel like *such* an *idiot*. But I have no business asking you someth—"

"It's done," I said, holding up one hand. "I can't think of a good reason why I'd have to mention it anyway."

"But—"

"Forget it. I'm not talkin' and you can't make me."

She gave a small, nervous laugh.

"I really only came in here to get her e-reader—" I spotted it on the nightstand and pointed. The aide handed it to me somehow looking grateful, sheepish, and relieved all at once. Her name tag said she was Lily R. "Thanks. What's the *R* for?"

She stared, baffled.

"Lily R." I nodded at her name tag. "*R* for . . . ?"

"Romano," she said, and rolled her eyes. "You must think I'm a real clown."

"Hardly." As I went back outside to my mother, I couldn't help feeling a bit guilty for leaving Lily *R*-for-Romano to remake the bed by herself. Then Mom asked me to read to her and I put it out of my mind. I might never have given it another thought if I hadn't found a pill in the sole of one of my very expensive athletic shoes.

I wore them not because I was particularly sporty but because walking in them felt so good. Plus, they came in bright, jazzy colors, which I had a new fondness for in my old age. And what the hell—if I ever decided to defy my old age and run a marathon, I was ready.

Running a marathon was probably the only thing that could have been farther from my mind than Lily R. when I felt something stuck to the sole of my shoe. Pausing at the kitchen door, I took it off before I scarred the tile flooring for life. A tiny rock—I used an ice pick to flip it out the open door, then checked the other shoe, just in case. The pill was about the same size as the rock but wedged in more deeply. Maybe that was why it was still intact, I thought, carefully working it free. Although I had no idea why I was bothering—I was hardly going to give it to Lily Romano next time I saw her. *Hey, girlfriend, found this on the bottom of my shoe, thought you'd want it back anyway.* Now *who's kind of stupid?*

I put it in an empty ring box on my bureau. As Mom always said, waste not; in a cluster-headache emergency, I'd be glad I'd saved it. Stranger things had happened; were happening now.

A week later, Jill Franklyn called in the middle of the afternoon, apologizing so much I couldn't get a word in edgewise. The I heard her say something about death being harder for some people, especially the first death.

"The *first* death?" I interrupted. "Are you talking about my mother?"

"Oh, no, no, no, your mother is fine!" she said quickly. "It's your sister—"

"My *sister?*" Suddenly the pit of my stomach was filling with ice water. "Something happened to *Gloria?*"

"No, no, no, she's fine," Jill Franklyn said. "Well, not *fine,* exactly—"

"Is she still alive?" I demanded.

"Yes, of *course* she's still *alive.*" Bewilderment crept into her apologetic tone. "But—well—you need to come and get her, she shouldn't drive home."

I said I was on my way and hung up without telling her that would be a bit longer than either of us would have liked, because I'd have to take a cab, and although this wasn't the middle of nowhere or darkest suburbia, it wasn't Manhattan, either. I got there in half an hour, which was actually sooner than I'd expected.

Jill Franklyn was waiting for me at the reception desk, looking a bit flustered. "I'm so glad you're here," she told me, smiling, but I could hear the admonition in her voice. The receptionist pretended not to eavesdrop by studying something intently on her desk.

"Sorry, I had to get a cab." I tried to look contrite or at least sheepish. "I'm not sure I understand what's going on. You said my mother's all right—"

"Yes, just fine." Jill Franklyn nodded vigorously as she ushered me through the entry gate and down the corridor leading directly to my mother's room. "Gloria's with her right now."

I found the two of them sitting side by side on Mom's bed. Mom had her arm around my sister, who had obviously been crying. Lily Romano was there as well, looking concerned and fidgeting. She left as soon as I came in, nodding a silent hello as she rushed past. I frowned, wishing she'd stay, but I had no chance to ask and no good reason to do so.

"What kept you?" my mother was saying, a bit impatient.

"There's only one car between us," I said, "and Gloria has it. I don't usually need it. What's up, Glow-bug?"

Gloria looked up at me and I thought she was furious at my using her childhood nickname so publicly. Then she got up, flung her arms around me, and sobbed.

By the time we got to the car, she had quieted down and stayed quiet all the way home, for which I was grateful. Rush hour had started and I didn't want to fight the traffic to the soundtrack of Gloria's heartbroken sobs. A dozen years ago, never driving in rush hour again had been one more good reason to leave the local tax-preparation firm in favor of a home business; now I decided that it had been the best reason.

We made it home alive; in lieu of kissing the ground in thanksgiving, I put a pizza in the oven and joined Gloria in the living room. I found her wedged into the far corner of the sofa, hugging her knees to her chest as if to make herself as small as possible. A joke about never having a white-knuckle ride on the couch crossed my mind, but for once I actually thought before speaking.

"I don't know what happened today," I said after a bit. "Jill Franklyn didn't have a chance to tell me and I thought I'd better just get you home rather than hang around."

She flicked a glance at me but neither spoke nor moved. I waited a little longer, then went into the kitchen to check on the pizza. I was taking it out of the oven when I heard Gloria say, "I couldn't save her."

I turned to see her sitting at the table. I cut the pizza into eight slices, grabbed a couple of plates, and put the platter on a heat pad within easy reach before taking the chair on her right.

"They gave me coffee with, like, six sugars." She frowned at the plate in front of her as if she were seeing something other than a Currier-and-Ives style winter scene in blue and white. We'd grown up with these dishes; in thirty or more years, we'd only lost two. "They said it was good for shock. I didn't think I was in shock but I guess I was." She raised her face to me. "I never, ever, *ever* imagined what it would be like to do CPR on someone and not . . . not w—" She swallowed hard. "Not have it work."

"Oh, sis, I'm so sorry." I got up and put my arms around her. She sat passively for a little while; then I felt her slowly move to hug me back. "I can't even imagine."

"It's not how it should've happened. Mrs. Boudreau should be playing bridge with her son and her friends right now. Watching a movie tonight. Getting up for breakfast tomorrow morning and then . . . just . . . having a few more years to be happy. Like Mr. Santos and the others."

The last three words clunked in my ear, but I was too busy trying to remember the dead woman. Still keeping hold of both her hands, I sat down again after a bit and said, "I'm sorry, Gloria, but I can't place her. The lady who died. Mrs. Boudreau?"

My sister nodded sadly. "She only moved in a couple of weeks ago; I don't think you ever even saw her." She took a shuddery breath. "I promised her son I'd look after her. I promised *her* I'd take care of her. And then her son had to watch while I broke that promise."

"You're a good person, sis." My thoughts shifted around like puzzle pieces trying to fit themselves together. "You *did* take care of her, as best you could. But no matter how well you do it, CPR isn't a get-out-of-death-free card."

As soon as the words were out of my mouth, I wanted to kick myself. Gloria frowned and I waited for her to tear me a new one for making stupid jokes again. Instead she said, "You don't understand. Mrs. Boudreau *really shouldn't be dead*. She wasn't even long-term. She was only there till the end of the month," she added in response to my questioning look. "Then she was gonna live with her son and his family. They're adding another room to their house for her. It isn't ready yet. And now they'll just have an extra room with nobody in it."

It was on the tip of my tongue to say that no extra space in any home ever went unused under any circumstances, but then I didn't. Having grown up in a decidedly uncrowded house, Gloria's experience was limited, and it was beside the point anyway.

Little by little, I got the story out of her; it was pretty much Mr. Santos all over again, with a slightly different cast and an unhappy ending that even a portable defibrillator couldn't change. "The defib's the last of the last resorts," Gloria said as she started on a slice of pizza. That had to be a good sign, I thought. "It's too easy to screw it up even if you're trained. I'm trained to defib, but I've never done it." She paused, head tilted to one side. "Jesus, I just heard myself. 'I'm trained to defib but I've never done it.' Like it's routine. Until I started volunteering, I'd never done any CPR for real. Not even once."

I was trying to think of something to say when she dropped the slice of pizza she'd been holding and put a hand to her mouth. "And I never even thought anyone would actually *die*. Mr. Santos and his daughter were calling me a heroine, the head nurse put a letter in my file, I got my name in the newsletter as this month's MVV—Most Valuable Volunteer. I didn't think, *What if somebody dies?* because nobody did. So I didn't think for one second that Mrs. Boudreau might die. I just waited for the nurses to say she had a pulse."

I frowned. Had Gloria performed CPR on someone else besides Mr. Santos? "Gloria, how many times—"

She didn't hear me. "Even after they shocked her, I was still waiting for someone to say she was back." She put her hand to mouth again. "Omigod, deep down I'm *still* waiting for Jill to call and say someone at the hospital decided to give it one last try and brought Mrs. Boudreau back after all."

And I was waiting for her to burst into tears again or even get sick all over the table. Instead, Gloria finished the slice and reached for another. Good to see she was recovering from the experience, I thought. My own appetite was history.

The head nurse who called the next morning to check on Gloria was new. Celeste Akintola had that friendly but no-nonsense voice all RNs above a certain level of experience seem to have. Jill Franklyn didn't have it, and I couldn't imagine that she ever would. I shook the thought away and focused on getting acquainted with the new head nurse. More specifically, on trying to find out how often Gloria had used her mad CPR skillz, but without sounding like I was prying. Or like I had to.

Celeste Akintola made friendly but no-nonsense noises about patient confidentiality, adding that she expected all staff, including volunteers, to respect the privacy of the residents. I gave up, handed the phone to Gloria, and stood by, blatantly eavesdropping; all I heard was *yes* and *okay*. After hanging up, Gloria said she had strict orders to take a full two weeks off before she even considered coming back. Even then, it would be for no more than three days a week, at least to begin with. My sister didn't mind going along with that, which was a relief. Also a little amazing— or perhaps not. She was subdued, obviously deep in thought.

If I were honest, I had to do some thinking of my own about taking Gloria seriously. As the older, supposedly wiser sister, I'd never saved a life or seen a person die right in front of me. Gloria had saved one person and had another die practically in her arms just in the space of a few weeks. Life and death—it didn't get any more serious than that.

I wanted to tell her as much, but I couldn't figure out how to begin. Whatever I said came out trite, if not weaselish. Gloria by contrast had a new eloquence. Or maybe it was only new to me.

"I was scared of what you'd say," she told me later. "I was doing so good, you know? Everybody needed me—*me*, personally. Me *specifically*. And then *this* happened. I needed you to come and be Mom, Jr., so much, but at the same time I was thinking how pathetic it was to be such a mess at thirty-eight. Then you came in and just—" She shrugged. "All you cared about was me. And I realized there's only one person in the whole world who'll always show up, no matter how pathetic I am. You didn't go all smarter or older or wiser on my ass and you didn't act like it was all a big joke." She paused. "Although the get-out-of-death-free-card thing was kinda cool."

"Some people make jokes when they're nervous," I said.

"Yeah, I get that now," she said. "See? I'm growing up."

But, I hoped, not so much that she'd ever realize how utterly and completely she'd pwned her big sister.

It was a nice two weeks. I took some time off and let Gloria introduce me to the quirky world of hard-core flea-market shopping, including lessons in haggling for the reserved soul. She even got me to admit it was fun, which it was, although I didn't see myself doing it without her. She said she felt the same way about *Red Dawn*.

I visited Mom alone and quickly learned to come in the mornings, when she was sharper, upbeat, and much more like her old self. After mid-day, her energy flagged and she had a hard time concentrating, whether she'd had a nap after lunch or not. Jill Franklyn said this was called *sun-downing*. Her sympathetic expression wasn't perfunctory, but there was something *professional* about it, almost rehearsed. Maybe it was all the training she'd had in how to discuss these things with the family.

Or maybe, I thought, suddenly ashamed, it was repetition. How many times had she explained this to anxious relatives? I really had to work on giving credit where credit was due, I thought, or I'd end up yelling *Get off my lawn!* at everyone under sixty.

After her two-week break, Gloria was ready to go back to work—or "work"—and I was happy to let her, despite being tempted to drop hints about looking for a paying job. Then I thought of Mom; having Gloria around again would probably be good for her, even if it wasn't as often as before.

After the first week, however, Gloria announced she'd be going every day again. "Akintola said I can only *volunteer* three days a week," she said when I questioned her. "So, fine. The rest of the time, I'll just visit Mom." She smiled like she'd just cut the Gordian knot with blunt-end scissors.

"I'm not trying to go all older, wiser, or smarter on your ass," I said, wincing, "but I'm pretty sure that violates the spirit of the order."

"She doesn't want me to volunteer, I won't volunteer," Gloria said stubbornly. "Four days out of seven, I'll sit around like a lady of leisure."

"I don't think you should go seven days in a row—"

Gloria huffed impatiently. "Have you seen Mom lately?"

My heart sank. "I know what you—"

"You always go in the morning, right? Who told you about sundowning—was it Jill?" I tried to say something but she talked over me. "It's code for Mom gets worse as the day goes on. They use *sundowning* with the families because the word makes them think of things like pretty sunsets after a nice day—as if the person started out good in the morning. But they don't. They're *better* in the morning—that's not the same as *good*."

I stared at her, slightly awestruck, then tried to cover it by saying the first thing that came into my head. "I thought you weren't volunteering today."

She frowned. "I'm not."

"So if Mr. Santos has another heart attack—or someone else has a coronary—you'd stand back and let the pros handle it?"

"Are you insane?" she demanded. "You think I'd just watch someone die just because it's my day off?"

"No, only if they were DNR. Like Mom."

She looked so stricken, I wanted to bite my tongue off and let her throw it away. "When you don't know for sure, you assume they want to live until you know otherwise for sure," she said in a stiff little voice, and I could have sworn she was trying to do Celeste Akintola's no-nonsense voice.

"And if it *is* otherwise?" I asked, trying not to sound argumentative.

She didn't answer.

"You know you can get into big trouble for doing CPR when you're not supposed to? Not just you, but the doctors and nurses and everyone else who works there, including all the other volunteers." I wasn't sure exactly how true that was, but it wasn't a complete lie. "*You* could even get arrested for assault, and I don't think the family has to wait till you're out of jail to sue you."

Gloria gave me the most severe Eyebrow I'd ever seen. "The box set of *Law & Order* doesn't come with a law degree. I do what I know is right."

"I just asked what if you knew for sure—"

"Like *Mom?*" she said, almost spitting the word. "Go ahead, say it: *Mom.* What's the matter, can't say who you really mean? Why? Things get too cold-blooded for you all of a sudden? Or are you really afraid Mom would sue me? Press charges? Both?" Gloria gave a single, short laugh. "Have I asked you for bail money? *Lately?*" she added. "No, I haven't. Case closed."

"So, what—you always guessed right?" I frowned. "Just how many times *was* that?"

She hesitated. "Counting Mr. Santos and Mrs. Boudreau? Five."

My jaw dropped. "Why didn't you tell me?"

"I was mad at you."

"Then why didn't *Mom*—no, scratch that. Why didn't *anybody* tell me?"

"Maybe they thought you knew." She shrugged. "I mean, they kept calling me a heroine."

I wanted a desk to pound my head on. "Don't you think I'd have said something if I *had* known?"

"I was mad at you," she said again. "Remember?"

"Yeah. I also remember why: I asked you why you thought there was something wrong at the home." I gave her a sideways look. "Does this mean you've changed your mind about that?"

She shifted her weight from one foot to the other and huffed. "Do you *really* have to make a big deal out of it?"

"Hey, it was *your* idea," I called after her as she left.

If Gloria had changed her mind, so had I, although I didn't realize it right away. It crept up on me in chilly slow motion. My visits went from three a week to daily. I thought it was intimations of mortality—specifically, my mother's—brought on by the revelation of how many times Gloria had used her mad CPR skillz. No, I corrected myself: *how many times Gloria had performed CPR in an emergency situation.* Taking her seriously meant swearing off funny terms for matters of life and death.

I was even ready to confess that I had a case of the jitters—not eager but willing—except that she didn't ask. Baffling—surely she was wondering why I'd rearranged my schedule so drastically . . . wasn't she? I waited, but she didn't try to talk to me during visits or at home, where I was now working through evening hours we had previously spent together.

After a week, I couldn't stand it anymore and called in one of my temps. Gloria raised her eyebrows—it wasn't the first half of April—but didn't ask. In fact, she didn't say a word on the drive in.

"Are you picking me up or should I get a ride with Lily?" she asked as I pulled into an empty space in the visitor's lot.

I made an exasperated noise. "You're gaslighting me, aren't you?"

"What is that?" Gloria looked genuinely baffled.

"Okay, not a fan of old movies. You're trying to drive me crazy," I said.

"And what happened to make you think that?" she asked politely. The strong urge I had to smack her must have been obvious. "Come on, seriously," she added. "You're the one who's gotten all weird, working all night so you can be here every day—"

"And you've never asked me why. Aren't you even a little bit curious?"

"Well, yeah," she said, like she'd never heard a stupider question. "But I figured I'd just be wasting my breath. You don't tell me a goddam thing till you feel like it. If you ever do."

I felt my face getting hot again.

"What's the matter?" she said, a little impatient now. "It's true, isn't it?"

I gave up. "Okay, okay. I'm nervous about Mom. Finding out how many times you'd done CPR kinda . . ." I shrugged. "It kinda freaked me out, I guess."

"Really." My sister gave me the skeptical Eyebrow. "When? After you considered the legal ramifications of my possibly keeping Mom alive?"

"I never did CPR on anyone—I don't even know how—so it took a while for the reality to sink in, that Mom could . . . you know. Die." I barely managed not to choke on the word.

My sister let out a long breath, staring through the windshield at nothing in particular. Then: "If it makes you feel any better, Mom isn't too likely to have a coronary anytime real soon. Her heart's in pretty good shape. To be honest, I worried more about her falling—the dizzy spells. Fortunately, she doesn't fight using the wheelchair as much as she did, so it's less of a worry than it was. But if you want to keep coming every day, I'm not gonna stop you," she added with a sudden smile. "Because it really seems to help her stay clear."

"What about the sundowning?"

"That's what I mean." Gloria's smile grew even brighter. "Some days, I can barely tell it's happening."

"New medication?" I asked.

"Nope, same stuff, same dose. Some of the other residents take a lot more and don't do as well."

"Maybe it's because she's eating better?" I said.

Gloria shrugged. "It doesn't hurt. Now, are we going in, or do you want to sit here and, as Mom says when she thinks no one's listening, fret like a motherfucker all day?"

She was right—Mom *was* better. But Dr. Li had warned me that these periods of near recovery, when patients somehow seemed to shake off the fog that had been rolling in, weren't signs of genuine improvement, only the erratic nature of the disease showing itself—one of dementia's special cruelties.

But it didn't make Mom any less lucid. She started telling me to go on vacation again and was annoyed when I refused, occasionally getting so agitated with me that I had to leave so she'd calm down.

"You want to know the truth," Lily Romano said as she walked me out one afternoon, "she's kinda scared that you're coming every day. She's afraid maybe it means that she's dying and the doctor won't tell her."

"Really?" I was shocked. "I'd never have thought of that. Gloria never said anything."

Lily Romano shrugged. "She doesn't know. Residents don't always tell their families everything. Sometimes it's easier for them to confide in someone they aren't so close to, especially when–"

"When . . . ?" I prodded after a moment.

She winced. "When it's something where they think their family will, like, just say they're being silly or paranoid."

When the family doesn't take them seriously, I thought, wincing a little myself. "So does my mother confide in you a lot?" She looked so uncomfortable, I went on quickly, "Forget I asked, it's not important. How're your headaches?"

She looked blank for a moment. "Oh, yeah, fine—I haven't had any in a while."

I might have mentioned finding the pill in my shoe just for the hell of it, but we were nearly at the entry gate and she was making gotta-get-back-to-work noises. I made a mental note to talk to Gloria later about Mom's possible anxieties. Then the day got busy; Gloria was getting a lift home with another aide, so I did the grocery shopping, and somewhere between the deli counter and the perennial choice between paper or plastic, a gust of tedium blew all the mental notes off the front of my mental refrigerator.

Only much later, after several hours into another night at the computer, did it come back to me. My work ethic said it could wait; my procrastinator said it was a golden opportunity. For once, I went with the latter.

I opened the door to find Gloria standing there with one hand raised, about to knock. "I'm sorry, I know I'm not supposed to interrupt you—"

"It's okay," I said. "I think I'm off tonight. What's up?"

"I've got a dilemma," she said, her face troubled, "and I need some advice."

"I'll get the Shiraz, you save me a seat on the couch."

"You'll probably think it's silly," she said as I poured wine into her glass.

"Apparently that's going around. Never mind," I added when she looked bewildered. "Just tell me. We'll decide if it's silly later."

She hesitated, gazing at me with uncertainty. Then she took a deep breath. "Okay, there are certain things that everybody at Brightside has to do—certain rules, I mean, that everybody has to obey, no matter what, or get terminated. Even the nurses. Even the janitorial staff. Even the gardening service people."

I nodded.

"Those are the strictest rules, and if you see an *infraction*"—she made a face at the word—"you're supposed to report it. Which is, like"—she rolled her eyes—"who wants to be a snitch? I mean, if I ever saw someone *hurt* a resident, I'd yell at the top of my lungs. But—"

"Did you see something?" I asked gently.

She nodded. "It was one of those things you can actually get away with if you're careful. And probably everyone there's done it at least once, but they'll fire you on the spot for it, even if nothing bad happens."

I shook my head. "What is this incredibly evil thing?"

"Having any unauthorized medication on you during your shift." She frowned. "I thought I told you that. We can't even have aspirin in our pants pocket."

"Why not?" I asked.

"Because it's a hazard to the residents."

"Only if they get into your pants pockets," I said, laughing a little.

"They don't care." Gloria was shaking her head. "Zero tolerance. The only way to be absolutely certain a resident doesn't take anything they're not supposed to is if there *isn't* anything."

"That's even stricter than a hospital, isn't it?" I said, thinking out loud.

"Beats me. And it doesn't matter anyway—it's their policy."

"So you saw someone—" I cut off, already knowing who it would be.

"Lily Romano," she said with a mournful sigh. "I caught her so redhanded, I couldn't even pretend that I didn't see anything. She was doing the rounds with water pitchers–"

I put up a hand. "Been there, sis."

"What are you talking about?" she asked, unsure again and about to get angry.

"I caught Lily Romano with pills," I said sadly. I gave her a quick rundown of our encounter in Mom's room, adding, "I can't remember if you told me about the no-drugs rule. If you did, I forgot it that day."

"Did she beg you not to tell?" Gloria asked, still unhappy.

"Yes, but not about that." I told her the rest.

"That's weird. Why would she ask you to keep quiet about her having to change the bed but not about the pills?"

I thought for a moment. "Because she realized that I didn't know the rule and she didn't want to tip me off. Making me think I was just saving her some embarrassment was pretty clever. Really clever."

"She kind of took a chance, though," Gloria said.

I shook my head. "I didn't even tell *you*, did I?"

Gloria sighed again. "She made me go with her to her locker and watch her put the pills in her purse, all the time begging me not to tell and promising she'd never do it again. I feel bad for her—cluster headaches really are murder—"

"Yeah, that's what she told me," I said. "But when I asked her this afternoon, she said she hadn't had any lately." I fetched the pill from my room. "It got stuck in my shoe," I explained, holding it out to her on a fingertip. "Is it the same as what you saw?"

"I didn't actually see the pills, just the bottle," she said, picking it up between thumb and forefinger. "This isn't a headache pill. It's methylphenidate."

I frowned. "Is that meth as in *meth*?" I asked, uneasy now.

"Methylphenidate as in Ritalin," she said. "You know, ADHD? No, you don't. Pardon me for saying so, Val, but you're too old. You grew up before they started trying to cure childhood. At least half the kids I went to school with were on Ritalin or Adderall or whatever."

I was aghast. "Did Mom and Dad—"

"Oh, hell, no." Gloria laughed. "But plenty of kids supplemented their allowance by selling anything they didn't need to kids without prescriptions. They'd buy it to lose weight or study all night before a test, and I heard that a sixth-grader was supplying a couple of teachers." She frowned. "You'd never take this for a headache. It would *give* you one."

"Okay, pointing out the obvious now: Lily Romano isn't a schoolkid. So why would she take it?" I asked.

"Adult ADHD, I guess?"

"Never mind, I think we'd better go back to the home right now and talk to whoever's on duty."

Gloria caught my arm as I stood up. "Okay, but what do we tell them?"

"We'll start with what we know and let them figure it out."

———

Gloria was as surprised as I was to find Jill Franklyn in charge of the graveyard shift. I supposed it figured: unremarkable but competent enough that no one would lose any sleep. Jill Franklyn was a hell of a lot more surprised to see us. We were heading down the main corridor in the residential area toward the nurses' station when a door on the left opened suddenly but very quietly and she stepped into the dim, shadowy hallway. She had her back to us but I knew that thin silhouette and ballerinaesque posture. She paused with her back to us. Gloria and I stopped dead in our tracks and looked at each other. I shrugged, then cleared my throat.

Jill Franklyn whirled and snapped on her flashlight, blinding both of us. "Omigod!" The word came out in a screechy whisper. The light went off again, leaving me and Gloria no less blind as Jill came toward us, her shoes making tiny squeak-squeak-squeak sounds. "What are you two *doing* here at this hour? It must be after midnight. Are you out of your minds?"

"Which question should we answer first?" I gave a nervous laugh and Jill Franklyn shushed me. She herded us down the hall toward the nurses' station, I thought, but before we reached it, she shoved us through a door on the right, hurriedly and with a strength I'd never imagined she had in those skinny ballerina arms. Gloria seemed equally taken aback; she was rubbing her upper arm.

"Sorry about that," Jill Franklyn said, not sounding very apologetic. "If anyone else sees you, they'll call Akintola and we'll all be in trouble. What are you doing here?"

I blinked rapidly, trying to clear my vision, and saw we were in Celeste Akintola's office. Jill Franklyn surprised me by sitting down behind her desk and motioned for us to take the chairs on the other side. Gloria and I traded looks as we sat down; she gave me a *you-first* nod.

Jill Franklyn sat straight up in the high-backed chair, listening to me with a troubled expression, nodding from time to time but saying nothing. I finished and turned to Gloria, who hesitated, waiting for some kind of response, but the nurse remained silent, not even looking at my sister.

Gloria spoke in a small, uncertain voice, occasionally pausing to look at me. Each time I made a small, keep-going gesture. She did, but any confidence she'd had had deserted her, and I had no idea why. Maybe she was having trouble with the whole snitching thing, I thought. Except this wasn't just tattling to teacher—Lily Romano was carrying around more pills than she needed. A *lot* more.

When Gloria was done, I sat forward in my chair and said, "What would happen if someone gave that stuff to a patient here?"

Jill Franklyn finally lifted her gaze to meet mine. "It would depend on the patient," she said, sounding calm and logical, like we were discussing the amount of caffeine in a cup of coffee. "And the dosage. And, of course, what other medications they might be on at the time. Someone taking vasopressin, for example, might be less drowsy. Depending on the dosage. It would probably have to be twenty or thirty milligrams, I think.

"Dementia patients respond best, though. Early dementia, I mean. Dexedrine's a lot better than methylphenidate but you have to work with what you've got." She sighed. "I don't suppose either of you have access to Dexedrine? It's practically impossible to get nowadays."

Gloria and I looked at each other. "Did you hear anything we just told you?" I asked.

Jill Franklyn wrinkled her nose. "Yeah, Lily Romano's screwed. And so am I, right?" She sat forward, putting her arms on the desk. "Or instead of being Girl Scouts, you could be part of advancing medicine and making life better for dementia patients everywhere."

"How?" I asked, wondering why her eyes weren't crazy.

"By going home and catching up on your sleep, and when you get up tomorrow, we'll all just have business as usual. You"—she pointed at Gloria with one hand—"can volunteer as much as you want, whenever you want; I'll get Akintola to sign off on it. I don't see why she wouldn't, considering you're four for five. That was pretty nice, wasn't it—getting to be a hero? Heroine, whatever. It was too bad about Mrs. Boudreau, but that'll happen—every so often, one of them won't come back for you, no matter how healthy they look. And you"—she pointed at me and frowned—"I can't remember what you do, but I remember your mother's always talking about how you never take a vacation. So take one. She won't lose much ground while you're away. Maybe none."

"How many people are in on this?" I asked incredulously.

Jill Franklyn looked up for a moment. "Hard to say. Here, it's just me and Lily."

"Are you saying this is a—a conspiracy?" My sister practically squeaked on the last word.

"What conspiracy?" Jill Franklyn looked at us like we were crazy. "You're on the Internet, does that mean you're in a conspiracy?" She looked from me to Gloria and back again, then stood up abruptly. "I should have known you wouldn't go for it." She began edging toward the door. "You two Girl Scouts're probably like most middle-aged women—not too physical. I know I don't look like much, but I've got nurse muscles—I can lift almost any resident here unassisted. Or subdue them if they get violent. So I'll just fold my tent now and you can call the—"

I never even saw Gloria move. One moment Jill Franklyn was opening the door; I felt something brush past me. A framed picture of Celeste Akintola's children skidded off the top of the desk into my lap. I barely had time to register that Gloria was crouched on the desk before she sprang forward, landing on top of Jill Franklyn as they fell through the open door into the hallway.

The next minute or so was chaos. Jill Franklyn was on her belly, screaming in outrage and calling for help while Gloria sat on her back, holding her arm so that she couldn't move without breaking it. I stood in the doorway, blinking down at them.

"I'm calling the police!" yelled a woman, presumably Deirdre, from the nurses' station.

"Tell them to hurry," Gloria yelled back. "No security guard?"

"Cost-cutting," Jill Franklyn grunted. "See how safe your mother is? No on-site security guard—"

"Shut up," Gloria said and twisted her arm slightly. "I'll show you who's middle-aged, bitch."

Now, I would like to say that Gloria kept Jill Franklyn subdued until the police arrived, and after hearing what we had to tell them, they immediately sent a car to pick up Lily Romano and they were prosecuted and got long prison sentences and so on and so forth. But Deirdre—yes, it was Deirdre—only saw my sister assaulting another nurse and, after summoning more staff via the PA, did something about it. Deirdre was closer to my age but her nurse muscles were more well developed and more experienced. She knocked me flat on my ass when I tried to get in her way. I still might have had a chance, except, of course, we woke everyone up and they all came out to see what was going on.

Except that it wasn't just a lot of half-asleep people opening their doors to see what all the noise was about—it was a lot of very disoriented elderly people who couldn't see or hear properly, all bumping into each other, stepping on me, falling over Gloria and Jill Franklyn, and crying out in pain or panic or both. In all the confusion, Jill Franklyn managed to get away several minutes before the police arrived.

They arrested me and Gloria, of course.

We didn't end up going to jail, but it was a very near thing. Fortunately, Celeste Akintola believed us.

There was little evidence—methylphenidate leaves the body relatively quickly. Metabolizes efficiently was how Celeste Akintola put it, I think. By the time she got a doctor to order blood tests, it was too late. I turned Lily Romano's pill over to the police but I couldn't prove it was hers; when I told the cop taking my statement how I had come by it, she just shook her head. Needless to say, both Lily and Jill were long gone. Celeste Akintola resigned.

I had to take a second mortgage on the house to cover our legal expenses, and yet I still felt funny about telling Gloria that she had to get a job. She started looking, which, in her case, meant uploading her somewhat padded résumé to a few job-hunters' websites and checking her e-mail before she went to see Mom. There was no more volunteering, but she still went to see our mother every day.

Interestingly enough, the firm that owned the nursing home saw fit to give me a nice break on the bill—apparently, their legal department advised that, despite the lack of hard evidence, the disappearance of both alleged wrongdoers might be enough for civil proceedings. I signed all the papers happily, including the confidentiality agreement and the waiver of responsibility (theirs, of course). With a second mortgage to feed, I was short on resources.

The change in Mom was undeniable, though not as dramatic as I'd feared it would be. She complained about not having any energy, of feeling slow. A number of other residents seemed to feel something similar, including some whom I knew weren't dementia patients.

I asked Gloria one night if there were any new heroes or heroines at the home, now that she was a civilian again. She said she hadn't heard anything. "But then, I probably wouldn't," she added. "They replaced most of the staff and all the volunteers. I'm out of the loop."

Gloria found a health club that needed an aqua-aerobics teacher, but still found a way to squeeze in a visit to Mom almost daily. Apparently aerobics in water was less exhausting than the dry-land variety. Or maybe exercise really was energizing—I didn't remember being able to maintain such a high level of activity in my late thirties.

And even then, it was six months after the fact before I really began to wonder. Mom's decline had come to another of its periodic plateaus, but she was still having slightly more good days than bad, or so I thought. Or so I wanted to think. And then I finally started thinking about Gloria and her energetic lifestyle.

It was a stupid idea, I decided, which was why it hadn't occurred to me before. But still, a small voice in my mind insisted that it actually had occurred to me and I'd deliberately refused to consider it. So it had simmered on the back-most of back burners in the back-most area of my mind until I was ready to jump at shadows.

Which made me think of how Gloria had leaped up onto Celeste Akintola's desk and from there across half the room to land on Jill Franklyn. With my own eyes, I'd seen her sitting on Jill Franklyn's back with her arm in a bone-breaker hold. We had both suffered through everything that followed. How could I think that Gloria would go through all of that with me only to turn around and do the same thing?

Not *the same*, nagged that mental voice. *Gloria's messiah complex is strictly limited—just her and Mom, no one else, not even you. Not yet anyway.*

The only way to kill shadows was to turn on all the lights. I got as far as opening the door to her room, but I couldn't go any farther. I'm not sure what I was more afraid of—that I *would* find Ritalin or Adderall or even Dexedrine, or that I wouldn't. If I did, I'd know what to do—I just didn't know if I could.

But if I didn't, no one would ever have to know . . . except *me,* of course. Because that's what I would find instead. I decided I would rather wonder about my sister than know for sure about myself, and closed the door.

It's been the same every night since for the past year and a half. Intellectually, I know I might as well stop, because I'm not going to do anything different. But on a gut level, I don't dare. I'm afraid of what could happen if I don't stand there and deliberately choose not to be a bad, sneaky, dangerous woman.

Caroline Spector

Caroline Spector has been an editor and writer in the science fiction, fantasy, and gaming fields for the last twenty-five years. She is the author of three novels, *Scars, Little Treasures,* and *Worlds Without End,* and her short fiction has appeared in the Wild Cards collections *Inside Straight* and *Busted Flush.* In the gaming world, she has written and edited several adventure modules and sourcebooks for several TSR game lines, notably Top Secret/S.I. and the Marvel Superheroes advanced role-playing game, both on her own and coauthored with her husband, gaming legend Warren Spector.

Here she gives us a deadly cat-and-mouse game between a woman with superhuman abilities and a faceless, enigmatic adversary who may be able to use her own powers against her, a game that she can't afford to lose, where the highest stakes of all are on the table, waiting for the next turn of a card.

LIES MY MOTHER TOLD ME

Zombie brains flew through the air, leaving a trail of blood and ichor on the throne riser of Michelle's parade float. She smiled as another bubble formed in her hand. This one was larger and heavier—the size of a base-ball. She let it fly, and it caught the zombie full in the chest and exploded. The zombie fell backwards off the float and was trampled by the panick-ing crowd.

Michelle saw more zombies moving toward her. They clambered over the floats in front of hers, pushing people aside as they flowed up the street. Another zombie crawled up onto her float, using the papier-mâché arbor for purchase. The arbor came loose, and Michelle watched in dismay as the sign reading "The Amazing Bubbles, Savior of New Orleans" broke off and fell into the street. Her daughter, Adesina, who'd been hiding under Mi-chelle's throne, let out a frightened shriek. Michelle released the bubble, knowing it would fly unerringly where she wished. When it hit, it would explode and leave a big, gooey zombie smear all over the decorations. Her beautiful float was getting ruined, and it really pissed her off.

There were three things Michelle hated about Mardi Gras: the smell, the noise, and the people. Add in a zombie attack, and it was going to put her off appearing in parades altogether.

To make sure she could bubble as much as needed during the parade, she spent the morning throwing herself off the balcony of her hotel room . . . until the hotel manager came up and made her stop.

"But I'm doing the Bacchus parade," she explained. "I won't be able to bubble through the whole parade if I don't get fat on me. And the only way to do that is to take damage. A lot of damage. A fall from a fourth story is good, but not great."

At this point, the manager turned an interesting shade of green.

"Look, Miss Pond," he said. "We're all grateful that you saved us from that nuclear explosion three years ago, but you're starting to scare the other guests. It just isn't normal."

Michelle stared at him, nonplussed. *Of course it isn't normal,* she thought. *If I were normal, New Orleans would be a radioactive hole in the ground and you'd be a black shadow against some wall. I didn't ask for this. None of us wild carders did.*

"Well," she said, thinking if she just explained it to him, he'd be less freaked out. "It isn't as if when I get hit, or slam into the ground, or even when I absorbed that explosion that it hurts me. I just turn that energy into fat. Actually, it feels pretty good." *Too good sometimes,* she thought. "So you don't have to worry that I'm in pain or anything like that."

But his expression said he really didn't want to hear about her wild card power. He just wanted her knock it off. So she stopped trying to explain and said, "I'm sorry I frightened the other guests. It won't happen again." It meant she didn't have as much fat on her as she wanted, but she'd make it work.

Adesina was still watching TV when Michelle closed the door after talking to the manager. She was perched on the foot of the bed, her iridescent wings folded against her back and her chin propped on her front feet. Just seeing Adesina made Michelle smile. Michelle had loved the child from the moment she'd pulled her from a charnel pit in the People's Paradise of Africa a year and a half ago.

Michelle still couldn't believe that Adesina had survived being injected with the wild card virus, much less being thrown into a pit of dead and dying children when her wild card had turned her into a joker instead of an ace. She shook her head to clear it. The memory of rescuing the children who were being experimented on in that camp in the African jungle was too fresh and raw. And her own failure to save all of them haunted her.

And Michelle wasn't certain how Adesina might develop. Right now she was small—medium-dog size. Her beautiful little girl's face was perched atop an insect body. But there was no telling if she would stay in this shape forever. She'd gone into chrysalis form after her card had turned and come out of that in her current state. It was possible she might change again—it all depended on how the virus had affected her.

"What on earth are you watching?" Michelle asked.

"*Sexiest and Ugliest Wild Cards*," Adesina replied. "You're on both lists. One for when you're fat and one for when you're thin."

Christ, Michelle thought. *I saved an entire city, and they're really judging me on how "hot" I am? Seriously?*

"You know, these lists are really stupid," Michelle began. "Everybody likes something different."

Adesina shrugged. "I guess," she replied. "But you *are* prettier when you're thin. They always want you to do pictures when you're thin."

Shit, Michelle thought. *That didn't take long. We've been in the States a year, and already she's thinking about who's prettier. And who's fat and thin.*

"Do you think a boy will ever like me?" Adesina asked. She turned her head and looked at Michelle. Her expression was serious. *Oh God*, Michelle thought. *It's too soon for this conversation. I'm not ready for this conversation.*

"Well," she began as she sat down next to Adesina. The bedsprings gave an unhappy groan under her weight. "I . . . I . . . I don't know." *Oh, great.* This was going well. "I don't see why not. You're beautiful."

"You have to say that," Adesina said. "You're my mother." She rubbed her back pair of legs together and made a chirping noise.

"Well, no one falls in love with you just because of how you look," Michelle said.

Adesina turned back to the TV. "Don't be dumb, Momma," she said. "Everyone loves the pretty girls."

A lump formed in Michelle's throat. She swallowed hard, refusing to cry. There was no way to ignore it. Every TV show, magazine, billboard, and website had some pretty, young, skinny, half-naked girl selling something. And up until a couple of years ago, a lot of the time that girl had been Michelle—but that was before her card had turned. And now Adesina was worrying about this crap. Michelle was at a loss.

She stared at the TV. The bumper coming in from the commercial break flashed a rapid succession of images. There was footage from the various seasons of *American Hero*. There were some still black-and-white photos from the forties when the Wild Card virus had first hit. And then there were pictures of Golden Boy testifying before the House Un-American Activities Committee. Shots of Peregrine at the height of her modeling days, looking like the ultimate disco chick—with wings. *Of course they have pictures of her*, Michelle thought. *She's gorgeous.*

"Since 1946, when the alien bomb carrying the wild card virus exploded over Manhattan, they've walked among us," the voice-over began. "The lucky few Aces and the hideously maimed Jokers. But who cares about that? We're here to determine the hottest of the hot and grossest of the gross—Wild Card style!"

Michelle grabbed the remote. "Okay, that's it," she said, snapping off the TV. "Look, honey, America is a stupid place sometimes. We get all caught up in unimportant junk like that show, and we forget the stuff that really means something. And I am really sucking at this mom thing right now. The truth is that the world is going to be unkind sometimes because you're different. But that doesn't have anything to do with you, honey. It's just that the world is full of idiots."

Adesina crawled into Michelle's lap—such as it was when she was in bubbling mode—and put her front two feet on either side of Michelle's face, pushing away Michelle's long, silvery hair. "Oh Momma," she said. "I already *knew* that. I just get scared sometimes."

Michelle kissed Adesina on top of her head. "I know, sweetie. I do, too."

It wasn't so bad up on the float. *Lots of sight lines,* Michelle thought. *That's good and bad.* Good because she could see anything coming, bad because it put Adesina at risk. But being Michelle's daughter was going to put Adesina at risk no matter what.

The crowd was especially boisterous in this section of the parade route. Maybe it was because they'd had longer to drink. The parade had been going on for a couple of hours, and now it was heading into the French Quarter.

Michelle's float was decorated in silver and green. A riser with a throne was at the rear, and a beautiful arbor of papier-mâché flowers arched over the throne. Adesina had commandeered the throne for herself while Michelle stayed out on the lower platform to toss beads, wave, and bubble. Michelle thought Adesina looked adorable in her pale lavender dress—even if it did have six cutouts for her legs and another pair for her wings. Michelle's dress was the same color, but made of a spandex blend. As she bubbled off fat, the dress would shrink along with her.

A couple of drunken blondes yelled at her, "Bubbles! Hey, Bubbles! Throw me some beads!" They pulled up their tops, revealing perky breasts. Michelle was unimpressed, but she threw them beads anyway.

"Momma," Adesina said. "Why do they keep doing that?"

"Got me," Michelle replied. "I guess they think they'll get more beads."

"That's dumb."

Michelle tossed more beads, then started bubbling soft, squishy bubbles that she let drift into the crowd. "You said it. Sadly, I think it works. I just tossed them some myself."

There was a commotion up ahead on the parade route. Michelle stopped bubbling and tried to see what was happening. The crowd was panicking—people were shoving, and others were caught in between, unable to move.

The frenzy moved toward Michelle's float like a tidal wave. Some of the crowd spilled off the sidewalks into the street, knocking down the containment barricades, and then they began clambering onto the floats in front of hers. Cops tried to calm the crowd and started pulling people off the floats, but they were soon overwhelmed.

And that's when she saw them: zombies coming up the street.

Joey, she thought. *What the hell are you doing?*

Then she saw a zombie grab a guy in an LSU T-shirt and snap his neck. Michelle was horrified. But she immediately slammed that feeling down. She couldn't help him—she had a job to do.

As she scanned the crowd, she saw the zombies brutalizing anyone in their way. A couple of cops tried to stop one of the zombies, and they each got a broken arm for their trouble before Michelle blasted the thing. And then she realized that the zombies were heading for her float.

"Momma!" Adesina's frightened voice came from behind Michelle. She spun around and saw a red-faced, pudgy man and a skinnier man in a striped polo shirt climbing onto the float.

"Hey!" Michelle shouted at them. "It isn't safe here. They're coming for me."

"Behind you is the safest place to be right now," the pudgy one said. "We're not going."

Michelle sighed. "You're leaving me no choice here, guys." The bubbles were already forming in her hands, and she let them fly. The bubbles—big as a medicine ball and just as heavy—bowled the men off the float. Michelle heard them cursing. "Hey," she yelled. "Language! There's a child here!" She picked up Adesina, tucking her under her left arm.

"Momma," Adesina complained, "you're embarrassing me."

"Sorry, sweetie," Michelle replied. "Now behave while I take Aunt Joey's zombies out."

Michelle let a tiny, bullet-size bubble fly at the closest zombie. Its head exploded, sending bits of brain, skull, and decaying flesh into the air. It was immensely satisfying. Unfortunately, this only made some of the people in the crowd even more panicked. And now Michelle could feel her dress getting looser. *Dammit,* she thought. *I knew I needed more fat.*

Michelle spotted another zombie and let a bubble go. There were more shrieks as its brains and pieces of its skull splattered everywhere. The float rocked as the crowd pressed against it, and she struggled to keep her balance.

"Momma, please, put me down."

"Not on your life," Michelle replied, yelling to be heard over the commotion. "Zombies and panicking nats are not a good combination. It would be too dangerous, so, yeah, that is not going to happen."

Adesina let out an exasperated sigh. "You're mean," she said.

Michelle destroyed another zombie. She felt her dress get a little looser. The zombies were coming faster, and one-handed bubbling wasn't getting the job done fast enough. "Oh darnit," she said, putting Adesina down. "Go stay under the throne. And let me know if anyone—anything—tries to get up here."

If there was anything Dan Turnbull liked better than blowing shit up in a first-person shooter, it was making a mess that someone else would have to clean up. His mother had left his father six months ago, and since she'd been gone, neither of them had cleaned up much of anything. Stacks of dirty laundry were piled like Indian burial mounds in different parts of the house. A variety of molds were growing on plates in the kitchen—and in the fridge, heads of lettuce were now the size of limes. Rancid, greasy water filled the sink, and Dan wasn't sure if the sink had stopped draining or if the stopper at the bottom needed to be pulled. What he knew was that he wasn't putting his hand down there to find out.

But lying up here on the roof of the St. Louis Hotel looking down on the mess he'd made just now, well, *that* made him seriously happy. Zombies were breaking up the Bacchus parade, and that Bubbles chick was trying to stop it.

He watched her pick up the freak she called her daughter while at the same time she methodically blasted the shit out of the zombies. And he had a grudging admiration for how cool she was, given the situation. She didn't get hysterical or spaz out the way most women would. No, she just mowed those zombies right down without ever hitting a single civilian. And he wondered what it would be like when he grabbed her power.

It had been a rush when he'd grabbed Hoodoo Mama's power. Of course, he'd only taken one other ace's power before, and that had been an accident.

He'd been walking down the street and had bumped into a teenage girl. Reflexively, he grabbed her bare arm to steady himself. The expression on her face when Dan's touch had taken her power was high-larious. He'd been so surprised that she had a power, he'd used it without thinking and teleported himself across the street, slamming into a wall as he materialized.

When Dan realized that he'd almost teleported into the wall, he started shaking. In a few moments, after the adrenaline rush of fear had passed, he looked around to find the girl. But she'd vanished. *Of course she had*, he thought. *What else would she do?*

Unlike the teleporting girl, Hoodoo Mama's power about blew his skull off. But he was only going to get one chance at using it before it reverted back to Hoodoo Mama, and he had orders to make a mess. What was happening out on the street was megaplus cool. He'd done his job well.

There were all kinds of local news video filming the parade, but this was the view he wanted. A nice long shot of the whole scene. He'd brought a video camera to get it, but he knew that there would be plenty of civilians making recordings, too. Those would be on YouTube before the end of the day. What mattered was having a lot of videos of all hell breaking loose. And the one that showed it all in perfect detail would be the icing on the cake.

It didn't matter to Dan why his employers wanted a mess. For 5K and an hour's work, it was a no-brainer. He didn't even care how they knew about his power. His father had started demanding rent, and Dan had no job. And he had no intention of giving up his status as top shooter on his server. It had taken way too long for him to get there, and his team needed him. A job would just get in the way of that.

With his video camera tucked into the pocket of his baggy jeans, he climbed down the fire escape and slipped down the back alley. A couple of stragglers from the parade came toward him. As they got closer, he saw that they were girls. They were trying to run, but drunk as they were, it was more like fast staggering.

"Oh my God," one of them said to him. She was wearing what looked like a pound of beads. Long dark hair framed her face, and he wondered if she was drunk enough to fuck him. "Did you see what happened back there?"

He shrugged. "Looked like a bunch of drunk assholes. Like every Mardi Gras."

They gave him a baffled look. "No," the other one said. She wasn't as pretty as her companion. *There's always a dog and a pretty one,* he thought. "I mean Bubbles. She was so incredible, like, she just demolished those zombies. Oh shit, I think I have some zombie on me." She wiped at her shirt.

"Looked like she just made a mess of things to me," Dan replied. Neither girl had looked at him with anything like interest, and it annoyed him. He'd been the one who'd made everything go crazy, not Bubbles. He'd made her look bad, too. It was his job to make her look bad. These chicks were drunk and stupid. He started past them, then impulsively grabbed the one with dark hair by the arm.

"Asshole!" she yelped, yanking away from him. But he hadn't wanted to cop a feel—he was checking whether she had a power. But there was nothing. She was an empty battery. It made him sad—and he hated that feeling more than anything.

"Jerk!" The uglier one snarled at him and looked like she might actually do something.

But then he put his hand up, using the universal gesture for a gun. He sighted down his finger at the girls.

"Bang," he said.

The zombies were nothing more than piles of dead flesh now. Zombie goo was splattered everywhere, but that couldn't be helped. *You kill zombies, it's gonna make a mess,* Michelle thought.

The parade had stopped, and some of the crowd who had climbed up onto the floats to get away from the zombies were making no effort to get down now. The rest of the crowd had poured into the street and surrounded the floats as well. It was a compete logjam. People were sitting on the ground crying. Some of them were wounded.

Adesina crawled out from under the throne, and Michelle picked her up. "You okay?" Michelle asked, kissing her on the top of her head. Adesina nodded. "Will you be okay sitting on the throne?"

"Yes," Adesina replied. "But there are some men trying to get up here." Michelle put Adesina on the throne, then spun around. A couple of different men were pulling themselves up.

"Guys, other people are going to be needing this space," she said, growing a bubble her hand. She'd lost most of her fat during the parade and zombie fight, but there was still enough on her to deal with a couple of drunken douches.

"Hey, it's really crowded down here," complained one of them.

Michelle shrugged. "I don't care," she said. "Right now, this isn't a democracy. I'm queen of this float, and I refuse."

"Bitch."

"That's Queen Bitch, and there's a child here. Watch your language. Besides, the people who are injured need to be up here more than you do." The men grumbled, but dropped down and began pushing their way back through the crowd.

The cops were trying to restore order. Michelle called out to them, and they began bringing the wounded to her float. One of them stayed and started triage. Then Michelle heard sirens and a surge of relief went through her. Blowing things up and taking damage was the sort of thing she excelled at. But the aftermath was always more complicated and messy than she liked.

Now that things were starting to calm down, one of the krewe running the parade got on the loudspeaker for the float in front of hers and encouraged people to get out of the street and back up on the sidewalks. A couple of teenage boys helped the police reset the barricades.

Michelle pulled her phone out of her dress pocket as she moved away from the wounded. Michelle hated purses, and because her clothes were specially made, she always had pockets added. Though why women's clothes never had pockets was a mystery to her. She scrolled through her favorites and then hit dial when she found Joey's number.

"What the hell is wrong with you," Michelle hissed as Joey answered. "Do you have any idea what a fu . . . freaking mess you made here today?"

There was a long pause on the other end of the line. "What are you talking about?"

A fine red curtain of rage descended on Michelle. "I'm talking about zombies attacking a parade," she whispered. "Killing people in the crowd—and they were coming for me and Adesina."

"You fucking think I'd do something like that, Bubbles?" Joey's voice was tremulous. It sounded worse than when they'd been in the People's Paradise of Africa and Joey had been running a hundred-and-four-degree fever. The hairs on Michelle's arms rose.

"Are you saying there's another wild carder who can raise the dead? Am I going to have to deal with two of you?" The red veil lifted, just long enough that another horrible thought slipped in. What if this had been just the first wave? *Honestly,* she thought. *Enough with the goddamn zombies already.*

The laugh that came over the line was hollow and mirthless. "For a smart bitch, you're awful fucking stupid. Obviously, we need to fucking talk. When can you get to my house?"

"I'm stuck here," Michelle replied. She looked around at the wounded on the float and the cops trying to get the crowd cleared out. There was zombie ick all over the sidewalks, and Michelle really wanted to smack Joey hard. "I'm kinda busy."

"Just get here quick as you can."

The connection went dead. Michelle stared at the blank screen.

"Are we going to Aunt Joey's now?" Adesina asked, tugging on Michelle's dress.

"Soon," Michelle replied, surveying the ruins of the parade. "Soon."

If there was one thing Joey hated, it was nosey cocksuckers sniffing about her business. Not that Bubbles was usually a nosey cocksucker. Given what she said had happened at the parade, Joey could even understand her being fucking pissed. But now she had to explain what was going on with her children.

The problem was that she had no idea.

One minute she'd been making her way back from the bakery up the street—early, because it was Mardi Gras, and there would be tons of tourist dickweeds otherwise—and the next thing she knew, it was as if a light had just shut off inside her head. Usually, she knew where every dead body lay for miles around, and she often had zombie bugs and birds moving about keeping an eye on things. And today had been no different, until the lights went out.

She'd been "blind" for a few hours, and then, just as abruptly, her power was back. Truth be told, she'd been out of her mind while her power was gone. And she'd been scared. Really scared. She couldn't remember the last time she'd been this frightened. *Yes, you can remember that time,* whispered a voice in the back of her mind. But Joey shut that thought down hard and fast—or tried to. *What did your mother say about lying?* the voice persisted. *Well, she'd lied, too,* Joey reminded herself. Her mother had lied, and left Joey alone, and what had happened after that . . .

Then Bubbles had shown up on her caller ID, and Joey had been relieved. Bubbles was the most powerful person she knew. Bubbles would keep her safe.

But when Joey picked up the phone, Bubbles started giving her shit. But Joey didn't know what had happened. And if she was being honest with herself, she was scared. What if she was losing her power?

Without her children, she wasn't safe. Without them, she was just Joey Hebert, not Hoodoo Mama. Without Hoodoo Mama, no one, not even Bubbles, could protect her.

And when she thought about what not being Hoodoo Mama anymore would mean, she began to shake.

There wasn't much that Adesina didn't like. She liked American ice cream, American TV, and American beds. Ever since Momma had brought her to America, Adesina had been making a list of all the things she liked.

She liked Hello Kitty, the Cartoon Network, and taking classes from a tutor (even though sometimes she missed being in school with other kids). She even liked the way the cities looked. They were so big and shiny, and everyone talked so fast and moved around like they were all in a big rush to get somewhere important. Even if it was just to go to the grocery store.

And she liked Momma's friends. Aunt Joey (even though when they'd

lived together in the PPA, Momma had kept yelling at Aunt Joey about
her language), Aunt Juliette, Drake (even though he was a god now and
they never saw him anymore), and Niobe. Sometimes they were invited to
American Hero events, and she got to meet even more wild carders. But she
liked Joker Town the best of all because no one there ever turned around
and stared at her.

And she had liked being in the Joker Town Halloween parade with
Momma, but she didn't like this parade now at all. Aunt Joey's zombies
had attacked, and people were hurt. So they were going to Aunt Joey's, and
Adesina knew Momma was mad. She didn't need to go into Momma's
mind to know that. It was pretty obvious.

Once, she and Momma had had a conversation about her ability to
enter Momma's mind. Momma had made her promise she wouldn't do it
anymore, but it was difficult to control. Once she'd gone into someone's
mind, it became easier. She couldn't go into nats' minds—only people
whose card had turned. She'd discovered that while they were still in the
PPA.

And she wasn't going to tell Momma that she had already been in more
people's minds than Momma knew. Sometimes it just happened when she
was dreaming, but mostly it happened if she liked someone. The next thing
she knew, she was sliding into their thoughts.

The police and ambulances came. The ambulance took the wounded
away, and the police cleared out the crowd so the parade could head back
to the storage facility. There was no more music, no more beads thrown,
and no more bubbles.

Adesina didn't mean to, but she found herself in Momma's mind.
Momma was worried. Worried about Aunt Joey and what she might have
to do to her if Aunt Joey really had made her zombies attack. She was
worried about Adesina and how much violence she was around. And she
was worried about the people who'd been hurt at the parade.

Adesina wanted to tell her that zombies weren't as bad as being in the
charnel pit. And that that wasn't as bad as what had happened to her after
she'd been injected with the virus and her card had turned. Even though
Adesina's mind wanted to skitter away from that memory, it rose up. She
couldn't—wouldn't—forget what had happened.

The doctors had grabbed her and strapped her down to the table with
brown leather straps that were stained almost black in places. Then they

slid a needle full of the wild card virus into her arm. She'd looked away and stared up at the sweet, fairy-tale pictures they'd put on the stark white walls. But the girls in the pictures were all pale, not at all like Adesina.

The virus burned as it rocketed through her veins. She looked away from the smiling children in the pictures and stared at the ceiling. There were reddish-brown splatter marks there. Then blinding pain swallowed her and she was wracked with convulsions. Her body bowed up from the table. She tried not to, but she screamed and screamed and screamed. And then there was darkness and relief when she'd gone into chrysalis form.

The doctors didn't want Jokers, they wanted only Aces, and so they threw her body into the pit with the other dead and dying children. But she wasn't dying. She was changing. And while she was cradled in her cocoon, she found that she could slip into the minds of other people infected with the virus.

That was how she'd found Momma. Both of them were floating in a sea of darkness. But Adesina wasn't lonely anymore, not now that she had Momma.

But if she said anything about that time, Momma would know she'd been in her mind. So she grabbed Momma and made her sit on the throne and cuddled in her lap until the parade came to its final stop.

Bullets flew across the smoking landscape, past the charred and burned wreckage of tanks and jeeps. A grenade exploded next to Dan, and he took a massive amount of damage. His health bar was blinking red, and he was out of bandages.

"Jesus, RocketPac, you were supposed to take that bitch with the grenade launcher out," Dan snarled into his mic. He'd logged on as soon as he'd gotten home from the parade. "You fucking faggot."

"Suck my dick, CF," Rocket replied. Feedback screamed into Dan's headset. "If you'd given me the suppressing fire, I could have gotten close enough to get a shot off. Go blow a goat, you asshole."

"Turn down your fucking outbound mic, bitch," Teninchrecord said to Rocket. "And your goddamn speakers, you big homo. CF, tell me again why the fuck we let this useless scrub onto the team."

Dan fell back. He's been using a bombed-out building for cover, but it was clear it wasn't doing any good. And he needed to find some bandages. If they made it out of this without losing, he was going to kick that useless POS RocketPac off the team. He couldn't figure out how this team he'd never heard of was pwning them. Especially since they had the utterly fag team name We Know What Boys Like.

A shadow passed in front of the TV. Dan jumped and dropped his controller. "What the fuck!"

"Mr. Turnbull, we need to talk," Mr. Jones said as he picked up the controller and handed it to Dan. He wore a sleek dark grey suit, a white shirt, and a black tie. No one Dan knew ever wore anything like that. Dan was certain Jones wasn't his real name, but he could identify with not wanting everyone to know who you were. And Dan didn't want any more information than necessary about Mr. Jones.

He was afraid of Mr. Jones because Mr. Jones looked like he could snap Dan's neck without blinking an eye. Mr. Jones reminded Dan of a coiled rattlesnake.

Dan ripped off his headphones and yanked the headphone jack out of his computer. "That's a voice-activated mic," he snapped, but his hands were trembling. "I don't want those dipshits knowing who I am in real life. And I told my dad no one was supposed to come down here when the sign was up."

Mr. Jones shrugged. "Your father isn't home and I don't care about your little game," he said.

"I did what you asked," Dan said more defensively than he wanted. "I've got the video here on this USB drive." He stood up and dug around in his pocket until he came up with the lint-speckled drive.

Mr. Jones plucked it from Dan's fingers, then delicately blew off the lint. "I doubt we'll need it," Mr. Jones said, slipping the drive into the breast pocket of his suit. "There are already more than fifty YouTube videos up. More going up by the minute. And the local news interrupted programming to report on it. CNN and Fox are running breaking-news tickers, and we know they're working up their own spin on things. You did well."

Dan didn't know what to say. He was both flattered and scared. "Uh, thanks," he replied, and jammed his hands into his pockets. Out of the corner of his eye, he saw that his CntrlFreak avatar was down. *Shit.*

"We may need you to do another small task for us," Mr. Jones said. He held out a thick manila envelope. "The payment. And a little extra."

A tingle slid up Dan's spine as he took the envelope. He thought about touching Mr. Jones's fingers to see if he was an Ace but, for the first time, it occurred to him that he might be out of his depth. "Sure, dude, whatever," he said. "But coming to my house, uh, maybe we could meet somewhere else?"

Mr. Jones's smile was shockingly white against his dark skin. "Looks like your team lost," he said, nodding at the monitor. "Combat Over" flashed on the screen. "I'll see myself out."

Dan took a long, shuddering breath when he heard the front door close. Then he opened the envelope and started counting.

The cab pulled to a stop in front of Joey's house. Michelle paid the driver, and she and Adesina got out. The house was a dilapidated Victorian with peeling paint and an overgrown garden surrounded by a wrought-iron fence. Dead birds nested in the trees and perched on the utility lines. In unison, they all cocked their heads to the left.

"Knock it off, Joey," Michelle said as she opened the gate. It gave a screeching complaint. *Has she never heard of WD-40? Even I know about that.* "Save it for the tourists."

"Caw," said one of the birds.

"Jerk," Michelle muttered.

A relatively fresh female zombie answered the door. She wore a cheerful floral print dress and was less filthy than most of Joey's corpses. *The dead don't groom*, Michelle thought. *They are so nasty.*

"Follow me," the zombie said. But it was Joey's voice Michelle heard. All the zombies had Joey's voice, and that was okay when the zombie was a woman. But it was weird as hell coming from a six-foot-tall former linebacker, as it sometimes happened.

"For crying out loud, Joey," Michelle said. "I know every inch of this house. You in the living room?"

The zombie nodded and Michelle pushed past it. Adesina flew up to Michelle's shoulder. "Momma, don't be too mad," she whispered.

"I'm just the right amount of mad," Michelle replied. Then she sighed, paused, and tried to get her mood under control. Adesina was right. Joey never responded well to an angry confrontation. Angry was Joey's stock-in-trade.

The living room was mostly bare. There were tatty curtains on the windows and a sagging couch against one wall. The new addition to the room was a large flat-screen TV. Across from the TV was Joey's Hoodoo Mama throne with Joey perched on it. She was slightly built and was wearing a shapeless Joker Plague T-shirt and skinny jeans. There was a shock of red in her dark brown hair and her skin was a beautiful caramel color. A zombie dog lay at her feet, and two huge male zombies flanked her chair.

Michelle and Adesina flopped on the couch. Joey frowned, but Michelle ignored it. "So, you want to explain what happened?"

The zombies growled, and then Joey said, "I had fuck-all to do with it." Her hands were gripping the arms of her throne, and her knuckles had turned white. "I can't believe you think I'd do something like that."

"Are you saying there's another person whose card has turned, who lives in New Orleans, and who can raise the dead just like you?" Michelle gave Joey her very best "Seriously, what the hell?" look. "That's a lot of coincidences, Joey."

"No, there's not a new fucking wild card who can control zombies," Joey said leaning forward on her throne. "There's one who can fucking well snatch powers."

"Jesus, Joey, language." Michelle glanced at Adesina, but she was already engrossed in a game on her iPad.

"Oh, fuck you, Bubbles," Joey said. "Adesina has heard it all and more. Haven't you, Pumpkin?"

Adesina glanced up and shrugged. "Yep. You cuss. A lot. But I'm not going to."

For a moment, Joey looked hurt. "Michelle, are you planting weird fucking ideas in my girl there?"

"No, just normal ones."

"That's a goddamn fool's errand for a Joker."

Michelle glared at Joey. "Back to your mystery wild card," she said. "What makes you think your powers were snatched? Maybe you just lost control."

The two big male zombies started across the room towards Michelle. Calmly, she dispatched them with a couple of tiny, explosive bubbles to the head. It took her last reserves of fat, but she wasn't putting up with any more of Joey's aggressive zombie shit.

"Motherfucker! Goddamnit, Bubbles, look at this dick-licking mess! Christ!" The female zombie came in and began cleaning up the remains. "I'm fucking fine," Joey continued. "What happened wasn't my cocksucking fault. I went out to get some pastries at the bakery. On my way home, I bumped into someone, then bang, my power just went away and I couldn't see any of my children anymore."

Her voice trailed off, and she looked so sad and scared that Michelle believed her. Michelle knew that Joey's card had turned because she'd been raped. But she didn't know any details and really didn't want to know them. She imagined that Joey must have felt as helpless now as she had then.

"Do you remember anything specific about how your powers were stolen?" Michelle asked. A wild card who could grab powers was frightening to contemplate. They needed to figure out who it was. But even more, she needed to protect Joey from having her powers stolen again. Joey had never been especially emotionally stable—Michelle reminded herself that a lot of the wild carders she knew were just shy of permanent residence in Crazytown—but seeing Joey's reaction now worried Michelle. Whatever having her power grabbed was triggering in Joey was bad. And Michelle was beginning to think it might be more important to help Joey deal than to get the person yanking her power.

Joey shook her head. "Fuck me, I've tried. I just remember being jostled, then . . . nothing."

Adesina tugged on Michelle's arm. "Momma, look," she said, pointing at the TV.

There was a long shot of the Bacchus parade as the zombies were attacking. The image zoomed in on Michelle as she began killing zombies. Joey turned up the volume on the TV.

"—ack on today's Bacchus parade. Michelle Pond, the Amazing Bubbles, was on one float and was the apparent target of the zombie attack. More horrifying is that Miss Pond had her seven-year-old daughter with her. Though Miss Pond managed to stop the attack, it is troubling that she had her daughter at an event where she would be exposed to such adult sights as women showing their naked breasts for beads. This isn't the first time that a public event featuring Miss Pond has turned violent. It does make one wonder about her choices."

Michelle jumped up from the couch. "What the fuck!" she yelled.

"Language," Joey said.

Adesina was worried. Momma was looking at videos of the parade on her laptop. Aunt Joey had switched off the TV after the news report, but Momma had pulled her laptop out of her bag and started looking for more reports online.

She'd found a lot of them. And even though Adesina tried not to, she couldn't help slipping into Momma's mind. And what she saw there was fear and anger and worry.

So she slipped out and started playing *Ocelot Nine* on her iPad again. Getting Organza Sweetie Ocelot out of the clutches of the Cherry Witch was easier than understanding the workings of the adult world.

Michelle's cell was buzzing. It had been buzzing since the attack on the parade. But she'd been ignoring the calls—she already knew things were screwed. The old adage "There's no such thing as bad publicity" was complete crap in her experience.

But she hadn't realized just how bad it was until she saw the news reports at Joey's house. And then she'd gone on YouTube and saw all the amateur videos.

It made her sick. *Of course there is going to be video everywhere, you idiot. It was Mardi Gras. Hell, it's just the way things are now. Not a moment unobserved.*

And there was still the issue of how Joey had lost her powers. More to the point, Joey's reaction to losing her powers was preying on Michelle's mind. She couldn't leave Joey alone in that state. Michelle decided she and Adesina would stay with Joey tonight and try to figure out what had happened. Much as she hated even considering it, Michelle thought she might have to ask Adesina for help. But God, she didn't want to do that. She didn't want to send her baby into Joey's mind. There were things Adesina did *not* need to see at her age—or any other age, as far as Michelle was concerned.

Since Michelle had decided that Joey shouldn't be alone for even an hour, the three of them cabbed it back to Michelle's hotel. Both Joey and Adesina were hungry, so Michelle left them in the hotel coffee shop while she went up to the room to pack a bag.

She slipped out of her dress and tossed it onto the bed. Then she pulled on a pair of baggy drawstring pants and a T-shirt. She needed to get fatter—throwing herself off Joey's roof hadn't done much—and her clothes needed to cooperate with a variety of sizes.

As she was packing an overnight bag, her cell began to ring again. She grabbed it off the bed and glanced at the number. It looked familiar, so she answered it saying, "Michelle here." She threw underwear, baggy pants, and T-shirts for herself into the bag, and then tossed in Adesina's favorite dress and nightgown.

There was a pause on the other end of the line. "Hey, Michelle. It's me." For a moment, Michelle's stomach lurched. It was Juliette. They hadn't spoken much since Juliette had left the PPA. And when they had, it was awkward. Sleeping with Joey had ruined Michelle's relationship with Juliette. And no matter how she tried, Michelle knew that there were some mistakes that couldn't be forgiven. "I saw some of the footage from the parade online," Juliette said.

Michelle's hands started shaking. *Crap, crap, crap.* She thought. *This is not the time to get emotional.*

"Yeah, it, uh, was intense."

"Was it really Joey?"

Michelle went into the bathroom and started grabbing toiletries. "She says no and I believe her," Michelle said. "This just isn't her style. She says someone stole her power, and right after the attack, her power came back."

There was another long pause. "So, you've been seeing her while you're there?"

Crap, Michelle thought again as she dumped the toiletries into a travel case. Then she released a stream of rubbery bubbles into the bathtub. A couple bounced out and rolled around the bathroom floor. Michelle kicked them, and they ricocheted off the wall. One hit her hard in the thigh.

"Yes, I went to see her," Michelle replied, reflexively rubbing her leg. *Stupid bubbles.* "Hello? Zombie attack. Who else am I going to see?" She went to the mirror and looked into it. *Stupid girl.* "We're not screwing, if that's what you're asking. And we haven't since that one time. And you

broke up with me and I'm pretty sure that means I'm allowed to see anyone I like. And I'm really sorry."

Shit.

"You done?" Juliette asked.

"Yes," Michelle said meekly.

"I'm glad you went to see her. This thing is a PR disaster for both of you."

This flummoxed Michelle. "I thought, well, I mean . . ."

"Look, Michelle, this isn't about you and Joey and me. This is about
Adesina. You suck as a girlfriend, but you've been a good mother to her.
And I really hate the idea that someone's playing a political game that'll
impact on Adesina's life."

Michelle slid down the bathroom wall and sat on the floor. The tiles
were cold against her butt.

"I'm not sure what you mean. Why would this affect Adesina?"

An exasperated sigh, not unlike the one Adesina often gave, escaped
Juliette. "How can you still be this naive? You're too damn powerful and
too damn popular. They can't do much about the powerful, but they will
happily destroy people's fondness for you. They need to marginalize you."

Michelle opened her left palm and let a light bubble form in it. She let
it go and it floated around the bathroom. "Well, who would do that? And
why use Joey?"

"Oh, it could be a lot of people: the NSA, CIA, and the PPA, for
starters. Also, the Committee might be involved, though that's less
likely. It could even be an entirely new group with their own agenda. And
it's tough to come at you directly, but going through people you love . . ."

"I don't love Joey," Michelle said emphatically. What she wanted to say
was "I love you. Please come back." Instead she said, "I've been off the
radar for almost a year. It doesn't make any sense." Michelle rubbed her
middle finger between her eyebrows.

"But you're back and already you're doing parades that remind people
how you saved New Orleans. Not to mention that you adopted Adesina,
who is just about the most adorable Joker in the world."

Michelle smiled. "Yeah, she is filled with adorableness, isn't she? I think
she has a creamy chocolate center, too."

Juliette laughed, and Michelle thought her heart might break. "I'm
gonna e-mail you a link to something," Juliette said. "This is what's at
stake and how far they're willing to go to marginalize you."

Will this bullshit never stop? Michelle thought. *I'm just trying to have a life.* "Thanks for the help, Juliette. And . . . I'm sorry. I know it's not enough, but I'm really sorry."

There was another long pause. "Yeah, I know," Juliette said. Then the line went dead. *Great,* Michelle thought, rubbing away tears. *Just great. You're never going to make the Joey thing up to her, so stop trying. You're lucky she even called.*

But Michelle knew Juliette hadn't called for her sake. She got up and ran cold water over a washcloth and held it against her face for a few minutes. The last thing she needed was Adesina seeing that she'd been crying. Her daughter saw too much anyway.

Even though her power was back, Joey was still grateful that Michelle was spending the night. She had her children, of course. But now there was the nagging fear that at any moment someone could grab her power.

Adesina was sitting on the coach playing that goofy game. *What the fuck are ocelots, anyway?* Joey thought as she sat down next to her. "So, you really like this game?" Joey asked. She wasn't a fan of video games, but she'd played a few here and there.

Adesina nodded. "The ocelots are really cute, and Organza Sweetie Ocelot is amazing. She has these cool powers and she just goes right after the Cherry Witch who wants to take all the ocelots' food and land . . ."

Joey tuned Adesina out. It was something she did on occasion. She just stopped listening and let herself slide into her children. There were dead dogs and cats. Dead people. Dead insects. She moved into them all, seeing through their dead eyes. Her children were the reason she was safe. No one could escape the dead. They were all around. So no one could get the drop on her.

But losing her powers for a few hours had been horrible. She tried to push away the memory of losing control—but that made another, darker, memory come to the surface. Bile rose in her throat, and sweat broke out across her back. No, she wouldn't let it come back. She was Hoodoo Mama. She'd already killed that motherfucker. That was over and done—he couldn't touch her anymore.

"Aunt Joey! Aunt Joey!"

Joey opened her eyes. It took a moment for her to snap out of the memory. Adesina was sitting on her lap, and her front feet were on Joey's face. Tears were streaming down Adesina's cheeks. "Aunt Joey, please stop!" she cried.

"What the fuck?" Joey said. "What are you doing, Pumpkin?"

"You were stuck," Adesina replied. She slid off Joey's lap and wiped at her tears and runny nose with her feet the way a praying mantis might groom itself.

Joey got up. "I'll get you a Kleenex," she said, running for the bathroom. She grabbed the box off the back of the commode and headed to the living room. She saw Michelle running into the room from the other side.

"What the heck is going on here?" Michelle asked. "I could hear Adesina crying from upstairs." *What the ever-fucking hell?* Joey thought. *Am I really losing it? Fuck me!*

Michelle went to console Adesina. Awkwardly, Joey held out the box of tissues. A withering glance was all Joey got from Michelle as she pulled tissues out and started dabbing Adesina's face.

"You want to tell me what happened?" Michelle asked Adesina. But Adesina wouldn't answer. She just curled up in Michelle's lap and closed her eyes.

When Michelle looked up, Joey wished she weren't on the receiving end of that look—and despite herself, Joey took a step back. *What happened?* Michelle mouthed silently. Joey shrugged and shook her head. And then Joey was pissed. Michelle *knew* she'd never do anything to hurt Adesina.

"Adesina," Michelle said softly. "Look at me."

For a moment, Adesina just lay there, but then she slowly opened her eyes. There was a stern expression on Michelle's face, and it struck Joey as mean. "Adesina," Michelle continued. "Did you go into Aunt Joey's mind without permission?"

"What the fuck are you talking about, Bubbles?" Joey asked. There were too many things she didn't want anyone to know about, much less have the Pumpkin see.

"Adesina can go into the minds of people who have the virus," Michelle said. "And I know she's been in yours before. Adesina, I told you about doing that, didn't I?"

Adesina nodded, and a tear slipped down her cheek. "I'm sorry, Momma," she said in a quavering voice.

"There are grown-up things you shouldn't be seeing, and it's an invasion of the other person's privacy. Like when you don't want me going into your room without asking."

That made Adesina burst into tears. Michelle hugged her. "It's okay, you just have to be more careful, honey." She looked up at Joey. "I think I'm putting Adesina to bed. It's been a long day."

"Yeah," Joey said. "Yeah, it really has."

After Michelle got Adesina settled for the evening, she went back downstairs to talk to Joey. She found her in the kitchen, pulling bottles of beer out of the fridge.

"You wanna tell me why the ever-lovin' fuck you never mentioned that Adesina can get into my cocksucking mind?" Joey demanded, handing Michelle a beer.

Michelle twisted off the bottle cap, flipped the cap in the trash, and then took a long swig. "She's knows she's not supposed to. And the one time before when she ended up in your head, it upset her so much she swore to me it would never happen again." What Michelle wanted to tell Joey was that being in her mind had made Adesina violently ill. That the garbage Joey was dragging around was toxic to Adesina and most likely to Joey, too. But Michelle knew that telling Joey anything was a losing proposition.

Another hard pull of the beer made Michelle's head swim a little. Aside from jumping off Joey's roof before they went back to the hotel, she hadn't done anything to bulk up again even though she'd meant to. She was thinner now, even more so than when she'd been a model. It meant she got buzzed much more quickly. And that wasn't feeling like a bad thing at all at the moment.

"Did she tell you what she saw?" Joey asked.

Michelle shook her head. "I didn't really ask her much about it. She's only seven. But really, how much of what's in your head does she need to see?" It was a cruel thing to say, but Michelle didn't much care. No, that wasn't true. She was just worn out.

"I don't want the Pumpkin seeing . . . things." Joey chugged her beer, plunked the empty bottle on the counter, then went to one of the cabinets and pulled out a bottle of Jack Daniel's. "Best fucking way I can think of to forget. You want a shot?"

Michelle shook her head, then killed the rest of her beer. Golden warmth encased her. Her lips went a little numb. "That's not going to help us figure out what happened to you. And I actually thought about having Adesina go into your mind to try to find out what happened. But that's obviously a terrible idea." Michelle took another beer out of the fridge. *Screw it*, she thought. *So I get hammered. My life is rapidly going into the toilet.* "Oh, and I talked to Juliette when we were at the hotel. And then she sent me some links. The new meme out there is that I'm a terrible mother who routinely endangers the life of her child."

"What the fuck is a meme?" Joey asked after she took a swig of the JD.

Dan jammed dirty laundry into the washer, then dumped laundry soap on top. Laundry pissed him off. If his mother hadn't left, the house would be clean, there would be food in the fridge, dinner on the table, and he would have clean clothes when he needed them. Instead, he was going commando in some ratty jeans (and he hated that commando shit), and his T-shirt was so smelly it grossed him out.

But the day wouldn't be a complete loss. He and Teninchrecord had booted RocketPac from the team, and they were interviewing replacements in an hour. He knew that they needed someone good, but weeding out the noobs and scrubs was going to be hilarious. After starting the washer, he headed back down to the basement. He'd replaced his old sofa with a tricked-out gaming chair using some of the money he'd gotten for grabbing Hoodoo Mama's power. The chair had built-in speakers and an ergonomic design in black leather that perfectly cradled his ass. His dad was at work, and Dan was looking forward to settling in for a nice long gaming session.

Except when he got to the bottom of the stairs, he saw that Mr. Jones was ensconced in his chair. *Son of a bitch*, Don thought. "Most people might start by knocking on the front door."

Mr. Jones smiled, and Dan didn't like it at all. "Dan, you might remember I told you the other day we might have need of you again. It appears we need you sooner than we expected."

For a moment, Dan thought about trying to get more money this time. But Mr. Jones's persistent smile made him leery. "What are you looking for? More of the same? There's all kinds of Mardi Gras stuff happening."

Mr. Jones had Dan's controller in his hands. He hit the start button, and Dan wished he could just kill him. The password page came up, and Mr. Jones punched in Dan's password.

"What the fuck?" Dan said.

"Do you seriously think we don't know everything there is to know about you, Dan? Your password is nothing. The location of your mother? That was simple, too. In fact, Dan, with the exception of your power, you're just not that complicated."

Mr. Jones was putting Dan's CntrlFreak avatar through his paces. And he was kicking major amounts of ass. It made Dan feel sick.

"Then why not just have me take Bubbles's power and then kill her?" Dan asked.

"Because we may have need of her in the future," Mr. Jones replied. "In your scenario, you could use her power once—and then, if she were dead, it would be gone and you couldn't take it again. A matchless resource would be lost."

Mr. Jones executed a perfect jump and roll with CntrlFreak, then single-head-shotted two combatants. "Perfect!" flashed on the screen.

"Not everyone is as uncomplicated as you are, Dan," Mr. Jones continued. "Take the lovely Miss Pond, for instance. She's ridiculously powerful, and yet, she cares little for that. But her friends, well, they're what matter to her.

"I could have had you steal her power, but that wouldn't have mattered to her. And we're not in the business of destroying people. We're in the business of managing them."

Watching Mr. Jones play the game made Dan want to jump straight out of his skin. And he didn't really give a shit about why Mr. Jones was doing anything he was doing—or why he was asking Dan to do anything. Just so long as they paid him. But he itched for Mr. Jones to put down the controller, get out of Dan's new chair, and tell him what the hell he wanted this time. The rest was just jacking off as far as Dan was concerned.

"But tormenting her friend," Mr. Jones said smiling beatifically, "well, that's another matter. That will teach her the lesson I mean for her to learn. That no one she loves is safe. That she can't protect them. There are a lot of people in the world now who are extremely powerful, Dan. Controlling them isn't always about their personal peril. It's about explaining to them the limits of their power. The world may be changed because of the virus, but people, well, they're still the same."

Mr. Jones made CntrlFreak do a diving jump over several dead bodies, then he rolled up into a perfect kneeling position, gun extended, and squeezed off a single-bullet killing shot.

"We'll need you tomorrow morning," Mr. Jones said as he put another bullet into the head of another player's avatar. "I'll send a van to get you at six a.m."

"Winner!" flashed on the screen. Mr. Jones got out of Dan's chair and tossed him the controller. "Have fun playing," he said.

Michelle woke up feeling muzzy-headed. She'd only had two beers, but at her current weight, it had hit her like a Mack truck. Actually, it wasn't that bad. She'd been hit by a couple of Mack trucks. And even a bus once. It was frustrating that there wasn't a large vehicle handy at the moment. She'd have to make do with having Joey's zombies pound on her for a while to get fat.

She rolled over and saw Adesina curled up in the center of the extra pillow. Michelle smiled. She reached out and touched Adesina's new braids. They'd been experimenting with different hairstyles, trying to find one Adesina liked. But Michelle suspected Adesina just enjoyed having her hair done.

"Stop playing with my braids, Momma," Adesina said.

Michelle pulled her close, saying, "But they're so awesome! I'm jealous!"

Adesina giggled, opening her eyes. "We could braid your hair. It's long enough."

"Yes, but it would look like crap the next day, and yours looks amazing. Let's go downstairs and see if Aunt Joey has anything for breakfast in the fridge besides beer."

But when they got downstairs, Joey was gone. There were no zombies in the parlor and none in the kitchen. And when Michelle went outside, there wasn't a single dead pigeon in sight.

Dammit, Michelle thought as she pushed open the gate, left the yard, and began looking up and down the street. *I told her not to go off alone. And now I've got to do something I really don't want to do. I am so going to kick her ass when we find her.*

"Adesina," Michelle said, "I know I told you not to go into Aunt Joey's mind, but we need to find her fast."

"It's okay, Momma," Adesina replied, flying into Michelle's arms. As Michelle cradled her, Adesina closed her eyes.

A minute later, her eyes snapped open. She squirmed out of Michelle's arms and floated down to the ground. Then she began running. Adesina could only fly short distances, but she ran fast. Michelle followed, wishing again that she'd piled on some fat.

Adesina ran down the street, turned right, then left. Then she ducked into an alleyway. The stink of puke and rotting garbage hit Michelle in a wave. A large Dumpster squatted at the end of the alley. Adesina slowed as she reached it, and Michelle heard sobbing. She stopped running and hesitantly approached the far side of the Dumpster.

Joey was sitting on ground with her back against the building's brick wall. Her arms were clasped around her legs, hugging them tight against her body.

"Joey," Michelle said softly as she crept forward. *Oh God*, she thought. *I should have been there for her.* "Joey, honey, it's me. It's Michelle."

Joey's shoulders shuddered, and then she looked up at Michelle. "Jesus, Bubbles," she said, her voice jerky from crying. "I shouldn't have come out here alone. They took my power again. I can't see any of my children."

Adesina flew to Joey's shoulder and gave her a quick kiss on the cheek, then hopped to the ground. "It's okay, Aunt Joey, we're here now," she said.

"I just wanted to get some pastries for breakfast," Joey said, wiping her nose on her sleeve. "Croissants, maybe a few turnovers. I know the Pumpkin likes turnovers. I just wanted to get something for breakfast. And then everything went dark."

Michelle reached out and took Joey's hands. They were shaking and cold. "C'mon," she said, pulling Joey to her feet. "Let's go home."

"But I didn't get the goddamn pastries," Joey said stubbornly. "There's nothing for breakfast. The Pumpkin needs breakfast."

"We can get breakfast later, Joey," Michelle said as she slowly pulled Joey down the alley. "Adesina will be fine without breakfast for a little while longer, won't you, sweetie?"

Adesina flew back up and into Joey's arms. Joey reflexively caught her. "I'm not hungry at all, Aunt Joey."

"But you need something to eat," Joey said stubbornly. "I was going to get pastries." Joey toyed with Adesina's braids. "My mother used to braid my hair."

Holy hell, Michelle thought. *She's unspooling. We've got to find whoever is stealing her powers. And, barring that, figure out a way for her to cope with losing them. And why steal Joey's power? Why not mine?* She'd rarely felt this helpless. She couldn't figure out a way to help Joey and she couldn't stop the person stealing Joey's power. It was infuriating. *When I find the person who's doing this to Joey, I will end them.* But she knew that was a lie. She'd give up ever finding them if she could only keep Joey safe.

"We could stop and get some turnovers on the way home," Joey said. She hugged Adesina tight. "You want something for breakfast, Pumpkin?" Adesina glanced at Michelle.

"We should get you home," Michelle said. "I'll go out after and get something."

Joey shifted Adesina into one arm, then grabbed Michelle's wrist. "No," she said. "You can't fucking leave me alone. Please. Not while my children are gone."

"It's okay," Michelle said, gently pulling Joey's hand away. "I won't go anywhere if you don't want me to. We'll figure it out." Michelle put her arm around Joey and led her home.

"So, where do you want me to use the zombies?" Dan asked. He was sitting in the paneled van with Mr. Jones and some other dude who was driving. It felt like his head was about to come off. Hoodoo Mama's power was kicking around in his skull and rattling his bones. It sang in his blood. It wanted to *move*.

"Dan," Mr. Jones said in a bored voice. "Don't be impatient."

Dan scratched at his arms. The power felt different this time. Angrier. This was the first time he'd grabbed a big Ace power more than once. He'd assumed it would be the same, but it wasn't. It felt like its own entity. As if he'd swallowed a bowl of bees.

"Mr. Jones," he said. "I'm not feeling so good."

Jones turned and looked at Dan. "Would you care to be more specific?" he asked in a flat voice.

"I . . . I . . . I'm not sure," Dan stuttered out. "Hoodoo Mama's power feels different this time. I'm having a hard time keeping it in. I've never grabbed a power like hers more than once." He didn't want Mr. Jones to know how strange the power felt this time.

Mr. Jones's cold, dark eyes appraised Dan. Normally, this would have scared Dan, but the power felt bad and was getting worse by the second.

"How annoying," Mr. Jones said. "We didn't anticipate your power would be so . . . inconsistent. He turned back around, and then said to the driver, "It's early, but let's do the drop."

The van jerked forward. Dan's head hit the side window. "Ow," he said, but neither Mr. Jones nor the driver said anything.

A few minutes later, the van stopped. Dan looked around. Victorian houses lined the street. Most were shabby looking and run-down.

"Bring me a zombie," Mr. Jones said as he pulled an envelope out of his breast pocket. Gratefully, Dan reached out and found a wealth of dead all around. "What do you want?" he asked. "Rats, dogs, cats?"

Mr. Jones glanced over his shoulder with an expression of contempt on his face. "Bring me a dead person, Dan."

Dan got the closest one he could find. It was a relief to be using the power. He could feel it starting to drain away from him. The buzzing died down to a dull hum. "Where do you want it?" Dan asked.

"Bring it here, have it take this note, and send it to that house two doors down across the street. Have it ring the bell and give the note to whomever answers the door."

"The one with the wrought-iron fence?" Dan asked to be sure. He didn't want to make Mr. Jones mad.

"Yes."

Dan did as he had been instructed.

The doorbell rang. Joey jumped, and Michelle reached out and patted her on the arm. It didn't help. She felt Joey trembling.

There was a zombie standing on the porch when Michelle answered the door. It held out an envelope. Michelle took the envelope, and then the zombie fell over in a heap.

The envelope was addressed to Michelle. *Okay,* she thought warily. *This isn't weird at all.*

There was a single sheet of paper inside the envelope.

> *Miss Pond,*
>
>   *We haven't been introduced, but my employers are big fans of yours. They've admired your many good works for years now. That said, they think you've had quite a nice run, but it might be time for you to retire and take a long vacation from the public eye.*
>
>   *The incidents with Joey Hebert are just a small sample of what we can do to people you care about. Persist in having such a public profile, and we will take more drastic measures. Perhaps something having to do with your child.*
>
>   *I look forward to meeting you soon.*
>
>

Sincerely Yours,
Mr. Jones
>

Michelle stared at the letter, trying to figure out who sent it. "Mr. Jones" was a transparent pseudonym.

Was Juliette right? Was this whole thing designed to marginalize her? And why target Joey? Joey helped the people who needed it who lived on the fringes of New Orleans society—why would anyone want to shut that down? Sure, some of them were grifters and other shady types, but some were homeless people who just needed looking after.

And me, Michelle thought. *What the hell? I'm not affiliated with any agency anymore. I don't try any of that vigilante bullshit. Why would anyone even care?*

"Michelle!" Joey said as she came running down the hall. "My children! I can fucking see them again!" She danced gleefully around Michelle, then glanced outside. "Why is that body on the porch?" The body sat up as Joey possessed it.

Michelle held the letter out to Joey, who took it and read it quickly.

"Is this Mr. Jones the motherfucker who's been taking my power?" Joey was jumping from one leg to another as if she'd been hitting the Red Bull hard all day.

"I'm not sure," Michelle said. "He could just be an errand boy. There's no way of knowing. My guess is that they're going to do something again—I just don't know why they're going after you." She looked at Joey and didn't like what she saw.

Joey's eyes were wide, and she was jittery as hell. Losing her power wasn't just making her nervous—it was making her angry, too.

"Joey," Michelle said. "I know losing your power is horrible, but you told me when we were in the PPA that knowing where all the nearby dead bodies were all the time made you kinda crazy. Wasn't it a little bit of a relief when it went away?"

Hands shaking, Joey gave the letter back to Michelle. "No, yes, no," she said. "In the PPA there were so many bodies. And so many of them were dead children. You remember, Bubbles. And at first, when my powers vanished, I was just me. And that was nice. But then I started remembering how it was before I turned into Hoodoo Mama . . ." Her voice trailed off.

Michelle frowned as she closed the door. "I don't know what to do. It's clear they want me to stay the hell out of the public eye, and they're willing to fu . . . mess with you to get me to do it. Maybe I should reach out to someone from the Committee."

"No!" Joey exclaimed. "No! I don't want anyone to know this is happening. What if they take my powers away forever? Jesus, Bubbles, what the fuck would I do then?" Her face began to crumple as if she was about to cry, and then a furious expression replaced it. "And, Bubbles, I want the fucker who's been yanking my power. This Mr. Jones motherfucking turd prick-ass bastard is going to pay."

"I'd like nothing more than to see him pay, too," Michelle said. She needed Joey to remember what had happened when her powers were taken. That was the most important thing right now. "This time was like the last time, right?"

Joey nodded, but she was still shaking.

"So," Michelle said. "They grab your power, use it, and then you get it back?"

"Yeah."

"Then my guess is they *can't* keep it. Otherwise, they'd just grab both our powers and be done with it. That's what I'd do. And you were out both times they took your powers, so maybe there needs to be line of sight, or proximity?"

Joey nodded and looked relieved. "I'm glad you're here, Bubbles," she said, with just a hint of a smile. "I mean, you know I still think you're a cocksucking bitch, right?"

"Well," Michelle replied. "You got that half right."

"Let's see what the Pumpkin wants for breakfast," Joey said as they went into the living room.

"Unless it's beer and bourbon," Michelle replied, "we've got to make a grocery run."

"You go make the run," Joey said. "I'll be okay here for that long. But I'm pretty sure I heard her saying she loooves bourbon for breakfast. Girl after my own heart."

Momma and Aunt Joey were laughing. Adesina felt the knot in her stomach loosen a little—until they came into the room. Then it was clear to her that they were putting a nice face on things. She didn't need to slip into their minds to know that.

There was a smile on Momma's face, but it wasn't one of her real smiles. And Aunt Joey was smiling, too, but Adesina could see the ghosts in her eyes.

"You up for some breakfast?" Momma asked as she sat on the couch next to Adesina.

"Your mom says you're not down with bourbon for breakfast," Aunt Joey put in. "I keep telling her you're my homegirl, but she doesn't believe me."

Adesina made her sincere face. "I'd love bourbon for breakfast, Momma."

"Okay," Momma replied. "But I'm going to pour it over your cereal. Yum."

"Gah," Adesina said. Once she'd been very bad and snuck a taste of Aunt Joey's bourbon. It was disgusting. "I want French toast."

"I'll go to the market," Michelle said as she leaned over and kissed the top of Adesina's head.

"Be careful, Bubbles. They could grab your power," Joey said. She bent down to tie the laces of her ratty Converse sneakers. Her hands shook as she did so. "It was bad when they took my power. It'd be much fucking worse if they got yours."

Momma shrugged. "I've been out in public and they could've already gotten my powers. So I don't think they're interested in it, Joey." She leaned over and kissed Adesina. "Don't let Aunt Joey do anything stupid like go out of the house, sweetie."

"I won't, Momma," Adesina replied.

Dan rubbed his face. He'd been about to explode when he'd had Hoodoo Momma's power. Even after using it, he was still jittery as hell. But maybe that was because he was stuck in a van with Mr. Jones and the creepily silent driver.

"Uhm, can you drop me back at my house?" he asked as he fidgeted in his seat.

"Yes, Dan, we will drop you off at your house," Mr. Jones said with barely concealed distaste. "I'm very disappointed in you, Dan. These things need to be timed properly and you didn't do your part."

A cold, slippery feeling slid into Dan's gut. "Uh, I know," he replied. "It's like I told you. I've never grabbed a big Ace power twice. And I didn't know it would be so weird the second time. I just don't know what happened. I'm sure it was nothing."

Mr. Jones didn't reply. Dan rubbed his palms on his pants. A silent Mr. Jones was worse than a talking one.

He decided that the next time Mr. Jones wanted him for anything, he'd just say no. It'd never occurred to him that there might be limitations on what he could do, or that yanking a big power more than once might have blowback. He needed to figure out what the real parameters of his ability were. And there was no way Mr. Jones was interested in helping him with that. Mr. Jones was interested in whatever weird-ass mind-fuck shit he was up to. And nothing else.

The van slowed in front of Dan's house. Dan was reaching for the door handle before it came to a stop. But before he could open the door, Mr. Jones's hand was clasped hard around his wrist.

"Just a moment, Dan," he said. "I forgot to give you your pay." He held out a fat manila envelope.

For a fleeting moment, Dan thought about turning it down. But then he took it.

"I'll be in touch," Mr. Jones said.

Dan nodded. What he wanted to say was "Fuck no, you crazy prick. I'd rather eat ground glass than deal with you again."

And it wasn't until he got to the front door that he realized Mr. Jones had no wild card abilities in him at all.

I'm not afraid, Michelle thought. *Well, not much anyway.* The streets were still pretty empty despite the fact that it was Mardi Gras. She went into the local corner store and began grabbing what she needed to make French toast.

"Hey, you're the Amazing Bubbles, aren't you?"

Michelle looked up and saw a young girl. She was maybe sixteen with hair dyed black, black clothes, black Doc Martens, and a wealth of silver studded and spiked jewelry. A pale face with heavy black eyeliner and crimson lips completed the look. Michelle wondered how she hadn't sweated through everything, including the heavy Pan-Cake makeup.

"Yeah," she replied. "I am." She dropped a loaf of bread into her basket and started to the dairy section. The girl followed.

"I thought what you did at the parade was awesome," the girl said. "I mean, you were really great."

Eggs, half-and-half, and butter went into Michelle's basket. "Thanks," she said as she walked to the produce section. "Just doing what I can."

What if this is the wild card who can grab powers? Michelle thought. *What kind of sick asshole would send a girl after me?* But then she realized that if this was the wild card who'd grabbed Joey's power, she would be just as helpless as Joey had been.

"Well," the girl said, "I just wanted you to know I really admire you. You've been my favorite wild card since *American Hero*."

Michelle smiled at the girl. If they were going to grab her power, they would be doing it soon. "Would you like an autograph?" she asked.

"Oh, I couldn't ask for that," the girl said. "But would you mind a picture of us together?" She held up her phone.

"Sure," Michelle replied. Michelle put her arm around the girl and smiled as the picture was snapped. "And what's your name?"

"Dorothy," the girl said as she looked at the image. "Hey, this came out amazing."

Michelle laughed. "Well, I am a professional. Or I was."

"Hey, thanks," Dorothy said. "Uhm, I just want you to know I don't think you're a lousy mother. I don't care what anyone is saying."

Michelle tried to keep her expression neutral, but she was irritated. And then she reminded herself that this was the way it was. You become famous, and you give up part of yourself. And Michelle knew she was lucky. Even with all the weird crap in her life, she could pay the bills and give herself and Adesina a decent life. So she made herself smile brightly and say, "I really appreciate that, Dorothy. It was nice to meet you."

"Mr. Jones would like to see you and Joey Hebert in two days, nine in the morning, at Jackson Square," Dorothy said. "He thinks it's time for you to meet in person." She gave Michelle a bright smile, then vanished.

For a moment, Michelle just stared at the spot where Dorothy had been. *Yeah, I was not expecting that,* she thought. Then she went and grabbed a bottle of vanilla extract. It was going to be one of those lives.

Joey was washing the breakfast dishes while Michelle dried. It was nice. Nice and normal, and that made Joey mad. She didn't know why. But she knew it wasn't the way she should be feeling.

After they'd finished eating, Michelle had asked for a couple of Joey's zombies to knock her around and fatten her up. It took a while, but eventually Michelle stopped looking like a horrific thinspiration photo and was pleasantly plump. Joey thought Michelle looked especially pretty when she was plump. Joey liked her girls curvy.

Then they'd come back inside and started cleaning up the kitchen. Adesina was flopped on the couch, playing her game, so Joey didn't bother to have her help. Sure, her mother might have said they were spoiling the child, but Joey didn't see it that way.

"I had another message from Mr. Jones," Michelle said softly while wiping a dish.

Joey looked over her shoulder to see if Adesina had heard. But she was still engrossed in her game. "What the fuck did he want?"

"He wants us to meet him in Jackson Square day after tomorrow morning at nine," Michelle replied. "Oh, and the messenger was a sixteen-year-old girl who can teleport."

"We're not going to go, right?" Joey asked. "That would be fucking insane." Joey wanted to hit something. Hard.

"I'm going," Michelle whispered. She kept drying dishes as if it were the most normal thing in the world to do while talking about some thug who wanted to steal your powers. "It's the only real choice we have. Unless you want to go underground, leave your home, and assume a new identity. Avoiding these people—whoever they are—just gives them power over you."

"But they've already got power over us, Michelle," Joey hissed, soapy water splashing on the floor as she angrily dumped the frying pan into it. "In case you've forgotten, they've yanked my power twice. Maybe they'll yank yours next."

Michelle nodded, then opened the silverware drawer and began putting utensils away. "They might," she said. "But if that happened, it wouldn't be the end of my life. I'd go back to what I was before. It wouldn't change what I've done and it wouldn't change who I am." Michelle slid the drawer shut.

"Well, it's fucking easy for you to say, Bubbles," Joey replied. "You had a life before your card turned. I had jack shit. Except for my mother." The thought of her mother made a hideous lump form in the back of Joey's throat. She swallowed and tried not to cry. "I was just a kid when my card turned."

And even though Joey had banished almost every moment of that day, flashes of what had happened would still swim to the surface. And she knew if she hadn't turned into Hoodoo Mama, she would have died then.

"I know it's easy for me," Michelle replied gently. She dropped the towel on the counter and turned to face Joey. "And that's why I need to do something to help you. If you'll let me."

Joey threw her sponge into the sink. "And what the fuck do you think you can do?"

Michelle grabbed Joey's hands. "I can have Adesina go into your mind—into your memories—and she can . . . help you."

Joey grew very still. "What do you mean?" she asked.

"You know that Adesina can go into your mind? Well, when we were in the PPA, after all the fighting had stopped and we stayed to help the children we'd found there, Adesina went into some of their minds and she . . . she took their pain away. She made them forget what had happened to them." Michelle paused and then she dropped Joey's hands. She picked up the dishtowel, folded it, and then hung it on the rack. "I stopped her from doing it because I didn't like how depressed she got afterward."

"Well, why would you fucking let her into my mind knowing that she's already been in there once before and it wasn't a fucking fun time?" Joey's hands were shaking and she jammed them into the pockets of her jeans. "I don't want her in my head. And I don't want to remember. I *won't* remember. Why should I?"

"I've been giving this a lot of thought," Michelle said. "And I talked to Adesina about it—to see if my plan would even work. She'll be in your mind, but not in the way she usually goes into someone's mind. I'm going in for her. Well, more like with her." Michelle rubbed her forehead and sighed. "I'm not describing this well. Adesina has linked two separate minds together before—by accident. So it'll be difficult. But she wants to help. And given our time frame, I don't see that there are any other solutions. So, yeah, I'm not going to be winning Mother of the Year anytime soon."

"Fuck," Joey said rocking back on her heels. She shook her head. "I don't think I can let Adesina do that. What if she sees . . . something a kid shouldn't see? What if *you* see?"

"Joey," Michelle said, exasperation hard in her voice. "We can't go on the run from these people. Christ, I can't even figure out who they work for. You freak when your power is lifted. I think I have a way to fix that—or at least a way to make the memory this is triggering go away. You have to be okay with not having your power. Otherwise, they can get to you. And I can't be here all the time. You need to deal with this. Yeah, it's a suck solution, but it's the only one we have. Do you really think I'd do this to my daughter if I could think of any other option? And may I remind you that Adesina is in danger from these assholes, too?"

"Honestly, Bubbles," Joey replied as she rocked back and forth on the balls of her feet. "I've seen you do some pretty bad shit."

"Yeah?" Michelle replied as she turned away from Joey and began putting dishes in the cupboard. "Welcome to the working world."

It took another two hours of arguing before Joey finally agreed to let Michelle and Adesina into her mind—and then only with the understanding that if Joey gave the word, the experiment ended.

"Where do you want to do this?" Joey asked. They were in the living room, and Joey had cleared out the usual zombie guard because Adesina mentioned that they were stinky.

"It easiest when the other person is asleep," Adesina said. "That's how I found Momma. When she was in the coma."

"Well, I'm not tired," Joey said.

"We could go upstairs and use the guest bedroom," Michelle suggested. "You could lie down and just try to relax."

"Fuck," Joey muttered as she turned and stomped out of the room. Michelle and Adesina followed her. And Joey couldn't help noticing that Michelle didn't say anything about her bad language in front of the child.

Adesina had a fluttery feeling in her tummy. She was pretty sure she could bring Momma into Aunt Joey's mind. But once they were there, could Momma really protect her? Adesina loved Aunt Joey, but there were things lurking in the dark corridors and rooms there that scared her.

Aunt Joey lay down on the bed, and Momma lay down beside her. Adesina hopped up and snuggled between them. Aunt Joey's body was rigid, her arms stiff and tight against her side. Momma rolled onto her side, reached out, and took Aunt Joey's left hand. Aunt Joey sighed, then relaxed a little. And then Adesina slid into Momma's mind.

It was a comfortable place for Adesina. Momma's mind was like a big, open house. There were pretty views out the windows and lots of bright, airy rooms. There were a couple of rooms Momma wouldn't let her go into, but Adesina didn't mind. Momma had explained that some of it was grown-up stuff, and some of it was private.

And there were bunnies in Momma's mind, too. Adesina liked the bunnies, but never could figure out why Momma had so many of them.

"Hey there, kiddo," Momma said. She was standing next to the windows looking out at the view holding a fat rabbit. "You ready to do this?" She turned toward Adesina, put the bunny down, and Adesina ran and jumped into her arms.

"I'm ready, Momma," Adesina said. And then she reached out for Aunt Joey.

One moment Michelle was in her own mind, or at least Adesina's interpretation of her mind—and the next, she and Adesina were in the front entryway of a version of Joey's house. But it was bigger than Joey's actual house. There were corridors that spawned from the main hallway. Michelle saw that they were lined with closed doors.

"Joey?" Michelle yelled. She tried not to shout in Adesina's ear, even though she knew she wasn't really carrying the child in the crook of her arm. "Where are you, Joey?"

"Here," Joey replied from behind her. Startled, Michelle spun around. There, in the multicolored light from the stained-glass windows in the front door, was Joey. She looked frailer and younger than she did in real life.

"You scared the crap out of me," Michelle said. She reached out and touched the intricately carved chair rail that ran the length of the hall. "Your house looks different in here."

"Yeah, I don't know if that's me doing it or the Pumpkin," Joey replied as she slowly turned around and took in the front entrance and hallway. "I guess if I ever got around to sprucing the place up, it might look like this. And that front door is really fucking cool."

Michelle kissed Adesina on the head and then put her down. "End of the line for you, kiddo," she said. "I want you to stay here, okay? Aunt Joey and I need to go the rest of the way alone."

"Wait," Joey said. She brushed by Michelle and opened the first door on the left. "I did something for the Pumpkin."

Adesina and Michelle turned and peered through the doorway. Inside the room were overstuffed couches upholstered in a faded chrysanthemum print. The couches were positioned in front of a large flat-screen TV. A couple of burly zombies played checkers on a table under the bay window. Several otters sat on the couches eating popcorn and watching cartoons on the TV. Adesina gave a squeal of delight, then ran into the room and hopped up on the couch next to the smallest otter.

Michelle looked at Joey and then cocked her head. "Really? Do otters even eat popcorn?"

"My head, my rules," Joey replied with a grin that surprised Michelle. "Besides, Adesina really loves those otters."

"I know," Michelle said. "Weird, huh? I guess we should get going."

Joey's smile faded. "Yeah, I guess we should."

"You're going to have to lead," Michelle said. "I have no idea where to start."

"I do," Joey replied. Her voice was sad. "It's this way." Then, much to Michelle's surprise, Joey took her hand.

They went to the second to the last corridor leading off the main hallway and turned into it. There were sconces lining the walls here, but several of the bulbs had burned out. The walls were painted a dull grey, and the hall runners sported an undulating pattern in chartreuse, smoke, and brown. There were three doors along each wall in this hallway, and there was a door at the far end as well. Joey slowed, and Michelle had to tug her hand to get her to move forward again.

"I know you don't want to do this," Michelle said. "But it's the only choice."

Joey stopped in front of the first door on the right. "I know," she said as she reached out and threw open the door.

Sunlight spilled into the hallway. They stepped through the doorway. The light was so bright that, for a moment, Michelle was blinded. She blinked, and blurry images turned into people.

Michelle and Joey stood at the top of a hill. Below them, a tall, willowy woman in a blue sundress was laughing at something a bandy-legged man standing beside her had said. She took a long drink from the tallboy in her hand. Around them ran a short, skinny, young girl.

"Mommy," Joey whispered. Then she pointed at the little girl. "And that's me down there, too."

"How old were you?" Michelle asked. She couldn't take her eyes away from the scene. Everything about it was golden and warm.

"Eleven," Joey replied, her voice wavering. Michelle glanced at her.

"Why are you crying?" Michelle asked, perplexed. "You look so happy here."

"It's the last fucking happy memory I have."

Michelle looked back to the scene. Joey's hair was done up in braids, and she wore a pink T-shirt and overalls. She threw head back and laughed and laughed, the perfect image of her mother.

"Screw this," Joey said. She yanked them out of the room, then slammed the door shut. The golden light was gone, and they were back in the gloomy hallway.

Joey dropped Michelle's hand, then ran to another door and yanked it open. Michelle sprinted to catch up with her. Inside, Joey's mother was sitting on a bed with Joey. Joey's mother wore a tatty floral housedress and her hair hadn't been combed. Joey was wearing a blue T-shirt with faded but clean jeans.

"I'm never gonna leave you, baby girl," Joey's mother said, her words slurring. She patted Joey's head and toyed with her braids. "I don't know where you get these crazy ideas."

There was a sick look on Joey's face. "You've been spending a lot of time in bed, Mommy," Joey said, touching her mother's cheek. "And you forget stuff. And you never want to eat anymore . . ." Joey's voice trailed off.

"Oh, baby girl, you know your mother has a bad memory," her mother said as she lay back against the pillows. Michelle saw now that Joey's mother's belly was distended and her skin was ashy. Even the whites of her eyes were yellow. Joey's mother was ill—very ill. "Always have had a poor memory," Joey's mother continued. "There's nothing to that. Your uncle Earl John is here to help me remember things."

"Mommy," Joey said, inching closer to her mother. "I don't like Uncle Earl John. I don't understand why you're with him."

"Baby girl," her mother said as she pushed herself up again. It looked like it took an effort. "When you get older you'll understand that it's hard to make a living. Your uncle Earl John takes care of us. He buys us what we need."

"I don't fucking want what he buys," Joey said in a surly voice.

Her mother slapped her across the face.

"Don't you take that tone with me," Joey's mother said. Her tone was angry, but her eyes were scared. "And don't you use that nasty language."

Young Joey rubbed her cheek, and adult Joey mimicked her. Michelle wanted to say something to help, but she was at a loss. Her parents had been horrible, but at least they had never hit her.

Then Joey's mother began to cry.

"Oh God," she said, pulling young Joey into her arms. "I'm so sorry, baby girl. I love you and I just want you to be safe after . . . I just want you to be safe. Uncle Earl John will keep you safe. He promised."

"It was the only time she ever hit me," adult Joey said, her voice hitching with tears. "She never let *anyone* touch me. Not ever. None of those cocksuckers she married. None of the ones she just fucked. They could beat the hell out of her, but never once did she let them hit me." She pulled Michelle out into the hall again and slammed the door shut.

"Where to now?" Michelle asked. At the dead end of the hall was a door flanked by flickering sconces. She pointed at it. "What about that one?"

"No," Joey said, taking a step backward while wiping the tears from her cheeks.

"Maybe it's what we're looking for," Michelle said, grabbing Joey's hand and pulling her toward the door.

"Michelle, don't!" Joey cried.

But it was too late. Michelle was already opening the door. She stepped through the doorway, dragging Joey along, and found herself on a rise overlooking a cemetery. A small knot of mourners was gathered around one of the small crypts.

Michelle saw young Joey. She as wearing a dark blue dress and was sobbing. Next to her was the man from the first room. He was rubbing Joey's back, and the sight of that action made the hairs on Michelle's neck stand up.

Abruptly, Michelle found herself in the living room of a shotgun house. There were casserole dishes laid out on card tables, and a group of women were fussing over the dishes and Joey. Michelle could see into the kitchen where a group of men were talking and drinking. The women in the living room clucked over the men's boozing between attempts to get Joey to eat. But Joey just sat curled up on the ratty sofa and cried.

The scene shifted again. It was dark outside, and in the back of the house Michelle heard someone banging around. Joey was still on the sofa, her legs pulled up under her chin. Her face was vacant. The guests had left, and someone had cleaned up the living room.

"Hey, baby girl," came a loud, slurred voice. Joey didn't respond, but Michelle turned. The short man with bandy legs leaned against the doorjamb. There were sweat stains on his shirt, and he'd pulled his tie loose. It was the man from the funeral. Joey's uncle Earl John.

"Baby girl!" he said louder. Michelle could smell the liquor on his breath. "You hear me?"

For a moment Joey didn't answer, but then she turned toward him. "Don't call me that," she said in a flat voice. "No one but my mother calls me that."

"Well, your drunk-ass, junkie momma is dead as a doornail," he said, pushing himself from the doorjamb. He staggered into the living room. "All the money I spent on that lush, down the drain. But you, well, you're going to fix it. Goin' to clean my house, goin' to fix my dinner, and goin' to get in my bed."

He grabbed her. Joey shrieked and tried to yank her arm away. But he held on tight and jerked her off the sofa.

Michelle instinctively tried to bubble—but nothing happened.

Of course not. This was Joey's memory, and Michelle was just a spectator. And then Michelle realized that her Joey—grown-up Joey—was gone.

"Let me go!" Joey screamed, but her voice and face switched back and forth from child to adult Joey. "Let me go!" She kicked, but it didn't do any good. Joey was just a skinny slip of a thing.

No. No. No. No. I don't want to see this, Michelle thought. *God, I don't want to.*

The memory began to fragment. Michelle found herself in a bedroom. A slice of light fell across the bed from the open bathroom door. The heavy smell of bourbon was everywhere.

The ceiling had a stain on it, a brown water stain from a roof leak. Joey remembered exactly how it looked. The edges were darker than the center. And then he was grabbing her legs and forcing them open. Joey screamed, and he released one of her legs and fumbled with his pants. The stain looked like Illinois.

There was a heavy weight on Joey's chest. She couldn't move. The world spun, and she thought she was going to be sick. She rolled over and started gagging. Earl John pushed her off the bed.

"You puke in the bathroom," he said.

Joey crawled to the bathroom. The floor tiles were blue, and until today Joey had always loved the color of them. She lifted the seat on the toilet and dry heaved. Nothing came up because she hadn't eaten in two days.

Something ran down her leg. She wiped at it. Her hand came away sticky and smelled like the river.

The memory jumped again. Earl John was holding Joey facedown on the bed. Joey pushed her face into the pillow and breathed in her mother's smell that still lingered there. It was Mommy's favorite rose perfume. Joey heard her own pathetic cries and Earl John's grunting, but it sounded as if it were coming from somewhere else. Somewhere far away.

Then he was done and he rolled off Joey and went into the kitchen. There was the sound of the refrigerator opening, and a glass being filled with ice cubes.

Joey wanted to die. She could die here with Mommy's smell in her nose. They'd be together, and she wouldn't have to feel the disgusting stickiness between her legs anymore.

"You just stay like you are, baby girl," Earl John said. "I'm going to break all your cherries tonight."

Joey didn't know what he meant. But she knew Mommy wouldn't want him to touch her. Mommy never let any of them touch her. Ever!

Earl John threw back his drink and set the glass on the dresser. He started toward Joey and there was another jump in time.

Someone was banging on the front door. Then there was the sound of wood smashing. Earl John jumped up, went to the side table, and pulled a gun out of the drawer.

"What the hell?" he said as he turned around. Then he gave a high-pitched shriek. Joey rolled over and saw Mommy in the doorway.

"You hurt my baby," Mommy said. But it was Joey's voice that came out of her mouth. "I told you to take care of her."

Earl John shot Mommy twice in the chest.

But Mommy just smiled.

"Can't hurt us no more, Earl John," she said. Joey mouthed the words, too. "Can't hurt us no more, you fucker."

And then Mommy ripped Earl John's head off.

Joey sat in the middle of the bed, her knees pulled up under her chin. She hurt all over. Mommy came and sat on the bed, too.

"I'm sorry, baby girl, I shouldn't have left you alone," she said. Her voice was still Joey's.

"It's okay, Mommy," Joey said. She crawled to Mommy and put her arms around her. Then she laid her head on Mommy's shoulder. "You're here now." Then Joey looked around the room. Earl John was scattered everywhere. The sheets were gross and streaked with blood. Then she looked at herself. There were bruises on her legs and arms and blood on her thighs. She started to shake. "What do I do?" she asked. "I gotta do something."

Mommy laughed. "Well, baby girl, you need to get dressed. But before you do that, you should wash up. Use my shower."

Joey slid off the bed, but her legs were weak and barely held her. Mommy grabbed her and helped her get to the bathroom. Mommy ran the water in the shower until it was warm—almost hot. She helped Joey into the shower, and then Joey lathered herself over and over until all she could smell was Mommy's soap.

Then Mommy helped her get dressed and braided her hair again. And together they went into Joey's room and packed a suitcase. Then Mommy went back into her own bedroom and rifled through all of Earl John's things until she came up with all the cash he had. Joey waited for Mommy to finish.

"Where are we going, Mommy?" Joey asked when Mommy returned.

"Wherever you want, baby girl," Mommy said in Joey's voice. "Wherever you want."

After Joey's mother saved her, the memories fragmented.

But the one constant from that terrible night onward were the zombies. After reanimating her mother, Joey began to raise more and more of the dead. They were often in different stages of decomposition, but the smell didn't bother Joey at all. And the more zombies Joey raised, the stronger she felt. And Mommy was proud of her.

But, like all zombies, Mommy began to fall apart. It was then that Joey realized her mother was really gone.

Joey put her mother back into her crypt and left her there. Then she plunged into the underworld of New Orleans and turned herself into Hoodoo Mama. As Hoodoo Mama she ruled the grifters, the street hustlers, and the people who were lost and stuck on the fringes. Joey was a queen in this world, and her justice against men who hurt women was swift and terrible.

And Hoodoo Mama never let anyone hurt Joey again.

And as she watched all of this, Michelle realized she'd been wrong. Even though Michelle wanted nothing more than to erase the horror of what had happened that night from Joey's mind, it wouldn't be right to do it.

What had happened was part of Joey now. It had made her who and what she was. There were ways for Joey to deal with her pain, but having Adesina just cut that part out was wrong. To do so would banish Hoodoo Mama forever.

They'd have to deal with Mr. Jones and his power-stealing Ace some other way.

As soon as she realized that, Michelle found herself back in the hall with Joey and Adesina. Joey was sitting on the floor.

"Sweetie, how did you get here?" Michelle asked Adesina. "I thought we said you were going to stay back in the otter room."

"I know, Momma," Adesina replied. She was sitting on her back legs with her front legs in Joey's hands. Tears were running down Joey's cheeks. "But Aunt Joey needed me, and you were stuck."

"Did you see anything?" Michelle asked nervously.

Adesina shook her head. "No, just some zombies. But they're everywhere in here."

Michelle plopped down on the floor next to Joey. "You okay?" she asked.

Joey shook her head. "I don't know," she said. She looked at Michelle. Tears stained her cheeks, and her eyes were red and puffy. "My mother came back for me and she made him pay. She told me she'd keep me safe." Tears ran down her cheeks. "Fuck, I hate crying," she said. "And I never, ever, wanted to think about that again. Hoodoo Mama shut it away."

"Look," Michelle began as she reached out and wiped the tears from Joey's face. "What happened to you was unspeakable. And you were just a child. You did what you needed to in order to survive."

"Fucker asked for it," Joey said with a hiss.

"Oh, I think that barely begins to cover it," Michelle said. She sat down in front of Joey and took her hands. "But you were just a little girl then. Even if they steal your power, you're a grown woman now. They can't control you."

"But if I'm not Hoodoo Mama, who am I?" Joey asked with a plaintive cry. "You saw what happened to me. If I'm not Hoodoo Mama, how can I stop those fuckers?"

"You're Joey fucking Hebert," Michelle replied. "And Joey fucking Hebert *is* Hoodoo Mama whether she has a wild card power or not. That's who the hell you are. And day after tomorrow we're going to tell this Mr. Jones he's gonna stop fucking with *both* of us."

"Momma," Adesina said. "Language."

It was muggy and hot the morning they were to meet Mr. Jones. Joey's eyes were gritty from lack of sleep, and she rubbed them. She'd heard Michelle get up in the middle of the night and go downstairs. Then she'd come back up to bed around four. Joey had assumed she couldn't sleep, either.

At 8 a.m. there was a knock on the front door. Joey went to the door flanked by two linebacker-sized zombies. She found a blond woman wearing a neat navy blue suit on the porch. Then she saw a black SUV with tinted windows parked in front of the house.

"Good morning. I'm Clarice Cummings, and I'm here to pick up Miss Pond's daughter," the blond woman said politely. "Will you tell her I'm here?"

Another one of Mr. Jones's scams, Joey immediately thought. Her zombies stepped toward the Cummings woman. "Yeah, I call bullshit, lady. You can tell Mr. Jones to fuck all the hell off. Or I could just send you back to him in pieces."

"Joey, it's okay," Michelle said as she ran to the front door. "I called in a favor. Thank you for the help, Miss Cummings. Adesina will be right here."

Miss Cummings smiled, and Joey decided she liked her just a little. "I'm happy to help. Adesina is one of my favorite pupils."

"Miss Cummings!" Adesina exclaimed, pushing herself between Joey and Michelle's legs. "Momma, you didn't tell me Miss Cummings was going to be here!"

Michelle grinned. "I wanted it to be a surprise. Besides, you've missed too much school this week. Now you're going to go with her, and I'll come to get you later this afternoon."

"I don't have my school bag," Adesina fretted.

"That won't be a problem," Miss Cummings said. "Everything today is on the computer."

Adesina jumped up and down excitedly. Miss Cummings laughed, then turned and started down the steps. Adesina followed her.

"Don't I get a kiss?" Michelle asked, her voice mock sad.

Adesina spun around, and then flew up into Michelle's arms. "Sorry, Momma," she said, planting a big kiss on Michelle's cheek.

Michelle kissed Adesina's forehead. "I'll see you soon," she said, and then she put Adesina down.

Adesina ran back to Miss Cummings and began chattering excitedly about lessons.

Joey shook her head. "I don't fucking get it," she said. "I hated school."

"Well, Adesina loves it," Michelle said. "And I needed someplace safe for her today. Before we came back to the States, I talked to Juliette about how to approach Adesina's education. I didn't want to send her to regular school, and it would have been dumb for me to homeschool her. I even thought about moving to Joker Town and having her go to school there, but I was worried everything there would be about being a Joker. And I wanted her to have as normal an education as possible."

Joey laughed. "You mean as normal as possible for a Joker who can go into other wild cards' minds? With a mother who's one of the most powerful Aces on earth?" She turned and went inside. "You coming?"

"I guess," Michelle replied. She followed Joey inside and then shut the front door. "Anyway, Juliette found out about this program for kids with wild cards. They monitor their development, they get classes, and they give them a place where they're not the only wild card. And it's a mix of Deuces, Aces, and Jokers. They also allow a really flexible schedule. Adesina started there when we got back from Africa."

Michelle and Joey went down the hall into the kitchen. Joey pulled out her coffeepot and Michelle got the coffee from the cupboard. She toyed with the edge of the bag.

"There's one more thing," Michelle began. "Miss Cummings knows that Juliette gets Adesina if anything happens to me."

"But nothing is going to happen to you," Joey said. "I mean, what can they do to you?"

Michelle shrugged. "Who knows?"

But they both knew. If Michelle's power could be stolen, she could be killed.

Michelle hadn't been back to Jackson Square since she'd absorbed Little Fat Boy's nuclear blast. There was a shrine to her in one corner of the park. Flowers and handmade signs decorated a small official placard.

She knew Mr. Jones had chosen Jackson Square to screw with her. Absorbing that blast had done something terrible to Michelle. It had driven her half-mad and had caused her to fall into a coma where she'd wandered alone for over a year. That is, until Adesina had found her and pulled her out of that dark, insane place.

The Square and surrounding area were oddly vacant, and Michelle didn't like that at all. She and Joey were the only people there. Even Café Du Monde was bizarrely vacant. And there were usually a least a couple of homeless people camped out on the benches. But not this morning. No doubt part of Mr. Jones's preparations.

She scanned the area. Mr. Jones hadn't arrived yet, but she and Joey were a little early. Joey was keeping watch on the whole square using zombie birds and insects. They'd agreed that Joey wouldn't make a big display of zombie power. Not only because they wanted Mr. Jones to see they were cooperating, but in case Joey's power got taken again, there would be fewer dead things for the other wild card to use.

"How the hell did they clear everyone out of here?" Joey asked. She jammed her hands into her jeans pockets and rocked back on her heels.

Michelle shrugged. "I have no idea," she replied. "But they must have clout to clear it during Mardi Gras."

"You're early," Mr. Jones said.

Michelle jumped, and then turned. Dorothy and a young man in a hooded sweatshirt were standing next to him. A bubble formed in her hand. She made it heavy. When it released, it would be fast as hell. When it hit, there would be carnage. They might nab her power, but she was going to get one last bubble off. And make it count.

"Hello, Michelle," Dorothy called out brightly. Today she was wearing a pale blue dress with a striped apron, and her hair was done up in pigtails.

"You're running with a bad crowd," Michelle replied. The bubble quavered in her hand. "But cute outfit."

Dorothy grinned and smoothed her skirt. "Thanks! My mother always said I'd end up in trouble."

It was an odd group: the girl, the boy in the hoodie, and the man who was so obviously a kill-first-ask-questions-later type. Michelle knew

Dorothy's power was teleportation, so she wasn't the power thief. That just left Mr. Jones and the kid with the unfortunate complexion.

"I'm just here for a little conversation," Mr. Jones said with a toothy smile. Despite the mugginess and rapidly rising heat, he looked cool. Michelle wondered how that was possible. Even his suit was crisp and impeccable.

"Dorothy you already know. This is Dan. He's the one who's been lifting Miss Hebert's power."

"Fucker!" Joey yelled.

"Oh, most likely not," Mr. Jones said. "If you were downwind of him, you'd know why."

"Hey!" Hoodie Boy said.

"Why are you telling us this?" Michelle asked. "I mean, can you not see this bubble? Can your boy yank both our powers before I get this bubble off?"

Mr. Jones smiled, and Michelle really wished she hadn't seen it. She'd battled crazy people before. She'd even fought people she was convinced were evil. But Mr. Jones was worse. His eyes were cold and dead. And the suit and all of his smiles couldn't disguise that he was devoid of humanity.

"I thought I was clear, Miss Pond," he said. "Killing me—or even all three of us—won't stop my organization. Consider me an errand boy. I make deliveries, send messages, take out the trash. In the great scheme of things, I am unimportant."

He smiled again. It didn't improve upon repetition.

"For instance," he said. "I could kill young Dan here." Then, in one swift motion, he reached into his jacket, pulled out a Glock, and held it to Hoodie Boy's head.

"Fuck!" Joey said.

"Shit!" Hoodie Boy said.

Michelle let her bubble fly—but Dorothy touched Mr. Jones and Hoodie Boy, and they teleported ten feet to the left. The bubble hit the wrought-iron fence surrounding the park and blew an enormous hole in it.

"Settle down, Miss Pond," Mr. Jones said. "I'm just trying to explain that even useful people reach an end to their usefulness. Dan's been handy, but his power, unlike yours, now appears to be unpredictable. But we adapt."

"Jesus, dude," Hoodie Boy said his voice quavering. "I'll do whatever you want, just don't shoot me."

"Miss Hebert has a very nice power, but her psychological profile is . . . subpar," Mr. Jones continued with a slight smile, ignoring Dan. "She's too unstable to be of any real use to us other than to manipulate you."

Michelle wanted to blow a hole in him but knew that Dorothy would just teleport them again.

That's when Michelle heard it. A faint rustling noise above her.

She looked up and there—spiraling down towards them—were hundreds of zombie birds. Dan, Mr. Jones, and Dorothy followed her gaze.

"How irritating," Mr. Jones said. "Dorothy . . ."

The girl grabbed the back of Dan's hoodie, and they ported. They reappeared next to Joey, and Dan grabbed her hand. Joey shrieked.

The zombie birds suddenly started flying erratically, crashing into one another.

Then Dan screamed, and his face turned red. Veins bulged out from his neck.

"Dan," Mr. Jones said calmly. "You're such a disappointment." He grimaced and leveled his Glock at Dan again. One moldy pigeon flew into Mr. Jones's face, and then Dan and Joey gasped at the same time.

The flock of zombie birds coalesced again and began to lower onto Mr. Jones and Dan.

"You played with my pain, fucker," Joey said. "That wasn't nice."

Dan scrambled to his knees and lunged at Michelle. He touched her bare arm, and there was a terrible wrenching inside her. The world tilted and went grey for a moment. Then the contact was broken, and Michelle staggered backwards. She was empty inside, as if someone had scooped out part of her. It was awful.

Dan made a whimpering noise and fell to his knees as bubbles filled his hands and rose into the zombie birds coming for him. But instead of exploding, the bubbles just kept floating upward as if made from soapy water.

Then Michelle's power flowed back into her like a tidal wave. It filled her up and made her whole. Relief surged into her. She was Bubbles again.

Dan was still on the ground. It was clear to Michelle that his power-snatching ability was spent. So that just left Dorothy and her teleportation, and Mr. Jones and his Glock.

"Little girl," Joey said, her voice cold, "Dorothy's your name? I suggest you bounce back to the fuckers who sent you and you tell them that we're off-limits. Or there will be more of *this*."

And then, in an eyeblink, the zombie flock descended on Mr. Jones and Dan.

Dan just lay there, twitching and crying, as the birds blanketed him. Michelle had a momentary twinge of guilt at seeing him buried under the birds, but then she remembered how she felt when he lifted her power and a cold anger filled her.

Mr. Jones pulled his Glock and began firing, but his bullets were useless against the zombie flock. Then he lowered his gun and aimed at Joey, but it was too late.

The birds engulfed him, and he shrieked as they ripped his flesh. He dropped his gun and began yanking the birds away from his face, tearing them to pieces as he did. But there were too many. And still they rained down on him.

"I'm Hoodoo Mama, fuckers," Joey said. Her tone was icy and imperious. "And this is *my* parish."

Dorothy squeaked, then vanished.

It grew dark, and Michelle looked up again. The sky was filled now with thousands of dead birds blotting out the sun. Crows, pigeons, waterfowl, sparrows, and more that she didn't recognize. She'd never seen Joey resurrect so many dead things at once before.

And when Michelle looked back at Joey, she was filled with awe. The scared and nervous girl Michelle had been trying to protect was gone. Joey's eyes had turned solid black, and her face was filled with rage. It seemed as if she were growing larger and larger. As if she had become a force of nature.

No. She had become a force *beyond* nature.

A force stronger than death.

She had become Hoodoo Mama.

And God help anyone who messed with her.

In the next instant Mr. Jones vanished, enveloped by the zombie flock. He screamed and screamed and screamed. Blood pooled under the mass of birds.

"Oh Jesus!" he shrieked. "Help me! Jesus, help me!"

"Jesus can't save you, fucker," Joey said in a cold voice. "No one can."

Then the mass of birds collapsed as Mr. Jones crumpled to the ground. Even then he kept kicking and screaming.

"Mommy," he cried. "Mommy!" His voice rose up into a high-pitched keen.

Then he fell silent. For almost a minute, one of his feet would pop out of the mass of birds as he kicked and flailed.

But after a while, Mr. Jones stopped doing even that.

And Dan was already still and silent.

Joey turned then and looked at Michelle with a beatific smile on her face.

"I think you were right, Bubbles," she said. "I think I *am* going to be okay."

With that, Joey threw her arms wide open and spun around. Ten thousand zombie birds swirled around her and rose back up to the sky.

George R. R. Martin

Hugo, Nebula, and World Fantasy Award–winner George R. R. Martin, *New York Times* bestselling author of the landmark A Song of Ice and Fire fantasy series, has been called "the American Tolkien."

Born in Bayonne, New Jersey, George R. R. Martin made his first sale in 1971, and soon established himself as one of the most popular SF writers of the seventies. He quickly became a mainstay of the Ben Bova *Analog* with stories such as "With Morning Comes Mistfall," "And Seven Times Never Kill Man," "The Second Kind of Loneliness," "The Storms of Windhaven" (in collaboration with Lisa Tuttle, and later expanded by them into the novel *Windhaven*), "Override," and others, although he also sold to *Amazing, Fantastic, Galaxy, Orbit*, and other markets. One of his *Analog* stories, the striking novella "A Song for Lya," won him his first Hugo Award, in 1974.

By the end of the seventies he had reached the height of his influence as a science fiction writer, and was producing his best work in that category with stories such as the famous "Sandkings," his best-known story, which won both the Nebula and the Hugo in 1980 (he'd later win another Nebula in 1985 for his story "Portraits of His Children"); "The Way of Cross and Dragon," which won a Hugo Award in the same year (making Martin the first author ever to receive two Hugo Awards for fiction in the same year): "Bitterblooms"; "The Stone City"; "Starlady"; and others. These stories would be collected in *Sandkings,* one of the strongest collections of the period. By now he had mostly moved away from *Analog*, although he would have a long sequence of stories about the droll interstellar adventures of Haviland Tuf (later collected in *Tuf Voyaging*) running throughout the eighties in the Stanley Schmidt *Analog,* as well as a few strong individual pieces such as the novella "Nightflyers." Most of his major work of the late seventies and early eighties, though, would appear in *Omni.* The late seventies and eighties also saw the publication of his memorable novel *Dying of the Light,* his only solo SF novel, while his stories were collected in *A Song for Lya, Sandkings, Songs of Stars and Shadows, Songs the Dead Men Sing, Nightflyers,* and *Portraits of His Children.* By the beginning of the eighties he'd moved away from SF and into the horror genre, publishing the big horror novel *Fevre Dream,* and winning the Bram Stoker Award for his horror story "The Pear-Shaped Man" and the World Fantasy Award for his werewolf novella "The Skin Trade." By the end of that decade, though, the crash of the horror market and the commercial failure of his ambitious horror novel *The Armageddon Rag* had driven him out of the print world and to a successful career in television instead, where for more than a decade he worked as story editor or producer on such shows as the new *Twilight Zone* and *Beauty and the Beast.*

After years away, Martin made a triumphant return to the print world in 1996 with the publication of the immensely successful fantasy novel *A Game of Thrones,* the start of his Song of Ice and Fire sequence. A freestanding novella taken from that work, "Blood of the Dragon," won Martin another Hugo Award in 1997. Further books in the Song of Ice and Fire series—*A Clash of Kings, A Storm of Swords, A Feast for Crows,* and *A Dance with Dragons,* have made it one of the most popular, acclaimed, and bestselling series in all of modern fantasy. Recently, the books were made into an HBO TV series, *Game of Thrones,* which has become one of the most popular and acclaimed shows on television, and made Martin a recognizable figure well outside of the usual genre boundaries, even inspiring a satirical version of him on *Saturday Night Live.* Martin's most recent books are the latest book in the Ice and Fire series, *A Dance with Dragons;* a massive retrospective collection spanning the entire spectrum of his career, *GRRM: A RRetrospective;* a novella collection, *Starlady and Fast-Friend;* a novel written in collaboration with Gardner Dozois and Daniel Abraham, *Hunter's Run;* and, as editor, several anthologies edited in collaboration with Gardner Dozois, including *Warriors, Songs of the Dying Earth, Songs of Love and Death,* and *Down These Strange Streets,* and several new volumes in his long-running Wild Cards anthology series, including *Suicide Kings* and *Fort Freak.* In 2012, Martin was given the Life Achievement Award by the World Fantasy Convention.

Here he takes us to the turbulent land of Westeros, home to his Ice and Fire series, for the bloody story of a clash between two very dangerous women whose bitter rivalry and ambition plunges all of Westeros disastrously into war.

THE PRINCESS AND THE QUEEN, OR, THE BLACKS AND THE GREENS

Being A History of the Causes, Origins, Battles, and Betrayals of that Most Tragic Bloodletting Known as the Dance of the Dragons, as set down by Archmaester Gyldayn of the Citadel of Oldtown

(here transcribed by GEORGE R. R. MARTIN)

The Dance of the Dragons is the flowery name bestowed upon the savage internecine struggle for the Iron Throne of Westeros fought between two rival branches of House Targaryen during the years 129 to 131 AC. To characterize the dark, turbulent, bloody doings of this period as a "dance" strikes us as grotesquely inappropriate. No doubt the phrase originated with some singer. "The Dying of the Dragons" would be altogether more fitting, but tradition and time have burned the more poetic usage into the pages of history, so we must dance along with the rest.

There were two principal claimants to the Iron Throne upon the death of King Viserys I Targaryen: his daughter Rhaenyra, the only surviving child of his first marriage, and Aegon, his eldest son by his second wife. Amidst the chaos and carnage brought on by their rivalry, other would-be kings would stake claims as well, strutting about like mummers on a stage for a fortnight or a moon's turn, only to fall as swiftly as they had arisen.

The Dance split the Seven Kingdoms in two, as lords, knights, and smallfolk declared for one side or the other and took up arms against each other. Even House Targaryen itself became divided, when the kith, kin, and children of each of the claimants became embroiled in the fighting. Over the two years of struggle, a terrible toll was taken of the great lords of Westeros, together with their bannermen, knights, and smallfolk. Whilst the dynasty survived, the end of the fighting saw Targaryen power much diminished, and the world's last dragons vastly reduced in number.

The Dance was a war unlike any other ever fought in the long history of the Seven Kingdoms. Though armies marched and met in savage battle, much of the slaughter took place on water, and . . . especially . . . in the air, as dragon fought dragon with tooth and claw and flame. It was a war marked by stealth, murder, and betrayal as well, a war fought in shadows and stairwells, council chambers and castle yards, with knives and lies and poison.

Long simmering, the conflict burst into the open on the third day of third moon of 129 AC, when the ailing, bedridden King Viserys I Targaryen closed his eyes for a nap in the Red Keep of King's Landing, and died without waking. His body was discovered by a serving man at the hour of the bat, when it was the king's custom to take a cup of hippocras. The servant ran to inform Queen Alicent, whose apartments were on the floor below the king's.

The manservant delivered his dire tidings directly to the queen, and her alone, without raising a general alarum; the king's death had been anticipated for some time, and Queen Alicent and her party, the so-called greens*, had taken care to instruct all of Viserys's guards and servants in what to do when the day came.

Queen Alicent went at once to the king's bedchamber, accompanied by Ser Criston Cole, Lord Commander of the Kingsguard. Once they had confirmed that Viserys was dead, Her Grace ordered his room sealed and placed under guard. The serving man who had found the king's body was taken into

---

* In 111 AC, a great tourney was held at King's Landing on the fifth anniversary of the king's marriage to Queen Alicent. At the opening feast, the queen wore a green gown, whilst the princess dressed dramatically in Targaryen red and black. Note was taken, and thereafter it became the custom to refer to "greens" and "blacks" when talking of the queen's party and the party of the princess, respectively. In the tourney itself, the blacks had much the better of it when Ser Criston Cole, wearing Princess Rhaenyra's favor unhorsed all of the queen's champions, including two of her cousins and her youngest brother, Ser Gwayne Hightower.

custody, to make certain he did not spread the tale. Ser Criston returned to White Sword Tower and sent his brothers of the Kingsguard to summon the members of the king's small council. It was the hour of the owl.

Then as now, the Sworn Brotherhood of the Kingsguard consisted of seven knights, men of proven loyalty and undoubted prowess who had taken solemn oaths to devote their lives to defending the king's person and kin. Only five of the white cloaks were in King's Landing at the time of Viserys's death; Ser Criston himself, Ser Arryk Cargyll, Ser Rickard Thorne, Ser Steffon Darklyn, and Ser Willis Fell. Ser Erryk Cargyll (twin to Ser Arryk) and Ser Lorent Marbrand, with Princess Rhaenyra on Dragonstone, remained unaware and uninvolved as their brothers-in-arms went forth into the night to rouse the members of the small council from their beds.

Gathering in the queen's chambers as the body of her lord husband grew cold above were Queen Alicent herself; her father Ser Otto Hightower, Hand of the King; Ser Criston Cole, Lord Commander of the Kingsguard; Grand Maester Orwyle; Lord Lyman Beesbury, master of coin, a man of eighty; Ser Tyland Lannister, master of ships, brother to the Lord of Casterly Rock; Larys Strong, called Larys Clubfoot, Lord of Harrenhal, master of whisperers; and Lord Jasper Wylde, called Ironrod, master of laws.

Grand Maester Orwyle opened the meeting by reviewing the customary tasks and procedures required at the death of a king. He said, "Septon Eustace should be summoned to perform the last rites and pray for the king's soul. A raven must needs be sent to Dragonstone at once to inform Princess Rhaenyra of her father's passing. Mayhaps Her Grace the queen would care to write the message, so as to soften these sad tidings with some words of condolence? The bells are always rung to announce the death of a king, someone should see to that, and of course we must begin to make our preparations for Queen Rhaenyra's coronation—"

Ser Otto Hightower cut him off. "All this must needs wait," he declared, "until the question of succession is settled." As the King's Hand, he was empowered to speak with the king's voice, even to sit the Iron Throne in the king's absence. Viserys had granted him the authority to rule over the Seven Kingdoms, and "until such time as our new king is crowned," that rule would continue.

"Until our new *queen* is crowned," Lord Beesbury said, in a waspish tone.

"*King,*" insisted Queen Alicent. "The Iron Throne by rights must pass to His Grace's eldest trueborn son."

The discussion that followed lasted nigh unto dawn. Lord Beesbury spoke on behalf of Princess Rhaenyra. The ancient master of coin, who had served King Viserys for his entire reign, and his grandfather Jaehaerys the Old King before him, reminded the council that Rhaenyra was older than her brothers and had more Targaryen blood, that the late king had chosen her as his successor, that he had repeatedly refused to alter the succession despite the pleadings of Queen Alicent and her greens, that hundreds of lords and landed knights had done obeisance to the princess in 105 AC, and sworn solemn oaths to defend her rights.

But these words fell on ears made of stone. Ser Tyland pointed out that many of the lords who had sworn to defend the succession of Princess Rhaenyra were long dead. "It has been twenty-four years," he said. "I myself swore no such oath. I was a child at the time." Ironrod, the master of laws, cited the Great Council of 101 and the Old King's choice of Baelon rather than Rhaenys in 92, then discoursed at length about Aegon the Conquerer and his sisters, and the hallowed Andal tradition wherein the rights of a trueborn son always came before the rights of a mere daughter. Ser Otto reminded them that Rhaenyra's husband was none other than Prince Daemon, and "we all know that one's nature. Make no mistake, should Rhaenyra ever sit the Iron Throne, it will be Daemon who rules us, a king consort as cruel and unforgiving as Maegor ever was. My own head will be the first cut off, I do not doubt, but your queen, my daughter, will soon follow."

Queen Alicent echoed him. "Nor will they spare my children," she declared. "Aegon and his brothers are the king's trueborn sons, with a better claim to the throne than her brood of bastards. Daemon will find some pretext to put them all to death. Even Helaena and her little ones. One of these Strongs put out Aemond's eye, never forget. He was a boy, aye, but the boy is the father to the man, and bastards are monstrous by nature."

Ser Criston Cole spoke up. Should the princess reign, he reminded them, Jacaerys Velaryon would rule after her. "Seven save this realm if we seat a bastard on the Iron Throne." He spoke of Rhaenyra's wanton ways and the infamy of her husband. "They will turn the Red Keep into a brothel. No man's daughter will be safe, nor any man's wife. Even the boys . . . we know what Laenor was."

It is not recorded that Lord Larys Strong spoke a word during this debate, but that was not unusual. Though glib of tongue when need be, the master of whisperers hoarded his words like a miser hoarding coins, preferring to listen rather than talk.

"If we do this," Grand Maester Orwyle cautioned the council, "it must surely lead to war. The princess will not meekly stand aside, and she has dragons."

"And friends," Lord Beesbury declared. "Men of honor, who will not forget the vows they swore to her and her father. I am an old man, but not so old that I will sit here meekly whilst the likes of you plot to steal her crown." And so saying, he rose to go.

But Ser Criston Cole forced Lord Beesbury back into his seat and opened his throat with a dagger.

And so the first blood shed in the Dance of the Dragons belonged to Lord Lyman Beesbury, master of coin and lord treasurer of the Seven Kingdoms.

No further dissent was heard after the death of Lord Beesbury. The rest of the night was spent making plans for the new king's coronation (it must be done quickly, all agreed), and drawing up lists of possible allies and potential enemies, should Princess Rhaenyra refuse to accept King Aegon's ascension. With the princess in confinement on Dragonstone, about to give birth, Queen Alicent's greens enjoyed an advantage; the longer Rhaenyra remained ignorant of the king's death, the slower she would be to move. "Mayhaps the whore will die in childbirth," Queen Alicent said.

No ravens flew that night. No bells rang. Those servants who knew of the king's passing were sent to the dungeons. Ser Criston Cole was given the task of taking into custody such "blacks" who remained at court, those lords and knights who might be inclined to favor Princess Rhaenyra. "Do them no violence, unless they resist," Ser Otto Hightower commanded. "Such men as bend the knee and swear fealty to King Aegon shall suffer no harm at our hands."

"And those who will not?" asked Grand Maester Orwyle.

"Are traitors," said Ironrod, "and must die a traitor's death."

Lord Larys Strong, master of whisperers, then spoke for the first and only time. "Let us be the first to swear," he said, "lest there be traitors here amongst us." Drawing his dagger, the Clubfoot drew it across his palm. "A blood oath," he urged, "to bind us all together, brothers unto death." And so each of the conspirators slashed their palms and clasped hands with one another, swearing brotherhood. Queen Alicent alone amongst them was excused from the oath, on the account of her womanhood.

Dawn was breaking over the city before Queen Alicent dispatched the Kingsguard to bring her sons to the council. Prince Daeron, the gentlest of her children, wept for his grandsire's passing. One-eyed Prince Aemond, nineteen, was found in the armory, donning plate and mail for his morning practice in the castle yard. "Is Aegon king," he asked Ser Willis Fell, "or must we kneel and kiss the old whore's cunny?" Princess Helaena was breaking her fast with her children when the Kingsguard came to her . . . but when asked the whereabouts of Prince Aegon, her brother and husband, said only, "He is not in my bed, you may be sure. Feel free to search beneath the blankets."

Prince Aegon was with a paramour when he was found. At first, the prince refused to be a part of his mother's plans. "My sister is the heir, not me," he said. "What sort of brother steals his sister's birthright?" Only when Ser Criston convinced him that the princess must surely execute him and his brothers should she don the crown did Aegon waver. "Whilst any trueborn Targaryen yet lives, no Strong can ever hope to sit the Iron Throne," Cole said. "Rhaenyra has no choice but to take your heads if she wishes her bastards to rule after her." It was this, and only this, that persuaded Aegon to accept the crown that the small council was offering him,

Ser Tyland Lannister was named master of coin in place of the late Lord Beesbury, and acted at once to seize the royal treasury. The crown's gold was divided into four parts. One part was entrusted to the care of the Iron Bank of Braavos for safekeeping, another sent under strong guard to Casterly Rock, a third to Oldtown. The remaining wealth was to be used for bribes and gifts, and to hire sellswords if needed. To take Ser Tyland's place as master of ships, Ser Otto looked to the Iron Islands, dispatching a raven to Dalton Greyjoy, the Red Kraken, the daring and bloodthirsty sixteen-year-old Lord Reaper of Pyke, offering him the admiralty and a seat on the council for his allegiance.

A day passed, then another. Neither septons nor silent sisters were summoned to the bedchamber where King Viserys lay, swollen and rotting. No bells rang. Ravens flew, but not to Dragonstone. They went instead to Oldtown, to Casterly Rock, to Riverrun, to Highgarden, and to many other lords and knights whom Queen Alicent had cause to think might be sympathetic to her son.

The annals of the Great Council of 101 were brought forth and examined, and note was made of which lords had spoken for Viserys, and which for Rhaenys, Laena, or Laenor. The lords assembled had favored the male claimant over the female by twenty to one, but there had been dissenters, and those same houses were most like to lend Princess Rhaenyra their support should it come to war. The princess would have the Sea Snake and his fleets, Ser Otto judged, and like as not the other lords of the eastern shores as well: Lords Bar Emmon, Massey, Celtigar, and Crabb most like, perhaps even the Evenstar of Tarth. All were lesser powers, save for the Velaryons. The northmen were a greater concern: Winterfell had spoken for Rhaenys at Harrenhal, as had Lord Stark's bannermen, Dustin of Barrowton and Manderly of White Harbor. Nor could House Arryn be relied upon, for the Eyrie was presently ruled by a woman, Lady Jeyne, the Maiden of the Vale, whose own rights might be called into question should Princess Rhaenyra be put aside.

The greatest danger was deemed to be Storm's End, for House Baratheon had always been staunch in support of the claims of Princess Rhaenys and her children. Though old Lord Boremund had died, his son Borros was even more belligerent than his father, and the lesser storm lords would surely follow wherever he led. "Then we must see that he leads them to our king," Queen Alicent declared. Whereupon she sent for her second son.

Thus it was not a raven who took flight for Storm's End that day, but Vhagar, oldest and largest of the dragons of Westeros. On her back rode Prince Aemond Targaryen, with a sapphire in the place of his missing eye. "Your purpose is to win the hand of one of Lord Baratheon's daughters," his grandsire Ser Otto told him, before he flew. "Any of the four will do. Woo her and wed her, and Lord Borros will deliver the stormlands for your brother. Fail—"

"I will not fail," Prince Aemond blustered. "Aegon will have Storm's End, and I will have this girl."

By the time Prince Aemond took his leave, the stink from the dead king's bedchamber had wafted all through Maegor's Holdfast, and many wild tales and rumors were spreading through the court and castle. The dungeons under the Red Keep had swallowed up so many men suspected of disloyalty that even the High Septon had begun to wonder at these disappearances, and sent word from the Starry Sept of Oldtown asking after some of the missing. Ser Otto Hightower, as methodical a man as ever served as Hand, wanted more time to make preparations, but Queen Alicent knew they could delay no longer. Prince Aegon had grown weary of secrecy. "Am I a king, or no?" he demanded of his mother. "If I am king, then crown me."

The bells began to ring on the tenth day of the third moon of 129 AC, tolling the end of a reign. Grand Maester Orwyle was at last allowed to send forth his ravens, and the black birds took to the air by the hundreds, spreading the word of Aegon's ascension to every far corner of the realm. The silent sisters were sent for, to prepare the corpse for burning, and riders went forth on pale horses to spread the word to the people of King's Landing, crying, "King Viserys is dead, long live King Aegon." Hearing the cries, some wept whilst others cheered, but most of the smallfolk stared in silence, confused and wary, and now and again a voice cried out, "Long live our queen."

Meanwhile, hurried preparations were made for the coronation. The Dragonpit was chosen as the site. Under its mighty dome were stone benches sufficient to seat eighty thousand, and the pit's thick walls, strong roof, and towering bronze doors made it defensible, should traitors attempt to disrupt the ceremony.

On the appointed day Ser Criston Cole placed the iron-and-ruby crown of Aegon the Conquerer upon the brow of the eldest son of King Viserys and Queen Alicent, proclaiming him Aegon of House Targaryen, Second of His Name, King of the Andals and the Rhoynar and the First Men, Lord of the Seven Kingdoms, and Protector of the Realm. His mother Queen Alicent, beloved of the smallfolk, placed her own crown upon the head of her daughter Helaena, Aegon's wife and sister. After kissing her cheeks, the mother knelt before the daughter, bowed her head, and said, "My queen."

With the High Septon in Oldtown, too old and frail to journey to King's Landing, it fell to Septon Eustace to anoint King Aegon's brow with holy oils, and bless him in the seven names of god. A few of those in attendance, with sharper eyes than most, may have noticed that there were but four white cloaks in attendance on the new king, not five as heretofore. Aegon II had suffered his first defections the night before, when Ser Steffon Darklyn of the Kingsguard had slipped from the city with his squire, two stewards, and four guardsmen. Under the cover of darkness they made their way out a postern gate to where a fisherman's skiff awaited to take them to Dragonstone. They brought with them a stolen crown: a band of yellow gold ornamented with seven gems of different colors. This was the crown King Viserys had worn, and the Old King Jaehaerys before him. When Prince Aegon had decided to wear the iron-and-ruby crown of his namesake, the Conquerer, Queen Alicent had ordered Viserys's crown locked away, but the steward entrusted with the task had made off with it instead.

After the coronation, the remaining Kingsguard escorted Aegon to his mount, a splendid creature with gleaming golden scales and pale pink wing membranes. Sunfyre was the name given this dragon of the golden dawn. Munkun tells us the king flew thrice around the city before landing inside the walls of the Red Keep. Ser Arryk Cargyll led His Grace into the torchlit throne room, where Aegon II mounted the steps of the Iron Throne before a thousand lords and knights. Shouts rang through the hall.

On Dragonstone, no cheers were heard. Instead, screams echoed through the halls and stairwells of Sea Dragon Tower, down from the queen's apartments where Rhaenyra Targaryen strained and shuddered in her third day of labor. The child had not been due for another turn of the moon, but the tidings from King's Landing had driven the princess into a black fury, and her rage seemed to bring on the birth, as if the babe inside her were angry too, and fighting to get out. The princess shrieked curses all through her labor, calling down the wroth of the gods upon her half brothers and their mother the queen, and detailing the torments she would inflict upon them before she would let them die. She cursed the child inside her too. "*Get out*," she screamed, clawing at her swollen belly as her maester and her midwife tried to restrain her. "*Monster, monster, get out, get out, GET OUT!*"

When the babe at last came forth, she proved indeed a monster: a stillborn girl, twisted and malformed, with a hole in her chest where her heart should have been and a stubby, scaled tail. The dead girl had been named Visenya, Princess Rhaenyra announced the next day, when milk of the poppy had blunted the edge of her pain. "She was my only daughter, and they killed her. They stole my crown and murdered my daughter, and they shall answer for it."

And so the dance began, as the princess called a council of her own. "The black council," setting it against the "green council" of King's Landing. Rhaenyra herself presided, with her uncle and husband Prince Daemon. Her three sons were present with them, though none had reached the age of manhood (Jace was fifteen, Luke fourteen, Joffrey twelve). Two Kingsguard stood with them: Ser Erryk Cargyll, twin to Ser Arryk, and the westerman, Ser Lorent Marbrand. Thirty knights, a hundred cross-bowmen, and three hundred men-at-arms made up the rest of Dragonstone's garrison. That had always been deemed sufficient for a fortress of such strength. "As an instrument of conquest, however, our army leaves somewhat to be desired," Prince Daemon observed sourly.

A dozen lesser lords, bannermen and vassals to Dragonstone, sat at the black council as well: Celtigar of Claw Isle, Staunton of Rook's Rest, Massey of Stonedance, Bar Emmon of Sharp Point, and Darklyn of Duskendale amongst them. But the greatest lord to pledge his strength to the princess was Corlys Velaryon of Driftmark. Though the Sea Snake had grown old, he liked to say that he was clinging to life "like a drowning sailor clinging to the wreckage of a sunken ship. Mayhaps the Seven have preserved me for this one last fight." With Lord Corlys came his wife Princess Rhaenys, five-and-fifty, her face lean and lined, her silver hair streaked with white, yet fierce and fearless as she had been at two-and-twenty—a woman sometimes known among the smallfolk as "The Queen Who Never Was."

Those who sat at the black council counted themselves loyalists, but knew full well that King Aegon II would name them traitors. Each had already received a summons from King's Landing, demanding they present themselves at the Red Keep to swear oaths of loyalty to the new king. All their hosts combined could not match the power the Hightowers alone could field. Aegon's greens enjoyed other advantages as well. Oldtown, King's Landing, and Lannisport were the largest and richest cities in the realm; all three were held by greens. Every visible symbol of legitimacy belonged to Aegon. He sat the Iron Throne. He lived in the Red Keep. He wore the Conquerer's crown, wielded the Conquerer's sword, and had been anointed by a septon of the Faith before the eyes of tens of thousands. Grand Maester Orwyle sat in his councils, and the Lord Commander of the Kingsguard had placed the crown upon his princely head. And he was male, which in the eyes of many made him the rightful king, his half sister the usurper.

Against all that, Rhaenyra's advantages were few. Some older lords might yet recall the oaths they had sworn when she was made Princess of Dragonstone and named her father's heir. There had been a time when she had been well loved by highborn and commons alike, when they had cheered her as the Realm's Delight. Many a young lord and noble knight had sought her favor then . . . though how many would still fight for her, now that she was a woman wed, her body aged and thickened by six childbirths, was a question none could answer. Though her half brother had looted their father's treasury, the princess had at her disposal the wealth of House Velaryon, and the Sea Snake's fleets gave her superiority at sea. And her consort Prince Daemon, tried and tempered in the Stepstones, had more experience of warfare than all their foes combined. Last, but far from least, Rhaenyra had her dragons.

"As does Aegon," Lord Staunton pointed out.

"We have more," said Princess Rhaenys, the Queen Who Never Was, who had been a dragonrider longer than all of them. "And ours are larger and stronger, but for Vhagar. Dragons thrive best here on Dragonstone." She enumerated for the council. King Aegon had his Sunfyre. A splendid beast, though young. Aemond One-Eye rode Vhagar, and the peril posed by Queen Visenya's mount could not be gainsaid. Queen Helaena's mount was Dreamfyre, the she-dragon who had once borne the Old King's sister Rhaena through the clouds. Prince Daeron's dragon was Tessarion, with her wings dark as cobalt and her claws and crest and belly scales as bright as beaten copper. "That makes four dragons of fighting size," said Rhaenys. Queen Helaena's twins had their own dragons too, but no more than hatchlings; the usurper's youngest son, Maelor, was possessed only of an egg.

Against that, Prince Daemon had Caraxes and Princess Rhaenyra Syrax, both huge and formidable beasts. Caraxes especially was fearsome, and no stranger to blood and fire after the Stepstones. Rhaenyra's three sons by Laenor Velaryon were all dragonriders; Vermax, Arrax, and Tyraxes were thriving, and growing larger every year. Aegon the Younger, eldest of Rhaenyra's two sons by Prince Daemon, commanded the young dragon Stormcloud, though he had yet to mount him; his little brother Viserys went everywhere with his egg. Rhaenys's own she-dragon, Meleys the Red Queen, had grown lazy, but remained fearsome when roused. Prince Daemon's twins by Laena Velaryon might yet be dragonriders too. Baela's dragon, the slender pale green Moondancer, would soon be large enough to bear the girl upon her back . . . and though her sister Rhaena's egg had hatched a broken thing that died within hours of emerging from the egg, Syrax had recently produced another clutch. One of her eggs had been given to Rhaena, and it was said that the girl slept with it every night, and prayed for a dragon to match her sister's.

Moreover, six other dragons made their lairs in the smoky caverns of the Dragonmont above the castle. There was Silverwing, Good Queen Alysanne's mount of old; Seasmoke, the pale grey beast that had been the pride and passion of Ser Laenor Velaryon; hoary old Vermithor, unridden since the death of King Jaehaerys. And back of the mountain dwelled three wild dragons, never claimed nor ridden by any man, living or dead. The smallfolk had named them Sheepstealer, Grey Ghost, and the Cannibal. "Find riders to master Silverwing, Vermithor, and Seasmoke, and we will have nine dragons against Aegon's four. Mount and fly their wild kin, and we will number twelve, even without Stormcloud," Princess Rhaenys pointed out. "That is how we shall win this war."

Lords Celtigar and Staunton agreed. Aegon the Conquerer and his sisters had proved that knights and armies could not stand against the fire of dragons. Celtigar urged the princess to fly against King's Landing at once, and reduce the city to ash and bone. "And how will that serve us, my lord?" the Sea Snake demanded of him. "We want to rule the city, not burn it to the ground."

"It will never come to that," Celtigar insisted. "The usurper will have no choice but to oppose us with his own dragons. Our nine must surely overwhelm his four."

"At what cost?" Princess Rhaenyra wondered. "My sons would be riding three of those dragons, I remind you. And it would not be nine against four. I will not be strong enough to fly for some time yet. And who is to ride Silverwing, Vermithor, and Seasmoke? You, my lord? I hardly think so. It will be five against four, and one of their four will be Vhagar. That is no advantage."

Surprisingly, Prince Daemon agreed with his wife. "In the Stepstones, my enemies learned to run and hide when they saw Caraxes's wings or heard his roar . . . but they had no dragons of their own. It is no easy thing for a man to be a dragonslayer. But *dragons* can kill dragons, and have. Any maester who has ever studied the history of Valyria can tell you that. I will not throw our dragons against the usurper's unless I have no other choice. There are other ways to use them, better ways." Then the prince laid his own strategies before the black council. Rhaenyra must have a coronation of her own, to answer Aegon's. Afterward they would send out ravens, calling on the lords of the Seven Kingdoms to declare their allegiance to their true queen.

"We must fight this war with words before we go to battle," the prince declared. The lords of the Great Houses held the key to victory, Daemon insisted; their bannermen and vassals would follow where they led. Aegon the Usurper had won the allegiance of the Lannisters of Casterly Rock, and Lord Tyrell of Highgarden was a mewling boy in swaddling clothes whose mother, acting as his regent, would most like align the Reach with her overmighty bannermen, the Hightowers . . . but the rest of the realm's great lords had yet to declare.

"Storm's End will stand with us," Princess Rhaenys declared. She herself was of that blood on her mother's side, and the late Lord Boremund had always been the staunchest of friends.

Prince Daemon had good reason to hope that the Maid of the Vale might bring the Eyrie to their side as well. Aegon would surely seek the support of Pyke, he judged; only the Iron Islands could hope to match the strength of House Velaryon at sea. But the ironmen were notoriously fickle, and Dalton Greyjoy loved blood and battle; he might easily be persuaded to support the princess.

The north was too remote to be of much import in the fight, the council judged; by the time the Starks gathered their banners and marched south, the war might well be over. Which left only the riverlords, a notoriously quarrelsome lot ruled over, in name at least, by House Tully of Riverrun. "We have friends in the riverlands," the prince said, "though not all of them dare show their colors yet. We need a place where they can gather, a toehold on the mainland large enough to house a sizeable host, and strong enough to hold against whatever forces the usurper can send against us." He showed the lords a map. "Here. Harrenhal."

And so it was decided. Prince Daemon would lead the assault on Harrenhal, riding Caraxes. Princess Rhaenyra would remain on Dragonstone until she had recovered her strength. The Velaryon fleet would close off the Gullet, sallying forth from Dragonstone and Driftmark to block all shipping entering or leaving Blackwater Bay. "We do not have the strength to take King's Landing by storm," Prince Daemon said, "no more than our foes could hope to capture Dragonstone. But Aegon is a green boy, and green boys are easily provoked. Mayhaps we can goad him into a rash attack." The Sea Snake would command the fleet, whilst Princess Rhaenys flew overhead to keep their foes from attacking their ships with dragons. Meanwhile, ravens would go forth to Riverrun, the Eyrie, Pyke, and Storm's End, to gain the allegiance of their lords.

Then up spoke the queen's eldest son, Jacaerys. "*We* should bear those messages," he said. "Dragons will win the lords over quicker than ravens." His brother Lucerys agreed, insisting that he and Jace were men, or near enough to make no matter. "Our uncle calls us Strongs, and claims that we are bastards, but when the lords see us on dragonback they will know that for a lie. Only *Targaryens* ride dragons." Even young Joffrey chimed in, offering to mount his own dragon Tyraxes and join his brothers.

Princess Rhaenyra forbade that; Joff was but twelve. But Jacaerys was fifteen, Lucerys fourteen; strong and strapping lads, skilled in arms, who had long served as squires. "If you go, you go as messengers, not as knights," she told them. "You must take no part in any fighting." Not until both boys had sworn solemn oaths upon a copy of *The Seven-Pointed Star* would Her Grace consent to using them as her envoys. It was decided that Jace, being the older of the two, would take the longer, more dangerous task, flying first to the Eyrie to treat with the Lady of the Vale, then to White Harbor to win over Lord Manderly, and lastly to Winterfell to meet with Lord Stark. Luke's mission would be shorter and safer; he was to fly to Storm's End, where it was expected that Borros Baratheon would give him a warm welcome.

A hasty coronation was held the next day. The arrival of Ser Steffon Darklyn, late of Aegon's Kingsguard, was an occasion of much joy on Dragonstone, especially when it was learned that he and his fellow loyalists ("turncloaks," Ser Otto would name them, when offering a reward for their capture) had brought the stolen crown of King Jaehaerys the Conciliator. Three hundred sets of eyes looked on as Prince Daemon Targaryen placed the Old King's crown on the head of his wife, proclaiming her Rhaenyra of House Targaryen, First of Her Name, Queen of the Andals, the Rhoynar, and the First Men. The prince claimed for himself the style Protector of the Realm, and Rhaenyra named her eldest son, Jacaerys, the Prince of Dragonstone and heir to the Iron Throne.

Her first act as queen was to declare Ser Otto Hightower and Queen Alicent traitors and rebels. "As for my half brothers, and my sweet sister Helaena," she announced, "they have been led astray by the counsel of evil men. Let them come to Dragonstone, bend the knee, and ask my forgiveness, and I shall gladly spare their lives and take them back into my heart, for they are of my own blood, and no man or woman is as accursed as the kinslayer."

Word of Rhaenyra's coronation reached the Red Keep the next day, to the great displeasure of Aegon II. "My half sister and my uncle are guilty of high treason," the young king declared. "I want them attainted, I want them arrested, and I want them dead."

Cooler heads on the green council wished to parlay. "The princess must be made to see that her cause is hopeless," Grand Maester Orwyle said. "Brother should not war against sister. Send me to her, that we may talk and reach an amicable accord."

Aegon would not hear of it. Septon Eustace tells us that His Grace accused the grand maester of disloyalty and spoke of having him thrown into a black cell "with your black friends." But when the two queens—his mother Queen Alicent and his wife Queen Helaena—spoke in favor of Orwyle's proposal, the king gave way reluctantly. So Grand Maester Orwyle was dispatched across Blackwater Bay under a peace banner, leading a retinue that included Ser Arryk Cargyll of the Kingsguard and Ser Gwayne Hightower of the gold cloaks, along with a score of scribes and septons.

The terms offered by the king were generous. If the princess would acknowledge him as king and make obeisance before the Iron Throne, Aegon II would confirm her in her possession of Dragonstone, and allow the island and castle to pass to her son Jacaerys upon her death. Her second son, Lucerys, would be recognized as the rightful heir to Driftmark, and the lands and holdings of House Velaryon; her boys by Prince Daemon, Aegon the Younger and Viserys, would be given places of honor at court, the former as the king's squire, the latter as his cupbearer. Pardons would be granted to those lords and knights who had conspired treasonously with her against their true king.

Rhaenyra heard these terms in stony silence, then asked Orwyle if he remembered her father, King Viserys. "Of course, Your Grace," the maester answered. "Perhaps you can tell us who he named as his heir and successor," the queen said, her crown upon her head. "You, Your Grace," Orwyle replied. And Rhaenyra nodded and said, "With your own tongue you admit I am your lawful queen. Why then do you serve my half brother, the pretender? Tell my half brother that I will have my throne, or I will have his head," she said, sending the envoys on their way.

Aegon II was two-and-twenty, quick to anger and slow to forgive. Rhaenyra's refusal to accept his rule enraged him. "I offered her an honorable peace, and the whore spat in my face," he declared. "What happens now is on her own head."

Even as he spoke, the Dance began. On Driftmark, the Sea Snake's ships set sail from Hull and Spicetown to close the Gullet, choking off trade to and from King's Landing. Soon after, Jacaerys Velaryon was flying north upon his dragon, Vermax, his brother Lucerys south on Arrax, whilst Prince Daemon rode Caraxes to the Trident.

Harrenhal had already once proved vulnerable from the sky, when Aegon the Dragon had overthrown it. Its elderly castellan Ser Simon Strong was quick to strike his banners when Caraxes lighted atop Kingspyre Tower. In addition to the castle, Prince Daemon at a stroke had captured the not-inconsiderable wealth of House Strong and a dozen valuable hostages, amongst them Ser Simon and his grandsons.

Meanwhile, Prince Jacaerys flew north on his dragon, calling upon Lady Arryn of the Vale, Lord Manderly of White Harbor, Lord Borrell and Lord Sunderland of Sisterton, and Cregan Stark of Winterfell. So charming was the prince, and so fearsome his dragon, that each of the lords he visited pledged their support for his mother.

Had his brother's "shorter, safer" flight gone as well, much bloodshed and grief might well have been averted.

The tragedy that befell Lucerys Velaryon at Storm's End was never planned, on this all of our sources agree. The first battles in the Dance of the Dragons were fought with quills and ravens, with threats and promises, decrees and blandishments. The murder of Lord Beesbury at the green council was not yet widely known; most believed his lordship to be languishing in some dungeon. Whilst sundry familiar faces were no longer seen about court, no heads had appeared above the castle gates, and many still hoped that that the question of succession might be resolved peaceably.

The Stranger had other plans. For surely it was his dread hand behind the ill chance that brought the two princelings together at Storm's End, when the dragon Arrax raced before a gathering storm to deliver Lucerys Velaryon to the safety of the castle yard, only to find Aemond Targaryen there before him.

Prince Aemond's mighty dragon Vhagar sensed his coming first. Guardsman walking the battlements of the castle's mighty curtain walls clutched their spears in sudden terror when she woke, with a roar that shook the very foundations of Durran's Defiance. Even Arrax quailed before that sound, we are told, and Luke plied his whip freely as he forced him down.

Lightning was flashing to the east and a heavy rain falling as Lucerys leapt off his dragon, his mother's message clutched in his hand. He must surely have known what Vhagar's presence meant, so it would have come as no surprise when Aemond Targaryen confronted him in the Round Hall, before the eyes of Lord Borros, his four daughters, septon, and maester, and two score knights, guards, and servants.

"Look at this sad creature, my lord," Prince Aemond called out. "Little Luke Strong, the bastard." To Luke he said, "You are wet, bastard. Is it raining, or did you piss yourself in fear?"

Lucerys Velaryon addressed himself only to Lord Baratheon. "Lord Borros, I have brought you a message from my mother, the queen."

"The whore of Dragonstone, he means." Prince Aemond strode forward, and made to snatch the letter from Lucerys's hand, but Lord Borros roared a command and his knights intervened, pulling the princelings apart. One brought Rhaenyra's letter to the dais, where his lordship sat upon the throne of the Storm Kings of old.

No man can truly know what Borros Baratheon was feeling at that moment. The accounts of those who were there differ markedly one from the other. Some say his lordship was red-faced and abashed, as a man might be if his lawful wife found him abed with another woman. Others declare that Borros appeared to be relishing the moment, for it pleased his vanity to have both king and queen seeking his support.

Yet all the witnesses agree on what Lord Borros said and did. Never a man of letters, he handed the queen's letter to his maester, who cracked the seal and whispered the message into his lordship's ear. A frown stole across Lord Borros's face. He stroked his beard, scowled at Lucerys Velaryon, and said, "And if I do as your mother bids, which one of my daughters will you marry, boy?" He gestured at the four girls. "Pick one."

Prince Lucerys could only blush. "My lord, I am not free to marry," he replied. "I am betrothed to my cousin Rhaena."

"I thought as much," Lord Borros said. "Go home, pup, and tell the bitch your mother that the Lord of Storm's End is not a dog that she can whistle up at need to set against her foes." And Prince Lucerys turned to take his leave of the Round Hall.

But Prince Aemond drew his sword and said, "Hold, Strong!"

Prince Lucerys recalled his promise to his mother. "I will not fight you. I came here as an envoy, not a knight."

"You came here as a craven and a traitor," Prince Aemond answered. "I will have your life, Strong."

At that Lord Borros grew uneasy. "Not here," he grumbled. "He came an envoy. I want no blood shed beneath my roof." So his guards put themselves between the princelings and escorted Lucerys Velaryon from the Round Hall, back to the castle yard where his dragon Arrax was hunched down in the rain, awaiting his return.

Aemond Targaryen's mouth twisted in rage, and he turned once more to Lord Borros, asking for his leave. The Lord of Storm's End shrugged and answered, "It is not for me to tell you what to do when you are not beneath my roof." And his knights moved aside as Prince Aemond rushed to the doors.

Outside, the storm was raging. Thunder rolled across the castle, the rain fell in blinding sheets, and from time to time great bolts of blue-white lightning lit the world as bright as day. It was bad weather for flying, even for a dragon, and Arrax was struggling to stay aloft when Prince Aemon mounted Vhagar and went after him. Had the sky been calm, Prince Lucerys might have been able to outfly his pursuer, for Arrax was younger and swifter . . . but the day was black, and so it came to pass that the dragons met above Shipbreaker Bay. Watchers on the castle walls saw distant blasts of flame, and heard a shriek cut the thunder. Then the two beasts were locked together, lightning crackling around them. Vhagar was five times the size of her foe, the hardened survivor of a hundred battles. If there was a fight, it could not have lasted long.

Arrax fell, broken, to be swallowed by the storm-lashed waters of the bay. His head and neck washed up beneath the cliffs below Storm's End three days later, to make a feast for crabs and seagulls. Prince Lucerys's corpse washed up as well.

And with his death, the war of ravens and envoys and marriage pacts came to an end, and the war of fire and blood began in earnest.

On Dragonstone, Queen Rhaenyra collapsed when told of Luke's death. Luke's young brother Joffrey (Jace was still away on his mission north) swore a terrible oath of vengeance against Prince Aemond and Lord Borros. Only the intervention of the Sea Snake and Princess Rhaenys kept the boy from mounting his own dragon at once. As the black council sat to consider how to strike back, a raven arrived from Harrenhal. "An eye for an eye, a son for a son," Prince Daemon wrote. "Lucerys shall be avenged."

In his youth, Daemon Targaryen's face and laugh were familiar to every cut-purse, whore, and gambler in Flea Bottom. The prince still had friends in the low places of King's Landing, and followers amongst the gold cloaks. Unbeknownest to King Aegon, the Hand, or the Queen Dowager, he had allies at court as well, even on the green council . . . and one other go-between, a special friend he trusted utterly, who knew the wine sinks and rat pits that festered in the shadow of the Red Keep as well as Daemon himself once had, and moved easily through the shadows of the city. To this pale stranger he reached out now, by secret ways, to set a terrible vengeance into motion.

Amidst the stews of Flea Bottom, Prince Daemon's go-between found suitable instruments. One had been a serjeant in the City Watch; big and brutal, he had lost his gold cloak for beating a whore to death whilst in a drunken rage. The other was a rat-catcher in the Red Keep. Their true names are lost to history. They are remembered as Blood and Cheese.

The hidden doors and secret tunnels that Maegor the Cruel had built were as familiar to the rat-catcher as to the rats he hunted. Using a forgotten passageway, Cheese led Blood into the heart of the castle, unseen by any guard. Some say their quarry was the king himself, but Aegon was accompanied by the Kingsguard wherever he went, and even Cheese knew of no way in and out of Maegor's Holdfast save over the drawbridge that spanned the dry moat and its formidable iron spikes.

The Tower of the Hand was less secure. The two men crept up through the walls, bypassing the spearmen posted at the tower doors. Ser Otto's rooms were of no interest to them. Instead they slipped into his daughter's chambers, one floor below. Queen Alicent had taken up residence there after the death of King Viserys, when her son Aegon moved into Maegor's Holdfast with his own queen. Once inside, Cheese bound and gagged the Dowager Queen whilst Blood strangled her bedmaid. Then they settled down to wait, for they knew it was the custom of Queen Helaena to bring her children to see their grandmother every evening before bed.

Blind to her danger, the queen appeared as dusk was settling over the castle, accompanied by her three children. Jaehaerys and Jaehaera were six, Maelor two. As they entered the apartments, Helaena was holding his little hand and calling out her mother's name. Blood barred the door and slew the queen's guardsman, whilst Cheese appeared to snatch up Maelor. "Scream and you all die," Blood told Her Grace. Queen Helaena kept her calm, it is said. "Who are you?" she demanded of the two. "Debt collectors,"

said Cheese. "An eye for an eye, a son for a son. We only want the one, t'
square things. Won't hurt the rest o' you fine folks, not one lil' hair. Which
one you want t' lose, Your Grace?"

Once she realized what he meant, Queen Helaena pleaded with the
men to kill her instead. "A wife's not a son," said Blood. "It has to be a
boy." Cheese warned the queen to make a choice soon, before Blood grew
bored and raped her little girl. "Pick," he said, "or we kill them all." On
her knees, weeping, Helaena named her youngest, Maelor. Perhaps she
thought the boy was too young to understand, or perhaps it was because
the older boy, Jaehaerys, was King Aegon's firstborn son and heir, next in
line to the Iron Throne. "You hear that, little boy?" Cheese whispered to
Maelor. "Your momma wants you dead." Then he gave Blood a grin, and
the hulking swordsman slew Prince Jaehaerys, striking off the boy's head
with a single blow. The queen began to scream.

Strange to say, the rat-catcher and the butcher were true to their word.
They did no further harm to Queen Helaena or her surviving children,
but rather fled with the prince's head in hand.

Though Blood and Cheese had spared her life, Queen Helaena cannot
be said to have survived that fateful dusk. Afterward she would not eat, nor
bathe, nor leave her chambers, and she could no longer stand to look upon
her son Maelor, knowing that she had named him to die. The king had no
recourse but to take the boy from her and give him over to his mother, the
Dowager Queen Alicent, to raise as if he were her own. Aegon and his wife
slept separately thereafter, and Queen Helaena sank deeper and deeper into
madness, whilst the king raged, and drank, and raged.

Now the bloodletting began in earnest.

The fall of Harrenhal to Prince Daemon came as a great shock to His
Grace. Until that moment, Aegon II had believed his half sister's cause to
be hopeless. Harrenhal left His Grace feeling vulnerable for the first time.
Subsequent rapid defeats at the Burning Mill and Stone Hedge came as
further blows, and made the king realize that his situation was more perilous than it had seemed. These fears deepened as ravens returned from
the Reach, where the greens had believed themselves strongest. House
Hightower and Oldtown were solidly behind King Aegon, and His Grace
had the Arbor too . . . but elsewhere in the south, other lords were declaring for Rhaenyra, amongst them Lord Costayne of Three Towers, Lord

Mullendore of Uplands, Lord Tarly of Horn Hill, Lord Rowan of Gold-engrove, and Lord Grimm of Greyshield.

Other blows followed: the Vale, White Harbor, Winterfell. The Black-woods and the other river lords streamed toward Harrenhal and Prince Daemon's banners. The Sea Snake's fleets closed Blackwater Bay, and every morning King Aegon had merchants whining at him. His Grace had no answer for their complaints, beyond another cup of strongwine. "Do something," he demanded of Ser Otto. The Hand assured him that something *was* being done; he had hatched a plan to break the Velaryon blockade. One of the chief pillars of support for Rhaenyra's claim was her consort, yet Prince Daemon represented one of her greatest weaknesses as well. The prince had made more foes than friends during the course of his adventures. Ser Otto Hightower, who had been amongst the first of those foes, was reaching across the narrow sea to another of the prince's ene-mies, the Kingdom of the Three Daughters, hoping to persuade them to move against the Sea Snake.

The delay did not sit well with the young king. Aegon II had run short of patience with his grandfather's prevarications. Though his mother the Dowager Queen Alicent spoke up in Ser Otto's defense, His Grace turned a deaf ear to her pleading. Summoning Ser Otto to the throne room, he tore the chain of office from his neck and tossed it to Ser Criston Cole. "My new Hand is a steel fist," he boasted. "We are done with writing let-ters." Ser Criston wasted no time in proving his mettle. "It is not for you to plead for support from your lords, like a beggar pleading for alms," he told Aegon. "You are the lawful king of Westeros, and those who deny it are traitors. It is past time they learned the price of treason."

King Aegon's master of whisperers, Larys Strong the Clubfoot, had drawn up a list of all those lords who gathered on Dragonstone to attend Queen Rhaenyra's coronation and sit on her black council. Lords Celtigar and Velaryon had their seats on islands; as Aegon II had no strength at sea, they were beyond the reach of his wroth. Those "black" lords whose lands were on the mainland enjoyed no such protection, however.

Duskendale fell easily, taken by surprise by the King's forces, the town sacked, the ships in the harbor set afire, Lord Darklyn beheaded. Rook's Rest was Ser Criston's next objective. Forewarned of their coming, Lord Staunton closed his gates and defied the attackers. Behind his walls, his lordship could only watch as his fields and woods and villages were burned, his sheep and cattle and smallfolk put to the sword. When provisions inside the castle began to run low, he dispatched a raven to Dragonstone, pleading for succor.

Nine days after Lord Staunton dispatched his plea for help, the sound of leathern wings was heard across the sea, and the dragon Meleys appeared above Rook's Rest. The Red Queen, she was called, for the scarlet scales that covered her. The membranes of her wings were pink, her crest, horns, and claws bright as copper. And on her back, in steel and copper armor that flashed in the sun, rode Rhaenys Targaryen, the Queen Who Never Was.

Ser Criston Cole was not dismayed. Aegon's Hand had expected this, counted on it. Drums beat out a command, and archers rushed forward, longbowmen and crossbowmen both, filling the air with arrows and quarrels. Scorpions were cranked upwards to loose iron bolts of the sort that had once felled Meraxes in Dorne. Meleys suffered a score of hits, but the arrows only served to make her angry. She swept down, spitting fire to right and left. Knights burned in their saddles as the hair and hide and harness of their horses went up in flames. Men-at-arms dropped their spears and scattered. Some tried to hide behind their shields, but neither oak nor iron could withstand dragon's breath. Ser Criston sat on his white horse shouting, "Aim for the rider," through the smoke and flame. Meleys roared, smoke swirling from her nostrils, a stallion kicking in her jaws as tongues of fire engulfed him.

Then came an answering roar. Two more winged shapes appeared: the king astride Sunfyre the Golden, and his brother Aemond upon Vhagar. Criston Cole had sprung his trap, and Rhaenys had come snatching at the bait. Now the teeth closed round her.

Princess Rhaenys made no attempt to flee. With a glad cry and a crack of her whip, she turned Meleys toward the foe. Against Vhagar alone she might have had some chance, for the Red Queen was old and cunning, and no stranger to battle. Against Vhagar and Sunfyre together, doom was certain. The dragons met violently a thousand feet above the field of battle, as balls of fire burst and blossomed, so bright that men swore later that the sky was full of suns. The crimson jaws of Meleys closed round Sunfyre's golden neck for a moment, till Vhagar fell upon them from above. All three beasts went spinning toward the ground. They struck so hard that stones fell from the battlements of Rook's Rest half a league away.

Those closest to the dragons did not live to tell the tale. Those farther off could not see, for the flame and smoke. It was hours before the fires guttered out. But from those ashes, only Vhagar rose unharmed. Meleys was dead, broken by the fall and ripped to pieces upon the ground. And Sunfyre, that splendid golden beast, had one wing half torn from his body, whilst his royal rider had suffered broken ribs, a broken hip, and burns that covered half his body. His left arm was the worst. The dragonflame had burned so hot that the king's armor had melted into his flesh.

A body believed to be Rhaenys Targaryen was later found beside the carcass of her dragon, but so blackened that no one could be sure it was her. Beloved daughter of Lady Jocelyn Baratheon and Prince Aemon Targaryen, faithful wife to Lord Corlys Velaryon, mother and grandmother, the Queen Who Never Was lived fearlessly, and died amidst blood and fire. She was fifty-five years old.

Eight hundred knights and squires and common men lost their lives that day as well. Another hundred perished not long after, when Prince Aemond and Ser Criston Cole took Rook's Rest and put its garrison to death. Lord Staunton's head was carried back to King's Landing and mounted above the Old Gate . . . but it was the head of the dragon Meleys, drawn through the city on a cart, that awed the crowds of smallfolk into silence. Thousands fled King's Landing afterward, until the Dowager Queen Alicent ordered the city gates closed and barred.

King Aegon II did not die, though his burns brought him such pain that some say he prayed for death. Carried back to King's Landing in a closed litter to hide the extent of his injuries, His Grace did not rise from his bed for the rest of the year. Septons prayed for him, maesters attended him with potions and milk of the poppy, but Aegon slept nine hours out of every ten, waking only long enough to take some meagre nourishment before he slept again. None was allowed to disturb his rest, save his mother the Queen Dowager and his Hand, Ser Criston Cole. His wife never so much as made the attempt, so lost was Helaena in her own grief and madness.

The king's dragon, Sunfyre, too huge and heavy to be moved, and unable to fly with his injured wing, remained in the fields beyond Rook's Rest, crawling through the ashes like some great golden wyrm. In the early days, he fed himself upon the burned carcasses of the slain. When those were gone, the men Ser Criston had left behind to guard him brought him calves and sheep.

"You must rule the realm now, until your brother is strong enough to take the crown again," the King's Hand told Prince Aemond. Nor did Ser Criston need to say it twice. And so one-eyed Aemond the Kinslayer took up the iron-and-ruby crown of Aegon the Conquerer. "It looks better on me than it ever did on him," the prince proclaimed. Yet Aemond did not assume the style of king, but named himself only Protector of the Realm and Prince Regent. Ser Criston Cole remained Hand of the King.

Meanwhile, the seeds Jacaerys Velaryon had planted on his flight north had begun to bear fruit, and men were gathering at White Harbor, Winterfell, Barrowton, Sisterton, Gulltown, and the Gates of the Moon. Should they join their strength with that of the river lords assembling at Harrenhal with Prince Daemon, even the strong walls of King's Landing might not be able to withstand them, Ser Criston warned the new Prince Regent.

Supremely confident in his own prowess as a warrior and the might of his dragon Vhagar, Aemond was eager to take the battle to the foe. "The whore on Dragonstone is not the threat," he said. "No more than Rowan and these traitors in the Reach. The danger is my uncle. Once Daemon is dead, all these fools flying our sister's banners will run back to their castles and trouble us no more."

East of Blackwater Bay, Queen Rhaenyra was also faring badly. The death of her son Lucerys had been a crushing blow to a woman already broken by pregnancy, labor, and stillbirth. When word reached Dragonstone that Princess Rhaenys had fallen, angry words were exchanged between the queen and Lord Velaryon, who blamed her for his wife's death. "It should have been *you*," the Sea Snake shouted at Her Grace. "Staunton sent to you, yet you left it to my wife to answer, and forbade your sons to join her!" For as all the castle knew, the princes Jace and Joff had been eager to fly with Princess Rhaenys to Rook's Rest with their own dragons.

It was Jace who came to the fore now, late in the year 129 AC. First he brought the Lord of the Tides back into the fold by naming him the Hand of the Queen. Together he and Lord Corlys began to plan an assault upon King's Landing.

Mindful of the promise he had made to the Maiden of the Vale, Jace ordered Prince Joffrey to fly to Gulltown with Tyraxes. Munkun suggests that Jace's desire to keep his brother far from the fighting was paramount in this decision. This did not sit well with Joffrey, who was determined to prove himself in battle. Only when told that he was being sent to defend the Vale against King Aegon's dragons did he grudgingly consent to go. Rhaena, the thirteen-year-old daughter of Prince Daemon by Laena Velaryon, was chosen to accompany him. Known as Rhaena of Pentos, for the city of her birth, she was no dragonrider, her hatchling having died some years before, but she brought three dragon's eggs with her to the Vale, where she prayed nightly for their hatching. The Prince of Dragonstone also had a care for the safety of his half brothers, Aegon the Younger and Viserys, aged nine and seven. Their father Prince Daemon had made many friends in the Free City of Pentos during his visits there, so Jacaerys reached across the narrow sea to the prince of that city, who agreed to foster the two boys until Rhaenyra had secured the Iron Throne. In the waning days of 129 AC, the young princes boarded the cog *Gay Abandon*— Aegon with Stormcloud, Viserys clutching his egg—to set sail for Essos. The Sea Snake sent seven of his warships with them as escort, to see that they reached Pentos safely.

With Sunfyre wounded and unable to fly near Rook's Rest, and Tessarion with Prince Daeron in Oldtown, only two mature dragons remained to defend King's Landing . . . and Dreamfyre's rider, Queen Helaena, spent her days in darkness, weeping, and surely could not be counted as threat. That left only Vhagar. No living dragon could match Vhagar for size or ferocity, but Jace reasoned that if Vermax, Syrax, and Caraxes were to descend on King's Landing all at once, even "that hoary old bitch" would be unable to withstand them. Yet so great was Vhagar's repute that the prince hesitated, considering how he might add more dragons to his attack.

House Targaryen had ruled Dragonstone for more than two hundred years, since Lord Aenar Targaryen first arrived from Valyria with his dragons. Though it had always been their custom to wed brother to sister and cousin to cousin, young blood runs hot, and it was not unknown for men of the House to seek their pleasures amongst the daughters (and even the wives) of their subjects, the smallfolk who lived in the villages below the Dragonmont, tillers of the land and fishers of the sea. Indeed, until the reign of King Jaehaerys and Good Queen Alysanne, the ancient law of the first night had prevailed on Dragonstone, as it did throughout Westeros, whereby it was the right of a lord to bed any maiden in his domain upon her wedding night.

Though this custom was greatly resented elsewhere in the Seven Kingdoms, by men of a jealous temperament who did not grasp the honor being conferred upon them, such feelings were muted upon Dragonstone,
where Targaryens were rightly regarded as being closer to gods than the
common run of men. Here, brides thus blessed upon their wedding nights
were envied, and the children born of such unions were esteemed above
all others, for the Lords of Dragonstone oft celebrated the birth of such
with lavish gifts of gold and silk and land to the mother. These happy
bastards were said to have been "born of dragonseed," and in time became
known simply as "seeds." Even after the end of the right of the first night,
certain Targaryens continued to dally with the daughters of innkeeps and
the wives of fishermen, so seeds and the sons of seeds were plentiful on
Dragonstone.

Prince Jacaerys needed more dragonriders, and more dragons, and it
was to those born of dragonseed that he turned, vowing that any man
who could master a dragon would be granted lands and riches and dubbed
a knight. His sons would be ennobled, his daughters wed to lords, and he
himself would have the honor of fighting beside the Prince of Dragonstone against the pretender Aegon II Targaryen and his treasonous supporters.

Not all those who came forward in answer to the prince's call were
seeds, nor even the sons or grandsons of seeds. A score of the queen's own
household knights offered themselves as dragonriders, amongst them the
Lord Commander of her Kingsguard, Ser Steffon Darklyn, along with
squires, scullions, sailors, men-at-arms, mummers, and two maids.

Dragons are not horses. They do not easily accept men upon their backs,
and when angered or threatened, they attack. Sixteen men lost their lives
during an attempt to become dragonriders. Three times that number were
burned or maimed. Steffon Darklyn was burned to death whilst attempting to mount the dragon Seasmoke. Lord Gormon Massey suffered the
same fate when approaching Vermithor. A man called Silver Denys, whose
hair and eyes lent credence to his claim to be a bastard son of King Maegor the Cruel, had an arm torn off by Sheepstealer. As his sons struggled
to staunch the wound, the Cannibal descended on them, drove off Sheepstealer, and devoured father and sons alike.

Yet Seasmoke, Vermithor, and Silverwing were accustomed to men and
tolerant of their presence. Having once been ridden, they were more ac-

cepting of new riders. Vermithor, the Old King's own dragon, bent his neck to a blacksmith's bastard, a towering man called Hugh the Hammer or Hard Hugh, whilst a pale-haired man-at-arms named Ulf the White (for his hair) or Ulf the Sot (for his drinking) mounted Silverwing, beloved of Good Queen Alysanne.

And Seasmoke, who had once borne Laenor Velaryon, took onto his back a boy of ten-and-five known as Addam of Hull, whose origins remain a matter of dispute amongst historians to this day. Not long after Addam of Hull had proved himself by flying Seasmoke, Lord Corlys went so far as to petition Queen Rhaenyra to remove the taint of bastardy from him and his brother. When Prince Jacaerys added his voice to the request, the queen complied. Addam of Hull, dragonseed and bastard, became Addam Velaryon, heir to Driftmark.

Dragonstone's three wild dragons were less easily claimed than those that had known previous riders, yet attempts were made upon them all the same. Sheepstealer, a notably ugly "mud brown" dragon hatched when the Old King was still young, had a taste for mutton, swooping down on shepherd's flocks from Driftmark to the Wendwater. He seldom harmed the shepherds, unless they attempted to interfere with him, but had been known to devour the occasional sheepdog. Grey Ghost dwelt in a smoking vent high on the eastern side of the Dragonmont, preferred fish, and was most oft glimpsed flying low over the narrow sea, snatching prey from the waters. A pale grey-white beast the color of morning mist, he was a notably shy dragon who avoided men and their works for years at a time.

The largest and oldest of the wild dragons was the Cannibal, so named because he had been known to feed on the carcasses of dead dragons, and descend upon the hatcheries of Dragonstone to gorge himself on newborn hatchlings and eggs. Would-be dragontamers had made attempts to ride him a dozen times; his lair was littered with their bones.

None of the dragonseeds were fool enough to disturb the Cannibal (any who were did not return to tell their tales). Some sought the Grey Ghost, but could not find him, for he was ever an elusive creature. Sheepstealer proved easier to flush out, but he remained a vicious, ill-tempered beast, who killed more seeds than the three "castle dragons" together. One who hoped to tame him (after his quest for Grey Ghost proved fruitless) was Alyn of Hull. Sheepstealer would have none of him. When he stumbled from the dragon's lair with his cloak aflame, only his brother's swift action saved his life. Seasmoke drove the wild dragon off as Addam used his own cloak to beat out the flames. Alyn Velaryon would carry the scars of the encounter on his back and legs for the rest of his long life. Yet he counted himself fortunate, for he lived. Many of the other seeds and seekers who aspired to ride upon Sheepstealer's back ended in Sheepstealer's belly instead.

In the end, the brown dragon was brought to heel by the cunning and persistence of a "small brown girl" of six-and-ten, named Netty, who delivered him a freshly slaughtered sheep every morning, until Sheepstealer learned to accept and expect her. She was black-haired, brown-eyed, brown-skinned, skinny, foul-mouthed, filthy, and fearless . . . and the first and last rider of the dragon Sheepstealer.

Thus did Prince Jacaerys achieve his goal. For all the death and pain it caused, the widows left behind, the burned men who would carry their scars until the day they died, four new dragonriders had been found. As 129 AC drew to a close, the prince prepared to fly against King's Landing. The date he chose for the attack was the first full moon of the new year.

Yet the plans of men are but playthings to the gods. For even as Jace laid his plans, a new threat was closing from the east. The schemes of Otto Hightower had borne fruit; meeting in Tyrosh, the High Council of the Triarchy had accepted his offer of alliance. Ninety warships swept from the Stepstones under the banners of the Three Daughters, bending their oars for the Gullet . . . and as chance and the gods would have it, the Pentoshi cog *Gay Abandon,* carrying two Targaryen princes, sailed straight into their teeth. The escorts sent to protect the cog were sunk or taken, the *Gay Abandon* captured.

The tale reached Dragonstone only when Prince Aegon arrived desperately clinging to the neck of his dragon, Stormcloud. The boy was white with terror, shaking like a leaf and stinking of piss. Only nine, he had never flown before . . . and would never fly again, for Stormcloud had been terribly wounded as he fled, arriving with the stubs of countless arrows embedded in his belly and a scorpion bolt through his neck. He died within the hour, hissing as the hot blood gushed black and smoking from his wounds. Aegon's younger brother, Prince Viserys, had no way of escaping from the cog. A clever boy, he hid his dragon's egg and changed into ragged, salt-stained clothing, pretending to be no more than a common ship's boy, but one of the real ship's boys betrayed him, and he was made a captive. It was a Tyroshi captain who first realized who he had, but the admiral of the fleet, Sharako Lohar of Lys, soon relieved him of his prize.

When Prince Jacaerys swept down upon a line of Lysene galleys on Vermax, a rain of spears and arrows rose up to meet him. The sailors of the Triarchy had faced dragons before whilst warring against Prince Daemon in the Stepstones. No man could fault their courage; they were prepared to meet dragonflame with such weapons as they had. "Kill the rider and the dragon will depart," their captains and commanders had told them. One ship took fire, and then another. Still the men of the Free Cities fought on . . . until a shout rang out, and they looked up to see more winged shapes coming around the Dragonmont and turning toward them.

It is one thing to face a dragon, another to face five. As Silverwing, Sheepstealer, Seasmoke, and Vermithor descended upon them, the men of the Triarchy felt their courage desert them. The line of warships shattered as one galley after another turned away. The dragons fell like thunderbolts, spitting balls of fire, blue and orange, red and gold, each brighter than the next. Ship after ship burst asunder or was consumed by flames. Screaming men leapt into the sea, shrouded in fire. Tall columns of black smoke rose up from the water. All seemed lost . . . all *was* lost . . .

. . . till Vermax flew too low, and went crashing down into the sea.

Several differing tales were told afterward of how and why the dragon fell. Some claimed a crossbowman put an iron bolt through his eye, but this version seems suspiciously similar to the way Meraxes met her end, long ago in Dorne. Another account tells us that a sailor in the crow's nest of a Myrish galley cast a grapnel as Vermax was swooping through the fleet. One of its prongs found purchase between two scales, and was driven deep by the dragon's own considerable speed. The sailor had coiled his end of the chain about the mast, and the weight of the ship and the power of Vermax's wings tore a long jagged gash in the dragon's belly. The dragon's shriek of rage was heard as far off as Spicetown, even through the clangor of battle. His flight jerked to a violent end, Vermax went down smoking and screaming, clawing at the water. Survivors said he struggled to rise, only to crash headlong into a burning galley. Wood splintered, the mast came tumbling down, and the dragon, thrashing, became entangled in the rigging. When the ship heeled over and sank, Vermax sank with her.

It is said that Jacaerys Velaryon leapt free and clung to a piece of smoking wreckage for a few heartbeats, until some crossbowmen on the nearest Myrish ship began loosing quarrels at him. The prince was struck once, and then again. More and more Myrmen brought crossbows to bear. Finally one quarrel took him through the neck, and Jace was swallowed by the sea.

The Battle in the Gullet raged into the night north and south of Dragonstone, and remains amongst the bloodiest sea battles in all of history. The Triarchy's admiral Sharako Lohar had taken a combined fleet of ninety Myrish, Lysene, and Tyroshi warships from the Stepstones; only twenty-eight survived to limp home.

Though the attackers bypassed Dragonstone, no doubt believing that the ancient Targaryen stronghold was too strong to assault, they exacted a grievous toll on Driftmark. Spicetown was brutally sacked, the bodies of men, women, and children butchered in the streets and left as fodder for gulls and rats and carrion crows, its buildings burned. The town would never be rebuilt. High Tide was put to the torch as well. All the treasures the Sea Snake had brought back from the east were consumed by fire, his servants cut down as they tried to flee the flames. The Velaryon fleet lost almost a third of its strength. Thousands died. Yet none of these losses were felt so deeply as that of Jacaerys Velaryon, Prince of Dragonstone and heir to the Iron Throne.

A fortnight later, in the Reach, Ormund Hightower found himself caught between two armies. Thaddeus Rowan, Lord of Goldengrove, and Tom Flowers, Bastard of Bitterbridge, were bearing down on him from the northeast with a great host of mounted knights, whilst Ser Alan Beesbury, Lord Alan Tarly, and Lord Owen Costayne had joined their power to cut off his retreat to Oldtown. When their hosts closed around him on the banks of the river Honeywine, attacking front and rear at once, Lord Hightower saw his lines crumble. Defeat seemed imminent . . . until a shadow swept across the battlefield, and a terrible roar resounded overhead, slicing through the sound of steel on steel. A dragon had come.

The dragon was Tessarion, the Blue Queen, cobalt and copper. On her back rode the youngest of Queen Alicent's three sons, Daeron Targaryen, fifteen, Lord Ormund's squire.

The arrival of Prince Daeron and his dragon reversed the tide of battle. Now it was Lord Ormond's men attacking, screaming curses at their foes, whilst the queen's men fled. By day's end, Lord Rowan was retreating north with the remnants of his host, Tom Flowers lay dead and burned amongst the reeds, the two Alans had been taken captive, and Lord Costayne was dying slowly from a wound given him by Bold Jon Roxton's black blade, the Orphan-Maker. As wolves and ravens fed upon the bodies of the slain, Lord Hightower feasted Prince Daeron on aurochs and strongwine, and dubbed him a knight with the storied Valryian longsword Vigilance, naming him "Ser Daeron the Daring." The prince modestly replied, "My lord is kind to say so, but the victory belongs to Tessarion."

On Dragonstone, an air of despondence and defeat hung over the black court when the disaster on the Honeywine became known to them. Lord Bar Emmon went so far as to suggest that mayhaps the time had come to bend their knees to Aegon II. The queen would have none of it, however. Only the gods truly know the hearts of men, and women are full as strange. Broken by the loss of one son, Rhaenyra Targaryen seemed to find new strength after the loss of a second. Jace's death hardened her, burning away her fears, leaving only her anger and her hatred. Still possessed of more dragons than her half brother, Her Grace now resolved to use them, no matter the cost. She would rain down fire and death upon Aegon and all those who supported him, she told the black council, and either tear him from the Iron Throne or die in the attempt.

A similar resolve had taken root across the bay in the breast of Aemond Targaryen, ruling in his brother's name whilst Aegon lay abed. Contemptuous of his half sister Rhaenyra, Aemond One-Eye saw a greater threat in his uncle, Prince Daemon, and the great host he had gathered at Harrenhal. Summoning his bannermen and council, the prince announced his intent to bring the battle to his uncle and chastise the rebellious river lords.

Not all the members of the green council favored the prince's bold stroke. Aemond had the support of Ser Criston Cole, the Hand, and that of Ser Tyland Lannister, but Grand Maester Orwyle urged him to send word to Storm's End and add the power of House Baratheon to his own before proceeding, and Ironrod, Lord Jasper Wylde, declared that he should summon Lord Hightower and Prince Daeron from the south, on the grounds that "two dragons are better than one." The Queen Dowager favored caution as well, urging her son to wait until his brother the king and his dragon Sunfyre the Golden were healed, so they might join the attack.

Prince Aemond had no taste for such delays, however. He had no need of his brothers or their dragons, he declared; Aegon was too badly hurt, Daeron too young. Aye, Caraxes was a fearsome beast, savage and cunning and battle-tested . . . but Vhagar was older, fiercer, and twice as large. Septon Eustace tells us that the Kinslayer was determined that this should be his victory; he had no wish to share the glory with his brothers, nor any other man.

Nor could he be gainsaid, for until Aegon II rose from his bed to take up his sword again, the regency and rule were Aemond's. True to his resolve, the prince rode forth from the Gate of the Gods within a fortnight, at the head of a host four thousand strong.

Daemon Targaryen was too old and seasoned a battler to sit idly by and let himself be penned up inside walls, even walls as massive as Harrenhal's. The prince still had friends in King's Landing, and word of his nephew's plans had reached him even before Aemond had set out. When told that Aemond and Ser Criston Cole had left King's Landing, it is said that Prince Daemon laughed and said, "Past time," for he had long anticipated this moment. A murder of ravens took flight from the twisted towers of Harrenhal.

Elsewhere in the realm, Lord Walys Mooton led a hundred knights out of Maidenpool to join with the half-wild Crabbs and Brunes of Crackclaw Point and the Celtigars of Claw Isle. Through piney woods and mist-shrouded hills they hastened, to Rook's Rest, where their sudden appearance took the garrison by surprise. After retaking the castle, Lord Mooton led his bravest men to the field of ashes west of the castle, to put an end to the dragon Sunfyre.

The would-be dragonslayers easily drove off the cordon of guards who had been left to feed, serve, and protect the dragon, but Sunfyre himself proved more formidable than expected. Dragons are awkward creatures on the ground, and his torn wing left the great golden wyrm unable to take to the air. The attackers expected to find the beast near death. Instead they found him sleeping, but the clash of swords and thunder of horses soon roused him, and the first spear to strike him provoked him to fury. Slimy with mud, twisting amongst the bones of countless sheep, Sunfyre writhed and coiled like a serpent, his tail lashing, sending blasts of golden flame at his attackers as he struggled to fly. Thrice he rose, and thrice fell back to earth. Mooton's men swarmed him with swords and spears and axes, dealing him many grievous wounds . . . yet each blow only seemed to enrage him further. The number of the dead reached three score before the survivors fled.

Amongst the slain was Walys Mooton, Lord of Maidenpool. When his body was found a fortnight later by his brother Manfyrd, nought remained but charred flesh in melted armor, crawling with maggots. Yet nowhere on that field of ashes, littered with the bodies of brave men and the burned and bloated carcasses of a hundred horses, did Lord Manfyrd find King Aegon's dragon. Sunfyre was gone. Nor were there tracks, as surely there would have been had the dragon dragged himself away. Sunfyre the Golden had taken wing again, it seemed . . . but to where, no living man could say.

Meanwhile, Prince Daemon Targaryen himself hastened south on the wings of his dragon, Caraxes. Flying above the western shore of the Gods Eye, well away from Ser Criston's line of march, he evaded the enemy host, crossed the Blackwater, then turned east, following the river downstream to King's Landing. And on Dragonstone, Rhaenyra Targaryen donned a suit of gleaming black scale, mounted Syrax, and took flight as a rainstorm lashed the waters of Blackwater Bay. High above the city the queen and her prince consort came together, circling over Aegon's High Hill.

The sight of them incited terror in the streets the city below, for the smallfolk were not slow to realize that the attack they had dreaded was at last at hand. Prince Aemond and Ser Criston had denuded King's Landing of defenders when they set forth to retake Harrenhal . . . and the Kinslayer had taken Vhagar, that fearsome beast, leaving only Dreamfyre and a handful of half-grown hatchlings to oppose the queen's dragons. The young dragons had never been ridden, and Dreamfyre's rider, Queen Helaena, was a broken woman; the city had as well been dragonless.

Thousands of smallfolk streamed out the city gates, carrying their children and worldly possessions on their backs, to seek safety in the countryside. Others dug pits and tunnels under their hovels, dark dank holes where they hoped to hide whilst the city burned. Rioting broke out in Flea Bottom. When the sails of the Sea Snake's ships were seen to the east in Blackwater Bay, making for the river, the bells of every sept in the city began to ring, and mobs surged through the streets, looting as they went. Dozens died before the gold cloaks could restore the peace.

With both the Lord Protector and the King's Hand absent, and King Aegon himself burned, bedridden, and lost in poppy dreams, it fell to his mother the Queen Dowager to see to the city's defenses. Queen Alicent rose to the challenge, closing the gates of castle and city, sending the gold cloaks to the walls, and dispatching riders on swift horses to find Prince Aemond and fetch him back.

As well, she commanded Grand Maester Orwyle to send ravens to "all our leal lords," summoning them to the defense of their true king. When Orywle hastened back to his chambers, however, he found four gold cloaks waiting for him. One man muffled his cries as the others beat and bound him. With a bag pulled down over his head, the grand maester was escorted down to the black cells.

Queen Alicent's riders got no farther than the gates, where more gold cloaks took them into custody. Unbeknownest to Her Grace, the seven captains commanding the gates, chosen for their loyalty to King Aegon, had been imprisoned or murdered the moment Caraxes appeared in the sky above the Red Keep . . . for the rank and file of the City Watch still loved Daemon Targaryen, who had commanded them of old.

The queen's brother Ser Gwayne Hightower, second in command of the gold cloaks, rushed to the stables intending to sound the warning; he was seized, disarmed, and dragged before his commander, Luthor Largent. When Hightower denounced him as a turncloak, Ser Luthor laughed. "Daemon gave us these cloaks," he said, "and they're gold no matter how you turn them." Then he drove his sword through Ser Gwayne's belly and ordered the city gates opened to the men pouring off the Sea Snake's ships.

For all the vaunted strength of its walls, King's Landing fell in less than a day. A short, bloody fight was waged at the River Gate, where thirteen Hightower knights and a hundred men-at-arms drove off the gold cloaks and held out for nigh on eight hours against attacks from both within and without the city, but their heroics were in vain, for Rhaenyra's soldiers poured in through the other six gates unmolested. The sight of the queen's dragons in the sky above took the heart out of the opposition, and King Aegon's remaining loyalists hid or fled or bent the knee.

One by one, the dragons made their descent. Sheepstealer lighted atop Visenya's Hill, Silverwing and Vermithor on the Hill of Rhaenys, outside the Dragonpit. Prince Daemon circled the towers of the Red Keep before bringing Caraxes down in the outer ward. Only when he was certain that the defenders would offer him no harm did he signal for his wife the queen to descend upon Syrax. Addam Velaryon remained aloft, flying Seasmoke around the city walls, the beat of his dragon's wide leathern wings a caution to those below that any defiance would be met with fire.

Upon seeing that resistance was hopeless, the Dowager Queen Alicent emerged from Maegor's Holdfast with her father Ser Otto Hightower, Ser Tyland Lannister, and Lord Jasper Wylde the Ironrod. (Lord Larys Strong was not with them. The master of whisperers had somehow contrived to disappear.) Queen Alicent attempted to treat with her stepdaughter. "Let us together summon a great council, as the Old King did in days of old," said the Dowager Queen, "and lay the matter of succession before the lords of the realm." But Queen Rhaenyra rejected the proposal with scorn. "We both know how this council would rule." Then she bid her stepmother choose: yield, or burn.

Bowing her head in defeat, Queen Alicent surrendered the keys to the castle, and ordered her knights and men-at-arms to lay down their swords. "The city is yours, princess," she is reported to have said, "but you will not hold it long. The rats play when the cat is gone, but my son Aemond will return with fire and blood."

Yet Rhaenyra's triumph was far from complete. Her men found her rival's wife, the mad Queen Helaena, locked in her bedchamber . . . but when they broke down the doors of the king's apartments, they discovered only "his bed, empty, and his chamber pot, full." King Aegon II had fled. So had his children, the six-year-old Princess Jaehaera and two-year-old Prince Maelor, along with the knights Willis Fell and Rickard Thorne of the Kingsguard. Not even the Dowager Queen herself seemed to know where they had gone, and Luthor Largent swore none had passed through the city gates.

There was no way to spirit away the Iron Throne, however. Nor would Queen Rhaenyra sleep until she claimed her father's seat. So the torches were lit in the throne room, and the queen climbed the iron steps and seated herself where King Viserys had sat before her, and the Old King before him, and Maegor and Aenys and Aegon the Dragon in days of old. Stern-faced, still in her armor, she sat on high as every man and woman in the Red Keep was brought forth and made to kneel before her, to plead for her forgiveness and swear their lives and swords and honor to her as their queen.

The ceremony went on all through that night. It was well past dawn when Rhaenyra Targaryen rose and made her descent. "And as her lord husband Prince Daemon escorted her from the hall, cuts were seen upon Her Grace's legs and the palm of her left hand. Drops of blood fell to the floor as she went past, and wise men looked at one another, though none dared speak the truth aloud: the Iron Throne had spurned her, and her days upon it would be few."

All this came to pass even as Prince Aemond and Ser Criston Cole advanced upon the riverlands. After nineteen days on the march, they reached Harrenhal . . . and found the castle gates open, with Prince Daemon and all his people gone.

Prince Aemond had kept Vhagar with the main column throughout the march, thinking that his uncle might attempt to attack them on Caraxes. He reached Harrenhal a day after Cole, and that night celebrated a great victory; Daemon and his "river scum" had fled rather than face his wroth, Aemond proclaimed. Small wonder then that when word of the fall of King's Landing reached him, the prince felt thrice the fool. His fury was fearsome to behold.

West of Harrenhal, fighting continued in the riverlands as the Lannister host slogged onward. The age and infirmity of their commander, Lord Lefford, had slowed their march to a crawl, but as they neared the western shores of the Gods Eye, they found a huge new army athwart their path.

Roddy the Ruin and his Winter Wolves had joined with Forrest Frey, Lord of the Crossing, and Red Robb Rivers, known as the Bowman of Raventree. The northmen numbered two thousand, Frey commanded two hundred knights and thrice as many foot, Rivers brought three hundred archers to the fray. And scarce had Lord Lefford halted to confront the foe in front of him when more enemies appeared to the south, where Longleaf the Lionslayer and a ragged band of survivors from the earlier battles had been joined by the Lords Bigglestone, Chambers, and Perryn.

Caught between these two foes, Lefford hesitated to move against either, for fear of the other falling on his rear. Instead he put his back to the lake, dug in, and send ravens to Prince Aemond at Harrenhal, begging his aid. Though a dozen birds took wing, not one ever reached the prince; Red Robb Rivers, said to be the finest archer in all Westeros, took them down on the wing.

More rivermen turned up the next day, led by Ser Garibald Grey, Lord Jon Charlton, and the new Lord of Raventree, the eleven-year-old Benji-cot Blackwood. With their numbers augmented by these fresh levies, the queen's men agreed that the time had come to attack. "Best make an end to these lions before the dragons come," said Roddy the Ruin.

The bloodiest land battle of the Dance of the Dragons began the next day, with the rising of the sun. In the annals of the Citadel it is known as the Battle by the Lakeshore, but to those men who lived to tell of it, it was always the Fishfeed.

Attacked from three sides, the westermen were driven back foot by foot into the waters of the Gods Eye. Hundreds died there, cut down whilst fighting in the reeds; hundreds more drowned as they tried to flee. By nightfall two thousand men were dead, amongst them many notables, including Lord Frey, Lord Lefford, Lord Bigglestone, Lord Charlton, Lord Swyft, Lord Reyne, Ser Clarent Crakehall, and Ser Tyler Hill, the Bastard of Lannisport. The Lannister host was shattered and slaughtered, but at such cost that young Ben Blackwood, the boy Lord of Raventree, wept when he saw the heaps of the dead. The most grievous losses were suffered by the northmen, for the Winter Wolves had begged the honor of leading the attack, and had charged five times into the ranks of Lannister spears. More than two thirds of the men who had ridden south with Lord Dustin were dead or wounded.

At Harrenhal, Aemond Targaryen and Criston Cole debated how best to answer the queen's attacks. Though Black Harren's seat was too strong to be taken by storm, and the river lords dared not lay siege for fear of Vhagar, the king's men were running short of food and fodder, and losing men and horses to hunger and sickness. Only blackened fields and burned villages remained within sight of the castle's massive walls, and those foraging parties that ventured further did not return. Ser Criston urged a withdrawal to the south, where Aegon's support was strongest, but the prince refused, saying "Only a craven runs from traitors." The loss of King's Landing and the Iron Throne had enraged him, and when word of the Fishfeed reached Harrenhal, the Lord Protector had almost strangled the squire who delivered the news. Only the incession of his bedmate, Alys Rivers, had saved the boy's life. Prince Aemond favored an immediate attack upon King's Landing. None of the queen's dragons were a match for Vhagar, he insisted.

Ser Criston called that folly. "One against six is a fight for fools, my prince," he declared. Let them march south, he urged once more, and join their strength to Lord Hightower's. Prince Aemond could reunite with his brother Daeron and his dragon. King Aegon had escaped Rhaenyra's grasp, this they knew, surely he would reclaim Sunfyre and join his brothers. And perhaps their friends inside the city might find a way to free Queen Helaena as well, so she could bring Dreamfyre to the battle. Four dragons could perhaps prevail against six, if one was Vhagar.

Prince Aemond refused to consider this "craven course."

Ser Criston and Prince Aemond decided to part ways. Cole would take command of their host and lead them south to join Ormund Hightower and Prince Daeron, but the Prince Regent would not accompany them. Instead he meant to fight his own war, raining fire on the traitors from the air. Soon or late, "the bitch queen" would send a dragon or two out to stop him, and Vhagar would destroy them. "She dare not send *all* her dragons," Aemond insisted. "That would leave King's Landing naked and vulnerable. Nor will she risk Syrax, or that last sweet son of hers. Rhaenyra may call herself a queen, but she has a woman's parts, a woman's faint heart, and a mother's fears."

And thus did the Kingmaker and the Kinslayer part, each to their own fate, whilst at the Red Keep, Queen Rhaenyra Targaryen set about rewarding her friends and inflicting savage punishments on those who had served her half brother.

Huge rewards were posted for information leading to the capture of "the usurper styling himself Aegon II," his daughter Jaehaera, his son Maelor, the "false knights" Willis Fell and Rickard Thorne, and Larys Strong, the Clubfoot. When that failed to produce the desired result, Her Grace sent forth hunting parties of "knights inquisitor" to seek after the "traitors and villains" who had escaped her, and punish any man found to have assisted them.

Queen Alicent was fettered at wrist and ankle with golden chains, though her stepdaughter spared her life "for the sake of our father, who loved you once." Her own father was less fortunate. Ser Otto Hightower, who had served three kings as Hand, was the first traitor to be beheaded. Ironrod followed him to the block, still insisting that by law a king's son must come before his daughter. Ser Tyland Lannister was given to the torturers instead, in hopes of recovering some of the crown's treasure.

Neither Aegon nor his brother Aemond had ever been much loved by the people of the city, and many kingslanders had welcomed the queen's return . . . but love and hate are two faces of the same coin, as fresh heads began appearing daily upon the spikes above the city gates, accompanied by ever more exacting taxes, the coin turned. The girl that they once cheered as the Realm's Delight had grown into a grasping and vindictive woman, men said, a queen as cruel as any king before her. One wit named Rhaenyra "King Maegor with teats," and for a hundred years thereafter "Maegor's Teats" was a common curse amongst kingslanders.

With the city, castle, and throne in her possession, defended by no fewer than six dragons, Rhaenyra felt secure enough to send for her sons. A dozen ships set sail from Dragonstone, carrying the queen's ladies and her son Aegon the Younger. Rhaenyra made the boy her cupbearer, so he might never be far from her side. Another fleet set out from Gulltown with Prince Joffrey, the last of the queen's three sons by Laenor Velaryon, together with his dragon Tyraxes. Her Grace began to make plans for a lavish celebration to mark Joffrey's formal installation as Prince of Dragonstone and heir to the Iron Throne.

In the fullness of her victory, Rhaenyra Targaryen did not suspect how few days remained to her. Yet every time she sat the Iron Throne, its cruel blades drew fresh blood from her hands and arms and legs, a sign that all could read.

Beyond the city walls, fighting continued throughout the Seven Kingdoms. In the riverlands, Ser Criston Cole abandoned Harrenhal, striking south along the western shore of the Gods Eye, with thirty-six hundred men behind him (death, disease, and desertion had thinned the ranks that had ridden forth from King's Landing). Prince Aemon had already departed, flying Vhagar. No longer tied to castle or host, the one-eyed prince was free to fly where he would. It was war as Aegon the Conquerer and his sisters had once waged it, fought with dragonflame, as Vhagar descended from the autumn sky again and again to lay waste to the lands and villages and castles of the river lords. House Darry was the first to know the prince's wroth. The men bringing in the harvest burned or fled as the crops went up in flame, and Castle Darry was consumed in a firestorm. Lady Darry and her younger children survived by taking shelter in vaults under the keep, but her lord husband and his heir died on their battlements, together with two score of his sworn swords and bowmen.

Three days later, it was Lord Harroway's Town left smoking. Lord's Mill, Blackbuckle, Buckle, Claypool, Swynford, Spiderwood . . . Vhagar's fury fell on each in turn, until half the riverlands seemed ablaze.

Ser Criston Cole faced fires as well. As he drove his men south through the riverlands, smoke rose up before him and behind him. Every village that he came to he found burned and abandoned. His column moved through forests of dead trees where living woods had been just days before, as the river lords set blazes all along his line of march. In every brook and pool and village well, he found death: dead horses, dead cows, dead men, swollen and stinking, befouling the waters. Elsewhere his scouts came across ghastly tableaux where armored corpses sat beneath the trees in rotting raiment, in a grotesque mockery of a feast. The feasters were men who had fallen in battle, skulls grinning under rusted helms as their green and rotted flesh sloughed off their bones.

Four days out of Harrenhall, the attacks began. Archers hid amongst the trees, picking off outriders and stragglers with their longbows. Men died. Men fell behind the rearguard and were never seen again. Men fled, abandoning their shields and spears to fade into the woods. Men went over to the enemy. In the village commons at Crossed Elms, another of the ghastly feasts was found. Familiar with such sights by now, Ser Criston's outriders grimaced and rode past, paying no heed to the rotting dead . . . until the corpses sprang up and fell upon them. A dozen died before they realized it had all been a ploy.

All this was but prelude, for the Lords of the Trident had been gathering their forces. When Ser Criston left the lake behind, striking out overland for the Blackwater, he found them waiting atop a stony ridge; three hundred mounted knights in armor, as many longbowmen, three thousand archers, three thousand ragged rivermen with spears, hundreds of northmen brandishing axes, mauls, spiked maces, and ancient iron swords. Above their heads flew Queen Rhaenyra's banners.

The battle that followed was as one-sided as any in the Dance. Lord Roderick Dustin raised a warhorn to his lips and sounded the charge, and the queen's men came screaming down the ridge, led by the Winter Wolves on their shaggy northern horses and the knights on their armored destriers. When Ser Criston was struck down and fell dead upon the ground, the men who had followed him from Harrenhal lost heart. They broke and fled, casting aside their shields as they ran. Their foes came after, cutting them down by the hundreds.

On Maiden's Day in the year 130 AC, the Citadel of Oldtown sent forth three hundred white ravens to herald the coming of winter, but this was high summer for Queen Rhaenyra Targaryen. Despite the disaffection of the Kingslanders, the city and crown were hers. Across the narrow sea, the Triarchy had begun to tear itself to pieces. The waves belonged to House Velaryon. Though snows had closed the passes through the Mountains of the Moon, the Maiden of the Vale had proven true to her word, sending men by sea to join the queen's hosts. Other fleets brought warriors from White Harbor, led by Lord Manderly's own sons, Medrick and Torrhen. On every hand Queen Rhaenyra's power swelled whilst King Aegon's dwindled.

Yet no war can be counted as won whilst foes remain unconquered. The Kingmaker, Ser Criston Cole, had been brought down, but somewhere in the realm Aegon II, the king he had made, remained alive and free. Aegon's daughter, Jaehaera, was likewise at large. Larys Strong the Clubfoot, the most enigmatic and cunning member of the green council, had vanished. Storm's End was still held by Lord Borros Baratheon, no friend of the queen. The Lannisters had to be counted amongst Rhaenyra's enemies as well, though with Lord Jason dead, the greater part of the chivalry of the west slain or scattered, Casterly Rock was in considerable disarray.

Prince Aemond had become the terror of the Trident, descending from the sky to rain fire and death upon the riverlands, then vanishing, only to strike again the next day fifty leagues away. Vhagar's flames reduced Old Willow and White Willow to ash, and Hogg Hall to blackened stone. At Merrydown Dell, thirty men and three hundred sheep died by dragonflame. The Kinslayer then returned unexpectedly to Harrenhal, where he burned every wooden structure in the castle. Six knights and two score men-at-arms perished trying to slay his dragon. As word of these attacks spread, other lords looked skyward in fear, wondering who might be next. Lord Mooton of Maidenpool, Lady Darklyn of Duskendale, and Lord Blackwood of Raventree sent urgent messages to the queen, begging her to send them dragons to defend their holdings.

Yet the greatest threat to Rhaenyra's reign was not Aemond One-Eye, but his younger brother, Prince Daeron the Daring, and the great southron army led by Lord Ormund Hightower.

Hightower's host had crossed the Mander, and was advancing slowly on King's Landing, smashing the queen's loyalists wherever and whenever they sought to hinder him, and forcing every lord who bent the knee to add their strength to his own. Flying Tessarion ahead of the main column, Prince Daeron had proved invaluable as a scout, warning Lord Ormund of enemy movements and entrenchments. Oft as not, the queen's men would melt away at the first glimpse of the Blue Queen's wings rather than face dragonflame in battle.

Cognizant of all these threats, Queen Rhaenyra's Hand, old Lord Corlys Velaryon, suggested to Her Grace that the time had come to talk. He urged the queen to offer pardons to Lords Baratheon, Hightower, and Lannister if they would bend their knees, swear fealty, and offer hostages to the Iron Throne. The Sea Snake proposed to let the Faith take charge of Queen Alicent and Queen Helaena, so that they might spend the remainder of their lives in prayer and contemplation. Helaena's daughter, Jaehaera, could be made his own ward, and in due time married to Prince Aegon the Younger, binding the two halves of House Targaryen together once again. "And what of my half brothers?" Rhaenyra demanded, when the Sea Snake put this plan before her. "What of this false king Aegon, and the kinslayer Aemond? Would you have me pardon them as well, them who stole my throne and slew my sons?"

"Spare them, and send them to the Wall," Lord Corlys answered. "Let them take the black and live out their lives as men of the Night's Watch, bound by sacred vows."

"What are vows to oathbreakers?" Queen Rhaenyra demanded to know. "Their vows did not trouble them when they took my throne."

Prince Daemon echoed the queen's misgivings. Giving pardons to rebels and traitors only sowed the seeds for fresh rebellions, he insisted. "The war will end when the heads of the traitors are mounted on spikes above the King's Gate, and not before." Aegon II would be found in time, "hiding under some rock," but they could and should bring the war to Aemond and Daeron. The Lannisters and Baratheons should be destroyed as well, so their lands and castles might be given to men who had proved more loyal. Grant Storm's End to Ulf White and Casterly Rock to Hard Hugh Hammer, the prince proposed . . . to the horror of the Sea Snake. "Half the lords of Westeros will turn against us if we are so cruel as to destroy two such ancient and noble houses," Lord Corlys said.

It fell to the queen herself to choose between her consort and her Hand. Rhaenyra decided to steer a middle course. She would send envoys to Storm's End and Casterly Rock, offering "fair terms" and pardons . . . *after* she had put an end to the usurper's brothers, who were in the field against her. "Once they are dead, the rest will bend the knee. Slay their dragons, that I might mount their heads upon the walls of my throne room. Let men look upon them in the years to come, that they might know the cost of treason."

King's Landing must not be left undefended, to be sure. Queen Rhaenyra would remain in the city with Syrax, and her sons Aegon and Joffrey, whose persons could not be put as risk. Joffrey, not quite three-and-ten, was eager to prove himself a warrior, but when told that Tyraxes was needed to help his mother hold the Red Keep in the event of an attack, the boy swore solemnly to do so. Addam Velaryon, the Sea Snake's heir, would also remain in the city, with Seasmoke. Three dragons should suffice for the defense of King's Landing; the rest would be going into battle.

Prince Daemon himself would take Caraxes to the Trident, together with the girl Nettles and Sheepstealer, to find Prince Aemond and Vhagar and put an end to them. Ulf White and Hard Hugh Hammer would fly to Tumbleton, some fifty leagues southwest of King's Landing, the last leal stronghold between Lord Hightower and the city, to assist in the defense of the town and castle and destroy Prince Daeron and Tessarion.

Prince Daemon Targaryen and the small brown girl called Nettles long hunted Aemond One-Eye without success. They had based themselves at Maidenpool, at the invitation of Lord Manfryd Mooton, who lived in terror of Vhagar descending on his town. Instead Prince Aemond struck at Stonyhead, in the foothills of the Mountains of the Moon; at Sweetwillow on the Green Fork and Sallydance on the Red Fork; he reduced Bowshot Bridge to embers, burned Old Ferry and Crone's Mill, destroyed the motherhouse at Bechester, always vanishing back into the sky before the hunters could arrive. Vhagar never lingered, nor did the survivors oft agree on which way the dragon had flown.

Each dawn Caraxes and Sheepstealer flew from Maidenpool, climbing high above the riverlands in ever-widening circles in hopes of espying Vhagar below . . . only to return defeated at dusk. Lord Mooton made so bold as to suggest that the dragonriders divide their search, so as to cover twice the ground. Prince Daemon refused. Vhagar was the last of the three dragons that had come to Westeros with Aegon the Conquerer and his sisters, he reminded his lordship. Though slower than she had been a century before, she had grown nigh as large as the Black Dread of old. Her fires burned hot enough to melt stone, and neither Caraxes nor Sheepstealer could match her ferocity. Only together could they hope to withstand her. And so he kept the girl Nettles by his side, day and night, in sky and castle.

Meanwhile, to the south, battle was joined at Tumbleton, a thriving market town on the Mander. The castle overlooking the town was stout but small, garrisoned by no more than forty men, but thousands more had come upriver from Bitterbridge, Longtable, and farther south. The arrival of a strong force of river lords swelled their numbers further, and stiffened their resolve. All told, the forces gathered under Queen Rhaenyra's banners at Tumbleton numbered near nine thousand. The queen's men were greatly outnumbered by Lord Hightower's. No doubt the arrival of the dragons Vermithor and Silverwing with their riders was most welcome by the defenders of Tumbleton. Little could they know the horrors that awaited them.

The how and when and why of what has become known as the Treasons of Tumbleton remain a matter of much dispute, and the truth of all that happened will likely never be known. It does appear that certain of those who flooded into the town, fleeing before Lord Hightower's army, were actually part of that army, sent ahead to infiltrate the ranks of the defenders. Yet their betrayals would have counted for little, had not Ser Ulf White and Ser Hugh Hammer also chosen this moment to change their allegiance.

As neither man could read nor write, we shall never know what drove the Two Betrayers (as history has named them) to do what they did. Of the Battle of Tumbleton we know much and more, however. Six thousand of the queen's men formed up to face Lord Hightower in the field, and fought bravely for a time, but a withering rain of arrows from Lord Ormund's archers thinned their ranks, and a thunderous charge by his heavy horse broke them, sending the survivors running back toward the town walls. When most of the survivors were safe inside the gates, Roddy the Ruin and his Winter Wolves sallied forth from a postern gate, screaming their terrifying northern war cries as they swept around the left flank of the attackers. In the chaos that ensued, the northmen fought their way through ten times their own number to where Lord Ormund Hightower sat his warhorse beneath King Aegon's golden dragon and the banners of Oldtown and the Hightower. As the singers tell it, Lord Roderick was blood from head to heel as he came on, with splintered shield and cracked helm, yet so drunk with battle that he did not even seem to feel his wounds. Ser Bryndon Hightower, Lord Ormund's cousin, put himself between the northman and his liege, taking off the Ruin's shield arm at the shoulder with one terrible blow of his longaxe . . . yet the savage Lord of Barrowton fought on, slaying both Ser Bryndon and Lord Ormund before he died. Lord Hightower's banners toppled, and the townfolk gave a great cheer, thinking the tide of battle turned. Even the appearance of Tessarion across the field did not dismay them, for they knew they had two dragons of their own . . . but when Vermithor and Silverwing climbed into the sky and loosed their fires upon Tumbleton, those cheers changed to screams.

Tumbleton went up in flame: shops, homes, septs, people, all. Men fell burning from gatehouse and battlements, or stumbled shrieking through the streets like so many living torches. The Two Betrayers scourged the town with whips of flame from one end to the other. The sack that followed was as savage as any in the history of Westeros. Tumbleton, that prosperous market town, was reduced to ash and embers, never to be rebuilt. Thousands burned, and as many died by drowning as they tried to swim the river. Some would later say they were the fortunate ones, for no mercy was shown the survivors. Lord Footly's men threw down their swords and yielded, only to be bound and beheaded. Such townswomen as survived the fires were raped repeatedly, even girls as young as eight and ten. Old men and boys were put to the sword, whilst the dragons fed upon the twisted, smoking carcasses of their victims.

It was about this time that a battered merchant cog named *Nessaria* came limping into the harbor beneath Dragonstone to make repairs and take on provisions. She had been returning from Pentos to Old Volantis when a storm drove her off course, her crew said . . . but to this common song of peril at sea, the Volantenes added a queer note. As *Nessaria* beat westward, the Dragonmont loomed up before them, huge against the setting sun . . . and the sailors spied two dragons fighting, their roars echoing off the sheer black cliffs of the smoking mountain's eastern flanks. In every tavern, inn, and whorehouse along the waterfront the tale was told, retold, and embroidered, till every man on Dragonstone had heard it.

Dragons were a wonder to the men of Old Volantis; the sight of two in battle was one the men of *Nessaria* would never forget. Those born and bred on Dragonstone had grown up with such beasts . . . yet even so, the sailors' story excited interest. The next morning some local fisherfolk took their boats around the Dragonmont, and returned to report seeing the burned and broken remains of a dead dragon at the mountain's base. From the color of its wings and scales, the carcass was that of Grey Ghost. The dragon lay in two pieces, and had been torn apart and partially devoured.

On hearing this news Ser Robert Quince, the amiable and famously obese knight whom the queen had named castellan of Dragonstone upon her departure, was quick to name the Cannibal as the killer. Most agreed, for the Cannibal had been known to attack smaller dragons in the past, though seldom so savagely. Some amongst the fisherfolk, fearing that the killer might turn upon them next, urged Quince to dispatch knights to the beast's lair to put an end to him, but the castellan refused. "If we do not trouble him, the Cannibal will not trouble us," he declared. To be certain of that, he forbade fishing in the waters beneath the Dragonmont's eastern face, where the dragon's body lay rotting.

Meanwhile, on the western shore of Blackwater Bay, word of battle and betrayal at Tumbleton had reached King's Landing. It is said the Dowager Queen Alicent laughed when she heard. "All they have sowed, now shall they reap," she promised. On the Iron Throne, Queen Rhaenyra grew pale and faint, and ordered the city gates closed and barred; henceforth, no one was to be allowed to enter or leave King's Landing. "I will have no turncloaks stealing into my city to open my gates to rebels," she proclaimed. Lord Ormund's host could be outside their walls by the morrow or the day after; the betrayers, dragonborne, could arrive even sooner than that.

This prospect excited Prince Joffrey. "Let them come," the boy announced, "I will meet them on Tyraxes." Such talk alarmed his mother. "You will not," she declared. "You are too young for battle." Even so, she allowed the boy to remain as the black council discussed how best to deal with the approaching foe.

Six dragons remained in King's Landing, but only one within the walls of the Red Keep: the queen's own she-dragon, Syrax. A stable in the outer ward had emptied of horses and given over for her use. Heavy chains bound her to the ground. Though long enough to allow her to move from stable to yard, the chains kept her from flying off riderless. Syrax had long grown accustomed to chains; exceedingly well fed, she had not hunted for years.

The other dragons were all kept in the Dragonpit, the colossal structure that King Maegor the Cruel had built for just that purpose. Beneath its great dome, forty huge undervaults had been carved from the bones of the Hill of Rhaenys in a great ring. Thick iron doors closed these man-made caves at either end, the inner doors fronting on the sands of the pit, the outer opening to the hillside. Caraxes, Vermithor, Silverwing, and Sheepstealer had made their lairs there before flying off to battle. Five dragons remained: Prince Joffrey's Tyraxes, Addam Velaryon's pale grey Seasmoke, the young dragons Morghul and Shrykos, bound to Princess Jaehaera (fled) and her twin Prince Jaehaerys (dead) . . . and Dreamfyre, beloved of Queen Helaena. It had long been the custom for at least one dragonrider to reside at the pit, so as to be able to rise to the defense of the city should the need arise. As Queen Rhaenyrs preferred to keep her sons by her side, that duty fell to Addam Velaryon.

But now voices on the black council were raised to question Ser Addam's loyalty. The dragonseeds Ulf White and Hugh Hammer had gone over to the enemy . . . but were they the only traitors in their midst? What of Addam of Hull and the girl Nettles? They had been born of bastard stock as well. Could they be trusted?

Lord Bartimos Celtigar thought not. "Bastards are treacherous by nature," he said. "It is in their blood. Betrayal comes as easily to a bastard as loyalty to trueborn men." He urged Her Grace to have the two baseborn dragonriders seized immediately, before they too could join the enemy with their dragons. Others echoed his views, amongst them Ser Luthor Largent, commander of her City Watch, and Ser Lorent Marbrand, Lord Commander of her Queensguard. Even the two White Harbor men, that fearsome knight Ser Medrick Manderly and his clever, corpulent brother Ser Torrhen, urged the queen to mistrust. "Best take no chances," Ser Torrhen said. "If the foe gains two more dragons, we are lost."

Only Lord Corlys spoke in defense of the dragonseed, declaring that Ser Addam and his brother Alyn were "true Velaryons," worthy heirs to Driftmark. As for the girl, though she might be dirty and ill-favored, she had fought valiantly in the Battle of the Gullet. "As did the two betrayers," Lord Celtigar countered.

The Hand's impassioned protests had been in vain. All the queen's fears and suspicions had been aroused. She had been betrayed so often, by so many, that she was quick to believe the worst of any man. Treachery no longer had the power to surprise her. She had come to expect it, even from those she loved the most.

Queen Rhaenyra command Ser Luthor Largent to take twenty gold cloaks to the Dragonpit and arrest Ser Addam Velaryon. And thus did betrayal beget more betrayal, to the queen's undoing. As Ser Luthor Largent and his gold cloaks rode up Rhaenys's Hill with the queen's warrant, the doors of the Dragonpit were thrown open above them, and Seasmoke spread his pale grey wings and took flight, smoke rising from his nostrils. Ser Addam Velaryon had been forewarned in time to make his escape. Balked and angry, Ser Luthor returned at once to the Red Keep, where he burst into the Tower of the Hand and laid rough hands on the aged Lord Corlys, accusing him of treachery. Nor did the old man deny it. Bound and beaten, but still silent, he was taken down into the dungeons and thrown into a black cell to await trial and execution.

All the while tales of the slaughter at Tumbleton were spreading through the city . . . and with them, terror. King's Landing would be next, men told one another. Dragon would fight dragon, and this time the city would surely burn. Fearful of the coming foe, hundreds tried to flee, only to be turned back at the gates by the gold cloaks. Trapped within the city walls, some sought shelter in deep cellars against the firestorm they feared was coming, whilst others turned to prayer, to drink, and the pleasures to be found between a woman's thighs. By nightfall, the city's taverns, brothels, and septs were full to bursting with men and women seeking solace or escape and trading tales of horror.

A different sort of chaos reigned in Tumbleton, sixty leagues to the southwest. Whilst King's Landing quailed in terror, the foes they feared had yet to advance a foot toward the city, for King Aegon's loyalists found themselves leaderless, beset by division, conflict, and doubt. Ormund Hightower lay dead, along with his cousin Ser Bryndon, the foremost knight of Oldtown. His sons remained back at the Hightower a thousand leagues away, and were green boys besides. And whilst Lord Ormund had dubbed Daeron Targaryen "Daeron the Daring" and praised his courage in battle, the prince was still a boy. The youngest of King Aegon's sons, he had grown up in the shadow of his elder brothers, and was more used to following commands than giving them. The most senior

Hightower remaining with the host was Ser Hobert, another of Lord Ormund's cousins, hitherto entrusted only with the baggage train. A man "as stout as he was slow," Hobert Hightower had lived sixty years without distinguishing himself, yet now he presumed to take command of the host by right of his kinship to Queen Alicent.

Seldom has any town or city in the history of the Seven Kingdoms been subject to as long or cruel or savage a sack as Tumbleton after the Treasons. Prince Daeron was sickened by all he saw and commanded Ser Hobert Hightower to put a stop to it, but Hightower's efforts proved as ineffectual as the man himself.

The worst crimes were those committed by the Two Betrayers, the baseborn dragonriders Hugh Hammer and Ulf White. Ser Ulf gave himself over entirely to drunkenness, drowning himself in wine and flesh. Those who failed to please were fed to his dragon. The knighthood that Queen Rhaenyra had conferred on him did not suffice. Nor was he surfeit when Prince Daemon named him Lord of Bitterbridge. White had a greater prize in mind: he desired no less a seat than Highgarden, declaring that the Tyrells had played no part in the Dance, and therefore should be attainted as traitors.

Ser Ulf's ambitions must be accounted modest when compared to those of his fellow turncloak, Hugh Hammer. The son of a common blacksmith, Hammer was a huge man, with hands so strong that he was said to be able to twist steel bars into torcs. Though largely untrained in the art of war, his size and strength made him a fearsome foe. His weapon of choice was the warhammer, with which he delivered crushing, killing blows. In battle he rode Vermithor, once the mount of the Old King himself; of all the dragons in Westeros, only Vhagar was older or larger. For all these reasons, Lord Hammer (as he now styled himself) began to dream of crowns. "Why be a lord when you can be a king?" he told the men who began to gather round him.

Neither of the Two Betrayers seemed eager to help Prince Daeron press an attack on King's Landing. They had a great host, and three dragons besides, yet the queen had three dragons as well (as best they knew), and would have five once Prince Daemon returned with Nettles. Lord Peake preferred to delay any advance until Lord Baratheon could bring up his power from Storm's End to join them, whilst Ser Hobert wished to fall back to the Reach to replenish their fast-dwindling supplies. None seemed concerned that their army was shrinking every day, melting away like morning dew as more and more men deserted, stealing off for home and harvest with all the plunder they could carry.

Long leagues to the north, in a castle overlooking the Bay of Crabs, another lord found himself sliding down a sword's edge as well. From King's Landing came a raven bearing the queen's message to Manfryd Mooton, Lord of Maidenpool: he was to deliver her the head of the bastard girl Nettles, who was said to have become Prince Daemon's lover and who the queen had therefore judged guilty of high treason. "No harm is to be done my lord husband, Prince Daemon of House Targaryen," Her Grace commanded. "Send him back to me when the deed is done, for we have urgent need of him."

Maester Norren, keeper of the *Chronicles of Maidenpool,* says that when his lordship read the queen's letter he was so shaken that he lost his voice. Nor did it return to him until he had drunk three cups of wine. Thereupon Lord Mooton sent for the captain of his guard, his brother, and his champion, Ser Florian Greysteel. He bade his maester to remain as well. When all had assembled, he read to them the letter and asked them for their counsel.

"This thing is easily done," said the captain of his guard. "The prince sleeps beside her, but he has grown old. Three men should be enough to subdue him should he try to interfere, but I will take six to be certain. Does my lord wish this done tonight?"

"Six men or sixty, he is still Daemon Targaryen," Lord Mooton's brother objected. "A sleeping draught in his evening wine would be the wiser course. Let him wake to find her dead."

"The girl is but a child, however foul her treasons," said Ser Florian, that old knight, grey and grizzled and stern. "The Old King would never have asked this, of any man of honor."

"These are foul times," Lord Mooton said, "and it is a foul choice this queen has given me. The girl is a guest beneath my roof. If I obey, Maidenpool shall be forever cursed. If I refuse, we shall be attainted and destroyed."

To which his brother answered, "It may be we shall be destroyed whatever choice we make. The prince is more than fond of this brown child, and his dragon is close at hand. A wise lord would kill them both, lest the prince burn Maidenpool in his wroth."

"The queen has forbidden any harm to come to him," Lord Mooton reminded them, "and murdering two guests in their beds is twice as foul as murdering one. I should be doubly cursed." Thereupon he sighed and said, "Would that I had never read this letter."

And up spoke Maester Norren, saying, "Mayhaps you never did."

What was said after that is unknown. All we know is that the maester, a young man of two-and-twenty, found Prince Daemon and the girl Nettles at their supper that night, and showed them the queen's letter. After reading the letter, Prince Daemon said, "A queen's words, a whore's work." Then he drew his sword and asked if Lord Mooton's men were waiting outside the door to take them captive. When told that the maester had come alone and in secret, Prince Daemon sheathed his sword, saying, "You are a bad maester, but a good man," and then bade him leave, commanding him to "speak no word of this to lord nor love until the morrow."

How the prince and his bastard girl spent their last night beneath Lord Mooton's roof is not recorded, but as dawn broke they appeared together in the yard, and Prince Daemon helped Nettles saddle Sheepstealer one last time. It was her custom to feed him each day before she flew; dragons bend easier to their rider's will when full. That morning she fed him a black ram, the largest in all Maidenpool, slitting the ram's throat herself. Her riding leathers were stained with blood when she mounted her dragon, Maester Norren records, and "her cheeks were stained with tears." No word of farewell was spoken betwixt man and maid, but as Sheepstealer beat his leathery brown wings and climbed into the dawn sky, Caraxes raised his head and gave a scream that shattered every window in Jonquil's Tower. High above the town, Nettles turned her dragon toward the Bay of Crabs, and vanished in the morning mists, never to be seen again at court or castle.

Daemon Targaryen returned to the castle just long enough to break his fast with Lord Mooton. "This is the last that you will see of me," he told his lordship. "I thank you for your hospitality. Let it be known through all your lands that I fly for Harrenhal. If my nephew Aemond dares face me, he shall find me there, alone."

Thus Prince Daemon departed Maidenpool for the last time. When he had gone, Maester Norren went to his lord to say, "Take the chain from my neck and bind my hands with it. You must need deliver me the queen. When I gave warning to a traitor and allowed her to escape, I became a traitor as well." Lord Mooton refused. "Keep your chain," his lordship said. "We are all traitors here." And that night, Queen Rhaenyra's quartered banners were taken down from where they flew above the gates of Maidenpool, and the golden dragons of King Aegon II raised in their stead.

No banners flew above the blackened towers and ruined keeps of Harrenhal when Prince Daemon descended from the sky to take up the castle for his own. A few squatters had found shelter in the castle's deep vaults and undercellars, but the sound of Caraxes's wings sent them fleeing. When the last of them was gone, Daemon Targaryen walked the cavernous halls of Harren's seat alone, with no companion but his dragon. Each night at dusk he slashed the heart tree in the godswood to mark the passing of another day. Thirteen marks can be seen upon that weirwood still; old wounds, deep and dark, yet the lords who have ruled Harrenhal since Daemon's day say they bleed afresh every spring.

On the fourteenth day of the prince's vigil, a shadow swept over the castle, blacker than any passing cloud. All the birds in the godswood took to the air in fright, and a hot wind whipped the fallen leaves across the yard. Vhagar had come at last, and on her back rode the one-eyed prince Aemond Targaryen, clad in night-black armor chased with gold.

He had not come alone. Alys Rivers flew with him, her long hair streaming black behind her, her belly swollen with child. Prince Aemond circled twice about the towers of Harrenhal, then brought Vhagar down in the outer ward, with Caraxes a hundred yards away. The dragons glared balefully at each other, and Caraxes spread his wings and hissed, flames dancing across his teeth.

The prince helped his woman down from Vhagar's back, then turned to face his uncle. "Nuncle, I hear you have been seeking us."

"Only you," Daemon replied. "Who told you where to find me?"

"My lady," Aemond answered. "She saw you in a storm cloud, in a mountain pool at dusk, in the fire we lit to cook our suppers. She sees much and more, my Alys. You were a fool to come alone."

"Were I not alone, you would not have come," said Daemon.

"Yet you are, and here I am. You have lived too long, nuncle."

"On that much we agree," Daemon replied. Then the old prince bid Caraxes bend his neck, and climbed stiffly onto his back, whilst the young prince kissed his woman and vaulted lightly onto Vhagar, taking care to fasten the four short chains between belt and saddle. Daemon left his own chains dangling. Caraxes hissed again, filling the air with flame, and Vhagar answered with a roar. As one the two dragons leapt into the sky.

Prince Daemon took Caraxes up swiftly, lashing him with a steel-tipped whip until they disappeared into a bank of clouds. Vhagar, older and much the larger, was also slower, made ponderous by her very size, and ascended more gradually, in ever widening circles that took her and her rider out over the waters of the Gods Eye. The hour was late, the sun was close to setting, and the lake was calm, its surface glimmering like a sheet of beaten copper. Up and up she soared, searching for Caraxes as Alys Rivers watched from atop Kingspyre Tower in Harrenhal below.

The attack came sudden as a thunderbolt. Caraxes dove down upon Vhagar with a piercing shriek that was heard a dozen miles away, cloaked by the glare of the setting sun on Prince Aemond's blind side. The Blood Wyrm slammed into the older dragon with terrible force. Their roars echoed across the Gods Eye as the two grappled and tore at one another, dark against a blood red sky. So bright did their flames burn that fisher-folk below feared the clouds themselves had caught fire. Locked together, the dragons tumbled toward the lake. The Blood Wyrm's jaws closed about Vhagar's neck, her black teeth sinking deep into the flesh of the larger dragon. Even as Vhagar's claws raked her belly open and Vhagar's own teeth ripped away a wing, Caraxes bit deeper, worrying at the wound as the lake rushed up below them with terrible speed.

And it was then, the tales tell us, that Prince Daemon Targaryen swung a leg over his saddle and leapt from one dragon to the other. In his hand was Dark Sister, the sword of Queen Visenya. As Aemond One-Eye looked up in terror, fumbling with the chains that bound him to his saddle, Daemon ripped off his nephew's helm and drove the sword down into his blind eye, so hard the point came out the back of the young prince's throat. Half a heartbeat later, the dragons struck the lake, sending up a gout of water so high that it was said to have been as tall as Kingspyre Tower.

Neither man nor dragon could have survived such an impact, the fisherfolk who saw it said. Nor did they. Caraxes lived long enough to crawl back onto the land. Gutted, with one wing torn from his body and the waters of the lake smoking about him, the Blood Wyrm found the strength to drag himself onto the lakeshore, expiring beneath the walls of

Harrenhal. Vhagar's carcass plunged to the lake floor, the hot blood from the gaping wound in her neck bringing the water to a boil over her last resting place. When she was found some years later, after the end of the Dance of the Dragons, Prince Aemond's armored bones remained chained to her saddle, with Dark Sister thrust hilt-deep through his eye socket.

That Prince Daemon died as well we cannot doubt. His remains were never found, but there are queer currents in that lake, and hungry fish as well. The singers tell us that the old prince survived the fall and afterward made his way back to the girl Nettles, to spend the remainder of his days at her side. Such stories make for charming songs, but poor history.

It was upon the twenty-second day of the fifth moon of the year 130 AC when the dragons danced and died above the Gods Eye. Daemon Targaryen was nine-and-forty at his death; Prince Aemond had only turned twenty. Vhagar, the greatest of the Targaryen dragons since the passing of Balerion the Black Dread, had counted one hundred eighty-one years upon the earth. Thus passed the last living creature from the days of Aegon's Conquest, as dusk and darkness swallowed Black Harren's accursed seat. Yet so few were on hand to bear witness that it would be some time before word of Prince Daemon's last battle became widely known.

Back in King's Landing, Queen Rhaenyra was finding herself ever more isolated with every new betrayal. The suspected turncloak Addam Velaryon had fled before he could be put to the question. By ordering the arrest of Addam Velaryon, she had lost not only a dragon and a dragon-rider, but her Queen's Hand as well . . . and more than half the army that had sailed from Dragonstone to seize the Iron Throne was made up of men sworn to House Velaryon. When it became known that Lord Corlys languished in a dungeon under the Red Keep, they began to abandon her cause by the hundreds. Some made their way to Cobbler's Square to join the throngs gathered there, whilst others slipped through postern gates or over the walls, intent on making their way back to Driftmark. Nor could those who remained be trusted.

That very day, not long after sunset, another horror visited the queen's court. Helaena Targaryen, sister, wife, and queen to King Aegon II and mother of his children, threw herself from her window in Maegor's Holdfast to die impaled upon the iron spikes that lined the dry moat below. She was but one-and-twenty.

By nightfall, a darker tale was being told in the streets and alleys of King's Landing, in inns and brothels and pot shops, even holy septs. Queen Helaena had been murdered, the whispers went, as her sons had been before her. Prince Daeron and his dragons would soon be at the gates, and with them the end of Rhaenyra's reign. The old queen was determined that her young half sister should not live to revel in her downfall, so she had sent Ser Luthor Largent to seize Helaena with his huge rough hands and fling her from the window onto the spikes below.

The rumor of Queen Helaena's "murder" was soon on the lips of half King's Landing. That it was so quickly believed shows how utterly the city had turned against their once-beloved queen. Rhaenyra was hated; Helaena had been loved. Nor had the common folk of the city forgotten the cruel murder of Prince Jaehaerys by Blood and Cheese. Helaena's end had been mercifully swift; one of the spikes took her through the throat and she died without a sound. At the moment of her death, across the city atop the Hill of Rhaenys, her dragon Dreamfyre rose suddenly with a roar that shook the Dragonpit, snapping two of the chains that bound her. When Queen Alicent was informed of her daughter's passing, she rent her garments and pronounced a dire curse upon her rival.

That night King's Landing rose in bloody riot.

The rioting began amidst the alleys and wynds of Flea Bottom, as men and women poured from the wine sinks, rat pits, and pot shops by the hundreds, angry, drunken, and afraid. From there the rioters spread throughout the city, shouting for justice for the dead princes and their murdered mother. Carts and wagons were overturned, shops looted, homes plundered and set afire. Gold cloaks attempting to quell the disturbances were set upon and beaten bloody. No one was spared, of high birth or low. Lords were pelted with rubbish, knights pulled from their saddles. Lady Darla Deddings saw her brother Davos stabbed through the eye when he tried to defend her from three drunken ostlers intent on raping her. Sailors unable to return to their ships attacked the River Gate and fought a pitched battle with the City Watch. It took Ser Luthor Largent and four hundred spears to disperse them. By then the gate had been hacked half to pieces and a hundred men were dead or dying, a quarter of them gold cloaks.

At Cobbler's Square the sounds of the riot could be heard from every quarter. The City Watch had come in strength, five hundred men clad in black ringmail, steel caps, and long golden cloaks, armed with short swords, spears, and spiked cudgels. They formed up on the south side of the square, behind a wall of shields and spears. At their head rode Ser Luthor Largent upon an armored warhorse, a longsword in his hand. The mere sight of him was enough to send hundreds streaming away into the wynds and alleys and side streets. Hundreds more fled when Ser Luthor ordered the gold cloaks to advance.

Ten thousand remained, however. The press was so thick that many who might gladly have fled found themselves unable to move, pushed and shoved and trod upon. Others surged forward, locked arms, and began to shout and curse, as the spears advanced to the slow beat of a drum. "Make way, you bloody fools," Ser Luthor roared. "Go home. No harm will come to you. Go home!"

Some say the first man to die was a baker, who grunted in surprise when a spearpoint pierced his flesh and he saw his apron turning red. Others claim it was a little girl, trodden under by Ser Luthor's warhorse. A rock came flying from the crowd, striking a spearman on the brow. Shouts and curses were heard, sticks and stones and chamber pots came raining down from rooftops, an archer across the square began to loose his shafts. A torch was thrust at a watchman, and quick as that his golden cloak was burning.

The gold cloaks were large men, young, strong, disciplined, well armed and well armored. For twenty yards or more their shield wall held, and they cut a bloody road through the crowd, leaving dead and dying all around them. But they numbered only five hundred, and tens of thousands of rioters had gathered. One watchman went down, then another. Suddenly smallfolk were slipping through the gaps in the line, attacking with knives and stones, even teeth, swarming over the City Watch and around their flanks, attacking from behind, flinging tiles down from roofs and balconies.

Battle turned to riot turned to slaughter. Surrounded on all sides, the gold cloaks found themselves hemmed in and swept under, with no room to wield their weapons. Many died on the points of their own swords. Others were torn to pieces, kicked to death, trampled underfoot, hacked apart with hoes and butcher's cleavers. Even the fearsome Ser Luthor Largent could not escape the carnage. His sword torn from his grasp, Largent was pulled from his saddle, stabbed in the belly, and bludgeoned to death with a cobblestone, his helm and head so crushed that it was only by its size that his body was recognized when the corpse wagons came the next day.

During that long night, chaos held sway over half the city, whilst strange lords and kings of misrule squabbled o'er the rest. A hedge knight named Ser Perkin the Flea crowned his own squire Trystane, a stripling of sixteen years, declaring him to be a natural son of the late King Viserys. Any knight can make a knight, and when Ser Perkin began dubbing every sellsword, thief, and butcher's boy who flocked to Trystane's ragged banner, men and boys appeared by the hundreds to pledge themselves to his cause.

By dawn, fires were burning throughout the city, Cobbler's Square was littered with corpses, and bands of lawless men roamed Flea Bottom, breaking into shops and homes and laying rough hands on every honest person they encountered. The surviving gold cloaks had retreated to their barracks, whilst gutter knights, mummer kings, and mad prophets ruled the streets. Like the roaches they resembled, the worst of these fled before the light, retreating to hidey-holes and cellars to sleep off their drunks, divvy up their plunder, and wash the blood off their hands. The gold cloaks at the Old Gate and the Dragon Gate sallied forth under the command of their captains, Ser Balon Byrch and Ser Garth the Harelip, and by midday had managed to restore some semblance of order to the streets north and east of Rhaenys's Hill. Ser Medrick Manderly, leading a hundred White Harbor men, did the same for the area northeast of Aegon's High Hill, down to the Iron Gate.

The rest of King's Landing remained in chaos. When Ser Torrhen Manderly led his northmen down the Hook, they found Fishermonger's Square and River Row swarming with Ser Perkin's gutter knights. At the River Gate, "King" Trystane's ragged banner flew above the battlements, whilst the bodies of the captain and three of his serjeants hung from the gatehouse. The remainder of the "Mudfoot" garrison had gone over to Ser Perkin. Ser Torrhen lost a quarter of his men fighting his way back to the Red Keep . . . yet escaped lightly compared to Ser Lorent Marbrand, who led a hundred knights and men-at-arms into Flea Bottom. Sixteen returned. Ser Lorent, Lord Commander of the Queensguard, was not amongst them.

By evenfall, Rhaenyra Targaryen found herself sore beset on every side, her reign in ruins. The queen raged when she learned that Maidenpool had gone over to the foe, that the girl Nettles had escaped, that her own beloved consort had betrayed her, and she trembled when Lady Mysaria warned her against the coming dark, that this night would be worse than the last. At dawn, a hundred men attended her in the throne room, but one by one they slipped away.

Her Grace swung from rage to despair and back again, clutching so desperately at the Iron Throne that both her hands were bloody by the time the sun set. She gave command of the gold cloaks to Ser Balon Byrch, captain at the Iron Gate, sent ravens to Winterfell and the Eyrie pleading for more aid, ordered that a decree of attainder be drawn up against the Mootons of Maidenpool, and named the young Ser Glendon Goode lord commander of the Queensguard. (Though only twenty, and a member of the White Swords for less than a moon's turn, Goode had distinguished himself during the fighting in Flea Bottom earlier that day. It was he who brought back Ser Lorent's body, to keep the rioters from despoiling it.)

Aegon the Younger was ever at his mother's side, yet seldom spoke a word. Prince Joffrey, ten-and-three, donned squire's armor and begged the queen to let him ride to the Dragonpit and mount Tyraxes. "I want to fight for you, Mother, as my brothers did. Let me prove that I am as brave as they were." His words only deepened Rhaenyra's resolve, however. "Brave they were, and dead they are, the both of them. My sweet boys." And once more, Her Grace forbade the prince to leave the castle.

With the setting of the sun, the vermin of King's Landing emerged once more from their rat pits, hidey-holes, and cellars, in even greater numbers than the night before.

At the River Gate, Ser Perkin feasted his gutter knights on stolen food and led them down the riverfront, looting wharfs and warehouses and any ship that had not put to sea. Though King's Landing boasted massive walls and stout towers, they had been designed to repel attacks from outside the city, not from within its walls. The garrison at the Gate of the Gods was especially weak, as their captain and a third their number had died with Ser Luthor Largent in Cobbler's Square. Those who remained, many wounded, were easily overcome by Ser Perkin's hordes.

Before an hour had passed, the King's Gate and the Lion Gate were open as well. The gold cloaks at the first had fled, whilst the "lions" at the other had thrown in with the mobs. Three of the seven gates of King's Landing were open to Rhaenyra's foes.

The most dire threat to the queen's rule proved to be within the city, however. By nightfall, another crowd had gathered in Cobbler's Square, twice as large and thrice as fearful as the night before. Like the queen they so despised, the mob was looking to the sky with dread, fearing that King Aegon's dragons would arrive before the night was out, with an army close behind them. They no longer believed that the queen could protect them.

When a crazed one-handed prophet called the Shepherd began to rant against dragons, not just the ones who were coming to attack them, but all dragons everywhere, the crowd, half-crazed themselves, listened. "When the dragons come," he shrieked, "your flesh will burn and blister and turn to ash. Your wives will dance in gowns of fire, shrieking as they burn, lewd and naked underneath the flames. And you shall see your little children weeping, weeping till their eyes do melt and slide like jelly down their faces, till their pink flesh falls black and crackling from their bones. The Stranger comes, *he comes, he comes,* to scourge us for our sins. Prayers cannot stay his wroth, no more than tears can quench the flame of dragons. Only blood can do that. Your blood, my blood, *their* blood." Then he raised the stump of his right arm, and pointed at Rhaenys's Hill behind him, at the Dragonpit black against the stars. "There the demons dwell, up *there.* This is their city. If you would make it yours, first must you destroy them! If you would cleanse yourself of sin, first must you bathe in dragon's blood! For only blood can quench the fires of hell!"

From ten thousand throats a cry went up. *"Kill them! Kill them!"* And like some vast beast with ten thousand legs, the Shepherd's lambs began to move, shoving and pushing, waving their torches, brandishing swords and knives and other, cruder weapons, walking and running through the streets and alleys toward the Dragonpit. Some thought better and slipped away to home, but for every man who left, three more appeared to join these dragonslayers. By the time they reached the Hill of Rhaenys, their numbers had doubled.

High atop Aegon's High Hill across the city, the Queen watched the attack unfold from the roof of Maegor's Holdfast with her sons and members of her court. The night was black and overcast, the torches so numerous that it was as if all the stars had come down from the sky to storm the

Dragonpit. As soon as word had reached her that the enraged crowd was on the march, Rhaenyra sent riders to Ser Balon at the Old Gate and Ser Garth at the Dragon Gate, commanding them to disperse the mob and defend the royal dragons . . . but with the city in such turmoil, it was far from certain that the riders had won through. Even if they had, what loyal gold cloaks remained were too few to have any hope of success. When Prince Joffrey pleaded with his mother to let him ride forth with their own knights and those from White Harbor, the queen refused. "If they take that hill, this one will be next," she said. "We will need every sword here to defend the castle."

"They will kill the *dragons*," Prince Joffrey said, anguished.

"Or the dragons will kill them," his mother said, unmoved. "Let them burn. The realm will not long miss them."

"Mother, what if they kill *Tyraxes*?" the young prince said.

The queen did not believe it. "They are vermin. Drunks and fools and gutter rats. One taste of dragonflame and they will run."

At that the court fool Mushroom spoke up, saying, "Drunks they may be, but a drunken man knows not fear. Fools, aye, but a fool can kill a king. Rats, that too, but a thousand rats can bring down a bear. I saw it happen once, down there in Flea Bottom." Her Grace turned back to the parapets.

It was only when the watchers on the roof heard Syrax roar that it was noticed that the prince had slunk sullenly away. "No," the queen was heard to say, "I forbid it, I *forbid* it," but even as she spoke, her dragon flapped up from the yard, perched for half a heartbeat atop the castle battlements, then launched herself into the night with the queen's son clinging to her back, a sword in hand. "After him," Rhaenyra shouted, "all of you, every man, every boy, to horse, *to horse*, go after him. Bring him back, bring him back, he does not know. My son, my sweet, my son . . ."

But it was too late.

We shall not pretend to any understanding of the bond between dragon and dragonrider; wiser heads have pondered that mystery for centuries. We do know, however, that dragons are not horses, to be ridden by any man who throws a saddle on their back. Syrax was the queen's dragon. She had never known another rider. Though Prince Joffrey was known to her by sight and scent, a familiar presence whose fumbling at her chains excited no alarm, the great yellow she-dragon wanted no part of him astride her. In his haste to be away before before he could be stopped, the prince had vaulted onto Syrax without benefit of saddle or whip. His intent, we must presume, was either to fly Syrax into battle or, more likely, to cross the city to the Dragonpit and his own Tyraxes. Mayhaps he meant to loose the other pit dragons as well.

Joffrey never reached the Hill of Rhaenys. Once in the air, Syrax twisted beneath him, fighting to be free of this unfamiliar rider. And from below, stones and spears and arrows flew at him from the hands of the rioters below, maddening the dragon even further. Two hundred feet above Flea Bottom, Prince Joffrey slid from the dragon's back and plunged to the earth.

Near a juncture where five alleys came together, the prince's fall came to its bloody end. He crashed first onto a steep-pitched roof before rolling off to fall another forty feet amidst a shower of broken tiles. We are told that the fall broke his back, that shards of slate rained down about him like knives, that his own sword tore loose of his hand and pierced him through the belly. In Flea Bottom, men still speak of a candlemaker's daughter named Robin who cradled the broken prince in her arms and gave him comfort as he died, but there is more of legend than of history in that tale. "Mother, forgive me," Joffrey supposedly said, with his last breath . . . though men still argue whether he was speaking of his mother the queen, or praying to the Mother Above.

Thus perished Joffrey Velaryon, Prince of Dragonstone and heir to the Iron Throne, the last of Queen Rhaenyra's sons by Laenor Velaryon . . . or the last of her bastards by Ser Harwin Strong, depending on which truth one chooses to believe.

And even as blood flowed in the alleys of Flea Bottom, another battle raged round the Dragonpit above, atop the Hill of Rhaenys.

Mushroom was not wrong: swarms of starving rats do indeed bring down bulls and bears and lions, when there are enough of them. No matter how many the bull or bear might kill, there are always more, biting at the great beast's legs, clinging to its belly, running up its back. So it was that night. These human rats were armed with spears, longaxes, spiked clubs, and half a hundred other kinds of weapons, including both longbows and crossbows.

Gold cloaks from the Dragon Gate, obedient to the queen's command, issued forth from their barracks to defend the hill, but found themselves unable to cut through the mobs, and turned back, whilst the messenger sent to the Old Gate never arrived. The Dragonpit had its own contingent of guards, but they were few in number, and were soon overwhelmed and slaughtered when the mob smashed through the doors (the towering main gates, sheathed in bronze and iron, were too strong to assault, but the building had a score of lesser entrances) and came clambering through windows.

Mayhaps the attackers hoped to take the dragons within whilst they slept, but the clangor of the assault made that impossible. Those who lived to tell tales afterward spoke of shouts and screams, the smell of blood in the air, the splintering of oak-and-iron doors beneath crude rams and the blows of countless axes. "Seldom have so many men rushed so eagerly onto their funeral pyres," Grand Maester Munkun later wrote, "but a madness was upon them." There were four dragons housed within the Dragonpit. By the time the first of the attackers came pouring out onto the sands, all four were roused, awake, and angry.

No two chronicles agree on how many men and women died that night beneath the Dragonpit's great dome: two hundred or two thousand, be that as it may. For every man who perished, ten suffered burns and yet survived. Trapped within the pit, hemmed in by walls and dome and bound by heavy chains, the dragons could not fly away, or use their wings to evade attacks and swoop down on their foes. Instead they fought with horns and claws and teeth, turning this way and that like bulls in a Flea Bottom rat pit . . . but these bulls could breathe fire. The Dragonpit was transformed into a fiery hell where burning men staggered screaming through the smoke, the flesh sloughing from their blackened bones, but for every man who died, ten more appeared, shouting that the dragons must need die. One by one, they did.

Shrykos was the first dragon to succumb, slain by a woodsman known as Hobb the Hewer, who leapt onto her neck, driving his axe down into the beast's skull as Shrykos roared and twisted, trying to throw him off. Seven blows did Hobb deliver with his legs locked round the dragon's neck, and each time his axe came down he roared out the name of one of the Seven. It was the seventh blow, the Stranger's blow, that slew the dragon, crashing through scale and bones into the beast's brain.

Morghul, it is written, was slain by the Burning Knight, a huge brute of a man in heavy armor who rushed headlong into the dragon's flame with spear in hand, thrusting its point into the beast's eye repeatedly even as the dragonflame melted the steel plate that encased him and devoured the flesh within.

Prince Joffrey's Tyraxes retreated back into his lair, we are told, roasting so many would-be dragonslayers as they rushed after him that its entrance was soon made impassable by their corpses. But it must be recalled that each of these man-made caves had two entrances, one fronting on the sands of the pit, the other opening onto the hillside, and soon the rioters broke in by the "back door," howling through the smoke with swords and spears and axes. As Tyraxes turned, his chains fouled, entangling him in a web of steel that fatally limited his movement. Half a dozen men (and one woman) would later claim to have dealt the dragon the mortal blow.

The last of the four pit dragons did not die so easily. Legend has it that Dreamfyre had broken free of two of her chains at Queen Helaena's death. The remaining bonds she burst now, tearing the stanchions from the walls as the mob rushed her, then plunging into them with tooth and claw, ripping men apart and tearing off their limbs even as she loosed her terrible fires. As others closed about her she took wing, circling the cavernous interior of the Dragonpit and swooping down to attack the men below. Tyraxes, Shrykos, and Morghul killed scores, there can be little doubt, but Dreamfyre slew more than all three of them combined.

Hundreds fled in terror from her flames . . . but hundreds more, drunk or mad or possessed of the Warrior's own courage, pushed through to the attack. Even at the apex of the dome, the dragon was within easy reach of archer and crossbowman, and arrows and quarrels flew at Dreamfyre wherever she turned, at such close range that some few even punched through her scales. Whenever she lighted, men swarmed to the attack, driving her back into the air. Twice the dragon flew at the Dragonpit's great bronze gates, only to find them closed and barred and defended by ranks of spears.

Unable to flee, Dreamfyre returned to the attack, savaging her tormenters until the sands of the pit were strewn with charred corpses, and the very air was thick with smoke and the smell of burned flesh, yet still the spears and arrows flew. The end came when a crossbow bolt nicked one of the dragon's eyes. Half-blind, and maddened by a dozen lesser wounds, Dreamfyre spread her wings and flew straight up at the great dome above in a last desperate attempt to break into the open sky. Already weakened by blasts of dragonflame, the dome cracked under the force of impact, and a moment later half of it came tumbling down, crushing both dragon and dragonslayers under tons of broken stone and rubble.

The Storming of the Dragonpit was done. Four of the Targaryen dragons lay dead, though at hideous cost. Yet the queen's own dragon remained alive and free . . . and as the burned and bloody survivors of the carnage in the pit came stumbling from the smoking ruins, Syrax descended upon them from above.

A thousand shrieks and shouts echoed across the city, mingling with the dragon's roar. Atop the Hill of Rhaenys, the Dragonpit wore a crown of yellow fire, burning so bright it seemed as if the sun was rising. Even the queen trembled as she watched, the tears glistening on her cheeks. Many of the queen's companions on the rooftop fled, fearing that the fires would soon engulf the entire city, even the Red Keep atop Aegon's High Hill. Others took themselves to the castle sept to pray for deliverance. Rhaenyra herself wrapped her arms about her last living son, Aegon the Younger, clutching him fiercely to her bosom. Nor would she loose her hold upon him . . . until that dread moment when Syrax fell.

Unchained and riderless, Syrax might have easily have flown away from the madness. The sky was hers. She could have returned to the Red Keep, left the city entirely, taken wing for Dragonstone. Was it the noise and fire that drew her to the Hill of Rhaenys, the roars and screams of dying dragons, the smell of burning flesh? We cannot know, no more than we can know why Syrax chose to descend upon the mobs, rending them with tooth and claw and devouring dozens, when she might as easily have rained fire on them from above, for in the sky no man could have harmed her. We can only report what happened.

Many a conflicting tale is told of the death of the queen's dragon. Some credit Hobb the Hewer and his axe, though this is almost certainly mistaken. Could the same man truly have slain two dragons on the same night and in the same manner? Some speak of an unnamed spearman, "a blood-soaked giant" who leapt from the Dragonpit's broken dome onto the dragon's back. Others relate how a knight named Ser Warrick Wheaton slashed a wing from Syrax with a Valyrian steel sword. A crossbowman named Bean would claim the kill afterward, boasting of it in many a wine sink and tavern, until one of the queen's loyalists grew tired of his wagging tongue and cut it out. The truth of the matter no one will ever know—except that Syrax died that night.

The loss of both her dragon and her son left Rhaenyra Targaryen ashen and inconsolable. She retreated to her chambers whilst her counselors conferred. King's Landing was lost, all agreed; they must need abandon the city. Reluctantly, Her Grace was persuaded to leave the next day, at dawn. With the Mud Gate in the hands of her foes, and all the ships along the river burned or sunk, Rhaenyra and a small band of followers slipped out through the Dragon Gate, intending to make their way up the coast to Duskendale. With her rode the brothers Manderly, four surviving Queensguard, Ser Balon Byrch and twenty gold cloaks, four of the queen's ladies-in-waiting, and her last surviving son, Aegon the Younger.

Much and more was happening at Tumbleton as well, and it is there we must next turn our gaze. As word of the unrest at King's Landing reached Prince Daeron's host, many younger lords grew anxious to advance upon the city at once. Chief amongst them was Ser Jon Roxton, Ser Roger Corne, and Lord Unwin Peake . . . but Ser Hobert Hightower counseled caution, and the Two Betrayers refused to join any attack unless their own demands were met. Ulf White, it will be recalled, wished to be granted the great castle of Highgarden with all its lands and incomes, whilst Hard Hugh Hammer desired nothing less than a crown for himself.

These conflicts came to a boil when Tumbleton learned belatedly of Aemond Targaryen's death at Harrenhal. King Aegon II had not been seen nor heard from since the fall of King's Landing to his half sister Rhaenyra, and there were many who feared that the queen had put him secretly to death, concealing the corpse so as not to be condemned as a kinslayer. With his brother Aemond slain as well, the greens found themselves kingless and leaderless. Prince Daeron stood next in the line of succession. Lord Peake declared that the boy should be proclaimed as Prince of Dragonstone at once; others, believing Aegon II dead, wished to crown him king.

The Two Betrayers felt the need of a king as well . . . but Daeron Targaryen was not the king they wanted. "We need a strong man to lead us, not a boy," declared Hard Hugh Hammer. "The throne should be mine."

When Bold Jon Roxton demanded to know by what right he presumed to name himself a king, Lord Hammer answered, "The same right as the Conquerer. A dragon." And truly, with Vhagar dead at last, the oldest and largest living dragon in all Westeros was Vermithor, once the mount of the Old King, now that of Hard Hugh the bastard. Vermithor was thrice the size of Prince Daeron's she-dragon Tessarion. No man who glimpsed them together could fail to see that Vermithor was a far more fearsome beast.

Though Hammer's ambition was unseemly in one born so low, the bastard undeniably possessed some Targaryen blood, and had proved himself fierce in battle and open-handed to those who followed him, displaying the sort of largesse that draws men to leaders as a corpse draws flies. They were the worst sort of men, to be sure: sellswords, robber knights, and like rabble, men of tainted blood and uncertain birth who loved battle for its own sake and lived for rapine and plunder.

The lords and knights of Oldtown and the Reach were offended by the arrogance of the Betrayer's claim, however, and none more so than Prince Daeron Targaryen himself, who grew so wroth that he threw a cup of wine into Hard Hugh's face. Whilst Lord White shrugged this off as a waste of good wine, Lord Hammer said, "Little boys should be more mannerly when men are speaking. I think your father did not beat you often enough. Take care I do not make up for his lack." The Two Betrayers took their leave together, and began to make plans for Hammer's coronation. When seen the next day, Hard Hugh was wearing a crown of black iron, to the fury of Prince Daeron and his trueborn lords and knights.

One such, Ser Roger Corne, made so bold as to knock the crown off Hammer's head. "A crown does not make a man a king," he said. "You should wear a horseshoe on your head, blacksmith." It was a foolish thing to do. Lord Hugh was not amused. At his command, his men forced Ser Roger to the ground, whereupon the blacksmith's bastard nailed not one but three horseshoes to the knight's skull. When Corne's friends tried to intervene, daggers were drawn and swords unsheathed, leaving three men dead and a dozen wounded.

That was more than Prince Daeron's loyalist lords were prepared to suffer. Lord Unwin Peake and a somewhat reluctant Hobert Hightower summoned eleven other lords and landed knights to a secret council in the cellar of a Tumbleton inn, to discuss what might be done to curb the arrogance of the baseborn dragonriders. The plotters agreed that it would be a simple matter to dispose of White, who was drunk more oft than not and had never shown any great prowess at arms. Hammer posed a greater danger, for of late he was surrounded day and night by lickspittles, camp followers, and sellswords eager for his favor. It would serve them little to kill White and leave Hammer alive, Lord Peake pointed out; Hard Hugh must needs die first. Long and loud were the arguments in the inn beneath the sign of the Bloody Caltrops, as the lords discussed how this might best be accomplished.

"Any man can be killed," declared Ser Hobert Hightower, "but what of the dragons?" Given the turmoil at King's Landing, Ser Tyler Norcross said, Tessarion alone should be enough to allow them to retake the Iron Throne. Lord Peake replied that victory would be a deal more certain with Vermithor and Silverwing. Marq Ambrose suggested that they take the city first, then dispose of White and Hammer after victory had been secured, but Richard Rodden insisted such a course would be dishonorable. "We cannot ask these men to shed blood with us, then kill them." Bold John Roxton settled the dispute. "We kill the bastards now," he said. "Afterward, let the bravest of us claim their dragons and fly them into battle." No man in that cellar doubted that Roxton was speaking of himself.

Though Prince Daeron was not present at the council, the Caltrops (as the conspirators became known) were loath to proceed without his consent and blessing. Owen Fossoway, Lord of Cider Hall, was dispatched under cover of darkness to wake the prince and bring him to the cellar, that the plotters might inform him of their plans. Nor did the once-gentle prince hesitate when Lord Unwin Peake presented him with warrants for the execution of Hard Hugh Hammer and Ulf White, but eagerly affixed his seal.

Men may plot and plan and scheme, but they had best pray as well, for no plan ever made by man has ever withstood the whims of the gods above. Two days later, on the very day the Caltrops planned to strike, Tumbleton woke in the black of night to screams and shouts. Outside the town walls, the camps were burning. Columns of armored knights were pouring in from north and west, wreaking slaughter, the clouds were raining arrows, and a dragon was swooping down upon them, terrible and fierce.

Thus began the Second Battle of Tumbleton.

The dragon was Seasmoke, his rider Ser Addam Velaryon, determined to prove that not all bastards need be turncloaks. How better to do that than by retaking Tumbleton from the Two Betrayers, whose treason had stained him? Singers say Ser Addam had flown from King's Landing to the Gods Eye, where he landed on the sacred Isle of Faces and took counsel with the Green Men. The scholar must confine himself to known fact, and what we know is that Ser Addam flew far and fast, descending on castles great and small whose lords were loyal to the queen, to piece together an army.

Many a battle and skirmish had already been fought in the lands watered by the Trident, and there was scarce a keep or village that had not paid its due in blood . . . but Addam Velaryon was relentless and determined and glib of tongue, and the river lords knew much and more of the horrors that had befallen Tumbleton. By the time Ser Addam was ready to descend on Tumbleton, he had near four thousand men at his back.

The great host encamped about the walls of Tumbleton outnumbered the attackers, but they had been too long in one place. Their discipline had grown lax, and disease had taken root as well; the death of Lord Ormund Hightower had left them without a leader, and the lords who wished to command in his place were at odds with one another. So intent were they upon their own conflicts and rivalries that they had all but forgotten their true foes. Ser Addam's night attack took them completely unawares. Before the men of Prince Daeron's army even knew they were in a battle, the enemy was amongst them, cutting them down as they staggered from their tents, as they were saddling their horses, struggling to don their armor, buckling their sword belts.

Most devastating of all was the dragon. Seasmoke came swooping down again and yet again, breathing flame. A hundred tents were soon afire, even the splendid silken pavilions of Ser Hobart Hightower, Lord Unwin Peake, and Prince Daeron himself. Nor was the town of Tumbleton reprieved. Those shops and homes and septs that had been spared the first time were eugulfed in dragonflame.

Daeron Targaryen was in his tent asleep when the attack began. Ulf White was inside Tumbleton, sleeping off a night of drinking at an inn called the Bawdy Badger that he had taken for his own. Hard Hugh

Hammer was within the town walls as well, in bed with the widow of a knight slain during the first battle. All three dragons were outside the town, in fields beyond the encampments.

Though attempts were made to wake Ulf White from his drunken slumber, he proved impossible to rouse. Infamously, he rolled under a table and snored through the entire battle. Hard Hugh Hammer was quicker to respond. Half-dressed, he rushed down the steps to the yard, calling for his hammer, his armor, and a horse, so he might ride out and mount Vermithor. His men rushed to obey, even as Seasmoke set the stables ablaze. But Lord Jon Roxton was already in the yard.

When he spied Hard Hugh, Roxton saw his chance, and said, "Lord Hammer, my condolences." Hammer turned, glowering. "For what?" he demanded. "You died in the battle," Bold Jon replied, drawing Orphan-Maker and thrusting it deep into Hammer's belly, before opening the bastard from groin to throat.

A dozen of Hard Hugh's men came running in time to see him die. Even a Valyrian steel blade like Orphan-Maker little avails a man when it is one against ten. Bold Jon Roxton slew three before he was slain in turn. It is said that he died when his foot slipped on a coil of Hugh Hammer's entrails, but perhaps that detail is too perfectly ironic to be true.

Three conflicting accounts exist as to the manner of death of Prince Daeron Targaryen. The best known claims that the prince stumbled from his pavilion with his night clothes afire, only to be cut down by the Myrish sellsword Black Trombo, who smashed his face in with a swing of his spiked morningstar. This version was the one preferred by Black Trombo, who told it far and wide. The second version is more or less the same, save that the prince was killed with a sword, not a morningstar, and his slayer was not Black Trombo, but some unknown man-at-arms who like as not did not even realize who he had killed. In the third alternative, the brave boy known as Daeron the Daring did not even make it out at all, but died when his burning pavilion collapsed upon him.

In the sky above, Addam Velaryon could see the battle turning into a rout below him. Two of the three enemy dragonriders were dead, but he would have had no way of knowing that. He could doubtless see the enemy dragons, however. Unchained, they were kept beyond the town walls, free to fly and hunt as they would; Silverwing and Vermithor oft coiled about one another in the fields south of Tumbleton, whilst Tessarion slept and fed in Prince Daeron's camp to the west of the town, not a hundred yards from his pavilion.

Dragons are creatures of fire and blood, and all three roused as the battle bloomed around them. A crossbowman let fly a bolt at Silverwing, we are told, and two score mounted knights closed on Vermithor with sword and lance and axe, hoping to dispatch the beast whilst he was still half-asleep and on the ground. They paid for that folly with their lives. Elsewhere on the field, Tessarion threw herself into the air, shrieking and spitting flame, and Addam Velaryon turned Seasmoke to meet her.

A dragon's scales are largely (though not entirely) impervious to flame; they protect the more vulnerable flesh and musculature beneath. As a dragon ages, its scales thicken and grow harder, affording even more protection, even as its flames burn hotter and fiercer (where the flames of a hatchling can set straw aflame, the flames of Balerion or Vhagar in the fullness of their power could and did melt steel and stone). When two dragons meet in mortal combat, therefore, they will oft employ weapons other than their flame: claws black as iron, long as swords, and sharp as razors, jaws so powerful they can crunch through even a knight's steel plate, tails like whips whose lashing blows have been known to smash wagons to splinters, break the spine of heavy destriers, and send men flying fifty feet in the air.

The battle between Tessarion and Seasmoke was different.

History calls the struggle between King Aegon II and his sister Rhaenyra the Dance of the Dragons, but only at Tumbleton did the dragons ever truly dance. Tessarion and Seasmoke were young dragons, nimbler in the air than their older brothers had been. Time and time again they rushed one another, only to have one or the other veer away at the last instant. Soaring like eagles, stooping like hawks, they circled, snapping and roaring, spitting fire, but never closing. Once the Blue Queen vanished into a bank of cloud, only to reappear an instant later, diving on Seasmoke from behind to scorch her tail with a burst of cobalt flame. Meanwhile, Seasmoke rolled and banked and looped. One instant he would be below his foe, and suddenly he would twist in the sky and come around behind her. Higher and higher the two dragons flew, as hundreds watched from the roofs of Tumbleton. One such said afterward that the flight of

Tessarion and Seasmoke seemed more mating dance than battle. Perhaps it was.

The dance ended when Vermithor rose roaring into the sky.

Almost a hundred years old and as large as the two young dragons put together, the bronze dragon with the great tan wings was in a rage as he took flight, with blood smoking from a dozen wounds. Riderless, he knew not friend from foe, so he loosed his wroth on all, spitting flame to right and left, turning savagely on any man who dared to fling a spear in his direction. One knight tried to flee before him, only to have Vermithor snatch him up in his jaws, even as his horse galloped on. Lords Piper and Deddings, seated together atop a low rise, burned with their squires, servants, and sworn shields when the Bronze Fury chanced to take note of them. An instant later, Seasmoke fell upon him.

Alone of the four dragons on the field that day, Seasmoke had a rider. Ser Addam Velaryon had come to prove his loyalty by destroying the Two Betrayers and their dragons, and here was one beneath him, attacking the men who had joined him for this fight. He must have felt duty-bound to protect them, though surely he knew in heart that his Seasmoke could not match the older dragon.

This was no dance, but a fight to the death. Vermithor had been flying no more than twenty feet above the battle when Seasmoke slammed into him from above, driving him shrieking into the mud. Men and boys ran in terror or were crushed as the two dragons rolled and tore at one another. Tails snapped and wings beat at the air, but the beasts were so entangled that neither was able to be able to break free. Benjicot Blackwood watched the struggle from atop his horse fifty yards away. Vermithor's size and weight were too much for Seasmoke to contend with, Lord Blackwood said many years later, and he would surely have torn the silver-grey dragon to pieces . . . if Tessarion had not fallen from the sky at that very moment to join the fight.

Who can know the heart of a dragon? Was it simple bloodlust that drove the Blue Queen to attack? Did the she-dragon come to help one of the combatants? If so, which? Some will claim that the bond between a dragon and dragonrider runs so deep that the beast shares his master's loves and hates. But who was the ally here, and who the enemy? Does a riderless dragon know friend from foe?

We shall never know the answers to those questions. All that history tells us is that three dragons fought amidst the mud and blood and smoke of Second Tumbleton. Seasmoke was first to die, when Vermithor locked his teeth into his neck and ripped his head off. Afterward the bronze dragon tried to take flight with his prize still in his jaws, but his tattered wings could not lift his weight. After a moment he collapsed and died. Tessarion, the Blue Queen, lasted until sunset. Thrice she tried to regain the sky, and thrice failed. By late afternoon she seemed to be in pain, so Lord Blackwood summoned his best archer, a longbowman known as Billy Burley, who took up a position a hundred yards away (beyond the range of the dying dragon's fires) and sent three shafts into her eye as she lay helpless on the ground.

By dusk, the fighting was done. Though the river lords lost less than a hundred men, whilst cutting down more than a thousand of the men from Oldtown and the Reach, Second Tumbleton could not be accounted a complete victory for the attackers, as they failed to take the town. Tumbleton's walls were still intact, and once the king's men had fallen back inside and closed their gates, the queen's forces had no way to make a breach, lacking both siege equipment and dragons. Even so, they wreaked great slaughter on their confused and disorganized foes, fired their tents, burned or captured almost all their wagons, fodder, and provisions, made off with three-quarters of their warhorses, slew their prince, and put an end to two of the king's dragons.

On the morning after the battle, the conquerers of Tumbleton looked out from the town walls to find their foes gone. The dead were strewn all around the city, and amongst them sprawled the carcasses of three dragons. One remained: Silverwing, Good Queen Alysanne's mount in days of old, had taken to the sky as the carnage began, circling the battlefield for hours, soaring on the hot winds rising from the fires below. Only after dark did she descend, to land beside her slain cousins. Later, singers would tell of how she thrice lifted Vermithor's wing with her nose, as if to make him fly again, but this is most like a fable. The rising sun would find her flapping listlessly across the field, feeding on the burned remains of horses, men, and oxen.

Eight of the thirteen Caltrops lay dead, amongst them Lord Owen Fossoway, Marq Ambrose, and Bold Jon Roxton. Richard Rodden had taken an arrow to the neck and would die the next day. Four of the plotters remained, amongst them Ser Hobert Hightower and Lord Unwin Peake. And though Hard Hugh Hammer had died, and his dreams of kingship with him, the second Betrayer remained. Ulf White had woken from his drunken sleep to find himself the last dragonrider, and possessed of the last dragon.

"The Hammer's dead, and your boy as well," he is purported to have told Lord Peake. "All you got left is me." When Lord Peake asked him his intentions, White replied, "We march, just how you wanted. You take the city, I'll take the bloody throne, how's that?"

The next morning, Ser Hobert Hightower called upon him, to thrash out the details of their assault upon King's Landing. He brought with him two casks of wine as a gift, one of Dornish red and one of Arbor gold. Though Ulf the Sot had never tasted a wine he did not like, he was known to be partial to the sweeter vintages. No doubt Ser Hobert hoped to sip the sour red whilst Lord Ulf quaffed down the Arbor gold. Yet something about Hightower's manner—he was sweating and stammering and too hearty by half, the squire who served them testified later—pricked White's suspicions. Wary, he commanded that the Dornish red be set aside for later, and insisted Ser Hobert share the Arbor gold with him.

History has little good to say about Ser Hobert Hightower, but no man can question the manner of his death. Rather than betray his fellow Caltrops, he let the squire fill his cup, drank deep, and asked for more. Once he saw Hightower drink, Ulf the Sot lived up to his name, putting down three cups before he began to yawn. The poison in the wine was a gentle one. When Lord Ulf went to sleep, never to awaken, Ser Hobert lurched to his feet and tried to make himself retch, but too late. His heart stopped within the hour.

Afterward, Lord Unwin Peake offered a thousand golden dragons to any knight of noble birth who could claim Silverwing. Three men came forth. When the first had his arm torn off and the second burned to death, the third man reconsidered. By that time Peake's army, the remnants of the great host that Prince Daeron and Lord Ormund Hightower had led all the way from Oldtown, was falling to pieces as deserters fled Tumbleton by the score with all the plunder they could carry. Bowing to defeat, Lord Unwin summoned his lords and serjeants and ordered a retreat. The accused turncloak Addam Velaryon, born Addam of Hull, had saved King's Landing from the queen's foes . . . at the cost of his own life.

Yet the queen knew nothing of his valor. Rhaenyra's flight from King's Landing had been beset with difficulty. At Rosby, she found the castle gates were barred at her approach. Young Lord Stokeworth's castellan granted her hospitality, but only for a night. Half of her gold cloaks deserted on the road, and one night her camp was attacked by broken men. Though her knights beat off the attackers, Ser Balon Byrch was felled by an arrow, and Ser Lyonel Bentley, a young knight of the Queensguard, suffered a blow to the head that cracked his helm. He perished raving the following day. The queen pressed on toward Duskendale.

House Darklyn had been amongst Rhaenyra's strongest supporters, but the cost of that loyalty had been high. Only the intercession of Ser Harrold Darke persuaded Lady Meredyth Darklyn to allow the queen within her walls at all (the Darkes were distant kin to the Darklyns, and Ser Harrold had once served as a squire to the late Ser Steffon), and only upon the condition that she would not remain for long.

Queen Rhaenyra had neither gold nor ships. When she had sent Lord Corlys to the dungeons she had lost her fleet, and she had fled King's Landing in terror of her life, without so much as a coin. Despairing and fearful, Her Grace grew ever more grey and haggard. She could not sleep and would not eat. Nor would she suffer to be parted from Prince Aegon, her last living son; day and night, the boy remained by her side, "like a small pale shadow."

Rhaenyra was forced to sell her crown to raise the coin to buy passage on a Braavosi merchantman, the *Violande*. Ser Harrold Darke urged her to seek refuge with Lady Arryn in the Vale, whilst Ser Medrick Manderly tried to persuade her to accompany him and his brother Ser Torrhen back to White Harbor, but Her Grace refused them both. She was adamant on returning to Dragonstone. There she would find dragon's eggs, she told her loyalists; she must have another dragon, or all was lost.

Strong winds pushed the *Violande* closer to the shores of Driftmark than the queen might have wished, and thrice she passed within hailing distance of the Sea Snake's warships, but Rhaenyra took care to keep well out of sight. Finally the Braavosi put into the harbor below the Dragonmont on the eventide. The queen had sent a raven to give notice of her coming, and found an escort waiting as she disembarked with her son Aegon, her ladies, and three Queensguard knights, all that was left of her party.

It was raining when the queen's party came ashore, and hardly a face was to be seen about the port. Even the dockside brothels appeared dark and deserted, but Her Grace took no notice. Sick in body and spirit, broken by betrayal, Rhaenyra Targaryen wanted only to return to her own seat, where she imagined that she and her son would be safe. Little did the queen know that she was about to suffer her last and most grievous treachery.

Her escort, forty strong, was commanded by Ser Alfred Broome, one of the men left behind when Rhaenyra had launched her attack upon King's Landing. Broome was the most senior of the knights at Dragonstone, having joined the garrison during the reign of the Old King. As such, he had expected to be named as castellan when Rhaenyra went forth to seize the Iron Throne . . . but Ser Alfred's sullen disposition and sour manner inspired neither affection nor trust, so the queen had passed him over in favor of the more affable Ser Robert Quince.

When Rhaenyra asked why Ser Robert had not come himself to meet her, Ser Alfred replied that the queen would be seeing "our fat friend" at the castle. And so she did . . . though Quince's charred corpse was burned beyond all recognition when they came upon it, hanging from the battlements of the gatehouse beside Dragonstone's steward, master-at-arms, and captain of guards. Only by his size did they know him, for Ser Robert had been enormously fat.

It is said that the blood drained from the queen's cheeks when she beheld the bodies, but young Prince Aegon was the first to realize what they meant. "Mother, flee!" he shouted, but too late. Ser Alfred's men men fell upon the queen's protectors. An axe split Ser Harrold Darke's head before his sword could clear its scabbard, and Ser Adrian Redfort was stabbed through the back with a spear. Only Ser Loreth Lansdale moved quickly enough to strike a blow in the queen's defense, cutting down the first two men who came at him before being slain himself. With him died of the last of the Queensguard. When Prince Aegon snatched up Ser Harrold's sword, Ser Alfred knocked the blade aside contemptuously.

The boy, the queen, and her ladies were marched at spearpoint through the gates of Dragonstone to the castle ward. There they found themselves face-to-face with a dead man and a dying dragon.

Sunfyre's scales still shone like beaten gold in the sunlight, but as he sprawled across the fused black Valyrian stone of the yard, it was plain to see that he was a broken thing, he who had been the most magnificent dragon ever to fly the skies of Westeros. The wing all but torn from his body by Meleys jutted from his body at an awkward angle, whilst fresh scars along his back still smoked and bled when he moved. Sunfyre was coiled in a ball when the queen and her party first beheld him. As he stirred and raised his head, huge wounds were visible along his neck, where another dragon had torn chunks from his flesh. On his belly were places where scabs had replaced scales, and where his right eye should have been was only an empty hole, crusted with black blood.

One must ask, as Rhaenyra surely did, how this had come to pass.

We now know much and more that the queen did not. It was Lord Larys Strong, the Clubfoot, who spirited the king and his children out of the city when the queen's dragons first appeared in the skies above King's Landing. So as not to pass through any of the city gates, where they might be seen and remembered, Lord Larys led them out through some secret passage of Maegor the Cruel, of which only he had knowledge.

It was Lord Larys who decreed the fugitives should part company as well, so that even if one were taken, the others might win free. Ser Rickard Thorne was commanded to deliver two-year-old Prince Maelor to Lord Hightower. Princess Jaehaera, a sweet and simple girl of six, was put in the charge of Ser Willis Fell, who swore to bring her safely to Storm's End. Neither knew where the other was bound, so neither could betray the other if captured.

And only Larys himself knew that the king, stripped of his finery and clad in a salt-stained fisherman's cloak, had been concealed amongst a load of codfish on a fishing skiff in the care of a bastard knight with kin on Dragonstone. Once she learned the king was gone, the Clubfoot reasoned, Rhaenyra was sure to send men hunting after him . . . but a boat leaves no trail upon the waves, and few hunters would ever think to look for Aegon on his sister's own island, in the very shadow of her stronghold.

And there Aegon might have remained, hidden yet harmless, dulling his pain with wine and hiding his burn scars beneath a heavy cloak, had Sunfyre not made his way to Dragonstone. We may ask what drew him back to the Dragonmont, for many have. Was the wounded dragon, with his half-healed broken wing, driven by some primal instinct to return to his birthplace, the smoking mountain where he had emerged from his egg? Or did he somehow sense the presence of King Aegon on the island, across long leagues and stormy seas, and fly there to rejoin his rider? Some go so far as to suggest that Sunfyre sensed Aegon's desperate *need*. But who can presume to know the heart of a dragon?

After Lord Walys Mooton's ill-fated attack drove him from the field of ash and bone outside Rook's Rest, history loses sight of Sunfyre for more than half a year. (Certain tales told in the halls of the Crabbs and Brunes suggest the dragon may have taken refuge in the dark piney woods and caves of Crackclaw Point for some of that time.) Though his torn wing had mended enough for him to fly, it had healed at an ugly angle, and remained weak. Sunfyre could no longer soar, not remain in the air for long, but must needs struggle to fly even short distances. Yet somehow he had crossed the waters of Blackwater Bay . . . for it was Sunfyre that the sailors on the *Nessaria* had seen attacking Grey Ghost. Ser Robert Quince had blamed the Cannibal . . . but Tom Tangletongue, a stammerer who heard more than he said, had plied the Volantenes with ale, making note of all the times they mentioned the attacker's golden scales. The Cannibal, as he knew well, was black as coal. And so the Two Toms and their "cousins" (a half-truth, as only Ser Marston shared their blood, being the bastard son of Tom Tanglebeard's sister by the knight who took her maidenhead) set sail in their small boat to seek out Grey Ghost's killer.

The burned king and the maimed dragon each found new purpose in the other. From a hidden lair on the desolate eastern slopes of the Dragonmont, Aegon ventured forth each day at dawn, taking to the sky again for the first time since Rook's Rest, whilst the Two Toms and their cousin Marston Waters returned to the other side of the island to seek out men willing to help them take the castle. Even on Dragonstone, long Queen Rhaenyra's seat and stronghold, they found many who misliked the queen for reasons both good and ill. Some grieved for brothers, sons, and fathers slain during the Sowing or during the Battle of the Gullet, some hoped for plunder or advancement, whilst others believed a son must come before a daughter, giving Aegon the better claim.

The queen had taken her best men with her to King's Landing. On its island, protected by the Sea Snake's ships and its high Valyrian walls, Dragonstone seemed unassailable, so the garrison Her Grace left to defend it was small, made up largely of men judged to be of little other use: greybeards and green boys, the halt and slow and crippled, men recovering from wounds, men of doubtful loyalty, men suspected of cowardice.

Over them Rhaenyra placed Ser Robert Quince, an able man grown old and fat.

Quince was a steadfast supporter of the queen, all agree, but some of the men under him were less leal, harboring certain resentments and grudges for old wrongs real or imagined. Prominent amongst them was Ser Alfred Broome. Broome proved more than willing to betray his queen in return for a promise of lordship, lands, and gold should Aegon II regain the throne. His long service with the garrison allowed him to advise the king's men on Dragonstone's strengths and weaknesses, which guards could be bribed or won over, and which must need be killed or imprisoned.

When it came, the fall of Dragonstone took less than an hour. Men traduced by Broome opened a postern gate during the hour of ghosts to allow Ser Marston Waters, Tom Tangletongue, and their men to slip into the castle unobserved. While one band seized the armory and another took Dragonstone's leal guardsmen and master-at-arms into custody, Ser Marston surprised Maester Hunnimore in his rookery, so no word of the attack might escape by raven. Ser Alfred himself led the men who burst into the castellan's chambers to surprise Ser Robert Quince. As Quince struggled to rise from his bed, Broome drove a spear into his huge pale belly, the thrust delivered with such force that the spear went out Ser Robert's back, through the featherbed and straw mattress, and into the floor beneath.

Only in one respect did the plan go awry. As Tom Tangletongue and his ruffians smashed down the door of Lady Baela's bedchamber to take her prisoner, the girl slipped out her window, scrambling across rooftops and down walls until she reached the yard. The king's men had taken care to send guards to secure the stable where the castle dragons had been kept, but Baela had grown up in Dragonstone, and knew ways in and out that they did not. By the time her pursuers caught up with her, she had already loosed Moondancer's chains and strapped a saddle onto her.

So it came to pass that when King Aegon II flew Sunfyre over Dragonmont's smoking peak and made his descent, expecting to make a triumphant entrance into a castle safely in the hands of his own men, with the queen's loyalists slain or captured, up to meet him rose Baela Targaryen, Prince Daemon's daughter by the Lady Laena, and fearless as her father.

Moondancer was a young dragon, pale green, with horns and crest and wingbones of pearl. Aside from her great wings, she was no larger than a warhorse, and weighed less. She was very quick, however, and Sunfyre, though much larger, still struggled with a malformed wing, and had taken fresh wounds from Grey Ghost.

They met amidst the darkness that comes before the dawn, shadows in the sky lighting the night with their fires. Moondancer eluded Sunfyre's flames, eluded his jaws, darted beneath his grasping claws, then came around and raked the larger dragon from above, opening a long smoking wound down his back and tearing at his injured wing. Watchers below said that Sunfyre lurched drunkenly in the air, fighting to stay aloft, whilst Moondancer turned and came back at him, spitting fire. Sunfyre answered with a furnace blast of golden flame so bright it lit the yard below like a second sun, a blast that took Moondancer full in the eyes. Like as not, the young dragon was blinded in that instant, yet still she flew on, slamming into Sunfyre in a tangle of wings and claws. As they fell, Moondancer struck at Sunfyre's neck repeatedly, tearing out mouthfuls of flesh, whilst the elder dragon sank his claws into her underbelly. Robed in fire and smoke, blind and bleeding, Moondancer's wings beat desperately as she tried to break away, but all her efforts did was slow their fall.

The watchers in the yard scrambled for safety as the dragons slammed into the hard stone, still fighting. On the ground, Moondancer's quickness proved of little use against Sunfyre's size and weight. The green dragon soon lay still. The golden dragon screamed his victory and tried to rise again, only to collapse back to the ground with hot blood pouring from his wounds.

King Aegon had leapt from the saddle when the dragons were still twenty feet from the ground, shattering both legs. Lady Baela stayed with Moondancer all the way down. Burned and battered, the girl still found the strength to undo her saddle chains and crawl away as her dragon coiled in her final death throes. When Alfred Broome drew his sword to slay her, Martson Waters wrenched the blade from his hand. Tom Tangletongue carried her to the maester.

Thus did King Aegon II win the ancestral seat of House Targaryen, but the price he paid for it was dire. Sunfyre would never fly again. He remained in the yard where he had fallen, feeding on the carcass of Moondancer, and later on sheep slaughtered for him by the garrison. And

Aegon II lived the rest of his life in great pain . . . though to his honor, this time His Grace refused the milk of the poppy. "I shall not walk that road again," he said.

Not long after, as the king lay in the Stone Drum's great hall, his broken legs bound and splinted, the first of Queen Rhaenyra's ravens arrived from Duskendale. When Aegon learned that his half sister would be returning on the *Violande*, he commanded Ser Alfred Broome to prepare a "suitable welcome" for her homecoming.

All of this is known to us now. None of this was known to the queen, when she stepped ashore into her brother's trap.

Rhaenyra laughed when she beheld the ruin of Sunfyre the Golden. "Whose work is this?" she said. "We must thank him."

"Sister," the King called down from a balcony. Unable to walk, or even stand, he had been carried there in a chair. The hip shattered at Rook's Rest had left Aegon bent and twisted, his once-handsome features had grown puffy from milk of the poppy, and burn scars covered half his body. Yet Rhaenyra knew him at once, and said, "Dear brother. I had hoped that you were dead."

"After you," Aegon answered. "You are the elder."

"I am pleased to know that you remember that," Rhaenyra answered. "It would seem we are your prisoners . . . but do not think that you will hold us long. My leal lords will find me."

"If they search the seven hells, mayhaps," the King made answer, as his men tore Rhaenyra from her son's arms. Some accounts say it was Ser Alfred Broome who had hold of her arm, others name the two Toms, Tanglebeard the father and Tangletongue the son. Ser Marston Waters stood witness as well, clad in a white cloak, for King Aegon had named him to his Kingsguard for his valor.

Yet neither Waters nor any of the other knights and lords present in the yard spoke a word of protest as King Aegon II delivered his half sister to his dragon. Sunfyre, it is said, did not seem at first to take any interest in the offering, until Broome pricked the queen's breast with his dagger. The smell of blood roused the dragon, who sniffed at Her Grace, then bathed her in a blast of flame, so suddenly that Ser Alfred's cloak caught fire as he leapt away. Rhaenyra Targaryen had time to raise her head toward the sky and shriek out one last curse upon her half brother before Sunfyre's jaws closed round her, tearing off her arm and shoulder.

The golden dragon devoured the queen in six bites, leaving only her left leg below the shin "for the Stranger." The queen's son watched in horror, unable to move. Rhaenyra Targaryen, the Realm's Delight and Half-Year Queen, passed from this veil of tears upon the twenty-second day of tenth moon of the 130th year after Aegon's Conquest. She was thirty-three years of age.

Ser Alfred Broome argued for killing Prince Aegon as well, but King Aegon forbade it. Only ten, the boy might yet have value as a hostage, he declared. Though his half sister was dead, she still had supporters in the field who must need be dealt with before His Grace could hope to sit the Iron Throne again. So Prince Aegon was manacled at neck, wrist, and ankle, and led down to the dungeons under Dragonstone. The late queen's ladies-in-waiting, being of noble birth, were given cells in Sea Dragon Tower, there to await ransom. "The time for hiding is done," King Aegon II declared. "Let the ravens fly that the realm may know the pretender is dead, and their true king is coming home to reclaim his father's throne." Yet even true kings may find some things more easily proclaimed than accomplished.

In the days following his half sister's death, the king still clung to the hope that Sunfyre might recover enough strength to fly again. Instead the dragon only seemed to weaken further, and soon the wounds in his neck began to stink. Even the smoke he exhaled had a foul smell to it, and toward the end he would no longer eat. On the ninth day of the twelfth moon of 130 AC, the magnificent golden dragon that had been King Aegon's glory died in the yard of Dragonstone where he had fallen. His Grace wept.

When his grief had passed, King Aegon II summoned his loyalists and made plans for his return to King's Landing, to reclaim the Iron Throne and be reunited once again with his lady mother, the Queen Dowager, who had at last emerged triumphant over her great rival, if only by outliving her. "Rhaenyra was never a queen," the king declared, insisting that henceforth, in all chronicles and court records, his half sister be referred to only as "princess," the title of queen being reserved only for his mother Alicent and his late wife and sister Helaena, the "true queens." And so it was decreed.

Yet Aegon's triumph would prove to be as short-lived as it was bittersweet. Rhaenyra was dead, but her cause had not died with her, and new "black" armies were on the march even as the king returned to the Red Keep. Aegon II would sit the Iron Throne again, but he would never recover from his wounds, would know neither joy nor peace. His restoration would endure for only half a year.

The account of how of the Second Aegon fell and was succeeded by the Third is a tale for another time, however. The war for the throne would go on, but the rivalry that began at a court ball when a princess dressed in black and a queen in green has come to its red end, and with that concludes this portion of our history.